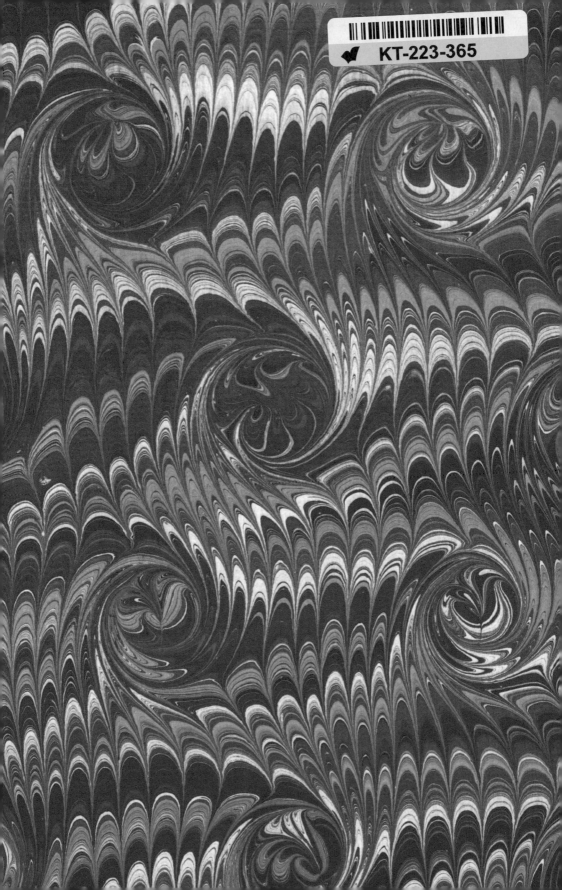

THE CRIMSON PETAL
AND THE WHITE

The
CRIMSON
PETAL
and the
WHITE

MICHEL FABER

CANONGATE

First published in Great Britain in 2002 by
Canongate Books Ltd, 14 High Street, Edinburgh EH1 1TE

1 3 5 7 9 10 8 6 4 2

The publisher acknowledges subsidy
from the Scottish Arts Council towards
the publication of this volume

British Library Cataloguing-in-Publication Data
A catalogue record for this book is available on
request from the British Library

ISBN 1 84195 323 7

Text design by James Hutcheson
Typeset in Van Dijck by Palimpsest Book Production Limited
Polmont, Stirlingshire

Printed and bound by
Creative Print and Design, Ebbw Vale, Wales

www. canongate.net

To Eva, with love and thanks

The girls that are wanted are good girls
Good from the heart to the lips
Pure as the lily is white and pure
From its heart to its sweet leaf tips.

The girls that are wanted are girls with hearts
They are wanted for mothers and wives
Wanted to cradle in loving arms
The strongest and frailest lives.

The clever, the witty, the brilliant girl
There are few who can understand
But, oh! For the wise, loving home girls
There's a constant, steady demand.

from 'The Girls that are Wanted'
J. H. Gray, *c.* 1880

CONTENTS

PART I

The Streets

ONE

atch your step. Keep your wits about you; you will need them. This city I am bringing you to is vast and intricate, and you have not been here before. You may imagine, from other stories you've read, that you know it well, but those stories flattered you, welcoming you as a friend, treating you as if you belonged. The truth is that you are an alien from another time and place altogether.

When I first caught your eye and you decided to come with me, you were probably thinking you would simply arrive and make yourself at home. Now that you're actually here, the air is bitterly cold, and you find yourself being led along in complete darkness, stumbling on uneven ground, recognising nothing. Looking left and right, blinking against an icy wind, you realise you have entered an unknown street of unlit houses full of unknown people.

And yet you did not choose me blindly. Certain expectations were aroused. Let's not be coy: you were hoping I would satisfy all the desires you're too shy to name, or at least show you a good time. Now you hesitate, still holding on to me, but tempted to let me go. When you first picked me up, you didn't fully appreciate the size of me, nor did you expect I would grip you so tightly, so fast. Sleet stings your cheeks, sharp little spits of it so cold they feel hot, like fiery cinders in the wind. Your ears begin to hurt. But you've allowed yourself to be led astray, and it's too late to turn back now.

It's an ashen hour of night, blackish-grey and almost readable like undisturbed pages of burnt manuscript. You blunder forward into the haze of your own spent breath, still following me. The cobblestones beneath your feet are wet and mucky, the air is frigid and smells of sour spirits and slowly dissolving dung. You hear muffled drunken voices from somewhere nearby, but what little you can understand doesn't sound like the carefully chosen opening speeches of a grand romantic drama; instead, you find yourself hoping to God that the voices come no closer.

The main characters in this story, with whom you want to become intimate, are nowhere near here. They aren't expecting you; you mean nothing to them. If you think they're going to get out of their warm beds and travel miles to meet you, you are mistaken.

You may wonder, then: why did I bring you here? Why this delay in meeting the people you thought you were going to meet? The answer is simple: their servants wouldn't have let you in the door.

What you lack is the right connections, and that is what I've brought you here to make: connections. A person who is worth nothing must introduce you to a person worth next-to-nothing, and that person to another, and so on and so forth until finally you can step across the threshold, almost one of the family.

That is why I've brought you here to Church Lane, St Giles: I've found just the right person for you.

I must warn you, though, that I'm introducing you at the very bottom: the lowest of the low. The opulence of Bedford Square and the British Museum may be only a few hundred yards away, but New Oxford Street runs between there and here like a river too wide to swim, and you are on the wrong side. The Prince of Wales has never, I assure you, shaken the hand of any of the residents of this street, or even nodded in passing at anyone here, nor even, under cover of night, sampled the prostitutes. For although Church Lane has more whores living in it than almost any other street in London, they are not of the calibre suitable for gentlemen. To connoisseurs, a woman is more than a carcass after all, and you can't expect them to forgive the fact that the beds here are dirty, the décor is mean, the hearths are cold and there are no cabs waiting outside.

In short, this is another world altogether, where prosperity is an exotic dream as distant as the stars. Church Lane is the sort of street where even the cats are thin and hollow-eyed for want of meat, the sort of street where men who profess to be labourers never seem to labour and so-called washerwomen rarely wash. Do-gooders can do no good here, and are sent on their way with despair in their hearts and shit on their shoes. A model lodging-house for the deserving poor, opened with great philanthropic fanfare twenty years ago, has already fallen into the hands of disreputables, and has aged terribly. The other, more antiquated houses, despite being two or even three storeys high, exude a subterranean atmosphere, as if they have been excavated from a great pit, the decomposing archaeology of a lost civilisation. Centuries-old buildings support themselves on crutches of iron piping, their wounds and infirmities poulticed with stucco, slung with clothes-lines, patched up with rotting wood. The roofs are a crazy jumble, the upper windows cracked and black as the brickwork, and the sky above seems more solid than air, a vaulted ceiling like the glass roof of a factory or a railway station: once upon a time bright and transparent, now overcast with filth.

However, since you've arrived at ten to three in the middle of a freezing November night, you're not inclined to admire the view. Your immediate concern is how to get out of the cold and the dark, so that you can become what you'd thought you could be just by laying your hand on me: an insider.

Apart from the pale gas-light of the street-lamps at the far corners, you can't see any light in Church Lane, but that's because your eyes are accustomed to stronger signs of human wakefulness than the feeble glow of two candles behind a smutty windowpane. You come from a world where darkness is swept aside at the snap of a switch, but that is not the only balance of power that life allows. Much shakier bargains are possible.

Come up with me to the room where that feeble light is shining. Let me pull you in through the back door of this house, let me lead you through a claustrophobic corridor that smells of slowly percolating carpet and soiled linen. Let me rescue you from the cold. I know the way.

Watch your step on these stairs; some of them are rotten. I know which ones; trust me. You have come this far, why not go just a little farther? Patience is a virtue, and will be amply rewarded.

Of course – didn't I mention this? – I'm about to leave you. Yes, sadly so. But I'll leave you in good hands, excellent hands. Here, in this tiny upstairs room where the feeble light is shining, you are about to make your first connection.

She's a sweet soul; you'll like her. And if you don't, it hardly matters: as soon as she's set you on the right path, you can abandon her without fuss. In the five years since she's been making her own way in the world, she has never got within shouting distance of the sorts of ladies and gentlemen among whom you'll be moving later; she works, lives and will certainly die in Church Lane, tethered securely to this rookery.

Like many common women, prostitutes especially, her name is Caroline, and you find her squatting over a large ceramic bowl filled with a tepid mixture of water, alum and sulphate of zinc. Using a plunger improvised from a wooden spoon and old bandage, she attempts to poison, suck out or otherwise destroy what was put inside her only minutes before by a man you've just missed meeting. As Caroline repeatedly saturates the plunger, the water becomes dirtier — a sure sign, she believes, that the man's seed is swirling around in it rather than in her.

Drying herself with the hem of her shift, she notes that her two candles are dimming; one of them is already a guttering stub. Will she light new ones?

Well, that depends on what time of night it is, and Caroline has no clock. Few people in Church Lane do. Few know what year it is, or even that eighteen and a half centuries are supposed to have passed since a Jewish troublemaker was hauled away to the gallows for disturbing the peace. This is a street where people go to sleep not at a specific hour but when the gin takes effect, or when exhaustion will permit no further violence. This is a street where people wake when the opium in their babies' sugar-water ceases to keep the little wretches under. This is a street where the weaker souls crawl into bed as soon as the sun sets and lie awake listening to the rats. This is a street reached only faintly, too faintly, by the bells of church and the trumpets of state.

Caroline's clock is the foul sky and its phosphorescent contents. The words 'three a.m.' may be meaningless to her, but she understands perfectly the moon's relationship with the houses across the street. Standing at her window, she tries for a moment to peer through the frozen grime on the panes, then twists the latch and pushes the window open. A loud snapping noise makes her fear momentarily that she may have broken the glass, but it's only the ice breaking. Little shards of it patter onto the street below.

The same wind that hardened the ice attacks Caroline's half-naked body too, eager to turn the sheen of perspiration on her pimpled breast into a sparkle of frost. She gathers the frayed collars of her loose shift into her fist and holds them tight against her throat, feeling one nipple harden against her forearm.

Outside it is almost completely dark, as the nearest street-lamp is half a dozen houses away. The cobbled paving of Church Lane is no longer white with snow, the sleet has left great gobs and trails of slush, like monstrous spills of semen, glowing yellowish in the gas-light. All else is black.

The outside world seems deserted to you, holding your breath as you stand behind her. But Caroline knows there are probably other girls like her awake, as well as various scavengers and sentinels and thieves, and a nearby pharmacist staying open in case anyone wants laudanum. There are still drunkards on the streets, dozed off in mid-song or dying of the cold, and yes, it's even possible there's still a lecherous man strolling around looking for a cheap girl.

Caroline considers getting dressed, putting on her shawl and going out to try her luck in the nearest streets. She's low on funds, having slept most of the day away and then passed up a willing prospect because she didn't like the look of him; he had a poxy air about him, she thought. She regrets letting him go now. She ought to have learned before today that it's no use waiting for the perfect man to come along.

Still, if she goes out again now, that would mean lighting another two candles, her last. The harsh weather must be considered, too: all that thrashing about in bed raises your temperature and then you go out in the cold and lose it all; a medical student once told her, as he was pulling on his trousers, that that was the way to catch pneumonia. Caroline has a healthy respect for pneumonia, although she confuses it with cholera and thinks gargling plenty of gin and bromide would give her a good chance of survival.

Of Jack the Ripper she need have no fear; it's almost fourteen years too early, and she'll have died from more or less natural causes by the time he comes along. He won't bother with St Giles, anyway. As I told you, I'm introducing you at the bottom.

A particularly nasty gust of wind makes Caroline shut the window, sealing herself once more into the box-like room she neither owns nor, properly speaking, rents. Not wanting to be a lazy slut, she tries her best to imagine walking around out there with an enigmatic look on her face; tries to conjure up a picture of an eligible customer stepping out of the darkness to call her beautiful. It doesn't seem likely.

Caroline rubs her face with handfuls of her hair, hair so thick and dark that even the crudest men have been known to stroke it in admiration. It has a silky texture, and is warm and pleasant against her cheeks and eyelids. But when she takes her hands away she finds that one of the candles has drowned in its puddle of fat, while the other still struggles to keep its flaming head above it. The day is over, she must admit, and the day's earnings are in.

In the corner of the otherwise empty room sags the bed, a wrinkled and half-unravelled thing like a bandaged limb that has been unwisely used for a rough, dirty chore. The time has come, at last, to use this bed for sleeping. Gingerly, Caroline inserts herself between the sheets and blankets, taking care not to tear the slimy undersheet with the heels of her boots. She'll take her boots off later, when she's warmer and can face the thought of unhooking those long rows of buttons.

The remaining candle-flame drowns before she has a chance to lean over and blow it out, and Caroline rests her head back against a pillow fragrant with alcohol and foreheads.

You can come out of hiding now. Make yourself comfortable, for the room is utterly dark, and will remain that way until sunrise. You could even risk, if you wish, lying down beside Caroline, because once she's asleep she's dead to the world, and wouldn't notice you – as long as you refrained from touching.

Yes, it's all right. She's sleeping now. Lift the blankets and ease your body in. If you are a woman, it doesn't matter: women very commonly sleep together in this day and age. If you are a man, it matters even less: there have been hundreds here before you.

A while yet before dawn, with Caroline still sleeping beside you and the room barely warmer than freezing outside the blankets, you had better get out of bed.

It's not that I don't appreciate you have a long and demanding journey ahead of you, but Caroline is about to be jolted violently awake, and it's best you aren't lying right next to her at that moment.

Take this opportunity to engrave this room on your memory: its dismal size, its moisture-buckled wooden floor and candle-blackened ceiling, its smell of wax and semen and old sweat. You will need to fix it clearly in your mind, or you'll forget it once you've graduated to other, better rooms which smell of pot-pourri, roast lamb and cigar smoke; large, high-ceilinged rooms as ornate as the patterns of their wallpaper. Listen to the faint, fidgety scufflings behind the skirting-boards, the soft, half-amused whimper of Caroline's dreams . . .

A monstrous shriek, of some huge thing of metal and wood coming to grief against stone, rouses Caroline from her sleep. She leaps out of bed in terror, throwing her sheets into the air like a flurry of wings. The shrieking grinds on for several more seconds, then gives way to the less fearsome din of a whinnying animal and human curses.

Caroline is at her window now, like almost every other resident of Church Lane. She's squinting into the gloom, excited and confused, trying to find evidence of disaster. There's none at her own doorstep, but farther along the street, almost at the lamp-lit corner, lies the wreck of a hansom cab still shuddering and splintering as the cabman cuts loose his terrified horse.

Her view hampered by dark and distance, Caroline would like to lean further out of the window, but gusts of icy wind drive her back into the room. She begins a fumbling search for her clothes, under the scattered bed-sheets, under the bed; wherever the last customer may have kicked them. (She really needs spectacles. She will never own any. They turn up in street markets from time to time, and she tries them on but, even allowing for the scratches, they're never right for her eyes.)

By the time she's back at her window, rugged up and fully roused, events have moved on remarkably quickly. A number of policemen are loitering around the wreck with lanterns. A large sack or maybe a human body is being bundled into a wagon. The cabbie is resisting invitations to climb aboard, and instead circles his upended vehicle, tugging at bits of it as if to test how much more it can possibly fall apart. His horse, placid now, stands sniffing the behinds of the two mares yoked to the police-wagon.

Within minutes, as the pale sun begins to rise over St Giles, whatever can be done has been done. The living and the dead have trundled away, leaving the wrecked cab in their wake. Splintered wheel-spokes and window-frame glass shards hang still as sculpture.

Peeping over Caroline's shoulder, you may think there's nothing more to see, but she remains hypnotised, elbows on the window-sill, shoulders still. She isn't looking at the wreck anymore; her attention has shifted to the house-fronts across the street.

There are faces at all the windows there. The silent faces of children, individually framed, or in small groups, like shop-soiled sweetmeats in a closed-down emporium. They stare down at the wreck, waiting. Then, all at once, as if by communal agreement on the number of seconds that must pass after the cabman's disappearance around the corner, the little white faces disappear.

At street level, a door swings open and two urchins run out, quick as rats. One is dressed only in his father's boots, a pair of ragged knicker-bockers and a large shawl, the other runs barefoot, in a night-shirt and overcoat. Their hands and feet are brown and tough as dog's paws; their infant physiognomies ugly with misuse.

What they're after is the cab's skin and bone, and they're not shy in getting it: they attack the maimed vehicle with boyish enthusiasm. Their small hands wrench spokes from the splintered wheel and use them as chisels and jemmies. Metal edgings and ledges snap loose and are wrenched off in turn; lamps and knobs are beaten, tugged and twisted.

More children emerge from other filthy doorways, ready for their share. Those with sleeves roll them up, those without fall to work without delay. Despite their strong hands and wrinkled beetle-brows, none of them is older than eight or nine, for although every able-bodied inhabitant of Church Lane is wide awake now, it's only these younger children who can be spared to strip the cab. Everyone else is either drunk, or busy prepar-ing for a long day's work and the long walk to where it may be had.

Soon the cab is aswarm with Undeserving Poor, all labouring to remove something of value. Practically everything is of value, the cab being an object designed for a caste many grades above theirs. Its body is made of such rare materials as iron, brass, good dry wood, leather, glass, felt, wire and rope. Even the stuffing in the seats can be sewn into a pillow much superior to a rolled-up potato sack. Without speaking, and each according to what he has in the way of tools and footwear, the children hammer and gouge, yank and kick, as the sound echoes drily in the harsh air and the framework of the hansom judders on the cobblestones.

They know their time is likely to be short, but it proves to be even shorter than expected. Scarcely more than fifteen minutes after the first urchins' assault on the wreck, a massive two-horse brewer's dray turns the corner and rumbles up the lane. It carries nothing except the cabman and three well-muscled companions.

Most of the children immediately run home with their splintery armfuls; the most brazen persist for another couple of seconds, until angry shouts of 'Clear off!' and 'Thief!' send them scurrying. By the time the dray draws up to the wreck, Church Lane is empty again, its house-fronts innocent and shadowy, its windows full of faces.

The four men alight and walk slowly around the cab, clockwise and counter-clockwise, flexing their massive hands, squaring their meaty shoulders. Then, at the cabman's signal, they lay hands on the four corners of the wreck and, with one groaning heave, load it onto the dray. It settles more or less upright, two of its wheels having been plundered.

No time is wasted scooping up the smaller fragments. The horse snorts jets of steam as it's whipped into motion, and the three helpers jump on, steadying themselves against the mangled cab. The cabman pauses only to shake his fist at the scavengers behind the windows and yell, 'This 'ere was my *life*!' and then he, too, is carted away.

His melodramatic gesture impresses nobody. To the people of Church Lane, he is a lucky man, a survivor who ought to be grateful. For, as the dray rattles off, it exposes a pattern of dark blood nestled between the cobbles, like a winding crimson weed.

From where you stand you can actually see the shiver of distaste travelling down between Caroline's shoulder-blades: she's not brave about blood, never has been. For a moment it seems likely she'll turn away from the window, but then she shudders exaggeratedly, to shake off the goose-flesh, and leans forward again.

The dray has gone, and here and there along the house-fronts doors are swinging open and figures are emerging. This time it's not children but adults – that is, those hardened souls who've passed the age of ten. The ones who have a moment to spare – the bill-poster, the scrubber, and the fellow who sells paper windmills – dawdle to examine the blood-spill; the others hurry past, wrapping shawls or scarves around their scrawny necks, swallowing hard on the last crust of breakfast. For those who work in the factories and slop-shops, lateness means instant dismissal, and for those who seek a day's 'casual' labouring, there's nothing casual about the prospect of fifty men getting turned away when the fittest have been chosen.

Caroline shudders again, this time from the chill of a distant memory. For she was one of these slaves herself once, hurrying into the grey dawn every morning, weeping with exhaustion every night. Even nowadays, every so often when she has drunk too much and sleeps too deeply, a brute vestige of habit wakes her up in time to go to the factory. Anxious, barely conscious, she'll shove her body out of bed onto the bare floor just the way she used to. Not until she has crawled to the chair where her cotton smock ought to be hanging ready, and finds no smock there, does she remember who and what she's become, and crawl back into her warm bed.

Today, however, the accident has shocked her so wide awake that there's no point trying to get more sleep just yet. She can try again in the afternoon – indeed, she'd *better* try again then, to reduce the risk of falling asleep next to some snoring idiot tonight. A simple fuck is one thing, but let a man sleep with you just once and he thinks he can bring his dog and his pigeons.

Responsibilities, responsibilities. To get enough sleep, to remember to comb her hair, to wash after every man: these are the sorts of things she must make sure she doesn't neglect these days. Compared to the burdens she once shared with her fellow factory slaves, they aren't too bad. As for the work, well . . . it's not as dirty as the factory, nor as dangerous, nor as dull. At the cost of her immortal soul, she has earned the right to lie in on a weekday morning and get up when she damn well chooses.

Caroline stands at the window, watching Nellie Griffiths and old Mrs Mulvaney trot down the street on their way to the jam factory. Poor ugly biddies: they spend their daylight hours drudging in the scalding heat for next to nothing, then come home to drunken husbands who knock them from one wall to the other. If this is what it means to be 'upright', and Caroline is supposed to be 'fallen' . . . ! What did God make cunts for, if not to save women from donkey-work?

There is one small way, though, in which Caroline envies these women, one modest pang of nostalgia. Both Nellie and Mrs Mulvaney have children, and Caroline had a child once upon a time, and lost it, and now she'll never have another. Nor was her child an illegitimate wretch: it was born in loving wedlock, in a beautiful little village in North Yorkshire, none of which things exists in Caroline's world anymore. Maybe her blighted insides couldn't even sprout another baby, and all that flushing with alum and sulphate of zinc is as pointless as prayer.

Her child would have been eight years old now, had he lived – and indeed he might have lived, had Caroline stayed in Grassington Village.

Instead, the newly widowed Caroline chose to take her son to London, because there was no dignified work in the local town of Skipton for a woman who'd not had much schooling, and she couldn't stand living on the charity of her mother-in-law.

So, Caroline and her son boarded a train to a new life together, and instead of going to Leeds or Manchester, which she had reason to suspect were bad and dangerous places, she bought tickets to the capital of the civilised world. Pinned inside her provincial little bonnet was eight pounds, a very substantial sum of money, enough for months of food and accommodation. The thought of it ought to have comforted her, but instead she was plagued by headache all the way into London, as if the massive weight of those bank-notes was bearing down hard on her neck. She wished she could spend this fortune right away, to be rid of the fear of losing it.

Within days of arriving in the metropolis she was offered help with her dilemma. A famous dress-making firm was so impressed with her manner that it commissioned her to make waistcoats and trousers in her own home. The firm would provide her with all the necessary materials, but required the sum of five pounds as a security. When Caroline ventured the opinion that five pounds seemed a great deal to ask, the man who was engaging her agreed, and assured her that the sum was not of his choosing. No doubt the manager of the firm, his own superior, had become disillusioned by the dishonest behaviour of the folk he'd taken on in more lenient times: yards and yards of the best quality cloth stolen, hawked in street markets, only to end up in tatters on the bodies of street urchins. A chastening picture for any businessman of a generous and trusting nature, did not Caroline agree?

Caroline *did* agree, then; she was a respectable woman, her boy was no urchin, and she considered herself a citizen of that same world her employer was trying to keep safe. So, she handed him the five pounds and began her career as a manufacturess of waistcoats and trousers.

The work proved to be tolerably easy and (it seemed to her) well-paid; in some weeks she earned six shillings or more, although from this must be deducted the cost of cotton, coals for pressing, and candles. She never skimped on candles, determined not to become one of those half-blind seamstresses squinting over their work by a window at dusk; she pitied the shirt-makers eulogised in 'The Song of the Shirt' in the same way that a respectable shop-keeper might pity a ragged costermonger. Though keenly aware of how much she'd come down in the world, she was not dissatisfied: there was enough to eat for her and her boy, their lodgings in Chitty Street were clean and neat, and Caroline, being husbandless, was free to spend her money wisely.

Then winter came and of course the child fell ill. Nursing him lost Caroline valuable time, particularly in the daylight hours, and when at last he rallied she had no choice but to engage his help.

'You must be my big brave man,' she told him, her face burning, her eyes averted towards the single candle lighting their shadowy labours. No proposal she would ever make in later years could be more shameful than this one.

And so mother and son became workmates. Propped up against Caroline's legs, the child folded and pressed the garments she had sewn. She tried to make a game of it, urging him to imagine a long line of naked, shivering gentlemen waiting for their trousers. But the work fell further and further behind and her drowsy boy fell forwards more and more often, so that in order to prevent him burning himself (or the material) with the pressing iron she had to pin the back of his shirt to her dress.

This dismal partnership didn't last very long. With dozens of waist-coats still waiting, the tugs at her skirts became so frequent it was obvi-ous the boy was more than merely tired: he was dying.

And so Caroline went to retrieve her bond from her employer. She came away with two pounds and three shillings and a sick, impotent fury that lasted for a month.

The money lasted slightly longer than that and, with her child in marginally better health due to medical attention, Caroline found work in a sweater's den making hats, jamming squares of cloth onto steaming iron heads. All day she was handing dark, shiny, scalding hats farther along a line of women, as if passing on plates of food in an absurdly steamy kitchen. Her child (forgive this impersonality: Caroline never speaks his name anymore) spent his days locked in their squalid new lodgings with his painted ball and his Bristol toys, stewing in his sickliness and fatherless misery. He was always fractious, whimpering over small things, as if daring her to lose patience.

Then one night at the end of winter he began coughing and wheezing like a demented terrier pup. It was a night very like the one we are in now: bitter and mucky. Worried that no doctor would agree, at such an hour and in such weather, to accompany her unpaid to where she lived, Caroline conceived a plan. Oh, she'd heard of doctors who were kind and devoted to their calling, and who would march into the slums to combat their ancient foe Disease, but in all her time in London Caroline had not met any such doctor, so she thought she'd better try deception first. She dressed in her best clothes (the bodice was made of felt stolen from the factory) and dragged her boy out into the street with her.

The plan, such as it was, was to deceive the nearest physician into believing she was new to London, and hadn't a family doctor yet, and had been all evening at the theatre, and only realised her son was ill when she returned and found the nurse frantic, and had hailed a cab immediately, and was not the sort of person to discuss money.

'Doctor won't send us away?' asked the child, scoring a bull's-eye, as always, on her worst fear.

'Walk faster,' was all she could reply.

By the time they found a house with the oval lamp lit outside, the boy was wheezing so hard that Caroline was half insane, her hands trembling with the urge to rip his little throat open and give him some air. Instead she rang the doctor's bell.

After a minute or two, a man came to the door in his night-gown, looking not at all like any doctor Caroline had met before, nor smelling like one.

'Sir,' she addressed him, doing her best to keep both the desperation and the provincial burr out of her voice. 'My son needs a doctor!'

For a moment he stared her up and down, noting her outmoded monochrome dress, the frost on her cheeks, the mud on her boots. Then he motioned her to come in, smiling and laying his broad hand on her boy's shivering shoulder as he said:

'Well now, this *is* a happy coincidence. *I* need a woman.'

Five years later, moving sleepily through her bedroom, Caroline stubs her toes on the ceramic basin and is provoked to clean up her bedroom. She transfers the stagnant contraceptive bouillon carefully into the chamber pot, watching, as she pours, the germs of another man's offspring combine with piss. She heaves the full pot onto her window-sill, and pushes the window open. There's no crack of ice this time, and the air is still. She'd like to toss the liquid into the air, but the Sanitary Inspector has been sniffing around lately, reminding everyone that this is the nineteenth century, not the eighteenth. Threats of eviction have been made. Church Lane is infested with Irish Catholics, spiteful gossips the lot of them, and Caroline doesn't want them accusing her of soliciting cholera on top of everything else.

So, she tips the chamber-pot slowly forwards and lets the mixture trickle discreetly down the brickwork. For a while the building will look as though God relieved Himself against it, but then the problem will get solved one way or another, before the neighbours wake up — either the sun will dry it or fresh snow will rinse it.

Caroline is hungry now, a sharp belly-hunger, despite the fact that she doesn't normally wake until much, much later. She's noticed that before: if you wake up too early, you're famished, but if you wake later, you're all right again, and then later still you're famished again. Needs and desires must rise and fall during sleep, clamouring for satisfaction at the door of consciousness, then slinking away for a while. A deep thinker, that's what her husband used to call her. Too much education might have done her more harm than good.

Caroline's guts make a noise like a piglet. She laughs, and decides to give Eppie a surprise by paying an early-morning visit to The Mother's Finest. Put a smile on his ugly face and a pie in her belly.

In the cold light of day, the clothes she hastily threw on in order to see the wrecked cab don't pass muster. Rough hands have wrinkled the fabric, dirty shoes have stepped on the hems, there are even speckles of blood from the scabby shins of old Leo the dyer. Caroline strips off and starts afresh with a voluminous blue and grey striped dress and tight black bodice straight out of her wardrobe.

Getting dressed is much easier for Caroline than it is for most of the women you will meet later in this story. She has made small, cunning alterations to all her clothing. Fastenings have been shifted, in defiance of fashion, to where her hands can reach them, and each layer hides short-cuts in the layer beneath. (See? — her seamstressing skills did come in useful in the end!)

To her face and hair Caroline affords a little more attention, scrutinising the particulars in a small hand-mirror tacked upside-down to the wall. She's in fair repair for twenty-nine. A few pale scars on her forehead and chin. One black tooth that doesn't hurt a bit and is best left alone. Eyes a little bloodshot, but big and sympathetic, like those of a dog that's had a good master. Decent lips. Eyebrows as good as anyone's. And, of course, her splendid nest of hair. With a wire brush she untangles the fringe and fluffs it out over her forehead, squaring it just above the eyes with the back of her hand. Too impatient and hungry to comb the rest, she winds it up into a pile on top of her head and pins it fast, then covers it up with an indigo hat. Her face she powders and pinks, not to conceal that she's old, ugly or corrupt in flesh, for she isn't any of these yet, but rather to brighten the pallor of her sunless existence – this for her own sake rather than for her customers.

Arranging her shawl now, smoothing down the front of her dress, she resembles a respectably well-to-do woman in a way she never could have managed when she slaved in the steam of the hat factory, suffering for her virtue. Not that an *authentic* lady could so much as fasten a garter in less than five minutes, let alone dress completely without a maid's assistance. Caroline knows very well she's a cheap imitation, but fancies herself a cheekily good one, especially considering how little effort she puts into it.

She slips out of her room, like a pretty moth emerging from a husk of dried slime. Follow discreetly after her. But you are not going anywhere very exciting yet: be patient a while longer.

On the landing and the stairs, all of last night's candles have burnt out. No new ones will be lit until the girls start bringing the men home in the afternoon, so there's not much light to see Caroline downstairs. The landing receives a lick of sunshine from her room, which she's left open to distribute the smell more evenly around the house, but the stairs, corkscrewed as they are inside a windowless stairwell, are suffocatingly gloomy. Caroline has often thought that this claustrophobic spiral is really no different from a chimney. Maybe one day the bottom-most steps will catch fire while she's on her way down and the stairwell will suck up the flames just like a chimney, the rest of the house remaining undisturbed while she and the spiral of dark stairs shoot out of the roof in a gush of smoke and cinders! Good riddance, some might say.

The first thing Caroline sees when she emerges into the light of the entrance hall is Colonel Leek seated in his wheelchair. Though he is berthed very near the foot of the stairs, he faces the front door, his back to Caroline, and she hopes that this morning he might, for once, be asleep.

'Think I'm asleep, don't you girlie?' he promptly sneers.

'No, never,' she laughs, though it's far too early in the day for her to be a convincing liar. She squeezes past the Colonel and lets him examine her for a moment, so as not to be rude, for he never forgets an insult.

Colonel Leek is the landlady's uncle, a pot-bellied stove of a man, keeping the warmth in with overcoats, scarves and blankets, stoking up on gossip, and puffing out smoke through a stunted pipe. Concealed under all the layers, Colonel Leek still wears his military uniform complete with medals, though these have a handkerchief sewn over them to prevent them catching. In the last war he went to, the Colonel accepted a bullet in the spine in exchange for a chance to take pot-shots at mutineering Indians, and his niece has cared for him ever since, installing him as her 'toll-collector' when she opened the empty rooms of her house to prostitutes.

Colonel Leek performs his job with grim efficiency, but his true passion remains war and other outbursts of violence and disaster. When he reads his daily newspaper, happy events and proud achievements fail to capture his interest, but as soon as he comes across a calamity he cannot contain himself. It often happens that Caroline, hard at work in her room, must suddenly croon more loudly in a customer's ear to cover the noise of a hoarsely shouted recitation from downstairs, such as:

'Six thousand Tartars have invaded the Amoor Province, wrested fifteen years ago from China!'

Now the Colonel fixes his bloodshot eyes on Caroline, and whispers meaningfully: '*Some* of us don't sleep through disaster. *Some* of us knows what goes on.'

'You mean that cab this mornin'?' guesses Caroline, well accustomed to his turn of mind.

'I *saw*,' the Colonel leers, trying to raise himself up off his perennially festering rear. 'Death and damage.' He falls back on the cushions. 'But that was only the *beginning*. A small part of what's afoot. The local manifestation. But everywhere! everywhere! Disaster!'

'*Do* let us go, Colonel. I'll drop if I don't 'ave a bite to eat.'

The old man looks down at his blanketed lap as if it were a newspaper and, raising his forefinger periscopically, recites:

'Disastrous overturn of train at Bishop's Itchington. Gunpowder explosion on the Regent's Canal. Steamer gone down off the Bay of Biscay. Destruction by fire of the *Cospatrick*, half-way to New Zealand, four hundred and sixty lost, mere days ago. Think of it! These are *signs*. The whirlpool of disaster. And at the centre of it – what there, eh? What there?'

Caroline gives it a couple of seconds' thought, but she has no idea what there. Alone of the three women who use Mrs Leek's house as their lay and lodgings, she's oddly fond of the old man, but not enough to prefer his demented prophesies to a hearty breakfast.

'Goodbye, Colonel,' she calls as she swings open the door and sweeps out into the street, closing him in behind her.

Now prepare yourself. You have not much longer with Caroline before she introduces you to a person with slightly better prospects. Watch her bodice swell as she inhales deeply the air of a new day. Wait for her to plot her safe passage through Church Lane, as she notes where the dung is most densely congregated. Then watch your step as you follow her towards Arthur Street, walking briskly along the line of litter left in the wake of the cab: first the blood, then a trail of seat-stuffing and wood-splinters. Perhaps they'll lead all the way to The Mother's Finest tavern, where hot pies are served from dawn and no one is going to ask you if you knew the woman who died.

TWO

ll along the burnished footpaths of Greek Street, the shop-keepers are out already, the second wave of early risers. Of course they regard themselves as the first wave. The grim procession of slop-workers and factory drudges Caroline looked down on from her window, though it happened only a few hundred yards from here less than an hour ago, might as well have happened in another country in another age. Civilisation begins at Greek Street. Welcome to the real world.

Getting up as early as the shop-keepers do is, in their view, stoic heroism beyond the understanding of lazier mortals. Any creature scurrying about earlier than themselves must be a rodent or an insect which traps and poisons have regrettably failed to kill.

Not that they are cruel, these industrious men. Many of them are kinder souls than the people you came here to meet, those exalted leading players you're so impatient to be introduced to. It's just that the shop-keepers of Greek Street care nothing about the shadowy creatures who actually manufacture the goods they sell. The world has outgrown its quaint rural intimacies, and now it's the modern age: an order is put in for fifty cakes of Coal Tar Soap, and a few days later, a cart arrives and the order is delivered. How that soap came to exist is no question for a modern man. Everything in this world issues fully formed from the loins of a benign monster called manufacture; a never-ending stream of objects – of graded quality, of perfect uniformity – from an orifice hidden behind veils of smoke.

You may point out that the clouds of smut from the factory chimneys of Hammersmith and Lambeth blacken all the city alike, a humbling reminder of where the cornucopia really comes from. But humility is not a trait for the modern man, and filthy air is quite good enough for breathing; its only disadvantage is the film of muck that accumulates on shop windows.

But what use is there, the shop-keepers sigh, in nostalgia for past times? The machine age has come, the world will never be clean again, but oh: what compensation!

Already they're working up a sweat, their only sweat for the day, as they labour to open their shops. They ease the tainted frost from the windows with sponges of lukewarm water and sweep the slush into the gutter with stiff brooms. Standing on their toes, stretching their arms, they strip off the shutters, panels, iron bars and stanchions that have kept their goods safe another night. All along the street, keys rattle in key-holes as each shop's ornate metal clothing is stripped away.

The men are in a hurry now, in case someone with money should come along and choose a wide-open shop over a half-open one. Passers-by are few and often queer at this hour of the morning, but all types may stray into Greek Street and there's no telling who'll spend.

An embarrassment of produce becomes available to Caroline as she walks towards The Mother's Finest; it's offered up to her in an indecent manner by the shop-keepers who, having thrown open their strongholds, now busy themselves selecting the most tempting wares to display on the footpaths outside. It's as if, having unlocked the chastity of shutters and doors, they can't see the point in maintaining any shred of modesty. Trays of books are shoved into Caroline's path, some of the volumes laid salaciously open to show off their colour plates. Stuffed manikins hold out their stitched hands, imploring Caroline to buy the clothes off their backs. Heavily curtained windows disrobe without warning.

'Morning, madam!' yelps more than one of the men as Caroline hurries by. They all know she's no lady – the mere fact that she's up at this hour makes that clear – but then they aren't exactly *gentlemen* of business either, and can't afford to scorn custom. Acutely aware how many rungs lower they are than the grand proprietors – *never* shop-keepers – of Regent Street, they'll as gladly sell their buns, boots, books or bonnets to a whore as to anyone else.

Indeed, there is an essential similarity between Caroline and the shop-keepers of Greek Street who woo her: much of what they hope to sell is far from virgin. Here you may find books with pages made ragged by a previous owner's paper-knife; there stands furniture discarded as outmoded, still bold as brass, still serviceable, and cheap – daring anyone fallen on hard times to fall just a little farther. A nice soft landing, ladies and gents! Here are beds already slept in – by the cleanest persons on earth, sir, the very cleanest. (Or perhaps by a diseased wretch, whose corruption might yet be lurking inside the mattress. Such are the morbid fantasies of those whom bankruptcy, swindles or dissolution have brought so low that furnishing their lodgings fresh from Regent Street is no longer possible.)

In much more dubious taste still are the clothes. Not only are they all reach-me-downs (that is, made for nobody in particular) but some of them have *already been worn* – and not just once, either. The shop-keepers will, of course, deny this; they like to fancy that Petticoat Lane and the rag-and-bone shop are as far beneath them on the ladder as Regent Street is above.

But enough of these men. You're in danger of losing sight of Caroline as she walks faster, spurred on by hunger. Already you hesitate, seeing two women ahead of you, both shapely, both with black bodices, both with voluminous bows bobbing on their rumps as they trot along. What colour was Caroline's skirt? Blue and grey stripes. Catch her up. The *other* whore, whoever she is, won't introduce you to anyone worth knowing.

Caroline has almost reached her goal; she's fixed her eyes on the dangling wooden sign of The Mother's Finest, a blistered painting of a busty girl and her hideous mam. One last obstacle – a stack of newspapers skidding onto the footpath right in front of her – and she's picking up the irresistible smell of hot pies and fresh-poured beer, and pushing open the old blue door with its framed motto, *PLEASE DON'T BANG DOOR, DRUNKARDS SLEEPING.* (The publican likes a laugh, and he likes others to laugh with him. When he first put up that sign, he recited it to Caroline so often she was almost convinced he'd taught her to read. But soon enough she was confusing the please with the don't, and the drunkards with the sleeping.)

Follow Caroline inside, and you'll notice there are no sleeping drunkards here after all. The Mother's Finest is a couple of rungs above the lowest drinking-houses and, despite its waggish motto, has a policy of ejecting sots as soon as they threaten to brawl or vomit. It's a solid, scrubbed sort of pub, all brass and poorly stained wood, with a variety of ornamental beer kegs suspended from the ceiling (despite not serving more than the one kind of beer), and a collection of coasters and bottle-tops on the wall behind the bar.

Of the forty-nine eyes in the room, only eight or ten turn to observe Caroline's entrance, for serious drinking and grumbling are the order of the day here. Those who do look at her, look just long enough to figure out who or at least *what* she is, then return to staring down into the gold froth on their bitter brown ale. By late tonight they may lust after her, but at this head-sore hour of morning the idea of paying for physical exertion lacks appeal.

It's a shabby crowd of men resting their elbows on The Mother's Finest's tables at this time of day; none of them exactly good-for-nothings, but certainly not good for much. Their coats and shirts have most of the buttons sewn on securely; the knitted scarves around their necks show signs of recent washing; and the boots on their feet are sturdy and, if not exactly shiny, no worse than dull. The majority of these men are not long out of work, and most of them are married to women who've not yet despaired of them. Caroline's presence here by no means offends or surprises them; you have a very long way to go before you set foot in the kind of establishment where only men are admitted.

''Ello, Caddie,' says the publican, raising a hairy hand glistening with beer. 'Cock wake you?'

'Never, Eppie,' says Caroline. 'The smell of your pies and ale.'

The exchange is a formality, as he's already filling a mug for her, and motioning to his wife for the pie. Of all the customers, Caroline can eat and drink on credit, because she's the only one he can trust to pay him later. What man, whose presence in a public house at this time of day trumpets his unemployed state, can claim that though he's penniless now, he'll have money tonight? Caroline, since losing her virtue, has gained respect where she needs it most.

That's not to say she's wise with money. Like most prostitutes, she spends her pay as soon as she's left alone with it. Apart from meals and rent, she buys fancy cakes, drinks, chocolates, clothes sometimes, hokey-pokey in the summer, visits to warm places in the winter – taverns, music halls, freak shows, pantomimes – anything to get her out of the cold, really. Oh yes, and she buys the ingredients for her douche, and firewood and candles, and every Sunday a penny sparkler, a firework she has loved since she was a child, and which she lights in her room late at night like a Papist lighting a votive candle. None of these vices costs very much – not compared with a man's gambling or medicines for a child – yet Caroline never saves a shilling. A reach-me-down dress, a penny sparkler, a fancy cake, a sixpenny entertainment . . . how can such things use up so much money? There must be other expenses, but she's damned if she can remember what they are. Never mind: her income is liquid, so she's never hard up for long.

Caroline devours her pie with an unselfconscious zest she would have found difficult to tolerate in others when she was a respectable Yorkshire wife. Fork and knife are not needed for the quivering assemblage of flour, sheep ankle, ox-tail and hot gravy she cups in her palm. She chews open-mouthed, to let the cooling air in. Within minutes she's licking her own hand.

'Thanks, Eppie, that was just what I needed.' She finishes her beer, stands up and shakes pastry crumbs off her skirts. The publican's wife will sweep up after her, sour-faced. Caroline mimes a goodbye kiss and leaves.

Outside, the civilised world hasn't quite woken up yet. The shop-keepers are still laying out their wares, while thieves, bill-stickers, beggars and delivery boys look on. There are no women about except two black-shrouded flower-sellers arguing quietly over territory. The loser trundles her barrow nearer to where the dray-horses stand, her swarthy back bent almost double over her stock of dubious posies.

Caroline isn't used to being on the streets so early, and feels almost intimidated by the sheer quantity of day left to be lived through. She wonders if she should offer her body to someone, to pass the time, but she knows she probably won't bother unless the opportunity leaps into her lap. The need isn't urgent yet. She can buy candles at her leisure. Why worry about being penniless when she can earn more in twenty minutes than she used to earn in a day?

She knows it's pig-laziness and moral weakness that prevent her from saving money as she ought to. The earnings of her trade could, if she'd been frugal over the years, have filled her old bonnet to bursting with bank-notes, but she's lost the knack of frugality. With no child or immortal soul left to save, the hoarding of coins in the hope of one day exchanging them for coloured paper seems pointless. All sense of purpose, of responsibility, indeed of any imaginable future, were removed from her by the deaths of her husband and child. It was they who used to make her life a *story*; they who seemed to be giving it a beginning, a middle and an end. Nowadays, her life is more like a newspaper: aimless, up-to-date, full of meaningless events for Colonel Leek to recite when no one's paying attention. For all the use she is to Society, beyond intercepting the odd squirt of sperm that would otherwise have troubled a respectable wife, she might as well be dead. Yet she exists, and, against the odds, she is happy. In this, she has a clear advantage over the young woman you are about to meet.

'Shush?'

Caroline has paused in front of a poky, gloomy stationer's on her way back down Greek Street, because inside the shop she's caught sight of — is it really? — yes, it's Shush, or Sugar as she's known to the world at large. Even in the gloom — *especially* in the gloom — that long body is unmistakable: stick-thin, flat-chested and bony like a consumptive young man, with hands almost too big for women's gloves. Always this same first impression of Sugar: the queasy surprise of seeing what appears to be a tall, gaunt boy wreathed from neck to ankle in women's clothes; then, with the first glimpse of this odd creature's face, the realisation that this boy is female.

At the sound of her nickname, the woman turns, clutching to her dark green bodice a ream of white writing paper. There's a bosom in that bodice after all. Not enough to nourish a child perhaps, but enough to please a certain kind of man. And no one has hair quite as golden-orange as Sugar's, or skin quite as luminously pale. Her eyes alone, even if she were wrapped up like an Arabian odalisque with nothing else showing, would be enough to declare her sex. They are naked eyes, fringed with soft hair, glistening like peeled fruits. They are eyes that promise everything.

'Caddie?'

The shadowy woman raises a green glove to her brow and squints at the sunlight beaming in from the street; Caroline waves, slow to realise that her friend is blinded. Her waving arm causes shafts of light to sweep back and forth over the cluttered rows of shelving, and Sugar squints all the more. Her head sways from side to side on its long neck, straining to find who has called out to her through the thorny confusion of quills, pencils and fountain pens. Shyly — for she has no business here — Caroline steps into the shop.

'Caddie!'

The younger woman's expression, in recognising her old friend, glows with what so many men have found irresistible: an apparent ecstasy of gratitude to have lived to experience such an enounter. She rushes up to Caroline, embraces and kisses her, while behind the counter the stationer grimaces. He's embarrassed not so much by the display of affection but by the blow to his pride: serving Sugar, he had taken her for a lady and been rather obsequious to her, and now it appears, from the commonness of her companion, that he was wrong.

'Will that be all, madam?' he harrumphs, affectedly sweeping a small feather duster over a rack of ink bottles.

'Oh yes, thank you,' says Sugar in her sweet fancy vowels and scrupulous consonants. 'Only, please . . . if you'd be so kind . . . I wonder if it could be made a little easier for me to carry?' And she transfers the ream of paper – slightly rumpled from the bosom-to-bosom embrace – into his hands. Scowling, he wraps the purchase in pin-striped paper and improvises a carry-handle of twine around it. With an ingratiating coo of thanks Sugar accepts the parcel from him, admiring his handiwork, demonstrating with a sensuous stroke of her gloved fingers what a good job he has done. Then she turns her back on him and takes her friend by the arm.

Out in the sun, up close, Caroline and Sugar appraise each other while pretending not to. It's months since they last met. A woman's looks can crumble irreparably in that time, her skin eaten away by smallpox, her hair fallen out with rheumatic fever, her eyes blood-red, her lips healing crookedly from a knife wound. But neither Caroline nor Sugar is much the worse for wear. Life has been kind, or at least has been sparing with its cruelty.

Shush's lips, the older woman notes, are pale and dry and flaking, but weren't they always? In Sugar's poorer days, before the move to smarter premises, she and Caroline lived three doors apart in St Giles, and even then customers would occasionally knock on the wrong door and ask for 'the girl with the dry lips'. Caroline knows, too, that underneath Sugar's gloves there's something wrong with her hands: nothing serious, but an unsightly skin ailment which, again, men have always seemed happy to forgive. Why men should tolerate such defects in Sugar was, and still is, mysterious to Caroline; indeed there's not a single physical attribute of which she could honestly say that Sugar's is better than hers.

There must be more to her than meets the eye.

'You're lookin' awful well,' Caroline says.

'I feel wretched,' says Sugar quietly. 'God damn God and all His horrible filthy Creation.' Her face and voice are calm; she might be commenting on the weather. Her hazel eyes radiate – or appear to radiate – gentle good humour. 'Bring on Armageddon, what do you think?'

Caroline wonders if she's missing a joke, the kind which Sugar shares with educated men now that she's relocated to Silver Street. Sugar used to be good for a laugh, back in the Church Lane days. Her parlour piece – a great favourite with all the whores – still makes Caroline smile, remembering it. Not that she remembers it very well, mind; it involved not just play-acting but words, hundreds of 'em, and the words were the best part. Sugar pretending to seduce an invisible man, begging him in a voice almost hysterical with lust. 'Oh, you *must* let me stroke your balls, they are so *beautiful* – like . . . like a *dog* turd. A *dog* turd nestling under your . . .' Your what? Shush had such a good word for it. A word to make you wet yourself. But Caroline has forgotten the word, and now's not the time to ask.

The fact that Sugar should be so much more desired and sought-after a whore than herself has always puzzled her, but that's the way it is and, judging by gossip in the trade, it's more true lately than ever. Certainly there's no doubt that the relocation of Mrs Castaway's from St Giles to Silver Street – a hop, skip and jump from the widest, richest, grandest thoroughfare in London – was as much due to the demand for Sugar as to the madam's ambition.

Which raises the question: what's Sugar doing here in a dingy Greek Street stationer's, when she now lives so close to the splendid shops of the West End? Why risk dirtying the hems of that beautiful green dress on carriage-ways where no one's in a hurry to sweep up the horse-shit? Indeed, why even bother to get out of bed (a bed Caroline imagines to be royally luxurious) before midday?

But when Caroline asks, 'What are you doin' all the way down 'ere?' Sugar just smiles, her whitish lips dry as moth's wings.

'I was . . . visiting a friend,' she says. 'All of last night.'

'Oh yes,' smirks Caroline.

'No, really,' says Sugar earnestly. 'An old friend. A woman.'

'So how is she, then?' says Caroline, angling for a name.

Sugar closes her eyes for a second. Her lashes, unusually for a red-haired person, are thick and lush.

'She's . . . gone away now. I was saying goodbye.'

They make an odd pair, Caroline and Sugar, as they walk up the street together: the older woman small-boned, round-faced, swell-bosomed, so neat and shapely in comparison to her companion, a long, lithe creature wreathed in a *peau-de-soie* dress the colour of moss. Although she has no bosom to speak of, this Sugar, and bones that poke alarmingly through the fabric of her bodice, she nevertheless moves with more poise, more feminine pride than Caroline. Her head is held high, and she appears to be wholly at one with her clothing, as if it were her own fur and feathers.

Caroline wonders if it's this animal serenity that men find so attractive. That, and the expensive clothes. But she is wrong: it's all to do with Sugar's ability to make conversation with men like the one you will meet very shortly. That, and never saying 'No.'

Now Sugar asks Caroline, 'How far out from home do you mean to start today?'

'Not 'ere,' the older woman replies, frowning, and gesturing back towards St Giles. 'Crown Street, maybe.'

'Really?' says Sugar, concerned. 'You were doing all right a few months ago, weren't you, around Soho Square?' (Here you see another reason why Sugar has done so well in her profession: her ability to recall the less than fascinating minutiae of other people's lives.)

'I lost me nerve,' says Caroline with a sigh. 'It was a good day, that day I ran into you and was all excited about Soho Square; I'd landed meself two champion customers in a row, and I was finkin': this is the patch for me from now on! But it was beginner's luck, Shush. I just don't belong this far into the good parts. I should know me place.'

'Nonsense,' says Sugar. 'They can't tell the difference, half these men. Put a black dress on, take a deep breath, puff your cheeks out and they'll mistake you for the Queen.'

Caroline grins dubiously. In her experience, the great jaded world is not so easy to impress.

'They see through me, Shush. You can't make a silk purse out of a sow's arse.'

'Oh, I think you can,' says Sugar, suddenly serious. 'It all depends who's buying it.'

Caroline sighs. 'Well, if I keep to *my* part of town, I find there's more

buyin' and less refusin'. Every time I try me luck any further west than
Crown Street, it's a struggle.' She squints up Greek Street in the direction of Soho Square, as if everything that lies beyond the Jews' School and
the house of charity is too steep to climb. 'Oh, I get foreigners, right
enough, and boys from the country, I get a few of those, that don't know
no better than to follow on and on. You keep 'em talkin' all the way there,
"Oh yes, and what brings a man like you to London, sir?" and 'fore they
know it they're in Church Lane and there's no backin' out. So they 'as
their pound o' flesh, pays you well for it and just puts it down to experience. But then you also get the ones that keeps on at you: "Is it far, is it
far, are we there yet? – you'd better not be one of those *Old City* sluts."
When they're like that, sometimes you can still steer 'em into an alley,
make 'em settle for a soot-arse, but sometimes they just shakes you off
'alf-way, really wild, and says, "Why don't you solicit from your own kind?"
I tell you, Shush, it really takes it out of you when they do that. You feel
so low, you want to go 'ome and weep . . .'

'No, no,' protests Sugar, shaking her head. 'You mustn't look at it that
way. You've brought *them* low, that's what you've done. They thought they
were Prince Glorious, and you've made them see they don't cut the figure
they thought they did. If their rank was obvious for all to see, why would
a woman like you approach them in the first place? I tell you, it's *they* who
go home and weep – pompous trembling little worms. Ha!'

The women laugh together, but Caroline only for a moment.

'Well, 'owever they see it,' she says, 'it can get me snivelling. And in
public too.'

Sugar takes Caroline's hand, grey and green gloves locking together,
and says, 'Come with me to Trafalgar Square, Caddie. We'll buy some
cakes, feed the pigeons – and watch the undertakers' ball!'

They laugh again. The 'undertakers' ball' is a private joke between
them, jokes being the main thing to have survived the three years since
they were neighbours and daily confidantes.

Soon they're walking together through a maze of streets neither of
them has any use for – streets they know only as the locales of other
women's brothels and introducing-houses, streets already marked for
destruction by town planners dreaming of a wide avenue named after the
Earl of Shaftesbury. Crossing the invisible boundary between St Anne
and St Martin-in-the-Fields, they see no evidence of saints, and no fields

unless one counts the tree-lined lawn of Leicester Square. Instead, they keep their eyes open for the same pastry-shop they visited last time they met.

'Wasn't it here?' (Shops appear and disappear so quickly in these modern times.)

'No, farther.'

London's pastry-shops (or 'patisseries', as they tend to style themselves lately) – poky little establishments that look like prettified ironmongers, displaying a variety of squat objects named after gateaux – may appal the French on their visits to England, but France is far away across a distant channel, and the patisserie in Green Street is quite exotic enough for such as Caroline. When Sugar leads her through the door, her eyes light up in simple pleasure.

'Two of those please,' says Sugar, pointing to the stickiest, sweetest, creamiest cakes on show. 'And that one too. Another two – yes, two of each.' The two women giggle, emboldened by that old girls-together chemistry. For so much of their lives, they have to be careful to avoid any word or gesture that might hinder the fickle swell of men's pride; what a relief it is to throw away inhibition!

'In the same scoop, *maydames*?' The shop-keeper, aware that they're as much ladies as he's a Frenchman, leers smarmily.

'Oh yes, thank you.'

Caroline gently cradles both of the thick paper scoops by their coned undersides and compares the four creamy lumps within, trying to decide which she'll eat first. Paid in full, the shop-keeper sees them off with a cheery '*Bon jewer*.' If two cakes each is what prostitutes buy, then bring on more prostitutes! Pastry will not stay fresh waiting for the virtuous, and already the icing is beginning to sweat. 'Come again, *maydames*!'

Onwards now to the next amusement. As they approach Trafalgar Square – what excellent timing – the fun has just begun. The unseen colossus of Charing Cross Station has discharged its most copious load of passengers for the day, and that flood of humanity is advancing through the streets. Hundreds of clerks dressed in sombre black are spilling into view, a tumult of monochrome uniformity swimming towards the offices that will swallow them in. Their profusion and their haste make them ridiculous, and yet they all wear grave and impassive expressions, as though their minds are fixed on a higher purpose – which makes them funnier still.

'The *un*-dertakers' ball, the *un*-dertakers' ball,' sings Caroline, like a child. The wit of the joke has long gone stale, but she cherishes it for its familiarity.

Sugar is not so easy to please; to her, all familiar responses smell of entrapment. Sharing an old joke, singing an old song – these are admissions of defeat, of being satisfied with one's lot. In the sky, the Fates are watching, and when they hear such things, they murmur amongst themselves: Ah yes, *that* one is quite content as she is; changing her lot would only confuse her. Well, Sugar is determined to be different. The Fates can look down any time they please, and find her always set apart from the common herd, ready for the wand of change to christen her head.

So, these clerks swarming before her cannot be undertakers anymore; what can they be? (Of course the banal truth is that they're clerks – but that won't do: no one ever escaped into a better life without the aid of imagination.) So . . . they're an enormous party of dinner guests evacuating a palatial hotel, that's what they are! An alarm has been raised: Fire! Flood! Every man for himself! Sugar glances down at Caroline, wondering whether to communicate this new perception to her. But the older woman's grin strikes her as simple-minded, and Sugar decides against it. Let Caroline keep her precious undertakers.

The clerks are everywhere now, piling out of omnibuses, marching off in a dozen directions, clutching packed lunches in parcels tied with string. And all the while still more omnibuses rattle into view, their knife-boards covered with more clerks shivering in the wind.

'I wish it'd rain,' smirks Caroline, recalling the last occasion when she and Sugar stood under cover, squealing with delight as the omnibuses ferried the clerks through a merciless downpour. The ones on the inside were all right, but the unfortunates riding on the knife-boards were hunched miserably under a jostling canopy of umbrellas. 'Oh, what a sight!' she'd crowed. Now she clasps her gloved hands as if in prayer, wishing the skies would open so she could see that sight again. But today, the heavens stay closed.

Under benign sunshine, the streets grow busier still, a chaos of pedestrians and vehicles making little distinction between street and footpath. Riding slowly through the hordes of clerks, like farmers trying to drive hay-carts through a flock of sheep, are the Jewish commission agents in their flashy broughams. Displayed at their sides are the ladies of mercantile nobility, lapdogs shivering in their laps. Wholesale merchants, holding their heads visibly higher than retail merchants, alight from cabs and clear a path with a sweep of their walking sticks.

It is from inside Trafalgar Square, however, that the scale of the parade can best be appreciated, as the crowds of clerks stream around and about like a great army surrounding Nelson. All Sugar and Caroline have to do is push through into the Square proper, holding their cakes and parcel aloft. With every step, despite the press of bodies, men make way for them, some falling back in ignorant deference, others in knowing disgust.

Suddenly Caroline and Sugar seem to have all the space in the world. They lean against the pedestal of one of the stone lions, eating cake with their heads thrown back and licking flecks of cream off their gloves. By the standards of respectability, they might as well be licking at gobs of ejaculate. A decent woman would eat cake only on a plate in a hotel, or at least in a department store – although there's no telling who, or what, one might risk meeting in such a universally hospitable place.

But in Trafalgar Square shocking manners are less conspicuous; it is, after all, a popular haunt for foreigners and an even more popular haunt for pigeons, and who can observe perfect propriety in amongst so much filth and feather-flutter? The class of people who worry about such things (Lady Constance Bridgelow is one of them, but you are far from ready to meet her yet) will tell you that in recent years these miserable creatures (by which she would mean the pigeons, but possibly also the foreigners) have only been encouraged by the official sanctioning of a stall selling paper cones of birdseed at a halfpenny each. Sugar and Caroline, having finished their cakes, buy themselves a seed cone at this stall, for the fun of seeing each other flocked all about with birds.

It was Caroline's idea; the stream of clerks is thinning now, swallowed up by the embassies, banks and offices; in any case, she's already bored with them. (Before she fell from virtue, Caroline could be entranced by embroidery or the slow blinking of a baby for hours at a time: these days she can barely keep her attention on an orgasm – admittedly not hers – happening in one of her own orifices.)

As for Sugar, what amuses her? She's regarding Caroline with a benign smile, like a mother who can't quite believe what simple things delight her child, but it's Caroline who's the mother here, and Sugar a girl still in her teens. If scattering seed to a flock of badly behaved old birds gives her no pleasure, what does? Ah, to know that you'd have to get deeper inside her than anyone has reached yet.

I can tell you the answers to simpler questions. How old is Sugar? Nineteen. How long has she been a prostitute? Six years. You do the arithmetic, and the answer is a disturbing one, especially when you consider that the girls of this time commonly don't pubesce until fifteen or sixteen. Yes, but then Sugar was always precocious – and remarkable. Even when she was newly initiated into the trade, she stood out from the squalor of St Giles, an aloof and serious child amongst a hubbub of crude laughter and drunken conviviality.

'She's a strange one, that Sugar,' her fellow whores said. 'She'll go far.' And indeed she has. All the way to Silver Street, a paradise compared to Church Lane. Yet, if they imagine her swanning up and down The Stretch under a parasol, they are wrong. She's almost always indoors, shut in her room, alone. The other whores of Silver Street, working in adjacent houses, are scandalised by the small number of Sugar's rendezvoux: one a day, or even none. Who does she think she is? There are rumours she'll charge one man five shillings, another two guineas. What's her game?

On one thing everyone's agreed: the girl has peculiar habits. She stays awake all night, even when there are no more men to be had; what's she *doing* in there with the lights on, if she's not sleeping? Also, she eats strange things – someone saw her eat a raw tomato once. She applies tooth powder to her teeth after each meal, and rinses it with a watery liquid that she buys in a bottle. She doesn't wear rouge, but keeps her cheeks terrible pale; and she never takes strong drink, except when a man bullies her into it (and even then, if she can get him to turn his back for an instant, she often spits out her mouthful or empties her glass into a vase). What *does* she drink, then? Tea, cocoa, water – and, judging by the way her lips are always peeling, in precious small quantities.

Peculiar? You haven't heard the half of it, according to the other whores. Not only is Sugar *able* to read and write, she actually enjoys it. Her reputation as a lover may be spreading among men-about-town, but it can't compare with the reputation she has among her fellow prostitutes as 'the one who reads all the books'. And not tuppenny books, either – *big* books, with more pages than even the cleverest girl in Church Lane could hope to finish. 'You'll go blind, you will,' her colleagues keep telling her, or, 'Don't you never think: enough's enough, this one's me last one?' But Sugar

never has enough. Since moving to the West End, Sugar has taken to crossing Hyde Park, over the Serpentine into Knightsbridge, and paying frequent
visits to the two Georgian houses in Trevor Square, which may look like
high-class brothels, but are in fact a public library. She buys newspapers
and journals too, even ones with hardly any pictures in them, even ones
that say they're for gentlemen only.

Her main expense, though, is clothes. Even by the standards of the
West End, the quality of Sugar's dresses is remarkable; in the squalor of
St Giles, it was astonishing. Rather than buying a discarded old costume
off a butcher's hook in Petticoat Lane, or a serviceable imitation of the
current fashion from a dingy Soho shop, her policy is to save every sixpence
until she can afford something that looks as though the finest lady's dressmaker might have made it especially for her. Such illusions, though they're
on sale in department stores, don't come cheap. The very names of the
fabrics – Levantine *folicé*, satin *velouté* and Algerine, in colours of lucine,
garnet and smoked jade – are exotic enough to make other whores' eyes
glaze over when Sugar describes them. 'What a lot of trouble you go to,'
one of them once remarked, 'for clothes that are stripped off in five minutes,
for a man to tread on!' But Sugar's men stay in her room for a great deal
longer than five minutes. Some of them stay for hours, and when Sugar
emerges, she looks as though she hasn't even been undressed. What does
she *do* with them in there?

'Talk,' is her answer, if anyone is bold enough to ask. It's a teasing
answer, delivered with a grave smile, but it's not the whole truth. Once
she has chosen her man, she'll submit to anything. If it's her cunt they
want, they can have it, although mouth and rectum are her preferred
orifices: less mess, and more peace of mind afterwards. Her husky voice is
the result of a knife-point being pressed to her throat just a little too hard
when she was fifteen, by one of the few men she ever failed to satisfy.

But it isn't simple submission and depravity that Sugar provides.
Submission and depravity come cheap. Any number of toothless hags will
do whatever a man asks if they're given a few pennies for gin. What makes
Sugar a rarity is that she'll do anything the most desperate alley-slut will
do, but do it with a smile of child-like innocence. There is no rarer treasure in Sugar's profession than a virginal-looking girl who can surrender to
a deluge of ordure and rise up smelling like roses, her eyes friendly as a
spaniel's, her smile white as absolution. The men come back again and

again, asking for her by name, convinced that her lust for their particular vice must equal their own; Sugar's fellow prostitutes, seeing the men so taken in, can only shake their heads in grudging admiration.

Those who are inclined to dislike her, Sugar strives to charm. In this, her freakish memory is useful: she's able, it seems, to recall everything anybody has ever said to her. 'So, how did your sister fare in Australia?' she will, for example, ask an old acquaintance a year after they last met. 'Did that O'Sullivan fellow in Brisbane marry her or not?' And her eyes will be full of concern, or something so closely resembling concern that even the most sceptical tart is touched.

Sugar's acute memory is equally useful when dealing with her men. Music is reputed to soothe the savage breast, but Sugar has found a more effective way to pacify a brutish man: by remembering his opinions on trade unions or the indisputable merits of black snuff over brown. 'Of course I remember you!' she'll say to the loathsome ape who, two years before, twisted her nipples so hard she almost fainted in pain. 'You are the gentle-man who believes that the Tooley Street fire was started by Tsarist Jews!' A few more such regurgitations, and he's ready to praise her to the skies.

A pity, really, that Sugar's brain was not born into a man's head, and instead squirms, constricted and crammed, in the dainty skull of a girl. What a contribution she might have made to the British Empire!

'Excu-*hoo*se me, ladies!'

Caroline and Sugar turn on their heels, and discover a man with a tripod and camera pursuing his hobby not far behind them in Trafalgar Square. He's a fearsome-looking creature with dark brows, Trollopean beard and a tartan overcoat, and the women jump to the conclusion that he wants them out of the way of his tripod-mounted ogre eye.

'Oh no no *n-o-o*, ladies!' he protests when they move aside. 'I would be honoured! Honoured to preserve your image for all time!'

They look at each other and share a smile: here is another amateur photographer just like all the rest, as fervent as a spiritualist and as mad as a hatter. Here is a man sufficiently charismatic to charm the pigeons down into his chosen tableau – or if he isn't, then sufficiently generous to buy lucky passers-by a halfpenny cone of birdseed. Even better when they provide their own!

'I am truly grateful, ladies! If you could but dispose yourselves a *little* farther apart . . . !'

They giggle and fidget as the pigeons flutter all around, alighting on their bonnets, clawing at their outstretched arms, settling on their shoulders – anywhere the seed has spilled. Despite the flurry of movement so near their eyes, they do their best not to blink, hoping the decisive moment will catch them in a good light.

The photographer's head moves to and fro beneath his hood, he tenses his entire body, and then there's a shudder of release. Inside his camera, a chemical image of Sugar and Caroline is born.

'A thousand thanks, ladies,' he says at last, and they know that this means goodbye: not *au revoir*, but farewell. He has taken all he wants from them.

'Did you 'ear what 'e said?' says Caroline as they watch him carry his trophies towards Charing Cross. 'For all time. *All time*. It couldn't be true, could it?'

'I don't know,' says Sugar, pensively. 'I've been to a photographer's studio once, and I've stood next to him in the dark room while he made the pictures appear.' Indeed she remembers holding her breath in the red light, watching the images materialising in their shallow font of chemicals, like stigmata, like spirit apparitions. She considers telling Caroline all this, but knows the older woman would require each word explained. 'They come out of a bath,' she says, 'and I'll tell you what: they *stink*. Anything that stinks so much can't last forever; I'm sure.' Her frown is hidden under her thick fringe: she isn't sure, at all.

She's wondering if the photographs taken of her at that photographer's salon will last forever, and hoping they don't. At the time, while the business was being done, she felt no qualms, and posed naked beside potted plants, in stockings by a curtained bed, and up to her waist in a tub of tepid bathwater. She didn't even have to touch anyone! Lately, however, she's come to regret it – ever since one of her customers produced a thumb-worn photograph of an awkward-looking naked girl and demanded that Sugar strike exactly the same pose with exactly the same kind of hand-brush, of which he'd thoughtfully brought his own. It was then that Sugar understood the permanence of being Sugar or Lotty or Lucy or whoever you might be, trapped on a square of card to be shown at will to strangers. Whatever violations she routinely submits to in the privacy of her bedroom, they vanish the moment they're over, half-forgotten with the drying of sweat. But to be chemically fixed in time and passed hand to hand forever: *that* is a nakedness which can never be clothed again.

You would probably think, if I showed you photographs of Sugar, that she needn't have worried. Oh, but they're charming, you'd say – innocuous, quaint, even strangely dignified! A mere century and a bit – or say, eleven dozen years later – and they're suitable for reproduction anywhere, without anyone thinking they might deprave and corrupt the impressionable. They may even be granted an artistic halo by that great leveller of past outrages, the coffee-table book. *Unidentified prostitute, circa 1875*, the book might say, and what could be more anonymous than that? But you would be missing the point of Sugar's shame.

'Imagine, though,' says Caroline. 'A picture of you still bein' there, 'undreds of years after you've died. An' if I pulled a face, that's the face I'd 'ave for ever . . . It makes me shiver, it does.'

Sugar strokes the edge of her parcel absently as she thinks up a way to steer the conversation into less tainted waters. She stares across the square at the National Gallery, and her painful memory of the hand-brush man fades.

'What about painted portraits?' she says, recalling Caroline's exaggerated admiration for an art student who once fobbed her off, in lieu of payment, with a sketch he claimed was of the Yorkshire dales. 'Don't *they* make you shiver?'

'That's different,' says Caroline. 'They're . . . you know . . . of kings and people like that.'

Sugar performs a chuckle of catty mischief from her encyclopaedic repertoire of laughs. 'Kitty Bell had her portrait done, don't you remember, by that old goat from the Royal Academy who fell for her? It was even hung at an exhibition; Kitty and I went to see it. "Flower Seller", they called it.'

'Ooo, you're right too – the slut.'

Sugar pouts. 'Jealous. Just think, Caddie, if you had a painter begging you to let him do your portrait. *You* sit still, *he* works, and then at the end of it, he gives you a painting in oils, like . . . like a reflection of how you'd see yourself in a looking-glass on the one day of your life when you were prettiest.'

Caroline licks the inside of the paper scoop, thoughtful, half-seduced by the mental picture Sugar has painted for her, half-suspecting she's being gulled. But, teasing aside, Sugar sincerely believes Caroline would make a fine subject for a painting: the small, pretty face and compact body of the older woman are so much more classically picturesque than her own bony physique. She imagines Caddie's shoulders swelling up out of an evening gown, smooth and flawless and peachy, and compares this rose-tinted vision with her own pallid torso, whose collar-bones jut out from her freckled chest like the handles of a grid-iron. To be sure, the fashions of the Seventies are growing ever more sylph-like, but what's in fashion and what a woman believes in her heart to be womanly may not be the same thing. Any print-shop is stocked to the rafters with 'Carolines', and her face is everywhere, from soap-wrappers to the stone carvings on public buildings – isn't that proof that Caroline is close to the ideal? Sugar thinks so. Oh, she's read about the Pre-Raphaelites in journals, but that's as far as it goes; she wouldn't know Burne-Jones or Rossetti if they fell on top of her. (Nor is such a collision likely, given the statistical improbability: two painters, two hundred thousand prostitutes.)

There's a fleck of cream on Caroline's chin when her face emerges from the paper scoop. Having savoured the fantasy of being an artist's muse and scorning mere money for the greater glory of her very own painted portrait, she's decided not to swallow it.

'No fanks,' she says in a nobody's-fool voice. 'If there's onc fing I've learnt, it's that if you join in games you don't understand, you finish up fleeced, wivout even knowin' 'ow you got that way.'

Sugar tosses her crumpled paper scoop to the ground and shakes her skirts free of cake-crumbs and birdseed. 'Shall we go?' she suggests and, reaching over to Caroline's face, she gently wipes the fleck of cream off her chin. The older woman recoils slightly, startled at this unexpected physical intimacy outside working hours.

It's half past eight. The undertakers' ball is over and the streets are once again sparsely peopled. First the garret-shop slaves, casual labourers and factory workers, now the clerks: the city swallows armies of toilers and is still not satisfied. All day there will be fresh deliveries from all over England, from all over the world. And tonight, the Thames will swallow what wasn't wanted.

Caroline yawns, exposing the one blackened tooth among the white ones, and Sugar yawns in response, covering her mouth demurely with her gloved hand.

'Lord, I could drop into bed now and snore me 'ead off,' declares the older woman.

'Me too,' says Sugar.

'I got woken early. A cab got smashed up, in Church Lane, as close to my window as . . .' (she points to King George) 'as that there statue.'

'Was anyone hurt?'

'I fink a woman died. The police carried a body away, wiv skirts on.'

Sugar considers tickling Caddie with a description of her faulty grammar made flesh: a procession of earnest moustachioed policemen, pretty skirts frou-frouing under their sombre overcoats. Instead she asks, 'Anyone you knew?'

Caroline blinks stupidly. The thought hadn't even occurred to her.

'Gaw, I don't *know*! Fancy it bein' . . .' She screws her face up, trying to imagine any one of her prostitute friends being on the street at that time of morning. 'I'd best go 'ome.'

'Me too,' says Sugar. 'Or Mrs Castaway's may lose its reputation.' And she smiles a smile that isn't for the likes of Caroline to understand.

Briefly they embrace and, as always when they do, Caroline is surprised by how awkward and tentative Sugar is; how the girl's body, so notorious for its pliability in the hands of men, feels gawky and stiff in the arms of a friend. The heavy parcel of paper, dangling from Sugar's fist, bumps against Caroline's thigh, hard as a block of wood.

'Come and visit me,' says Caroline, releasing Sugar from the clasp.

'I will,' promises Sugar, a blush of colour coming to her face at last.

Who to follow? Not Caroline – she'll only take you where you've come from, and what a shabby place that was. Stay with Sugar now. You won't regret it.

Sugar wastes no time watching Caroline go, but hastens out of the Square. As hurriedly as if she's being pursued by ruffians intent on garrotting her, she makes her way to the Haymarket.

'I'll get you there faster, missie!' shouts a cabman from one of the hotel stands, his raucous tone making clear he's seen through her fancy clothes.

'You can 'ave a ride on me 'orse, too!' he whoops after her as she ignores him, and other cabmen on the rank guffaw with mirth, and even their horses snort.

Sugar advances along the footpath, face impassive, back straight. The other people on the streets do not exist for her. The men loitering around the coffee-stall step back from her advance, lest her swinging parcel clip their knees. A bill-poster moves his bucket closer to the pillar on which he's pasting his placard, lest she kick his gluey liquid all over the paving-stones. A bleary-eyed gent – a new arrival from America, by the look of his hat and trousers – appraises her from head to hurrying feet; his innocence will wear off by this evening, when a flock of harlots will flutter into the Haymarket and proposition him every dozen steps.

'Begging your pardon, ma'am,' he mutters as Sugar pushes past him.

Up Great Windmill Street Sugar goes, past Saint Peter's where the best of the child prostitutes will later congregate, past the Argyll Rooms where even now the cream of male aristocracy lies drunk and snoring, interleaved with snoozing whores damp with champagne. Unerringly she turns corners, ducks through alleyways, crosses busy streets with barely a glance, like a cat with an idea glowing in its catty brain.

She doesn't stop until she's in Golden Square, with the rooftop and smoking chimneypots of Mrs Castaway's, and the desultory traffic of Silver Street, already in view. Then, with only a few yards to go, she cannot bring herself to walk those last steps and knock at the door of her own house. Under her green silks, she's sweating, not just from her haste, but in fresh distress. She turns about, hugs her parcel to her bosom, and dawdles towards Regent Street.

On the stone steps of the Church of Our Lady of the Assumption in Warwick Street, a small child of uncertain sex lies huddled in a pale-yellow blanket that twinkles with melted frost. In the pale sunlight, the drizzle of snot on the child's lips and mouth shines like raw egg-yolk, and Sugar, disgusted, looks away. Alive or dead, this child is doomed: it's not possible to save anyone in this world, except oneself; God gets His amusement from doling out enough food, warmth and love to nourish a hundred human beings, into the midst of a jostling, slithering multitude of millions. One loaf and one fish to be shared among five thousand wretches – that's His jolliest jape.

Sugar has already crossed the street, when she's stopped by a voice – a feeble, wheezy bleat, making a sound that could be wordless nonsense, could be 'Money', could be 'Mama'. She turns, and finds the child alive and awake, gesturing from its swaddle of dirty wool. The grim façade of the chapel, new red brick with no windows down below, and spy-holes in dark locked door, flaunts its imperviousness to anti-Catholic rioters and children seeking charity.

Sugar hesitates, rocking on the balls of her feet, feeling the sweat inside her boots prickle and simmer between her toes. She cannot bear going backwards when she's made up her mind to go forwards; she's crossed this street now, and there's no crossing back. Besides, it's hopeless; she could fuck a hundred men a day and give all the proceeds to destitute children, and still make no lasting difference.

Finally, when her heart begins to labour in her breast, she fetches a coin from her reticule and throws it across the street. Her aim is true, and the shilling lands on the pale-yellow blanket. She turns away again, still unsure of the child's sex; it doesn't matter; in a day or a week or a month from now, the child will be dragged down into oblivion, like a lump of refuse flushed into London's sewers. God damn God and all His horrible filthy creation.

Sugar walks on, her eyes fixed on the grand thoroughfare of Regent Street shimmering through her stinging eyes. She needs sleep. And, yes, if truth be told, if you really must know, she is suffering, suffering so much that she'd be relieved to die, or else kill. Either would do. As long as a decisive blow is struck for disengagement.

It's not Caroline's company that's brought this on. Caroline, as you already know, is inconsequential; she asks nothing.

No, what has tested Sugar so unbearably is this: having to be patient and kind all yesterday and last night, sitting up with a dying friend called Elizabeth in a fetid slum in Seven Dials. How long Elizabeth took to die, clutching Sugar's hand all the while! Such a clammy, cool, claw-like hand it was too, for all those hours! At the thought of it, Sugar's own hands sweat even more inside her gloves, itching and stinging against the powdered lining.

But being a fallen woman has its small advantages, and she claims one of them now. The rules governing outdoor dress are clear, for those who can understand them: men may wear gloves or not wear gloves, as they please; poor shabby women must not wear them (the thought alone is ridiculous!) or the police are likely to demand where they got them; respectable women of the lower orders, especially those with babes in arms, can be forgiven for not wearing them; but ladies must wear them at all times, until safely indoors. Sugar is dressed like a lady, therefore she must on no account bare her extremities in public.

Nevertheless, glove-tip by glove-tip, finger by finger, Sugar strips, even as she walks, the soft green leather off her hands. Unsheathed, her sweating white skin glistens in the sunshine. With a deep sigh of relief, indistinguishable from the one she uses when a man has done to her all he can do, she flexes in the cool air her intricately cracked and flaking fingers.

Follow Sugar now into the great open space, the grandiose vacancy of Regent Street – admire those towering honeycombs of palatial buildings stretching into the fog of architectural infinity, those thousands of identically shaped windows tier upon tier; the glassy expanse of roadway swept clear of snow; all of it is a statement of intent: a declaration that in the bright future to come, places like St Giles and Soho, with their narrow labyrinths and tilting hovels and clammy, crumbling nooks infested with human flotsam, will be swept away, to be replaced by a new London that's entirely like Regent Street, airy, regular and clean.

The Stretch at this hour of morning is already alive with activity – not the insane profusion it will bear in the summer Season, but enough to impress you. Cabs are trotting backwards and forwards, thickly bearded gentlemen in dark clothing dash across their path, sandwich-board men patrol the gutters and, over there, a trio of street-sweepers are standing over a drain, cramming the accumulated porridge of snow-slush, dirt and horse-dung down through the grille with jabs of their brooms. Even as they toil, an equipage bristling with provincial businessmen jingles by, leaving a steamy festoon of turd in its wake.

An omnibus is reined to a halt, and half a dozen passengers alight. One of them, a soberly dressed man of average height and build, is in an indecent hurry, and almost runs into the shit-spill: just in time he reels backwards, like a street clown performing for whinnying onlookers in Seven Dials. Mortified, he whips off his hat, and advances with a cringing gait. His hair, thus released into the atmosphere, is remarkable in how it sits, or more accurately jumps around, on his head. From the forehead down, he looks terribly serious, even anxious, as if he's late for work and may expect a reprimand, but from the forehead up he is a comic delight: a flip-flopping crest of curly golden hair, like a small furry animal fallen out of the sky onto the head of a man, and determined to keep its purchase there no matter what.

Sugar smiles, relieved to see something amusing in the world at last; then she hugs her parcel once more, and starts to idle along the Stretch.

Just a few more minutes, here on the cobbled shore of London's tomorrow, and she'll be ready to go home.

Leave Sugar to herself now; she longs to walk alone, anonymous. She's already forgotten about the man with the ridiculous hair, whom you took to be just another passer-by, a flash of local colour distracting you from your quest to find the people you came here to meet. Stop daydreaming now; cross the shiny Rubicon of Regent Street, avoiding the traffic and the mounds of muck; and seek out that clownish man.

Whatever you do, don't let him melt into the crowd, for he's really a very important man, and he'll take you further than you can possibly imagine.

THREE

illiam Rackham, destined to be the head of Rackham Perfumeries but rather a disappointment at present, considers himself to be in *desperate* need of a new hat. That's why he is hurrying so. That's why you had better stop staring at the gently bobbing bustle of Sugar's dress as she moves away from you, stop staring at her sharp shoulder-blades and wasp waist and the wisps of orange hair fluttering under her bonnet, and run after William Rackham instead.

You hesitate. Sugar is going home, to a bawdy-house with the most peculiar name of 'Mrs Castaway's'. You'd like to see the insides of such a place, wouldn't you? Why should you miss whatever is about to happen, just to pursue this stranger, this . . . man? Admittedly his bouncing mop of golden hair was comical, but he was otherwise not very fascinating – especially compared to this woman you're only just getting to know.

But William Rackham is destined to be the head of Rackham Perfumeries. Head of Rackham Perfumeries! If you want to get on, you can't afford to linger in the company of whores. You must find it in you to become extraordinarily interested in why William Rackham considers himself to be in desperate need of a new hat. I will help you as much as I can.

His old hat he carries in his hand as he walks along, for he'd rather go bareheaded in a world of hatted men than wear it a minute longer, so ashamed is he of its unfashionable tallness and its frayed brim. Of course, whether he wears it or doesn't wear it, people will be staring at him in pity, just as they stared at him in the omnibus . . . do they truly imagine he can't see them smirking? Oh God! How is it possible things have come to this! Life has conspired . . . but no, he has no right to make so all-embracing an accusation . . . Rather say, there are *unfriendly elements* in Life conspiring against him, and he can't yet see his way clear to victory.

In the end, though, he will triumph; he *must* triumph, because his happiness is, he believes, essential to a larger scheme of things. Not that he necessarily deserves to be happier than other men, no. Rather, his fate is a sort of . . . a sort of *hinge* on which much else depends, and if he should be crushed by misfortune, something greater will collapse along with him, and surely Life wouldn't risk that.

William Rackham has come . . .

(Are you still paying attention?)

William Rackham has come into the city because he knows that in Regent Street he can put an end to his humiliation by buying a new hat. Which isn't to imply he couldn't buy just as good a hat at Whiteley's in Bayswater and save himself the journey, but he has an ulterior reason for coming here, or two ulterior reasons. Firstly, he'd rather not be seen in Whiteley's, which he's been heard to disparage, in the course of those smart dinner parties to which he always used to be invited, as hopelessly vulgar. (Where he's heading now is vulgar too, of course, but he's less likely to meet anyone he knows.) Secondly, he wishes to keep a careful eye on Clara, his wife's lady's-maid.

Why? Oh, it's all very sordid and complicated. Having recently forced himself to make a few calculations of his household's expenses, William Rackham has concluded that his servants are stealing from him – and not just the odd candle or rasher of bacon, but on an outrageous scale. No doubt they're taking advantage of his wife's illness and his own disinclination to dwell on his financial woes, but they're damned mistaken if they think he notices nothing. Damned mistaken!

And so, yesterday afternoon, as soon as his wife finished describing to Clara what she wished bought in London the next morning, William (eavesdropping outside the door) smelled avarice. Watching Clara descend the stairs, looking down on her from the shadowy landing, he fancied he could see plans for embezzlement already simmering in her stocky little body, simmering towards the boil.

'I trust Clara with my life,' Agnes objected, with typical exaggeration, when he told her privately of his misgivings.

'That may be so,' he said. 'But I don't trust her with my money.' An uneasy moment followed then, as Agnes's face was subtly contorted by the temptation to point out that the money wasn't his but his father's, and that if he would only comply with his father's demands, they'd have a lot more of it. She behaved herself, though, and William felt moved to reward her with a compromise. Clara would be trusted with the actual purchase, but William would, by sheer 'chance', accompany her into the city.

And so it is that the master and the lady's-maid have travelled down from Notting Hill together on the omnibus, a cab being 'out of the question, of course' – not (Rackham hoped the servant would understand) because he can ill afford cabs nowadays, but because people might gossip.

A vain hope. The servant naturally chose to believe she was seeing yet more evidence of her master coming down in the world. (She'd also noticed how worn and outmoded his hat has become; in fact, she was the *only* person who'd noticed it, for he has been avoiding all his fashionable friends in shame.) Every change in the household routine, no matter how trifling, and every suggestion of economy, no matter how reasonable, Clara interprets as further proof that William Rackham is being squashed under his father's boot like a slug.

In her delight at his humiliation, it doesn't occur to her that if he isn't rescued from his predicament he might eventually be unable to keep her employed: her insights are of a different kind. She's detected, for example, a cowardly retreat on the matter of the coachman, whose coming has been foretold for years, but who has never yet materialised. Lately there appears to be an unspoken agreement that there should be no further mention of this fabled advent. But Clara doesn't forget! And what about Tilly, the downstairs housemaid? Dismissed for falling pregnant, she has never been replaced, with the result that Janey is doing far more than should be expected of a scullery maid. Rackham says it's only temporary, but the months pass and nothing is done. Good lady's-maids like Clara may be hard to find, but surely downstairs housemaids are plentiful as rats? Rackham could have one within the hour if he was willing to pay for it.

All in all it's a disgraceful situation, which Clara handles to the best of her abilities – that is, by making her displeasure felt in every way she can think of short of outright insolence.

Hence the pained expression she maintained on her face all the way into London on the omnibus, an expression which the miserable Rackham didn't even notice until the horses pulled the vehicle through Marble Arch.

Perhaps *all* members of the female sex are sickly, he thought then, guessing that the servant must be in some sort of pain.

Perhaps (he tried to reassure himself) *my poor sick Agnes is not so unusual after all.*

William has deliberately made an early start in the city, so that he'll have plenty of time to study, on his return home, the long-avoided progress papers and accounts of Rackham Perfumeries. (Or at least take them out of the envelopes his father sent them in.) Then tomorrow (perhaps) he will visit the lavender farm, if only to be seen there, so that report of it may reach the old man's ears. It would probably be as well to ask the farm workers a few pertinent questions, if he can think of any. Reading the documents will help, no doubt − if it doesn't drive him insane first.

Madhouse or poorhouse: is that what his choices have been reduced to? Is there no way forward but to . . . to sell a false image of himself to his own father, faking enthusiasm for something loathsome? How, in the name of . . . But he mustn't dwell on the deeper implications: that's the curse of higher intellect. He must meet the day's demands one by one. Buy a new hat. Keep an eye on Clara. Go home and make a start on those papers.

William Rackham does not imagine he will master the family business in a day, no: his aims are modest. If he shows a *little* interest, his father may surrender a little more money. How long can it possibly take to read a few papers? One afternoon wasted on it ought to be enough, surely? Granted, he once opined in a Cambridge undergraduate magazine that 'a single day spent doing things which fail to nourish the soul is a day stolen, mutilated, and discarded in the gutter of destiny.' But, as his recent haircut proves, the Cambridge life can't last for ever. He's made it last a good few years as it is.

So, light-headed and blinking in the sun, legs still stiff from the long omnibus journey, William hurries along the Stretch. At his side, clutched in his gloved fingertips, swings the detestable hat; a few yards ahead of him walks his detested servant; and immediately behind him follows his shadow. Feel free, now, to follow him every bit as close as that shadow, for he is determined never to look back.

There, up ahead, its grand mysterious interior glowing with a thousand lights, is the place where he'll put an end to his misery. Buying a new hat should take no more than an hour or so, and Clara's errand had better take less, if she knows what's good for her. Straight in, get what's wanted, then straight out, that's how it'll be. Back home by midday.

William Rackham's view of the enormous glass-fronted Billington & Joy emporium, unobstructed by the crowds through which he had to usher Agnes last time he was here, is panoramic. Dozens of display windows, huge by comparison with most shops' humble panes, proclaim the store's grand scale and modernity. Behind each of the windows is a showcase, offering for public admiration (the possibility of sale is not alluded to) a profusion of manufactures. These are artfully displayed against painted *trompe-l'œils* of their settings in rooms of a fashionable house. Clara is moving past the dining-room display just now, a thick pane of glass separating her from the sumptuously laid table of silverware, china and wine-filled glasses. In the painted backdrop behind the table, a hearth glows convincingly with life-like flame and, to the side, poking through a slit in a real curtain, two porcelain hands with white cuffs and a hint of black sleeve hold aloft a papier-mâché roast.

So impressive are these displays, so diverting, that William almost careers into a headlong fall. There are hooks jutting out of the wall at ankle-level, provided for the tethering of dogs, and he very nearly trips. It's just as well Clara has already entered Billington & Joy's great white doors slightly ahead of him, at his instruction. How she would adore to see him fall!

Once inside, William tries to catch sight of her, but she's already lost in the wonderland of mirrored brightness. Glass and crystal are everywhere, mirrors hung at every interval, to multiply the galaxy of chandeliered gas-light. Even what is not glass or crystal is polished as if it were; the floor shines, the lacquered counters shimmer, even the hair of the serving staff is brilliant with Macassar oil, and the sheer profusion of merchandise is a little dazzling too.

Mind you, as well as selling many elegant and indispensable things, Billington & Joy also sells magnetic brushes for curing bilious headaches in five minutes, galvanic chain-bands for imparting life-giving impulses, and glazed mugs with the Queen's face scowling out of them in bas-relief, but even these objects seem already to have the status of eccentric museum exhibits, as though showcased for public wonderment alone. The whole effect, indeed, is so suggestive of the great Crystal Palace Exhibition on which the store is modelled, that *some* visitors, in their awe, are reluctant to buy anything, lest they mar the display. The fact that no prices are attached only adds to their timorousness, for they fear to ask and discover themselves insufficiently affluent.

Therefore less is sold than might be sold – but at least not much gets stolen. To the urchins and thieves of Church Lane, Billington & Joy is Heaven – that is, not for the likes of them. They could no more hope to pass through its great white doors than through the eye of a needle.

As for breakages, the most fragile displays endure safely for months at a time, because even prosperous children are rarely seen here, and on a tight leash when they are. Also, more crucially, the evolution of ladies' fashions has meant that stylish female shoppers can move through a shop without knocking things over. Indeed, it would be fair to say that Billington & Joy, and other establishments of its kind, have expanded in celebration of the crinoline's demise. The modern woman has been streamlined to permit her to spend freely.

Once more before mounting the stairs to the hat department, William looks around the store for Clara. Though she was a dozen footsteps ahead of him at most, she has disappeared like a rodent. The only thing resembling a servant he can see is the dummy serving-maid behind the display curtain, but there's nothing to her except disembodied plaster arms that end abruptly at the elbows, mounted on metal stands.

Clara's errand, which she is to complete unsupervised while William Rackham chooses his new hat, is to procure for her mistress eighteen yards of ochre silk, plus matching trimmings, to be made into a dress when Mrs Rackham feels well enough to apply herself to the pattern and the machine. Clara likes this errand very much. In performing it, she experiences not only the thrill of saying, 'Well, my man, I'll need eighteen yards of it,' and handling all that money, but she also executes a neat swindle whereby an additional item is bought – ostensibly for her mistress. This is the beauty of working for the Rackhams: *he* pays but has no stomach to understand what he's paying for, *she* has needs but has no idea what they ought to cost, and the accounts disappear in a chasm between the two. And there's no housekeeper! That's the most convenient thing of all. There was a housekeeper once upon a time, a tubby Scotchwoman to whom Mrs Rackham attached herself, limpet-like, until it ended in tears: thereafter, a ban on the very subject.

'We can run the house perfectly well between us, can't we, Clara?'
Oh, yes, ma'am. We surely can!

Clara already decided yesterday, while discussing the purchase of the dress material with Mrs Rackham ('The prices lately, ma'am – you wouldn't believe them!') to buy herself a little something. A figure, if you must know.

Clara hates her dowdy servant's uniform fervently, and she knows only too well that for Christmas this year she'll get exactly the same gift parcel she got *last* Christmas. Every year the same insult! – seven yards of double-width black merino, two yards of linen, and a striped skirt. Just what's needed to make a new uniform – well, fancy that. Damn William Rackham and his stinginess – he deserves everything that befalls him!

All year she slaves to make her mistress beautiful, breaking her fingernails on the clasps of Mrs Rackham's corsets, simpering in feigned admiration, and now, five years on, what has she to show for it? Her own body is thickening in the middle, and grievance is etching lines in her face. She possesses nothing that would make a man look at her once, let alone twice. Nothing, that is, until now. With her heart in her mouth, she hurries back towards the corsetry department, where she'll duck behind a curtain and stuff her illicit purchase, parcel and all, into her capacious drawers.

Although it was partly for fear of such wickedness that he insisted on chaperoning Clara today, there's really nothing William can do to prevent it. All he can verify, without soiling his mind with money matters, is that Clara does indeed, as agreed, emerge from the store with one big parcel in her arms. The theft she's now committing, easily detected and mercilessly punished in stricter households than the Rackhams', will go unnoticed.

For all his chagrin at his wife's frailty, William hasn't quite grasped just how ignorant Agnes has become, with every passing month of her seclusion, of what's what in the world at large. He would never guess, for example, that she could possibly entrust the costing of eighteen yards of material to a servant. Instead, he's relieved that she's no longer having dresses made for her, because that indulgence cost him a fortune in the past – a fortune wasted, given how little of her life Agnes spends out of bed.

Luckily, Agnes seems to agree. In giving up her dressmaker for a mechanical toy, she has side-stepped social disgrace as deftly as possible, by claiming genteel boredom as her excuse. The tedium of convalescence can be whiled away so much more agreeably, she says, with a diverting (never to mention money-saving) invention like the sewing-machine. Anyway, she's a modern woman, and machines are part of the modern landscape – or so William's father keeps declaring.

She's putting on a brave face, William knows that. In her more reproachful moments, Agnes lets him know how humiliating it is to maintain a pretence of genteel boredom when anyone can see she's economising. Couldn't he make a gesture to appease his father – write a letter or something – that would make everything all right again? Then they could have a coachman at last, and she could – but No, William warns her. Rackham Senior is an unreasonable old man and, having failed to bully his first-born, he has turned his bullying on William. If Agnes feels she's suffering, can she not spare a thought for what her husband must endure!

To which Agnes responds with a forced smile, and a declaration that the silvery Singer really is an amusing novelty, and she'd best be getting back to it.

Agnes's willingness to save money on clothes pleases William well enough, but he's less pleased with having to buy his new hat from Billington & Joy and pay for it on the spot, as if it were a roasted chestnut or a shoeshine, rather than having it fitted at a prestigious hatter's and adding its cost to a yearly account. Why, the top-notch gentleman visits his hatter every few days just to have his hat ironed! How has it come to this? Penury, penury and piecemeal disgrace, for a man by rights so rich! Isn't it true that Billington & Joy stock shelves full of Rackham perfumes, soaps and cosmetics? The name Rackham is everywhere! And yet he, William Rackham, heir to the Rackham fortune, must loiter around hat stands, waiting for other men to replace hats he wishes to try on! Can't the Almighty, or the Divine Principle, or whatever is left now that Science has flushed out the stables of the universe, see there's something wrong here?

But if It does, It snubs him regardless.

At a quarter to eleven, William Rackham and Clara meet briefly outside the emporium. Clara has a large, crackling parcel clasped to her bosom, and walks more stiffly than usual. William has his new hat screwed firmly on his head, the old one now removed to that hidden store-room where the unwanted hats, umbrellas, bonnets, gloves and a thousand other orphaned things are banished. Where do they go, in the end? To Christian missions in Borneo, perhaps, or a fiery furnace. Certainly not to Church Lane, St Giles.

'It suddenly occurs to me,' says William, squinting into the servant's eyes (for he is exactly her height), 'that I have some other business to attend to. In town, I mean. So, I think it would be best if you returned alone.'

'As you wish, sir.' Clara dips her head meekly enough, but still William thinks he detects a note of sly mockery, as if she thinks he's lying. (For once, she isn't thinking that at all: she's merely savouring how convenient it will be not to have the secret package squashed against her itchy buttocks all the way home in the omnibus.)

'You won't lose that, will you?' says William, pointing at Agnes's bounty of silk.

'No, sir,' Clara assures him.

William tugs his watch out of his fob-pocket into his palm and pretends to consult it, so that he has an excuse for looking away from the irritating little minx he pays £21 a year to be his wife's closest companion.

'Well, off you go then,' he says, and 'Yes, sir,' she replies, and off she goes, mincing as if she's straining not to fart. But William doesn't notice. In fact, much later today, when he sees Clara flitting around his house with a waist she didn't possess before, he won't notice that either.

It wasn't always thus. In the past, William Rackham was very much the sort of man to notice small, even tiny, differences in dress and personal appearance. In his University prime, he was quite a dandy, with silver-handled cane and a shoulder-length mane of golden hair. In those days it was perfectly normal for him to dawdle in front of the flower vases in his own 'set' for half an hour at a time, selecting a particular flower for a particular buttonhole; he might spend even longer matching silk neckties of one colour with waistcoats of another, and his most dearly beloved trousers were dark blue with mauve checks. On one memorable occasion, he instructed his tailor to shift a waistcoat's buttonhole to discourage one troublesome button from peeping out indiscreetly behind the overcoat. 'A quarter of an inch to the right, no more, no less,' he said, and God help the fellow if it weren't done just so.

In those days, William was proud to correct faults of dress few people had the good taste to perceive in the first place. Now his shrinking fortunes make him prey to faults which anyone, even his servants, can perceive all too clearly.

Nervously, William feels above his head, to check that everything is still in place. It is, but he has good reason to worry. Only an hour ago, in a mirror, he saw a vision so shocking that he still can't erase it from his mind. For the first time since rashly whipping off his old hat in Regent Street, he was made aware of the anarchy that had broken out on his scalp.

Once upon a time William's hair was his proudest feature: all through his childhood it was soft and golden-bronze, cooed over by aunts and passing strangers. As a student at Cambridge, he wore it long, to his shoulders, brushed back without oil. He was slender then, and his flowing hair disguised the pear shape of his head. Besides, long hair stood for Shelley, Liszt, Garibaldi, Baudelaire, individualism – that sort of thing.

But if his intention, in getting those long locks cut shorter a few days ago, was to retreat into anonymity, it had all gone terribly wrong. Reflected in the looking-glass, he saw what his hair had done in defiance of the ruthless barbering; it had sprung loose from oily restraint, and risen up in outright rebellion against him. God in Heaven, how many onlookers witnessed him in this state, a clown with a ludicrous crown of tufts and crinkles! With a spasm of embarrassment, right there in Billington & Joy's hat department, William hid his fleecy halo under the nearest hat he could lay his fingers on. And that was the hat, despite many subsequent tentative choices, he finally bought.

Since then, he's combed the halo flat, and applied more oil, but has it learned its lesson? With his fingertips he touches it nervously, smoothing it under the hat-brim. His bushy sideboards prickle. 'I want it like Matthew Arnold,' he told his barber, but instead he got the Wild Man of Borneo. What has he done? He'd convinced himself (well, almost) that a modest new exterior would help him stride forwards into the final quarter of the century, but does his hair have other ideas?

As William walks in the general direction of the Thames, he keeps an eye out for an alley in which, hidden from judgemental eyes, he can run a comb through his hair again. He has offended against decent manners quite enough for one morning.

At last a suitable alley offers itself, an alley so narrow it doesn't merit a name. William slips inside it immediately. Standing there in the dimness between the filthy walls, only a few steps from Jermyn Street, he has to be careful not to tread in maggoty garbage as he chastises himself with his ivory-handled comb.

A voice behind him – an ugly, nasal sound – makes him jump.

'Are you kind, master?'

William spins around. A mousy-haired little whore, easily forty or even more, is toddling out of the gloom towards him, wrapped in what appears to be an old tablecloth. What the devil's she doing in this part of town, so close to the palaces and the best hotels?

Speechless with disgust, William retreats. Four hasty steps take him back into the sunshine. A prickle of sweat has broken out on the scalp he's just combed, and against all reason he imagines his hair springing up, popping his hat off like a cork.

Minutes later, not far short of Trafalgar Square, William Rackham passes a pastry shop. It occurs to him that he would enjoy a small treat.

Of course, what he *really* ought to do, if he wishes to dine, is make his way to the Albion or the London or the Wellington, where his old school chums are probably sitting even now, lighting up their first cigar of the day – that is, if they're not still sleeping in the arms of their mistresses. But William is in no mood to go to any of these places. At the same time he's afraid that if he eats a cake in Trafalgar Square, he might be spotted and shunned forever after by an important acquaintance.

Ah, to be a carefree student again! Was it really twelve years ago that he did all manner of outrageous things in the company of his laughing, fearless companions, without anyone ever doubting his status? Didn't he go to public houses, the working man's sort with no screens dividing the classes, and drink himself stupid, right there in amongst the toothless old women and tosspots? Didn't he buy oysters from street stalls and toss them into his mouth? Didn't he wink saucily at promenading matrons just to scandalise them? Didn't he sing bawdy songs, in a louder and fruitier baritone than any of his friends, while dancing bareheaded on the Waterloo Bridge?

Oh, my love is a thing of airs and graces,
Her chins are held to her neck with laces,
Her hair is red, likewise her nose,
From out her skirts an ill wind blows . . .

Why, he could still sing it now!

Everyone in the patisserie is all ears, ready. 'Yes, that one please,' he mouths, *sotto voce*. He'll risk it, yes he'll risk it (the cake, that is, not the bawdy song), if only out of nostalgia for his old abandoned self.

And so William takes his chocolate and cherry confection into the Square with him and nurses it, worrying. The lower half of his body is only just

beginning to respond to the suggestion made to him by the alley prostitute and, since she's by now out of sight, out of mind and out of the question, he ogles a trio of French girls scampering gleefully among the pigeons.

'*Moi aussi! Moi aussi!*' they're shrieking, for there's a photographer
nearby, pretending to be taking pictures of things other than them. They
are pretty, their dresses are pretty, they move prettily, but William can't
give them the attention they merit. Instead he broods on a glowing memory
of the photograph that was taken of him a week ago, just prior to getting
his locks cut shorter. The last photograph, in other words, of the old (the
young) William Rackham.

This photograph is already hidden away in a drawer at home, like
pornography. But the image is sharp in his mind: in it he is still a Cambridge
gallant, quite the cocky scholar, wearing the canary-yellow waistcoat which
even the current generation of swells wouldn't dare to wear. The facial
expression, too, is a relic of the past, in the sense that he no longer wears
that either; it's the one that Downing College put on his face, contrary to
the hopes of his father: good-humoured contempt for the workaday world.

The difficult part was explaining to the photographer the reason for
the outdated clothes, namely that this picture should be regarded as a . . .
(how should one put it?) a retrospective record of history, a re-capturing
of the past. (He needn't have bothered: the walls of the photographer's
foyer were crowded with slightly faded debutantes in resurrected triumphal
gowns, tubby old men squeezed into slender military uniforms, and a
variety of other resurrected dreams.)

'*Moi aussi, oh ma*man!'

Back in Trafalgar Square, a silky white girl of about nine is given
permission to pose for the man with the camera. One sprinkle of seed and
she's deluged with pigeons, just in time for the exposure. She squeals excitedly, arousing the jealousy of her companions.

'*Et moi maintenant, moi aussi!*'

Another girl clamouring for her turn, and William is already bored.
Having finished his cake, he pulls on his gloves and continues on his way
to St James's Park, gloomily asking himself *how*, if such enchanting sights
bore him so soon, will he *ever* be able to stand being the head of Rackham
Perfumeries?

What a curse that his father can't see this! The old man, grown rich
working at the same thing daily from 8 a.m. to 8 p.m. for forty years, has

lost any natural sense of the pain that monotonous drudgery might inflict on a finer soul. To Henry Calder Rackham, even the recently introduced half-day holiday on Saturdays is a shameful waste of man-hours.

Not that Henry Calder Rackham is working as hard now as in earlier years, his involvement in the company being more deskbound now. He's still fit as a horse, mind you, but, with William's marriage prospects to consider, a change was needed. A better address, a respectably sedentary routine, a few offers of assistance to members of the aristocracy experiencing a spot of pecuniary bother: without these gestures on Rackham Senior's part, his son would never have won Agnes Unwin's hand. Had the old man still been striding up and down the lavender farm in his worsted jacket and boots, there would have been no point even asking Lord Unwin if Agnes was available.

Instead, by the time of the marriage negotiations, Rackham Senior was 'keeping an eye' on his business from a very presentable house, admittedly *in* Bayswater but *very near* Kensington, and his son William was *such* a promising young man, sure to become a notable figure in . . . well, some sphere or other.

Oh, certainly it was understood that the younger Rackham would eventually take charge of Rackham Perfumeries, but his grip on the reins would no doubt be all-but-invisible, and the public would see only his other, loftier accomplishments. At the time of his courtship of Agnes, William, though long out of university, still managed to glow with the graduate's aura of infinite promise and the vivacious charm of the contentedly idle. All sham? How dare you! Even now, William keeps up to date with the latest developments in zoology, sculpture, politics, painting, archaeology, novel-writing . . . everything, really, that is discussed in the better monthly reviews. (No, he will *not* cancel any of his subscriptions – none, do you hear!)

But how can he *possibly* make his mark in any of these (William frets as he finds his favourite bench in St James's Park) when he's being virtually blackmailed into a life of tedious labour? How can he *possibly* be expected . . .

But let me rescue you from drowning in William Rackham's stream of consciousness, that stagnant pond feebly agitated by self-pity. Money is what it boils down to: how much of it, not enough of it, when will it come next, where does it go, how can it be conserved, and so on.

The bald facts are these: Rackham Senior is getting tired of running Rackham Perfumeries, damn tired. His first-born, Henry, is no use whatsoever as an heir, having devoted himself to God from a young age. A decent enough fellow and, as a frugal bachelor, not much of a bother to support – although if he really means to make his career in the Church, he's taking a powerful long time deliberating over it. But never mind: the younger boy, William, will have to do. Like Henry, he's slow to show a talent for anything, but he has expensive tastes, a stylish wife and a fair-sized household – all of which suck hard at the nipple of paternal generosity. Stern lectures having failed to have the desired effect, Rackham Senior is now attempting to hasten Rackham Junior's halting steps towards the directorship of the business by reducing William's allowance, slowly and steadily. Each month he reduces it a little more, whittling away at the style to which his son is accustomed.

Already William has been obliged to reduce the number of his servants from nine to six; trips abroad are a thing of the past; travel by cab has become, if not a luxury, then certainly no longer a matter of course. William is no longer prompt to replace worn-out or outmoded possessions; and the dream of employing a male – the true yardstick of prosperity – remains emphatically a dream.

What grieves William most is how *unnecessary* his suffering is, given the value of the family assets. If his father would only sell his company, lock, stock and barrel, the sum it raised would be so enormous that the Rackhams could live off it for generations – What was the old man working for, all these years, if not for that?

The desire to make more money when more than enough has already been made disgusts William, a socialist by inclination. Besides, were Rackham Senior to sell up and invest the proceeds, the money would be self-replenishing; it might even last forever, and come, in time, to be regarded as 'old money'. And if it's sentimental attachment to the business that prevents the old man from selling, why oh why must it be William who accepts the burden of leadership? Why can't some capable trustworthy fellow be appointed from the ranks of Rackham Perfumeries itself?

In his grief, William resorts to a political philosophy of his own invention, a scheme he hopes might one day be imposed on English society. (Rackhamism, history might call it.) It is a theory he's toyed with for a decade or more, though he's sharpened it recently; it involves the abolition of what he terms 'unjustifiable capital', to be replaced with what he terms 'equity of fortune'. This means that as soon as a man has made a large enough fortune to support, perpetually, his household (defined as a family of up to ten persons, with no more than ten servants), he is banned from stockpiling any more. Speculative investments in Argentinian gold-mines and the like would be prohibited; instead, investment in safe and solid concerns would be overseen by Government, to ensure that the return, although unspectacular, was perennial. Any excess income flowing to the wealthiest men would be re-routed into the public coffers for distribution among society's unfortunates – the destitute and homeless.

A revolutionary proposal, he's well aware of that, and no doubt horri-fying to many, for it would erode the present distinctions between the classes; there would no longer be an aristocracy in the sense nowadays understood. Which, in William's view, would be a damn good thing, as he's tired of being reminded that Downing College was hardly Corpus Christi, and that he was lucky to get in at all.

So there you have it: the thoughts (somewhat pruned of repetition) of William Rackham as he sits on his bench in St James's Park. If you are bored beyond endurance, I can offer only my promise that there will be fucking in the very near future, not to mention madness, abduction, and violent death.

In the meantime, Rackham is jogged violently from his brooding by the sound of his own name.

'Bill!'

'Great God yes: Bill!'

William looks up, head still full of sludge, so that he can only stare dumbly at the sudden apparition of his two best friends, his inseparable Cambridge cronies, Bodley and Ashwell.

'Won't be long now, Bill,' cries Bodley, 'before it's time to celebrate!'

'Celebrate what?' says William.

'Everything, Bill! The whole blessed Bacchanalia of Christmas! Miraculous offspring popping out of virgins into mangers! Steaming mounds of pudding! Gallons of port! And before you know it, another year put to bed!'

'1874 well-poked and snoring,' grins Ashwell, 'with a juicy young 1875 trembling in the doorway, waiting to be treated likewise.'

(They are very similar, he and Bodley, in their ageless 'old boys' appearance. Immaculately dressed, excitable and listless all at once, slick-faced, and wearing hats superior to any sold by Billington & Joy. They are in fact *so* similar that William has been known, in moments of extreme drunkenness, to address them as Bashley and Oddwell. But Ashwell is distinguishable from Bodley by sparser side-whiskers, slightly less florid cheeks, and a smaller paunch.)

'Haven't seen you in *aeons*, Bill. What have you been up to? Apart from cutting all your hair off?'

Bodley and Ashwell sit heavily on the bench next to William, then perch forward, their chins and folded hands resting on the knobs of their walking sticks, grotesquely attentive. They are like architectural gargoyles carved for the same tower.

'Agnes has been bad,' Rackham replies, 'and there's that cursed business to take over.'

There, it's said. Bodley and Ashwell are trying to seduce him into frivolity: they may as well know he's not in the mood. Or at least that they must seduce him harder.

'Be careful the business doesn't take *you* over,' cautions Ashwell. 'You'd be such a bore gassing on about . . . oh, I don't know . . . crop yield.'

'No fear,' says William, fearing.

'Far better to make a trembling young beauty *yield* to the *crop*,' snarls Bodley theatrically, then looks to Rackham and Ashwell for praise.

'That's utterly feeble, Bodley,' says Ashwell.

'Maybe so,' sniffs Bodley. 'But you've paid pounds for worse.'

'At any rate, Bill,' pursues Ashwell, '– pornography aside – you mustn't let Agnes keep you out of the great stream of Life this way. The way you're worrying so much over a mere woman . . . it's dangerous. That way lies . . . uh . . . what's the word I'm looking for, Bodley?'

'Love, Ashwell. Never touch the stuff myself.'

A wan smile twitches on William's face. Stroke on, old friends, stroke on!

'Seriously, Bill, you mustn't let this problem with Agnes turn into a family curse. You know, like in those frightful old-fashioned novels, with the distracted female leaping out of cupboards. You have to realise you're not the only man in this position: there are *hordes* of mad wives about — half of London's females are positively *raving*. God damn it, Bill: you're a free man! There's no sense locking yourself up, like an old badger.'

'London out of Season is enough of a bore as it is,' chips in Ashwell. 'Best to waste it in style.'

'And how,' asks William, 'have the two of you been wasting it?'

'Oh, we've been hard at work,' enthuses Ashwell, 'on a simply superb new book — mostly *my* labour,' (here Bodley scoffs loudly) 'with Bodley polishing up the prose a bit — called *The Efficacy of Prayer*.'

'Awful lot of work involved, you know. We've been quizzing hordes of devout believers, getting them to tell us honestly if they ever got anything they prayed for.'

'By that we don't mean vague nonsense like "courage" or "comfort"; we mean actual *results*, like a new house, mother's deafness cured, assailant hit by bolt of lightning, et cetera.'

'We've been terrifically thorough, if I do say so myself. As well as hundreds of *individual* cases, we also examine the *general, formulaic* prayers that thousands of people have uttered every night for years. You know the sort of thing: delivery from evil, peace on Earth, the conversion of the Jews and so on. The clear conclusion is that sheer weight of numbers and perseverance don't get you anywhere either.'

'When we've chalked it all up, we're going to talk to some of the top clergy — or at least solicit correspondence from them — and get their view. We want to make it clear to everyone that this book is a disinterested, scientific study, quite open to comment or criticism from its . . . ah . . . victims.'

'We mean to hit Christ for six,' interjects Bodley, driving his cane into the wet earth.

'We've had some delightful finds,' says Ashwell. 'Superbly mad people. We talked to a clergyman in Bath (wonderful to see the place again, capital beer there) and he told us he's been praying for the local public house to burn down.'

'"Or otherwise perish".'

'Said he supposed God was deciding on the right time.'

'Completely confident of eventual success.'

'Three years he's been praying for this — nightly!'

Both men thump their canes on the ground in sarcastic ecstasy.

'Do you think,' says William, 'there's the slightest chance you'll find a publisher?' He's in better spirits now, almost seduced, yet feels compelled to mention the spoilsport realities of the world as it is. Bodley and Ashwell merely grin at each other knowingly.

'Oh yes. Sure to. There's a simply thundering call nowadays for books that destroy the fabric of our society.'

'That goes for novels, too,' says Ashwell, winking pointedly at William. 'Do keep that in mind if you still mean to produce anything in that field.'

'But honestly Bill – you really must show yourself more often. We haven't seen you at any of the old haunts for ages.'

'Got to preserve your bad name, you know.'

'Got to keep your hand in.'

'Mustn't be foiled by the march of time.'

'What do you mean?' says the startled William. His traumatic haircut has exposed strands of premature grey amongst the gold, so he's sensitive to any mention of advancing age.

'Pubescent *girls*, William. Time catches up with them. They don't stay ripe for ever, you know. Half a year makes all the difference. Indeed, you've already missed *some* girls that have passed into legend, Bill – *legend*.'

'To give just one example: Lucy Fitzroy.'

'Oh yes – Lord Almighty yes.'

The two men leap up from the bench as if on a pre-agreed signal.

'Lucy Fitzroy,' begins Ashwell, in the manner of a music-hall recital, 'was a new girl at Madame Georgina's in the Finchley Road, where there is chastisement a'plenty.' By way of illustration Ashwell brings his cane down hard on his calf several times. '*Down*, flesh! *Up*, flesh! *Down!*'

'Steady on, Ashwell.' Bodley lays a cautioning hand on his friend's arm. 'Remember, only a lord can make a limp look distinguished.'

'Well, as you may know, Bodley and I occasionally take a peek in Madame Georgina's to see what calibre of girl is wielding the whips. And late last year we came upon an absolute fizgig of a girl, introduced to us by the madam as Lucy Fitzroy, illegitimate daughter of Lord Fitzroy, with horse-riding consequently in her blood.'

'Well no doubt it's all bosh, but the *girl* seemed convinced of it! Fourteen years old, smooth and firm as a babe, with the most *glorious* pride. She had on all the riding gear, and she wore it so well – she'd come down the stairs, *sideways*, like this, one boot, then the other, as though she were *dismounting* from the steps. She'd be clutching a *very* short and quite *vicious* riding crop, and on her cheeks you could see those little spots of colour burning – genuine, I'll swear. And Madame Georgina told us that whenever a man was sent up to her, the girl would stand on the landing and wait there just so, and when the poor fool got close enough, *ssshwish!* she'd slash him across the cheek with the crop, and then point with it towards the bed and say—'

'Good God!' exclaims Ashwell, having chanced to look in the direction of Bodley's pointing stick. 'God almighty! Who would you say *that* is?' He shades his eyes with one hand and peers intently at the far end of St James's Park. Bodley falls into position at his side, peering likewise.

'It's Henry,' he proclaims delightedly.

'Yes, yes it is – and Mrs Fox!'

'Of course.'

The two men turn to face William once more and bow gravely.

'You must excuse us, Bill.'

'Yes, we wish to go and torment Henry.'

'You have my blessing,' says William, with a smirk.

'He avoids us, you know – avoids us like the plague, ever since . . . uh . . . how shall we put it . . . ?'

'Ever since his own personal angel alighted at the end of his bed.'

'Quite. Anyway, we must do our very best to catch him before he makes a run for it.'

'Oh, he couldn't, not with Mrs Fox in tow: she'd drop dead! They haven't a chance, I tell you.'

'Cheers, Willy.'

And with that they are off, pursuing their victims at high speed. Indeed, they run at such a furious pace, despite their formal dress, that they must pump their arms for balance, quite unconcerned about the impression they must be making on anyone watching – in fact, they exaggerate their ridiculous chuff-chuffing gait for their own amusement. Behind them they leave two long, wet, dark-green trails in the grass, and a rather dazed William Rackham.

It's always been very much Bodley and Ashwell's style to swoop in and out of conversations, and if one wishes to feel comfortable in their company, one must swoop alongside them. As William watches them dashing across the park, the burden of despondency descends on his shoulders once more. He has lost, through lack of use, his own nerve and agility for this sort of banter, this brand of exhibitionism. Could he even run as fast as his friends are running? It's as if he's watching his own body fleeing across the park, a younger self, speeding away.

Could he perhaps leap up and follow? No, it's too late. There's no catching up now. They are dark, fleet figures on a bright horizon. William slumps back on the bench, and his thoughts, briefly stirred up by Bodley and Ashwell, settle into their former stagnancy.

What grieves him most is how *unnecessary* his suffering is, given the value of the family assets. If his father would only sell the company . . .

But you have heard all this before. Your best course is to leave William to himself for ten minutes or so. In that time, while his brain forms a crust of reflective algae, the rest of him will feel the influence of all he's been plied with this morning: the alley whore's proposition, the sight of the French girls in Trafalgar Square, Bodley and Ashwell's talk of brothels, their own teasing courtship of him followed by their desertion, and (just in the last hour or so) the arrival in St James's Park of a number of beautiful young ladies.

A potent brew, all that. Once sufficiently intoxicated, William will rise from his seat and follow his desires, follow them along the path that leads, ultimately, to Sugar.

FOUR

aiting for William to stir, there's no need for you to gaze unblinking into his lap until he does. Instead, why not look at some of the objects of his desire? They've come to St James's Park to be looked at, after all.

If you've any love for fashion, this year is not a bad one for you to be here. History indulges strange whims in the way it dresses its women: sometimes it uses the swan as its model, sometimes, perversely, the turkey. This year, the uncommonly elegant styles of women's clothing and coiffure which had their inception in the early Seventies have become ubiquitous – at least among those who can afford them. They will endure until William Rackham is an old, old man, by which time he'll be too tired of beauty to care much about seeing it fade.

The ladies swanning through St James's Park this sunny November midday will not be required to change much between now and the end of their century. They are suitable for immediate use in the paintings of Tissot, the sensation of the Seventies, but they could still pass muster for Munch twenty years later (though he might wish to make a few adjustments). Only a world war will finally destroy them.

It's not just the clothes and the hairstyle that define this look. It's an air, a bearing, an expression of secretive intelligence, of foreign *hauteur* and enigmatic melancholy. Even in these bright early days of the style, there is something a little eerie about the women gliding dryad-like across these dewy lawns in their autumnal dresses, as if they're invoking the *fin de siècle* to come prematurely. The image of the lovely demon, the demi-ghost from beyond the grave, is already being cultivated here – despite the fact that most of these women are daft social butterflies with not one demonic thought in their heads. The haunted aura they radiate is merely the effect of tight corsets. Too constrained to inhale enough oxygen, they're ethereal only in the sense that they might as well be gasping the ether of Everest.

To be frank, some of these women were more at home in crinolines. Marooned in the centre of those wire cages, their need to be treated as pampered infants was at least clear, whereas their current affectation of *la ligne* and the Continental confidence that goes with it hints at a sensuality they do not possess.

Morally it's an odd period, both for the observed and the observer: fashion has engineered the reappearance of the body, while morality still insists upon perfect ignorance of it. The cuirass bodice hugs tight to the bosom and the belly, the front of the skirt clings to the pelvis and hangs straight down, so that a strong gust of wind is enough to reveal the presence of legs, and the bustle at the back amplifies the hidden rump. Yet no righteous man must dare to think of the flesh, and no righteous woman must be aware of having it. If an exuberant barbarian from a savage fringe of the Empire were to stray into St James's Park now and compliment one of these ladies on the delicious-looking contours of her flesh, her response would most likely be neither delight nor disdain, but instant loss of consciousness.

Even without recourse to feral colonials, a dead faint is not very difficult to provoke in a modern female: pitilessly tapering bodices, on any woman not naturally thin, present challenges above and beyond the call of beauty. And it must be said that a good few of the wraith-like ladies gliding across St James's Park got out of bed this morning as plump as the belles of the previous generation, but then exchanged their roomy nightgowns for a gruelling session with the lady's-maid. Even if (as is now becoming more common) there are no actual laces to be pulled, there are bound to be leather panels to strap and metal hooks to clasp, choking their wearer's breath, irreparably deforming her rib-cage, and giving her a red nose which must be frequently powdered. Even walking requires more skill than before, on the higher heels of the calf-length boots now fashionable.

Yet they *are* beautiful, these tubby English girls made willowy and slim, and why shouldn't they be? It's only fair they should take other people's breath away, suffering such constriction of their own.

And William — what is he up to? All these attractively clothed women circling his park bench (albeit at a distance) — have they made him ripe and ready for a naked one? Nearly.

He's been mulling over his financial humiliation so long now that he's been inspired to compose a metaphor for it: he imagines himself as a restless beast, pacing the confines of a cage wrought in sterling silver '£' symbols, all intertwining like so: £££££££££££££££££££££££. Ah, if only he could spring out!

Another young lady glides past from behind him, very close to his bench this time. Her shoulder-blades protrude from her satin thorax, her hourglass waist sways almost imperceptibly, her horse-hair bustle shakes gently to the rhythm of her walk. William's financial impotence shifts its focus, ceasing to be a challenge to his wits and becoming instead a challenge to his sex. Before the young lady in satin has trod twenty more paces, William is already convinced that something important — something *essential* — would be proved about Life if he could only have his way with a woman.

And so the passing strollers in St James's Park are transformed unwittingly into sirens, and each glowing body becomes suggestive of its social shadow, the prostitute. And to a blind little penis, swaddled in trousers, there is no difference between a whore and a lady, except that the whore is available, with no angry champions to duel with, no law on her side, no witnesses, no complaints. Therefore, when William Rackham finds himself possessed of an erection, his immediate impulse is to take it directly to the nearest whore.

Perversely, though, he's too proud of his newly conceived metaphor of financial entrapment — the cage of wrought-iron sterling symbols — to let it go so easily. There's something grand, ennobling even, about the hopelessness of his plight, the tragic unfairness of it. Bound and frustrated, he can be King Lear; granted a climax, he may find himself the Fool. And so William's mind conjures up ever more fearsome pictures of his cage, l£rg£r and l£rg£r and l£rg£r. And, in response, his lust suggests ever more vivid fantasies of sexual conquest and revenge. By turns, he rapes the world into submission, and cowers under its boot in piteous despair — each time more ferocious, each time more fawning.

At last he springs up from his seat, completely sure that to quell his turmoil nothing less will do — *nothing* less, do you hear? — than the utter subjugation of two very young whores simultaneously. What's more, he has a damn good idea of where he might find two girls ideally suited to the purpose. He'll go there at once, and the devil take the hindmost! (Only a manner of speaking, you understand.)

Inconveniently, the strategic redistribution of blood among William's bodily organs has no effect whatsoever on the rotation of the Earth, and he finds, when he returns to the centre of town, that it's lunch-time in London, and the clerks are out in force. William and his manhood are rudely jostled by a hungry crowd, a dark sea of functionaries, scribes and other nobodies, threatening to carry him along if he tries to swim against them. So he stands close to a wall and watches, hoping the sea will part for him soon.

Au contraire. The building against which he presses, distinguished only by the brass letters COMPTON, HESPERUS & DILL, suddenly throws open its doors and yet another efflux of clerks pushes him aside.

This is the last straw: dismissing his last pang of conscience, William raises his hand above the crowd and hails a cab. What does it matter now that he denied himself cab travel earlier this morning? He'll be a rich man soon enough, and all this fretting over petty expenses will be nothing more than a sordid memory.

'Drury Lane,' he commands, as he mounts the step of a swaying hansom. He slams the cabin door shut behind him, bumping his new hat on the low ceiling, and the abrupt jog of the horse throws him back in his seat.

No matter. He's on his way to Drury Lane, where (Bodley and Ashwell never cease reminding him) good cheap brothels abound. Well, cheap ones at least. Bodley and Ashwell enjoy 'slumming', not because they're short of money, but because it amuses them to pass from the cheapest to the most expensive whores in quick succession.

'Vintage wine and alehouse beer' is how Bodley likes to put it. 'In the pursuit of pleasure, both have their place.'

On this excursion to Drury Lane, William is only interested in the 'alehouse beer' class of girl — which is just as well, as that's all he can afford. The two particular girls he has in mind . . . well, to be honest he's never actually met them, but he remembers reading about them in *More Spreeds in London — Hints for Men About Town, with advice for greenhorns.* It seems an awfully long time since he consulted this handbook regularly (is he even sure of its current whereabouts? the bottom drawer of his study desk?) but he does have a distinct recollection of two very 'new' girls, included in the guide by virtue of their tender age.

'You know, it boggles the mind,' Ashwell has mused more than once. 'All those thousands of bodies on offer, and still it's a hellish job to find a truly succulent young one.'

'All the *really* young ones are dirt poor, that's the problem.' (Bodley's response.) 'By the time they come to bud, they've already had scabies, their front teeth are missing, their hair's got crusts in it . . . But if you want a little alabaster Aphrodite, you have to wait for her to become a fallen woman first.'

'It's a damn shame. Still, hope springs eternal. I've just read, in the latest *More Sprees*, about two girls in Drury Lane . . .'

William strains to recall the girls' names or that of their madam – tries to picture the page of text in the handbook – but finds nothing. Only the number of the house – engraved on his brain by the simple mnemonic of it comprising the day and month of his birth.

The brothel opens to William Rackham virtually as soon as he pulls the cord. Its receiving room is dim, and the madam old. She sits dwarf-like on a sofa, all in purple, her baroquely wrinkled hands clasped in her lap. William has not the faintest recollection of what she or any of her stable might be called, so he mentions *More Sprees in London* and asks for 'the two girls – the pair'.

The old woman's red eyes, which seem to swim in a honeyish liquid too thick for tears, fix William in a stare of sympathetic befuddlement. She smiles, exposing string-of-pearl teeth, but her powdered brow is frowning. She forms her hands into a steeple, lightly tapping her nose with it. A fat grey cat ventures out from behind the sofa, sees William, retreats.

Then suddenly the old woman unclasps her hands and holds her palms aloft excitedly, as if an answer is dropping, out of the heavens or at least through the ceiling, into each.

'Ah! The two girls!' she cries. 'The *twins*!'

William nods. He can't recall them being twins at the time of their inclusion in *More Sprees in London*; no doubt the first bloom of their youth has passed and further enticement has become necessary. The madam shuts her eyes in satisfaction, and her raw bacon eyelids glisten as she smiles.

'Claire and Alice, sir. I should have known – a man such as you, sir –

you would want my best girls – my most very special.' Her accent and phrasing are a bit on the foreign side, making it difficult to guess how well or ill bred she might be. 'I will see that they are prepared to receive you.'

She rises, hardly any taller for it, many yards of dark silk tumbling off the sofa with her, and makes as if to escort him directly to the stairs. She pauses theatrically, however, and casts her gaze at the floor, as if embarrassed to speak the words: 'Perhaps, sir, to save troubling you afterwards . . . ?" And she looks up at him once more, her eyes heavy with translucent fluid.

'Of course,' says William, and stares into her hideous smile for a full five seconds before prompting her. 'And . . . what *is* the price, madam?'

'Ah, yes, forgive me. Ten shillings, if you please.'

She bows as William hands her the coins, then tugs at one of three slender ropes which dangle beside the banister.

'A few moments, sir, is all they will need. Do make yourself easy in one of the *chaises-longues* – and be free to smoke.'

So it's *that* kind of brothel, thinks William Rackham, but it's too late now to withdraw, and in any case he wants satisfaction.

For no other reason than to rest his gaze on a cigar rather than on the madam's ugly face, William sits on a *chaise* and smokes while he waits for his predecessor to finish. No doubt there's another staircase at the back of the house, through which this fellow will leave, and then the dirty sheets will be changed, and then . . . William sucks sourly on his cigar, as if he has just bought a ticket for an inferior conjuring performance at which the magician's sleeves sag with devices and there's a stench of rabbits under the floorboards.

But while William broods, let me tell you about Claire and Alice. They are brothel girls in the truest and lowest sense: that is, they arrived in London as innocents and were lured into their fallen state by a madam who, resorting to the old stratagem, met them at the railway station and offered them a night's lodgings in the fearsome new metropolis, then robbed them of their money and clothing. Ruined and helpless, they were then installed in the house, along with several other girls similarly duped or else bought from parents or guardians. In return for snug new clothes and two meals a day, they've worked here ever since, guarded at the back-stair by a spoony-man and at the front by the madam, unable even to guess how much or little they are hired for.

Finally the time arrives for William Rackham to be shown upstairs. Claire and Alice's room, when he enters it, is small and square, draped all around with long red curtains puddling down onto dingy skirting boards. The lone window is shrouded by one of these drapes, so that the claustral little chamber is lit less by the sun than by candles, and is jaundice-tinged and overwarm. Flattened velvet cushions are strewn on the threadbare Persian carpet, and above the large rococo bed is displayed, in an ornate frame, a photograph of a naked woman dancing around an indoor maypole. Claire and Alice, dressed in plain white chemises, are sitting together on the bed, pretty little hands folded in their laps.

''Ow d'you do, sir,' they welcome him in unison.

But, unison or not, it's obvious they aren't twins. They aren't even, pedantically speaking, girls – as William verifies when he removes Alice's chemise. The undersides of her breasts no longer stand out from her midriff, but lie flat against it. The pink of her hairless vulva is tinged with tell-tale shadow, and her lips are no longer a rosebud, but a full-blown rose.

Worse than this, she moves like any other mediocre whore. A bit of puppyish curiosity would be delightful, but this practised submission, like a tame Labrador rolling over, is merely dispiriting. God damn it! Is there *never* such a thing as exceptional value for money? Does it always have to be a king's ransom that buys promise fulfilled? Is it the sole purpose of the modern world to disappoint ideals and breed cynicism?

As Alice begins to wrap her body around him in the waxy heat, William wishes suddenly to flee the house, never mind the money wasted. For a moment he pulls back, squirming to be free, but he cannot persuade his erection to accompany him. So, making the best of things, he pulls Claire's chemise off as well, and finds her to be younger than Alice, with cone-shaped breasts and subtle, welt-like nipples of hyacinth-pink.

Encouraged by this, William throws himself into the business at hand with a passion, a passion to exorcise his griefs and frustrations. There is an answer to be found, a solution to his suffering, if he can only break through the obstacles of the flesh. With such furious vehemence does he fuck that he loses, at times, all awareness of what he's doing, the way a frenzied fighter may become blind to his opponents. Yet these are, for him, the best moments.

Aside from such transcendent lapses, however, he is not to be pleased. The girls are no good: they don't move as he wishes, they are the wrong shape, the wrong size, the wrong consistency, they collapse under him when he requires them to bear his weight, they totter when he requires them to stand firm, they wince and flinch and all the while keep so damnably silent. Too much of the time, William feels himself to be alone in the room with his own breathing, alone with the faintly absurd sound of his foot sliding a cushion along a carpet, the dull musical twang of the bed-springs, the comical *ugh-ugh* of his own allergic cough.

The blame he lays entirely on Claire and Alice. Hasn't he had the most sublime, the most joyous times with prostitutes in the past? Especially in Paris. Ah, Paris! Now *there* was a breed of girl that knew how to please a man! As William presses down heavily on these glum English girls, themselves lying crushed breast to breast, he can't help reminiscing. In particular, about one occasion when he ventured out on his own to the Rue St Aquine, leaving Bodley, Ashwell and the others still drinking at The Cul-de-Sac. By some strange chance, God knows how (he was squiffed to the gills) he ended up in a room full of *exceptionally* friendly whores. (Is there anything more delightful than the laughter of tipsy young women?) Anyway, inspired by their boisterous vulgarity, William invented a hilarious erotic game. The girls were to squat in a circle close around him, legs spread apart, and he would toss coins, gently and carefully aimed, at their slits. The rule was that if the coin lodged, the girl was allowed to keep it.

The long years since that extraordinary night haven't dimmed its sights and sounds: even now he can hear the ecstatic giggles and the cries all around him of '*Ici, monsieur! Ici!*' Ah! to think that those girls are probably lying idle at the Rue St Aquine at this very moment, while *he* toils here, hundreds of miles away from them, straining to extract an ounce of enthusiasm from these dull English pretenders.

'Do try to do your best for me,' he urges Claire and Alice as he prises apart their squashed bodies, noticing that each of their clammy torsos bears the flushed imprints of the ribs of the other. He turns them over, over and over, as if hoping to find an orifice not yet detected by previous customers. His lust has become almost somnambulistic; he demands ever greater liberties, in a voice he hardly recognises as his own, and the girls obey like figments of his own sluggish dream.

He hardly knows what he's saying, then, when at last he takes Alice by the wrists and gives her the command which will transform many lives.

The girl shakes her head.

'I don't do that, sir. I'm sorry.'

William releases her wrists, one by one. With the first hand freed, Alice tucks a lock of her hair nervously behind one ear. William flips it back onto her cheek.

'What do you mean, you don't do that?' He looks from Alice to Claire who, sensing that the ordeal is over, is surreptitiously pulling her night-dress up over her shoulders.

'Me neiver, sir.'

William rests his hands on his naked knees, speechlessly outraged. His blood, redistributed from below, flushes his cheeks and neck.

'We would if we could, sir,' says Alice, taking up her position next to Claire on the edge of the bed once more. 'But we can't.'

William reaches for his trousers, as if in a dream.

'It seems odd,' he says, 'to draw the line at *that* rather than at . . . well, something else.'

'I'm sorry, sir,' replies the elder (for so she obviously is), 'And so is Claire, I'm sure. You know it ain't nuffink to do wif *you*, sir. Troof is, we wouldn't do it for nobody, sir. Troof is, it would put us off, sir, put us off altogevver, and then we'd not be wurf a farvin' to you, sir.'

'Oh, but,' pursues William, catching sight of a glimmer of hope, 'I wouldn't blame you for that, oh no. And it wouldn't matter, you see. You'd not have to do anything more after that, just that one thing, and with your eyes closed if you liked.'

The girls' faces are by now ugly with embarrassment.

'Please, sir,' begs Alice, 'don't press on us; we can't do it and there it is, and we are very sorry to 'ave offended you. All I can do for you, sir, is give you a name – the name of a person as'd do what you ask.'

William, huffily dressing, and preoccupied with locating a lost garter, is not sure he has heard correctly.

'*What* did you say?'

'I can tell you 'oo'll do it for you, sir.'

'Oh yes?' He sits taut, ready to vent his fury on yet more whore-bluff. 'Some poxy hag in Bishopsgate?'

Alice seems genuinely abashed.

'Oh *no*, sir! A very '*igh*-class girl in *ever* such a good 'ouse – in Silver Street, sir, just off The Stretch. Mrs Castaway is the madam there – and it's said this girl is the best girl in the 'ouse. She's the madam's own daughter, sir, and 'er name is Sugar.'

William is by now fully dressed and self-possessed: he might be a charity worker or a parson come to inspire them to seek a better life.

'If . . . If this girl is so high-class,' he reasons, 'why would she be prepared to . . . do such a thing?'

'Ain't *nuffink* Sugar won't do, sir. *Nuffink.* It's common knowledge, sir, that special tastes as can't be satisfied by the ordinary girl, Sugar will satisfy.'

William voices a grunt of sulky mistrust, but in truth he's struck by the name.

'Well,' he smiles wearily. 'I'm sure I'm most grateful for your advice.'

'Oh, I 'ope you may be, sir,' responds Alice.

Standing alone in the stinking alley behind the brothel, William clenches his fists. It's not Claire and Alice he's angry with; they're already forgiven and half-forgotten, shut away like unwanted lumber in a dark attic to which he will never return. But his frustration remains.

I must not be denied, he says aloud – well, almost. The words are loud in his mind, and on the tip of his tongue, withheld only for fear that to proclaim 'I must not be denied!' in an alleyway off Drury Lane might attract mockery from uncouth passers-by.

It's blindingly clear to William that he must proceed directly to Silver Street and ask for Sugar. Nothing could be simpler. *He* is in town; *she* is in town: now is the time. There isn't even any need to squander money on a cab; he'll take the omnibus along Oxford Street, and then another down Regent Street, and he'll be almost there!

Rackham strides forth, hurries to New Oxford Street and, as if the universe is impressed – no, *cowed* – by the sheer strength of his resolve, an omnibus turns up almost instantaneously, allowing him to board without breaking his pace.

Mrs Castaway. Sugar. Give me Sugar and no excuses.

Once William is actually seated in the omnibus, however, and the solid street outside the soot-speckled windows becomes a moving panorama, his resolve begins to weaken. For a start, paying the fare reminds him of how much money he has already spent on his new hat (not to mention the lesser expense of Alice and . . . whatever the other one's name was). Who can say how much this girl Sugar will cost? The streets around Golden Square contain a mixed assortment of houses, some grand, some shabby. *What if this girl demands more than he has on his person?*

William stares across at the passengers opposite him – dozing old fossils and overdressed matrons – and notes how vividly real they are compared to the blurry world beyond the window-glass. Has he really any choice but to stay in his seat, a passenger among other passengers, until the omnibus horses have pulled him all the way back to Notting Hill?

And shouldn't he be getting home, anyway? The responsibilities awaiting him there are most urgent – so much more deserving of his attention than this secret ember of lust glowing inside him. This Sugar, whoever or whatever she may be, can only make him poorer, whereas a few hours spent in duteous study could well rescue him from ruin.

William is staring sightlessly ahead of him, deep in thought; suddenly he notices a prune-faced dowager staring back at him. *What an ill-mannered creature you are!* she seems to be thinking. Chastised, he lowers his head, and stays stoically seated, even as the omnibus rattles past Regent Circus. He's had his extravagance for the day; he has made his stand. Now he sinks back, closes his eyes, and dozes for the remainder of the journey.

'Chepstow Villas cor-*nerrr!*' warbles the conductor. William jolts back to life. The world has turned greener; the buildings have thinned. It's sleepy Notting Hill in the sunny glow of afternoon. London is gone.

Blinking and groggy, William dismounts the omnibus right behind a lady he doesn't know. Indeed, he almost blunders into her, trapped in the wake of her black and terracotta striped skirts. In better circumstances, he might find her enticing, but she's too close to home and he is still hankering after Sugar.

'Forgive me, madam,' he says as he circles free of her snail's-pace.

She glares at him as if he has treated her shabbily, but William feels a second apology would be excessive. There ought to be a limit to how much allowance men make for the delicate speed of women.

Forging ahead, William hurries past the long ornate fence of the park to which he is one of the private key-holders. Where that key might be, he has forgotten; he's in the habit nowadays of ignoring the pale flowers, evergreens and marble fountains that twinkle so fetchingly behind the wrought-iron bars. Oh, granted, in the beginning, when Agnes was still well, he did occasionally take the air with her in this park, to prove to her how nice a place Notting Hill could be despite everything, but now . . .

He slows his pace, for the handsome house directly up ahead is the Rackham house – his own house, so to speak – in which lie waiting for him his problematical wife, his ungrateful servants, and a stack of unreadable business papers on which (outrageously!) his entire future depends. He draws a deep breath and approaches.

But already there is an obstacle, before he's even set foot on his own grounds. Just outside the front gate sits a dog – a fairly small dog, admittedly – at fully erect attention, as if volunteering its services as gatekeeper. It wags its tail and nods its head as William steps near. It's a mongrel, of course. All the proper dogs are indoors.

'Get away,' growls William, but the dog doesn't budge.

'Get *away*,' William growls again, but the animal is stubborn, or confused, or stupid. Who knows what goes on in a dog's brain? (Well, actually, William did publish a monograph, during his time at Cambridge, called *Canines and the Canaille: The Differences Explained*. But Bodley wrote some of it.) William pulls the gate open and hastens through, in the process shoving the dog's body aside with the great hinged grille.

Locked out, the animal takes offence at the rebuff. It rears up against the gate, paws scratching at the wrought-iron curlicues, and barks clamorously as William walks up the steep path towards his own front door.

These last few steps of his homeward journey tire him more than all the rest. The lawn on either side of the path hasn't been cut for months. His private carriage-way leads to a coach-house with no coach and a stable with no horses, and serves only to remind him of the Sisyphean challenge ahead.

And all the while, the dog barks tirelessly on.

It should never be necessary to ring a doorbell more than once – especially if it's one's own. Principles like that should damn well be tattooed on servants' thumbs, to help them remember. Nevertheless, William's arm is raised for his third tug on the bell-pull when Letty's face finally appears in the doorway.

'Good arfernoon Mr Rackham,' she beams.

He brushes past her, resisting the urge to dress her down in case she protests it's the heavy weight of her new duties that's to blame. (Not that such a complaint could ever come from Letty, and William would do well to accept her ovine placidity for what it is, rather than mistaking it for Clara's grudging acquiescence.)

As Rackham clumps towards the stairs, Letty's smile falters; she has disappointed her master yet again. He was so full of praise for her when Tilly was dismissed, but ever since then . . . She bites her lip, and shuts the front door as gently as she can.

In truth, there's nothing she can do to make William happy. Her new status has transformed her from a human being, albeit of a lower order, to a walking, breathing sore point. There's simply no escaping the fact that before Tilly was dismissed, he had an upstairs *and* a downstairs housemaid, and now he has only one. This, Rackham knows, is basic social arithmetic that a child could understand – so what, then, must he make of Letty's cheerful simper? She's either stupider than a child, or else she's faking it.

Every time William speaks to her, he recalls his words of encouragement when he first told her the way things would be from now on – his insistence that she was very privileged to be 'promoted' with a pound extra on her wage, because 'that naughty Tilly' did nothing Letty can't do better alone. And, after all, isn't the Rackham house much easier to maintain nowadays, with its master rarely at home and its mistress rarely leaving her bed? (What hogwash! But Letty seemed to lap it all up and, despite his relief, how William despised her for swallowing!)

So: *that* is why William now refrains from demanding an explanation for her tardiness in answering the door.

(Are *you* curious to know, though? No, she wasn't snoozing, or gossiping, or stealing from the pantry. It's just that when a housemaid is summoned by a bell in the middle of cleaning out a fireplace, she must wash her hands, roll down her sleeves, and descend two flights of stairs, all of which can't be done in less than two minutes.)

However, our Rackham, given a moment to reflect, is not an unreasonable man. In his doleful heart, he knows very well that prompt service can only be expected in a house stuffed to the rafters with servants, each with very little to do. Letty's bearing up well, under the circumstances, and at least she always has a smile for him.

He'll probably keep her, when things improve.

In the meantime, he's growing almost accustomed to slow service. Lately he has even taken it upon himself to perform such menial tasks as drawing a curtain, opening a window, or adding wood to a fire. In a tight spot, everyone must do his bit.

He's adding more wood to the fire now, in his smoking-room. Clara has been summoned, but she too is taking some time to arrive, and he's impatient to be warmer. So, he's thrown a faggot on the flames. It's not so difficult, really. In fact, it's *so* easy he wonders why the damn servants don't do it a damn sight more often.

When Clara finally turns up, she finds him installed in his favourite armchair, pushing his head wearily against the antimacassar, calming his nerves with a cigar. The girl's hands are demurely folded in front of her new twenty-inch waist, and she looks very much as if she has something to hide.

'Yes sir?' Her tone is cool and a little defiant. She has already rehearsed an ingenious response to the challenge, 'Where did you get that waist?' – a rather far-fetched tale involving a non-existent niece.

Instead, William merely enquires, 'How has Mrs Rackham been?' and looks away.

Clara clasps her hands behind her back, like a schoolchild about to recite a poem.

'Nothing out of the usual, sir. She has read a book. She has read a journal. She has done some embroidery. She has asked once for a cup of cocoa. Otherwise she is in perfect health.'

'Perfect health.' William raises his eyebrows in the general direction of the not sufficiently dusted bookcases. No wonder Agnes claims she trusts Clara with her life. The two of them are in clammy female collusion, cooking up the notion that the decline of the Rackham house is not the fault of its mistress – for isn't she a fine lady in perfect health? – but solely due to her husband's want of will, his fear of his appointed destiny. Oh no, there was never anything wrong with the small, perfect woman upstairs, yet still her cruel and ineffectual husband persists in demanding round-the-clock accounts of her behaviour. William can picture Agnes now, doing her bit to prop up this lie by sitting in her bed, her cameo face innocent, reading *Great Thoughts Made Plain for Young Ladies* or some such book, while he, the villain, slumps down here in his oily armchair.

'Anything else?' he enquires sourly.

'She says she doesn't wish to see the doctor today, sir.'

William clips the end off another cigar and flicks it into the fireplace.

'Doctor Curlew will come today, as always.'

'Very well, sir. But you are a spineless fool and that's the only thing making your wife sick.' Well, no, actually Clara doesn't say that last sentence. Not aloud.

What time remains before dinner, William whiles away with a book. Why not? He can't very well get started on the Rackham proprietary papers, can he, if he's going to be called away shortly to the dining-room?

The book of his choice is *Exploits of a Seasoned Traveller, or, Around the World in Eighty Maidenheads,* and he makes no attempt to hide it or even obscure its title when Letty enters the room to stoke the fire. She can barely write her own name, so complicated words like 'fleshy orbs' and 'rampant member' are mysteries to her.

You see them there in the smoking-room together, William and Letty, and wonder if this is going to be a scene from a moralistic drama, a Samuel Richardson tale of seduction and ruin, for Letty is a servant with no means of defence or recourse to the law, alone in a room with her master as he reads inflammatory material. Nevertheless she finishes her tasks and leaves without being molested, for to the preoccupied William at that moment she's merely the means by which his lamps are lit, no more alive than the wires and switches which light yours.

William carries on reading his book with the nonchalance that men like to affect when contemplating pornography. In his own mind, he is a picture of roguish sophistication sitting there in his armchair, but still there's a fierce little fire raging inside him, converting the words that pass under his level gaze into a smouldering punk of fragmented anatomies.

'Dinner is served, sir,' a servant informs him, and he folds closed his book, pressing it down on his lap, half to caress and half to suppress his desire.

'I'll be there shortly.'

Seated at one end of the long mahogany dining-table, William samples his first mouthful of yet another of the cook's excellent meals (ah, but how long will they remain so?) She really is a treasure – the only female in the house whose worth has never been in doubt, since the very first day he got her. Informing her that she can't have quite so much sirloin in future is going to be difficult. Especially since, by rights, it should be the mistress of the house who passes on such news.

William stares down the length of the table, along the glowing white trail of table-cloth leading all the way to the empty other end. As always, cutlery, glassware and gleaming vacant plates are laid out for Mrs Rackham, should she feel up to attending. In the kitchen, there is still the bulk of a chicken's warm and juicy carcass she could have if she wanted it. William has consumed one thigh and a leg, no more.

Not long after dinner, Doctor Curlew arrives at the Rackham house. William, ensconced once more in the smoking-room, consults his watch, to measure how much time elapses between the sound of the doorbell and the sound of the doctor being admitted.

Better, he thinks. Better.

There is a creak of banister as Dr Curlew climbs the stairs to Agnes's room. Then a silent quarter-hour is scalpelled from the evening.

Afterwards, the doctor visits William in the smoking-room, as he does each and every week. He proceeds directly to a particular armchair which he knows to be the most firm and resilient. Flaccidity of all kinds is his bugbear.

Uncommonly tall without being bony, he cuts an impressive figure, as if his frame has expanded, over time, to make room for the growth of experience within. His long, strong-browed face, his dark eyes, his fastidiously sculpted beard, hair and moustache, and his austerely dashing dress sense, make him a more distinguished-looking specimen than Rackham.

He's also highly skilled, with a long list of initials after his name. To give but one example, he can dissect a pregnant rabbit for the purposes of anatomical study in ten minutes and can, if required, pretty well sew it back together again. He enjoys the reputation, at least among general physicians, of being something of an expert on feminine illness.

Puffing thoughtfully on one of William's cigars, he speaks for a few minutes on this subject as far as it applies to his host's wife. The atmosphere is thick with smoke and alcohol, and you may be forgiven for losing the thread of the good doctor's thesis, but do rouse yourself for his conclusion:

'I'll admit she's tolerably lucid just now, and no great trouble. I suspect the improvement is due to the time of the month. I certainly don't think we should be lulled into thinking there won't be another relapse: in fact,

I'm expecting one very soon. With every visit I observe more clearly how strenuously she must fight to compose herself. It's like a quantity of vomit that *will* not be kept down. This is not a healthy state of affairs . . . Not for *anyone*.' Here Curlew pauses in order that William may be struck squarely by his point. 'I must emphasise, my dear Rackham, that you continue to show the unmistakable signs of mental strain.'

William grins. 'Perhaps I'm trying to maintain some consistency of mood in the family, doctor.'

Curlew frowns impatiently and uncrosses his legs. He knows William well enough to forgo decorum. 'Don't joke about it, man,' he says, leaning closer. 'You should know that mental illness in the male has nothing to do with nature. Every man has his breaking-point. Once the suffering is beyond endurance, madness strikes, and note that I say *strikes*, for often it comes suddenly, and it is *not* reversible. You and I have no womb that can be taken out if things get beyond a joke — for God's sake remember that.'

William glances up at the ceiling, looking for a way to cut short the argument.

'I don't believe the continued presence of my wife in this house is likely to drive me mad just yet, Doctor Curlew. Perhaps the strain you detect is merely . . . tiredness.'

'My dear Rackham,' sighs the doctor, as if seeing through a brave falsehood to the fearful truth beneath. 'I understand, of course I understand, that having Agnes committed to an asylum would cause you pain and shame. But you must trust me: I've seen other men wrestling with the same decision. And once they make it, they are relieved beyond words.'

'Well, not quite beyond words, it seems,' demurs William sardonically, 'if they can give you their testimonial.'

Doctor Curlew narrows his eyes in disapproval. Too clever for their own good, these men with literary pretensions; they can split hairs, but fail to see what's in front of their faces.

'Think about what I've said,' the doctor says, rising from his chair.

'Oh, I shall, I shall,' William assures him, rising likewise. The two of them shake hands, with nothing agreed, and William squeezing harder and harder to prove he's not the weaker man.

But enough of this. There's a limit to how long William can be a disappointment to all who observe him. He's not so spineless as everyone supposes! True to his earlier resolve, he finally climbs the stairs to his study, where the Rackham Perfumeries documents lie in wait for him. It's time to take the bull by the horns.

Seated at his desk, William grasps the Manila envelopes by the scruffs of their sealed ends and empties out their contents. His plan, when he sees the documents spread like this before him, is to pick them up one by one, in no particular order, and scan them as quickly as possible. All that's needed is a vague sense of how the business holds together. An inkling is better than nothing. Getting bogged in the details is what's fatal: better to read everything half-comprehendingly, to get the gist of the thing. He coped with far worse than this at school, didn't he?

William takes the topmost paper from the nearest pile and peruses it with an ill-humoured squint, impatient for it to make itself clear. There's a fearsome density of words here . . . Who would have thought the old man had so many words in him? Many of them misspelled, too – how embarrassing! But that's not the worst of it: how is it possible that so many nouns can conjure up so few pictures? How can so many verbs suggest so few actions worth attempting? It beggars belief. But he struggles on.

Ten lines down, half-way through the eleventh, William's eye is caught by the interesting word 'juices'. This gets him thinking about this woman in Silver Street, Sugar, and how she'll gasp, perhaps, at his demand. Well, *let* her gasp, as long as she submits! What, after all, is she—

But he is straying from the task at hand. Breathing deeply, he returns to the beginning, this time reading each word aloud in his mind.

Utilisable cuttings down 15% from last year. Many would not div. at the root but crumbld. 4 gross ordered from Copley. Only 60 of the 80 acres prime.
?Buy more prime from Copley. ?Rackhams good name. First gallons will tell.
Drying House needs new roof – ?Saturday afternoon if workers will stretch to it. Rumour of trade union infiltraitor.
2% rise in cost of manure.

At this, William lets the page flutter through his knees to the floor. This tabulation of mucky stratagems, this intimacy with manure – he cannot bear it – he must be free of it.

Yet there is no escape. His father has told him that if he doesn't wish to be head of an empire he's free to get a job elsewhere – either that, or surprise everyone with sudden success in one of those 'gentlemanly' pursuits he's always talking about.

Stung by the memory, William girds himself for another assault on the Rackham papers. Perhaps the problem is not so much the content as his father's cryptic shorthand. And if it must be this incoherent scrawl, could it *please* be in black ink, rather than faded blue or pale brown? Would proper ink cost the old skinflint ninepence more per gallon, perhaps?

William rummages through the papers, and at the bottom of the pile he finds what appears to be a more substantial document bound into sturdy pamphlet form. To his astonishment, it proves to be *More Sprees in London – Hints for Men about Town, with advice for greenhorns.* So this is where it's been hiding!

He lays it on his lap, turns it over and opens it. The pocket in the back still contains half a dozen condoms made of animal intestine. They've dried out now, poor withered things, like pressed leaves or flowers. In his prime, in France, they were a daily necessity. The whores swore by them, in a manner that was friendly but allowed for no excuses. *'Mieux pour nous, mieux pour vous.'* Ah, those girls, those times! Far away and long ago.

William flips through the pages. He bypasses the 'Trotters' section (street girls) and flicks through 'Hocks' (the cheapest brothels). 'Prime Rump', at the back of the book, is out of his range, being the class of establishment where one is expected to call for first-rate wines on top of everything else. Thankfully, Mrs Castaway's is listed in 'Mid Loin (For Moderate Spenders)'.

This Good Lady's Establishment contains an Embarrassment of Pulchritude, viz, Miss Lester, Miss Howlett, and Miss Sugar. These Ladies may be found at home from the middle of the afternoon; after six o'clock they are wont to take Entertainment at 'The Fireside', an unpretentious but convivial place for Nocturnals, and will leave with any suitable Escort at a time of mutual choosing.

Miss Lester is of middling stature, with . . .

William pursues Miss Lester no further, but proceeds directly to:

We can presume that 'Sugar' was not the name our third Lady bore at her christening, but it is the name under which she rejoices now, should any man wish to baptize her further. She is an eager Devotee of <u>every</u> known Pleasure. Her sole purpose *is to put the demanding Connoisseur at his ease and far Exceed his expectations. She boasts tresses of fiery red which may fall to the midriff, hazel eyes of rare pene-tration, and (despite some angularity) a graceful enough carriage. She is especially accomplished in the Art of Conversation, and is most assuredly a fit companion for any True Gentleman. Her one shortcoming, which to Some may well be a piquant virtue, is that her Bosom scarcely exceeds the size of a child's. She will ask for 15s., but will perform Marvels for a guinea.*

William feels for his watch in his waistcoat pocket and fingers it into his palm. For a long time he stares at it, then folds warm fingers shut, enclosing the golden time-piece ticking in his fist.

'I'd better make a start,' he says to himself.

But hours later, Letty, alerted by a loud, unidentifiable snore in the stillness of the night, tiptoes into the study and finds William asleep in his chair.

'Mr Rackham?' she whispers, ever-so-gently. 'Mr Rackham?'

He snores on, his big pale hands hanging loose at his sides, his golden hair ruffled and wayward, like an urchin's. Letty, at a loss what to do, tiptoes out again. Obviously, her master has been working too hard today.

FIVE

he following evening, William alights from a cab in Silver Street, ready to stride across the threshold of his destiny and claim whatever lies on the other side. His travails begin immediately.

'I ain't hacquainted wiv the pertickler plice,' says the cab-man, when William asks him to point out Mrs Castaway's. 'Somewhere in back a' vese buildins 'ere, I speck.' And with his whip he makes a sweep-ing motion across the entire street, a crowded thoroughfare with a wide assortment of humanity on show, but no giant bills advertising Mrs Castaway's or sandwichboard-men saddled with signs saying 'This Way To Sugar'. William turns back to the cabman to complain, but the black-guard's already driving off, having pocketed a more generous fare than he deserves.

God damn it! Is there *never* such a thing as value for money? Does it always have to be a king's ransom . . . But no, William has thought all this before. Nothing is gained by thinking it all again. Sugar is waiting for him very nearby: all he need do is make enquiries.

Silver Street is crawling with hawkers, barrow-boys and curious pedes-trians straying eastwards from The Stretch. William raises his hand to his brow, to survey the likeliest prospects, but before he can choose, he's accosted by a tiny lad selling cigars.

'Best cigars, sir, tuppenny a piece, real Cubers, lights for nuffing.'

William looks down – steeply down – at the half-dozen miserable speci-mens in the boy's grubby fingers. The likelihood that they're genuinely smuggled from Cuba, rather than from a pickpocketed cigar-case, is small indeed.

'I don't need cigars. I'll give you tuppence if you tell me where Mrs Castaway's is.'

The lad's wizened little face screws up with disappointment at not knowing this lucrative piece of information. Tuppence for nothing, if he only knew one thing! His mouth opens to utter a lie.

'Never mind, never mind,' says William. He's always been ill-at-ease around small children, especially when they want something from him. 'Here's a penny.' And he hands it over.

'God bless you, sir.'

Ruffled by this exchange, William hesitates towards a pipe-smoking pedestrian, then loses nerve and cringes back. He can't go asking every passer-by for directions to a whorehouse: what will they take him for? If he were back in Cambridge, or in France, a bachelor without a care in the world, he might have cried his request for all ears to hear, without a hint of a blush on his cheeks. Fearless, he was then! Oh, see what penury and the cares of marriage have done to him! He hurries along the footpath, his eyes scanning the lamp-lit house-fronts for clues. *More Sprees* supplied no exact address for Mrs Castaway's, implying either that it ought to be known to every serious sophisticate, or that Silver Street is a nondescript strip in which an establishment as illustrious as Mrs Castaway's must shine out like a pearl on a chain. It does no such thing.

He spies a girl in a doorway who impresses him as a whore, though she has a babe in arms.

'Do you know where Mrs Castaway's is?' he asks her, after a quick to-and-fro glance.

'Never 'eard of her, sir.'

William walks on before she can speak more, then stops under a street-lamp to consult his watch. It's almost six o'clock; yes! he knows what he'll do: he'll go to The Fireside and hope that Sugar turns up there, as she is 'wont' to do! Or if she doesn't, someone there will know where Mrs Castaway's is. Steady, Rackham: a rational mind can solve all problems.

He proceeds straight to the nearest public house, and peers up at its inn-sign. No luck. He walks a few dozen steps farther, to the next pub on the next corner. Again, no luck. He makes the mistake of pausing to scratch the back of his head, and is immediately hailed by a street vendor with a bulging knapsack. A cheerful-looking old rogue, whose woollen-gloved fist bristles with pencils.

'Beau'iful pencils, sir,' he cries, his mouth full of donkeyish teeth so black-edged he might almost have been scribbling on them in his idle moments. 'Stay sharp seven times longer than the usual kind.'

'No, thank you,' says William. 'I'll give you sixpence if you tell me where The Fireside is.'

'The Fireside?' echoes the cheap-john, grinning and frowning at the same time. 'I've 'eard of it, I've surely 'eard of it.' Stowing the pencils in his coat pocket, he extracts a shiny tin salver from his knapsack, a glittering oval like a Roman gladiator's puny shield, and wiggles it to catch the lamp-light. 'While I rummages me brains, sir, would you cast yer eye over this tea-tray, nuffing inferior to silver.'

'I don't need a tea-tray,' says Rackham. 'Especially not one made of—'

'Yer muvver, then, sir. Fink 'ow a tray like this would bring a sparkle to 'er eye.'

'I don't have a mother,' retorts William testily.

'Everyone's got a muvver, sir,' grins the cheap-john, as though enlightening an innocent imbecile with the facts of generation.

William is dumbstruck with offence; it's bad enough that this ugly ruffian imagines himself to be addressing a person who might be tempted by the rubbish in that grubby knapsack, but does he expect an explanation of the Rackham family history too?

'Here's a bargain,' leers the old man, 'I'll frow in a pocket-comb. Very best Britannia metal.'

'I *have* a pocket-comb,' says William, whereupon, to his mortification, the cheap-john raises one wiry eyebrow in disbelief. 'What I *don't* have,' he growls, his scalp prickling nervously under its mop of unruly hair, 'is reliable directions to The Fireside.'

'I'm still finkin', sir, still finkin',' the old scoundrel assures him, shoving the tea-tray back into his sack and rooting around in its nether reaches up to his armpit.

And what's this? Dear Heaven, it's beginning to rain! Great heavy raindrops are being tossed down from the sky, hitting the shoulders of William's coat so hard that they spatter up against his jaw and into his ears, and he realises that, in his eagerness to reach his goal, he has left lying inside the cab an almost-new *parapluie* for the cabman to sell in his idle hours. In an instant, William's mood darkens to despair: this is Fate, this is God's will: the rain, the lost umbrella, the alien indifference of a street he doesn't know, the mockery of strangers, the obstinate cruelty of his own father, the damnable ache in his shoulder from sleeping half the night in his chair . . .

(A truly modern man, William Rackham is what might be called a superstitious atheist Christian; that is, he believes in a God who, while He may no longer be responsible for the sun rising, the saving of the Queen or the provision of daily bread, is still the prime suspect when anything goes wrong.)

Another street vendor approaches William, attracted by the smell of unfulfilled desires. 'The Fireside!' he says, elbowing the other cheap-john aside. He's dressed in a flaccid grey jacket and corduroy trousers, with a frayed billycock on his lugubrious head. 'Let me 'elp you, sir!'

William glances at what the fellow is selling: dog collars, a dozen of them arrayed all up his shabby grey arm. God damn it, will it be necessary to buy a dog collar in order to be pointed in the right direction?

But 'That way, sir,' says the fellow. 'Carry on, all the way up Silver Street. Then you'll see the Lion Brewery: that's New Street. Then turn . . .' – he clenches alternate fists, reminding himself of the difference between right and left, and the dog collars slide down to his gnarly wrist – 'right, until you comes to 'Usband Street. And that's where it is.'

'Thank you, my man,' says William, and gives him the sixpence.

The dog-collar seller tips his billycock and disappears, but his luckless companion, having fetched a small black object out of his knapsack, lingers.

'You look like a gentleman of business, sir,' he chirrups. 'Can I interest you in a diary? It's for 1875, sir, what's comin' upon us fast as a train. It's got an almanac in the back, a golden string for marking your place, and everyfing you'd wish to find in a diary is in it, sir.'

William ignores the fellow and strides up Silver Street.

'Pair of larvely scissors to cut all yer bits off, sir!' the man yells after him.

The impertinence runs off William's back like the rain. Nothing can injure him now; his mood has lifted; he is on the right track at last. The world has consented to be friendly after all. The lights shine brighter, and he hears music, whisked into carillon incoherence by the wind. From one direction come the cries of the pedlars, from another come flurries of excited chatter. He sees the flash of gathered skirts as women hurry through the gaslit drizzle; he smells roasting meats, wine, and even perfume. Doors open and close, open and close, each time releasing a gust of music, a glimpse of orange-yellow conviviality, a haze of smoke. He'll get his way now, he's sure of it: God has relented. Yesterday William Rackham was humbled by two Drury Lane trollops; tonight he will snatch victory from the orifice of defeat.

Ah, but what if Sugar, too, should refuse him?

Kill her, is his first thought.

Immediately he feels a stab of shame. What a base and unworthy impulse! Is this how low the goad of his own suffering has driven him? To the contemplation of murder? He is by nature a gentle and sympathetic soul: if this girl, this Sugar, refuses, she refuses, and that's that.

If she refuses, what will he do? What *can* he do? Where can he find the woman who'll do what he requires? It's out of the question for him to go roaming the streets of St Giles – some ruffian will bash him on the skull. Nor should he even contemplate loitering in the parks after dark, where ageing dryads specialise in the rankest depravities – and the rankest diseases. No, what he needs is the surrender of a woman befitting his own station, in surroundings of comfort and taste – his humiliation in Drury Lane has taught him *that* much.

He turns the corner into New Street, cheered to see the Lion Brewery just where he was told it would be. In his head, he is already inventing his own Sugar, in advance of meeting the real one: he pictures her huge-eyed, slightly afraid, but compelled to submit. William passes this vision down to his penis, and it swells in anticipation.

Husband Street, when he comes to it, is a dubious place, an insalubrious place, but at least it's cheerful. Or so it seems to him. Everyone's smiling, the whores giggle, and even that toothless old beggar over there is smiling as she gums a saliva-covered apple.

There now: The Fireside. Is it *too* far beyond the pale? Should he turn back while he still can? As he narrows the distance between his quick-breathing breast and the lustrous, lantern-orange inn-sign that hangs from a cast-iron spike, he tells himself he mustn't judge until he sees what it's like inside.

'*Upon the woild woild ocean!*' sings a loud voice startlingly close to William's left ear. '*Far away from 'ooome!*'

He turns his head to find himself waylaid by a sheet-music-seller, singing pugnaciously on: '*'Ow bitterly the sailor croid! Amid the surgin' fooooooam!* Missis play the pianner, sir?'

William tries to wave the music vendor aside with one gloved hand, but the fellow is not so easily deterred; he limps into William's way, thrusting his plywood tray of songs out before him like a ripe bosom framed by *décolletage*.

'Missis *don't* play the pianner, then, sir?'

'Not for years,' says Rackham, annoyed to be reminded of Agnes at a time like this.

'This tune'll put 'er right back in the mood, sir,' persists the music seller, and abruptly resumes his song:

'*May God protect moi mother!*
She will break 'er 'eart for me!
When she 'ears that Oi yam sleepin'
In the deep, deep sea!' — Noice, eh sir? The very latest tune, sir. 'S called "The Shipwrecked Sailor".'

William has been pressing closer to his objective, but this bothersome fellow has limped backwards along with him. At the very doorway of The Fireside, William glares him in the eye and says,

'The latest tune? What nonsense. It's "No Treasure Like a Mother" with different words.'

'Nah, sir,' the man begs to differ, waving a sheet of creamy paper, suitably embellished with nautical designs, in William's face. 'Entoirely different. Take it 'ome, sir, and you'll see.'

'I don't wish to take it home,' says William. 'I wish to enter The Fireside, unaccompanied by *you*, sir, and to enjoy music *there* — without charge I might add.'

At this, the vendor steps aside theatrically, bows and grins. But not in defeat.

'If you 'ear a tune you pertickly loike in there, sir, do tell me, won't you sir: I'll be *sure* to 'ave it.' And with that he melts away, determined to make the most of the next hour, the next year, the next ten centuries plying his indispensable trade.

William Rackham closes his fist around the ornate brass bar of The Fireside's door and swings it open, breathing deeply. The smell of good beer and the babble of friendly voices envelops him immediately and, stepping inside, he feels the cold flesh of his face tingle with warmth radiating from chandeliers and, yes, a roaring fireside. And what a surprise! The patrons aren't shabby at all! Why, some of them are even smartly dressed! This is the sort of pub that a better sort of person is glad to discover, a well-kept secret in the midst of poverty, a gathering-place for those in the know. The regulars, many of whom clearly don't live anywhere near Husband Street themselves, turn to look at William for a moment, then return to their conversations. They are merry, but not drunk; this is not the sort of place where patrons drink in silence waiting for the alcohol to do its job. William sighs with relief, removes his hat, and walks into the company of his peers.

'*In, one by one, the casuals crawl,*' a tenor voice greets him. '*In filthy tatters, raiment called . . .*'

The singer is standing on a narrow strip of stage at the far end of the room, almost hidden behind the smoky throng of tables and patrons. His sombre evening dress is augmented by a crudely knotted red scarf meant to symbolise the neckerchief of a labourer. Striking a piteous pose, he sings to a florid piano accompaniment.

'*Bags of hay laid on the floor,*
For fretful wretches on to snore;
For one, but holding three or four
All night in a London workhouse.'

The muted crash of glass on the floor provokes laughter and the excited woof of a dog. A uniformed barmaid, shaking her head in exasperation, hurries out from behind the bar.

It's a cheerful sight, The Fireside's bar: bosomy women busy at the bottles and beer pumps, their frilly finery reflected in the huge mirrors lining the wall behind them. Over their heads, a hundred handbills, prints and placards hang jumbled almost to the ceiling, advertising all sorts of ales and stouts and porters.

William doesn't have to search for a table; a smiling serving-maid motions him to follow her, and she installs him at a table which has room for at least two others – evidently no one drinks alone here. Smiling, William puts his order in, and she flits off to do his bidding.

Lively little place, this, thinks Rackham, momentarily forgetting why he's come. A bit on the warm side, though! As the singer warbles on and the rubato hurly-burly of the piano is half-submerged in waves of laughter, William does what he can – pulling off his gloves, unbuttoning his coat, smoothing down his hair. His table is right next to a cast-iron column, and affixed to that column is a notice saying: 'GENTLEMEN ARE PARTICULARLY REQUESTED NOT TO PLACE CIGARS ON THE TABLE, AND NOT TO TAKE LIGHTS FROM THE CHANDELIERS, BUT FROM THE GAS-LIGHTS FIXED FOR THAT PURPOSE.' William has no desire to smoke, but vapour issues from his person nonetheless: his damp clothing is beginning to steam. His skin prickles with sweat and his ample ears are, he knows, glowing red. How grateful he is when the serving-maid hurries back to him, bearing aloft a big tumbler of beer! She can obviously tell how thirsty he must be, bless her heart!

'Capital!' he exclaims above the song, then cranes his head around, wondering why the singing is growing louder: are there more tenors up there than he thought? But no, it's the Fireside regulars joining in.

'*Swearing, yelling, all the throng*,' they croon, between sips of beer.

'*With jest obscene and ribald song,*
They pass the weary hours long,
Of a night in a London workhouse . . .'

You who, like William, are visiting The Fireside for the first time, may wonder: how can these revellers sing of horror in such jolly voices? See them tap their feet and nod their heads to the plight of the destitute – is no other part of them moved? Why yes, of course it is! They fairly worship at the altar of pity! But what can be done? Here in The Fireside, no one is to blame (except perhaps God, in his infinite wisdom). Wrapped up in a good tune, poverty takes its place of honour amongst all the other sing-along calamities: the military defeats, the shipwrecks, the broken hearts – Death itself.

A little nervously William scans The Fireside for female clientele. There are plenty of women in the place, but all of them seem to be taken; perhaps Sugar is one of these, a worm caught by an early bird. (Or should that be the other way around?) He surveys the assortment a second time, sizing up the physiques as best he can through the haze of cigar smoke and whatever else is in the way. None of the bodies he sees fits Sugar's description, even allowing for the fact that *More Sprees* may have stretched the truth.

William prefers to believe Sugar isn't here yet. That's good: his ears have stopped burning now, and should fade (God willing) by the time he has to make a good impression. He sips at his glass of ale, finds it so much to his liking that he pours it down his throat and immediately orders another. The serving-maid has a pretty body; he hopes Sugar's, when he uncovers it, is at least half as nice.

'Thank you, thank you,' he winks, but she's already gone, serving someone else. *Così fan tutti*, eh? William leans back, listening to the words of the tenor's next song.

'One day I'll dine on pheasants and grouse
And cocktails in fine crystal glasses
And roast pigs with apples stuck in their mouths
And silver spits shoved up their arses . . .'

The Fireside regulars chortle: this one's the latest favourite from the bawdy sheet-music sellers of Seven Dials.

'Me spotted dick puddin' will be such a size
Four footmen will carry it in!
But for now I'll survive on porter and pies
For me ship ain't quite come in.'
'Oh!' the audience joins in, *'me ship ain't quite come in,*
It's subject to delay;
Me ship ain't quite come in,
It's expected any day.
When me ship comes in, the grin on me chin
Will never go away
But me ship ain't quite — me ship ain't quite —
Me ship ain't quite come in!'

William chuckles. Not bad, not bad! Why has he never heard of The Fireside before? Do Bodley and Ashwell know of it? And if not, how would he describe it to them?

Well . . . of course it's a few rungs below top class – a good few rungs. But it's a damn sight better than some of the sorry establishments Bodley and Ashwell have dragged him along to. ('This is the place, Bill, I'm almost sure of it!' '*Almost* sure?' 'Well, to be wholly sure, I'd have to lie down on the floor and study the ceiling.') The Fireside is innocent of anything *too* common: there's not a pewter mug in sight, but all good glass, and the beer is light and frothy. The floors are tiled rather than wooden, and there's no fake marble anywhere. Most tellingly of all, unlike the haunts of low men, it doesn't stay open all hours, but closes, demurely, at midnight. Which suits Rackham: all the shorter will he have to wait for his sweet Cinderella.

'Millie, me wife, will be chuffed with 'er life
She'll change 'er name to Octavia
There won't be no strife, no need for me knife
In our smart new abode in Belgravia.
We'll 'ave fat tums, we'll bring all our chums,
I can't 'ardly wait to begin
But I'm twiddlin' me thumbs in these 'ere slums
For me ship ain't quite come in.'

It's time for the chorus, and the regulars sing it with gusto. William merely hums, not wishing to attract attention. (Ah, but didn't he once sing bawdy songs, in a louder and fruitier baritone than . . . Oh, sorry, you've heard that already . . .)

When the song is over, William joins in the applause. There's a reshuffling of patrons as people stand to leave and others venture in the door. Leaning over his beer-glass, Rackham tries to keep track of anything in skirts, hoping to catch his first glimpse of the girl with the 'hazel eyes of rare penetration'. However, his own gaze must be more penetrating than he imagines, for when his eyes alight briefly on a trio of unattached young women, they rear up, all three, from their seats.

He tries to look away, but it's too late: they're moving directly towards him, a phalanx of taffeta and lace. They're smiling – showing too many teeth. In fact, they have too much of everything: too much hair spilling out from under their too-elaborate bonnets, too much powder on their cheeks, too many bows on their dresses, and overly flaccid Columbine cuffs swirling around their clutching pink hands.

'Good evenin', sir, may we sit down?'

William cannot refuse them as he refused the sheet-music seller: the laws of etiquette – or the laws of anatomy – won't allow it. He smiles and nods his head, shifting his new hat onto his lap for fear it might get sat on. One of the whores swings into the space thus vacated, and her two companions jostle for the remainder.

'A honour, sir.'

They're pretty enough, though William would like them better if they didn't appear to be dressed for a box at the opera, and if their combined scent weren't quite so pungent. Pressed close together like this, they smell like a barrowful of cut flowers on a humid day; William wonders if it's a Rackham perfume that's responsible. If so, his father has more to answer for than parsimony.

Still, he reminds himself, these girls are better-looking than most, peach-firm and unblemished – more expensive, possibly, than Sugar. There's just . . . rather a surfeit of them, that's all, crammed into such a small space.

'You're too 'andsome to sit alone, sir.'

'You're the kind of man as should 'ave a pretty woman on 'is arm – or three.'

The third girl only snorts, outdone by her comrades' wit.

William avoids meeting their stares openly, fearing to find in those bright eyes the presumption, the insolence, of inferiors seeking to wrest control from their master. Sugar won't behave this way, will she? She'd better not.

'You flatter me, ladies,' says William. He looks away, wishing for rescue.

The closest whore leans closer still, her lips pouting open not far from his, and whispers loudly,

'You're not waiting for a *man* friend, are you?'

'No,' says William, smoothing the back of his hair nervously. Does his tufty mop make him look like a sodomite? Should he have kept it long? Or should he get it cut shorter still? God, will he have to shave his head bald before his indignity is subdued? 'I'm waiting for a girl called Sugar.'

All three whores erupt in a pantomime of offence and disappointment.

'Won't I do, ducks?' 'You've broke my 'eart, sir!' and so forth.

Rackham doesn't respond, but continues to gaze at the door, hoping to make clear to The Fireside's other customers that these women have no connection with him. The more he leans away, however, the more they push to be near him.

'Sugar, eh?'

'A true connoisseur, you are.'

Crude laughter erupts from a nearby table, making William wince. The tenor is having a rest from singing; is the humiliation of the hapless Rackham now to be The Fireside's entertainment? William casts his eye over the throng of patrons, and locates the folk who are laughing – but they have their backs to him. The joke is on someone else.

'What do you like, then?' one of the whores asks, brightly, as though enquiring how he takes his tea. 'Come on, sir, you can tell me. Speak in riddles, I'll understand.'

'No need,' pronounces the closest one. 'I can see in his eyes what 'e wants.' Her companions turn to look at her, intrigued. She pauses with a music hall comic's sense of timing, then boasts simply: 'It's . . . a gift I 'ave. A *secret* gift.'

All three begin to laugh then, open-mouthed, indecent, and within moments their hilarity has escalated to the brink of hysteria.

'Well, what *does* 'e want then?' one of them manages to demand, but the soothsayer, convulsed in giggles, has trouble replying.

'Hurm . . . Huhurm . . . Hum . . .' – wiping her eyes – 'Oh-ho! You naughty, *naughty* girl – 'Ow could you even ask? A secret's a secret, innit, sir?'

William squirms, his ears once again flaming.

'Really now,' he mutters. 'I don't see that this is called for.'

'Quite right, quite right, sir,' she says and, to the delight of her companions, she mimes a furtive peek into William's hidden heart, then recoils in burlesque shock at what she spies there. 'Oh *no*, sir,' she gasps, covering her open mouth with slack fingers. 'P'raps you'd better wait for Sugar after all.'

'Don't take any notice of her, sir,' says one of the others. 'She talks tripe all day long. Now come on ducks, why not give *me* a try?' She strokes her throat with her fingertips. 'You wouldn't be getting second best, you know. I'm just as good as any of the Castaway girls.'

William again casts a longing glance towards the door. If he leaps up and storms out of The Fireside now, will every man, woman and beast in the place hoot with glee?

''Ere,' says one of the girls, folding her arms on the table, framing (as best she can with her fashionably tight bodice) her bosom in her forearms. ''Ere, tell us about yerself, sir.' The prankishness has abruptly vanished from her face; she's almost deferential.

'Let me guess,' says the one who had seemed shy. 'Writer.'

The casually aimed epithet lands on William's face like a blow, or a caress. What can he do but turn to face the girl, and, impressed, say 'Yes'?

'An extrawdry life, I'm sure,' opines the soothsayer.

All three whores are serious now, keen to make amends for ruffling his dignity.

'I write,' elaborates William, 'for the better monthly reviews. I'm a critic – and a novelist.'

'Cor. Wha's'name o' one o' yer books?'

William chooses from among the many he means, one day, to produce. '*Mammon O'erthrown*,' he says.

Two of the girls just grin, but the shy one mummels her lips like a fish, silently testing whether she could possibly repeat such an exotic title. None of the whores is about to mention that The Fireside is infested with critics and would-be novelists.

'Hunt's the name,' improvises William. 'George W. Hunt.' Inwardly, he cringes in shame, a four-legged creature in the shadow of his father's derision, a sham. *Go home and read about the cost of manure!* is the nagging command, but William quells it with a gulp of ale.

The most forward of the whores narrows her eyes pensively, as if bothered by a conundrum.

'And Mr 'Unt wants Sugar,' she says. 'And Sugar only. Now what, oh what, might Mr 'Unt . . . want? Hmmmm?'

Her nearest crony answers, quick as a flash.

''E might want to discuss books wiv 'er.'

'Cor.'

'Georgie got no critic friends, then?'

'Sad life.'

The beleaguered Rackham smiles stoically. No one new has entered The Fireside for what seems like a long time.

'Nice weather we're 'avin',' remarks the least forward of the whores, out of the blue. 'Not at all bad for November.'

'If yer like snow and rain,' mutters one of the others, idly picking up folds of her dress and making them stand up in little mountain peaks of serge.

'Special tastes, our Mr 'Unt's got, remember.'

'All set for Christmas, are yer, sir?'

'Fancy unwrappin' a present early?' Pink fingers pluck suggestively at a shawl, and William glances once again at the door.

'Maybe she won't come,' suggests the boldest whore. 'Sugar, I mean.'

'Sshhh, don't tease him.'

'You'd be better off with me, ducks. I know a thing or two about lidder-ature. I've 'ad all the great names. I've 'ad Charles Dickens.'

'Ain't 'e dead?'

'Not the bit *I* sucked on, dear.'

'Dead five years or more. Hignorant, you are.'

'It was 'im, I tell yer. I didn't say it was last week, did I?' She sniffs pathetically. 'I was no more than a babe.'

The others snicker. Then, as if by a mutually understood signal, they all three turn serious, and lean their faces towards him, fetchingly tilted. They look just like yesterday's counterfeit 'twins', with an extra sibling added, an inedible third scoop of gateau.

'All three of us together, for the one price,' says the soothsayer, lick-ing her lips. 'How about it?'

'Awf—' stammers Rackham, 'awfully tempting, I'm sure. But you see . . .'

At that moment The Fireside's door swings open and in walks a soli-tary woman. A whiff of fresh air comes in with her, as well as the sound of wild weather outside, cut off in mid-howl by the sealing of the door, like a cry stifled under a hand. The pall of cigar smoke parts momentar-ily, then mingles with the smell of rain.

The woman is all in black – no, dark green. Green darkened by the downpour. Her shoulders are drenched, the fabric of her bodice clinging tight to her prominent collar-bones, and her thin arms are sheathed in dappled chlorella. A sprinkling of unabsorbed water still glistens on her simple bonnet and on the filmy grey veil that hangs from it. Her abun-dant hair, not flame-red just now but black and orange like neglected coal embers, is all disordered, and loose curls of it are dripping.

For an instant she quivers, irritably, like a dog, then regains her compos-ure. Turning to the bar, she greets the publican, unheard over the clamour of conversation, and raises her arms to lift her veil. Sharp shoulder-blades writhe inside wet fabric as she bares her face, unseen as yet by Rackham. There is a long stain of wetness all down her back, shaped like a tongue or an arrowhead, pointing down towards her skirts.

'Who's that?' asks William.

The three whores sigh almost in unison.

'That's her, ducks.'

'Go to it, Mr 'Unt. 'Appy criticisin'.'

Sugar has turned, and is scanning The Fireside for a place to sit. The boldest whore, the soothsayer, stands up and waves, motioning her over to William's table.

'Sugar dear! Over here! Meet . . . Mr 'Unt.'

Sugar walks directly to William's table, as if it was her destination from the first. Although she must be responding to the whore's hello, she doesn't acknowledge her, and sets her sights on Rackham alone. Almost within arm's reach, she calmly regards William with those hazel eyes which, as promised in *More Sprees in London*, do indeed appear golden – at least in the lights of The Fireside.

'Good evening, Mr Hunt.' Her voice is not overly feminine, rather hoarse even, but wholly free of class coarseness. 'I don't wish to interrupt you and your friends.'

'We was just leavin',' says the soothsayer, rising and, as if on strings, pulling up her companions with her. 'It's *you* 'e's after.' And with that, gathering their surplus of taffeta together, they retreat.

Don't bother even to glance after them; they are persons of no consequence (is there no end to them?), and they have outlived their use. William stares at the woman he has come for, unable to decide whether her face is annoyingly imperfect (mouth too wide, eyes too far apart, dry skin, freckles) or the most beautiful he has ever seen. With every passing second, he is closer to making up his mind.

At his request, Sugar sits down at his side, her wet skirts rustling and squeaking, her upper body smelling of fresh rain and fresh sweat. She has been running, it seems – something that no reputable woman would ever, ever do. But the flush it has brought to her cheeks is damned attractive, and she smells divine. Several locks of hair have come loose from her elaborately styled fringe, and these sway in front of her eyes. With a languid motion of one gloved hand, she gently pushes them aside, to the furry edges of her eyebrows. She smiles, sharing with William the rueful understanding that there is a limit to what one may hope for once one's plans have gone awry.

The state she's in is certainly unladylike, but in all other respects she radiates surprisingly good breeding. And yet . . . a breed of what? She could be the daughter of foreign royalty, deposed in an unexpected revolt, driven through midnight forests in the pelting rain, head high, regal even while hair swirls round her face, shoulders erect while a wounded servant fusses to cover them with his fur-lined coat . . . (Do bear with William, if you can stand it, while he indulges himself a little here. He read a lot of racy French novels in the early Sixties when he was supposed to be studying the defeats of the Hittites.)

Sugar is starting to steam, a faint halo of vapour rising from her bonnet and outermost ringlets. She cocks her head slightly to one side, as if to ask, Well, what now? Her neck, William notices, is longer than the high collar of her bodice can hold. She has an Adam's apple, like a man. Yes, he has decided now: she is the most beautiful thing he has ever seen.

To his bemusement, he's made shy by her demeanour; she appears so *much* the lady that it's difficult to imagine how he could possibly soil that status. Her long, lithe body, beguiling though it is, only complicates matters, as she wears her attire like a second skin, seamless and, by implication, irremovable.

The way he phrases his dilemma is this: 'I don't know that I deserve this honour.'

Sugar leans forward slightly and, in a low tone, as if making a comment about a mutual acquaintance who has just walked in, says, 'Don't worry, sir. You have made the right choice. I'll do anything you ask of me.'

A simple exchange, murmured above the babble of a crowded drinking-house, but was there ever a marriage vow more explicit?

A serving-maid comes to deliver the drink Sugar ordered at the bar. Colourless, transparent and with scarcely any bubbles, it can't be beer. And if it's gin, the perennial favourite of whores, William can't smell it. Could it possibly be . . . water?

'What am I to call you?' wonders William, resting his chin on his locked hands the way he used to do as a student. 'There must be more to your name than . . .'

She smiles. Her lips are extraordinarily dry, like white tree-bark. Why does this strike him as beautiful rather than ugly? It's beyond him.

'Sugar is all there is to my name, Mr Hunt. Unless there's another name you particularly wish to know me by?'

'No, no,' William assures her. 'Sugar it is.'

'What's in a name, after all?' she remarks, and raises one furry eyebrow. Can it be that she's quoting Shakespeare? Coincidence, surely, but how sweet she smells!

The Fireside's tenor has resumed warbling. William feels the place becoming warmer and friendlier; the lights seem to burn more golden, the shadows turn a rich dark brown, and everyone in the great room seems to be smiling bright-eyed at a companion. The door swings open frequently now, admitting smarter and smarter folk. The noise of their arrivals, the chatter, and the singing which strains to soar above it, grows into such a din that William and Sugar must lean close to one another's faces in order to converse.

Gazing into her eyes, which are so large and shiny that he sees his face reflected, William Rackham rediscovers the elusive joy of being William Rackham. There is a will-o'-the-wisp of behaviours, alcohol-fuelled and fragile, that he singles out as being his *true* self, quite distinct from the thickening physical lump he sees in the looking-glass every morning. The mirror cannot lie, and yet it does, it does! It cannot reflect the flame-like destinies trapped inside the frustrated soul. For William *ought* to have been a Keats, a Bulwer Lytton, or even a Chatterton, but instead is transmogrifying, outwardly at least, into a gross copy of his own father. Rare indeed are the moments when he can illuminate a captivated audience with the glow of his youthful promise.

He and Sugar speak, and Rackham comes to life. He has been dead these past few years, dead! Only now can he admit that he has been underground, hiding in fear from anyone worth knowing, deliberately avoiding bright company. Any company, in fact, in which he might be tempted or called upon to . . . well, let's put it this way: what is audacious promise in a golden-haired youth can be mocked, in a man with greying sideboards and an incipient triple chin, as mere gasbagging. For a long time now, William has made do with his internal monologues, his fantasies on park benches and the lavatory, immune from the risk of sniggers and yawns.

In Sugar's company, however, it's different: he listens to himself talk, and is relieved to find that his own voice can still weave magic. Wreathed in the subtle haze of steam rising from her, Rackham holds forth: fluent, charming and intelligent, witty and full of sensibility. He imagines his face shining with youth, his hair smoothing itself out and flowing like Swinburne's.

Sugar, for her part, has not a fault; she is scrupulously respectful, gently good-humoured, thoughtful and flattering. It's even possible, thinks William, that she likes him. Surely her laughter is not the sort that can be faked, and surely the sparkle in her eyes – that same sparkle he inspired in Agnes long ago – cannot be counterfeited.

And, to William's surprise and deep satisfaction, he and Sugar *do* converse about books after all, just as the whores mischievously predicted. Why, the girl's a prodigy! She has an amazing knowledge of literature, lacking only Latin, Greek and the male's instinctive grasp of what is major and minor. In terms of sum total of pages she seems to have read almost as much as he (although some of it, inevitably, is the sort of piffle written for and by her own sex – novels about timid governesses and so forth). Yet she's well-versed in many of the authors he holds in high esteem – and she adores Swift! Swift, his favourite! To most women – Agnes among them, unfortunately – Swift is the name of a cough lozenge, or a bird to be worn stuffed on their bonnets. But Sugar . . . Sugar can even pronounce 'Houyhnhnms' – and God, doesn't her mouth make a pretty shape when she does! And Smollett! She's read *Peregrine Pickle*, and not only that, she can discuss it intelligently – certainly as intelligently as he could have done, at her age. (What *is* her age? No, he dares not ask.)

'But that's not possible!' she protests demurely, when he confesses that he hasn't yet read James Thomson's *The City of Dreadful Night*, even now, a full year after its publication. 'How terribly busy you must be, Mr Hunt, to be kept from such a pleasure so long!'

Rackham strains to recall the literary reviews.

'Son of a sailor, wasn't he?' he ventures.

'Orphan, orphan,' she enthuses, as if it were the grandest thing in the world. 'Became a teacher in a military asylum. But the poem is a miracle, Mr Hunt, a miracle!'

'I'll certainly endeavour to find time . . . no, I shall *make* time, to read it,' he says, but she leans close to his ear and saves him the bother:

'*Eyes of fire*,' she recites in a throaty whisper, loud enough nonetheless to surmount the singing and the chatter all around them.

'*Glared at me throbbing with a starved desire;*
The hoarse and heavy and carnivorous breath
Was hot upon me from deep jaws of death;
Sharp claws, swift talons, fleshless fingers cold
Plucked at me from the bushes, tried to hold:
   But I strode on austere;
   No hope could have no fear.'

Breathless with emotion, she lowers her eyes.

'Grim poetry,' comments William, 'for such a beautiful young woman to have as a special favourite.'

Sugar smiles sadly.

'Life can be grim,' she says. 'Especially when fit companions – like yourself, sir – are difficult to find.'

William is tempted to assure her that, in his opinion, *More Sprees in London* has not praised her accomplishments anywhere near highly enough, but he can't bring himself to say it. Instead, they talk on and on, about Truth and Beauty, and the works of Shakespeare, and whether there is any meaningful distinction to be made nowadays between a small hat and a bonnet.

'Watch,' says Sugar, and, with both her hands, pushes her bonnet well forward on her head. 'Now it's a hat! And watch again . . .' – she pushes it well back – 'Now it's a bonnet!'

'Magic,' grins William. And indeed it is.

Sugar's little demonstration of fashion's absurdity has left her hair even more disordered than before. Her thick fringe, quite dry by now, has tumbled loose, obscuring her vision. William stares, half in disgust, half in adoration, as she pouts her lower lip as far as it will go and blows a puff of air upwards. Golden-red curls flutter off her forehead, and her eyes are unveiled once more, mildly shocking in how far apart they are, *perfect* in how far apart they are.

'I feel as though we're courting,' he tells her, thinking that it may make her laugh.

Instead she says very solemnly, 'Oh, Mr Hunt, it so flatters me that I should inspire such treatment.'

This last word hangs in the smoky air a moment, reminding William why he came here tonight, and why he sought out Sugar specially. He imagines afresh the treatment he was raring – still *is* raring, damn it – to mete out to a woman. Can he still ask *that* of her? He recalls the way she said she would do anything, anything he asked of her; re-savours the exquisite gravity of her assurance . . .

'Perhaps,' he ventures, 'it's time you took me home and . . . introduced me to your family.'

Sugar nods once, slowly, her eyes half-closing as she does so. She knows when simple, mute assent is called for.

It is, in any case, almost closing time. Rackham could have guessed this even without consulting his watch, for, on The Fireside's stage, the singer is sharing a heaving chest full of sentiment with the last tipsy patrons. The patrons bray in approximate unison with his warble, a beery confraternity, as serving-maids remove empty glasses from slackening grasps. It's an old song, a rousing bit of doggerel almost universally (if the universe is considered to extend no further than England) sung at pub closing time:

> *'Hearts of oak are our ships,*
> *Jolly tars are our men:*
> *We are always ready,*
> *Steady, boys, steady,*
> *We'll fight and we'll conquer again and again!'*

'Last drinks, ladies and gentlemen, please!'

William and Sugar winch themselves out of their seats; their limbs are stiff from too much conversation. Rackham finds that his genitals have gone to sleep, though a faint galvanic tingling between his legs reassures him that the anaesthesia will pass away soon enough. In any case, he's no longer in a mad hurry to perform feats of lascivious heroics: he still hasn't asked her if she's read Flaubert . . .

Sugar turns to leave. The burden of rainwater having wholly evaporated, during the course of the evening, from her dress, she looks lighter in colour, all in green and pale grey. But sitting so long on her wet skirts has pressed anarchic pleats into them, crude triangles pointing up towards her hidden rump, and Rackham feels strangely protective towards her for her ignorance of this, wishing he could get Letty to iron Sugar's skirts for her and make them neat, before he removes them once and for all. Made awkward by these feelings of tenderness, he follows her through The Fireside, stumbling past empty tables and unpeopled chairs. When did all these people leave? He didn't notice their departures. How much has he drunk? Sugar is erect as a lance, walking straight towards the exit without a word. He hurries to catch up, breathing deeply of the air she lets in as she opens the door.

Outside in the streets, it's no longer raining. The gas-lights glow, the footpaths shine, and most of the hawkers have retired for the night. Here and there, women less beautiful than Sugar loiter under yellowish lamps, sour-faced, commonplace, and surplus to requirements.

'Is it far?' enquires Rackham as they turn the corner into Silver Street together.

'Oh no,' says Sugar, gliding two steps ahead of him, her hand trailing behind almost maternally, the gloved fingers wiggling in empty air as if expecting him to seize hold like a child. 'Close, very close.'

SIX

ust three words, if spoken by the right person at the moment, are enough to make infatuation flower with marvellous speed, popping up like a nub of bright pink from unfurling foreskin. Nor need those three magic words be 'I love you'. In the case of Miss Sugar and George W. Hunt, venturing out into dark wet streets after heavy rain, walking side by side under gas-lamps and a drained empty sky, the three magic words are these: 'Watch your step.'

It's Sugar who utters them; she's taken hold of her companion's hand and, for a moment, steers him closer to her, away from a puddle of creamy vomit quivering on the cobbles. (It's probably brown, but the gas-light adds a yellowish tinge.) William registers everything at once: the vomit, barely visible inside his own sprawling shadow; his feet, stumbling, almost tripping on the hems of Sugar's skirts; the gentle tug on his hand; the faint hubbub of strangers' voices nearby; the sobering chill of the air after the boozy warmth of The Fireside; and those three words: 'Watch your step.'

Spoken by anyone other than Sugar, they would be words of warning, or even threat. But, issuing from her slender throat, modulated by her mouth and tongue and lips, they are neither. They are *an invitation to be safe*, a murmured welcome into a charmed embrace that wards off all misfortune, an affectionate entreaty to keep firm hold of the woman who knows the way. William disengages his hand from hers, worried that a respectable person of his acquaintance might, even at this late and unlikely hour, chance upon him here. Yet his freed hand tingles, through the leather of his gloves, at the after-feel of her grip — strong as a cocky young man's handshake.

Watch your step. The words are still resounding in his head. Her voice

. . . husky, yes . . . but such a musical tone, an ascending trio of notes, *do re fa*, an imperfect but delightful arpeggio of feminine breath, an air played on the *flûte d'amour*. What must a voice like that sound like in the crescendo of passion?

Sugar is moving faster now, gliding over the dark cobbles at a speed he would reserve for daytime. Beneath her skirts, she must be taking deplorably unfeminine steps, to move at the same pace as him: all right, granted, he may not be the tallest of men, but his legs are surely no shorter than normal – indeed, if the stunted lower classes were admitted into the equation, might his legs not be longer than average? And what's that sound? He's not . . . panting, is he? Christ Almighty, he mustn't pant. It's all the beer he's drunk, yes, and the exhaustion he's been suffering lately, mounting up. Even as Sugar beckons him, with an almost imperceptible gesture, to follow her into a dark, narrow close, he turns his head back into the fresher air and sniffs deeply, trying to snatch a second wind.

Maybe the girl is hurrying because she fears he'll grow impatient, or that he'll baulk at following her into a dark passage of uncertain length harbouring God knows what. But William has entered many pleasure houses from alleys as dark and narrow as this one; he has, in his time, descended stone stairwells so deep that he began to wonder if his paramour's boudoir was burrowed straight into one of Bazalgette's great sewers. No, he is not unreasonably fastidious, and not the claustrophobic sort, although naturally he has a preference for bright, airy brothels (who wouldn't?). However, he's so smitten with Sugar that, to be honest, he'd willingly follow her into the rankest cloaca.

Or would he? Has he lost all reason? This girl is nothing more than a . . .

'This way.'

He hastens after her, following the words like a scent trail. Oh my, her voice is like an angel's! An exquisite whisper leading him through the dark. He would follow that whisper even if there was nothing attached to it. But she is more than a whisper – she is a woman with a brain in her head! He has never met anyone remotely like her, except himself. Like him, she thinks Tennyson isn't up to much lately and, like him, she believes trans-Atlantic cables and dynamite will change the world far more than Schliemann's rediscovery of Troy, despite all the fuss. And what a mouth and throat she has! 'Anything you ask of me': that's what she promised him.

'We're here,' she says now.

But where is 'here'? He looks all about him, trying to get his bearings. Where is Silver Street? Is Mrs Castaway's address yet another of *More Sprees'* falsifications? But no: aren't those the lights of Silver Street shining on the far side of this modest Georgian house? This is just a back entrance, yes? It's not a bad-looking place, solid and without any evidence of decay, although it's hard to tell in the dark. But the contours of the house look straight and symmetrical, defined by the lights of Silver Street beyond, a haze of gaseous radiance around the gables and rooftop like a . . . what's the word he's looking for? an aurora? an aura? – one is spiritualist nonsense, the other a scientific phenomenon, but which? . . . aur-aur-aur . . . The Fireside's deceptively frothy ale has numbed his brain's voice and given his thoughts a stutter.

'Home,' he hears Sugar say.

A complicated knock – the tattoo of secrecy – admits Sugar and her companion into Mrs Castaway's dimly lit hallway. William expects to see a spoony-man holding the inner doorknob, a leering stubbly-faced ape such as ushered him out the back door in Drury Lane, but he is wrong. Standing there, a good eighteen inches lower than his first gaze, is a small boy, blue-eyed and as innocent looking as a shepherd's lad from a Nativity scene.

'Hello, Christopher,' says Sugar.

'Please come into the front room, sir,' says the boy, reciting his line primly, casting a glance of infant collusion at Sugar. Intrigued, William allows himself to be led into the sombre but sumptuously papered vestibule, towards a door that stands ajar, emitting warmth and light. The child runs ahead, disappearing into the glow.

'Not yours, is he?' William asks Sugar.

'Of course not,' she replies, her eyebrows raised, mock-scandalised, her lips curving into a grin. 'I'm a spinster.'

In the dimness of the vestibule, the glow of the door they're approaching illuminates Sugar's mouth strangely, outlining the rough, peeling texture of her lips in pure white. William wants to feel those feathery lips closing around the shaft of his prick. More urgently, though, he wants to empty his bladder – no, not into her mouth, anywhere – and then lay himself down to sleep.

As he enters the parlour, it's as if he is already dreaming. An obscure

female figure sits in a far corner, face turned away from him, smoke rising
from her hair. A tentative violoncello is playing, invisible and plaintive,
then stops with an asthmatic scrape of catgut. The upper parts of the
walls, seamed with a dado rail, are painted lurid peach, and crowded with
framed miniatures; the lower parts are papered with a dense design of
strawberries, thorns and red roses. And, in the centre of the parlour,
directly under a bombastic bronze chandelier, sits Mrs Castaway.

She is an old woman, or badly preserved, or both. Dressed for going
out of doors, bonnet and all, she is clearly not about to do so, stationed
snug as a judge behind a narrow desk. The desk is strewn with snippets
of paper, cuttings from journals. A pair of oversized dressmaking scissors
snickers in her hand, paring away an almost substanceless rind of paper
which slips over her knuckles and flutters into her lap. She looks up, stops
scissoring, in honour of her guest's arrival; carefully she disentangles the
shears from her fingers and lays the gleaming metal to one side.

From head to hems she is decked out entirely in one colour: scarlet,
which William has never seen on any other English woman in his lifetime.
Her mouth, too, is painted the same hue, the hundred tiny wrinkles around
her lips tainted, so that when she smiles in welcome the effect is
disturbingly like a furry red caterpillar responding to stimulus.

At first William thinks she must be insane, a mad old witch compelled
to make bizarrely manifest her status as a 'scarlet' woman, but then he
detects a certain dignity about her, a self-possession, that makes him more
inclined to think her attire is an elaborate joke. She wouldn't be the first
madam he's met with her tongue planted in her cheek. In any case (he
notices now) the scarlet is softened by one dissenting shade, that of the
veil pinned back onto her bonnet. This is the same colour exactly as the
Rackham Perfumeries emblem, the dusty pink rose.

'Welcome to Mrs Castaway's, sir,' she says, white teeth seeming to
revolve like cogs behind her cochineal lips. '*I* am Mrs Castaway, and these
are my girls.' She waves one hand vaguely about, but William cannot yet
take his eyes off her. 'The use of the room upstairs will cost you five
shillings, though what happens there, and for how long, is for you and
Sugar to put a value to. If you wish, there can be good wine waiting for
you, for an additional two shillings.'

'Wine, then,' William says. Lord knows he has enough strong drink in
him, but he doesn't wish to impress the madam as tight-fisted. As he

stumbles forward to pay (What fool placed the edge of a rug just there, where a man must put his foot?) he surveys the old woman's body more analytically: she's an ugly old bird, he decides. And ugliness is not what he came here to see.

Freed from Mrs Castaway's spell, William is able to take in the rest of the room. Its giddying effect is not, he reassures himself, a symptom of his own inebriation: the whole parlour really *is* a grotesquerie. The framed prints, he notices now, all depict Mary Magdalen: a varied assortment of half-naked, half-clothed versions of her, repentant or otherwise, some of them painted by pious Christians, others sly caricatures intended as pornography. Dozens of replicas of that same expression of sad serenity, of renunciation of the all-too-wicked flesh, of surrender to a God who makes all other males redundant. Mary Magdalen in full colour, from Romish prayer cards; Mary Magdalen in black-and-white, from Protestant journals; Mary Magdalen with halo and without; Mary Magdalen large as the frontispiece of a penny magazine; Mary Magdalen tiny as a locket miniature. It's like Billington & Joy in here!

In the armchair by the hearth, still ignoring everybody, sits the young woman William is later to know as Amy Howlett. She's a compact thing, sloe-eyed and sulky, with pitch-black hair and a figure rather like . . . well, rather like Agnes's really, packed into a smart if severe black, white and silver dress. He can see her face now; she is, shockingly, smoking a cigarette, without even the mitigation of a holder, and if she has any inkling that, in England at least, a man may more often have seen a penis in a woman's mouth than a cigarette, she betrays no sign. Instead, frowning, she sucks, her eyes focused on the little glow-tipped cylinder of rice-paper and tobacco between her pretty fingers. In nonchalant defiance, she glances at him through a haze of smoke, as if to say, 'So?'

Nonplussed, William looks away towards the hearth, and catches sight of the polished neck of a violoncello, poking up over the back of an armchair facing the fire. There's a woman's neck showing, too, and a skull's-worth of mousy hair as thin as cobwebs.

'Do play on, Miss Lester,' says Mrs Castaway. 'This gentleman appreciates fine things, I'm sure.'

Miss Lester's head turns; she looks for William over the back of the armchair, her cheek resting on the antimacassar, her forehead wrinkled, her eyes deep-set in their sockets. But locating where in the world he might be costs her too much effort, and she turns again, back to the fire. The see-sawing moan of the 'cello resumes.

Just as he begins to wonder what these peculiar people would do with his unconscious body if he were to fall to the floor, William is much relieved to feel Sugar's hand slip into his. She squeezes once, to bid him come.

Mounting the stairs, William feels his ears burning red, his brow prickling with sweat. His bladder aches with every step, his balance is not the best, his vision requires regular eye-blinks to clear the gathering mists. Time is running out on his sexual coup.

'My room is the first upstairs,' whispers Sugar at his side. She is lighting their way with a candle; her posture is ramrod-straight and her arm holds the spear of wax without a tremble. The receding song of the 'cello provides the melody to the rhythm of their footfalls.

William, glancing back downstairs to make sure he is out of the madam's earshot, mutters, 'Your Mrs Castaway is a queer fish.'

He has quite forgotten the claim made by the Drury Lane 'twins', that Mrs Castaway is Sugar's own mother, though if reminded he would probably dismiss it as whores' claptrap anyway.

'Oh, very queer indeed,' agrees Sugar with a smile, and sweeps her skirts over the last steps and onto the landing. 'Try to think of her as a sort of Janus in red taffeta, and this door as . . . well, whatever door you most dearly wish to go through.' She opens it wide and beckons him across the threshold.

William sways after her, blinking sweat from his eyes. If only he could turn her off for just a few moments, like a machine, while he took the opportunity to wash his face, run a comb through his hair, empty his aching bladder. Mercifully, Sugar's bed-chamber is bright and airy, free of that waxy smell which so sickened him in Drury Lane. Higher-ceilinged than most upstairs rooms, it is lit by gas rather than candlelight and, though there's a fire glowing in the hearth, there's also a blessed whiff of fresh, ice-cold air filtering through from somewhere.

As soon as he has cast off his coat and waistcoat, William heads for the bed, a queen-sized and much augmented edifice much more impressive than his own at home (that is, the one he sleeps in, not the conjugal one in what's become, over the years, Agnes's private bedroom). Sugar's has a canopy of green silk mounted on it, an awning fit for a king. The drapes hang slightly parted, gathered in with golden cords, and all around the base is a sumptuous valence in a (sadly) unmatching shade of . . . what would one call it? . . . mint. A shame. He looks across the room at Sugar, who stands by the door still, hesitating to remove her gloves, waiting for his approval or the lash of his tongue. He smiles, signalling that she needn't fret; he'll overlook the mint valence. It's a mere hiccup of taste, a regrettable touch of 'make-do', no doubt forced upon the house by economy. Even in this, he and Sugar are soulmates of a kind: why, think of the humiliating hat he would have been wearing, if he'd met her only a few days earlier!

'Everything to your liking, Mr Hunt?'

'It will be,' he grins, narrowing his eyes meaningfully, 'soon enough.'

He reclines on the mattress, tests its firmness and softness with his elbows. Thirty seconds later he is fast asleep.

To fall asleep in the bed-chamber of a prostitute, unless you are the prostitute herself, is, as a general rule, either impossible or impermissible. Rackham has, in the past, been roughly taken in hand and brought to orgasm or, if that wasn't practical, to the brothel's back door and discharged into the chill of the night, shoved towards his own bed, however far away that might be.

Yet, Rackham sleeps on.

Sugar does not sleep with him. She sits at an escritoire near the window, fully dressed (though she has removed her gloves), writing. Her cracked and peeling fingers grip the pen tight. A journal not unlike a business ledger is scratched quietly, with long silences between certain words.

Rackham snores.

Just before dawn, Rackham wakes. He is sprawled on his back, his head sunk unpillowed into the soft surface of the undisturbed bed. He cranes his head further back, looking up towards the bed-head. Alarmingly, another man stares back at him, a wild-eyed, tousle-haired fellow reaching towards him across the sheets, keen (it would seem) to recommence abominable acts.

William sits up with a start, and so does the stranger. Mystery solved: the entire bed-head is a massive mirror.

The bed's drapes have been fully drawn, veiling him inside. Just as well: to his shame and consternation, he finds that his trousers are sodden with urine. This is what's woken him − not the emission from his bladder *per se*, which must have happened hours ago, but a maddening itch in his clammy groins. He peers into the mirror again, compiling a mental inventory of the damage. He doesn't seem to have vomited, nor is he queasy now. His head throbs considerably less than he expected (The Fireside's ale must agree with him – or perhaps he's still drunk . . . What time is it? Why the devil hasn't he been expelled?). His hair has come loose again, standing up from his scalp like greasy sheep's wool. He digs into a trouser pocket for a comb, finds only a tangle of sopping undergarments.

God Almighty, how is he going to get out of this?

He crawls to the foot of the bed, peeks through a gap in the drapes. A cast-iron stand is right outside, cradling a pewter ice bucket. The neck of a full wine-bottle rests against the rim, re-corked with the screw still in. On the floor, well out of his reach, lies the waistcoat that contains his watch. He can even see its silver chain, trailing out of the flaccid fob-pocket. (If this had been France, he wouldn't be seeing that chain, he has to admit.)

Where is Sugar? He holds his breath, listening hard. All he hears, apart from an unidentifiable scratching, is the sudden rustle of the hearth's contents, the sound of unstable half-burnt coals and embers collapsing.

Only one wall is visible through the slit in the veil. Fortunately it's the one with the window in it, offering valuable clues to the time of night. The panes are almost opaque with frost – thick frost such as accumulates over many hours. Beyond the frost, the sky is black and indigo, or seems so in contrast to the undimmed interior. The curtains stir almost imperceptibly: despite the freeze, Sugar has left the window open just the tiniest crack. But where is she? William leans further forward, nudging the fabric with his nose, insinuating one eye into the open.

Sugar's room is . . . homely. The walls are simply painted, a uniform flesh-pink as opposed to the rococo excesses of the parlour downstairs. A few small, framed prints, much faded from exposure, hang at strategic intervals. The furnishings are decent, comprising a freshly upholstered couch, two armchairs that don't quite match, and (he pushes his face further forward still) an escritoire complete with pens, inkwell, and . . . (he blinks in disbelief) Sugar herself, hunched over, lost in concentration.

'Ah . . . forgive me,' he announces.

She looks up, lowers her pen, and smiles – a disarming, companionable smile. She's dog-tired, he can tell.

'Good morning, Mr Hunt,' she says.

'Oh Lord . . .' he sighs, awkwardly running his hands through his hair. 'What . . . what time is it?'

She consults a clock beyond his range of vision. Her own hair, he suddenly notices, is absolutely glorious, a lush corona of golden-orange curls: she has taken the trouble to brush and shape it while he slept.

'Half past five.' She pouts roguishly. 'If anyone else is still up, they'll be much impressed by your prowess.'

William moves to dismount from the bed, then stiffens, blushing.

'I . . . I hardly know how to tell you this. I . . . I have . . . suffered a most regrettable, a most shameful loss of . . . ah . . . control.'

'Oh, I know,' she says, matter-of-factly, getting to her feet. 'Don't worry, I'll take care of it for you.'

She pads over to the hearth, where a kettle has been gently simmering on a grate above the embers. She sloshes a brilliant arc of steaming water into an earthenware tureen which, by the sound of it, is already partly filled, and carries it over to the bed. The skin of her hands, he notes, is dry and cracked, like peeling bark, yet the fingers are exquisitely formed. Michelangelo fingers, ringed with an exotic blight.

'Take your wet things off, please, Mr Hunt,' she says, kneeling on the floor, her skirts spreading out all around her. The tureen is almost brim-full of sudsy liquid, a sea sponge bobbing around in it like a peeled potato. Apparently Sugar has been waiting for this moment.

'Really, Miss Sugar,' William mumbles. 'This is quite beyond . . . How can I possibly expect you—'

She looks up at him, half-closes her eyes, shakes her head slowly, mimes the swollen-lipped supplication: 'Shu-u-u-sh.'

Together they manage to remove his trousers and underbreeches. The sharp stink of stewed piss wafts up, inches from Sugar's nose, but she doesn't flinch. For the all the effect the stench has on her unblinking gaze, her serene brow, her secret half-smile, it might as well be perfume.

'Lie back, Mr Hunt,' she croons. 'Everything will be set to rights soon.'

With the utmost gentleness, she washes him while he reclines, astounded, on the bed. A touch of her rough-textured knuckles is enough to make him part his legs wider, as she dabs the warm soapy sponge into his groin. She frowns in sympathy, to see excoriation in the clefts.

'Poor baby,' she murmurs.

The bed-sheets beneath him are soaked, so she nudges him to wriggle further up. Then, with a brushed cotton cloth wrapped around one hand like a mitten, she mops and dabs him dry. Nothing escapes her attention, even the ticklish hollow of his umbilicus. His penis she squeezes gently in her soft cottony palm, progressing in tiny increments as if its sheer length calls for a measure of patience.

'Really, Miss Sugar . . .' he protests again, but he has no words to follow.

'No "Miss" needed,' she corrects him, tossing the cloth aside. 'Just Sugar.' And she lowers her face to his perfumed belly and kisses his navel. He gasps as one of her knuckles pushes between the powdered cheeks of his arse, gently corkscrewing into him. A moment later, she lays her cheek on his thigh, hair sprawling all over his stomach, and secretes the whole of his sex into her mouth. Once she has it there, she lies still, neither sucking nor licking: just still, as if keeping him safe. All the while, she massages his anus, using her free hand to stroke his belly. His prick grows hard against her tongue, and when it's nestling snug she begins to suck, placidly, almost absentmindedly, as a child might suck its own thumb.

'No,' groans William, but of course he means the opposite.

Minute upon minute she lies on his thigh, milking him, slyly inserting her middle finger into his anus, deeper and deeper, pushing past the sphincter. When he comes, she feels the contractions squeezing her finger first, then clamps her lips firm around his cock as the warm gruel squirts into her throat. She swallows hard, sucks, swallows again. Slowly she extracts her finger, sucking still, sucking until there's nothing left to suck.

Later, the two of them discuss remuneration.

Dawn is on the horizon, a tarnished halo over Soho. The first horses are passing along Silver Street, their harnesses jingling, their hooves drubbing on the cobbles. Inside Sugar's bed-chamber, the gas-lamps are beginning to cast the faintly unreal hue so characteristic of artificial light when a natural alternative lies in wait. A subtle haze of steam is rising from a dark wad of male clothing, suspended on a rack near the fire.

The owner of those trousers and the owner of that rack are engaged in polite dispute over what the night's transpirations, considered *in toto*, have been worth. Rackham is inclined to be generous; he fears he has imposed on her while he slept.

'A man needs his sleep,' demurs Sugar. 'And it would have been cruel to condemn you to the streets in such a state. Besides, I occupied myself quite usefully while I was waiting.'

'You were waiting?'

'Of course I was waiting. You are a very interesting man, Mr Hunt.'

'Interesting?' William can scarcely believe his ears.

She smiles, exposing pearly-white teeth. Her lips are red now, no longer so dry. 'Very interesting.'

'Nevertheless I feel I must pay you for the time I lay here like a drunken fool. And for my disgraceful . . . incontinence. Unintentional though it was.'

'Whatever you wish,' she concedes graciously.

But Rackham is unable to divide the night's events into discrete services; to categorise them thus cheapens them somehow. Instead, gauchely, he fingers a number of coins out of his purse, heavy coins of a greater value than some of this city's inhabitants — say, the denizens of Church Lane — ever set eyes on.

'I — is this enough?' he asks, conferring the silver pieces into her palm.

'Exactly right,' she replies, closing her hand. 'Including a little extra' (she winks) 'for the sleeping.'

Outside, something massive is being delivered to the rear of a shop. Weary male voices chant 'One, two, free!', followed by a chain-clanking thump. William walks over to the window, naked from the waist down, and tries to descry through the frosty panes what's happening out there, but he can't make it out.

'You know,' he muses, 'I haven't even seen you naked.'

'Next time,' says Sugar.

He knows he ought to go home, but he's loath to leave. Besides, his trousers may not be dry yet. Solemnly, to buy another few minutes, he examines the prints on Sugar's walls, dawdling past them as he might at a Royal Academy exhibition. They are pornographic, depicting eighteenth-century gentlemen (his father's grandfathers, so to speak) contentedly fucking the harlots of their day. The men are amiable duffers, ruddy-faced and fat; the women are plump too, with Raphael breasts, puff sleeves, and faces like sheep. Phalluses twice the size of his are shown entering freakishly extruded vaginas, and yet the effect is no more erotic than a Bible illustration. In Rackham's judgement, these pictures are (what's the word he's looking for?) . . . *feeble*.

'You don't like them, do you?' Sugar's husky voice, at his shoulder.

'Not much. They're rather second-rate, I think.'

'Oh, without a doubt, you're right,' she says, wrapping one arm around his waist. 'They've been hanging there forever. They're insipid. In fact, I know the right word for them: feeble.'

He gapes at her, dumbfounded. Are his thoughts as naked to her as his legs and genitals?

'I'll replace them with something better,' she promises wistfully, 'if I can ever afford it.' Then she turns away, as though discouraged by the yawning gulf that separates her from being able to afford top-notch pornographic prints.

All of a sudden a far more vivid image springs into Rackham's mind: a recollection of Sugar just as she was when he first woke from his sleep: Sugar sitting hunched at the escritoire, scribbling, at half past five in the morning. His heart is jabbed with the awareness of her poverty – what could she possibly have been doing? Sweated labour of some kind, but what? Is there such a thing as secretarial piece-work? He's never read of it (it surely merits an article in one of the monthly reviews, along the lines of *Outrage Uncovered in the Very Heart of Our Fair City!*) but why else would a girl be toiling over a copy-book in the middle of the night? Doesn't she earn enough as a . . . as a prostitute, to keep body and soul together? Perhaps she's undervalued; perhaps most men spurn her, on account of her small breasts, her skin ailment, her masculine intellect. Well, it's their loss, thinks Rackham. *Honi soit qui mal y pense!*

This stab of sympathy he feels for Sugar he could never feel for the Drury Lane 'twins', much less for the shabby trollops who accost him in alleyways; those creatures are indivisible from the muck that surrounds them, like rats. One's heart does not go out to rats. But to see Sugar – this clever, beautiful young woman who shares his own low opinion of Matthew Arnold, and many things besides – slaving over an ink-stained ledger late at night, pricks his conscience. If the accounts of Rackham Perfumeries are cruel drudgery for a man of his temperament, what must this girl, barely past adolescence, brimful of life and promise, be suffering as she scribbles? How difficult Life is for those who deserve better!

'I must be going,' he says, brushing her cheek with his hand. 'But before I do, I . . . I have something more to give you.'

'Oh?' She raises her eyebrows, raises her own hand to grasp his.

'On the bed.' Explanation or command, her response is the same; she clambers onto the bed, boots and all, on her knees. William climbs after her, gathering up the skirts of her dress in big soft handfuls, tossing the silken greenery onto her back. The horse-hair hump of her bustle makes the pile absurdly large, so bulky it obscures her reflection in the bed-head.

'I can't see your face,' he says.

Even as he pulls her pantalettes down, she lifts her head high, straining as if for a Lamarckian feat of evolution, her jaw trembling slightly, her mouth falling open with effort. Over the mound of scrumpled dress material, he sees all this and more reflected back at him in the glass.

Her cunt is tight, and surprisingly dry. This girl's flesh needs more moisture altogether, it seems; perhaps her diet is lacking in oily foods or an essential nutrient. How strange that when she had him in her mouth, it felt as if she had no teeth, whereas now, inside her vagina, the tender nub of his prick is being nipped by unyielding tucks of flesh. However, he pushes through the discomfort, wincing once or twice, persisting until his organ and hers are accommodating each other perfectly, and he comes like a piston.

Minutes later, when he has already donned his hot, dampish trousers and is handing Sugar an additional coin, he is suddenly plagued by an anxiety that he'll never see her again. (Not without cause, either: wasn't there that girl in Paris, the one who liked rough treatment, who promised him '*A demain!*' and then was gone the next morning?)

'You'll be here tomorrow?' he asks.

Her brow furrows, as if he has just rekindled their Fireside conversation on the subject of Death, Fate and the Soul. 'God willing,' she concedes, with a glimmer of a smile.

He's standing in the threshold of her door now, lingering, knowing that if he stays any longer he's liable to make an ass of himself.

'Goodbye then, Mr Hunt.' She kisses him on the cheek, her lips dry as paper, her breath sweet as scented soap.

'Yes . . . I . . . but . . . but I must tell you . . . the name George Hunt. It's — I'm ashamed to tell you — a fiction. A white lie. To keep those nosy girls at The Fireside from becoming bothersome.'

'A man must be careful with his name,' Sugar agrees.

'Discretion is a much abused virtue,' says Rackham.

'You needn't tell me anything.'

'William,' he volunteers immediately. 'William is my name.'

She nods, accepts the intimacy with mute good grace.

'However,' he goes on, 'I would be most grateful if you could, at all times when you're in mixed company, refer to me as Mr Hunt.'

She opens her mouth to speak, stifles a yawn with the back of her hand. *Forgive me please, I'm so terribly sleepy*, her eyes plead, as she nods again. 'Anything you please.'

'But do call me William — here.'

'William,' she repeats. 'William.'

Rackham smiles, a beam of satisfaction that is still on his face when, a mere sixty seconds later, he's standing out in the street, alone, two guineas the poorer, horses snorting to his left, flakes of snow stinging his face. A stiff wind alerts him to the fact that his trousers needed more time in front of the fire; the odour of faeces at his feet reminds him that the sweet scent of a woman can be expunged all too soon.

Of course this is not the first time William Rackham has been smoothly and swiftly swept out into the street as soon as his tryst with a prostitute has been concluded. But it's certainly the first time he arrives at that juncture feeling perfectly content, begrudging not a penny of the expense, wishing not an instant of the experience undone. God, what a night! Nothing transpired as he imagined it might, and yet everything surpassed his dreams! Who would believe it! He feels like telling someone the whole exciting story, feels like rushing home and . . . well, perhaps not.

The snowfall thins and dwindles, and is abruptly gone, but this narrow street is a draughty place and William begins to shiver. Still he's reluctant to leave the scene of his remarkable adventure: it can't be over yet! Craning his head back, he stares up the rear of Mrs Castaway's, wondering which of those windows is Sugar's. Half-way up the building, a brightly lit window shows some movement: a silhouette passing. But it isn't Sugar, it's a child, moving slowly and haltingly, humping a large burden up a flight of unseen stairs.

'Excuse me, master,' says a voice behind him.

William almost jumps out of his skin, whirls round to face whoever dares intrude on his reverie.

It's a filthy old crone clutching a rusted bucket, her dark face like driftwood eaten away by the Thames, her lifeless hair indistinguishable from the threadbare shawl that covers it, her back bent like a rusted sickle wrapped in oily black rags. Her free hand is dangling low, an inch or two from the ground, her gnarled fingers clutching near his trouser-bottoms as if hoping to stroke them.

'Excuse me, master,' she says again, in an ancient, sexless voice that seems to issue from an abscess inside her scum-encrusted clothing. She smells repulsive. William steps aside.

Immediately she waddles forward and reaches down to the exact spot where he was standing, or damn near. With her blackened claws she picks up a large dog turd, fingering it carefully so that it doesn't crumble, and transfers it into her bucket, which is a quarter-full with ordure of the same kind, destined for the Bermondsey tannery where it will be used to dress morocco and kid leather. Rackham stares down at her, and the old woman mistakes his disbelief for pity; she looks up to him, wondering if the eight pence she hopes to get for her pail of 'pure' can be supplemented with an early-morning godsend.

'Ha'penny for a crust, master?'

Galvanised by disgust, Rackham fumbles in his purse and tosses her a coin. She knows better than to grasp his gloved hand and kiss it. Instead, bowing to his wish, she melts away into the first rays of the sun.

At the door of Sugar's bedroom, a knock. She opens it, her face arranged into her best 'serene' expression in case it's Mr Hunt – William – Prince Glorious, whatever his name is, coming back for a lost garter or a grope at her bosom. '*It suddenly occurs to me I haven't seen your breasts yet.*'

But no, it's not Mr Hunt.

'Up already, Christopher?'

The boy stands, veiled in steam, behind the great pail of fresh hot water he has carried up to her. He's only partly dressed, his mop of blond hair is disordered, and he has crystals in the corners of his eyes.

'I saw yer light,' he says.

Such a sweet boy, anticipating her needs like this. Unless he's just trying to get a chore out of the way.

'But weren't you asleep?'

'Amy wakes me,' he sniffs, flexing his tiny pink fingers to get the blood back into them. The dull iron rim of the pail reaches his knees and its circumference, Sugar estimates, equals his height.

'So early? What does she wake you for?'

'Nuffink. She yells in 'er sleep.'

'Really?' As a rule, Amy dispatches her last customer much earlier than Sugar, and doesn't rise again until the following noon. 'I never hear it.'

'She yells soft,' says Christopher, brow knitting. 'But I'm right up close. Next to 'er mouth, like.'

'Really?' From the way Amy talks when awake, it's difficult to believe she would tolerate her son in the same bed with her. 'I thought you had your own little closet to sleep in.'

'I do. But I come out when Amy's finished, an' get in next to 'er. She don't mind me when she's asleep. She don't mind nuffink.'

'She *does*n't mind *any*thing, Christopher.'

'What I said.'

Sugar sighs, lifts the pail and carries it inside her room, careful to acknowledge in her posture how heavy it is. What a little champion! She'd been resigned, at this irregular hour, to going down to the boiler room herself, no sign of life being evident by the time William – Mr Hunt – Emperor Pisspants – finally departed. She'd already dragged the hip-bath, and sundry other necessities, from their hiding-place inside the wardrobe, and was just trying to persuade herself to fetch the water when Christopher came knocking.

'I really am grateful,' she says, tipping the contents of the bucket into the tub.

'It's what I should be about,' he shrugs. 'I earn me keep.'

Looking back at him standing on the landing, Sugar notices the tell-tale marks of his struggle with the pail, lugged over-full up far too many stairs in his effort to save an extra trip. There are livid red crescents on his forearms, and his bare feet and trouser-cuffs are wet and steaming with hot spillage.

'Man of the house, you are,' she praises him, but she's forgetting that flattery rubs him up the wrong way. With a peevish twitch he turns from her, and runs back downstairs.

Shame, she thinks, but then again there are only so many hours on end that a woman can keep in mind all the needs and preferences of males. In the bleary light of dawn, Sugar is ready to be excused.

For the first time in thirty-three hours, she removes all her clothes. Her green dress smells of cigar smoke, beer and sweat. Her corset is stained with dye from the bodice, which is evidently not meant to be worn in the rain. Her camisole stinks, her pantalettes have the snot of male ecstasy all over them. She tosses everything into a pile, and steps naked into the tub. First her long legs, then her bruised buttocks, then finally that bosom whose immaturity those drooling swine who compile muck-rags like *More Sprees in London* never fail to remark upon – all sink beneath the bubbles.

Guffaws, chatter and the clanking din of goods deliveries grow louder outside her window; sleeping may prove difficult, though she'll probably drop off during the lull that always comes between the shops preparing themselves and the customers arriving. Her consciousness is already dissolving at the edges; she must take care not to fall asleep where she sits. She's so tired now that she can't even remember whether she has performed her prophylactic ritual or not.

Heavy locks of hair disentwine from her loosening chignon, unravelling onto her wet back, dropping hairpins into the water, as she turns to look for evidence of remembering or forgetting. The tureen of contraceptive is where she left it, and yes, she remembers now, she *has* used it. Thank God for that. Not that she can actually recall inserting the plunger, but there it lies (tipped not with cloth, like Caroline's, but with a real sea sponge), sopping wet beside the tureen.

How many hundred times has she performed this ceremony? How many sponges and swabs has she worn away? How many times has she prepared this witches' brew, measuring the ingredients with mindless precision? Granted, in her Church Lane days the recipe was slightly different; nowadays, as well as the alum and the sulphate of zinc, she adds a dash of *sal eratus*, or bicarbonate of soda. But in essence it's the same potion she's squatted over almost nightly since she began to bleed at sixteen.

A crucial hairpin gives way; the remainder of her waist-length hair threatens to unfurl into the tepid water. Shivering, she rises, standing above the froth, hands on her thighs. And, at long last, she is able to release the residue of urine, trifling but painful, that wouldn't come out earlier, before her bath. The yellow droplets patter down on the suds, writing dark nonsense into the white of the soap-scum. Is it only piddle draining out of her now? Could there really be anything else left in there? Sometimes she has walked along the street, a full half-hour after a wash, and suddenly felt a gush of semen soiling her underclothes. What could God, or the Force of Nature, or whatever is supposed to be holding the Universe together, possibly have in mind, by making it so difficult to be clean inside? What, in the grand scheme of things, is so uniquely precious about piss, shit or the makings of another pompous little man, that it should be permitted to cling to her innards so tenaciously?

'God damn God,' she whispers, tensing and untensing her pelvic muscles, 'and all His horrible filthy creation.'

As if in response to the trickle into her bathwater, there is a pattering against the frosty window, and then the gentle rush of rain, drowning out the noise of humans and horses. Sugar steps out of the tub, drying herself with a fresh white towel while, on the window, the frost crackles, turns milky and washes off, revealing rooftops silhouetted against a brightening sky. The fire in her hearth has gone out and she's shivering with cold as she pulls her night-gown over her head, half dead with exhaustion. But her patience with what's-his-name – with Do-Call-Me-William – has been plentifully rewarded: as much money as she would have had from three individual men. Mind you, she isn't greedy: she'd happily have done without getting fucked in the end.

Then she shuffles – yes, yes, *yes* – to her bed.

Grunting, she slaps aside the sagging drapes. Her reflection shows an angry young woman ready to murder anyone or anything that stands in her way. With a grunt of determination she seizes hold of the soiled sheets and tries to drag them off the mattress, but all strength is gone. So, slumping in defeat, she extinguishes the lights, crawls up to a dry corner of the bed right near the mirror, pulls a blanket over her body, and utters a cry of relief.

For a few seconds more she lies awake, listening to the downpour. Then she shuts her eyes and, as usual, her spirit flies out of her body, into the dark unknown, unaware that this time she is flying in a different direction. Down on earth, her dirty tub and her wet bed remain, shut inside a decaying building among other decaying buildings in this vast and intricate city; in the morning, it will all be waiting to swallow her back inside. But there is a greater reality: the reality of dreams. And, in those dreams of flying, Sugar's old life has already ended, like a chapter in a book.

PART 2

The House of Ill Repute

SEVEN

he heir to Rackham Perfumeries, in a fresh suit of clothes and light-headed from lack of sleep, stands in his parlour staring out at the rain, wondering if what he's feeling is love. He has been rudely drenched, he has been overcharged by the cabman who brought him home, no one received him until the fourth pull of the bell, his bathwater was an age in coming, and now he is being kept waiting for his breakfast – but none of it matters. *Out there*, he thinks, *is the girl of a lifetime.*

He pulls harder on the sash, and the curtains part wider – as wide as they can go. But the torrential downpour that has followed him from the city all the way to Notting Hill is letting precious little sunlight show; rather, a quantum of paleness filters through the French windows, settling on the lamp-lit parlour like a layer of dust. Half past nine, and the lamps still on! Ah, but it doesn't matter. The rain is beautiful: how beautiful rain can be! And think of all the muck it's washing off the streets! And think also: only a few miles south-east of here, housed under this self-same sky, in all probability still tucked up in bed, lies a naughty angel called Sugar. And inside *her*, glowing like silver on the lining of her womb, is *his* seed.

He lights a cigarette and inserts it between his pursed lips, reconfirming the decision he made almost immediately after leaving Mrs Castaway's: that he must have Sugar entirely to himself. An idle dream? Not at all. He need only be rich, and wealth, great wealth, is his for the claiming.

A haze of smoke on his side of the glass; a panorama of rain on the other. He imagines the metropolis seen from a great height, all of it bound together not just in a shimmering web of rain but in his own web as well, the web of his destiny. Yes, on this luminous grey day he will gather the Rackham empire into his grasp, while Sugar sleeps. Let her sleep, until the time is ripe for him to tug on a thread and wake her.

Obscure noises emanate from elsewhere in the house, not recognisable as footsteps and voices, scarcely audible above the din of the downpour. Rainy weather makes servants skittish, William has found. In fact, he's noticed it so often that he's toyed with the idea of writing an amusing article about it, for *Punch*, called 'Servants and the Weather'. The silly creatures dash back and forth aimlessly, standing very still for a few moments and then jerking into motion, disappearing suddenly under the stairs or into a corridor – just like kittens. Amusing . . . but they've kept him waiting so long for his breakfast this morning that he could almost have written the article already.

A slight dizziness, caused no doubt by hunger, prompts him to sit in the nearest armchair. He stares down, through his tobacco fog, at the polished parlour floor, and notes that a tiny trickle of water has entered the room through the French windows, from the sheer force and persistence of the rain. It's advancing unevenly along the floorboards, inching its way towards him; it has a long way to go yet, trembling, waiting on another gust of wind. With nothing better to do, William sits entranced and watches its progress, laying a mental wager on whether, by the time Letty comes to announce that breakfast is served, this trickle will have reached the tip of his left slipper. If it hasn't, he'll . . . what shall he do? He'll greet Letty nicely. And if it has . . . he'll chastise her. Her fate, therefore, is in her own hands.

But when the servant finally comes, it isn't Letty, but Clara.

'If you please, sir,' she says (managing to convey, in that delightful way she has, that she couldn't care less if he pleases or not), 'Mrs Rackham will be joining you at breakfast this morning.'

'Yes, I . . . what?'

'Mrs Rackham, sir . . .'

'My – wife?'

She looks at him as though he's an imbecile; what other Mrs Rackham could it be?

'Yes, sir.'

'She's . . . quite *well*, then?'

'I can't see anything wrong with her, sir.'

William ponders this, while his cigarette, forgotten between his fingers, slinks towards scorching him.

'Splendid!' he says. 'What a pleasant surprise.'

And so it is that William finds himself seated at a table laid for two, waiting for the empty chair opposite him to be filled. He blows on his tender burnt flesh, shakes his hand in the air. He'd like to dunk his fingers into ice-cold wine or water, but there's only tea, and a small jug of milk which he (and . . . Agnes?) will need shortly.

The dining-room, built for a family of Biblical proportions, appears cheerlessly spacious. To compensate, some servant or other has over-stoked the fire, so that surplus warmth is getting stowed under the table, trapped by the heavy linen tablecloth. Better they had spent their meagre brain-power on drawing the curtains wider: it's none too bright in here.

Letty arrives, carrying a platter of toast and muffins. She looks flustered, poor creature. Not at all the way she looked months ago when he told her she'd be earning an extra two pounds a year 'because Tilly isn't here anymore'. No frown on her face then! But he knows what the problem is: Agnes, as mistress of the house, was meant to decide exactly which tasks would devolve to which servants, and she's done no such thing. Instead, the servants seem to have carved up the new responsibilities themselves.

'Everything all right, Letty?' he murmurs, as she pours him a cup of tea.

'Yes, Mr Rackham.' A lock of her hair has fallen loose, and one white cuff of her sleeve is lower than the other. He decides to let it pass.

'Do dampen that fire a bit, Letty,' he sighs, when she has finished arranging the toast in its rack and is about to leave. 'We'll all burst into flames in a minute.'

Letty blinks uncomprehendingly. She spends much of her time hurrying through draughty corridors, and her bedroom is in the attic, so warmth is not something with which she's too familiar. Her gimcrack little hearth is prone to choking up, making her room colder still, and what with the recent increase of her duties, she hasn't had time to spoon out her flue.

William mops his brow with a napkin while the servant kneels to her task. Why has Agnes chosen this morning, of all mornings, to join him at breakfast? Has her lunacy granted her a glimmer of clairvoyance? A glimpse of him and Sugar *in delicto*? Lord knows she's slept peacefully through many adulteries, so is it his after-glow of elation she senses? Yes, that must be it: his elation is charging the house like static before a storm, and Agnes has been stimulated. One minute she was unconscious, her sick-room shrouded and still; the next, her eyes flipped open like a doll's, animated by the electric change in atmosphere.

Surreptitiously, William lifts the lid of the butter-dish, and scoops out a smidgen of the golden grease to soothe his fingers.

Let's leave William now, and follow Letty out of the dining-room. She herself is of no consequence, but on her way towards the long subterranean passage to the kitchen, she catches sight of Agnes coming down the stairs – and Agnes is one of the people you came here to meet. It will be *so* much better if you have a chance to observe her now, before she composes herself for her husband.

Here, then, is Agnes Rackham, gingerly descending a spiral of stairs, breathing shallowly, frowning, biting her lip. As she reluctantly entrusts her weight to each carpeted step, she clutches the banister with one white-knuckled hand, while the other hand is laid on her breastbone, just under the mandarin collar of her morning-gown. It's Prussian blue velvet, that gown, and so ample in comparison to her dainty body that its hems threaten to ensnare the toes of her soft grey slippers, and send her tumbling.

You wonder if you've seen her somewhere before: indeed you have. She is a high-Victorian ideal; perfection itself at the time William married her, ever-so-slightly quaint now that the Seventies are half-way over. The shapes and demeanours now at the height of fashion are not Agnes's, but she remains an ideal nonetheless; her ubiquity cannot be erased overnight. She graces a thousand paintings, ten thousand old postcards, a hundred thousand tins of soap. She is a paragon of porcelain femininity, five foot two with eyes of blue, her blonde hair smooth and fine, her mouth like a tiny pink vulva, pristine.

'Good morning, Letty,' she says, pausing at the banister while she speaks the words. With the challenge of facing her husband still ahead, there's no point tempting Fate, on this hazardous descent, by talking and walking at the same time.

★   ★   ★

William jumps to attention when his wife arrives.

'Agnes, dear!' he says, hastening to pull her chair out from the table.

'No fuss, please, William,' she replies.

Thus begins the fight, the old fight, to establish which of them has the superior claim to being normal. There is a standard to which all reasonable humans conform: which of them falls short more noticeably? Which will be found most wanting by the impartial judge hovering invisibly in the space between them? The starting-gun has been fired.

Having seated his wife, William walks stiffly back to his own chair. So deathly quiet do they sit then that they can hear, not far outside the room, anxious female voices hissing. Something about Cook throwing fits, and a disagreement between the hissers (Letty and Clara?) about which of them has more arms.

Agnes calmly butters a muffin, ignoring the to-do on her behalf. She takes a bite, confirms the thing is made of leftover breadcrumbs, replaces it on the plate. A slice of Sally Lunn, still warm from its swaddling of serviette, is more to her liking.

A minute or two later, a perspiring Letty arrives at the Rackhams' table.

'If you please . . .' she simpers, curtseying as well as she can manage with two large, heavy-laden trays balanced, trembling, one on each arm.

'Thank you, Letty,' says Agnes, leaning back, observing the reaction of her husband as the food is unloaded, dish by dish, onto the table: a *proper* breakfast, the sort that gets served only when the mistress of the house is on hand to inspire it.

Eggs still steaming, rashers of bacon crisp enough to spread butter with, sausages cooked so evenly that there isn't a line on them, mushrooms brown as loam, roulades, fritters, kidneys grilled to perfection: all this and more is set before the Rackhams.

'Well, I hope you've an appetite today, my dear,' quips William.

'Oh yes,' Agnes assures him.

'You're feeling well, then?'

'Quite well, thank you.' She decapitates an egg: inside it is saffron-yellow and as soft as anyone could possibly want.

'You're *looking* very well,' observes William.

'Thank you.' She searches the walls for inspiration to go on. And, though there's no window visible from where she sits, she thinks of the rain which kept her company all night, stroking against her own window upstairs. 'It must be the weather,' she muses, 'that has made me so well. It's very strange weather, don't you think?'

'Mmm,' agrees William. 'Very wet, but not nearly so cold. Don't you find?'

'True, the frozenness is gone. If there is such a word as frozenness.' (What a relief! On the damp foundations of the weather, a spindly conversation has been built.)

'Well, my dear, if there isn't such a word, you've just done the English language a good turn.'

Agnes smiles, but unfortunately William is looking down just then, investigating if his roulade is beef or mutton. So, she prolongs the smile until he looks up and notices it — by which time, although her lips are shaped exactly the same, there's something indefinably amiss.

'I take it you heard the . . . disagreement?' remarks William, pointing vaguely towards where the hissing occurred.

'I heard nothing, dear. Only the din of the rain.'

'I think the servants are lacking guidance in who should be doing what, now that Tilly is gone.'

'Poor girl. I liked her.'

'They look to *you*, my dear, for that guidance.'

'Oh, William,' she sighs. 'It's all so complicated and tiresome. They know perfectly well what needs doing; can't they sort it out amongst themselves?' Then she smiles again, happy to have retrieved a useful memory from their shared past. 'Isn't that what you always used to talk about: Socialism?'

William pouts irritably. Socialism is not the same thing as letting one's servants muddle towards anarchy. But never mind, never mind: on a day like today, it's not worth worrying over. Soon the servant question, at least in William Rackham's household, will be resolved beyond any ambiguity.

A more immediate problem: the conversation is dying. William racks his brains for something to interest his wife, but finds only Sugar there, Sugar in every nook and corner. Surely, in the three or four weeks since he last breakfasted with Agnes, he's met *someone* they both know!

'I . . . I ran into Bodley and Ashwell, on . . . Tuesday, I b'lieve it was.'

Agnes inclines her head to one side, doing her best to pay attention and be interested. She detests Bodley and Ashwell, but here's a valuable opportunity to get in practice for the coming London Season, during which she will be required to do a great deal of talking to, and feigning interest in, people she detests.

'Well now,' she says. 'What are they up to?'

'They've written a book,' says William. 'It's about prayer, the efficacy of prayer. I imagine it will cause quite a stir.'

'They'll enjoy that, I'm sure.' Agnes selects some mushrooms for a slice of toast, lays them on in careful formation. Small morsels of time are consumed, with an indigestible eternity remaining.

'Henry didn't come to visit us last Sunday,' she remarks, 'nor the week before.' She waits a moment for her husband to take up the thread, then adds, 'I do like him, don't you?'

William blinks, discomfited. What is she getting at, discussing his brother as though he were an amusing fellow they met at a party? Or is she implying she cares more for Henry than he does?

'Our door is always open to him, my dear,' he says. 'Perhaps he finds us insufficiently devout.'

Agnes sighs. 'I'm being as devout as I possibly can,' she says, 'in the circumstances.'

William thinks better of pursuing this subject; it can only lead to trouble. Instead, he eats his sausage while it's still warm. Inside his mind, a naked woman with flame-red hair is lying face-down on a bed, semen glistening white on her crimson-lipped vulva. It occurs to him that he has not yet seen her breasts. Staring deeper into his thoughts, he wills her to turn, to rotate at the waist, but nothing happens – until Agnes breaks the silence.

'I wonder if . . .' She puts one nervous hand to her forehead, then, catching herself, slides it over to her cheek. 'If this weather were to go for ever . . . Raining, I mean . . . Rain would become normal, and dry skies something rather queer?'

Her husband stares at her, demonstrating his willingness to wait as long as it may take for her to resume making sense.

'I mean,' she continues, inhaling deeply, 'What I imagine is . . . The whole world might so . . . *fit* itself around constant rain, that when a dry day finally came, hu-husbands and wives . . . sitting at breakfast just like this . . . might find it awf-awfully strange.'

William frowns, stops chewing sausage for a second, then lets it pass.

He cuts himself another mouthful; in the luminous dimness of the rain-shrouded dining-room, a silver knife scrapes against porcelain.

'Mmm,' he says. The hum is all-purpose, incorporating agreement, bemusement, a warning, a mouthful of sausage – whatever Agnes cares to glean from it.

'Do go on, dear,' she urges him weakly.

Again William racks his brains for news of mutual acquaintances.

'Doctor Curlew . . .' he begins, but this is not the best of subjects to share with Agnes, so he changes it as smoothly as he can. 'Doctor Curlew was telling me about his daughter, Emmeline. She . . . she doesn't ever wish to remarry, he says.'

'Oh? What does she wish to do?'

'She spends almost all her time with the Women's Rescue Society.'

'Working, then?' Disapproval acts like a tonic on Agnes's voice, giving it much-needed flavour.

'Well, yes, I suppose it can hardly be called anything else . . .'

'Of course not.'

'. . . for although it's a Charity, and she's a volunteer, she's expected to do . . . well, whatever she's asked to. The way Curlew describes it, I understand she spends entire days at the Refuge or even on the streets themselves, and that when she visits him afterwards, her clothes fairly stink.'

'That's hardly surprising – ugh!'

'They claim an amazing rate of success, though, to be fair – at least so the doctor tells me.'

Agnes peers longingly over his shoulder, as if hoping a giant-sized parent might come rushing in to restore decorum.

'*Really*, William—' she squirms. 'Such a topic. And at the *break*fast table.'

'Hm, yes . . .' Her husband nods apologetically. 'It *is* rather . . . hm.' And he takes a sip of his tea. 'And yet . . . And yet it is an evil that we must face, don't you think? As a nation, without quailing.'

'What?' Agnes is forlornly hoping the topic will disappear if she loses the thread of it irretrievably enough. 'What evil?'

'Prostitution.' He enunciates the word clearly, gazing directly into her eyes, *knowing*, God damn it, that he is being cruel. In the back of his mind, a kinder William Rackham watches impotently as his wife is penetrated by that single elongated word, its four slick syllables barbed midway with t's. Agnes's cameo face goes white as she gulps for air.

'You know,' she pipes, 'when I looked out of my window this morning, the rose bushes – their branches – were jogging up and down so – like an umbrella opening and closing, opening and closing, opening and . . .' She shuts her lips tight, as if swallowing back the risk of infinite repetition. 'I thought – I mean, when I say I thought, I don't mean I actually *believed* – but they *seemed* as if they were sinking into the ground. Flapping like big green insects being sucked down into a quicksand of grass.' Finished, she sits primly in her chair and folds her hands in her lap, like a child who has just recited a verse to the best of her ability.

'Are you quite well, my dear?'

'Quite well, thank you, William.'

A pause, then William perseveres.

'The question is, *Is reform the answer?* Or even possible? Oh, the Rescue Society may claim some of these women now live respectably, but who knows for certain? Temptation is a powerful thing. If a reformed wanton knows very well she can earn as much in an afternoon as a seamstress earns in a month, how steadfast will she be in honest work? Can you imagine, Agnes, sewing a great mound of cotton shifts for a pittance, when if you will but remove your *own* shift for a few minutes . . .'

'William, *please!*'

A trickle of remorse stings his conscience. Agnes's fingers are gripping the tablecloth, wrinkling the linen.

'I'm sorry, dear. Forgive me. I'm forgetting you haven't been well.'

Agnes accepts his apology with a quirk of the lips that could be a smile – or a flinch.

'Do let's talk about something else,' she says, almost in a whisper. 'Let me pour you some more tea.'

Before he can protest that a servant should be summoned to perform this task, she has grasped the teapot's handle in her fist, her wrist shaking with the effort of lifting it. He rears up in his seat to help her, but she's already standing, her petite frame poised to support the massive china pot.

'Today is a special day,' she says, leaning over William's tea-cup. 'I intend,' (slowly pouring) 'to put my heads together – Cook and I – our heads together, to bake you your favourite chocolate and cherry cake, that you haven't had in *so* long.'

William is touched by this – touched to his soul.

'Oh, Aggie,' he says. 'That would be simply wonderful.'

The vision of her standing there, so small and frail, pouring his tea, suddenly overwhelms him. How despicably, how unfairly, he has treated her! Not just this morning, but ever since she first began to loathe him. Is it really her fault that she turned against his love, began to treat him as if he were a brute, turned him, finally, into a brute? He ought to have conceded that she was a flower not designed to open, a hothouse creation, no less beautiful, no less worth having. He should have admired her, praised her, cared for her and, at close of day, let her be. Moved almost to tears, he reaches out his hand across the table.

Abruptly, Agnes's arm begins to shake, with mechanical vehemence, and the spout of the teapot rattles loudly against the rim of William's cup. In an instant the cup has jumped out of its saucer, and the white of the tablecloth erupts with brown liquid.

William leaps from his seat, but Agnes's hand has already shivered out of the teapot's grip, and she totters away from the table, eyes wild. The shoulders around which he tries to cast a comforting arm seem to convulse and deflate and, with a retching cry, she falls to the floor. Or sinks to the carpet, if you will. Whatever way she gets there, she lands without a thump, and her glassy blue eyes are open.

William stares down in disbelief, though this is not the first time he's seen her sprawled at his feet; he is sick with concern, and hatred too, for he suspects she conspired in her collapse. She, in turn, stares up at him, bizarrely calm now that she can fall no farther. Her hair is still neat, her body is arranged as if for sleep. Shallow breaths, lifting her bosom, reveal that the body underneath the blue dressing-gown is more adult than its tiny size suggests.

'I made a mistake, getting up today,' she reflects, spiritlessly, her gaze drifting from her husband to the plaster rosettes on the ceiling. 'I thought I could, but I couldn't.'

Fortuitously — for the Rackhams at least — it's at this moment that Janey enters the room, sent to clear the breakfast table.

'Janey!' William barks. 'Run to Doctor Curlew's house and tell him to come at once.'

The girl curtseys, primed to obey, but she's stopped in her tracks by the sound of her mistress's voice coming up from the floor.

'Janey can't go,' the recumbent Mrs Rackham points out, a little wheezy from carpet dust. 'She's needed in the kitchen. And Letty will be busy with the beds now. Janey, tell Beatrice she's to go; she's the only one we can spare.'

'Yes 'm.'

'And call Clara to me.'

'Yes 'm.' Without waiting for a word from the master, the girl hurries off.

William Rackham dawdles near his wife, awkwardly flexing his hands. Once upon a time, when Agnes's illness was still new, he used to lift her up into his arms, and carry her from room to room. Now he knows that merely picking her up is not enough. He clears his throat, straining to find a way of demonstrating his remorse and his forgiveness.

'You aren't hurt, are you, my dear? I mean, in your bones? Should I even have called for Doctor Curlew, d'you think? I did it without thinking, in my . . . my agitation. But I daresay you don't need a doctor, now. Do you?' He holds it out to her: a tempting offer, for her to take or leave as she chooses.

'It's kind of you to think so,' she responds wearily. 'But it's too late now.'

'Nonsense. I can call the girl back.'

'Out of the question. As if it weren't bad enough, what's become of this household, without you running about in your slippers, chasing after a servant.'

And she turns her head away from him, towards the door through which rescue will come.

Clara arrives a few seconds later. She takes one look at her master, and another at Mrs Rackham. It's only natural, this appraisal: natural to link, with a glance, the upright man and the supine woman. And yet William detects something more in Clara's glance, a glower of accusation, which outrages him: he has never struck anyone in his life! And if he ever does, by God this insolent little beast is likely to be the first!

Clara, however, is already ignoring him; she's pulling Agnes to her feet (or is Agnes rising by her own efforts? – the deed is done with remarkably little fuss) and, shoulder to shoulder, the two women walk out of the room.

Now, who shall we follow? William or Agnes? The master or the mistress? On this momentous day, the master.

Agnes's collapse, though dramatic, is of no great significance; she has collapsed before and will collapse again.

William, on the other hand, proceeds directly to his study and, once seated there, does something he's never done before. He reads his father's papers, and he re-reads them, and then he ponders them, peering out into the rain, until he begins to understand them. He has been shocked into a state of acute wakefulness; he is ready. The pages of Rackham Perfumeries' history glow on the desk before him, veined with vertical shadows: rivulets of rain running down his window. He reads, pen poised. This is the day, the stormy and significant day, when he will bring his unruly future to heel.

Fearlessly, he opens his mind to the mathematics of manure, the arithmetic of acreage, the delicate balances between distillation and dilution. If he encounters a word that's nonsense to him, he roots it out in the reference books his father has thoughtfully provided, such as *A Lexicon of Profitable Vegetation* and *The Cultivator's Cyclopædia of Perfumes and Essences*. As of last night, ignorance of the inner workings of Rackham Perfumeries is a luxury he can no longer afford.

Of course he wants to put Agnes out of her misery. Each time a new economy is imposed – another servant lost, another extravagance denied – she takes a turn for the worse. A coachman and carriage would do more to woo her back to health than any of Curlew's prescriptions.

But Agnes is not at the heart of why he squints over his father's smudged and faded handwriting, tolerating his father's crude provincial spelling and crude provincial mind, puzzling over the technicalities of extracting juice from dry leaves. At the heart lies this: if he's to have Sugar all to himself, the privilege is going to cost him dear. A small fortune, probably, which he has no choice but to defray with a *large* fortune.

He pauses in his labours, rubs his eyes, itchy from lack of rest. He flips backwards through the handwritten essay his father has prepared for his illumination, and re-reads a paragraph or two. There's a missing link in the life cycle of lavender as his father chronicles it (if life cycle is the correct term for what happens to a flower after it is cut). Here on this page, the newly filtered oil is described as having an undesirable 'still smell'; on the next page, the smell is apparently gone, with no mention of how it was removed. William passes one hand through his hair, feels it standing up from his scalp, ignores the feeling.

Still smell – quo vadis? he jots in the margin, determined to survive this ordeal with his sense of humour intact.

★   ★   ★

Downstairs in the dining-room, Janey has an important task of her own. She is to remove all evidence of what Miss Tillotson described as a 'disaster' on the breakfast table. Janey, too downtrodden to dare ask what exactly this word means (she'd always thought it had something to do with the Navy) has come here prepared for the worst, with bucket and mop, her pinafore weighed down with rags and brushes. She finds an abandoned but perfectly lovely-looking breakfast and, on closer examination, one spilled tea-cup. No debris on the floor. Only what Janey herself has brought in, on the bottom of her bucket: a few crumbs of dirt from the uncarpeted nether regions of the Rackham house.

Hesitantly, the girl reaches for a slice of cold bacon, one of three still glistening on the silver dish. She takes it between her stubby fingers, and begins to nibble on it. Theft. But the wrath of God shows no interest in coming down upon her head, so she grows bolder, and eats the whole rasher. It's so delicious she wishes she could post one home to her brother. Next, a muffin, washed down with a sip of stewed tea. Mrs Rackham's uneaten kidneys she leaves alone, not sure what they are. Her own diet is what Cook decides will agree with her.

Wicked just like everyone says she is, Janey lowers her weary body into Mrs Rackham's chair. Though only nineteen, she has legs as dense and varicose as rolled pork, and any opportunity to rest them is bliss. Her hands are lobster-red, in vivid contrast to white china as she inserts her finger into the handle of her mistress's cup. Shyly, she extends her pinkie, testing to see if this makes any difference to the way the cup lifts.

But this is as much as God is willing to tolerate. A bell tolls, making her jump.

'Come in, Letty,' says Rackham, but he's wrong: it's Clara again. What *are* these servants playing at? Has the house descended into utter chaos while he's been toiling here? But then he remembers: he himself has sent Letty on an errand to the stationers, fifteen minutes ago.

'I suppose Doctor Curlew has arrived?'

Wrong again. Clara explains to him that there is no sign yet of Beatrice and the good doctor, but that, instead, Mr Bodley and Mr Ashwell have come to visit. They are (quotes Clara with conscientious disdain)

challenging him to a duel, acting as each other's seconds, and demanding that Rackham choose his weapon.

'I'll see them shortly,' he says. 'Bid them make themselves at home.'

If there's one thing that Bodley and Ashwell can be relied upon to do, it's
to make themselves at home. When William reaches a natural breathing-
space in his work and goes downstairs, he finds them sunk deep in the
smoking-room armchairs, languidly kicking each other's feet in competition for the privilege of resting them on the bald head of a stuffed tiger
skin.

'*Ave, Rackhamus!*' hails Ashwell, the old school greeting.

'By God, Bill,' exclaims Bodley. 'Your eyes look worse than mine! Been
fucking all night?'

'Yes, but I'm turning over a new leaf,' William volleys back. He's ready
for this! On a day like today, whatever God may send to frustrate him –
lack of sleep, burnt fingers, Agnes on the floor, a mound of dreary documents to plough through, the wit of his bachelor friends – he will not
allow his glow of triumph to be overshadowed.

It helps that in Bodley and Ashwell's company, he is forever an honorary
bachelor. As far as they're concerned, Agnes does not exist until William
mentions her. Admittedly, here in the Rackham house, her existence is
more difficult to deny than in the streets of London or Paris, for there are
reminders of her everywhere. The antimacassars on the chairs were
crocheted by her; the tablecloths are adorned by her embroidery; and under
every vase, candle-holder and knick-knack is likely to lie some finely
wrought doily or place-mat beautified by Mrs Rackham's handicraft. Even
the cedar cigar case owes its little embroidered jacket (in five colours of
thread, replete with silken tassels) to Agnes. But ('Cigar, Bodley?') William
is so accustomed to his wife's rococo icing on every exposed surface that
he has become blind to it.

In a sense, this policy of Bodley and Ashwell's – of denying Mrs
Rackham's existence – is considerate rather than callous. It tactfully lets
the marriage rest for as long as it needs to, like an invalid whose recovery
cannot be hurried. William is grateful to them, really he is, for their willingness to act the part of the three wise monkeys (well, two), seeing no
evil, hearing no evil, and . . . well, he doesn't know if they speak evil of
Agnes when they're in other company. He hopes not.

'But you must tell us,' says Ashwell, after they've been chin-wagging and smoking for a few minutes. 'You must tell us the secret of Mrs Fox. Come now, Bill: what *are* her virtues? – besides Virtue, I mean.'

Bodley interposes: 'Can a woman who works with prostitutes be virtuous?'

'Surely the prime requisite, hmm?' says Ashwell, 'for a woman thus employed?'

'But contact with Vice corrupts!' protests Bodley. 'Haven't you found?'

William flicks his cigar into the hearth. 'I'm sure Mrs Fox is proof against all evil. God's deputy in a bonnet. That's the impression Henry gave me, from the day he first met her. Well, not *the* actual day, I suppose, since he doesn't visit me very often.' William leans back in his chair and stares at the ceiling, the better to read any bygone conversations that might still be floating up there. '"She's so *good*, William"– that's what he kept saying to me. "So very good. She'll make some lucky man a saint of a wife." '

'Yes, but what does he think of her rubbing shoulders with whores?'

'He hasn't told me. I can't imagine he likes it much.'

'Poor Henry. The dark shadow of Sin comes between him and his love."

William wags his finger in mock disapproval. 'Now now, Bodley, you know Henry would be horribly offended to hear that word used in connection with his feelings for Mrs Fox.'

'What word? Sin?'

'No no, Love!' chides William. 'Any suggestion that he's in love with Mrs Emmeline Fox . . .'

'Agh, it's as plain as the nose on his face,' scoffs Ashwell. 'What does he imagine brings them together so often? The irresistible charm of debating Scripture?'

'Yes, yes, precisely that!' exclaims William. 'You must remember they're both *furiously* devout. Every whisper of reform or lapse in the Church, here in England or abroad, is of *unbearable* interest to them.' ('Then why don't they want to hear about our new book?' mutters Bodley.) 'As for Mrs Fox's work with the Rescue Society, the way Henry describes it, she does it all for God. You know: souls brought back to the fold . . .'

'No no, old chap,' corrects Bodley. 'Souls to the *bosom*; *sheep* to the fold.'

'As for Henry,' perseveres William, 'He's still hell-bent on becoming a parson. Or is it a vicar, or a rector, or a curate? The more he explains the distinctions, the less difference I can see.'

'Tithes,' says Bodley with a wink, 'and what proportion of 'em you can pocket.'

Ashwell snorts and produces from inside his coat a squashed clump of Turkish Delight wrapped in tissue paper. 'It's *too* absurd,' he mumbles, after taking a bite and re-pocketing the remainder. 'A fine manly specimen like Henry – best rower in our set, champion swimmer, I can still see him running around Midsummer Common stripped to the waist. What's he thinking of, shuffling alongside a sickly widow? Don't tell me it's her snow-white soul – I know a man on heat when I smell one!'

'But how can he stand the sight of her?' groans Bodley. 'She looks like a greyhound! That long, leathery face, and that wrinkled forehead – and always so *terribly* attentive, *just* like a dog listening for commands.'

'Come now,' cautions William. 'Aren't you placing too much impor-tance on physical beauty?'

'Yes but damn it, William – would *you* marry a widow who looked like a dog?'

'But Henry has no *intention* of marrying Emmeline Fox!'

'Oooh! Scandalous!' mugs Bodley, clapping his hands to his cheeks.

'I can vouch for the fact,' pronounces William, 'that my brother wants nothing from Mrs Fox but conversation.'

'Oh *yes*,' sneers Ashwell, removing his coat, warming to his theme. 'Conver*sa*tion. Conversation while they go on walks together in the park, or in cosy tea rooms in town, or by the sea, gazing into each other's eyes constantly. I heard they even went boating on the Thames – in order to discuss Thessalonians, no doubt.'

'No *doubt*,' insists William.

Ashwell shrugs. 'And this mad desire to be a parson: how long has he had that?'

'Oh, years and years.'

'I never noticed it at Cambridge – did you, Bodley?'

'Beg pardon?' Bodley is rummaging in the pockets of Ashwell's discarded coat, looking for the Turkish Delight.

'Father forbade the idea ever to be discussed,' William explains. 'So Henry wished for it in secret – though it wasn't much of a secret from *me*,

I'm sorry to say. He was always frightfully pious, even when we were small. Always lamented that we were a prayers-once-a-day family and not a prayers-twice-a-day family.'

'He should've counted his blessings,' muses Bodley. ('He *was* counting his blessings,' quips Ashwell.) '*We* had prayers twice a day in our house. I owe my atheism to it. Once a day fosters piety, and poor fools like Henry wanting to be clerics.'

'It's been a great disappointment to my father, at any rate,' says William. 'He assumed for so long that it would be Henry, his precious namesake, who took the business over. And instead, of course,' (he stares them straight in the eye) 'it will be me.'

Bodley and Ashwell are struck silent, visibly surprised to hear him talking this way about Rackham Perfumeries, usually another unmentionable subject. Well, let them be surprised! Let them gain an inkling of the change that has come over him since yesterday!

He longs to tell them about Sugar, of course; to sing her praises and (all right: yes) revenge himself a little for the last few years, when Bodley and Ashwell's lives seemed always so gay in comparison with his own. But he can imagine only too well their response: 'Well then, let's try this Sugar!' And what could he do then? Retract everything? Begin falsely dispraising her, like a stammering old peasant trying to persuade a pillaging soldier that his daughter isn't worth raping? Futile. To such as Bodley and Ashwell, all female treasures are in the public domain.

'So,' he questions them instead, 'have you heard anything more about that amazing girl you were describing to me?'

'Amazing girl?'

'The fierce one — with the riding crop — supposed to be the illegitimate daughter of somebody or other . . .'

'Lucy Fitzroy!' Bodley and Ashwell ejaculate simultaneously.

'Yes, by God, odd you should mention that,' says Ashwell. The two of them turn to each other and raise an eyebrow each, their signal to slip into alternating raconteuring.

'Yes, damned odd.'

'We got the news about her, oh, barely three hours after we told you about her in the first place, didn't we, Bodley?'

'Two and three-quarter hours, no more.'

'The news?' prompts William. 'What news?'

'Not a very happy tale,' says Ashwell. 'One of Lucy's admirers took to her, apparently.'

'Took to her?' echoes William, his own feelings for Sugar causing him to construe the phrase benignly.

'Yes,' says Bodley. 'With her own riding crop.'

'Beat her very severely.'

'Particularly about the face and mouth.'

'I understand all the fight's gone out of her now.'

Bodley, noticing his cigar has gone out, removes it from his lips and examines its potential momentarily before tossing it into the fire.

'Well, as you can imagine,' he says. 'Madam Georgina doesn't have high hopes. Even if she's willing to wait, there will be scars.'

Ashwell, eyes downcast, is picking at the lint on his trousers. 'Poor girl,' he laments.

'Yes,' smirks Bodley. 'How are the fighty maulen!'

At this, Ashwell and Rackham both wince. 'Bodley!' one of them cries. 'That's *appalling*!'

Bodley grins and blushes at the chastisement like a schoolboy.

Just then the door of the smoking-room flies open and Janey bursts across the threshold, panting and distressed.

'I – I'm sorry,' she says, tottering on tiptoes in the doorway, as if a great filthy flood were surging against her back, threatening to spill past her into this smoky masculine domain.

'What *is* it, Janey!' (The girl's looking at *Bodley*, damn it: doesn't she even know which man is her master?)

'Sir – if you please – I mean—' Janey bobs up and down in a nervous dance, less a curtsey than a pantomime of needing to pee. 'Oh, sir – your daughter – she's – she's all *bloody*, Mr Rackham!'

'My daughter? All bloody? Good Lord, what? All bloody where?'

Janey cringes in an ecstasy of anxiety.

'All *over*, sir!' she wails.

'Well . . . uh . . .' flusters William, astounded that this emergency has landed in *his* lap rather than someone else's. 'Why isn't . . . uh . . . what's-her-name . . .'

Janey, feeling herself accused, is almost in a frenzy. 'Nurse ain't 'ere, sir, she went to fetch Doctor Curlew. And I can't find Miss Playfair, she must 'ave gone out too, and Miss Tillotson, she won't—'

'Yes, yes, I see now.' Social humiliation burns on Rackham's shoulders like Hercules' fatal shirt of Nessus. Inescapably, there are too few servants in his house just now, and those that are left are the wrong kind for this emergency, and – more embarrassing even than this – he has a wife who, alas, does not function. Therefore – guests or no guests – he must step down and see to this matter himself.

'My friends, I *am* sorry . . .' he begins, but Ashwell, sensitive to William's plight, takes the mood of the moment in hand and commands the sobbing Janey thus:

'Well, don't just stand there, Janey – bring the child down *here*.'

'Yes!' Bodley chips in. 'This is just what's needed on a rainy morning: drama, bloodshed – and feminine charm.'

At a nod from William the servant runs off, and yes, *now* they hear it: the animal wail of a child. Muted at first, then (presumably when the door of the nursery is opened) distinctly audible, even above the rain. Louder and louder it grows, heralding the child's progress down the stairs, until finally it is very loud indeed, and accompanied by a descant of anxious whisperings and shushings.

'*Please*, Miss Sophie,' whines Janey as she escorts into the smoking-room William and Agnes's only begotten infant. '*Please*.' But Miss Sophie Rackham cannot be persuaded to scream any softer.

Despite all the din, you are intrigued: fancy William being a father! All this time you've spent with him, in the most intimate of circumstances, and you'd no idea! What does this daughter of his look like? How old is she? Three? Six? But you can't tell. Her features are distorted and obscured by blood and weeping. There's a bulge under her bloodstained pinafore, which Sophie cradles through the cloth with one bloody hand, to keep it all in, but two flaccid rag-doll legs have slipped out already, dangling their crudely stitched feet. Sophie clutches and clutches, trying to gather the legs up, shrieking all the while. Blood bubbles out of her face, dripping off her tangled mop of blonde hair, spattering the Persian carpet and her pale, bare toes.

'What on Earth,' gasps William, but Bodley has already sprung up from his chair, waved Janey away, and knelt before the gory child, cupping the back of her skull in his hands.

'Wh-what's wrong with her, Bodley?'

There is a terrible pause, then Bodley gravely announces: 'I'm afraid it's . . . epistaxis! A proboscidiferous haemorrhage! Quickly, child: who is to have custody of the doll?'

William collapses back into his chair, struck by relief and anger. 'Bodley!' he yells over Sophie's ceaseless wailing. 'This is no laughing matter. A child's life is a fragile thing!"

'Nonsense,' tushes Bodley, still on his knees before the child. 'A biff on the nose, is it then? How did you get that, hmm? Sophie?' She screams on, so he tugs the legs of her doll to get her attention. Encouraged by her reaction, he lifts her pinafore, exposing her toy.

'Now, Sophie,' he cautions, 'you must put your little friend down. You're frightening him to death!' Instantly the pitch of Sophie's wailing drops considerably, and Bodley pushes through. 'From the way you're weeping he must think he's about to be orphaned – left all alone! Come now, put him down – or no, give him to *me* for a moment. Look, his eyes are wide with fright!' The doll, a Hindoo boy with 'Twinings' embroidered on his chest, is indeed wide-eyed, his chocolate-brown bisque head disturbingly lifelike in comparison with his limp rag body, a soft hemp skeleton swathed in cotton clout suggestive of smock and pantalettes. Sophie looks her coolie in the face, sees the fear there – and hands him over to the gentleman.

'Now,' Bodley goes on, 'you must prove to him that you're really all right, which you can't do with all that blood on your face.' (Sophie's wailing has been reduced to a snivel, though her nose is still bubbling crimson.) 'Ashwell, give me your handkerchief.'

'*My* handkerchief?'

'Be reasonable, Ashwell; mine is still fashionable.' Never taking his eyes off Sophie, and holding her doll in one arm, he extends his other arm behind him, wiggling the fingers impatiently until the handkerchief is surrendered. Then he sets to, mopping and dabbing at Sophie's face, so vigorously that she sways on her feet. As he wipes, he catches sight of Janey out of the corner of his eye, and instructs her, in a sing-song school-masterly tone:

'Come now, Janey. I shall need a wet cloth presently, shan't I?'

The servant gapes, too dazed to move.

'Wet cloth,' simplifies Bodley patiently. 'Two parts cloth, one part water.'

A nod from William frees Janey to run off on this errand, even as the handkerchief begins to unmask the features of his only child. She is merely sniffling now, lifting her head in rhythm with the stranger's strokes against her face, trusting him instinctively.

'Look!' says Bodley, directing her attention to the Hindoo boy. 'He feels much better, don't you see?'

Sophie nods, the last tears rolling out of her enormous red-rimmed eyes, and stretches out her arms for her doll.

'All right,' judges Bodley. 'But mind! You mustn't get him all bloody.' He takes a fold of her pinafore between two fingers and holds it up so she can see how wet it is. Without demur, she allows him to lift the offending garment over her head; he has it off with a swift one-handed motion.

'There now,' he says, tenderly.

Janey returns with the wet flannel, and makes as if to wipe Sophie's face with it, but Bodley takes the cloth from her and performs the task himself. Sophie Rackham, her features now uncamouflaged and her cheeks less swollen, is revealed a plain, serious-looking child, certainly no candidate for a Pears' Soap advertisement – or a Rackhams' one, at that. Her large eyes are china blue, but protruding and cheerless, and her curly blonde hair hangs limp. More than anything else she has the air of a domestic pet bought for a child who has since died; an obsolete pet that is given food, lodging, and even the occasional pat of affection, but no reason for living at all.

'Your little friend has a stain on him; we must wash it off,' Bodley is saying to her. 'Every second counts.'

She lays her tiny hand on his, and together they sponge at the blood on the Hindoo's back; she would do anything for this sympathetic stranger, anything.

'I once knew of a doll who got cranberry sauce all over her hair,' he tells her, 'and no one saw to it until much too late. By then, it was hard as tar – with the consequence that her hair had to be shaved off, and she caught pneumonia.'

Sophie looks at him anxiously, too shy to ask the question.

'No, she didn't die,' says Bodley. 'But she has remained, from that day onward, entirely bald.' And he raises his eyebrows as far as they will go, pouting in mock disappointment at the idea of one's eyebrows being the only hairs left on one's head. Sophie chuckles.

This chuckle, and the screams she came in with, are the only sounds you are going to hear her utter, here in her father's smoking-room. Nurse is always telling her she knows nothing, but she knows that well-behaved children are neither seen nor heard. Already she has caused a fuss for which she will no doubt be punished; she must become silent and invisible as soon as possible, to placate what's coming to her.

Yet, even as Sophie stands mute, hunching her shoulders to take up less room, William is amazed at how big she's grown. It seems like only last week that Sophie was a newborn babe, sleeping invisibly in her cot, while elsewhere in the house, a feverish Agnes lay sobbing in hers. Why, she's not even a toddler anymore, she's a . . . what would one call it? a girl! But how is it possible that he hasn't noticed the transformation? It's not as if he doesn't see her often enough to note her progress – he glimpses her, oh . . . several times a week! But somehow, she never impressed him as being quite so . . . *old*. God almighty: he remembers now the day when his father gave that hideous doll to the baby Sophie – something he picked up on a trade visit to India, a Twinings mascot originally meant to sit astride a tin elephant filled with tea. Wasn't it on that same day that his father loudly declared, in front of the servants, that William had better start 'boning up' on the perfume trade? Yes! And this child, this plain-faced girl with blood on her feet, this overgrown infant whose back is turned to him as she and his old chum Philip Bodley indulge in foolish-ness together . . . *she* is the living embodiment of the years since; years of veiled threats and enforced economies. How he would like to be the sort of father depicted in ladies' journals, lifting his smiling tot like a trophy in the air while his adoring wife looks on! But he hasn't an adoring wife anymore, and his daughter is tainted by misery.

He clears his throat. 'Janey,' he says, 'don't you think Mr Bodley has done quite enough?'

Who to follow now? Janey, I suggest. Mr Bodley and Mr Ashwell are about to leave anyway, and William Rackham will then immediately resume his study of the Rackham papers. He'll barely move for hours, so unless you are madly curious about the cost of unwoven Dundee jute as a cheap substitute for cotton wool, or the secrets of making pot-pourri-scented migraine sachets, you are likely to have a more interest-ing time with Janey and Sophie as they sit in the nursery, waiting for Beatrice to return.

Janey squats beside Sophie on the floor, clutching her abdomen, suffering the wickedest stomach pains she's ever had in her life. It must be the stolen morsels of the Rackhams' breakfast she ate . . . her punishment from God, a skewer going right through her guts. She rocks to and fro, arms wrapped around her knees, Sophie's blood-soaked pinafore folded in her lap. What on Earth is she supposed to do with it? Will she be punished by Cook for leaving the kitchen? Will she be punished by Nurse for allowing the Rackhams' child to come to harm? Punished by Miss Playfair, for rushing to investigate Sophie's screams instead of finishing the cleaning of the dining-room? Punished by Miss Tillotson for . . . whatever Miss Tillotson feels like punishing her for today? How did this happen to her, these bloody mishaps and tasks undone, and she to blame, and a thousand girls jostling to take her place? Oh please, let Mr Rackham not dismiss her! Where could she go? Home is too far away, and it's raining so hard! She'll end up on the streets, she will! Her honour is all she has to her name, but she *knows* she's not brave enough to starve for it! But no, please no: she'll work harder for the Rackhams, yes she will, harder than she's ever worked before; she just needs a little more time to learn what her new duties actually are.

'Who was that man?'

Janey turns towards the unfamiliar sound of Sophie Rackham's voice. She squints, trying not to look at Sophie's Bristol top spinning on the floor in front of the little girl's skirts, for fear it might make her feel more bilious.

'Beg pardon, Miss Sophie?'

'Who was that man?' the child repeats, as the top spins drunkenly on to its side.

'What man, Miss Sophie?' Janey's voice is squeezed thin with pain.

'The nice one.'

Janey struggles to remember a nice man.

'I din't know nobody there, I never seen them before,' she pleads. 'Except Mr Rackham.'

Sophie spins her top again. 'He's my father, did you know?' she says, frowning. She's keen to teach Janey the facts of life: servants deserve to learn things too, in her opinion. 'And *his* father, my father's father, is a very 'portant man. He has a long beard, and he goes to India, Liv'pool, everywhere. He's the same Rackham that you see on the soap and the perfume.'

Janey's soap is made of leftover slivers from the kitchen, doled out by

Cook on a weekly basis, and she has never in her life seen a bottle of perfume. She smiles and nods, in agony, pretending to understand.

'The nice man,' Sophie tries again. 'Has he never come to the house before?'

'I don't know, Miss Rackham.'

'Why not?'

'I . . . I used to work all the time only in the scullery. Now I work in the kitchen too — and I bring out the food sometimes, and . . . and other fings. But I ain't . . . I ain't been out in the 'ouse much yet.'

'Me neither.' It's a shy pleasure, this illicit comradeship with the lowliest of servants. Little Sophie peers directly into Janey's face, wondering if anything unusual is going to happen, now that they've shared such intimacy. This could be a special day, the beginning of a new life; why, this is the way friendships start in storybooks! Sophie opens her eyes as wide as she can and smiles, giving the servant permission to speak her heart, to propose (perhaps) a secret rendezvous after bedtime.

Janey smiles back, whey-faced, rocking on her heels. She opens her lips to speak, then suddenly pitches forward on her knees and spews a pale shawl of vomit onto the nursery floor. Two open-mouthed, silent-scream retches, and she spews again. Bile, stewed tea, Cook's morning gruel and glimmering bits of bacon puddle out onto the polished boards.

Seconds later, the nursery door swings open: it's Beatrice, returning at last. In the rest of the Rackham house, as by a wave of a magic wand, everything is back to normal: Doctor Curlew is climbing the stairs to Mrs Rackham's bedroom, Mr Rackham's old schoolfriends have left, Letty is back from the stationers, the rain is waning. Only here in the nursery — where, by rights, everything should always be perfectly under control — is anything amiss: a revolting stench; Sophie dishevelled, tangle-haired, barefoot; the scullery maid on her hands and knees, with no bucket or mop in sight, stupidly staring down at a pool of sick in the middle of the room, and . . . what's this? Sophie's pinafore, covered in blood!

Growing erect with fury, Beatrice Cleave brings the full power of her basilisk stare to bear on the Rackham child, the bane of her life, the sinful creature who cannot be trusted for five minutes, the useless daughter of an undeserving heir to an unworthy fortune. Under the weight of that stare, little Sophie cowers, points a trembling, grubby finger at Janey.

'*She* done it.'

Beatrice winces, but resolves to resume the war on the child's grammar later, *after* a few other mysteries have been solved.

'Now,' she says, hands on hips, even as the first rays of sunshine flicker in through the nursery window, turning the pool of vomit silver and gold. 'From the beginning . . . !'

EIGHT

efore we go on, though . . . Forgive me if I misjudge you, but I get the impression, from the way you're looking at the Rackhams' house – at its burnished staircases and its servant-infested passageways and its gaslit, ornately decorated rooms – that you think it's very old. On the contrary, it's quite new. So new that if, for example, William decides it really *will not do* to have a trickle of rain stealing through the French windows in the parlour, he only has to ferret out the business card of the carpenter who guaranteed the seal.

In the boyhood of Henry Calder Rackham, when Notting Hill was a still a rural hamlet in the parish of Kensington, cows grazed on the spot where you have seen, fifty years later, William and Agnes making their own less successful attempt to breakfast together. Porto Bello was a farm, as was Notting Barn. Wormwood Scrubs was scrub, and Shepherds Bush was a place where one might find shepherds. The raw materials of the Rackhams' dining-room were, in those days, still untouched in quarries and forests, and William's bachelor father was far too busy with his factories and his farms to give serious thought to housing, or even siring, an heir.

All the years leading up to his marriage, Henry Calder Rackham lived in a rather grand house in Westbourne, but liked to joke (especially when talking to intractable snobs whose friendship he couldn't win) that his true home was Paddington Station, for 'a man's business is liable to go to the dogs every day that he don't go and see how his workers are getting on.' Work has never been a dirty word to Henry Calder Rackham, although – bafflingly – this has never yet earned him the devotion of his own employees. To those that toil in his factories, the sight of him pacing the iron ramps above their heads in his black suit and top hat falls short of inspiring solidarity. But then, perhaps he's a simple country man at heart . . . although the workers in his lavender fields don't seem to have warmed to him much either. Could it be they labour under the misapprehension that the sturdy rustic clothes he wears whenever he visits them are an affectation, rather than his preferred garb?

Another thing for which he feels he's been given too little credit is his passionate nature. Gossips in both city and country were wont to mutter that he'd have more hope wooing a mechanical grinder than a human female. Imagine their surprise, then, when he suddenly married a damn fine-looking woman! Dumbstruck, they were, every time he showed her off.

Still, if the arrival of his wife took them unawares, her departure, nine years later, surprised no one. Indeed, her adultery seemed to be common knowledge long before he, its victim, learned of it; most galling, that. Then there was endless speculation about whether he disowned her, or if she ran off willingly. What did it matter? She evaporated from his life, leaving behind two infant boys. But, ever practical even in grief, he hired an additional servant to provide such services as his sons' mother had provided, and got on with his work.

Years went by, the boys grew up with no ill effects whatsoever, and business prospered, until eventually Rackham Senior must give some thought to where young Henry, his heir, was to live. By this time, the 1850s, the prime parts of Notting Hill were rural no longer. The Potteries to the west of the town were still infested with gypsies and piggeries, and the abortive attempts to turn half the parish into a race-course had tainted the character of the whole area, but there were signs that the cluster of houses around Ladbroke Square might become desirable residences. And, by the late 1860s, sure enough, the locale was recognised as a place where prominent men who did not aspire to the very *best* Society might be satisfied to live. Also, it was handy for the railways, which Henry the Younger would be needing to use often, once he'd assumed control of the business.

So, Henry Senior bought his heir a large and handsome house in Chepstow Villas, barely ten years old and in tip-top condition. As for where William, the second son, would eventually live, well . . . that was for the boy himself to sort out.

Now the future is here, and the history of the Rackham empire has run contrary to prospectus. Henry Senior's side of the bargain has been amply fulfilled: he has, by a combination of robust charm and discreet money-lending, lodged himself in polite Society, counting magistrates, peers and all manner of gentlefolk among his friends. But Henry Junior, his first-born, is living like a monk in a pokey cottage near Brick Field, while William, having enjoyed the best education money could buy, is content to occupy the house in Chepstow Villas, playing the gentleman without the independent means to do so. It's years now since the boy left university, and he still hasn't earned a penny of his keep! Is this how William means to go on, leaving his old father burdened with responsibility, while he writes unpublished poems for his own amusement? It's high time he noticed that the 'R' insignia is wrought into the very ironwork of the gates that surround him!

The house is showing signs of strain. The gardens are a disgrace, especially around the edges of the building and behind the kitchen. There's no carriage, no horse in the stable. The coachman's tiny bungalow, never yet inhabited by a coachman and converted by William, during a short-lived passion for painting, into a studio, now stands useless. The low greenhouses lie like glass coffins, filled to bursting with whatever weedy rubbish can grow without a gardener. All very regrettable, but only natural: Henry Senior, in his attempt to cure William, has inflicted on the household a series of traumatic shocks, and as a consequence all its servant blood has been drawn away from the peripheries to the beleaguered heart.

Inside, there's really nothing in particular to impress anyone, except a foreigner like you. You may admire the many high-ceilinged rooms, the dark polished floors, the hundreds of pieces of furniture destined for the antiques shops of your own time, and most of all, you may be impressed by the dumb industry of the servants. All these things are taken for granted here. To the Rackhams' dwindling circle of acquaintances, the house is tainted: it smells of cancelled *soirées*, dismal garden parties, the sound of Agnes breaking glass at dinner, embarrassed goodbyes, the glum exodus of guests. It smells of deserted rooms where tables stand groaning with delicacies, empty floors ringing with the heavy footfalls of a forsaken host. No, there's no reason why anyone should go back to the Rackhams' again, not after all that's happened.

In Agnes Rackham's bedroom, the curtains are thick and almost always drawn, a detail not lost on snoopers who peek across from Pembridge Mews.

Those drawn curtains have unfortunate consequences within: Agnes's room must be lit all through the daylight hours, and smells very strongly of burnt candle-fat (she doesn't trust gas). Also, on those rare occasions when she ventures out and the candles are snuffed (for she has a fear of the house burning down) her room is dark as a tomb on her return.

This is what we find on the morning when Agnes returns from her brave attempt at a connubial breakfast. She and her lady's-maid stand at the bedroom door, breathing heavily from the long ascent of the stairs. Clara cannot, at one and the same time, carry a candle and support her mistress, so the door is elbowed open, and the pair of them shuffle inside, lacking bearings in the gloom. By sheer chance, just as the door of Agnes's bedroom is opened, the main door downstairs is slammed shut, so that Agnes actually hears her husband leaving the house. Where to? she wonders, as she's led into a room that has become unrecognisable since she was last in it.

The white bed looms unambiguous, but what's that in the corner? A skeleton half-smothered in bandages? And next to that . . . a large dog?

Clara lights an oil-lamp, and the mysterious figures are clarified: a cast-iron dressmaker's dummy swathed in strips of dress material and, standing at the ready like a silver-plated Doberman, the sewing-machine.

'Give me your hands, Mrs Rackham.'

Agnes shuffles to obey, but not like an old woman – more like a child being taken back to bed after a nightmare.

'Everything will be all right now, Mrs Rackham.' Clara pulls back the bedclothes. 'You can have a peaceful little rest now.' To the tune of these and other perfunctory soothings, Clara undresses her mistress and puts her to bed. Then she gives Agnes her favourite brush, and Agnes automatically begins to groom her hair, worrying at the tangles caused by her fall.

'How do I look?'

Clara, who is folding her mistress's dressing-gown to pillow-slip size, pauses to make her appraisal.

'Beautiful,' she says, smiling, 'ma'am.'

Her smile is insincere. All her smiles are; Agnes knows that. But they're offered ungrudgingly in the line of duty, and have no harm hidden behind them, and Agnes knows this too, and is grateful. Between her and her maid there's an understanding that in return for life-long employment, Clara will satisfy any whim, be witness to any fiasco, without ever complaining. She will be a comfort from dawn to midnight, and occasionally at sticky moments in between. She will be a confidante to anything Agnes might confide, no matter how daft, and, if asked to forget it an hour later, will scrub it entirely from her mind as if it were a careless spill of milk.

Most importantly, she will aid and abet her mistress in the disobeying of all orders given by those two evil men, Doctor Curlew or William Rackham.

For Agnes, life with Clara provides her with a game she can play in perfect safety, a regimen of gentle exercise with a benign familiar. With Clara's help, she will re-learn the social skills she sorely needs for the London Season. For example, she sometimes bids Clara pretend to be this lady or that, and together they act out little dramas, so that Agnes can practise her responses. Not that Clara's play-acting is terribly convincing, but Agnes doesn't mind. Too real an imitation might unnerve her.

Heartened now by the sensation of soft tidy hair on her head, she lays down her brush and settles back against the pillows.

'Clara: my new toilet book,' she commands softly. The servant hands over the volume, and Agnes opens it to the chapter entitled 'Defending Yourself Against the Enemy' – the enemy in this case being old age. She rubs her cheeks and temples, obeying as closely as possible the text's instructions, although she has trouble rubbing 'in a direction contrary to that which the wrinkles threaten to take', because she hasn't any wrinkles yet. 'Change hands in case of fatigue', says the book – and she's certainly fatigued. But how, if she only has two hands, can she change them? And how does she know if she's touching herself correctly, with the right amount of 'firm, gentle pressure'; and what are the consequences of not using a lubricant, as the writer recommends? Books never address what one really needs to know.

Too weary to continue her exercises, she turns the page to see what's next.

The skin of the face wrinkles for the same reason and by the same mechanisms that the skin of an apple wrinkles. The pulp of the fruit under the skin shrinks and contracts as the juices dry up . . .

Agnes claps shut the book at once.

'Take it away, Clara,' she says.

'Yes, ma'am.' Clara knows what to do: there's a special room farther along the landing, where unwanted things go.

Next, Agnes glances surreptitiously at the sewing machine.

Clara misses nothing. 'P'raps, ma'am,' she says, 'we might carry on with your new dress? The most difficult part is over, isn't it, ma'am?'

Agnes's face lights up. What a blessing that there *is* something to do, something with which to fill the time – at a time like this. After all, she's not forgotten that very soon she'll have to receive Doctor Curlew.

For the love of God, why did she reject William's offer to stop Beatrice fetching him? He was willing to do it – willing to rush through the house, onto the street if need be, to undo the message! And she refused him! Madness! But, lying there on the floor, she had, for a brief moment, an intoxicating power over him – the power to scorn his offer of the olive branch. Standing up to him like that – admittedly, while lying at his feet – was revenge of sorts.

Agnes stares at the half-finished dress, imagines it wreathing her own body like silken armour. She smiles shyly at Clara, gets a smile in return.

'Yes,' she says, 'I do believe I'm well enough to go on.'

Within minutes, the whirring of the sewing-machine is muffling the ticking of the clock. With each seam and tuck they complete, the two women interrupt their labours, remove the dress from the machine, replace it on the dummy. Over and over, the sexless frame is clothed anew, each time appearing a little more shapely, a little more feminine.

'We are weaving magic!' chortles Mrs Rackham, almost forgetting that Doctor Curlew is on his way, satchel swinging in his gloved fist.

But her sewing is more than mere distraction. She needs at least four more dresses if she's to have any hope of taking part in the Season next year and, by Goodness, next year she *shall* take part. For, if there's one thing that has shaken Agnes's faith in her own sanity, it was being unable to participate in the Season this year. And if there's one thing that can restore her faith, it is (so to speak) redressing that lapse.

It's true that from birth she has been groomed to do nothing especially well except appear in public looking beautiful. But that's not the reason she's making these splendid dresses, these elaborate constructs in which she hopes to sweep across other people's floors. Taking part in the Season is, to her, the One Thing that will prove beyond doubt that she isn't mad.

For, in her uncertainty where exactly the borderline between sanity and madness is supposed to lie, Agnes has chosen a line for herself. If she can only keep on the right side of it, she will be sane, first in the eyes of the world, then in her husband's, and finally even in Doctor Curlew's.

And in her own eyes? In her own eyes she is neither sane nor insane; she is simply Agnes . . . Agnes Pigott, if you don't mind. Look into her heart, and you will see a pretty picture, like a prayer-card depicting the girlhood of the Virgin. It's Agnes, but not as we know her: it's an Agnes who's ageless, changeless, spotless, no step-daughter of any Unwin, no wife of any Rackham. Her hair is silkier, her dresses frillier, her bosom subsided to nothing, her very first Season still to come.

Agnes sighs. In reality, more years than she can bear to remember have passed since her first Season, and her ambitions for the next one are modest. Her dream of moving among the Upper Ten Thousand, which seemed perfectly achievable when she was Lord Unwin's step-daughter, has receded now it's clear that William, if he has any future at all, will never be the famous author she once imagined he would be. He'll be the head of a perfumery – when he finally stirs himself to accept the responsibility – and then, if he gets very, very rich, he may ascend slowly through the social firmament. But until then, the lower reaches of fashionable Society are the best the Rackhams can hope for. Agnes knows that. She doesn't like it, but she knows it, and she's determined to make the most of it.

So, what is she looking forward to? She has no wish to be considered beautiful by men. Such things lead only to unhappiness. Nor is she hoping for the admiration of other women; from them she expects only polite nonchalance, and spiteful gossip behind her back. To be honest, she doesn't really imagine engaging in intercourse of *any* sort next Season; on the contrary, she intends to glide through the entire affair barely noticing anyone, speaking only the emptiest formulae, and listening to nothing that requires more than the shallowest attention. This, she's learned from past experience, is by far the safest course. More than anything, she yearns for the bliss of being tolerated outside the confines of her own bedroom, dressed in nicer clothes than her much-stained, much-laundered nightgowns.

'You know, ma'am,' says Clara, 'Mrs Whymper will turn green when she sees you in this dress. I met her maid in town, and she said Mrs Whymper is pining to wear this style, but she's grown too fat for it.'

Agnes laughs childishly, knowing full well that this is almost certainly a lie. (Clara is always fabricating such things.) She is feeling better by the minute; the pain is fading from her head; she might even ask Clara to open the curtains . . .

But then comes the knock at the door.

Clara has no choice but to let her share of the dress slither to the floor, leaving her mistress marooned in silk. She gets up and, with an apologetic smile, hurries to admit the doctor. A long shadow flows into the room.

'Good day to you Mrs Rackham,' the doctor says, moving smoothly in. The perfumed air of this female sanctum is tainted by his unmistakable smell, displaced by his towering bulk. He deposits his satchel on the floor next to Agnes's bed and perches on the edge of the mattress, nodding to Clara. That nod means Clara is dismissed; that nod is a command.

Agnes, having turned her chair away from the sewing-machine and towards the doctor, knows, as she watches Clara leave, that the trap is shut, but still she can't help trying to wriggle against its jaws.

'I'm sorry you have been made to come all this way,' she says. 'Because unfortunately – I mean, fortunately for *me*, but not for you – I'm quite well now. As you can see.'

The good doctor makes no reply.

'It was kind of my husband to summon you, I'm sure . . .'

The doctor's brow wrinkles. He is not one to let an inconsistency pass unquestioned. 'Oh, but William gave me to understand that you yourself insisted on my being summoned.'

'Yes, well, I'm sure I'm very sorry,' says Agnes, noting with horror his habit of cocking his head slightly at anything she tells him, as if he's loath to miss even one of her preposterous lies. 'I suppose, in that moment of feeling so unwell, I . . . I feared the worst. At any rate, I'm quite myself now.'

Doctor Curlew rests his handsomely sculpted beard on his interlocking hands.

'You look very pale to me, Mrs Rackham, if I may say so.'

Agnes attempts to hide her rising panic with a coy half-smile. 'Ah, but that may be face powder, mayn't it?'

Doctor Curlew looks puzzled. Agnes knows that look well, considers it to be the nastiest, most maddening of all the looks in his repertoire.

'But had I not cautioned you,' he says, 'against the use of cosmetics, for the sake of your skin?'

Agnes sighs. 'Yes, Doctor, you had.'

'In fact, I thought—'

'—that they'd all been disposed of, yes,' she says.

'So . . .'

'So, yes,' she sighs, 'it cannot be powder on my face.'

The doctor presses his fingertips to his beard and inhales deeply.

'Please, Mrs Rackham,' he reasons. 'I know you don't like to be examined. But what you like and what's good for you are not always the same thing. Many a dire turn in an otherwise manageable illness can be averted if it's seen to immediately.'

Agnes leans back in her chair, allowing her eyes to fall shut. There is nothing she can say that hasn't failed many times before. *I am too tired to be examined.* 'Too tired? Then you must be ill.' *I am too ill to be examined.* 'But the examination will make you better.' *You examine me every week; what harm can it do to leave it undone just once?* 'You can't mean that; only a madwoman would willingly let her health decline.' *I am not a madwoman!* 'Of course not. That's why I'm asking your permission, rather than ignoring your wishes as I would ignore those of an asylum inmate.' *But I am too tired* . . . And so on.

Is she mad to imagine that Doctor Curlew is bullying her? That he's taking liberties no physician should? She's so out of touch with the world at large – has she missed momentous changes in the way doctors address their patients? Is the Queen herself bullied and threatened by *her* physician? She'd dismiss him, surely? How wonderful it would be to tell Doctor Curlew that she doesn't require his services any more, that he is *dismissed*.

Instead, as always, she acquiesces, and takes her position on the bed. The good doctor has opened the curtains, so that the sun can shine upon his work. Agnes fixes her attention on a clutch of extinguished candles, counting the drips of hardened wax on their shafts. She loses count, starts again, loses count again, all the while trying to ignore the electric apprehension travelling up through her body from her toes to the roots of her hair, as Doctor Curlew lifts her dressing-gown over her legs.

William Rackham, meanwhile, first knocks, then rings at the door of Mrs Castaway's, and waits impatiently for it to be opened. Wet gusts of wind tug at his trouser-legs; overdressed trollops eye him as they sweep by. His scalp prickles from all the oil he has combed through his hair. A minute passes: why, this is as bad as his own house!

After another minute, the sound of unlatching. A narrow slit offers him a glimpse of a female eye, glittering with mistrust.

'Sugar's not free.' The unfriendly voice of Amy Howlett. 'P'raps you'd care to come back later.'

'As a matter of fact, I wish to speak with your . . . Mrs Castaway,' says William. 'Strictly a business matter.'

'There's no matters here,' the girl sneers, 'but business matters.'

His mind boggling at how any man could kiss and embrace a creature so cynical, William tries again: 'I insist . . . I've something of great interest, I'm sure, to Mrs Castaway.'

Whereupon Miss Howlett swings the door wide, her back already turned.

In Mrs Castaway's parlour, everything is much as it was when William — when *Mr Hunt* last paid a visit. Just as before, he's struck by the scores of Mary Magdalen prints on the walls, the blazing fire, and Mrs Castaway herself, seated at her desk, dressed all in scarlet. Of Miss Lester and her 'cello, this time, there's no sign; her chair stands empty. Amy Howlett slouches back into her seat, settles with a *wumph* of wrinkled skirts, and slyly watches his approach. Hands hanging at her sides, head tilted back, she sucks smoke, then does a most startling thing: she opens her lips and performs a juggling trick with the cigarette adhering to the end of her tongue, almost swallowing it, then catching it, still lit, between her teeth. She sucks again. Her eyes do not blink.

'I *do* hope you'll try to forgive Amy's manners,' sighs Mrs Castaway, motioning William towards an armchair. 'Her ways have great charm for some of our visitors.'

Amy smirks.

'I'm sure I don't mean to cause offence, Mr . . . Mr . . .' Stuck for his name, she abandons her stab at good behaviour, and looks away with a shrug.

'Hunt,' says William. 'George W. Hunt.'

Mrs Castaway narrows her eyes, narrows them so much that the blood-shot whites almost entirely disappear, leaving the dark bits shining like sucked licorice. She is bigger than he remembered, more formidable.

'So, what can we do for you, Mr Hunt?' she croons, her painted mouth puckering with the vowels. 'We hadn't expected you back so soon.'

William takes a deep breath, leans forward, and launches into his proposal. He speaks earnestly, quickly, nervously. His Mr Hunt is a shy man, but a rich one. The source of his wealth? Oh, he's a somewhat retiring, not to say sleeping, partner in a giant publishing firm, gross income £20,000 a year, titles too numerous to name, but works by Macaulay, Kenelm Digby, Le Fanu and William Ainsworth are among them. As a matter of fact, he has an appointment to see his old chum Wilkie – Wilkie Collins – in . . . (he pulls his silver watch into view) four hours from now. But first . . .

He argues his case and, as well as arguing, he takes care to ask questions. Asking questions (or so Henry Calder Rackham keeps emphasising in the correspondence William has only just read) is essential in bending a prospective partner to one's will. *Ask questions*, urges the old man, *express simpathy for the differculties of the fellow you wish to do business with, then demenstrate you have the answer.* William steams ahead, sweat forming on his brow, words pouring from his lips. *Leave no silence for the other fellow to fill with quarms*, that's another thing the old man harps on. William leaves no silence. *Look into the other fellows eyes.* William looks into Mrs Castaway's eyes and, as the minutes pass, he judges he's getting through. She is increasingly frank when it comes to surrendering figures; she nods gravely when he tells her how he means to swell them.

'So,' he sums up at last. 'Exclusive patronage of Sugar by me: will you consider it?'

To which Mrs Castaway replies, 'I'm sorry, Mr Hunt. No.'

Shocked, William looks to Amy Howlett, as if expecting she'll leap to his defence. Amy, however, is slumped in her chair, picking at her fingernails, her sharp eyes, for the moment, benignly crossed.

'But whyever not?' he cries, striving to keep his voice down, for fear of being collared by a hidden strongman. 'I can't imagine any cause for objection.' (What would Henry Calder Rackham advise? *Say back to the fellow what the fellows just told you.*) 'You've told me that in an average evening, Sugar entertains one or two, at most three, gentlemen. Now, I am offering to meet whatever you say are the costs to you of those three engagements. Sugar I will pay whatever she considers fair. The profit to you remains the same, only it comes from one man and not several.'

Mrs Castaway, instead of clapping her wrinkled hand to her forehead in belated epiphany, responds to William's plea in a way that unnerves him. She begins to rummage in one of her desk drawers, and extracts a sheaf of unruly papers. Then she slips her fingers into the handles of her big brass scissors, and exercises the blades experimentally.

'These matters are more complex than you might think, Mr Hunt,' she murmurs, spreading the papers out before her on the desk. Her eyes flicker, dividing attention between William and the task she's plainly impatient to resume. 'To begin with, we are a small house and arithmetic is against us. If one third of what we're reputed to offer is perpetually unavailable—'

A ring of the doorbell makes them both quiver.

Amy Howlett groans, looks up at the ceiling. 'Where *is* that boy?' she sighs, then jerks up from her chair.

'Mr Hunt, I must apologise,' says Mrs Castaway as Amy flounces off, once again, to do the sleeping Christopher's work. 'One of our little customs here is that no gentleman should ever be seen by another. So, if you'd be kind enough to step into the next room' (she points with the shears) 'for *just* a moment . . .'

She nods maternally, and he obeys.

'The pain,' Doctor Curlew is saying just then, 'lies entirely in the resistance.'

He wipes his fingers with a white handkerchief, pockets it, bends down to try a second time. She makes him work hard, does Mrs Rackham, for his fee.

Not Sugar, not Sugar, you blackguard, you swine, thinks William, as he stands squirming in the next room, his ear pressed to the door. *She's not available. You've changed your mind. Your cockstand's gone soft.*

'. . . early in the day . . .' he hears Mrs Castaway saying.

'. . . Sugar . . .' is the masculine reply.

The hairs on William's neck tingle with loathing. He is tempted to rush out of his hiding-place and attack his rival, battering him right through the floor.

'. . . no shortage of alternative delights . . .'

His heart beats vehemently; his future, he feels, is poised on a vertiginous edge, waiting to be rescued or cast down. How can it be? A couple of days ago, Sugar didn't even exist. Now here he stands with fists clenched, half-willing to kill for her!

But it appears bloodshed won't be necessary after all. The man in the parlour has been fobbed off with Miss Howlett. Serves him right, the blackguard. William hopes she thrashes him within an inch of his life, for daring to ask for Sugar.

'. . . no wine, then . . . appreciate you are in a hurry . . . like a thousand-and-one nights squeezed into a few minutes . . .'

William hears the music of transaction. Strange how speech can be almost inaudible through a closed door, while the sound of coins chinking together is so clear!

'Mr Hunt?'

Thank God.

Only now does William notice what sort of room he's been hiding in: a tiny infirmary, well stocked with bandages and jars of medicine. Also bottles of strong spirits, abortifacients marked with crossbones and infant skulls, and perfumed antiseptics manufactured by . . . manufactured by . . . (he peers closer, just in case he should spot the rose insignia or the ornamental 'R') . . . Beechams.

'Mr Hunt?'

'Mrs Rackham?'

Agnes Rackham, lying on her bed miles away, rolls onto her side so that Doctor Curlew can reach deeper inside her.

'Good,' he murmurs abstractedly. 'Thank you.' He is trying to find Agnes's womb, which to his knowledge ought to be exactly four inches from the external aperture. His middle finger being exactly four inches long (for he has measured it), he is perplexed to be having no success.

'You alluded to . . . complications I hadn't considered?' William prompts.

'Many, many,' sighs Mrs Castaway. Rather off-puttingly, she's already busy with her cuttings, snipping into sheets of paper which, from where William sits, look like pages torn from books. 'Another has just occurred to me: our house has, if not precisely an agreement, then certainly a . . . bond of mutual regard, with The Fireside. You know The Fireside? Oh, yes, of course.' She takes her eyes off him again, and steers the scissors through a circuitous cut. 'Now you, Mr Hunt, who are so appreciative of

Sugar's merits; you can well understand that she is considered an attraction – a draw-card, if you will – for The Fireside. At least, the proprietors seem to think so. So, we are doing them a favour, not strictly measurable in terms of money, but valuable nonetheless. Now, if Sugar were to . . . disappear – for how*ever flat*tering a reason, Mr Hunt – I'm sure The Fireside would feel itself the poorer, d'you see?'

A tiny human figure has taken shape, blank on William's side, engraving-grey on Mrs Castaway's.

She is mad, he thinks, as he watches a haloed female saint, torn from a Papist picture-book, flutter to the table. How can one bargain with a madwoman? Might he convince her better if he revealed his true name? Which identity, from the point of view of a madwoman who cannibalises books for their Magdalens, might be the more impressive – an authentic heir to a renowned perfume concern, or a make-believe partner in a prestigious publishing house? And what the Devil does she mean about The Fireside? A simple bribe, or is he expected to buy the whole damn place?

Push the fellow to say, one time only, the word Yes – that's what his father keeps underlining in green ink. *All else is details.*

'Madam, these are mere details, surely,' he declares. 'Couldn't we . . .' (a happy inspiration) 'couldn't we call Sugar herself downstairs? It's *her* future that's at stake here – with all due respect to the matters you've been raising, madam . . .'

Mrs Castaway picks up another scrap of paper. This one bears, on its blank reverse, the unmistakable stamp of a circulating library.

'Mr Hunt, there is another thing you haven't allowed for. You don't consider the possibility that Sugar might prefer – forgive me, I don't wish to cause you offence – that she might prefer *variety*.'

William lets this pass; he can tell that indignation is of no use.

'Madam, I urge you – I implore you – allow Sugar to speak for herself.'

Give her over, give her over, he thinks, staring hard into the madam's eyes. He has never wished for anything more fervently than this; the fervour of his wishing astounds him. If he can have this one thing, he will ask God for nothing else, nothing, as long as he lives.

Mrs Castaway withdraws her fingers from the scissors, pushes her chair back, gets to her feet. Dangling from the ceiling are three silken ropes; she pulls one. Who does it summon? A strongman to eject him? Or Sugar? Mrs Castaway's eyes give nothing away.

God almighty, this is a damn sight more difficult than winning Agnes's hand in marriage, William thinks. If only this mad old bawd would be prepared to take a risk on him, the way Lord Unwin did!

Sitting there in Mrs Castaway's bawdy-house, waiting for Sugar or a burly spoony-man to appear, he remembers being invited to see the pickled old aristocrat in his smoking-room, and there, over port, being read the terms of the marriage of Agnes Unwin to William Rackham, Esquire. The legalities were, he recalls, quite beyond him, so when Lord Unwin had finished and archly asked something like 'Well, how does that suit?' he'd not known what to say. 'It means you've *got* her, God help you,' Lord Unwin had spelled out, pouring him another drink.

Now here's a shadow on the stairs . . . Is it . . . ? Yes! It's she! In a blue twilled dressing-gown and slippers, hair loose and tangled, still sleepy-eyed God bless her, and with a spattering of dark water-drops on the breast of her gown. His heart, so recently filled with murderous thoughts towards Mrs Castaway, is suddenly spilling over with tenderness.

'Why, Mr Hunt,' says Sugar, softly, pausing half-way down, 'What a pleasure to see you again so soon.' She motions apologetically at her *déshabillé*. A draught on the stairs sends strands of her hair floating across her cheeks and naked neck. How could he not have noticed before how abnormally thin that neck is? And her lips: they're so pale and dry, like scraps of lace – she doesn't drink enough! How he'd love to rub salve into her lips, while she kissed his fingers . . . !

'Mr Hunt has a proposition to make to you, Sugar,' says Mrs Castaway. 'Mr Hunt?'

Old witch! She hasn't even asked Sugar to take a seat – as if his offer is so preposterous the girl will be sure to refuse it before she reaches the bottom of the stairs. But a look passes between him and Sugar that gives him courage; it's a look that says, *We know each other, don't we, you and I?*

Courteously, he bids her be seated, and she is seated, in Miss Lester's chair. He repeats his little oration, but this time, freed from the odious necessity of addressing Mrs Castaway, he speaks directly into Sugar's face (her eyes are still sleepy; she licks her lips with a sharp red tongue, the same tongue that . . . Concentrate, Rackham!). He speaks less nervously than before; when repeating the fictions he's spun around George W. Hunt, he shares with her a secret smile, a mutual understanding of something that's already part of their intimate history. But when it comes to the arithmetic, he is emphatic and precise. For diplomacy's sake, he mentions Mrs Castaway's misgivings, and absorbs them into his account. Everyone, he declares reassuringly, is going to be the richer for this; no one will suffer the slightest inconvenience.

'But you haven't yet said,' objects the old woman from across the room. 'What will you pay Sugar?'

William flinches. The question seems to him crassly indelicate – and none of her business, either. This is not a low brothel!

'I will pay her,' he says, 'whatever makes her happy.' And he nods almost imperceptibly in Sugar's direction, to show her he means it.

Sugar blinks several times, runs one hand through the unruly orange fleece of her hair. The barrage of facts and figures has left her a little dazed, as if she's woken up this morning to a discussion of John Stuart Mill's *Principles of Political Economy* rather than to a boiled egg. At last she opens her mouth to speak.

'All right, Mr Hunt,' she says, with a sly smile. 'I am willing.'

Yes! She said yes! Rackham can scarcely contain himself. But he must, he must. Childish enthusiasm would ill become him; he's supposed to be a publisher!

So, bowing his head to Mrs Castaway's writing-desk, he watches her draw up the contract, *on this, the twenty-fourth day of November, 1874*. A waste of ink and effort: if only she knew that he'd sign anything, including a sheet of paper inscribed with just that one word, Anything! But she wants more. He reads what's flowing from her pen, written in (to give her credit) a most elegant and fluent script . . . *hereinafter known as 'the House'* . . . God almighty! She's going to pull the wool over his eyes, he can tell . . . but what does it matter? Measured against the wealth that will soon be his, the reach of her avarice will be Lilliputian.

In any case, if he should decide to renege, what could she possibly do? Pursue an imaginary man through the courts of Whoredom? *Regina* hears the case of 'Castaway' versus 'Hunt'? Stop scribbling, woman, and leave room for the signatures!

Looking back on it now, the contract for Agnes's hand was extraordinarily *laissez-faire* – much less demanding of him than this one here. In a marriage settlement, one might expect a degree of parental protectiveness, but Lord Unwin showed (now that William reflects on it) precious little for Agnes. Her dowry was no great fortune – nothing a young woman couldn't spend within a year or two – and no date was set for William's own succession to independent means. No mention, either, of how large a wardrobe of fashionable clothes William was obliged to ensure his wife maintained, or how Agnes's style of life was supposed to be safeguarded. For all that Lord Unwin seemed to care, his new son-in-law could dispose of Agnes's clothes, her jewellery, her books, her servants. Short of saying so, he was washing his hands of her – no doubt because he already knew (crafty old sot!) what poison was eating away at his step-daughter's sanity.

Faintly through the house, the slam of a door resounds: Miss Howlett's man, leaving. William looks askance at Sugar, but she's sunk into the armchair, her head nestled in the crook of her arm, eyes closed. The sleeve of her dressing-gown has fallen, exposing the white flesh of her forearm, bruised blue with finger-marks. His own, surely – *or are they*? With a jolt, he realises that this contract depends not merely on these women's trust in him, but his trust in them. What's to stop them conducting business as usual behind his back? Nothing, unless he takes care to be unpredictable, never letting them know the hour of his coming . . . Mad, he must be mad – yet a smile tempts the corners of his mouth as he signs, with a flourish, a false name to this bargain struck with a madam and a whore.

'It gives me great pleasure,' he says, bringing to light the ten guineas which the sale of some of Agnes's long-unused possessions has raised, 'to solemnise our agreement.'

Mrs Castaway accepts the money, and her face appears, all of a sudden, ancient and weary.

'I'm sure you can imagine greater pleasures than signing your name, Mr Hunt,' she says. 'Wake up, Sugar dear.'

Agnes stares at the small ivory knobs on the bedside cabinet, taking careful note of every tiny nick and scratch in each one. The shadow of the doctor's head falls across her face; his fingers are not inside her anymore.

'I'm afraid all is not as it should be.'

The words come to Agnes like overheard chatter from a railway platform opposite one's own. She is beginning to dream, her eyes shutting and her face shiny with perspiration, a dream she has already dreamed many times in her sleep, but never before while awake. The dream of the journey . . .

But Doctor Curlew is speaking, trying to summon her back. Gently but firmly he prods a spot on Mrs Rackham's naked abdomen.

'You feel this spot here? where I touch? That is where your womb has moved, much higher up than it ought to be, which is more . . . here.' His finger slides down towards the motte of blonde hair at which Agnes has glanced perhaps twenty times in her whole life, each time with shame. This time, however, there is no shame to feel, for the doctor's finger is sliding (as she perceives it in her dream) not on her body, but on a surface somewhere beyond it: a windowpane perhaps. She's in a train, and as it moves away from the station, someone on the platform outside is putting his finger against the window of her compartment.

Agnes closes her eyes.

Up in Sugar's room, William unpins his collars while Sugar kneels at his feet. She nuzzles the flies of his trousers with her face.

'R-r-r-r,' she purrs.

The buttons of William's shirt are stiff; he has worn his best to impress Mrs Castaway. While struggling to undo them, he glances at the escritoire, which is covered in papers as before. Masculine-looking papers, not leaves of tinted rice-paper and floral-patterned envelopes, not a bound volume of recipes and homilies illustrated with prissy watercolours, not puzzles or brain-teasers from the popular press. No, these papers lie on Sugar's desk in untidy stacks, scrawled and blotted on, crumpled, in amongst candle-stubs. And, on top of them all, a printed pamphlet, dense with text, scored in the margins with India-ink annotations.

'Whatever you're working on there, I can see it's no easy labour,' he remarks.

'Nothing to interest a man,' she murmurs, clawing gently at his buttocks with both hands. 'Come, take me.'

The bed's drapes are already tied back, like theatre curtains. In the bed-head mirror, William watches his reflection being led, stumbling, towards the rumpled sheets that still smell of him and Sugar.

'My little cunt is dripping for you, Mr Hunt,' she whispers.

'No, call me William, really,' he says. 'And please let me reassure you: you don't have to work at anything anymore, except . . .'

'Mmm, yes,' she says, pulling him onto the bed next to her. She gathers up the soft, loose fabric of her dressing-gown and tosses it over his head; he squirms, but she sheaths him snugly inside, trapping him against her midriff. His breath is hot and humid on her flesh; she feels him burrowing upwards, heading for the light at her neck.

'Oooh, not yet,' she croons, holding him back through the fabric. 'My breasts are burning for you.'

He begins to lick – gently, thank God. She's had men go after her nipples as if ducking for apples in a barrel. This one's lips are soft, his tongue is smooth, his teeth are barely noticeable. Harmless as any man can be, and with plenty of ready money. If he wants her name on a contract, well, why not?

But Holy Jesus, she'll have to keep him from seeing what's on her writing-desk. Her mother caught her by surprise, that's for sure, by pulling on the cord so early. Dead to the world she was, in a dream buried deep inside her pillow. How could she be expected, in her sleepy state, to think of clearing her desk? Getting herself downstairs without breaking her neck was as much as she could manage. And what for? No one could blame her, surely, for failing to guess it was to pledge eternal fidelity to a man . . .

Still, she'll have to be more careful in future: her papers can't be in the open like this, for him to sniff at. What's uppermost on her desk just now? She tries to picture it as she lifts her gown, to give her man some air . . . Could it be that horrid little pamphlet concerning . . . oh Lord, yes! She blenches at the thought of what, if she hadn't led him away, he might have stuck his nose into.

Open on her escritoire lies a medical tract, stolen from the public library's reading room in Trevor Square. The text itself would be no surprise to him; he's likely to have seen it all before:

No woman can be a serious thinker, without injury to her function as the conceiver and mother of children. Too often, the female 'intellectual' is a youthful invalid or virtual hermaphrodite, who might otherwise have been a healthy wife.

Let us close our ears, then, to siren voices offering us a quantity of female intellectual work at the price of a puny, enfeebled and sickly race. Healthy serviceable wombs are of more use to the Future than any amount of feminine scribbling.

No, it's not the text, but Sugar's handwritten comments in the margins that her new benefactor must at all costs not see: *Pompous oaf!* here; *Tyranny!* there; *Wrong, wrong, wrong!* over there and, scrawled under the conclusion in angry blotted ink: *We'll see about that, you poxy old fool! There's a new century coming soon, and you and your kind will be <u>DEAD!</u>*

As Doctor Curlew rummages in the compartments of his satchel for the leech box, he spies, under his patient's bed, the cover of a journal not sanctioned by him. (It's the *London Periodical Review*, which Agnes is reading for the perfectly innocent reason that she wishes to know what she's supposed to think of the new paintings she's not been able to see, the new poetry she hasn't read, and the recent history she hasn't witnessed, in case, next Season, she is put on the spot for an opinion.)

'Pardon me, Mrs Rackham,' he says, still unaware that she no longer hears him. He has the offending item in his hand, and holds it up for her unseeing eyes to recognise. 'Is this your journal?'

He doesn't wait for a reply; his admonition is impervious to excuses. Nor would it have made any difference if the item had not been the *London Periodical Review* but Mrs Henry Wood's *The Shadow of Ashlydyat* or some such rubbish. Excessively thrilling reading, excessively taxing reading, excessively pathetic reading, too much washing, too much sun, tight corsets, ice-cream, asparagus, foot-warmers: these and many more are causes of the womb's distress. But no matter, he has a remedy.

Doctor Curlew appraises for a moment the patch of white skin behind one of Agnes's ears, then places, with precision, the first of the leeches there. Agnes chooses this inopportune moment to venture out of her dream, in case the real world should, in the interim, have become safe again. She observes the leech being conveyed through the air towards her, clamped in the tongs. Before she can retreat into unconsciousness she has felt the cold touch of the instrument behind her ear, and though she cannot feel the leech begin to suck, she nevertheless imagines a watery spiral of blood swimming up through her innards towards her head, like a crimson worm in a viscous medium. But then she's back in her dream and, by the time Doctor Curlew applies the second leech, the passenger train is again in motion.

Gently, the doctor's hands turn her head one hundred and eighty degrees on the pillow, for the process must be repeated on the other side.

'Excuse me, Mrs Rackham.'

Agnes doesn't stir: her journey has vaulted forward to its end. Two old men are carrying her stretcher from the railway terminus, deep in the heart of the countryside, to the gates of the Convent of Health. A nun rushes to open the gates, giant iron gates that rustle with ivy and holly-hock. The old men gently put the stretcher down on the sunlit grass and doff their caps. The nun kneels beside Agnes and lays a cool palm on her brow.

'Dear, dear child,' she chides in loving exasperation. 'What are we going to do with you?'

Passion spent, William is able to examine his prize more closely, studying her in loving detail. She lies cradled in his arm, apparently asleep, her eyelashes still. He combs his fingers through her hair, admiring all the unexpected colours to be found in it, hidden inside the red: streaks of pure gold, wisps of blond, single strands of dark auburn. Her skin is like noth-ing he's ever seen: on every limb, and on her hips and belly, there are . . . what can he call them? Tiger stripes. Swirling geometric patterns of peel-ing dryness alternating with reddened flesh. They are symmetrical, as if scored on her skin by a painstaking aesthete, or an African savage. (Doctor Curlew, if he were here, could have told William, and Sugar for that matter, that she suffers from an unusually generalised psoriasis which, in places, crosses the diagnostic line into a rarer and more spectacular condition called ichthyosis. He might prescribe expensive ointments which would have no more effect on the cracks in Sugar's hands or the flaky stripes on her thighs than the cheap oil she's already using.) To William, the patterns are beguiling, a fitting mark of her animal nature. She smells like an animal too: or what he imagines animals smell like, for he's no animal lover. Her sex is luxuriantly aromatic, her shame-hair twinkles with sweat and semen.

He lifts his head slightly to get a better view of her breasts. Supine, she's almost flat-chested, but her nipples are full and unmistakably female. (And, when she's the other way around, there's enough for him to hold onto.) In truth, he's delighted with every inch of her; she might almost be a thing designed for no purpose but to bring him to orgasm.

He squeezes her shoulders, to rouse her enough for a question he has been wanting to ask her for the best part of an hour.

'Sugar?'

'Mmm?'

'Do you . . . Do you *like* me?'

She laughs throatily, turns her head against his, nuzzles his cheek.

'Oh William, yessss,' she says. 'You're my rescuer, aren't you? My champion . . .' She cups his genitals in her rough palm. 'I can scarcely believe my good fortune.'

He stretches, closes his eyes in languor. She chews surreptitiously at her peeling lips, worrying at a wedge-shaped flake of skin that's almost, but not quite, ready to come off. She must leave it alone, or it'll bleed. How much money will she ask for this time? His big soft hand is on her breast, his heart is beating against her sharp shoulder-blade. On his face, an expression of happiness. It occurs to her – well, no, she suspected it from the moment she first looked in his eyes – that for all his transgressive posturing he is an infant searching for a warm bed to sleep in. If she will but smooth his greasy golden curls off his sweaty brow, he'll give her anything she asks for in return.

He's breathing deeply now, almost unconscious, when there's a soft, hesitant knock at the door.

'What the devil?' he mutters.

But Sugar knows that knock.

'Christopher!' she calls, *sotto voce*. 'What's up?'

'I'm very sorry,' comes the child's voice through the key-hole. 'But I've a message from Mrs Castaway. For the gentleman. To remind 'im – in case it's slipped 'is mind, like – of 'is appointment. With a Mister Wilkie Collins.'

William turns to Sugar and smiles sheepishly.

'Duty calls,' he says.

Several hours later, Agnes Rackham feels the small feminine hands of Clara stroking her mechanically through the bedclothes, but she's too deeply inside her dream to recognise them.

The dream, having reached its heavenly conclusion, has started again from the very beginning. She's on her way to the Convent of Health: a train compartment has been specially prepared for her, to look as much like her own room as possible; she lies in a berth by the window, and on the walls there is proper wallpaper, and framed portraits of her mother and father.

She raises herself up from her pillow to look out onto the platform, which is bustling with activity, with passengers rushing to and fro, luggage-boys tottering under suitcases, pigeons fluttering up to the domed ceiling high above and, on the far platform nearest the street, the cab-horses stamping impatiently. The unsavoury man who had tapped on her window with his finger is gone, and in his place, a smiling old stationmaster strolls up and calls to her through the glass,

'Are you all right, Miss?'

'Yes, thank you,' she replies, settling back into her pillow. Outside, a whistle is blown, and with nary a jolt the train rolls into motion.

An hour or so later still, William Rackham, ensconced in his study, rummages in the drawers of his desk and realises, with a slight shock, that there are no more Rackham papers he hasn't read. He has finally ploughed through them all; he has extracted their essence. A large, leather-bound notebook lies open, and in it, in his own squarish handwriting, a number of unanswered questions. He'll have answers to those questions soon enough.

Light-headed with Madeira and achievement, he tears the brown wrapper off a virgin parcel of Rackham Perfumeries letterhead, extracts a sheet, positions it carefully on the desk, secures it with his elbow, dips pen in ink, and writes under the company's rose insignia:

Dear Father,

NINE

ome with me now, away from the filthy city streets, away from rooms that stink of fear and deceit, away from contracts forged in mucky cynicism. Love exists. Come with me to church.

It's a cold but sunny Sunday morning, four months later. The air is pure, with nothing added to it but a subtle scent of rain and, here and there, a sparrow in flight. All along the path to the church, the dark wet grass is dotted with tiny white buds that will soon be daffodils. Maturer blossoms are to be found—

(What? Sugar? Why are you thinking about Sugar? Don't worry about her anymore; she's spoken for! And try also to put William from your mind. Everything is in hand, I assure you. A series of increasingly cordial letters have been exchanged between father and son; the transfer of power was smooth. Oh, to begin with, the old man was a doubting Thomas, and mistrusted William's detailed description of the Rackham company, the duties of its director, and the exact manner in which William meant to discharge these duties, as nothing more than a ploy to wheedle the where-withal for an extravagant Christmas. Soon enough, however, the old man was convinced that a birth scarcely less miraculous than the Saviour's had occurred: the advent of William Rackham, captain of industry. Now everything has been made sweet, and William's humiliations are a thing of the past, so let's not dwell on them any longer.)

As I was saying, maturer blossoms are to be found inside the church: in translucent grey vases, and on the bonnets of some of the congregation. Not only flowers, but also stuffed birds and butterflies on the headgear of the more fashionable ladies here. They file out of the pews, eyeing each other's dresses and bonnets, and only that peculiar soul Emmeline Fox is unadorned. She holds her head as high as if she were beautiful, and holds her body as if she were strong. Walking at her side, as always, is Henry Rackham, the man who should by rights have been *the* Rackham of Rackham Perfumeries, but who (as everybody knows by now) has lost that claim for good.

Henry is a handsome man, taller than average – well, taller than his brother, anyway – bluer of eye and firmer of chin. Also, unlike his brother, his hair – no less gold – sits on his head most decorously, and his midriff is trim. In earlier years, before it became obvious he had no intention of claiming his birthright, he was sought out by a succession of eligible young ladies, each of whom found him to be a decent if over-serious man, each of whom hinted that the inheritor of a large concern would need a devoted wife, and each of whom melted away from him as soon as he spoke disparagingly of money. One of these ladies (present in church today, newly married to Arthur Gillow, the Ice Chest manufacturer) even kissed him on the brow, to see if it cured his shyness.

This is not the love I spoke of. The love I spoke of is real. It is the love of two friends for their God, and for each other.

Henry approaches the vestibule of his church – well, not a church of his *own*, sadly, but the church he attends – and sniffs the fresh air wafting in from outside. He has no interest in perfume, except to note that each week there seems to be more of it within these walls. Today it emanates as strongly from those ladies (within earshot of the rector) who are speaking of Scriptural matters, as from those, farther away, discussing the coming London Season.

He and Mrs Fox are loath to linger now that the service is over, scorning the opportunity to gossip with Notting Hill's other churchgoers. They shake the rector's hand, Henry commends him on his refutation of Darwinism, and they are on their way. The gossips stare after them but, having been thus snubbed every Sunday for months, don't bother passing comment. So much has already been said about Henry Rackham and Mrs Fox, that if neither of them will rise to the bait, despite everyone's best efforts to whisper as *clearly* as possible, well, what's the use?

Henry and Mrs Fox walk gingerly down the steep gravel path that leads to the churchyard, each using a furled umbrella as a walking stick, rather than taking each other by the arm. At the bottom of the slope the path curves sharply, running along the churchyard for a while before becoming part of the main road; that's the way they walk, with butter-yellow tombstones to the right of them, and black-trunked evergreens to the left.

'How beautiful this morning is,' says Emmeline Fox. (No, she means it! No, she is *not* making conversation! Your time in the streets and in houses of ill repute has made you cynical; it's a beautiful Sunday morning, and here is someone expressing her delight.) She is full of the love of God's creation, full to overflowing. The glories of God are copious, endless; they enter her from all directions . . . (What are you *thinking*? You've *definitely* been too long in the wrong company!)

'Beautiful, yes,' agrees Henry Rackham. He looks around, inviting the glory of Nature to flood into him, but Nature is reluctant to comply. He squints into the green-tinted light, yearning to feel the same as his enraptured companion.

The problem is, although the sun is beaming through the trees just like in Dyce's painting of *George Herbert in Bemerton*, it fails to impress him half as much as the quilting on Mrs Fox's bodice. And, although lively new sparrows are rustling through the leaves and hopping across the cobblestones, they cannot compete with Mrs Fox's grace as she walks. And as for the falling of light, that phenomenon is most admirable on her face.

How handsome she is! She dresses like an angel – an angel in grey serge. Try as he might to 'consider the lilies of the field', they are too common and gaudy for him; he cannot prefer them to Mrs Fox's sober finery. Her voice, too, is low and musical, like . . . like a softly-played bassoon; so much more soothing than the twitterings of sparrows or other women.

'Have I lost you, Henry?' she says suddenly.

He blushes. 'Do go on, Mrs Fox. I was merely admiring . . . the miracle of God's creation.'

Mrs Fox hooks the handle of her umbrella on her belt so she can lift both her gloved hands up to her forehead. The steep slope of the path has made her perspire; she dabs her skin under the thick frizz of her hair.

'I was merely saying,' she says, 'that I wish all this fighting over our origins would come to an end – *any* sort of end.'

'Pardon me, Mrs Fox, but what do you mean, "any sort of end"?' Henry's questions to her are always gently posed, for fear of offending her.

'Well,' she sighs, 'If only it could be resolved once and for all where we come from: from Adam, or from Mr Darwin's apes.'

Henry stops in his tracks, amazed. Each time they meet, just when he least expects it, she unveils something like this.

'But my dear Mrs Fox — you cannot be serious!'

She looks aside at him, licks her lips, but says nothing to soothe his alarm.

'My dear Mrs Fox,' he begins again, blinking at the sun-dappled road ahead of them. 'The difference between belief in the one descent rather than the other is the difference . . . why, between Faith and Atheism!'

'Oh Henry, it isn't, *really* it isn't.' Her voice is impatient now, passionate, alerting him to the fact that she's about to talk of her work with the Rescue Society. 'If only you could know the wretches I work among! You'd see that the debate that rages in our churches and town halls means nothing to them. It's seen as a spat between one set of stuffed shirts and another. "I know all about it, miss," they say. "We're to choose who was our grandparents: two monkeys or two naked innocents in a garden." And they laugh, for both strike them as equally ridiculous.'

'In *their* eyes, perhaps, but not in the eyes of God.'

'Yes but Henry, can't you see that they will not be brought to God by seeing us quarrelling. We must accept that they don't care where life comes from. What is far more important to address is that they despise our faith. *They*, Henry, who were once the backbone of the Church, in the days when the world was not yet blighted with cities and factories. How it saddens me to think of them as they were then, tilling the land, simple and devout . . . Look there!'

She points to a meadow some distance away which, on closer scrutiny, is a site of swarming industry. There are tiny workmen, cartloads of timber and earth, and a giant machine of mysterious function.

'Another house, I suppose,' sighs Mrs Fox, turning her back on it and leaning her bustle against a stile. 'First come the houses, then the shops, then finally . . .' (she rolls her eyes at the impiety of Commerce) 'the Universal Provider.' She rubs her gloved hands along her thin arms, shivering. 'Still, I suppose your father will be pleased.'

'My . . . father?' Henry is slow to catch her drift; the only father to whom he gives regular thought is in Heaven.

'Yes,' prompts Mrs Fox. 'More houses, more people — more business, yes?'

Henry leans gingerly against the nearest stile to hers. Discomfited though he is by his connection with the arch-profiteer who gave him his name, he feels constrained to defend him.

'My father likes Nature as much as anyone,' he points out. 'I'm sure he doesn't want any more of it despoiled. Anyway, perhaps you haven't heard? He's stepped down from the directorship of Rackham's, and William has taken charge.'

'Oh? Is he ill?'

Henry, unsure which Rackham she has in mind, replies: 'My father's fit as a whale. As for William, I don't know what's come over him.'

Mrs Fox smiles. The essential and irreconcilable differences between Henry and his brother are a source of secret pleasure to her. 'How very unexpected,' she declares. 'I always took your brother to be a man full of plans, but not much fruition.'

Henry blushes again, aware he's the sibling of a profligate, a ne'er-do-well. What has *he*, Henry, achieved in life? Does Mrs Fox look down her nose at him, too, for his failure to grasp his destiny? (And why are people always remarking that her nose is long? It's the perfect length for her face!)

She's still leaning against the stile, head back, eyes shut, so near to him that he can hear her breathing and see the breath coming out of her parted lips. He indulges a fantasy, despising himself for it, but indulging all the same. He imagines himself a vicar, digging in the rich dark earth of a vicarage garden, with Emmeline at his side, golden in the sunlight, holding a seedling tree ready for planting. 'Tell me when,' she says to him.

With effort, he leaves this blissful day-dream, and focuses on reality. Mrs Fox's demeanour has changed. She looks less spirited than before – almost dejected. A simple sequence of expressions, this, incalculably common in human history, yet they wrench at his heart.

'You look sad,' he finally succeeds in saying.

'Oh Henry,' she sighs, 'There's no stopping what has been begun; you know that, don't you?'

'B-begun?'

'The march of progress. The triumph of the machine. We are on a fast train to the twentieth century. The past cannot be restored.'

Henry ponders this for a moment, but finds he cares little for the past or the future as abstracts. Only two things glow clear in his brain: the fantasy of digging the vicarage garden with Mrs Fox, and the urgent desire to remove her unhappiness from her.

'The past is more than pasture,' he suggests, wincing at his own un-intended wit. 'It's standards of conduct, too. Don't you think we can keep those if we wish?'

'Oh, it would be nice to think so. But the modern world seduces right-eousness, Henry — in every conceivable way.'

He blushes, thinking of her flock of prostitutes, but she means more than that.

'Last week,' she says, 'I was in the city, on my way to visit a wretched family I'd visited before, to plead with them once more to listen to the words of their Saviour. I was tired, I felt disinclined to walk far. Before I knew what I was doing, I was in the Underground Railway, pulled by an engine, mesmerised by the alternation of darkness and light, speeding through the earth at the cost of a sixpence. I spoke to no one; I might as well have been a ghost. I enjoyed it so much, I missed my stop, and never saw the family.'

'I . . . I confess I don't quite divine the point you are making.'

'This is how our world will end, Henry! We're foolish to imagine the Last Days will be ushered in by a giant Antichrist brandishing a bloody battle-axe. The Antichrist is our own *desires*, Henry. With my sixpence, I absolved myself utterly of responsibility — for the welfare of the poor filthy wretches who slaved to dig out that railway, for the grotesque sum of money spent on it, for the violation of the earth that ought to be solid beneath my feet. I sat in my carriage, admiring the dark tunnels flashing by me, not having the foggiest notion where I was, mindless of every-thing except my pleasure. I ceased to be, in any meaningful sense, God's creature.'

'You are being hard on yourself. A single ride in the Underground isn't going to hasten Armageddon.'

'I'm not so sure,' she says, a smile tempting her lips. 'I think we're moving towards *such* a strange time. A time when all our moral choices will be complicated and compromised by our love of progress.' She looks up into the sky, as if checking her facts with God. 'I can see the world descending into chaos, and us just watching, not sure what we should, or could, have done about it.'

'And yet you work for the Rescue Society!'

'Because I must do *something* while I still can. Each soul is still in-calculably precious.'

Henry strives to recall how they reached this point. While he agrees wholeheartedly that each soul is precious, just now he can't help noticing that the stiles against which he and Mrs Fox have been leaning are cold and damp, and that Mrs Fox is protected from feeling this by her bustle whereas he is not. Politely he suggests they walk on.

'Forgive me, Henry,' she says, jerking stiffly into motion. 'Have I made us late again? My mind wanders while my body takes root.'

'Not at all! And I was a little tired myself!'

'That's sweet of you, Henry,' she says, gaining her stride once more. 'And you know, I really meant what I said about Darwin. The Church has been wrong before, after all – on details of science, I mean. Didn't it once maintain that the Sun revolved around the Earth? – and put people to death for suggesting otherwise? Now every school-book tells us that the Earth revolves around the Sun. Does it really matter? I shouldn't be surprised if the women I work with still believe it's the other way around. It's not my business to set them straight on cosmology, or the origin of man. I'm fighting to save them from the death of their bodies and souls!' Even as she walks, she clenches one delicate fist to her breast. 'Oh, if you could only know the state of moral anarchy in which they exist . . . !'

To his shame, Henry *longs* to know the state of moral anarchy in which Mrs Fox's prostitutes exist. Ah, the depravity she must be witness to! It's all he can do to refrain from asking her questions which, under the guise of an interest in urban sanitation, goggle for a glimpse of something else entirely. Sometimes he must clench the muscles in his jaw, to bite back a demand that she reveal more.

The strange thing is: even when he has himself firmly under control, and is communing with Mrs Fox on an unsullied plane, she *herself* moves the conversation – innocently, no doubt – into more sensual regions.

Not so long ago, for example, he and Mrs Fox were dawdling by the Serpentine, discussing the Afterlife.

'You know, Henry,' she was saying, 'I often doubt there is a Hell. Death itself is so cruel. Oh, I don't mean the sort of death you and I are likely to suffer, but the sort of death so often suffered by those wretches I work among. Our doctrine would have us believe they're bound for Hell, but what *is* Hell for such as they? When I see a woman dying of a vile disease, bitterly regretting every minute she's spent on this earth, I wonder if she hasn't already endured the worst.'

'But surely the righteous must have their reward!' he protested, alarmed at her heresy, not because he feared God would be angry with her (God couldn't fail to appreciate her good intentions) but in case the wrath of the Church should fall upon her exquisite head.

'Isn't Heaven reward enough,' she protested in turn, 'without needing to see the damned punished?'

'Of course, of course it is,' he said hastily. 'I didn't mean that *I* wish to see sinners suffer. But there are righteous folk who do; and surely in Heaven, we can't have any of the souls feeling resentful . . .'

Emmeline was leaning forward over the edge of the Serpentine's bank, waving at a fat, grey duck, which disappeared underwater.

'I don't know that our resurrected souls will have the capacity to feel resentment,' she said.

'A sense of . . . unfairness, then.'

She smiled, her face lit up by reflections off the rippling lake.

'Those seem awfully queer things for resurrected souls to be feeling.' And she extended one silky arm over the water, wiggling her fingers to attract whatever might be underneath.

'But . . . they must be capable of feeling *something* . . .' Henry persisted. 'We aren't Orientalists, expecting to disappear into our deity like a puff of smoke.' She seemed however to be no longer listening, staring at the brilliant water, waiting for the duck to resurface. He cleared his throat. 'What do *you* think, Mrs Fox? What will souls in Heaven feel?'

'Oh,' said Emmeline, eyes mysterious in the sun-dappled shade under her hat-brim, and mouth licked brilliant as the leaves on the water, 'I should think . . . Love. The most wonderful . . . endless . . . perfect . . . Love.'

That's how she always did it! With just a few words and a certain quality of voice, she artlessly penetrated his Platonic armour, and he was helpless with impure thoughts. All sorts of lurid scenarios would flash into his mind like *tableaux vivants*: Mrs Fox's skirts catching on the branches of a tree, and being torn right off; Mrs Fox being attacked by a degenerate ruffian, who might succeed in baring her bosom before Henry smote him down; Mrs Fox's clothing catching fire, necessitating his prompt action; Mrs Fox sleepwalking to his house, in the night, for him to restore to dignity with his own dressing-gown.

Once he was roused like this, prurience would start to whisper in his ear. He would press Mrs Fox to describe her work with fallen women, knowing perfectly well that while there were some things he wished to know, there were others he wished only to *imagine*.

'What . . . what do these poor creatures wear?' he asked her on one such occasion, when they were walking in St James's Park.

'The latest fashions, more or less,' she replied, suspecting nothing. 'Some affect a more old-fashioned appearance. I've seen several with their hair still parted down the middle, without a fringe. In general I should guess their colours are a few months behind, though I'm hardly the best judge of such things. Why do you ask?"

'Their attire . . . It isn't . . . loose?'

'Loose?'

'They don't . . . flaunt their bodies?'

She became pensive, giving the question serious thought. Eventually she replied, 'I suppose they do. But it isn't with their attire so much as with the way they wear it. A dress which on me might appear perfectly decent, might be a Jezebel's costume on them. The way they stand, and sit, and move, and walk, can be indecent in the extreme.'

Henry wondered how a whore might sit, that was so shamefully different from the method employed by a decent woman. How might she stand, and how might she move? Fortunately, on that particular occasion, he was saved from himself (however dubious the rescue) by Bodley and Ashwell, running across the park towards them.

Now, on this sunny Sunday morning, with the God-given miracle of Spring in evidence all around them, Henry Rackham is once more in turmoil under his stiff clothes. Mrs Fox has cried, 'Oh, if you could only know the state of moral anarchy in which they exist . . . !' and he is desperate to know. So, he asks her to elaborate, and she does.

As they stroll on, she recounts one of her Rescue Society stories. (There are never any unclothed bodies in these stories, never any embraces, but still he listens with ears aflame.) She speaks of a time not long ago, when she and her sisters in the Society were admitted into a bawdy-house, and found there a girl who quite plainly was not long for this world. When Mrs Fox expressed concern over the girl's health, the madam retorted that the girl was in good hands – better than any doctor's – and that, if truth be told, Mrs Fox didn't look so well herself, and would she like to lie down in one of the spare rooms?

'I was shocked, I must admit, at her perversity.'

'Yes, quite,' mutters Henry. 'A most sly and licentious suggestion.'

'No, no, it wasn't *that* that shocked me. It was her rejection of Medicine! What a topsy-turvy state these people are in: God and doctors bad; prostitution good!'

Henry grunts sympathetically. In his head, a vision of topsy-turviness is made flesh: a squirming heap of pink women flipping over and over, like frogs in a pond.

'Do I look ill to you?' Mrs Fox asks suddenly.

'Not at all!' he exclaims.

'Well, at any rate,' she says, 'it makes me ill in *here*' (palm on her breast) 'to think of the poor girls in that evil woman's clutches, and to imagine how cruelly they must be treated.'

Henry, doing his very best *not* to imagine how those poor girls might be treated, is relieved to observe a distraction coming up Union Street towards them.

'Look there, Mrs Fox,' he says. 'Isn't that someone we know?'

A short, plump lady sumptuously dressed in purple with black trimmings – the last tokens of mourning – is trotting towards them. Almost a whole bird's-worth of dyed feathers jigs up and down on her bonnet, and her parasol is of Continental proportions.

'*You* know her, perhaps,' says Mrs Fox. 'I'm sure I've never met her.'

(In point of fact, there are *two* women walking towards them, but the servant is of no consequence and doesn't warrant a name.)

'Good morning, Lady Bridgelow,' says Henry, as soon as she's within hailing distance. By way of response, she removes one purple-gloved hand from her black muff and motions it demurely.

'Good morning to *you*, Mr Rackham.' With eyes slightly narrowed she regards Mrs Fox. 'I do not believe I am acquainted with your companion.'

'Allow me to introduce Mrs Emmeline Fox.'

'*Enchantée.*' The lady nods, smiles, and without hesitation she and her lady's-maid pass, their black boots ticking on the cobblestones.

Henry waits until they are out of earshot, then turns to Mrs Fox and says, 'You have been slighted.' His voice is choked with vexation.

'I'm sure I'll survive, Henry. Remember I'm accustomed to having doors slammed in my face, and foul language thrown at me. And look! Here we are at William Street. Is it a message from Providence, d'you think, to turn right and visit your brother?'

Henry frowns, uneasy as always to hear her flirting with what more judgemental souls might consider blasphemy.

'I imagine it was from William's house that Lady Bridgelow came.'

'Certainly not from church,' remarks Mrs Fox. 'But tell me, Henry: I didn't know your brother was apt to receive visits from the aristocracy.'

'Well, they are neighbours, after a fashion.' (It's all coming back to him now; William has told him a great deal about this person, as though he ought to be fearfully interested in her.)

'Neighbours? There must be a dozen houses in between.'

'Yes, but . . .' Henry strains to recall the last conversation he had with his brother. Suicide was part of it, was it not? 'Oh yes: William is the only one who doesn't hold it against her that her husband did away with himself.'

'Did away with himself?'

'Yes, shot himself I believe.'

'Poor man. Couldn't he simply have divorced her instead?'

'Mrs Fox!'

A small dog stationed just outside the gate to William Rackham's property raises its mongrel head in hope, then begins to lick its genitals, unaware that this is not the way to earn respect.

'Don't look, Mrs Fox,' urges Henry, as he ushers her through.

Emmeline turns, but sees only a dog appealing to her with soulful brown eyes as the gate shuts in its face. *Poor thing*, she thinks.

'Could it be William's?' she says as they walk up the Rackham path together.

'William has no pets I know of.'

'He might have got one since we last visited.'

'In which case I don't imagine he'd settle for a mongrel.'

Henry stands at his brother's front door (the door that could have been his own, garlanded with an ornate brass 'R'), and pulls the bell. Even before the cord stops swinging, he is aware that much has changed in the Rackham house since he visited, *sans* Mrs Fox, several weeks ago. Maybe it's the way the brass 'R' gleams, transmuted almost into gold by vigorous polishing. Maybe it's the way the doorbell is answered in seconds rather than minutes, or the way Letty greets them so avidly, as though a fresh coat of obsequiousness has just been applied to her. Behind her, inside the receiving hall, everything is on show, sparkling and dust-free.

'Come in, come in!' exclaims William Rackham, half-way up the stairs, waving jovially. Henry scarcely recognises him: a dark curly fungus is sprouting from William's upper lip and chin, while the hair on his head has been cut even shorter, plastered flat to his scalp. Far from wearing his Sunday best, he's in a weekday suit minus the jacket, plus an ankle-length dressing-gown with quilted lapels. At his extremities, he brandishes a magnifying glass, a cigar, and the most peculiar two-tone shoes. Yet it's his beaming smile that is the most conspicuous novelty.

Thus begins the great exhibition. Mind you don't slip on the newly waxed floor!

'Step this way, step this way.'

Guided by the master of the house, brother Henry and his companion are shown everything. The melancholy atmosphere of the Rackham home, which had become like a characteristic odour, has been banished. All the windows have been replaced; the old steps have been removed from the garden; new French windows have been screwed into the parlour door. The whole place smells of paint, wallpaper paste and fresh air. To Henry's mortification, there are three workmen still at large in the hall, pasting up the last few strips of a new wallpaper, under the critical eye of Agnes, who has left her bed in order to supervise.

And did Henry not notice that the fence around the grounds is no longer rusty brown but fresh rose-pink? No? Ha!Ha! In a world of his own, this brother of mine, as always! And what about the grounds themselves? What a difference, eh? The gardener's name is Shears – really! Isn't that exquisite? Shears! Ha!Ha! A little mule of a man: just the fellow to bring the unruly wilds around the greenhouse back into Man's dominion.

Nor are the house and its environs the only things subject to reform. William Rackham has a great many other fish to fry, or at least to be fried for him. The servants, for example.

Everything that was wrong has been set to rights. Janey has been relieved of her extra duties and is a simple scullery maid again, overjoyed no doubt to be responsible only for mops, rags and brushes. A new kitchen-maid has been hired, who'll also assist Letty in some of her duties, so that Letty can be more prompt in her attention to the needs of visitors and the family. There's another housemaid on the way too. William now has a pretty full complement of females; he can't hire any more until he lives in a much grander house (the future, the future!) He could hire another male, but he's undecided what kind. The gardener is an impressive acquisition, and moreover essential, but the idea of a manservant doesn't particularly appeal. A coachman? Hmm . . . yes, but actually he's holding off hiring one of those until he gets a coach. And who knows? He may not get a coach after all. He's too busy nowadays to waste time riding around showing off. Though perhaps if Agnes has a need in the coming Season, he'll buy her a coach then.

Mind you, there's nothing like the prestige that comes with male servants. Female servants aren't the same: any shop-keeper or pennywise matron can afford one or two. Still, the gardener's a grand beginning, isn't he? The lawns will be rescued from anarchy yet!

Yes, William Rackham is a changed man: that's plain. He has now the air of a man for whom there's never enough time in the day: a twenty-four hour man. It's an Augean labour, this perfume business, but someone's got to do it, now that the old man is on the way out. (What? No, Father's quite well, it was just a figure of speech.) But it's a big job, that's the point, a seven-day-a-week job. (Don't scowl, dear brother: again, just a manner of speaking. How *was* church? Would've loved to attend, but had these workmen to supervise. What? The Sabbath? Oh, quite, quite. But the job was only a few sheets short of being finished, and these fellows begged to come today and be done with it. Jews, I shouldn't wonder.)

To discourage his brother from censure, William launches into a pan-egyric on perfume: the miracle of its mysterious mechanisms. Scents, like sounds (he explains) stroke our olfactory nerve in exquisite and exact degrees. There's an octave of odours like an octave in music. The top note is what we notice when the headiest element dies off the handkerchief; the middle note, or modifier, provides full, solid character to the fragrance; then, once the more volatile substances have flown, the base, or end, note is left resonating: and what is that end note, brother? Lavender, if you please!

Expansively, William plays the host to Henry and Mrs Fox. Tea and cake are served, perfectly on time, perfectly presented. And, while his guests make appreciative noises, he sizes them up in comparison to himself.

Of Mrs Fox he thinks: *Ashwell's right — her face is just like a greyhound's. I wonder if she's as ill as she looks.*

And of his brother Henry: *How ill-at-ease he appears, as if he has boils on his bum. Strange that it's come to this, when, of the two of us, it was always Henry who cut the better figure . . . yet here we are on this sunny Sunday afternoon, and lo and behold: it's left to me to demonstrate how a man may subjugate Life and make it do his bidding.*

'Thank you both for paying this visit,' he says to them, when it's time they were going.

Mrs Fox, thoughtlessly usurping Henry's right to speak first, replies, 'Not at all, Mr Rackham. The energy with which you've pursued the improvements to your house, why, it's . . . startling. The world sorely needs such energy – especially in other arenas.'

'You are too kind,' says William.

'Yes, too kind,' echoes Agnes, adding these three words to the approximately twenty she's contributed to the conversation. Beautifully turned out though she is, in powder blue and black, she hasn't yet regained the knack of conversing with the world.

'I hope,' says William as he passes his guests into Letty's care, 'that you find enjoyable diversions for the rest of the day.'

Henry, bristling at this suggestion that he and Mrs Fox might seek to use God's day for selfish entertainment, replies, 'I'm sure Mrs Fox and I will spend it as . . . fittingly as we can.'

And on this note, Henry and Mrs Fox are shown out.

Quiet descends on the Rackham house – or at least, such quiet as can prevail with the paperers packing up their tools in the hall. William, a little hoarse from his performance, lights a cigarette. Agnes sits nearby, staring with unfocused eyes at a biscuit she will not eat. The oxalate of cerium pill she swallowed with her tea is already disagreeing with her.

After a good five minutes, she says: 'It's Sunday, then?'

'Yes, dear.'

'I thought it was Saturday.'

'Sunday, dear.'

Another long pause follows. Surreptitiously, Agnes scratches at her wrists, which have grown unaccustomed to the tight sleeves of daywear and the texture of anything but cotton. She clasps her hands together, to stop herself scratching any more. Then:

'Are they really Jews?'

'Who, dear?'

'The workmen here today.'

'With what I'm paying them extra,' snorts William, 'they might as well be. But you know it pains me to keep my precious little wife waiting for anything she deserves.'

Agnes lowers her face and plays with her tiny fingers, confused. Her renovated husband is going to take getting used to. And, if she's going to take part in the Season this year, she'll have to get a firmer grip on what day it is.

Having said goodbye to Mrs Fox and watched her walk away, Henry returns to his own modest home in Gorham Place, on the very brink of Pottery-and-Piggery-land. The meeting with William has left him flustered, despite Mrs Fox's sensible parting advice not to judge his brother too harshly for his vulgar and impious behaviour. 'He's just a boy with a new toy,' she counselled him, and no doubt she's right, but still . . . what an embarrassment. And what a relief to go back to his own house, his own small retreat, where nothing ever changes, and everything is plain and functional, and there isn't a servant to be seen (except himself, servant to the Lord).

In truth, Henry's house is a little shabbier than modest. It's among the smallest in the district, with no grounds except a minuscule back garden, and a bedroom whose opposite walls can be touched by the fingertips of a man extending his arms Christ-wise. It's also poorly sealed and draughty, and at nights the smell of boiling pig fat is wont to come in through the windows, but this has never troubled Henry. The great mass of mankind must make do with much worse.

In any case, he's suspicious of too much comfort – it breeds thoughtlessness. Kneeling at his hearth, he prepares a nest of kindling, lights it, ladles lumps of coal into it one by one. Thus is he reminded of what he's taking from God's earth, and of how each twig and coal-lump is a privilege – an advantage he has over the unfortunates who shiver their lives away in perpetual subterranean damp. To help the reluctant flame rise, he adds a few pages from old copies of the *Illustrated London News*, screwing up engravings of rail disasters, fashionable ice-skaters and visiting Negro potentates. An article extolling the miracle of electricity crumples in his fist; he has read it and was not impressed. 'Professor Gallup astounded the audience with tales of a future in which we shall scarcely be able to distinguish day from night, and there will be nothing we do that is not dependent on electric machinery.' A vision of Hell.

As soon as the fire grows warm, Henry's cat saunters into the room from parts unknown. Her name is simply Puss, scrupulously to avoid treating her too much like a human being, or perhaps to soften the blow of her inevitable loss. She lies down on the ember-blackened rug, and allows her master to stroke her furry flank.

Soon, Henry has settled into a typical Sunday afternoon. While Puss sleeps in the sitting-room, he sits in the adjacent study, reading the Bible. Regrettably, the walls that divide his *sanctum sanctorum* from the outside world are thin, and true silence is difficult to come by. Life goes on, and isn't shy to let him know it.

At every sound that betrays someone nearby spending the Sabbath in ways other than those approved by God, Henry frowns in disappointment. He does nothing on the Lord's day but attend church twice, visit his brother, converse with Mrs Fox (if the opportunity arises), and read pious literature. But listen there, through the window! Isn't that the sound of a large object being loaded onto a cart, with shouted instructions? And isn't that the excited barking of a dog, encouraged by the whistle of its owner? And listen there! Wasn't that a child yelping 'Hoop-la'? Has the whole world become a mob of Sunday workers and merry-makers, dancing behind his brother William into a fog of self-gratification?

For Henry, the Sabbath is something far more profound than a test of obedience. Like so many of God's laws, it appears stern and arbitrary when really it's as kind and wise as a mother's nurture. (Not that Henry has very clear memories of maternal love, his own mother having vanished from his childhood like a snowman on a rainy night, but he's read testimonials.) The frantic pace of modern life permits us not a moment's peace; only by obeying the fourth Commandment are we enfolded in the blessed embrace of stillness. And let it not be said that Henry is too much the scholar to appreciate the urge to run with a dog or kick a ball; he is a man who once swam across the Cam fully-clothed in December on a dare, who rowed like a demon, fenced like a fiend, and ran cross-country as though powered by steam. But what did such exertions win him? His name inscribed on silver-plated trophies; the ruin of many shoes; the admiration of cronies he'd rather forget. The firm handshake of Bodley, congratulating him on a fine afternoon's cricket. ('Top-notch sportsman, that Rackham! Frightful bore when he gasses about the ills of the world, but get him off that subject and he's as decent a chap as ever lived!') Henry hopes God will forgive him for playing foolish games while England burned, and for accepting the friendship of blasphemers. Now he reads the Bible, murmuring the words to himself until the combined strength of his voice and the Lord's drowns out the noise of Sabbath-breakers.

During the week, Henry is still a restless man. He chops firewood into smaller pieces than he needs; he walks to Mrs Fox's street in Bayswater in case she should emerge from her house at the precise moment that he strolls past, then carries on to Hyde Park and beyond; it's nothing for him to walk all the way to Kensal Green Cemetery on no particular errand. But on Sunday, he rests, and he reads the Bible, and he wishes all men and women would do the same.

Let us leave Henry to his Book of Nehemiah now, and rejoin William Rackham in his hive of industry. He is wandering around his severely pruned grounds, smoking a pipe – oh no, that's not William, is it? It's another short-haired man of middling stature: Shears, the gardener. Where's William, then? The workmen have departed, and Mrs Rackham has retired upstairs. Where is the man of the house? Gone to town, if you ask Letty.

Sundays in the heart of London can be quite entertaining – more lively, anyway, than in Notting Hill. We find William walking in the Embankment Gardens, watching a variety of impious souls at play. In defiance of the by-laws, there are people boating on the Thames, fishing, playing football, flying pigeons. He's not implicated in their activities, as he merely walks a straight path through them, but they do amuse him in passing. No one could possibly mistake him for one of these poor toilers filling their one free day with strenuous pleasure; he's set apart by his superior attire and his purposeful stride.

What an agreeable circus the world is! he thinks, watching here the antics of the pigeon-fanciers, and there the struggles of weekend swells to launch their giggling lady-loves upon the Thames's dark waters. He has, after so long, rediscovered the simple pleasure of being a spectator rather than (what to call it?) a . . . an introspectator (jolly good, yes, he must use that somewhere).

No more brooding! Instead, look outward! Excellent mottos for any man, especially one whose bank has suddenly changed its tune from reproach to *rapprochement*. The experience of seeing his debts vaporise and his assets multiply, nought by nought and acre by acre, has taken William's mind off himself. Or, more precisely, he no longer seeks himself within himself; instead, he watches William Rackham, head of Rackham Perfumeries, doing this and doing that, causing effects, achieving results.

On another path from William's rides a man on a velocipede, the perspiration on his forehead brilliant in the sunlight, his eyes bulging with concentration on the path before him. His cap is jammed tight onto his head to discourage it blowing off, and under its brim there flaps a clownish fuzz of wind-mussed hair. Poor deluded fellow! He'd be better off getting it cut short, as the head of Rackham Perfumeries has done. Long hair is an affectation from a bygone age: this is the look of tomorrow.

As he walks, William touches his sideboards; they're joining up nicely with his newly-grown moustache and beard which, unlike the hair on his scalp, are not blond, but a rich dark brown. It isn't vanity that makes him look forward to seeing himself in a mirror: it's the lushness of the brown he likes, in a more abstract aesthetic sense; it needn't even be hair, it could be tobacco, tree-bark, a fresh coat of paint.

A football rolls onto the path before him, and without a second thought he shoots it back to the players with a swift kick: shoe-shines, after all, he can now afford by the thousand.

He's pleased, too, that the police have been bribed, with shillings and free beer, to allow a few ale-houses to break the Sabbath, for he finds he's getting thirsty walking. Perhaps he should have got a cab all the way to the bottling factory, rather than taking this detour through the park, but the weather was so superb, it seemed a shame to waste it. Then there's the matter of his digestion: he ate rather too much at lunch, and this constitutional will hasten an evacuation.

If there's one thing he doesn't want this afternoon, it's to be lying in Sugar's arms with a chamber pot full of his own faeces stinking under the bed. (Could he arrange to have a water closet installed in her room? Ah: the future, the future.)

The last half-mile to the bottling factory is a half-mile too far: he commandeers a cab. No sense tiring himself out and, besides, the factory is in unappealing surroundings. On either side of it, grimy rented lock-ups for costermongers' barrows and, all along the street, slimy remains of fruit and vegetables too far gone for scavenging.

However, in amongst the filth nestles this haven, a little castle of ingenious industry disguised in an unassuming outer mantle of blackened red brick. When Rackham the Elder recently took Rackham the Younger on a tour of all three of the Rackham factories, it was this bottling factory that interested William most. Its deceptive exterior, once entered, revealed a magical interior: a miniature Crystal Palace of glass and metal, in constant movement like a carousel. It had a superhuman allure which, to his surprise, was not incompatible with the highest aesthetic principles. Ever since that first visit, William has been wondering what the place looks like when it's empty of workers and its machinery is still.

Standing at last before the massive iron gate of the factory, he feels a thrill as he slides the key in. Another few steps, and he slides a second key into the great double doors.

His factory is as spacious and dark and quiet as a church. Seeing it without his father by his side, and without the distraction of the workers and the steam, he understands for the first time the sheer scale of what he has inherited. He treads reverently across the plaza-sized, sawdust-covered floor, staring up at the great balconies, the sloping chutes and jar-slides, the columnar pipes from furnace to ceiling, the dark grilles and gleaming tables; all the giant sculptures in perfume's honour. What beauty there is in the evenly spaced patterns of rivets, the precise geometry of pylon and crosspiece, the thousands of tiny glass bottles standing at the ready. What a playground this would have been for him when he was a boy! But his father only ever brought Henry here as a child, never William. And what did the infant Henry think of this palace, the crown of the empire laid out for him? William can't recall his brother ever mentioning the visit. No doubt Henry, even then, was aspiring to shrines of a different kind.

'Ach, I had high hopes for that boy.' (Thus William's father confessed when he and William were walking here together.) 'He had brains and brawn in plentiful supply, and I thought he might mature into . . . well, something better than a parson, anyway.'

A distillation of Henry's pious spirit into a more useful essence, eh? William thought of saying, but, knowing his father to be impervious to metaphor, he let it pass. Instead, he plumped for platitudinous diplomacy.

'Never mind, Father. We all mature in different ways. All for the best, eh? Here's to the future!' And he laid a hand on his father's back, a gesture of intimacy so rare and so bold that neither of them quite knew what to do with it. Fortunately the guilt of having allowed his son to suffer a miserable Christmas when he ought by rights to have rescued him was still fresh in the old man's mind, and he patted William's shoulder in return.

Now, alone, William wanders out into the yard behind his factory and surveys the mounds of coal, the massive carts with their reins and bridles lying in tangled heaps. He reaches out a gloved hand and touches, as one might touch a monument in a public park, a stack of crates ready for filling. What a pity it must all lie idle on a Sunday! Oh, not that William doubts that the workers need some rest and religion one day a week, but what a pity all the same. A short story is born in his brain then, called 'The Impious Automata', in which an inventor devises mechanical men to perform factory work on a Sunday. In the end, mechanical parsons roll into the factory and persuade the mechanical workers to observe the Sabbath. Ha!

Suddenly William is startled by a loud clatter behind him. He turns at once, only to find (once he's lowered his eyes to the ground) a small dog emerging from behind an unsoundly-stacked pile of firewood. It looks very like the dog that loiters around the Rackham house, except that it's a bitch.

The animal is nothing to William, but he's concerned it might cause mischief to his property. So he picks up one of the numerous charred pokers littering the grounds, and brandishes it threateningly. The dog flees in a cloud of sawdust and dirt. William's satisfaction at this result turns to chagrin when he realises that his own scrupulous locking of all doors and gates behind him has left the trespassing creature no escape.

Consulting his watch, William decides he's hungry, and makes his way back to the main gate. He half hopes to find the dog waiting there, meekly resigned to expulsion, but it's nowhere to be seen, and with some regret he shuts it inside with a clank of the key.

In her upstairs room at Mrs Castaway's, Sugar is writing her novel. In the room adjacent, Amy Howlett is inserting the handle of a Chinese fan into the anus of a schoolmaster who comes every Sunday for just this purpose. Downstairs, Christopher is playing rummy with Katy Lester, the cards laid out on a soft stack of ironed bed-sheets. Mrs Castaway is dozing, slumped at her desk, the sheen of viscous glue on her scrapbook slowly drying to a matt glaze. The noise from Silver Street is so muted that Sugar can hear the schoolmaster's frenzied babbling. She strains to hear the words, but their sense doesn't survive the passage through the wall.

Sugar leans her chin against the knuckles of the hand that holds the pen. Glistening on the page between her silk-shrouded elbows lies an unfinished sentence. The heroine of her novel has just slashed the throat of a man. The problem is how, precisely, the blood will flow. *Flow* is too gentle a word; *spill* implies carelessness; *spurt* is out of the question because she has used the word already, in another context, a few lines earlier. *Pour out* implies that the man has some control over the matter, which he most emphatically doesn't; *leak* is too feeble for the savagery of the injury she has inflicted upon him. Sugar closes her eyes and watches, in the lurid theatre of her mind, the blood issue from the slit neck. When Mrs Castaway's warning bell sounds, she jerks in surprise.

Hastily, she scrutinises her bedroom. Everything is neat and tidy. All her papers are hidden away, except for this single sheet on her writing-desk.

Spew, she writes, having finally been given, by tardy Providence, the needful word. The nib of the pen has dried out and the scrawl passes from inkless invisibility to clotted stain, but she'll make it more legible later. Into the wardrobe with it just now! Time enough left over for a quick piss, which she can immediately hurl out the window: her Mr Hunt is sensitive to bad smells, she's noticed.

Hours later, *many* hours later, William Rackham wakes from dreamless sleep in a warm and aromatic bed. He's sluggish and content, though rather confused about where he is and what time it might be. There is gas-light overhead, but suffused through gauzy fabric, and through the window he sees only darkness. A rustling of paper alerts him to the fact that he's not alone.

'What the Devil?' he mumbles.

Next to him in the bed, a body. He lifts his head, finds Sugar propped up on the pillows, apparently reading *The London Journal*. She has a camisole on, and there are ink stains on her fingers, but otherwise she is exactly as she was when he last saw her.

'What time is it?'

She leans right out of the bed, exposing the whole of her rump. Her flaky ichthyosis patterns radiate across the flesh of each buttock like scars from a thousand flagellations, but in perfect symmetry, as though inflicted by a deranged aesthete.

Rolling back to him, she hands him his waistcoat, from whose flaccid fob-pocket his watch-chain dangles.

'God almighty,' he says when he consults the time-piece. 'It's ten o'clock. At night!'

She pouts, strokes his cheek with one peeling, inky hand.

'You work too hard,' she croons. 'That's what it is. You don't get enough rest.'

Rackham blinks dazedly and rakes through his hair, startled (before he remembers) how little remains of it.

'I – I must go home,' he says.

Sugar lifts one long naked leg and rests it on the knee of the other, displaying her cunt to him.

'I hope,' she smiles, 'this is your home away from home.'

In the Rackham house, several clocks chime eleven. Everyone is in bed, except here and there a servant, still toiling to clean away the last fragments of dirt, wood-shavings, and other evidence of men's labour. It has been a noisy Sunday, but quiet reigns at last.

Agnes Rackham, sitting up in her bed, in darkness except for a window-square of moonlight draped across her knees like a luminous coverlet, wonders if God is angry. If so, she hopes He's angry with William, not with her. Had she known sooner that it was Sunday, she would have tried harder to do nothing, or as close to nothing as possible.

The salmon she ate for supper lies heavy on her stomach. It was intended for William, really, but he didn't come home for supper so Letty was going to take the shiny little creature back to the kitchen, where Cook would've mashed it all up and made it into something else for breakfast – pasties or suchlike. It seemed a shame to waste the flawless fish body, so Agnes ate it. Smallish salmon though it was, it proved too big for her, yet she couldn't stop. She wanted to see the backbone clean against the plate. Now here she lies, with stomach-ache. Gluttony. On a Sunday.

Where is William? In the early days of their marriage, he hardly went out at all. Then he took to going out and coming back drunk. More recently he's been going out and coming back sober. But where does he go? What is there to *do* out there in the cold, after the shops are shut? The Season hasn't even started yet . . .

There must be complicated engines that keep English civilisation humming, which men must minister to. Nothing happens of itself; even a simple grandfather clock, if left to carry on untended, runs down. Society as a whole would run down, she suspects, if men weren't oiling it constantly, winding it up, tinkering with it.

The doorbell sounds. He's come! Agnes pictures Letty hurrying, lamp-first, down the newly polished stairs and across the new hallway carpets to open the door for her master. It's so quiet she can hear her husband's voice in the hall: not the words, but the tone and the spirit. He sounds cheery and authoritative, as sober as a clergyman. Now he and Letty are on the stairs, and William is saying, 'Back to bed with you, you poor girl!' Plainly, he's not wanting supper; a lucky thing, since his gluttonous wife has eaten the salmon.

Agnes cannot understand the change that has come over him. Only a few months ago, his late arrival home might have meant the sound of stumbling and cursing on the stairs. And what about the rages he used to get into whenever she mentioned money or his father? Gone entirely, as if they were nothing but a bad dream. Rackham the Elder and Rackham the Younger are suddenly thick as thieves, and she, Agnes, is well-off again, and wants for nothing except health.

She hears his footsteps – feels them, almost – passing her door. This is not unusual; they haven't slept together for years. Indeed, the fear that tonight he might break their unspoken agreement and enter her bedroom is, momentarily, as sharp as ever. And yet, she must admit he has been good lately – almost as charming as he ever was. He consults her in all things, hardly ever says anything cruel, and only yesterday he declared that she doesn't have to make her own dresses if the sewing-machine has ceased to amuse her: she can have them made for her, as before.

But it's *good for her* to make them, she knows that. It's discipline for the mind, and keeps her fingers nimble, and is less wearisome than tapestry work. Although, speaking of tapestry work: if there's more money now, could she enlist some help with her embroidered copy of Landseer's *Monarch of the Glen*? It would look frightfully impressive finished, but it's been on her conscience so long now that she can't think of it without being reminded of the worst months of her illness. The greater part of the stag is done, as well as the more interesting features of the landscape; it's only the thought of all that sky and all those mountains that makes her heart sink. Couldn't someone else do it for her? One of those seamstresses who advertise in the ladies' journals (*ELSPETH, finishes woolwork, etc, at moderate prices. Address with editor*) perhaps? Yes, she'll raise the subject with William tomorrow.

Agnes's eyes are sore from lack of sleep. She looks at the pattern of the window on her eiderdown. The shadows of the window-frames, dividing the rectangle of light into four squares, suddenly appear to her like a Christian cross. Is it a sign? Is God cross with her for giving those workmen, those paperers, instructions? She only spoke; she didn't lift a finger herself! And if she'd kept silent, they would've put the dado rail back at quite the wrong height! And anyway, she didn't know it was Sunday, then!

Unnerved, she slips out of bed and draws the curtain, shutting out the cross, plunging the room into profound darkness. She leaps back under the eiderdown, pulls it up to her neck, and tries to pretend she's back in her old house, back in her innocent childhood. In the absence of visible evidence to the contrary, it should be easy to imagine nothing has changed in the years since she slept soundly in the bosom of her family.

But even in total darkness her memory of the old home is spoiled by reality. Try as she might, she cannot transport herself into her childhood as it *ought* to have been; she cannot purge Lord Unwin from her recollections and replace him with her real father. Every time she strives to envision her father's face, the familiar photograph refuses to come to life, and instead her step-father looms before her, sneering in gloomy silence.

Stifling a sob of fear, she seizes hold of a pillow from William's side of the bed and gathers it to her breast. She hugs it tightly, burying her face into its subtly perfumed linen.

All the lights in the house are now extinguished, except for one in William's study. All of the household, except for William, is under the sheets, like dolls in a doll's house. If the Rackham house were such a toy, and you could lift off its roof to peek inside, you would see William in shirt-sleeves at his desk, working on correspondence: nothing to interest you, I promise. In another compartment, at the far end of the landing, you would see a child's body huddled in a cot slightly too small for it: Sophie Rackham, who isn't yet of any consequence. In another compartment still, you would see Agnes swaddled in white bedding, with only her blonde head showing, like a cake-crumb half-submerged in cream. And inside the upended roof held in your hand, the servants would be upside-down in their attic honey-combs, thrown along with their meagre belongings against the rafters.

William burns the midnight candle for a little while longer, before closing his ledger and stretching his short limbs. He is satisfied: another tedious Sunday has been endured with as much recreation and as little religion as possible. He discards his day clothes, puts on his night-shirt, extinguishes the light, and inserts himself between the sheets. Within minutes he is snoring gently.

Agnes, too, has drifted off. One tiny, upturned hand slips off the pillow and glides towards the edge of the bed. Then, one of William's hands, in sleep, begins to move towards the edge of *his* bed, in Agnes's direction. Soon their hands are in perfect alignment, so that, if this really were a doll's house, we could imagine removing not only the roof, but some of the internal walls as well, and sliding the two bedrooms into each other, joining the couple's hands like the clasp of a necklace.

But then William Rackham begins to dream, and flips over onto his other side.

TEN

gnes Rackham's bedroom, whose windows are never opened and whose door is always closed, fills up every night with her breath. One by one, her exhalations trickle off her pillow onto the floor; then, breath by breath, they rise, piling on top of each other like invisible feathers, until they're nestling against the ceiling, growing denser by the hour.

It's morning now, and you can scarcely believe you are in a bedroom: it feels more like the world's smallest factory, which has been working all night for no purpose but to turn oxygen into carbon dioxide. You turn instinctively to the curtains; they're drawn, and as motionless as sculpture. A skewer-thin shaft of sunlight penetrates the dimness, through a slit in the velvet. It falls on Agnes's diary, open at yesterday's page, and illuminates a single line of her handwriting.

Really _must_ *get out more*, she exhorts herself, in tiny indigo letters you must squint to read.

You glance over to the bed, where you expect to see her body still huddled under the eiderdown. She is gone.

Agnes Rackham has a new routine. Every morning, if she can possibly manage it, she takes a walk in the street outside her house, alone. She is going to get well if it kills her.

The Season is drawing nigh, and there's frighteningly little time left to regain certain essential skills — like being able to walk, unsupported, further distances than are found inside her own home. Participating in Society is not a thing one can do naturally; one has to rehearse for it. Half a dozen circuits of a ballroom, if added end to end, could stretch to a mile.

So, Agnes is taking walks. And, surprisingly, Doctor Curlew has judged her decision a good one, as he says she's deficient in corpuscles. Unopposed, then, several mornings a week, she is escorted to the front gate by Clara, whereafter, parasol in hand, she totters out onto the footpath all by herself, listening anxiously for hoof-beats on the deserted cobbled street.

The mongrel dog which has made its camp at the Rackham front gate is there to meet her almost every time, but Agnes doesn't fear him. He's never given her any cause to, never once barked at her. Whenever she shuffles by, braced against the *ferocious* breezes that flap her skirts and pull her parasol askew, the dog reassures her, with lashings of his tail or a benevolent yawn, that he's friendly. He reminds her of an outsized Sunday roast, so roly-poly in his dark brown flesh, and his eyes are more benign than those of anyone she knows. Admittedly, she once almost soiled her boots on his droppings; she was disgusted with him then, but didn't let her disdain show, in case it hurt his feelings – or provoked him to viciousness. Another time, she saw him licking at a part of him that was red as a flayed finger, but she didn't recognise the organ, taking it to be an appendage peculiar to dogs, a sort of fin or spine, which in this dog's case had become painfully inflamed. She swept by him with an awkward smile of pity.

As for creatures of the human variety, Agnes meets very few. Notting Hill, though not nearly as quiet as it used to be, is by the same token not yet part of the metropolis. If one chooses one's streets with care, one can concentrate on putting one foot in front of the other without the additional challenge of meeting other pedestrians. Kensington Park Road is the busiest, for it's along this thoroughfare that the omnibus goes. She avoids it if she can.

Every morning, she walks a little farther. Every day, she gets a little stronger. Five new dresses are finished, with a sixth on the way. The garden looks awfully nice, thanks to Shears. And William is in *such* a good mood all the time, although (she can't help noticing) he does look quite a lot older all of a sudden, what with the beard and the moustache.

They haven't breakfasted together since her last collapse, but they've fallen into the habit of seeing each other at luncheon. It's altogether safer, Agnes feels. And the morning walk gives her a healthy appetite, so she doesn't risk the embarrassment of toying with a half-eaten morsel while William wolfs his portion and asks her if she is all right.

Today, they both eat with equal relish. Cook has outdone herself with an extraordinary galantine made of pork loin layered with ham, cooked tongue, mushrooms and sausage. It's a most elegant looking thing, and so delicious they have to call Letty back to the table twice, to cut more slices.

'I wonder what *this* is,' murmurs William, winkling an object out of the aspic.

'It's a fragment of pistachio kernel, dear,' Agnes informs him, proud to know something he doesn't.

'Fancy that,' he says, startling her by holding the glistening smithereen under his nose and giving it a good sniff. He's sniffing everything lately: new plants in the garden, wallpaper paste, paint, napkins, notepaper, his own fingers, even plain water. 'My nose must become my most sensitive organ, dear,' he'll tell her, before launching into an explanation of the almost imperceptible but (in the perfume business) crucial difference between one flower petal and another. Agnes is pleased he's so determined to master the subtleties of his profession, especially since it has made them suddenly so much more comfortably off, but she hopes he'll not be sniffing everything during the Season, when they're in mixed company.

'Oh, did I tell you?' William tells her. 'I'm going to see The Great Flatelli this evening.'

'Something to do with perfume, dear?'

He smirks. 'You might say that.' Then, digging into his plum suet pudding, he sets her straight. 'No, dear. He's a performer.'

'Anyone I should know about?'

'I very much doubt it. He's on at the Lumley Music Hall.'

'Oh, well then.'

There should be no need to say more, but Agnes is nagged by her awareness of being out of touch. After a minute she adds: 'The Lumley *is* still the Lumley, isn't it?'

'What do you mean, dear?'

'I mean, it hasn't been . . . elevated in any way?'

'Elevated?'

'Brought higher . . . Become more fashionable . . .' The word 'class' eludes her.

'I should think not. I expect I'll be surrounded by men in cloth caps and women with teeth missing.'

'Well, if that appeals to you . . .' she says, making a face. The suet pudding is too rich for her, and she's starting to feel bilious after all the galantine, but a small slice of the luncheon cake is irresistible.

'Man cannot live on high culture alone,' quips William.

Agnes chews her cake. It, too, is richer than she expected, and she's nagged by the suspicion that there's something she should know.

'If you . . .' she hesitates. 'If you *see* anyone there . . . at the Lumley . . . I mean anyone important, that I'm likely to meet in the Season . . . Do tell me, won't you?'

'Of course, dear.' He lifts a slice of the luncheon cake to his nose and sniffs. 'Currants, raisins, orange peel, steeped in sherry. Almonds. Nutmeg. Caraway . . . Vanilla.' He grins, as if expecting applause.

Agnes smiles wanly.

Less than half a mile to the west of the Rackham house, Mrs Emmeline Fox, dressed for going out but still in her kitchen, is coughing into a handkerchief. The weather doesn't agree with her today; there's something oppressive in the atmosphere that's giving her a headache and a tight chest. She'll have to make sure she's rallied by tomorrow, though, or she'll miss the rounds with the Rescue Society.

She considers nipping over to her father's house and asking him for a draught of medicine, but decides this would only worry him. Besides, who knows what emergencies he might need to attend to with his satchel of drugs and implements? For Emmeline's father is Doctor James Curlew, and he's a busy man.

Instead, she swallows a spoonful of liver salts followed by a sip of hot cocoa to take the taste away. The cocoa has the additional effect of warming her up, not just her cold hands as they cradle the cup, nor even her sensitive stomach hidden away in her belly, but the whole of her body. In fact, all of a sudden, she's *too* warm: her forehead prickles with sweat and her arms feel stifled inside her tight sleeves. Hastily, she passes through the kitchen door and into the garden.

Her house is bigger than Henry's, and her garden more substantial, though rather overgrown since its heyday when her husband pottered about in it. He had a taste for the bizarre, did Bertram, always trying to grow exotic vegetables for the table, which he'd give to the cook they had in those days. There are scorzonera growing here yet, half-hidden by weeds, and some strangled roots of salsify. Father sends his gardener round from time to time, to slash the worst of it away and expose the paving for Emmeline to walk on, but the weeds are busy all summer and merely lie waiting in winter. They're coming to life again now, lush green, while the great coffin-shaped enclosure in which Bertie grew those monstrous man-sized celeries (what were they called – cardoons?) is dense with dull exhausted earth.

Always indifferent, was Bertie, to anything that endures, fascinated instead by the ephemeral and the spectacular. A good man, though. The house they shared is too big for her alone, but she stays on for his sake – for the sake of his memory. He did so little that was memorable, and never spoke his profounder thoughts (if indeed he had any); the best way of recalling the marriage is to remain in his house.

Now she stands in the garden, her hands still cradling her cup of cocoa, her feverish brow cooled by the breeze. She'll be better very shortly. She is not ill. She ought to have opened the windows last night, to air the house after the unseasonal warmth of the day before. This headache is her own fault.

She drinks the rest of the cocoa. Already, it's perking her up, giving her a feeling of heightened alertness. What makes it do that? It must have a secret ingredient, she reckons, that adds to her sluggish blood a squirt of analeptic or even a stimulant. In her own small way, she's scarcely better than the dope fiends she sees in the course of her work with the Rescue Society – the addled morphine slaves, who can keep their attention on the words of Christ for no longer than two minutes before their pink eyes start rolling sideways. She smiles, tilting her head back in the breeze, pressing the rim of the cup against her chin. Emmeline Fox: cocoa fiend. She can imagine herself on the cover of a tuppenny dreadful, a masked villain dressed in men's trousers and a cape, evading police by leaping from rooftop to rooftop, her superhuman strength deriving entirely from the evil cacao seed. The earthbound constables stretch their stubby arms impotently towards her, open-mouthed in their rage and frustration. Only God can bring her down.

She opens her eyes, shivers. The sweat in her armpits has turned cold; there's a damp chill on her spine. Her windpipe itches, tempting her to cough, cough, cough. She refuses; she knows where that leads.

Back inside the house, she rinses out the milk-pan, wipes the stove-top, puts away the cocoa things. Few women of her acquaintance would have the faintest idea how to perform such tasks, even assuming they were forced at knife-point to attempt them; Mrs Fox performs them without thinking. Her maid-of-all-work, Sarah, doesn't live with her and won't be back till tomorrow, but Mrs Fox has a policy of helping the girl as much as she can. She and Sarah are, she feels, more like aunt and niece than mistress and servant.

Oh, Mrs Fox knows there is gossip about her, generated by ladies who judge her to be a disgrace to polite society, a *sansculotte* in disguise, a Jacobin with an ugly face. They would sweep her – or, preferably, have her swept – out of their sight if they could.

Such ill will from her sisters saddens Mrs Fox, but she makes no special effort to placate it nor to challenge it, for it is not in the households of fashionable ladies that she longs to be welcomed, but rather in the wretched homes of the poor.

In any case, all this *fuss* about a little work! In the future, she believes, all women will have some useful employment. The present system cannot endure; it goes against God and good sense. One cannot educate the lower classes, nourish them with better food and unpolluted water, improve their housing and their morals, and all the while expect them to continue aspiring to nothing but servitude. Nor can one fill newspapers with outrageous disclosures of human misery and expect no one to be outraged into action. If the same streets and rookeries are named daily, and if every detail of our brothers' and sisters' suffering is published, is it not inevitable that a growing army of Christians will roll their sleeves up and demand to render assistance? Even those ladies and gentlemen untroubled by conscience will, Mrs Fox is convinced, find their supply of servants drying up soon enough, and all but the wealthiest of them will then have to acquaint themselves with such exotic objects as mops and dishcloths.

By next century, predicts Mrs Fox, buttering a slice of bread, women like me will no longer be regarded as freaks. England will be *full* of ladies who labour for a fairer society, and who keep no servants under their roof at all. (Her own maid, Sarah, lives with an ailing grandfather, and comes in every other day to do the heavy work, for a fair wage which saves her from slipping back into prostitution. She's worth her weight in gold, is Sarah, but even such as she will disappear in time, as prostitution is eradicated.)

Emmeline wonders if a short walk would be good for her chest. She has a bag full of woollen gloves and another full of socks to deliver to Mrs

Lavers, who's organising something next month for the destitute of Ireland. (*Fenian*! the gossips would no doubt say, or *Papist*!) The Lavers' house is only a few minutes away, and she could carry a bag on each arm, providing they were of roughly equal weight.

All the rooms in Mrs Fox's home except her own small bed-chamber are cluttered with boxes, bags, books and parcels. Indeed her house is the unofficial warehouse of the Rescue Society, and of several other charities besides. Emmeline ascends the stairs, pokes her nose into what used to be the master bedroom, and confirms that what she's looking for isn't in there. On the landing, rather precariously balanced, is a stack of New Testaments translated into . . . into . . . She cannot recall the language just at the moment; a man from the Bible Dissemination Society is coming back for them shortly.

The socks and gloves are nowhere to be found, and she returns downstairs to butter another slice of bread – all she has in the house that's ready to eat. Usually on a Monday, there's a quantity of left-over Sunday roast, but yesterday Mrs Fox let Sarah eat as much as she liked, not expecting the girl to have the appetite of a labrador.

To those above me, she thinks, as she chews her bread, *I am a pitiable widow, paddling in the shallows of penury; to those below, I am a pampered creature in paradise. All of us are at once objects of repugnance and of envy. All of us except the very poorest, those who have nothing below them but the sewage pit of Hell.*

Freshly determined to find the socks and gloves, Emmeline searches in earnest. She even puts on her bonnet, to solemnise her intentions in case she's tempted to give up. To her delight, however, she finds the bags almost immediately, stacked on top of one another in a wardrobe. But pulling them out disturbs dust, and before she can steel herself against it, she's coughing, coughing, coughing. She coughs until she's on her knees, tears running down her cheeks, her trembling hands pressing her handkerchief hard against her mouth. Then, when it's over, she rests on the foot of the stairs, rocking herself for comfort, staring at the square of light beaming through the frosted glass in her front door.

Mrs Fox does not consider herself ill. In her estimation she is as healthy as any woman with a naturally weak chest can expect to be. Nor, while we're on the subject of her disadvantages, does she consider herself ugly. God gave her a long face, but it's a face she's satisfied with. It reminds her of Disraeli, but softer. It didn't stop her getting a husband, did it? And if she never has another, well, one husband is enough. And, returning to the subject of health, despite Bertie's ruddy cheeks and ready grin, in the end it wasn't *her* health that failed but *his*. Which just goes to prove that it's not gossips who decide the span of human life, but God.

Breathing carefully, she rises to her feet and walks over to the bags. She grasps one in each hand and tests their weight. Equal. She carries them to the door, pausing only a moment to check her hair in the glass before leaving.

A world away to the east, Henry Rackham walks the streets too. (What a day this is for walking! You couldn't have predicted how healthy you'd become, could you, following these people around?)

Henry is walking along a street where he has never walked before, a winding, shadowy street where he must watch his step lest his shoes slip in shit, where he must keep an eye on every alley and subterranean stairwell lest he be accosted. He walks stiffly, his determination only slightly stronger than his fear; he can only hope (for he has, in the circumstances, no right to *pray*) that no one of his acquaintance sees him entering this evil-smelling maze.

Henry knows which days Mrs Fox works for the Rescue Society and which days she's at home; her schedule is engraved on his memory, and on Mondays she rests. That is why he has chosen today to be walking in St Giles, just the sort of place where she might minister. He suppresses a cough against the stench, and wades deeper.

Within minutes, all pretence of decency is gone; the solidity and straight lines of Oxford Street are invisible and already half-forgotten, erased from the mind by a nightmare vision of subsidence – subsidence of the roadway itself, of the ramshackle houses shored on either side, of the flesh and moral character of the squalid inhabitants.

Truly, thinks Henry, this quarter of the city is an outer rim of Hell, a virtual holding area for the charnel-house. The newspapers say it is much improved since the Fifties, but how can that be? Already he has seen a severed dog's head rotting in the gutter, its protruding tongue swollen with lice; he has seen half-naked infants throwing cobble-stones at each other, their haggard faces distorted by rage and glee; he has seen a host of spectres staring out of broken windows, their eyes hollow, their sex indeterminate, their flesh scarcely less grey than the rags that clothe them.

A disturbing number of them seem to be housed underground, in basements accessible only by obscure stairwells or, in some cases, rickety ladders. Wet washing hangs from window to window, speckled with soot; here and there a tattered bed-sheet flaps in the breeze, like a flag whose distinguishing marks are posies of faded bloodstain brown.

Henry Rackham has come here with one purpose in mind: to make a difference. Not the kind of difference Mrs Fox makes, but a difference nonetheless.

Mere minutes after his arrival, he is approached by an ugly woman of middle age, or perhaps younger, wearing a voluminous dress in the Regency style, but much darned and patched. She is bare-headed and bare-necked, and her smile as she greets him displays all her remaining teeth: is she therefore a prostitute?

'Spare a few pennies, sir, for a poor nunfortunate.'

A beggar, then.

'Is it food you need?' says Henry, wary of being taken for a dupe. He aches to be generous, but fancies he detects a whiff of alcohol on her breath.

'You said it, sir. Food is the fing I want. 'Ungry, I am. I've 'ad nuffink since yesty.' Her eyes shine greedily; she wrings her swollen hands.

'Shall I . . .' He hesitates, resisting her predatory gaze, which tugs at his soul as if it were a juicy worm. 'Shall I accompany you to a place where food is sold? I'll buy you whatever you wish.'

'Oh *no*, sir,' she replies, apparently scandalised. 'My reputation, sir, is precious to me. I've got children to fink of.'

'Children?' He hadn't imagined she would have children; she looks too unlike the plump unwrinkled mothers he sees in church.

'I've five children, sir,' she assures him, her hands hovering in the air as if she might seize hold of his arm at any moment. 'Five; and two of 'em's babes, and they's awful squally, and me 'usband can't torrelate it, sir, on account of his sleep. So 'e whacks 'em, sir, whacks 'em in their cots, till they's quiet. And I was finkin', sir, if I could 'ave a few pennies from your kind self, sir, I could dose me babies wiv some Muvver's Blessing from the pharmasiss, sir, and they'd sleep like angels.'

Henry's hand is already in his pocket when the horror of it strikes him.

'But . . . but you must dissuade your husband from striking your children!' he declares. 'He could do them terrible harm . . .'

'Ah, yes, sir, but 'e's sich a tired soul, what wiv workin' all day, 'e needs 'is sleep at night, and the babes is awful squally, as I said; when one falls quiet the others set to screamin', an' it's impostible, sir, wiv six of 'em.'

'Six? You said you had five just now.'

'Six, sir. But one's so quiet, you 'ardly know she's there.'

A strange impasse settles between them, there in the sordid public street. He has a coin enclosed in his palm, hesitating. She licks her lips, afraid to say more, in case she prejudices his generosity.

'Children don't weep for mischief's sake,' says Henry, still wrestling with the vision of innocent babies battered in their cots. 'Your husband must understand that. Children weep because they're hungry, or sad.'

'You said it, sir,' she eagerly agrees, nodding her head, staring deep into his eyes. 'You understand. 'Ungry, they are. And awful, awful sa-ad.'

Henry sighs, letting go of his suspicions. There can be no charity without trust, or at least the willingness to take a risk. All right, so this woman has recently touched strong drink and is, in her manner, crudely ingratiating: what of it? Kindness will not spoil her further; nor is her family, whatever their true number may be, to blame for her sins.

'Here,' he says, transferring the money into her trembling grasp. 'Mind you use it for food.'

'Fank you, *fank* you, sir,' she crows. 'Wiv dis small coin, as is nuffink to you, sir, you've jest put a fine meal on the table for a poor widder and her family – jest fink on that, sir!'

Henry thinks on it, frowning, as she scurries into a dark cleft between two buildings.

'Widow?' he mutters, but she is gone.

In a more ideal world, Henry should have had a few minutes' grace in which to reflect upon this encounter and consider what to do next, for he is troubled by a jostle of conflicting emotions. However, the glint of his money has been observed by other citizens of the street, no less clearly than if it were a firework exploding in the sky above. From every nook and corner, ragged humans begin to converge upon him, their verminous eyes aglow with cunning. Henry strides forward, unnerved and yet at the same time queerly reckless. There's a substance coursing through his bloodstream, transforming his fear into something else altogether: a feeling of exaggerated readiness, of unaccustomed one-ness with his body.

First to reach him is a weasel-like fellow with a grotesque limp. In one bony hand he clutches a tanning-knife, held aloft so that Henry can see it

– but almost as if it's an innocuous article the newcomer has carelessly forgotten, and he is merely returning it. The air, for Henry, is charged not with danger but with a hallucinatory whiff of farce.

'Gi-hive me yer mu-huny,' the little man wheezes, grimacing like a chimpanzee, brandishing the grimy blade an arm's length from Henry's chest.

Henry stares into his assailant's eyes. The fellow is a head shorter then he, and half his weight.

'God forgive you,' growls Rackham, raising his fists, which compare favourably, in size, with the thief's stunted skull. 'And God forgive me too, for if you step any closer I swear I'll knock you down.'

Gurning fearsomely, the fellow backs off, almost stumbles on a loose cobble, turns and limps away. Several other denizens of St Giles halt their advance on Rackham and retreat likewise, deciding that he is not, in one way or another, the soft touch he appeared to be.

Only one person is not dissuaded; only one person continues to approach. It's a scrawny young woman, dressed in what to Henry looks like a white night-dress, a man's black overcoat, and a lace curtain for a shawl. Like the beggar-woman, she's bare-headed, but her elfin face is fresher, and her hair is red. She steps boldly into Henry's path, and unknots her shawl with a casual motion, revealing a freckled sternum.

'My hand is yours for a shillin', sir,' she declares, 'and any other part of me for two shillin's.'

There, it's said. She stands in his shadow and waits.

A feeling of wholly unexpected calm descends upon Henry Rackham, a disembodied serenity such as he's never experienced before, even at the threshold of dreamless sleep. This is the moment he has long dreaded and desired, his own initiation into the sensual underworld that Mrs Fox negotiates with such dignity and aplomb. So often in his imaginings he has seen this girl (or a girl vaguely like her); now here she stands before him, in the flesh. And, to his relief, he finds her to be not a siren at all, but a mere child – a child with crusts on her eyelids and a graze on her chin.

How he feared, before summoning the courage to come here today, that his good intentions were nothing but a sham, a fragile delusion preserved only by an accident of geography. How haunted he was by the anxiety that, if God should ever bless him with a parish of his own, his first act in exploring its poorer streets would be to fall upon just such a defenceless

wretch as stands before him now, and violate her. But here she is: a prostitute, a harlot, an abandoned creature who has just given him explicit
permission to do with her exactly as he wishes. And what does he wish?
She breathes shallowly, lips parted, looking up at him in his shadow, awaiting his approval, unaware that she has already passed on to him a gift of
incalculable value – a reflection of his own nature. He knows now: Whatever
he desires, whatever his sinful heart lusts after, it is not this small carcass
of scuffed flesh and bone.

'Your body parts aren't yours to sell, miss,' he says, gently. 'They belong
together, and the whole belongs to God.'

'*My* 'ole belongs to anyone that's got two shillin's, sir,' she insists.

He winces and digs his hand into his pocket.

'Here,' he says, handing her two shillings. 'And I'll tell you what I want
for it.'

She cocks her head, a flicker of apprehension disturbing the dead calm
of her eyes.

'I want you . . .' He hesitates, knowing this world is too intractably
wicked, and he too lacking in moral authority, for him to command her to
'Go and sin no more'. Instead, he does his best to smile and appear less
stern. 'I want you to regard these two shillings as an act that's no longer
necessary . . .' (Even as the words leave his mouth, her puzzled expression
lets him know he is losing her.) 'Ah . . . I mean, *in lieu* of whatever you
might otherwise have done to earn it . . .' (Still she frowns, uncomprehending, her bottom lip disappearing under her top teeth.) 'What I mean
is . . . For goodness' sake, miss, whatever you were going to do, don't do
it!'

Instantly she grins from ear to ear.

'Understood, sir!' And she saunters away – with rather more of a swing
to her undercarriage than he's ever observed on a decent woman.

By now, Henry has had enough. He is tired, and longs for the safety
and decorum of his own study in Gorham Place. The burst of adrenalin
which enabled him to defend himself against the weasel man has ebbed
now, and the foreign admixtures of emotion left in its wake are no longer
exhilarating but merely befuddling.

With a heavy tread, he walks back towards the better part of town,
where he'll be able to hail an omnibus and begin the daunting task of
disentangling what he has learned today. However, as he hurries through

.the labyrinthine streets, peering briefly into every alley and cul-de-sac in case it offers an early escape from St Giles, he happens to catch sight of ... is it not? Yes, it's the beggar-woman he gave money for food – the widow with the violent husband and five, or six, children.

She's sitting in the open doorway of a slum, side-on to public view, her skirts puddling over the filthy summit of a half-dozen stone steps. Behind her, just inside the house, slouches a man with hair as black and coarse as the bristles on a chimney-brush. He wears a knitted waistcoat, a blue scarf and a military jacket, and loose trousers against which the woman casually leans her head. The two of them are sharing a brand-new bottle of spirits, handing it back and forth between them, guzzling with great satisfaction.

Henry stops in his tracks and gapes at the scene, played out not twenty feet from his nose. Too dismayed to approach the couple, too outraged to flee, he stands his ground, fists clenched. The woman, in between gulps, notices his arrival and, recognising him at once, exclaims, 'Look, Dug! It's our saviour!' The pair of them convulse with laughter, wheezing and spluttering, their lips agleam with alcohol.

Speechless, Henry stands, cheeks burning, the nails of his fingers piercing the flesh of his palms, so hard does he clench his fists.

'Make 'im go away, Dug,' says the woman, evidently finding her enjoyment of the spirits hampered by this scowling booby. 'Make 'im go away.'

Clumsily, the bristly man climbs over her skirts, almost pitching forward onto the steps, and positions himself in front of his companion. 'Yaarr!!' he shouts. When this has no immediate effect on the intruder, he turns and yanks his trousers down, baring his bony pale buttocks to Henry's astounded gaze. He turns again, trousers slumped around his ankles, and assesses the effect upon the interloper. What next? Not suspecting that Henry is transfixed less by fear than by the sight of a stranger's penis, he snatches this flaccid organ from its thatch of black hair and begins to spray urine into the air.

Henry Rackham, several yards out of reach, leaps backwards nevertheless, with a cry of disgust. The woman cries out too, her hilarity souring abruptly into fury as the steaming liquid spatters back onto her skirts.

'Yer splashin' me, yer bloody fool!'

In moments the pair of them are fighting, he slapping her fiercely around the ears, she jabbing and kicking his legs. He attempts to control her struggles by stamping one boot down on her skirts while he hauls up his trousers; without hesitation, she clubs him with the gin bottle, a vigorous overarm blow against his bony forehead that sends him sprawling down the steps.

'Christ!' she cries, as a long silvery arc of spilled alcohol hits the ground. The (miraculously unbroken) flask is hastily turned upright, and, while the man writhes at her feet clutching his bloody forehead, she shoves the bottle's glistening neck deep into her mouth and sucks hard on what's left.

For Henry, the ghastly spell is broken, and he is finally able to turn his back on these, the first poor people he has ever been intimate with, and lurch towards home.

Sitting in the Lumley Music Hall that evening, surrounded by men in cloth caps and women with teeth missing, William Rackham savours the fact that he can once more show himself in a place like this without fearing to be mistaken for a lesser being than he is. Now that the foundations of his wealth have solidified, and his ascension to directorship has become common knowledge (at least among those who make it their business to know 'who's who'), he can scarcely go anywhere without *someone* whispering, 'That's William Rackham.' And, now that every stitch of his clothing is of the finest quality and the latest style, he can rest assured that even those humble souls who are ignorant of his identity must recognise him as a well-to-do gentleman – a gentleman who is sampling, for diversion's sake, the entertainments of the not-so-well-to-do.

Of course, he's not the only one here tonight who's slumming. The Lumley's audience is a curate's omelette of mostly plain folk seasoned with a speckling of well-to-do gentlemen. But William likes to think he stands out by virtue of his beaver-skin frock-coat, his doe-skin trousers and especially his new top hat, the shortest one in the place. (No, no, not his *old* new hat, his *new* new hat – can't you see it's shorter? And it's not a Billington & Joy job, either: Staniforth's, 'Hatters of Distinction since 1732', if you please.)

The Lumley isn't the kind of place where hats and cloaks are taken at the door, which makes it a sticky proposition for the overdressed, but at least it allows comparison of finery. Even so, it's difficult to estimate how many persons of William's own class are here tonight, as the hall is full, and any overview of the crowd is obscured by a froth of dowdy bonnets. The evening's proceedings are by now well advanced and, in the warmth generated by the audience and hundreds of gas-lights, common men are removing jackets to reveal bare shirts, while the females fan themselves with cheap paper and plywood.

The row immediately in front of William holds no such females – regrettably enough, for Rackham wouldn't mind catching a surplus breeze from a fluttering fan. He is, after all, not immune to what the ruder folk are feeling; his forehead is subject to the same sweat, and inside his layers of clothing he's beginning to simmer. Perspiration prickles in his new beard, giving rise to itches he must resist the urge to scratch. Too many bodies crammed into one establishment! Couldn't some have been turned away?

His new ulster hangs from the back of his seat, and his new cane lies across his knees, for he can imagine how desirable its silver knob might be to a thief. He also prefers to hold on to his triple-striped dog-skin gloves, even while applauding, unaware that this makes him look as if he's beating a helpless rodent to death.

To the left of him sit Bodley and Ashwell. They, too, are overdressed, though less so than Rackham, for they know the Lumley better. They, too, are secure in their distinction from the common herd; slightly bored, they were, on Mount Parnassus, and so they thought, well, why not saunter down and see what's on at the Lumley? And, having studied the bill, they really are looking forward to the Great Flatelli – 'The Sensation of Sensations: The Magician of Emissions: Hear Him and Swoon!! All Italy Scandalised! France at his Feet! A One-Man Wind Ensemble!!!'

Already they've sat through a pretty but unfashionably plump girl singing humorous ballads, followed by the 'London debut' of Mr Epiderm, an old man with the curious ability to pull his skin out from his naked torso in elastic handfuls, and suspend heavy objects from it by means of metal pegs. It's now a quarter past eight and the Great Flatelli has still not appeared. William and his two friends add their voices to the mutterings that accompany the efforts of a dapper little man on the faraway stage to reproduce the sounds of a bird being stalked, pursued and devoured by a variety of animals.

'Bring on Flatelli!' a brutish voice shouts, prompting William to reflect on how handy common people can be, when one wants something impolite said. Other hecklers join the cause, and the animal impressionist flails on under a thick cloud of ill-will.

Finally, at twenty-five to nine, the trumpeted Italian is brought on, to unanimous approval.

'*Buona sera*, London!' he bellows, scooping applause out of the air with his open hands and pressing it to his chest like invisible bouquets. Despite his oiled black moustache and black frock-coat, he's suspiciously tall for an Italian, and his continental accent, when the clapping has faded and he begins his preamble, rings false in the ears of such sophisticates as Ashwell. ('Jew. Wager anything you like: Jew,' he mutters to William.)

'My hunusual eenstrument,' the great Flatelli is explaining, 'ees 'ere be'ind me. I tike eet wiz me airvrywhere I go.' (Titters from the audience as he casts a pantomime glance over his shoulder.) 'Eet rhequires no blow-ing, touching, squeezing . . .' (Alto guffaws from a coterie of homosexuals at the back of the hall.) 'But eet is a vairy *dell*icayte sound. I ask-a you to leesten vairy vairy carefooly. My first-a piece is a be-*oo*tifool old-a Eenglish . . . *air*. Eetsacalled "Greensleeves".'

Index finger pressed to his lips to enforce absolute hush, Flatelli bends at the waist. A solemn-faced associate wheels a large brass amplification funnel, mounted on a trolley, across the stage until its burnished mouth is almost touching the great man's backside. One final flourish (a ceremo-nial flipping up of the frock-coat's tails) and the farting begins.

For several seconds, the unmistakable tune of 'Greensleeves' vibrates in the air, as accurate, in its reedy way, as anything played on comb-and-paper or even (stretching it a bit) bassoon. Then the laughter starts, swelling from a suppressed murmur to a raucous rumble, and William and his companions, seated far from the front, must lean forward, concentrat-ing intently.

At the chime of ten, in a house otherwise deathly quiet, Agnes Rackham is lying in bed. She knows, even without consulting the servants, that her husband has not yet returned from the city; she's abnormally sensitive to the shutting of any door in the house, feeling the vibration, she fancies, through the floor or the legs of her bed. She lies in darkness and silence, thinking, merely thinking.

In Agnes's head, inside her skull, an inch or two behind her left eye, nestles a tumour the size of a quail's egg. She has no inkling it's there. It nestles innocently; her hospitable head makes room for it without demur, as if such a diminutive guest could not possibly cause any trouble. It sleeps, soft and perfectly oval. No one will ever find it. Roentgen photography is twenty years in the future, and Doctor Curlew, whatever parts of Agnes Rackham he may examine, is not about to go digging in her eye-socket with a scalpel. Only you and I know of this tumour's existence. It is our little secret.

Agnes Rackham has a little secret of her own. She is lonely. In the closed-curtained, airless chamber of her room, in the thick invisible fog of perfume and her own exhaled breath, she is suffocating with loneliness. Looking back over her day, she can recall nothing that nourished her forlorn heart, only her greedy stomach which gets quite enough as it is – more than is good for it. At supper she ate (*over*-ate) alone, at dinner she ate (*much* too much) alone, tea and breakfast she couldn't face for biliousness, luncheon she shared with William, but felt even lonelier than when he wasn't there – *and* she ate too much, *again*.

Nor has this been a lonelier day than most: every day of her life is much the same. All through the long hours of sewing and staring out the window at what the gardener is up to, of making up her mind whether she'll comb her own hair or have Clara comb it for her, she is longing for true companionship and suffering the lack of it. Doctor Curlew has never diagnosed this secret disease of hers, though she's sure it makes her a great deal sicker than anything he claims to have found. What would he do, if he knew? What could he prescribe for her, to ease the pain of lying awake at night in an unkind world with not a soul to love her?

Oh, granted: her dreams, when they finally take her in, welcome her with open arms, but in the insomniac hours before sleep she lies marooned in her queen-sized bed, like the Lady of Shalott launched upon a dark lake in a vessel twice the size it need be.

What Agnes craves is not a man, nor even a female lover. She knows nothing of her body's interior, nothing; and there is nothing she wants to know. Her loneliness, though it aches, is not particularly physical; it hangs in the air, weighs on the furniture, permeates the bed-linen. If only there could be someone next to her in this great raft of a bed, someone who liked and trusted her, and whom she liked and trusted in turn! There is no such person in the world. Dear Clara is paid to be agreeable; when her day's work is done, she hurries upstairs for a well-earned rest from Mrs

Rackham. The other servants have little to do with her; they fear her and, unbeknownst to them, she is a little afraid of them, too. A dog is out of the question; maybe she'll get a kitten, if there's a variety without claws? William's brother Henry is terribly nice (she's thinking of possible friends now, not of someone to share her bed) but altogether too serious; Agnes likes to keep her mind on pleasant things, not on all the problems of the world. As for William, he's lost her trust forever. Whatever he does now, however wealthy he makes her, however courteously he addresses her over luncheon, however much freedom he offers her to accumulate more dresses, bonnets and shoes, however hard he tries to win her forgiveness, she can never forgive. One who sups with the Devil must use a long spoon; Agnes Rackham's spoon, in supping with her husband, is the length of an oar.

With so little hope of friendship in her waking life, is it any wonder that Agnes prefers the company of the nuns at the Convent of Health? They welcome her and care for her, without any reward but to see her smile. One nun in particular has such a sweet, kind face . . . Yet Agnes's visits to the Convent of Health are always over so soon: restricted, by an ungenerous God, to her short hours of sleep. The journey to the Convent, by train through an eternity of countryside, sometimes takes most of the night, so that the time left for the nuns to nurse her is pitifully brief — a few minutes only, before waking. On other nights, the journey there seems to take hardly any time at all — an express locomotive pulls her through a green blur — and she's enveloped in the Holy Sisters' care before her tears have even sunk into the pillow. But on those nights, the return journey must be long indeed, for by the time she reaches morning, she has forgotten everything.

Agnes doesn't believe there is any such thing as a dream. In her philosophy, there are events that happen when one is awake, and others that happen when one is sleeping. She is aware that some people — men, in particular — take a dim view of what happens when the eyes are closed and the sheets are still, but she has no such doubts. To dismiss the night's events as unreal would be to credit herself with the power of invention, and she knows instinctively that she is powerless to create. Creation out of nothing: only God can do that. How like men, in their monstrous conceit and their shameless blasphemy, to disagree! How like them to disown half their lives, saying none of it exists, it's all phantasmagoria!

The difference between men and women is nowhere plainer, thinks

Agnes, than in the novels they write. The men always pretend they are making everything up, that all the persons in the story are mere puppets of their imagination, when Agnes knows that the novelist has invented nothing. He has merely patchworked many truths together, collecting accounts from newspapers, consulting real soldiers or fruit-sellers or convicts or dying little girls – whatever his story may require. The lady novelists are far more honest: Dear Reader, they say, This is what happened to *me*.

For this reason, Agnes much prefers novels written by ladies. She gets *The London Journal* and *The Leisure Hour* every week, bringing her all the latest instalments from the pens of Clementine Montagu, Mrs Oliphant, Pierce Egan (not a man, surely?), Mrs Harriet Lewis, and all the rest. As a special treat, Mudie's Circulating Library brings her bound volumes of Mrs Riddell and Eliza Lynn Linton, so she can read a whole story without delay.

Even when Agnes is not bedridden, novels are *such* a boon, for they bring a steady supply of noble and attractive human beings into her life which, it must be said, the world at large is not generous with. A sympathetic heroine, she finds, is almost as good as a friend of flesh and blood. (What a repulsive expression 'flesh and blood' is, though, when one thinks about it!)

Lately, Agnes Rackham hasn't much time for reading. All her waking hours are spent preparing for the Season. Chiefly she's in thrall to her sewing-machine, constructing dress after dress, or else leafing through magazines in search of patterns. Acres of material have passed under the needle already; acres more are still to be done. Nine complete dresses hang on frames in her dressing-room; a tenth stands in the darkness of her bedroom, still half-finished on the dummy.

Ten won't be nearly enough, of course. How sincere is William *really* when he says she has his blessing to have 'any number of dresses' made for her by a dressmaker? What number does he have in mind? Is he aware how much she would cost him if she took him at his word? She dreads a return to the kind of intercourse they were having not so long ago, with him irritable and intolerant of the needs of her sex, barely able to control his exasperation and his disapproval, while she is perpetually close to tears.

It's a pity she can't do what many other ladies with sewing-machines are doing just now – altering beyond recognition gowns they wore in previous Seasons. In an afternoon of madness on New Year's Day, inspired by a novelty sewing pattern she chanced to find in a magazine, she ruined all her best dresses. She remembers clearly (how odd the things one remembers, and the things one forgets!) the fatal text: '*Fabric remnants and outmoded curtains need not lie idle. Turn them into an Effortless Amusement for you and a Delight for your Children.*' Neat diagrams and simple instructions imparted the knack of fashioning, '*with only a quarter-hour's stitching apiece*', life-like, three-dimensional humming-birds.

An irresistible mania, whose intensity she's even now chilled to recall, gripped her then. She had no remnants in the house, yet the desire to turn remnants into humming-birds raged in her like a fever. Despite Clara's pleas that if Madam could only wait until morning, she could have a pile of remnants from Whiteley's in Bayswater, the torture of waiting even a single minute was unbearable. So, she fell upon her 'old' dresses – 'I shan't be wearing these again,' she insisted – and sliced into them with her dress-making shears. By nightfall, the floor was a chaos of cannibalised ball-gowns and bodices, and dozens of humming-birds had been made: soft satin birds, drooping like sick things; hard spry birds made of stiff petticoat; white silken birds trembling in the breeze from Agnes's furious pedalling of the sewing-machine; dark velvet birds sitting quite still. Odd, how some of her dresses were ruined instantly, as if the scissors had punctured them like a bladder, while others more or less kept their shape and were merely . . . disfigured. To these she returned again and again with her scissors, to make more birds.

'I must,' sighs Agnes into her pillow now, 'have been mad.'

Her eyelids flutter shut in the darkness. Somewhere nearby, a train whistle blows. The sun rises – not slowly, according to its usual custom, but in a few seconds, as if fuelled by gas. The big wide world glows green and blue, the colours of travel, and everything disagreeable disappears.

Outside Agnes's bedroom, in what men and historians like to call 'the real world', the night is not yet over. In the poorer streets, the grocer, the cheese-monger and the chop-house man haven't shut up shop; their customers are match-sellers and cress-sellers and street-walkers, come to claim their reward for long hours of standing in the cold. Beggar children come too, pestering the merchants for unsaleable fragments of ham or

Dutch cheese to take back home for Father's supper. And for Father, there are countless drinking-houses open all night.

It is through the streets of this 'real' world – not far from the Lumley Music Hall – that three well-to-do, slightly drunk gentlemen, Messrs Bodley, Ashwell and Rackham, stroll, march and stagger. They scarcely notice the dark, the cold and the drizzle, except to note that their half-shouted altercation doesn't echo as it should.

'*Caput mortuum!*' cries Bodley, resorting to the old school insults.

'*Bathybius!*' retorts Ashwell.

'Stone-deaf cretin!' bawls Bodley.

'Unswabbed haven of earwax!' hisses Ashwell. 'It was "The Collier's Daughter", and *nothing* will convince me otherwise.'

'It was "Weep Not, My Pretty Bride", or I'm a Christ-killer. Shall I sing the chorus for you, idiot?'

'What difference would *that* make, fool? You'd have to *fart* it to convince me!'

William Rackham has not contributed a word to the debate, content merely to watch.

'What is *your* opinion, Bill?' says Bodley.

Rackham scowls in annoyance: he was so keen to show off his new cane tonight that he left his umbrella at home, and now the rain is setting in. 'God only knows,' he shrugs. 'The whole thing was a damn fiasco. I could barely hear a thing. The Lumley was *quite* the wrong place for such a performance. It should've been somewhere small and intimate. And with an audience well-bred enough to behave themselves.'

Bodley strikes himself on the forehead with his palm, and reels back.

'Lord Rackham has spoken!' he proclaims. 'Tremble, impresarios!'

'A church,' says Ashwell. 'That's the place for the Great Flatelli, eh, Bill? Smallish crowd, everyone on their best behaviour, superb acoustics . . .'

William spits into the gutter, whose sodden contents are just beginning to move. 'I'm glad *you* two are so easy to please. In *my* view, we've been shamefully short-changed tonight. Think of the poorer folk, who can ill afford to waste their wages on such a . . . such a puffed-up swindle!'

'D'you hear that, Ashwell? Think of the poorer folk!'

'Toiling all week to hear a good fart, and what do they get?'

'Fuck-all!'

'I'm going home,' says Rackham, peering through the gas-lit drizzle for a cab.

'Aww, no, Bill, don't leave us all alo-o-o-ne.'

'No, damn it, I'm going home. It's cold and it's raining.'

'There are plenty of warm dry places for a man to crawl into, aren't there, Ashwell?'

'Warm and wet, heh-heh-heh.'

Inspired, Bodley unbuttons his overcoat and begins to rummage in the pockets within. 'I just so happen to have on my person . . . Bear with me, friends, while I fumble . . .' – he whips out a crumpled tract the size of a cheap New Testament and waves it in the lamp-light – 'A brand, *spanking* new edition of *More Sprees in London*. A year in the making, no expense spared, all lies guaranteed true, all virgins guaranteed intact. I've been studying it ass . . . assiduously. Some of the houses have moved up a few rungs since the last edition. There was one in particular . . .' (he flips the already dog-eared pages) 'Ah! yes, this one here: Mrs Castaway's. Silver Street.'

'A hop, skip and a jump away!' says Ashwell.

'Sugar,' declares Bodley. 'That's the girl: Sugar. Words can't do her justice, it says here. Luxury for the price of mediocrity. A treasure. On and on in that vein. And the house is awarded four stars.'

'Four stars! Let's go this minute!' Ashwell wheels round and waves his cane in the air. 'Cab! Cab! Where's a cab!'

For a moment William's blood runs cold, as he imagines Sugar has betrayed him and is conducting business as usual. Then he reminds himself what a catalogue of fictions *More Sprees* is. The Sugar who exists in its pages is not the real one he knows.

While Bodley and Ashwell lurch backwards and forwards in the rain, singing 'Cab!' and 'Sugar!' in silly voices, William thinks of her as she was when he last saw her – only three days ago. He remembers the look on her face when he disabused her of her ignorance. 'I am William Rackham,' he told her. 'The head of Rackham Perfumeries.' Why shouldn't she know?

Once he'd let the cat out of the bag, however, and lapped up Sugar's surprise and admiration, he wished he had more cats to let out, to receive more of the same. Guessing that her good fortune must seem to her like a dream, he made it more real by telling her that anything she might desire (in the way of perfumes, cosmetics and soaps) was hers for the asking. To which she responded, naturally enough, with a request for a Rackham's brochure.

'Cab! Cab!' Ashwell is yelling still. 'Come, stout companions, let's try around the corner!'

'Steady on, Ashwell,' cautions William, 'Have you considered the possibility this girl you want may not be available?'

'Damn it, Bill; where's your sense of adventure? Let's take our chances!'

'*Our* chances?'

'Three men; three holes — the arithmetic of it is perfect!'

William smiles and shakes his head.

'My friends,' he says, bowing mock-solemnly. 'I wish you the best of luck finding this . . . what's her name? . . . this Sugar. I regret I'm too tired to go with you. You can tell me all about it when next we meet!'

'Agreed!' cries Bodley. '*Au revoir!*' And he reels off on Ashwell's arm, singing 'Off to Mrs Castaway's! Off to Mrs Castaway's!' all the way to the corner.

'*Au revoir!*' William calls out after them, but they're already gone.

The drizzle is drizzle no longer; heavy raindrops splash against his ulster, threatening to turn it into a water-logged burden, and there's still no cab in sight. Yet, oddly, his irritable mood is passing from him now that he's alone; Bodley and Ashwell, always such a tonic for him in the past, were tonight more like a dose of cod liver oil. What a tiresome thing it is to be a sober man among soused companions! Perhaps he should've drunk more, but damn it, he didn't wish to . . . Why drink half a dozen glasses when two are enough to warm the stomach? And why reel from woman to woman when one is enough to satisfy the loins? Or is he merely getting old?

'Are you needin' a numbrella, good sir?'

A female voice at his side. He whirls to face her; she is young and shabbily dressed, with comely brown eyes, well-shaped eyebrows, too spade-like a jaw — quite fuckable, really, all things considered. She shelters under an umbrella that's ragged and skeletal, but holds in her free hand a much more substantial looking one, furled.

'I suppose I am,' says Rackham. 'Show me what you have there.'

'Jus' one left, good sir,' she replies apologetically, rolling her eyes at the weather as if to say, 'I had dozens to begin with, but they've all been bought.'

William examines the parapluie, weighing it in his hands, running one gloved finger along its ivory handle, peeking into its waxy black folds. 'Very handsome,' he murmurs. 'And belonging, if I read this label correctly, to a Mr Giles Gordon. How peculiar that he should have discarded it! You know, miss, his address is *so* nearby, we could even ask him how well this umbrella served him, couldn't we?'

The girl bites her lip, her pretty eyebrows contorted in agitation.

'Please, sir,' she whines. 'Me ol' man give me that umbrella. I don't want no trouble. I don't usually do this sort o' fing, it's just the umbrella came me way, and . . .' She gestures helplessly, as if trusting him to understand the economics of it: a high-class umbrella is worth more than a low-class woman.

For a moment she and he are locked in an impasse. Her free hand squirms against her bosom: protective, suggestive.

Then, 'Here,' he says gruffly, handing her a few coins — less than the umbrella is worth, but more than she would have dared ask him for her body. 'You're too sweet a girl to go to gaol on my account.'

'Oh, *fank* you sir,' she cries, and runs off into the nearest alley.

William frowns, wondering if he's done the right thing. With gloriously perverse timing, a cab rolls jingling round the corner, rendering his purchase futile; nor does he want another man's parapluie lying about his house. With a pang of regret, he tosses the thing away: perhaps the girl will find it again, or if she doesn't, well . . . nothing goes to waste in these streets.

'What's yer pleasure, guv?' yells the cabman.

Home, Rackham is thinking, as he seizes hold of the hand-grip and pulls himself up out of the muck.

ELEVEN

ugar's forehead lands with a soft thud on the papers she has been toiling over. Half past midnight, Mrs Castaway's. Musty quiet and the smell of embers and candle-fat. The cobwebby mass of her own hair threatens to stifle her as she comes back to life with a gasp.

Raising herself from her writing-desk, Sugar blinks, scarcely able to believe she could have fallen asleep when, only an instant before, she was so seriously pondering what word should come next. The page on which her face landed is smudged, still glistening; she stumbles over to the bed and examines her face in the mirror. The pale flesh of her forehead is branded with tiny, incomprehensible letters in purple ink.

'Damn,' she says.

A few minutes later she's in bed, looking over what she has written. A new character has entered her story, and is suffering the same fate as all the others.

'Please,' he begged, tugging ineffectually at the silken bonds holding him fast to the bedposts. 'Let me go! I am an important man!' – and many more such pleas. I paid no heed to him, busying myself with my whet-stone and my dagger.

'But tell me, exalted Sir,' I said at last. 'Where is it your pleasure to have the blade enter you?'

To this, the man gave no reply, but his face turned gastly grey.

'The embarassment of choices has taken your tongue,' I suggested. 'But never fear: I shall explain them all to you, and their exquisite effects . . .'

Sugar frowns, wrinkling the blur of backwards text on her forehead.

There's something lacking here, she feels. But what? A long succession of other men, earlier on in her manuscript, have inspired her to flights of Gothic cruelty; dispatching them to their grisly fate has always been sheer pleasure. Tonight, with this latest victim, she can't summon what's needed – that vicious spark – to set her prose alight. Faced with the challenge of spilling his blood, she hears an alien voice of temptation inside her: *Oh, for God's sake, let the poor fool live.*

You're going soft, she chides herself. *Come on, shove it in, deep into his throat, into his arse, into his guts, up to the hilt.*

She yawns, stretches under the warm, clean covers. She has slept here alone for days now; it smells of no body but hers. As always, there are half a dozen clean sheets on the bed, interleaved with waxed canvas, so that each time a sheet is soiled she can whip it off, revealing a fresh layer of bedding. Before William Rackham came into her life, these layers were stripped off with monotonous regularity; now, they stay in place, all half-dozen of them, for days at a time. Christopher climbs the stairs every morning to collect soiled bedding, and finds nothing outside her door.

Luxury.

Sugar slides deeper under the covers, her manuscript weighing heavy on her breast. It's a rag-bag of a thing, made up of many different sized papers, sandwiched in a stiff cardboard folder on which are inscribed many titles, all crossed out. Underneath this inky roll-call of erasures, one thing survives: '*by "Sugar"*.'

Her story chronicles the life of a young prostitute with waist-length red hair and hazel eyes, working in the same house as her own mother, a forbidding creature called Mrs Jettison. Allowing for a few flights of fancy – the murders, for instance – it's the story of her own life – well, her early life in Church Lane, at least. It's the story of a naked, weeping child rolled into a ball under a blood-stained blanket, cursing the universe. It's a tale of embraces charged with hatred and kisses laced with disgust, of prac-tised submission and the secret longing for vengeance. It's an inventory of brutish men, a jostling queue of human refuse, filthy, gin-stinking, whisky-stinking, ale-stinking, scabrous, oily-nailed, slime-toothed, squint-eyed, senile, cadaverous, obese, stump-legged, hairy-arsed, monster-cocked – all waiting their turn to root out the last surviving morsel of innocence and devour it.

Is there any good fortune in this story? None! Good fortune, of the

William Rackham kind, would spoil everything. The heroine must see only poverty and degradation; she must never move from Church Lane to Silver Street, and no man must ever offer her anything she wants – most especially, rescue into an easier life. Otherwise this novel, conceived as a cry of unappeasable anger, risks becoming one of those 'Reader, I married him' romances she so detests.

No, one thing is certain: her story must not have a happy ending. Her heroine takes revenge on the men she hates; yet the world remains in the hands of men, and such revenge cannot be tolerated. Her story's ending, therefore, is one of the few things Sugar has planned in advance, and it's death for the heroine. She accepts it as inevitable, and trusts that her readers will too.

Her readers? Why, yes! She has every intention of submitting the manuscript for publication once it's finished. But who on Earth would publish it, you may protest, and who would read it? Sugar doesn't know, but she's confident it has a fighting chance. Meritless pornography gets published, and so do respectable novels politely calling for social reform (why, only a couple of years ago, Wilkie Collins published a novel called *The New Magdalen*, a feeble, cringing affair in which a prostitute called Mercy Merrick hopes for redemption . . . A book to throw against the wall in anger, but its success proves that the public is ready to read about women who've seen more than one prick in their lives . . .) Yes, there must be receptive minds out there in the world, hungry for the unprettified truth – especially in the more sophisticated and permissive future that's just around the corner. Why, she may even be able to live by her writing: A couple of hundred faithful readers would be sufficient; she's not coveting success on the scale of Rhoda Broughton's.

She snorts, startled awake again. Her manuscript has slid off her breast, spilling pages onto the bed-clothes. Page one is uppermost.

All men are the same, it says. *If there is one thing I have learned in my time on this Earth, it is this. All men are the same.*

How can I assert this with such conviction? Surely I have not known all the men there are to know? On the contrary, dear reader, perhaps I have!

My name is Sugar . . .

Sugar sleeps.

★   ★   ★

Henry Rackham removes the wrapping-paper from the red hearts, dark livers and pale pink necks of chicken he has bought from the pet-meat man, and throws a few morsels to the kitchen floor. His cat pounces instantly, seizing the meat in her mouth, her sleek shoulders convulsed with the effort of swallowing. Once upon a time, Henry would murmur pleas of restraint, for fear she'd make herself sick; now he looks on, acquiescent in the ravenous face of Nature. He knows that in a few minutes, she'll be lying in front of the fire, as serene and innocent as the moon. She will purr at his touch, licking his hand which, although he has washed it, still smells – to her – of his gift of bloody flesh.

What is there to be learned from cats? thinks Henry. Perhaps that all creatures can be peaceable and kind – if they're not hungry.

But how to explain the iniquity of those who have sufficient to eat? They hunger in a different way, perhaps. They are starving for grace, for respect, for the forgiveness of God. Feed them on that, and they will lie down with the Lamb.

Henry walks noiselessly in his thick knitted socks, into his sitting-room, and kneels at the hearth. Sure enough, no sooner has he stirred the fire than his cat comes to join him, purring and ready for sleep. Out of the blue he finds himself remembering, as he often does, his first meeting with Mrs Fox – or at least the first time he became aware of her. Inconceivable though it now seems that he could have failed to notice a woman of her beauty, she claims she was worshipping alongside him for weeks before the incident he so clearly recalls.

It was in 1872, in August of that year. She shone a bright fresh light into what had until then been the *camera obscura* of the North Kensington Prayer and Discussion Assembly. She was like the answer to his prayers, for he harboured in his heart the conviction that Christ never intended Christianity to be quite as Jesuitical as the N.K.P.D.A. would have it.

It was Trevor MacLeish who provoked her to make herself manifest on that day in August. A Bachelor of Science, and always abreast of the most recent developments in that sphere, he voiced his misgivings on the manner of receiving Holy Communion. 'It has been conclusively proven,' he said, 'that disease may be communicated from person to person when utensils and especially when drinking vessels are shared.' He argued for a new procedure of drinking Communion wine out of a number of individual cups, as many as there were Communicants. Someone asked if the wiping of a cup's rim were not sufficient to remove the Bacteria, but MacLeish insisted that it was impervious to such measures.

In fact, MacLeish had brought to the Assembly a petition on this matter, addressed to the Archbishop of Canterbury no less, and lacking only signatures. Henry was glum at the prospect of signing, believing the whole affair to be ridiculous, but fearing to say so, in case he were accused of Papist primitivism. Then up spoke a young lady, new to their midst, a Mrs Fox by name, saying,

'Really, gentlemen, this is a quibble, refuted by the Bible.'

MacLeish's countenance fell, but at Mrs Fox's direction, Bibles were opened to Luke, Chapter 11, *vv.* 37–41, and she read the lines aloud without even being invited to do so, putting especial emphasis on the words: *'Now do ye Pharisees make clean the outside of the cup and the platter; but your inward part is full of ravening and wickedness.'*

To see MacLeish folding his petition under the table, face red as a beetroot, was a pleasure; to be alerted to Mrs Fox's existence, a delight. That a person of the fair sex, and one additionally hampered in her religious growth by her beauty, should be so well versed in the Bible, was almost a miracle. Henry yearned to hear her speak again. He loves to hear her still.

The next time William visits Sugar, he brings with him two publications, both promised when last they met.

'Oh! You remembered!' she cries, with a puppyish embrace. She's dressed as if going out, in dark blue and black silk, not a hair out of place, not a crease out of line. Her soft sleeves whisper and rustle as she squeezes her arms around his waist, her hair is fragrant and slightly damp.

He notices, over her shoulder, that her bedroom is immaculately tidy: she always keeps it so for him. There are pale rectangles on the wallpaper, unstained by smoke, where those feeble pornographic prints used to hang, and although it's months since they disappeared, their absence never fails to thrill him, for it was to please him that Sugar removed them. How did she put it? Ah yes: 'This room is no one's business now but yours and mine!' A golden tongue she has, in more ways than one.

He seizes her by her bony shoulders and pushes her, affectionately, to arm's-length. She grins at him, twice as beautiful as last time. Dozens of times he's seen her, and each time it's as if he's seen her only dimly before, and this is the fully-lit reality! Her mouth is fuller, her nose is more perfect, her eyes are brighter, and her eyebrows have (how could he not have noticed this before?) bristles of dark purple within the auburn.

'Yes, yes of course I remembered,' he grins back. 'My God, you are a lovely thing.'

She lowers her face, blushing. Yes, that's a blush, he'll swear — and no one can fake a blush! She's genuinely flattered, he can tell!

'Which first?' he says, pulling both of the promised pamphlets into view.

'Whichever you wish,' she says, stepping back towards the bed.

He hands her his newly-cut copy of Mr Philip Bodley and Mr Edward Ashwell's book, *The Efficacy of Prayer*. This little tome, he explains, has already caused a sensation, principally among the dozens of clergymen with whom Bodley, son of Bishop Bodley, conducted his 'informal' chats. Libel actions aplenty have been threatened but as the book discloses initials and localities only (Reverend H. of Stepney: '*Why God should deem it so essential I suffer lumbago I cannot hope to understand*') they're likely to come to nothing.

Perched on the edge of the mattress, Sugar leafs through the slim volume, quickly appraising its thrust. She knows men like Bodley and Ashwell. They talk loudly, are subject to fits of sniggering, and pretend they wish to deflower virgins when what they secretly desire is a milky cuddle from a fat matron.

(*If, at a conservative estimate, 2,500,000 British infants per day pray for the health of their mamas and papas, can we conclude, from current mortality rates, that the Almighty's juvenile applicants would be better advised to safeguard their parents by other means?*)

Oh yes, she knows men like this all right. They're always half-drunk, half-stiff, they beaver away endlessly, they can't spend, they won't leave. Must she praise their handiwork now? Sugar re-plays, in her uncanny memory, the way William has talked about these friends of his, these cronies from his fading youth. Can she take a risk?

She smiles. 'How perfectly . . .' (she consults his face, decides to gamble) 'childish.'

For a moment William's brow creases; he hovers on the brink of disapproval — maybe even anger. Then he permits himself to savour his own superiority to his friends, his annoyance with their immature shenanigans.

The air between him and Sugar is suddenly sweet with lovers' concord.

'Yes,' he says, almost in wonder. 'Isn't it?'

She arranges herself more comfortably, leaning one elbow on the mattress, allowing her hip to rise up through her trailing skirts.

'Have they nothing better to do, do you think?'

'No, nothing,' he affirms. How odd that he never realised this before! His two oldest friends, and there's a gulf between him and them – a gulf he could bridge only if he resumed being as idle as they, or if they found something purposeful to do. What an insight! And it comes out of the mouth of this entrancing young woman whom it has been his good fortune to win. Truly, these are strange and significant times in his personal history.

A little shyly, in exchange for the Bodley and Ashwell book she's plainly losing patience with, he hands her the Winter 1874 catalogue of Rackham manufactures. (The Spring one isn't ready.) Again Sugar surprises him, by looking him square in the eyes, and saying, 'But tell me, William . . . how is business?'

No woman has ever asked him this question. It is a great deal more transgressive than talk of cocks and cunts.

'Oh . . . splendid, splendid,' he replies.

'No, really,' she says. 'How is it? The competition must be frightful.'

He blinks, nonplussed; clears his throat. 'Well, uh . . . Rackham's is on the ascendant, I'd venture to say.'

'And your rivals?'

'Pears and Yardley are unassailable, Rimmel and Rowland are in good health. Nisbett had a bad Season last year, and may be in decline. Hinton is ailing, perhaps fatally . . .'

How queer this conversation is becoming! Is there no limit to what's possible between him and Sugar? First literature, now this!

'Good,' she smirks. 'Here's to the decline of your rivals: may they expire one by one.' And she opens the catalogue and begins browsing. William sits close beside her, one arm around her back, his knees pressing into the warmth of her skirts.

'The end of Winter is always a good time for sales of soaps, bath oils and the like,' he informs her, to fill the silence.

'Oh?' she says. 'I suppose it's because people aren't so reluctant to wash.'

He chuckles. They've been together for fifteen minutes already, and are both still fully clothed, as proper a pair as any married couple.

'Maybe so,' he says. 'Mainly it's due to the London season. Ladies like to stock up early, so that when May comes and they have to brave the crowds, they've nothing left to buy but big things in showy parcels.'

Sugar reads on attentively. When Rackham strokes her cheek, she nudges her face against his hand affectionately and kisses his fingers, but her eyes don't leave the pages of the catalogue. Even when William kneels at her feet and lifts her skirts, she reads on, shifting forward on the bed to allow him greater freedom, but otherwise pretending not to notice what's happening to her. It is a game that Rackham finds arousing. Through the layers of soft fabric that shroud him in darkness, he hears, at once muffled and sharp, the sound of a page being turned; closer to his face, he smells the odour of female excitement.

When it's over, and she's belly-down on the bed, she is still reading. She reads aloud, reciting the entries, breathless from her exertions.

'Rackham's Lavender Milk. Rackham's Lavender Puffs. Rackham's Lavender Scented Moth Balls. Rackham's Damask Rose Drops. Rackham's Raven Oil . . .' She squints at the fine print, rolling onto her side. 'A high class and innocent Extract for giving instant and permanent Colour. Not a dye.' She raises her eyebrows over the edge of the catalogue.

'Of *course* it's a dye,' snorts William, at once embarrassed and slightly exhilarated by this frankness, this *intimacy* she's drawing him into.

'Rackham's Snow Dust,' Sugar continues. 'Are malodorous feet your Achilles' heel? Try Rackham's Foot Balm. Not a soap. A Medicinal Preparation to Scientific Specifications. Rackham's Aureoline. Produces the beautiful Golden Colour so much admired, ten shillings and sixpence, not a dye. Rackham's Poudre Juvenile . . .'

William notes that her French accent is not at all bad: better than most. From the waist up, she's as *soignée* as any lady he knows, reciting his company's products like poetry; from the waist down . . .

'Rackham's Cough Remedy. Free of poisons of any kind. Rackham's Bath Sweetener. One bottle lasts a year. Do your feet smell? To spare your blushes, use Rackham's Sulphur Soap, does not contain lead, one shilling and sixpence . . .'

Suddenly he frets: is she mocking him? Her voice is a soft purr, without any audible trace of disrespect. Her legs are still open, displaying the white abundance of Rackham semen slowly leaking out. And yet . . .

'Are you making fun of me?' he asks.

She puts the catalogue down, leans over to stroke his head.

'Of course not,' she says. 'All this is new to me. I want to learn.'

He sighs, flattered and shamed. 'If you're keen to fill gaps in your education, better you read Catullus than a Rackham catalogue.'

'Oh, but *you* didn't write this, did you, William?' she says. 'It was written in your father's time, yes?'

'By many hands, no doubt.'

'None as elegant as yours, I'm sure.' And she eyes him, a gentle challenge.

He reaches for his trousers. 'I wouldn't know where to begin.'

'Oh, but I could help you. Make suggestions.' She smiles lasciviously. 'I'm awfully good at making suggestions.' Fetching the catalogue up again, she lays her forefinger on one line of it. 'Now, I happened to notice you flinching when I read the words "Do your feet smell?" A rather low phrase, I must agree.'

'Ugh, yes,' he groans, hearing the old man's voice, picturing him writing those ugly words in that ridiculous green ink of his, tongue slightly protruding from his wrinkled mouth.

'So let's think of a phrase worthy of Rackham's,' says Sugar, tossing her skirts down to her ankles. '*William* Rackham's, that is.'

Bemused, he opens his lips to protest. Swift as a bird, she swoops on him, laying one flaky finger on his mouth.

Shush, she mimes.

Miles away, the woman whom William vowed before God to love, honour and cherish is examining her face in a mirror. A tight, throbbing blemish has appeared on her forehead, just below the wispy golden hairline. Unthinkable, given how often and how carefully she sponges her face, but there it is.

On impulse, Agnes squeezes the pimple between her thumb and forefinger. Pain spreads across her brow like a flame, but the pimple stays intact, only angrier. She should have been patient, and applied some Rackham's Blemish Balm. Now the thing is rooted fast.

In her hand-held mirror, she sees the fear in her eyes. She's had this pimple before, in exactly the same place, and it has proved a harbinger of something much, much worse. But surely God will spare her, on the eve of the Season? She imagines she can feel her poor brain pulsing against the pink seashell of her inner ear.

Why, oh why, is her health so bad? She has harmed no one, done nothing. What is she doing in this frail and treacherous body? Once upon a time, when she wasn't born yet, she must have had a choice between a number of different bodies in a number of different places, each destined to have its own retinue of friends, relations and enemies. Maybe *this* place, this body, caught her fancy for the silliest of reasons, and now here she is, stuck! Or maybe a mischievous imp distracted her when she was choosing . . . She imagines herself looking down, from Heaven, from the spirit world, at all the nice new bodies available, trying to decide whether Agnes Pigott might be an agreeable thing to be, while all around her other spirits jostled for their own return to human life. (Pray God Doctor Curlew never finds her hidden cache of books about Spiritualism and the Beyond. It'll be the death of her if he does!)

Ah, but all this sophisticated thought is no help at all. She must make peace with her body, however bad a choice it may have been, for if she's to manage the coming Season, she needs unhindered use of her body's faculties.

So, bravely, Agnes carries on with her day, forcing herself to perform small tasks – combing her hair, buffing her nails, writing her diary – doing her best to ignore clumsy mishaps. Small scratches and chafes appear on her skin without warning; bruises spread over her like measles; the muscles in her neck, arms and back are stretched to snapping-point, and on her forehead the shiny blemish throbs and throbs.

Please, no, please, no, please, no, she recites constantly, as if from a rosary. *I don't want to bleed again.*

To Agnes, bleeding from the belly is a terrifying and unnatural thing. No one has told her about menstruation; she has never heard the word nor seen it in print. Doctor Curlew, the only person who might have enlightened her, never has, because he assumes his patient can't possibly have married, borne a child and lived to the age of twenty-three without becoming aware of certain basic facts. He assumes incorrectly.

But it's not so very odd: when, at seventeen, Agnes married William, she'd only bled a few times, and ever since then she's been ill. Everyone knows that ill people bleed: bleeding is the manifestation of serious illness.

Her father (her *real* father, that is) bled on his deathbed, didn't he, despite not being in any way injured, and she remembers also, as a small child, seeing a baa-lamb lying in a pool of blood, and her nurse telling her that the animal was 'sickly'.

Well, now *she*, Agnes, is 'sickly'. And, from time to time, she bleeds.

She hasn't discerned any pattern. The affliction began when she was seventeen, was cured by prayer and fasting and, after her marriage, it stayed away for almost a year. Then it came at intervals of a month or two – or even three, if she starved herself. Always she hopes she's seen the last of it, and now she prays she might be spared until August.

'After the Season,' she promises the demons who wish her ill. 'After the Season, you can have me.' But she feels her belly swelling already.

A few days later, with William away on business in Dundee (wherever on Earth that might be), Sugar decides to take a peep at his house. Why not? She'll only sit idle in her little room at Mrs Castaway's otherwise, her novel stalling upon the latest man, unable to decide on his fate.

Her collaboration with William on the wording of future Rackham catalogues proved very fruitful – for her as well as for him. In his enthusiasm to jot down her suggestions, he pulled an old envelope from his pocket that happened to have his address written on it. 'How about . . . "Restore your hair to the luxuriance that is your birthright!"?' she said, simultaneously committing the address to memory.

Now Sugar sits among old folk and respectable young women, riding the omnibus from the city to North Kensington, on a changeable Monday afternoon, on her way to find out where William Rackham, Esquire, lays his head at nights. She's wearing her dowdiest dress – a loose-fitting woollen one in plain blue, so at odds with the latest fashions as to be pitiable on a woman under thirty. Indeed, Sugar has the impression she *is* pitied by one or two of the ladies, but at least no one suspects her of being a prostitute. That might have made things difficult, given that in the confines of the omnibus there's no choice but to sit face-to-face with one's fellow passengers.

'High Street already,' murmurs an old man to his wife very near Sugar. 'We've made good time.'

Sugar looks past their wrinkled heads at the world outside. It's sunny and green and spacious. The omnibus slows to a stop.

'Chepstow Villas *Cor-nerrr!*'

Sugar alights right behind the elderly couple. They don't hurry away from her, but accept her walking in their wake as if she's respectable, just like them. Her disguise, evidently, is perfect.

'Chilly, isn't it?' one old dear mutters to the other, while the sun beams down on Sugar's perspiring back.

I am young, she thinks. *It's a different sun shining on me from the one that shines on them.*

Sugar walks slowly, allowing the old folk to forge ahead. The ground beneath her feet is extraordinarily smooth, as near as cobble-stones can get to parquetry; she imagines an army of paviours patiently completing it like a jigsaw puzzle while the placid citizens look on. She walks on, sniffing the air and goggling at the handsome new houses, trying hard to absorb the Notting Hillness of Notting Hill, trying to imagine what the choice of such a place for a man's home reveals about him. *This, not the stench of the city, is the air my William breathes*, she reminds herself.

What she knows about William Rackham so far would hardly fill a book. She knows his preferences in orifices (conventional, unless he's in a bad mood) and how he feels about the size of his pego (it's a respectable size, isn't it, though some other men may be bigger?), and she's inscribed on her memory all his opinions in literature, down to the last witticism at George Eliot's expense. But William Rackham the family man and citizen? An elusive creature, not identifiable as the lover she embraces.

Now, she walks along his home street, determined to learn more. How quiet it is here! And how spacious! Moats of greenery everywhere, and trees! Pedestrians are few and far between; they have nothing to sell, they are pensive and unencumbered, they stroll. Carts roll into view very slowly, and take their own sweet time to amble away. There are no shrieks of laughter or distress, no vertiginous stacks of decaying housing, no din of industry or smell of faeces, only curtains in the windows and birds in the trees.

One large house, set well back from the street, is fenced all around in freshly painted cast-iron; as she walks past, Sugar runs her gloved hands along the knots and curls. It's only after a minute that she realises the dominant motif in the iron design is the letter 'R', repeated hundreds and hundreds of times, hidden among the curlicues.

'Eureka,' she whispers.

Adjusting her bonnet, she peers through the eye of the largest 'R' she can find. Her lips part, her mouth dilates in awe as she takes stock of the house, its pillars and porticos, its carriage-way and gardens.

'My God. You'll keep me better than you do now, my dear Willy,' she softly prophesies.

But then the Rackham house's front door swings open, and Sugar instantly pulls her hands away from the gate and retreats. She hurries around the corner into a different crescent, looking neither right nor left, wishing herself invisible. It's all she can do not to break into a run; her bustle bounces against her bottom as it is. A stiff wind springs up where there was no wind before (or was it at her back, gently pushing her on?), stinging her face, almost tearing her bonnet off, flapping the skirts of her dress. She shelters – hides – behind the first public monument she comes to: a marble column commemorating the fallen in the Crimean War.

She peeps from behind the plinth, her cheek brushing against the names of young men who are no longer alive, subtle absences in the smoothness of the marble. A woman is coming down Pembridge Crescent, a small blonde woman with a perfect figure and a chocolate-and-cream-coloured dress. She walks briskly, bobbing slightly as she advances. Her eyes are so big and blue that their beauty can be appreciated at twenty yards' distance.

This, Sugar is certain, is the wife of William Rackham.

He's alluded to her once or twice, by way of comparison, but stopped short of naming her, so Sugar has no name to put to this pretty young woman drawing near. 'Always-Sick', perhaps. Apart from her bosom, which is full, Mrs Rackham inhabits a body of remarkably infantile scale. Nor is her body the only childish thing about her: is she aware, Sugar wonders, that she's biting her lower lip as she walks?

Just as Mrs Rackham reaches the monument, a peculiar thing happens: the whole of North Kensington undergoes a remarkable meteorological phenomenon – the sun is covered over by sheets of dark-grey cloud, but continues to shine with such brilliance that the clouds themselves assume an intense luminosity. Down below, the crescent and everything in it is coated with a spectral light that lends an unnatural definition to each and every cobble, leaf and lamp-post. Everything stands out sharply and nothing recedes, at once revealed and obscured in a glow as treacherous as polar twilight.

Mrs Rackham stops dead. She looks up into the heavens in naked terror. From her hiding-place behind the column, Sugar can see the convulsive swallow in her white throat, the sheen of dread in her eyes, the angry red pimple on her forehead.

'Saints and angels preserve me!' she cries, then spins on her axis and flees. Her tiny feet all-but-invisible beneath her frothing hems, she glides back down the road like a bead sliding along a string, her progress unnaturally straight, unnaturally rapid. Then the pretty chocolate-coloured bead that is Mrs Rackham veers, and disappears, as if following a twist in its string, through the Rackham gates.

Moments later, the sun is unveiled again, and the world loses its eerie clarity. Everything is back to normal; the Gods are appeased.

Sugar gets to her feet, pats the dust off her skirts with her palms. She moves sluggishly, as though roused from a deep sleep. All she can think is: *Why has William never told me his wife has such a beautiful voice?* To Sugar's ear, Mrs Rackham, even in the grip of terror, sounds like a bird – a rare bird pursued for its song. What man, if he could hear that voice whenever he pleased, wouldn't listen to it as often as possible? What ear could tire of it? It's the voice she wishes she'd been born with: not hoarse and low like her own croak, but pure and high and musical.

Go home, you fool, she cautions herself, as the first few raindrops spatter against the plinth. *All this clean air is going to your head.*

A few days later still, Henry Rackham, desperate to confide, yet having not a single confidante in the world except Mrs Fox, to whom he can't possibly confess this particular secret, calls upon his brother William.

Intimacy hasn't always flowed smoothly, it must be said, between the Rackham brothers. Despite their blood ties, and despite Henry giving William the benefit of the doubt in many things, Henry can't help noticing their differences. Devoutness, for example, has never been William's strong point, although they do share – judging from past conversations – a passionate desire to improve the world, and reform English society.

From William's point of view, his older brother is dismal company indeed. As he put it once to Bodley and Ashwell: Henry has that werewolf look of someone who ought to be ravaging virgins, then scourging his flesh in remorse while the townspeople surround the castle with flaming torches, baying for his blood – but alas, no such racy scenario ever accompanies his fraternal visits. Instead, Henry always bemoans, in vague, irritatingly opaque terms, his unworthiness for anything he aspires to. What a pitiful head of Rackham Perfumeries he would have made! Surrendering his claim to William may well have been the only clever thing the poor dullard ever did!

Still, William has lately resolved to be generous and hospitable to his brother, and forgive him his shortcomings. It's all part and parcel of being the chief Rackham now: this receiving of visits from troubled family members, this imparting of advice.

On the rainy afternoon that Henry does finally cough up a secret, it's cold enough indoors for both men to regret that Spring has already been put into effect in the Rackham house. Granted, the banishing of Winter furnishings is a social obligation that must be obeyed, but Agnes has obeyed it rather earlier than necessary, and now, on her instruction, the fireplace in the parlour has been rendered wholly useless. Force of habit makes the men sit near it still, even though it's empty and brushed out, sporting a small philodendron where the flames ought to be, and lace curtains embroidered with crocuses, robins and other vernal symbols. Henry leans forwards, closer to his brother and the hearth, trying to warm himself on what's not there.

'William,' he is saying, the furrow in his brow identical to the one he already had as a boy of seven, 'Do you think it's wise for you to have so much to do with Bodley and Ashwell? They've published that book you know – *The Efficacy of Prayer* – Have you seen it?'

'They've given me a copy,' admits William. 'Boys will be boys, yes?'

'Boys, yes . . .' sighs Henry, 'but with the capacity of men to do harm.'

'Oh, I don't know,' says William, folding his arms against the chill and glancing at the clock. 'They're surely preaching to the . . . ah . . . *converted* is the wrong word here, isn't it? . . . to the *deconverted*, shall we say. How many people d'you *really* think are going to regard prayer any differently as a result of this book?'

'Every soul is precious,' fumes Henry.

'Ach, it'll all blow over,' counsels the younger brother. 'Ashwell's last book, *The Modern Dunciad*, was a scandal for two months, and then . . . ?' William flings a handful of fingers wide, to mime a puff of smoke.

'Yes, but they're taking *this* book all around England on a sort of . . . grand tour, showing it off at working men's clubs and so on, as if it were a two-headed giraffe. They read it aloud, taking parts, mimicking the voices of feeble old clerics and angry widows, and then they solicit questions from the audience . . .'

'How do you know all this?' asks William, for it's news to him.

'I'm forever running into them!' cries Henry, as though lamenting his own clumsiness. 'I'm convinced they follow me – it can't be mere chance. But *you*, William, you must be careful – no, don't smile – William, they're becoming notorious, and if you're seen to be thick with them, *you* may become notorious as well.'

William shrugs, unconcerned. He's too wealthy now to fear the gossip of the righteous, and in any case, he's noticed a tendency lately amongst the Best People to seek out the notorious, to add a bit of spice to parties.

'They are my *friends*, Henry,' he chides gently, 'from so long ago . . . the best part of twenty years.'

'Yes, yes, they were once my friends too,' groans the older Rackham. 'But I can't be loyal to them as you are, I can't! They cause me nothing but embarrassment.' Henry's large hands, one on each of his knees, are white-knuckled. 'There are times – I hardly dare confess it – there are times when I wish I could simply be rid of them and all their memories of the man I used to be; when I wish I could wake one day to a world of perfect strangers who knew me only as . . . as . . .'

'A man of the cloth?' prompts William, staring in pity at those hands of Henry's, clutching at his ungainly knees as if at the rim of a pulpit.

'Yes,' confesses Henry, and (*oh, for Heaven's sake!*) hangs his head.

'You haven't . . . taken Orders, have you?' enquires William, wondering if this is the oh-so-coy secret Henry has been struggling to divulge.

'No, no.' Henry fidgets irritably. 'I know I'm not ready for *that* yet. My soul is far from . . . ah . . . *any* sort of purity.'

'But isn't the idea of it – forgive me if I've got the wrong end of the stick here – Isn't the idea of it that you . . . ah . . . *become* pure *while* you're taking the Orders? I mean, that the process itself effects a sort of trans-formation?'

'That isn't the idea at all!' protests Henry.

But, inwardly, he fears that it is. The real truth of his reluctance to take the first steps towards becoming a clergyman, at least since he's known Mrs Fox, is that he's terrified his examiners will peer into his soul and tell him he is unfit not only for the collar and the pulpit, but for any sort of Christian life.

As a layman, he's spared that awful judgement, for although he's his own harshest critic, there's one respect in which he's lenient on himself:

he doesn't believe his sins disqualify him from striving to be a decent person. As long as he remains a layman, he can be impure in thought and word, or even in deed, and afterwards he can repent and resolve to do better in future, disappointing no one but himself and God. No one else is dragged down by his sins; he is the captain of his soul, and if he steers it into dark waters, no innocent person risks shipwreck along with him. But if he aspires to leadership of others, he cannot afford to be such a poor captain; he'll have to be a stronger and better man than he is now. Sterner judges even than himself will have the right – nay, the obligation – to condemn him. And surely his depravity is written all over his face? Surely anyone can guess that his soul is rotten with carnal desires?

Perhaps it's this belief that his secret must already be suspected by everyone except Mrs Fox, and all the more so by his brother, a man of the world, that finally makes it possible for Henry to confess, on this rainy afternoon in front of the frilly hearth.

'William, I . . . I spoke to a prostitute last week,' he says.

'Really?' says William, roused from near-somnolence by this promising titbit. 'Did Mrs Fox bring her along to a meeting?'

'No, no,' grimaces Henry. 'I spoke to her in the street. In fact, I . . . I have been speaking to prostitutes in the street for some time now.'

There is a pause while the brothers gaze first at each other, then at their shoes.

'Speaking only?'

'Of course, speaking only.' If Henry notices his brother's shoulders slump slightly in disappointment, he's not put off by it. 'I've fallen into the habit of walking in a wretched part of London – High Street – no, not the High Street *here*, the one in St Giles – and conversing with whoever addresses me.'

'Which, I take it, is mainly prostitutes.'

'Yes.'

William scratches the back of his head in bemusement. He wishes there were a fire he could stir with the poker, rather than this ridiculous philodendron.

'This is . . . a rehearsal, perhaps, for your future career? You have your eye on St Giles as your parish?'

Henry laughs mirthlessly. 'I am a mad fool, playing with fire,' he says, enunciating the words with bitter emphasis, 'and if I don't come to my

senses, I'll be consumed.' His fists are clenched, and his eyes shine angrily
– almost as if it's William, not his own desires, threatening his safety.

'Well . . . urm . . .' frowns William, crossing and uncrossing his legs.
'I've always known you to be a sensible chap. I'm sure you don't lack . . .
resolve. And anyway, you'll find that infatuations tend to run their course.
What enthrals us today may have no hold on us tomorrow. Urm . . . These
prostitutes, now. What are they to you?'

But Henry is staring sightlessly ahead of him, haunted.

'They're only children, some of them: children!'

'Well, yes . . . It's a disgrace, as I've often said . . .'

'And they stare at me as if I were to blame for their misery.'

'Well, yes, they're very good at that . . .'

'I try to convince myself that it's pity that moves me, that I wish only
to help them, as Mrs . . . as others help them. That I wish only to let them
know I don't despise them, that I believe they are God's creatures just as
I am. But, when I return home, and I lie in my bed, ready for sleep, it's
not any vision of aiding these wretched women that fills my mind. It's a
vision of an embrace.'

'An embrace?' Lord, here it is at last: the meat of the matter!

'I see myself embracing them . . . *all* of them at once; they are all em-
bodied in one faceless woman. I shouldn't call her faceless, for she has a
face, but it's . . . many women's faces at once. Can you understand that?
She is their . . .' (a comparison with the Trinity occurs to him, but he bites
his tongue on the brink of blasphemy) '. . . their common body.'

William rubs his eyes irritably. He's tired; he slept badly in the guest-
house in Dundee, and slept badly on the train, and he's been working late
hours since his return.

'So . . .' he rejoins, determined now, if it kills him, to get his brother
to the point. 'What *exactly* do you picture yourself doing to this . . . common
body?'

Henry raises his face, suffused with an alarming glow of inspiration (or
is it merely the sun beaming through the window at last?).

'The embrace is all!' he declares. 'I feel I could hold this woman for
a lifetime – pressed close to me – quite still, and doing nothing else but
holding, and reassuring her that everything will be all right from now
on. I swear it's not Lust!' He laughs incredulously. 'I know what Lust
feels like, and this is different . . .' He looks across at William, loses

courage as a result. 'Or perhaps that's what I delude myself to believe.'

William offers a smile which he hopes may pass for sympathy. This must be what it's like, he thinks, for Catholic priests when they have to endure the confessions of the very young. Reams of lurid wrapping-paper to be removed from a giant parcel of guilt, only to reveal a tiny trifle inside.

'So . . .' he sighs. 'Is there anything I can do for you, brother?'

Henry leans back in his chair, apparently exhausted. 'You have done it already, William, merely by listening to my ravings. I know I am a fool and a hypocrite, trying to dress my sins up as virtue. You see, I was on my way to St Giles today – instead, I stopped here.'

William grunts, nonplussed. All things considered, he would rather Henry had pursued his original inclination, and left his overburdened brother in peace. This visit has swallowed up valuable time. The freshly signed contract with those damned Jewish jute merchants, which seemed such a good idea up in Dundee, is looking less advantageous the more he thinks about it, and he needs every spare minute to reconsider it before those damned crates of sacking start arriving on the damned wharf.

'Well, I'm glad to have been of some use to you, Henry,' he mutters. Then his glance falls on Henry's bulbous Gladstone bag, which has been sitting at his brother's side, stuffed to bursting like a burglar's swag. 'But what, if you don't mind me asking, is all this?'

For one last time before he leaves, Henry blushes. Wordlessly, he unfastens the bag and allows its jumble of contents to protrude into the light. A Dutch cheese, some apples and carrots, a loaf of bread, a fat cylinder of smoked sausage, tins of cocoa and biscuits.

William stares into his brother's face, utterly baffled.

'They always say they're hungry,' Henry explains.

Later, much later, when brother Henry has gone home and the sun has long since set and the first draft of an important letter has been written, William lays his cheek on a warm pillow – a pillow with just the right amount of firmness, just the right amount of yield. Sleep follows inevitably.

A gentle, feminine hand strokes his cheek as he nuzzles deeper into the cotton-covered mound of duck feathers. Even in sleep, he knows it's not his mother. His mother has gone away. 'She's turned into a bad woman,' Father says, and so she's gone, gone to live with other bad people, and

William and Henry must be brave boys. So who is this female stroking him? It must be his nurse.

He burrows deeper into slumber, his head penetrating the shell of dreams. Instantly the room where he lies sleeping expands to a vast size, encompassing the whole universe, or at least all the known world. Ships sail into the docks, groaning with jute bags he doesn't want: that's bad, and the gloomy sky overhead reflects this. But, elsewhere, the sun is shining on his lavender fields, which this year are bound to surrender a juicier crop than they ever did in his father's time. All over England, in shops and homes alike, the unmistakable 'R' insignia is on prominent display. Aristocratic ladies, all of whom bear a remarkable resemblance to Lady Bridgelow, are perusing Rackham's Spring catalogue, uttering discreet sounds of approval over each item.

A loud snort – his own snore – half-rouses him. His prick is stiff, lolling aimlessly under the blankets, lost. He turns, huddles against the long hot body of the female, fitting himself against her back, comforting himself against her buttocks. With one arm, he hugs her close to him, breathes the perfume from her hair, sleeps on and on.

In the morning, William Rackham realises that this is the first time in six years he has slept all night with a woman at his side. So many women he's fucked, and so many nights he's slept, and yet so rarely the twain have met!

'Do you know,' he muses to Sugar, before he's even fully awake, 'this is the first time in six years I've slept all night with a woman at my side.'

Sugar kisses his shoulder. Almost says, 'You poor thing,' but thinks better of it.

'Well, was it worth the wait?' she murmurs.

He returns the kiss, ruffles her red mane. Through the fog of his contentment, the cares of his diurnal existence struggle to surface. Dundee. Dundee. A wrinkle dawns on his brow as he recalls the freshly penned letter he brought to show Sugar last night.

'I should get up,' he says, raising himself onto his elbows.

'It's an hour at least before the post gets collected,' remarks Sugar calmly, as if, for her, reading his thoughts is the most natural thing in the world. 'I have stamps and envelopes here. Rest your head a little longer.'

He falls back on his pillow, befuddled. Can it really be as early as that?

Silver Street is so noisy, with carts and dogs and chattering pedestrians, it feels like mid-morning. And what sort of creature is he in bed with, who can hold in her head the fine print of his contract with a firm of jute merchants, while stretching her naked body like a cat?

'The tone of my letter . . .' he frets. 'Are you sure it's not too fawning? They'll understand my meaning, won't they?'

'It's clear as crystal,' she says, sitting up to comb her hair.

'But not *too* clear? They can make trouble for me, these fellows, if I get on the wrong side of them.'

'It's exactly right,' she assures him, dragging the metal teeth in slow rhythm through her tangled orange halo. 'All it needed was a softer word here and there.' (She's referring to the changes he made, on her advice, before they went to bed.)

He turns on his side, watches her as she combs. With every flex of her muscles, the tiger-stripe patterns of her peculiar skin condition move ever-so-slightly – on her hips, on her thighs, on her back. With every sweep of her comb, a luxuriant mass of hair falls against her pale flesh, only to be swept up again a moment later. He clears his throat to tell her how . . . how very fond he is growing of her.

Then he notices the smell.

'*Paghh* . . .' he grimaces, sitting bolt upright. 'Is there a chamber-pot under the bed?'

Without hesitation, Sugar stops combing, bends over the edge of the mattress, and fetches out the ceramic tureen.

'Of course,' she says, tipping it sideways for his inspection. 'But it's empty.'

He grunts, impressed by her masculine continence, never guessing that she slipped away from his side during the night, performed a number of watery procedures, and disposed of the results. Instead, preoccupied with the task at hand – at nostril – William continues his search for the true source of the stench. He stumbles barefoot out of the bed, following his sensitive nose from one end of Sugar's bedroom to the other. He's embarrassed to find that the stink emanates from the soles of his own shoes, lying where he kicked them off the night before.

'I must have stepped in dog's mess on the way here,' he frowns, disproportionately shamed by the stiff sludge he can neither clean nor endure. 'There aren't enough lamps out there, damn it.' He's pulling on his socks now, looking for his trousers, preparing to take his disgraced shoes away with him, away from Sugar's immaculate boudoir.

'The city is a filthy place,' Sugar affirms, unobtrusively wrapping her body in a milk-white dressing-gown. 'There's muck on the ground, muck in the water, muck in the air. I find, even on the short walk between here and The Fireside – *used* to find, I should say, shouldn't I? – a layer of black grime settles on one's skin.'

William, buttoning himself into his shirt, appraises her fresh face, her bright eyes – the white gown.

'Well, you look very clean to me, I must say.'

'I do my best,' she smiles, folding the creamy sleeves across her breast. 'Though a little of your Rackham's Bath Sweetener wouldn't go amiss, I suppose. And do you have anything to purify drinking water? You don't want to see me carried off by cholera!'

Bull's-eye, she thinks, as a shudder passes through him.

'I wonder, though,' she goes on, in a dreamy, musing tone. 'Don't you ever get fed up, William, with living in the city? Don't you ever wish you lived somewhere pleasanter and cleaner?' She pauses, ready to feed him specifics ('like Notting Hill, perhaps, or Bayswater . . .') but biting her tongue on the words in case he should come out with them first.

'Well, actually, I live in Notting Hill,' he confesses.

Sugar allows her face to light up with the merest fraction of the joy she feels at this triumph in winning his confidence.

'Oh, how agreeable!' she cries. 'It's the ideal place, don't you think? Close to the heart of things, but so much more civilised.'

'It's all right, I suppose . . .' he says, fastening his collars. 'Some might call it unfashionable.'

'I don't think it's unfashionable at all! There are some grand parts to Notting Hill; everybody knows that. The streets between Westbourne Grove and Pembridge Square, for example, have a reputation for being awfully desirable.'

'But that's precisely where I live!'

At this, she throws her head back and chuckles, a rough low sound from her long white throat. In all things (says that chuckle) William Rackham can be depended upon to choose the best. 'I ought to have guessed,' she says.

'You guess damn near everything else,' he retorts ruefully.

She examines his eyes, weighs his tone, confirms he isn't angry with her, merely impressed. 'Feminine intuition,' she winks. 'I feel it, somehow.' (Her hands caress her bosom, stray down to her abdomen.) '*Deep* inside me.'

Then, judging she must let him go, she swings off the bed and walks over to the escritoire, from which all her own papers have been removed, leaving nothing but William's letter to the jute merchants. 'Now, we had better get this ready for the post.'

Fully dressed but for the shoes, William joins her at the writing-desk. Sugar stands demurely at his shoulder and watches as he re-reads the letter, watches as he judges it satisfactory, watches as he folds it into the envelope she hands him, watches as he addresses it and, without attempting to obscure her view, writes his home address on the reverse. Only then does she close her eyes in satisfaction. What so recently were the fruits of stealth have now been given to her freely. Nothing now remains for her to do but sink her teeth in.

'*Mercy,*' *he pleaded once more.*

William is gone, and Sugar sits at her desk, finishing the troublesome chapter at last.

I gripped the hilt of the dagger, but found I lacked the strength (the strength of will, perhaps, but also the strength of sinew, for slaughtering a man is no easy labour) to plunge the knife into this fellow's flesh and do my worst. I had performed the act so many times before; but that night, it was beyond me.

And yet, the man must die: he could not be released now that I had entrapped him! What, dear Reader, was I to do?

I put away my knife, and instead fetched up a soft cotton cloth. My helpless paramour ceased his struggle against his bonds, an expression of relief manifesting on his face. Even when I up-ended the flask of foul-smelling liquid into the cloth, he did not lose hope, imagining perhaps that I was about to swab his fevered brow.

Holding my own breath as if in sympathy, I pressed the poison rag to his mouth and nose, wholly sealing those orifices.

'Sweet dreams, my friend.'

TWELVE

Henry Rackham, unaccustomed as he is to ecstasy, is so happy he could die. He is in Mrs Fox's house, sitting in the chair which must have been her husband's, eating cake.

'Excuse me just a moment, Henry' was the last thing she said, before removing her exquisite self from the parlour. In his mind's eye, she still stands before him, her ginger dress brightening the room, her gentle manner warming the air. The very atmosphere is reluctant to let her go.

'More tea, Mr Rackham?'

Henry jerks, spilling cake crumbs into his lap. He'd forgotten about Mrs Fox's servant, Sarah; she'd ceased to exist for him. Yet there she stands, inconspicuous against the papery clutter of Mrs Fox's belongings, a stacked tea-tray on her forearms, a hint of a smirk on her face. In that smirk, Henry can see reflected what a moonstruck booby he must appear.

'I have sufficient, thank you,' he says.

All at once, his happiness has left him – or rather, he has pushed it to arm's length, the better to subject it to scrutiny. What *is* this happiness, really? Nothing more or less than captivation by a member of the fair sex. And captivation is a frightening thing.

Granted, he's not a Catholic: he could, if he wished, be both a clergyman *and* a husband. Mrs Fox, for her part, is a widow: that is, free. But, leaving aside the unlikelihood of her wanting a dull and awkward fellow like him, there remains, in Henry's mind, a religious obstacle.

This captivation . . . This infatuation . . . This *love*, if he dares call it that, in earshot of the Almighty . . . This *love* has the power to steal away so much time – whole hours and days – which might otherwise have been devoted to the work of God. Good works are frugal with time; love for a woman squanders it. It is possible to follow the example of Jesus on a dozen occasions in a single morning, and still have energy for more; yet dwelling upon the wishes – even the imagined wishes – of a beloved can swallow up all one's waking hours, and achieve nothing.

Henry knows! Too often, the time that elapses between one meeting with Mrs Fox and the next is a dream, a mere intermission. She need only smile at him, and he cherishes that smile to the exclusion of all else. Days pass, life goes on, yet the best part of him is given over to the memory of that smile. How can this be?

Henry sips his tea, uneasy under the gaze of Sarah. She gazes too directly, he feels; there's no hope of him picking the crumbs off his lap without her observing him at it. What's wrong with the girl? Perhaps, when it comes to servants, the rehabilitated fallen can never be quite as discreet as those who never fell in the first place. Sweat breaks out on Henry's forehead, explicable (he hopes) by the steam rising from his tea-cup. This girl – this protégée of the Rescue Society – is she essentially any different from the trollops he's seen in St Giles? Underneath her dowdy clothing, a quantity of naked flesh is contained, a living, breathing vessel of sinful history.

She's not beautiful, this Sarah – at least, not beautiful to him. She is a provocative reminder of the female sex in its fallen state, but as an individual she leaves him unmoved. The thought of Mrs Fox's gloved hand clasped momentarily inside his own is far more seductive than any fantasy this rescued wanton can give rise to. And yet she's a similar age to Mrs Fox, a similar size, a similar shape . . . How is it possible for him to be entranced by the one, and indifferent to the other? What is God trying to teach him?

The servant walks away, and Henry attends to his trousers. What do the great Christian philosophers have to say on this matter? A woman, they remind him, flourishes and dies like a flower. A decade or two sees the passing of her beauty, a few decades more the passing of its beholders, and finally the woman herself returns to dust. Almighty God, by contrast, lives for ever, and is the author of all beauty, having shaped it in his hands in the very first week of Creation.

And yet, how much more difficult it is to love God with the passion that a beautiful woman inspires! Can this truly be a part of God's plan?

Are desiccated woman-haters like MacLeish the only men suited for the cloth? And what's become of Mrs Fox? She said she'd only be a moment . . . the vision of her ginger dress has faded from the air in front of him, the warm traces of her voice have evaporated in the silence.

Henry smiles sadly, there in Bertie Fox's chair. What is he to do? His desire to impress Mrs Fox is the only thing that may lend him the courage to take Holy Orders; yet, if he were to win Emmeline's love, would he care a fig for anything else in the world? He was miserable all his life until he met her – could he resist the siren call of animal contentment if she were his? How shameful that he has always greeted the bounties of Providence with a heavy heart, but when given an opportunity to drink tea in the parlour of a pretty widow he feels such joy that he must suppress the urge to rock in his seat! God save from happiness the man who would better the world!

But what's that sound? From upstairs, muffled by the floors and passage-ways of Mrs Fox's little house . . . Is it . . . coughing? Yes: a horrifying, convulsive cough such as he has heard issuing from dark cellars in filthy slums . . . Can this be the same voice as he has grown to love?

For another couple of minutes, Henry sits waiting and listening, stiff with anxiety. Then Mrs Fox returns to the parlour, flushed in the cheeks, but otherwise quite well-looking and calm.

'I'm sorry to have kept you waiting, Henry,' she says, in tones as smooth as linctus.

Agnes lowers the latest issue of *The Illustrated London News* to her lap, offended and upset. An article has just informed her that the average Englishwoman has 21,917 days to live. Why, oh *why* must newspapers always be so disagreeable? Have they nothing better to do? The world is going to the dogs.

She rises, letting the newspaper fall to the floor, and walks to the window. After checking the sill for dirt (the first flying insects of the season have been spawned, unfortunately, and one cannot be too careful), she rests her hands on the edge and her hot clammy forehead against the frigid glass, and looks down into the garden. The old poplar tree is pimpled with buds, but afflicted also with green fungus; the lawn below is clean-shaven and, here and there, scraped down to the dark soil by scythe and hoe. It makes Agnes melancholy to see what Shears is doing to the garden. Not that she wasn't thoroughly ashamed of the Rackham grounds as they were before he came, but now that they've been brought to heel, she misses the bright daisies around the trees and the dark green sprouts of sword-grass among the paving-stones, especially as nothing has been put in their place yet. Shears is waiting, he says, for the grass to grow back 'right'.

Agnes can feel one of her bouts of tearfulness coming on, and grips the window-ledge hard to suppress it. But one by one, the tears for the daisies and the wild grass roll down her cheeks, and the more she blinks the more freely they flow.

21,917 days. Less in her case, as she's been alive for so long already. How many days are left to her? She has forgotten all the arithmetic she ever knew; the challenge is impossible. Only one thing is clear: the days of her life are, in the cruellest and crudest sense, numbered.

It wasn't always thus, she knows. Women in the time of Moses lived spans unheard-of now, at least in England. Even today, in the Orient and the further reaches of the Empire, there are to be found wise men (and wise women, surely?) who have solved the riddle of ageing and physical injury, and survived unscathed for generations. Their secrets are hinted at in the Spiritualism pamphlets Agnes has hidden inside her embroidery basket; there are authenticated drawings of miracles – holy men emerging spry and smiling from six months' burial, exotic black gentlemen dancing on flames, and so forth. No doubt there exist other books – ancient manuals of forbidden knowledge – which explain all the techniques in detail. Everything that's known to Man is published *somewhere* – but whether Mudie's Circulating Library will let a curious woman see it is another matter.

Oh, but what use is there in thinking about it! She's cursed, it's all too late for her, God has turned his back, the garden is ruined, her head aches, none of her dresses is the right colour, Mrs Jerrold scorned to reply to her letter, her hair-brush is always thick with hair, the sky darkens ominously when she so much as dares to set foot outside the house. Choking, Agnes slides the window open and thrusts her twisted face into the fresh air.

In the grounds below, Janey the scullery maid appears from a door directly beneath Agnes's window, to fetch a bucket-load of rich soil for the mushroom cellar. Agnes can see the flesh of the girl's back straining at the buttons of her plain black dress, straining at the white knot of her pinafore's bow. All at once she feels a flush of compassion for this poor little drudge in her employ. Two heavy tears fall from her eyes, straight down at the girl, but the wind blows them away before they reach the already retreating body.

It's only when Mrs Rackham draws back from the window-sill, and adjusts her legs for balance, that she appreciates she has begun to bleed.

Of Mrs Rackham's subsequent behaviour her husband will soon be informed, but in those few minutes before it comes to the attention of the servants, William sits oblivious in his study, not having thought about Agnes for hours.

Although he has illness very much on his mind, it doesn't happen to be his wife's. A worry has been planted in his brain, and is growing there at an alarming rate – a weed of anxiety. Sugar's innocent jest about cholera has reminded him of some grim statistics: every day, the diseases bred in the unhygienic conditions of inner London claim a certain number of lives – not least those of prostitutes. Yes, Sugar appears fresh as a rose, but by her own admission it isn't easy; all around her is filth and damp and decay. Who knows what foulness her stable-mates bring into the house? Who knows what contagions hang around the walls of Mrs Castaway's, threatening to seep into Sugar's bedroom? She deserves better – and so, of course, does he. Must he tramp through a quagmire of dung to reach his lover? It's clear what he must do – how simple the solution is! He has the funds, after all! Why, in the past two months, according to the books, sales of lavender water alone—

An erratic knocking at his door interrupts his calculations.

'Come in,' he calls.

The door swings open, and an agitated Letty is revealed.

'Oh Mr Rackham sir, I'm sorry sir, but, oh, Mr Rackham . . .' Her eyes swivel about in their sockets, looking back and forth from William to the stairs she's just run up; her body sways obsequiously.

'Well?' prompts William. 'What *is* it, Letty?'

'It's *Mrs* Rackham, sir,' she pipes. 'Doctor Curlew has already been sent for, sir, but . . . I thought you might wish to see for yourself . . . we closed the door at once . . . nothing's been disturbed . . .'

'Oh for goodness' sake!' exclaims William, as exasperated by all this intrigue as he is unnerved by it. 'Show me this disaster.' And he follows Letty hurriedly downstairs, buttoning his waistcoat as he goes.

★   ★   ★

In Mrs Fox's parlour, Mrs Fox is doing a rather impolite thing in plain view of her visitor. She is folding sheets of paper from a stack in her lap, inserting them in envelopes, and licking the edges, all the while continuing her conversation. The first time Henry Rackham witnessed this, months ago, he was no less taken aback than if she'd raised a mirror to her face and begun picking her teeth; now, he's used to it. There are simply not enough hours in the day for all of her activities, so some must be performed simultaneously.

'May I help you?' Henry suggests.

'Please,' she says, and hands him half the stack.

'What *are* these?'

'Bible verses,' she says. 'For night shelters.'

'Oh.' He glances at a sheet before folding it. The words of Psalm 31 are instantly recognisable: 'Have mercy upon me, O Lord, for I am in trouble: mine eye is consumed with grief, yea, my soul and my belly . . .' and so on, up to the exhortation to be of good courage. Mrs Fox's handwriting is remarkably legible, given the number of times she's had to transcribe the same few passages.

Henry folds, inserts, licks, presses tight.

'But can the unfortunates in the night shelters read?' he asks.

'Destitution can come to anyone,' she says, folding, folding. 'In any case, these verses are for the wardens and the visiting nurses to read aloud. They walk up and down the long aisles of beds, you know, reciting anything they think might comfort the sleepless.'

'Noble work.'

'*You* could do it, Henry, if you wished. They won't let *me* — they say they couldn't guarantee my safety. As if that were in anyone's hands but God's.'

Silence falls, except for the whispery sound of their folding and licking. The wordless simplicity of this shared activity is, to Henry, almost unbearably satisfying; he would be happy to spend the next fifty years sitting here in Mrs Fox's parlour, helping her with her correspondence. Sadly, there are only so many night shelters in Britain, and the envelopes are soon filled. Mrs Fox squints and licks her lips, miming her disgust at the acrid taste on her pink tongue — on his tongue, too.

'Cocoa is the answer,' she assures him.

★ ★ ★

Letty has led her master through passages he has not seen more than a half dozen times since taking on the house that bears his name; passages made for servants to scuttle along. Now she and William Rackham stand at the kitchen door. By dumb show she communicates to him that, if neither of them makes the slightest noise, and if they enter the kitchen with the utmost stealth, they're likely to observe an extraordinary thing.

William, sorely tempted to cast aside this foolishness and shove on through, resists the temptation and does as Letty suggests. Noiselessly, like a stage curtain parting, the door is nudged open, to reveal not just the harshly-lit, high-ceilinged cell in which all his food is prepared, but also (when he lowers his eyes) two women engaged in an act which shouldn't have shocked him in the least – had not one of the women been his wife.

For there, side by side on the stone floor, are Agnes and the scullery-maid Janey, both with their backs to him and their arses in the air, crawling along on their hands and knees, dipping scrubbing-brushes by turns into a large pail of soapy water. And conversing while they're at it.

Agnes scrubs with a less practised rhythm than Janey but with equal vigour, the tendons in her tiny hands standing out. The hems of her skirts are plastered to the wet floor, her bustled rear rocks to and fro, her slippered feet squirm for purchase.

'Well, ma'am,' Janey is saying. 'I *tries* to wash every dish the same, but the fing is, you don't expeck *fingerbowls* to be all that dirty, do yer?'

'No, no, of course not,' pants Agnes as she scrubs.

'Well, neiver did I,' rejoins the girl. 'Neiver did I. And so there I was, with Cook shoutin' and bawlin' at me, and wavin' these fingerbowls at me, and I carn't deny as they 'ad a cake o' grease all under 'em, but honest to crikey, ma'am, it was fingerbowls, and Cook must *know* they's normally always so *clean* . . .'

'Yes, yes,' sympathises the mistress. 'You poor girl.'

'And this . . . This 'ere's blood,' comments Janey, referring to an old stain on the wooden duckboard she and Mrs Rackham have before them now. 'Spilt ever so long ago but you can still see it, no matter 'ow many times I've scrubbed it.'

Mrs Rackham hunkers over to look, her shoulder touching Janey's.

'Let *me* try,' she urges breathlessly.

William chooses this moment to intervene. He strides into the kitchen, his shoes striking sharply on the wet floor, straight towards Agnes, who turns, still on her hands and knees, to face him. Janey doesn't turn, but squats petrified, like a dog caught in an act that warrants a beating.

'Hello, William,' says Agnes calmly, blinking at a strand of hair dangling in front of one sweaty eyebrow. 'Is Doctor Curlew here yet?'

But William doesn't respond with the impotent exasperation she expects. Instead, he reaches down and, sweeping one arm under her bustle and another against her back, he heaves her up, with a mighty grunt of effort, off the floor. As she slumps bewildered against his chest, he loudly declares,

'Doctor Curlew was sent for without my authority. I'll let him give you a sleeping draught, then ask him to leave. He's here too often and too long, in my opinion – and what good has it done you?'

And with that, he carries her out of the kitchen and through the several doors and passageways to the stairs.

'Inform me when Doctor Curlew arrives,' he orders the mortified Clara, who emerges from the shadows to trot up the stairs beside him. 'Tell him: a sleeping draught, no more! I shall be in my study.'

And that, once his wife is safely laid in her bed, is where William Rackham goes.

'You know, Henry,' muses Mrs Fox as she surveys the teetering pile of addressed envelopes between them, 'I feel blessed never to have had children.'

Henry almost inhales his mouthful of cocoa. 'Oh? Why is that?'

Mrs Fox leans back in her chair, allowing her face to be lit by a muted ray of sunlight filtering through the curtains. There are mauve veins on her temples that Henry has never noticed before, and a red flush on her Adam's apple – if women *have* Adam's apples, which he's not sure they do.

'I sometimes think I've only a finite measure of . . .' she closes her eyes, searching for the word '. . . of *juice* in me, to give to the world. If I'd had children, I would've given most of it to them, I imagine, whereas now . . .' She gestures at the philanthropic clutter all about, the charitable chaos of her house, half rueful, half contented.

'Does this mean,' ventures Henry, 'that you believe all Christian women ought to remain childless?'

'Oh, I'd never say "ought",' she replies. 'All the same, what an enormous power for Good it would unleash, don't you think?'

'But what of the Lord's commandment, "Be fruitful and multiply"?'

She smiles and looks out of the window, her eyes narrowed against the flickering afternoon light. It's probably only the clouds, but if one uses one's imagination, there might be a vast army marching past the house, numberless hordes blotting out the sun, a million-spoked wheel of bodies.

'I think there's been quite enough multiplication, don't you?' Mrs Fox sighs. 'We have filled the world up awfully well, haven't we, with frightened and hungry humans. The challenge now is what to *do* with them all . . .'

'Still, the miracle of new life . . .'

'Oh, Henry, if you could but see . . .' She is poised to speak of her experiences with the Rescue Society, but decides against it; evocations of pox-raddled infants stowed in prostitutes' cupboards and dead babies decomposing in the Thames are, over cocoa, too indecorous even for her.

'Honestly, Henry,' she says instead. 'There's nothing so very exceptional about bearing children. Acts of genuine charity, on the other hand . . . Perhaps you ought to try to see good works as eggs, and we women as hens. Fertilised, eggs are useless except to produce more chickens, but what a useful thing is a pure egg! And how very many eggs one hen can come up with!'

Henry blushes to the tips of his ears, the crimson flesh contrasting fetchingly with the gold of his hair. 'You are joking, surely.'

'Certainly not,' she smiles. 'Haven't you heard how your friends Bodley and Ashwell sum me up? I'm serious to the bone.' And she reclines suddenly in her chair, her head lolling back in apparent exhaustion. Henry watches, worried and fascinated, as she breathes deep, her bosom swelling out through her bodice, a subtle protuberance on either side growing visible through the soft fabric.

'M-Mrs Fox?' he stammers. 'Are you all right?'

When Doctor Curlew arrives at William Rackham's study, he finds himself greeted politely but without deference. This confirms in his mind the changes he's noticed in the Rackham household (and his place in it) over the last four or five visits. Gone are the armchair chats, the proffered cigars, the upward gaze of respect. Today Doctor Curlew feels as if he's been summoned as a mere dispenser of medicines, rather than invited as an eminent scholar of mental frailty.

'She will sleep now,' he says.

'Good,' says Rackham. 'You'll forgive me if we don't discuss the details of my wife's latest relapse. If relapse it is.'

'As you wish.'

Forgive me also, thinks William, *if I send you on your way before you suggest to me again that Agnes belongs in an asylum. I am a rich man and there is nothing I can't take care of in my own home. If Agnes goes mad and needs nurses, I shall employ them. If one day she is so beyond reason as to need strongmen to restrain her, I can afford them, too. I am above any man's pity, doctor: watch your place.*

William informs the doctor of the change henceforth from weekly to monthly visits, thanks him for coming, and hands him into Letty's care. He fancies, as Curlew is leaving, that he spots a glimmer of humiliation in the doctor's face – fancies mistakenly, for men like Doctor Curlew have so many human mirrors reflecting their importance back at them that when one mirror shows a less flattering image they simply turn to another. The doctor's next patient is an old woman who worships him; he'll look in the Rackhams' mirror again another time, when the light is different. Agnes Rackham is doomed; he need only wait.

With Curlew safely dispatched, William considers looking in on his wife, to make sure she's sleeping peacefully, but decides against it, for he knows she hates him coming into her bedroom. Nevertheless he wishes her well, and even conjures up a picture of her face wearing a tranquil expression.

Oddly enough, ever since he's known Sugar he has been able to spare Agnes many more affectionate and indulgent thoughts than before; she no longer weighs upon him as a burden, but rather as a sort of challenge. Just as the mastery of Rackham Perfumeries, once an odious impossibility, has become, with Sugar's encouragement, an interesting adventure, the vanquishing of Agnes's ills may likewise be a test of his powers. He knows what his little wife holds dear: he'll give her as much of it as she desires. He knows what she hates: he'll spare her the worst.

Serene and resolute, William returns to the work at hand: calculating exactly what's needed if he's to remove Sugar from the hazards of her current lodgings.

While her husband ponders the details, Agnes Rackham, brim-full of morphine, sleeps. A railway carriage, specially prepared for an Invalid, stands waiting in her dreams, wreathed in steam. She's tucked up inside it already, in a darling little bed by the window, and her head is raised up on pillows so that she can look out. The Station Master knocks at her window and asks her if she's all right and she replies 'I am'. Then the whistle blows, and she's on her way to the Convent of Health.

A fortnight later, we find William Rackham making his final inspection of the place where he intends, from this evening onwards, to spend as much time as his busy life will allow. The last of the hired men has left, having installed the last of the furniture; William is free now to survey the whole effect, and judge if these smart rooms in Priory Close, Marylebone, truly look as if they're worth the small fortune he's spent on them.

He loiters in the front passage, fussily rearranging a bunch of red roses in their crystal vase, clipping the stems of individual blooms where necessary, to achieve the perfect arrangement. He hasn't paid this much attention to aesthetic niceties since his dandy days at Cambridge. Sugar brings out the . . . Well, to be frank, she brings out the 'everything' in him. These elegant rooms are a fitting place for her – a jewel box to house the treasure she is.

The agreement with Mrs Castaway is already signed. The old woman complied without opposition; indeed, what else could she do? He's now ten times the man he was when he made the original contract with her, months ago – and she, by contrast, has diminished. In the creamy mid-morning sunshine of his most recent visit to her, she appeared less fearsome than in the red glare of firelight, her garish clothing paler, decked with motes of dust that swirled visibly in the sunbeams. He showed her receipts from the best furniture-makers, drapers, tilers, glass merchants, and many other craftsmen employed by George Hunt, Esq., as well as a bank account in Mr Hunt's name to the value of a thousand pounds. (Of course William knows he could, if he wished, abandon this pantomime now, but, seeing as it's effortless to maintain, why not spare himself the embarrassment? And as for the bank account in George W. Hunt's name – well, that might prove a damn good idea in its own right, if his researches into taxation are not mistaken!)

Mrs Castaway seemed mightily impressed with him, anyway, whatever name he bore, and she needed little persuasion (apart from an additional wad of money) to tear up the old contract and release Sugar into his sole proprietorship.

'I have cared for her as best I could, in the circumstances' were her final words. 'I have faith that you will do the same – to our everlasting benefit.'

Now, inspecting the rooms in Priory Close, William banishes the memory of her horrible, waxen, wrinkled old face, by confirming that everything is in order here – flawless and perfect. He assures himself of his love-nest's ideal location, its ideally appointed interior, its harmonious compromise between male and female tastes. He sits in each of the chairs and the *chaise-longue*, taking stock of all he can survey of the decor from each vantage point. He opens and closes all the little doors, windows, lids and ledges of all the cupboards, bookcases and whatnots to make sure they don't stick or creak.

The bathroom is a cause for concern. Has he done the right thing in having it plumbed for a hot bath? The pipes are ugly, resembling the elephantine apparatus in one of the Rackham factories; mightn't Sugar have been happier with a freestanding and opulent washtub? Ah, but he wants her to be clean, and these new 'Ardent' bathtubs are the very latest thing. The instructions for operating the hot water geyser may be a little complicated, and there *is* the risk of explosion, it's true, but Sugar is a clever girl, and won't allow herself to be blown to Kingdom Come by a bath, he's sure. And these new 'Ardent' designs are the safest yet. 'In the future, everyone will have one of these,' the salesman said. (To which William, tempted to give the fellow a lesson in business, almost responded: 'No, no, no, say rather: the common mortal will always wash in a glori-fied slop-pail – only the most fashionable and fortunate will have one of *these*.')

Then he walks slowly into the bedroom and, for the tenth time, scru-tinises the bed, feeling the sheets and coverlets between his fingers, reclin-ing momentarily against the pillows to take note of the prints on the walls (*chinoiserie*, not pornography) and the way the wallpaper's pattern glows in the light. All of it, he dares to be sure, will meet with her approval.

From the outside, the house is unremarkable; virtually identical to those on either side. The door into the front passage faces the street, but is half-hidden inside a dark guard-box of a porch, affording shelter from the scrutiny of the neighbours. There are no lodgers upstairs, as William has leased both floors and decided, for discretion's sake (though he could get a pretty penny for them in rent!), to leave the upper rooms empty.

William consults his watch. It is nine o'clock, on the evening of March seventeenth, 1875. Nothing remains but to visit Mrs Castaway's one last time, and fetch Sugar to her new home.

Henry Rackham is out walking in the half-developed fringes of civilisation, walking after bedtime, walking in the dark. He is not by nature a night owl, is Henry; he's the kind of man who wakes as soon as the sun rises and who has trouble suppressing his yawns once it sets. Yet tonight he has left his warm bed, hastily pulled some clothing over his night-shirt, and covered his dishevelled appearance with a long winter coat – and gone out walking.

For the first couple of miles there are lanes with houses and street-lamps, but these become sparser and sparser until they finally give way to the flickering campfires of distant gypsies, the eerie halo emanating from the Great Western Railway, and the natural illumination provided by God. A full moon shines down on him as he forges ahead. His enormous shadow runs along beside him, jumping nimbly over the uneven ground like a swarm of black rats. He ignores it, concentrating on his own clumsy feet, striding restlessly forward in unlaced shoes.

I am a monster, he is thinking.

In spite of the chill air and the challenge of finding his way through the dark, he still sees Emmeline Fox before his mind's eye – or whatever eye it is that can see her thus, splayed supine in a pillowy bower, naked and abandoned, inviting him to fall upon her. The vision is scarcely less vivid now than it was when he first cast his bed-sheets aside and repulsed the advances of lubricious sleep. Yet, for all its luminescent clarity, the picture of his dear friend is damnably false. He has never, in God's reality, glimpsed any of Mrs Fox's flesh except her face and hands; anything below the neck and above the wrists is his own wicked fantasy. He has given her a body of his own design, stitched seamlessly together from painted nudes of Greek goddesses and water nymphs, and grosser parts supplied to him by the Devil. Only the face is her own.

But, *Yes!* she whispers, her ghostly pale arms reaching languidly into the space between them. *Yes.*

Henry presses against the wooden railings of a low bridge over Grand Junction Canal, unbuttons his clothes, and cries for release.

'Where,' murmurs Sugar, 'are we going?'

The cab has rattled past all the likely places William might have intended for them to go when he commanded her (most unusually!) to dress for 'a little jaunt'. At first she thought he might have in mind a visit to The Fireside, for sentimental reasons; he's been queerly sentimental lately, reminiscing about their affaire as if they've known each other for years. But no, when she saw the cab waiting, she knew they weren't going to The Fireside. And now they've passed all the best pubs and eating houses, and have turned up the wrong road for the Cremorne Gardens.

'That's for me to know,' teases William gently, stroking her shoulder in the dimness of the cabin, 'and you to find out.'

Sugar loathes pranks and riddles of all kinds. 'How exciting!' she breathes, and presses her nose to the window.

William finds this child-like curiosity adorable – and a most pleasing contrast to the way the newly-married Agnes behaved on the day he took her to *her* new home. Agnes looked behind her all the way, however much he implored her not to; Sugar is looking ahead with naked anticipation. Agnes was so irksome (snivelling and fretting) that he wished he could knock her insensible, not to wake until snugly ensconced in the new house; Sugar he wants to lift onto his lap, right here in the cab, so that the vibrations of the carriage on the bumpy road help her ride his cockstand. But, apart from stroking her shoulder, he does nothing: this is a momentous occasion in her life – in both their lives – and must not be spoiled.

Meanwhile, Sugar sits watching the dark, eyes wide. Is William taking her to his home in Notting Hill? No, they've turned right at Edgware Road, instead of carrying straight on. Is he taking her to some deserted place outside the city, the better to murder her and dump her corpse? In her own novel she's described so many such murders that the possibility seems quite real to her; in any case, don't prostitutes die at the hands of their men all the time? Only last week, according to Amy, a woman was found headless and 'interfered with' on Hampstead Heath . . .

One sideways glance at Rackham reassures her: he's radiant with smugness and desire. So, she returns her nose to the glass, realigning her mouth with the expanding crest of condensation she has breathed there.

At the end of the journey, she is made to alight in a dark close, a very modern-looking terrace whose façades are all identical. Inadequate lamp-light is intercepted by a pair of massive stately trees, each with branches of Gothic complication. As the cab rattles away into the distance, a ceme-tery quiet descends, and Sugar is led by the arm into the pitch-black porch of one of these strange new buildings.

William Rackham is at her side, an obscure figure in the darkness; she can hear his breathing and the rustle of her skirts as he brushes against them in his search for the key-hole. How quiet it is here, for her to be able to hear such things! What sort of place is this, that leaves its air so vacant? All of a sudden she's under the sway of an unknown, but potent, emotion. Her heart thuds, her legs grow weak and begin to tremble – almost as if she were about to be murdered after all. A match is struck with a sound like fabric tearing; she sees William's face illuminated in the lucifer's flicker as he bends to unlock the door. His bewhiskered features are utterly un-familiar to her.

This man is changing my life, she thinks as the key turns and the door swings open. *My life is being tossed like a coin.*

William lights the hallway lamp and instructs Sugar to stand under-neath it while he hurries into each of the dark rooms beyond, lighting their lamps too. Then he returns and takes her gently by the arm.

'This,' he says, extending his arm theatrically, 'is yours. All yours.'

For a moment everything is silent and motionless, a *tableau vivant* made up of three elements: a man, a woman, and a vase of red roses.

Then, 'Oh William!' the astonished Sugar exclaims, as Rackham leads her into the sitting-room. 'Oh, dear God!' All the way here, she's been preparing herself to play-act, whatever his little surprise should prove to be; but now there's no need for play-acting, as she reels in stupefaction.

'You're trembling,' he observes, cupping her hand inside both of his, to authenticate the phenomenon. 'Why are you trembling?'

'Oh William!' Her eyes are wet as she looks back and forth between him and the unbelievably sumptuous room. 'Oh William!'

At first he's taken aback by this display of gratitude, shyly distrust-ing it in a way that he's never distrusted her displays of lust. As soon as he realises she's genuinely overwhelmed, he swells with pride, to have been the engineer of such a transport of delight. She seems in danger of swooning, so he takes her by the shoulders and turns her to face him. Adroitly he unknots the silken ribbon under her chin and, as he lifts her hat off, eases the pins out of her hair, so that her mass of golden-ochre curls spills down like newly-shorn wool out of a basket. He feels a pain in his heart: if only this instant could be spun out forever!

'Well?' he demands, teasingly. 'Aren't you going to explore your new home?'

'Oh *yes!*' cries the girl, springing away from him. He watches, beaming, as she dances around the room, acquainting herself physically with everything, laying claim to objects and surfaces with a touch of her palm, then dashing through the door to the next room. As she does so, William can't help recalling Agnes moving through the house in Chepstow Villas on her first day like a sick and petulant child, blind to everything, oblivious to all his preparations.

'I hope I've thought of everything,' he murmurs into her ear, having caught up with her as she stands, entranced, at the writing-desk in the study. She accepts his kisses in a daze, staring down at her reflection in the varnished wood.

'What *is* this room?' she asks.

He caresses her neck with his bearded jaw. 'Sewing-room, dressing-room, study – whatever you like. I didn't put much in it – thought you might need a thing or two from your old room at Mrs Castaway's.'

'She knows?'

'Of course she knows. It's all arranged.'

Sugar's face goes white. Nightmare visions are suddenly before her: a vision of an old woman in blood-red dress, mounting the staircase to Sugar's bedroom; a vision of a cupboard door swinging open to reveal the white manuscript of *The Fall and Rise of Sugar*. Mrs Castaway mustn't touch those pages! In those pages, a madam called 'Mrs Jettison' is blamed for many, many things – principally the violation of her own innocent daughter, the intrepid heroine.

'My room . . . my *old* room . . .' she falters. 'What . . . what arrangements . . .'

'Don't worry,' Rackham laughs. 'I have your privacy very much in mind. Nothing will be touched until you remove it. I'll arrange for that too, whenever you wish.' And he strokes her face, to soothe some colour back into it.

Bewildered, Sugar walks over to the French windows, watching her quartered reflection approach the glass. The panes are at fractionally different angles, so the four portions of her image don't quite meet, until she moves so near to the glass that she becomes transparent and disappears altogether. Outside, there's a tiny walled-in garden, difficult to make out in the darkness, but abundant with . . . well, *some* sort of greenery – living proof that her new home is at ground level, in far more verdant surrounds than Silver Street. Her doubts fall away from her, and the exhilaration returns.

'Oh, William,' she cries once more. 'Is all this really for me alone?'

'Yes, yes,' he laughs. 'For *us* alone. I've leased it for a lifetime.'

'Oh, William!'

And she's off again, tearing off her gloves and dropping them on the floor in order to run her hands along the spines of the books in the book-case and the embossed candy-stripe of the wallpaper. She skips from room to room with William following on behind, and in each she performs the same dance of celebration and tactile acquaintance. Such cart-loads of things Rackham has bought for her! The place is crammed with bric-a-brac: useless, useful, ugly, beautiful, ingenious, impractical: and all, as far as she can tell, expensive.

'Let me show you, let me show you!' he keeps saying. 'There's a bath, with warm water. It's simple to use. Even a child . . .'

And he demonstrates the procedures for enjoying all the luxury of the modern age without the risk of mishaps.

'Repeat the sequence,' he urges her, for she's rather dazed. 'Show me you understand.' And she does, she does.

As the wealth that William has invested in her sinks into Sugar's brain, she moves faster and faster, whirling from room to room, from table to cabinet to bookcase, sliding her back against the walls like an animal in heat. Instead of words she utters such a variety of appreciative squeals and moans that William seizes her wrist and leads her to the bed, a king-sized monster even more arabesque than the one they know so intimately.

He catches her appraising the bed-head, quizzical, even as she unbuttons her boots: there's no looking-glass affixed there, no reflection except what the polished grain of dark wood offers. William frowns, wondering if he's made the right decision: he couldn't bring himself to have a mirror rudely screwed into the lustrous teak. Oh, he considered it, calling to mind how much he liked to see, in the mirror on Sugar's old bed, his stiff manhood disappearing into her and emerging wet and slick. He even went so far as to say to the furniture-maker, 'I wonder, my good man, if it would be possible . . .'

But then he changed his mind in mid-sentence, and concluded, '. . . to carve a small, ornamental "R" just here, near the top?'

Now William carefully examines Sugar's face, even as she prepares her body for him.

'Do you miss the looking-glass?' he asks her.

She laughs. 'What do I need to look at myself for, when I have you to look at me?'

She's wearing only her camisole now, and his trousers are bulging. He pushes her down on the mattress, and observes her eyes widen as she stares up at the canopy of the bed – yes, that's finest Belgian lace! It's as much as William can manage, to resist the temptation to tell her everything: the trouble he went to in choosing the furnishings, the rare and elusive objects he found, the bargains he struck . . . But it's better this way, not to puncture the fairytale magic of his gift.

God almighty, her cunt is wetter than he's ever known it before! What a state she is in! And all because of him!

'But dear William,' she gasps as he enters her. 'There's no kitchen.'

'Kitchen?' He's seconds away from bursting. 'You don't need a kitchen, you goose,' he groans. 'I'll . . . give you . . . all you need . . .' And he spurts his seed inside her.

Afterwards, Sugar lies in his arms, kissing his chest a hundred times, asking forgiveness for appearing preoccupied at such a delicate moment. She was overwhelmed, she says, by his generosity – still is. It's too much to take in all at once, her poor head is in a spin, but her cunt knows what's what, as he can attest! And if he bears any regret that his climax was a solitary one, unaccompanied (for the first time since they met) by the simultaneous eruption of her own ecstasy, well, she's more than willing to wait until his manhood has revived. Or if he prefers, shall she take it in her mouth? The taste of it alone is enough, she assures him, to bring her to the brink of ecstasy.

No, William sighs, it's all right. He is tired; this has been a weighty day for him too. And she was right to wonder how she's to get fed in this new home of hers. But it's all taken care of. He – or rather his bank – will post her a weekly allowance, more than sufficient for her independence. There are a number of excellent establishments on Marylebone Road, including breakfast rooms at the Aldsworth Hotel that he has no hesitation recommending; the omelettes there are especially good. The Warwick is superb for fish: does she like fish? Yes, she adores fish. What fish in particular? Oh, all fish. And she's not to worry about keeping her rooms clean, either, or the laundry: he'll procure a girl for her . . .

'Oh no, William, that really isn't necessary,' Sugar protests. 'I am really *very* domesticated, you know, when I want to be.' (Completely untrue, she inwardly concedes – she's never done a stroke of housework in her life. But if these rooms are to be her own, let them *truly* be her own!)

Indeed, as she and William lie on their newly christened bed together, she's growing increasingly desperate to be alone. This gift of his . . . She won't be able to believe it exists until he disappears and it fails to disappear with him. What can she do to make him go! Her kisses on his chest increase in frequency, like a nervous tic; she pecks softly in a line towards his genitals, hoping to force the issue one way or the other.

'I must go,' he says, patting her between the shoulder-blades.

'So soon?' she croons.

'Duty calls.' He is already donning his shirt. 'In any case, I expect you'll be wanting to get familiar with your little nest.'

'*Our* little nest,' she demurs. (*There* are your trousers, you fool! *There*!)

Minutes later, as he's stroking her goodbye, she kisses his fingers, and says, 'It's as if all my birthdays have come at once.'

'Dear Heaven!' Rackham declares. 'I don't even know when your birthday is!'

Sugar smiles as she selects, from the jumble of contending responses in her head, the perfect sentence to send him on his way, *les mots justes* for the closure of this transaction.

'*This* will be my birthday from now on,' she says.

After the door shuts, Sugar lies unmoving for a minute or two, in case William returns. Then, slowly, she swings her legs over the side of the bed, finds her feet on the unfamiliar floor, and stands up. Her camisole, much rumpled, falls down over her breasts. Pensively she smooths it with her palms, wondering if William's boast that he has thought of 'everything' includes such a thing as an iron. Item by item she re-dresses herself. With a tiny clothes-brush from her reticule she brushes her skirts, which come up nicely. Exchanging the clothes-brush for a hand-mirror, she tidies her hair a little, and peels a flake or two of skin from her dry lips before leaving the bedroom.

'*Slowly, slowly*,' she cautions herself, aloud. 'You've all the time in the world now.'

First of all she goes to . . . her study. Yes, her study. She stands at the French windows, looking out at the garden. In the morning it will be sunlit, won't it, and dew will be twinkling on the neat beds of grass and the exotic plants she doesn't have names for. Through her one little window at Mrs Castaway's, there was never anything to see except dirty roof-tops and impatient human traffic; here, she has grass and . . . pretty green stuff.

The red roses in the hallway are another matter: they get up her nose, quite literally. How long ought she leave them there in that vase, before tossing them in the garbage where they belong? Always she has detested cut flowers, and roses in particular: their smell and the way they fall apart when past their bloom. The flowers she can tolerate – hyacinths, lilies, orchids – die firm on their stems, in one piece to the last.

Still, the bouquet is an emblem of the care with which William Rackham has prepared this place for her. What a lot of trouble he has gone to: how richly he has repaid the trouble *she* has gone to in cultivating him! The more she explores her rooms, the more evidence she finds of his thoughtfulness: the glove-stretcher and the glove-powderer, the shoe tree and the ring stand, the bellows for the fire, the bedwarming pans. Did he really think of all these things, or did he simply blunder through a Regent Street emporium and buy every damn thing in sight? Certainly there are some queer objects lying about. A magnetic brush, still in its box, claims to curl hair and cure bilious headaches. An expertly stuffed ermine lies curled up in front of her wardrobe as though waiting to be skinned, made into a stole, and hung up inside. Ornaments of silver, glass, pottery and brass jostle one another on the mantelpieces. Two dressing-tables stand side by side, one larger than the other but less attractively finished, inviting the conclusion that Rackham, after buying the one, had second thoughts and bought the other as well, leaving the final choice to her. Does this signal his blessing on any changes she wishes to make? Too soon to tell.

Damn those roses! They're filling the whole place with their stink . . . but no, that's not possible, not from one vase of blooms. There's a mysterious surfeit of perfume in the atmosphere, as if the entire building has been sponged with scented soap. Sugar wrenches the French windows open, and fresh night air shoots up her nostrils. She pokes her face out into the dark, breathing deeply, sniffing the subtle odour of wet grass and the unsubtle *absence* of all those smells she's so accustomed to: meat and fish, the droppings of cart-horses and ponies, sullied water gurgling down drainpipes.

A warm reflux of semen trickles down her thighs and into her pantalettes as she stands sniffing; she winces, clutches herself, pushes the windows shut with her free hand. What to do next? Wouldn't it be astonishing if she opened the door of this wardrobe here and found, just where she needed it to be, the big silvery bowl and the box of poison powders? She opens the wardrobe door. Empty.

She runs back to the bedroom, checks under the bed on both sides. No chamber-pot. What does Rackham think she is? A . . . ? The word she's looking for, if it exists, eludes her . . . In any case, she's just remembered that she has a bathroom. Sweet Jesus, a bathroom! She stumbles there immediately.

It's an eerie little chamber, with a burnished wooden floor the colour of stewed tea, and shiny tricoloured walls – glazed bronze tiles on the dado, then a band of black wallpaper like a ribbon round the room, then a satiny coat of mustard-yellow paint up to the ceiling. All this casts a most peculiar light on the ceramic bathtub, washbasin and lavatory.

Sugar sits on the privy. It's just like the one downstairs at Mrs Castaway's, except it smells absurdly of roses: an essence sprinkled in the water. *I'll soon fix that*, she thinks, and empties her aching bladder. She runs some water into the washbasin as she pisses, preparing to wash with a luxurious cotton towel. Every horizontal surface, she notes, is crowded with Rackham produce: soaps of all sizes and colours, bath salts, bottles of unguent, pots of cream, canisters of powder. The 'R's are all facing front, their orientation identical. She pictures William spending an age in here, arranging the containers thus, standing back to appraise the 'R's with narrowed eyes, and it makes her shiver in pleasure and fear. How he craves to please her! How insatiable is his need for recognition! She'll have to anoint herself with every damned thing here, and sing its praises to him afterwards, if she knows what's good for her.

But not tonight. Sugar flips the lavatory lever, and all her waste, magically, is swallowed into an underground Elsewhere.

Emerging from the bathroom, she notes that the rest of the place is still there, luxurious and silent, littered with shiny objects she's only just beginning to recognise as her own. Abruptly, her shoulders begin to shake and tears spring into her eyes.

'Oh dear God,' she sobs, 'I'm *free!*'

She bursts into motion once more, dashing from room to room again, but this time more badly behaved: not girlish, not squealing in musical delight, but rampaging like a gutter infant, grunting and crying in ugly jubilation.

'It's all *mine*! It's all for *me!*'

She snatches the roses from their vase, crushing their stems in her fist, and starts waving them around in a mad spilth of water. She whacks the blooms against the nearest doorjamb, crowing with angry satisfaction as the petals fly apart. She wheels about, whipping the disintegrating bouquet against the walls, until the floor is strewn with red and the stems are limp and splintered.

Then, ashamed and unnerved by her orgy, she stumbles over to the bookcase – the beautifully crafted, lustrously polished, glass-fronted, locked-with-a-brass-key bookcase that is *hers*, all hers – and swings its doors wide open. She selects from the shelves the most important-looking volume, carries it to the armchair in front of the fire, and, seating herself, begins to read. Or at least, pretends to; her mind has come too far adrift from its moorings for her to admit she's not actually reading. One elbow on the chair's arm, she sits demurely; she is buzzing with demureness. One hand cradles the book in her lap, the other presses knuckles against her cheek in a cosmetic pose of support. Sugar stares at the printed page, but what she pictures before her glassy eyes is not the words but herself sitting alone in an elegant, well-furnished room, Sugar demurely reading a book, anchored to this room of her own by a heavy volume.

For a measureless time she sits like this, every so often turning a page. She watches, from somewhere on high, the pale, intricately patterned fingers moving over the minute print. But for the ichthyosis afflicting them, they might be the hands of a well-born lady (and might there not be ladies afflicted by this condition?) moving across the pages. Sugar feels certain that somewhere, in a tranquil mansion, a genuine lady must at this very moment be sitting just as she is here, reading a book. The two of them are as one, reading together.

Eventually, however, the spell stretches thin, unfeasibly thin. She concedes she is not reading this book; that she has not the faintest idea what is in it nor even what it is called. In the same way as a painter, upon realising the light has failed, resignedly packs up his materials, Sugar shuts her book and lays it on the floor beside her chair. And, when she stands up, she finds she's preposterously weary, weak at the knees and damp with sweat from head to foot.

She staggers into the bedroom and sits heavily on the bed. A crystal jug of water and a glass tumbler stand side by side on the bedside table: Sugar snatches up the jug and pours water directly into her mouth, heedless of spillage, two pints of it at least. When she's satisfied, she sinks back on the pillows, her neck and breast plastered with wet hair.

'Yes, I *am* free,' she says again, but less ecstatically now. Her eyelids are falling shut; parts of her body feel numb, already asleep. She staggers to her feet in order to inspect the bedroom wardrobe. Empty. Of all the things Rackham has taken it upon himself to select for her, he has stopped short of nightwear. Couldn't he have told her, when he came to fetch her from Mrs Castaway's, to take a night-dress along! . . . Ah, but that would have given away his grand surprise.

Reeling with exhaustion, Sugar manages to extinguish all the lights and return to the bedroom, where she pulls off her clothing, lets it fall in a heap on the floor, and crawls into bed. After only a few moments, however, she crawls out again, her sleep-hungry body protesting against this delay at the very brink of sweet oblivion. Kneeling beside the bed, she lifts a corner of the sheet off the mattress, to verify what she knows already: that this bed, unlike her old bed at Mrs Castaway's, doesn't have several layers of clean sheets and waxed canvas. The sheet Rackham has soiled is the only sheet there is. She yanks it off the bed, and lays her naked body down on the bare mattress.

You can buy all the sheets you want tomorrow, she tells herself, as the warm luxurious covers settle over her. Gratefully she allows unconsciousness to spread up, like a tide, into her head. In the morning she will give thought to what she needs that Rackham hasn't provided; in the morning she will design the armour of an independent life.

In the morning she will discover she's forgotten to extinguish the fires, and the hearths will be black with exhausted ash, and there will be no warmth wafting up from Mrs Castaway's overheated parlour downstairs, and no Christopher waiting outside her door with a bucket of coals. Instead she will have to suffer, for the first time in her life, the unmitigated rawness of a new day.

PART 3

The Private Rooms and the Public Haunts

THIRTEEN

pproaching the city by an unfamiliar route, her vision clouded by morning fog and the steam snorting up from the cab-horse's mouth, the elegant young woman feels as though she's never been here before. She'd thought she knew these streets like the back of her hand but, admittedly, even her own hands are a little strange to her, tightly enclosed in a virgin pair of the whitest dogskin gloves.

The Season has almost begun, and more and more of the Best People are leaving their country seats for London; Oxford Street is clogging up with human traffic, so the cab-man has veered off into the smaller streets, nimbly negotiating the intricacies of the social maze. One minute the elegant young woman is being pulled past elegant young houses built for the *nouveaux riches*, the next she's craning her head at older, grander terraces owned by the old and grand, the next she's rattling past ancient tenements which once housed peers and politicians but now, in overcrowded squalor, house a vast troop of serfs. Hollow-eyed men and women stare from every mews and stairwell, half-starved from the long wait for the Season, hungry for the work that it will bring. They can barely wait to start sweeping horse-shit from the path of advancing ladies, and taking in young gentlemen's washing.

At last the cab-man steers his horse into Great Marlborough Street and everything looks suddenly familiar.

'This will do!' cries the young lady.

The cab-man reins the horse in. 'Didn't you say Silver Street, miss?'

'Yes, but this will do,' repeats Sugar. Her courage is failing, and she needs more time before facing Mrs Castaway's. 'I feel a little giddy – a walk will do me good.'

The cab-man eyes her slyly as she alights. Her easy candour with him counts against her; she cannot be what he at first took her to be.

'Watch yer step, miss,' he grins.

She smiles back as she hands him the fare, a saucy quip on the tip of her tongue – why not share, to the full, this moment of recognition, rogue to rogue? But no, she might meet him again one day, with William in tow.

'I sh'll take care,' she says primly, and turns on her heel.

The sun has shed its cover of clouds by now, beaming all over the West End. The chilly air turns mild, but Sugar shivers beneath her dress and coat, for her camisole and pantalettes, clumsily washed in the bath-tub and dried in front of the fire, are still damp. Also, she had a mishap ironing one of the bed-sheets and burned a hole in it; she'll have to judge if her allowance (the first envelope from Rackham's banker arrived in this morning's post) is enough to defray such mishaps. He's given her an awful lot of money – enough to get a less elegant-looking woman instantly arrested, unless she took the bank-notes to a fence for conversion into coin – but maybe he won't send her so much in future, and this is just to get her started. Perhaps, to spare herself the embarrassment of asking Rackham for a laundry maid after all, she could buy herself new sheets and under-clothes every week! The thought is seductive – and shameful.

Carnaby Street is littered with beggars, many of them children. Some clutch worthless posies or punnets of watercress; others make no pretences, extending grubby palms and naked forearms that are bruised and blood-scabbed. Sugar knows all the tricks: the putrid shank of meat hidden inside a raggedy shirt, seeping pitifully through; the fake sores created with oatmeal, vinegar and berry juice; the soot-shadows under the eyes. She also knows that human misery is only too real, and there are drunken parents waiting to beat a child who fetches too little money home.

'Ha'penny, miss, ha'penny,' pleads a stunted girl in mud-coloured clothes and oversized bonnet. But Sugar has no small change, only a couple of new shillings and Rackham's bank-notes. She hesitates, fingers pinched and clumsy inside her new gloves; she keeps walking; the moment is gone.

At Mrs Castaway's, she lets herself in the back way. Although it seems wrong to sneak into the house like a thief, it seems equally wrong to knock at the front door without a customer at her side. If only the house could be magically emptied of people for the duration of her visit! But she knows that her mother scarcely ever leaves the parlour, that Katy is too ill to go out, and that Amy sleeps till midday.

Sugar creeps up the stairs to her room. The house smells the same: musty and overbearing, a stale accumulation of bandaged water pipes and cosmetic repairs to the crumbling plaster, of cigar smoke and alcohol sweat, of soap and candle-fat and perfume.

In her bedroom, a surprise. Four large wooden crates, sitting ready to be filled, lids leaning up against them, generously hemmed with tacks. Rackham really has thought of everything.

'A big giant brought 'em,' says Christopher from the doorway, his childish voice making Sugar jerk. 'Said 'e'd come back for 'em when 'e got the word.'

Sugar turns to face the boy. He has shoes on and his hair is combed, but otherwise he's just as she would expect to see him, standing in her doorway with his bare arms ruddy and swollen, ready for the day's load of dirty linen.

'Hello, Christopher.'

'Carried 'em on one shoulder, 'e did, 'eld wiv one finger. Like they was straw baskets.' Plainly, it's important to the boy not to be dragged into awkward adult complications. Sugar's abrupt disappearance from his life is nothing to get excited about; not compared to the amazing strength of the giant stranger who carried big wooden crates with one finger. Christopher looks straight at her like the African explorer-man on the tea-tin staring down the savages; if Sugar took him for the sort of fellow that gets attached to anyone, she's got another think coming.

Sugar chews her lips miserably as the seconds pass and Christopher shows no sign of moving.

'Good boxes, them,' he comments, as if in his young life he's had to master carpentry along with everything else. 'Good wood.'

Turning her back to him to hide her distress, Sugar begins to pack. Her novel, she finds, is safe and sound, apparently untouched during her absence. She fetches it to her breast, transfers it as quickly as she can to the bottom of the nearest crate. Still the boy's eyes grow large at the sight of all that scribbled paper.

'Didn't you never send them letters?' he asks.

'Plenty of time yet,' sighs Sugar.

Next she loads her books in — the proper, printed books written by other people. Richardson, Balzac, Hugo, Eugène Sue, Dickens, Mary Wollstonecraft, Mrs Pratt. A Manila folder containing cuttings from newspapers. Handfuls of penny dreadfuls with lurid covers: swooning or dead women, furtive-looking men, roof-tops and sewers. Pamphlets on venereal disease, on the shapes and measures of the criminal brain, on the feminine virtues, on preventing skin discoloration and other marks of age. Pornography, in verse and prose. A volume of Poe clearly stamped on the flyleaf, *Property of W. H. Smith's Subscription Library*, with a stern warning that all books containing maps or pictures will be carefully checked to be sure they are 'perfect in number and condition'. A New Testament given to Katy Lester by the Rescue Society. A slim volume, *Modern Irish Poets, 1873* (unread, the gift of a customer from Cork). And on and on, half a crate full.

'' Ave you read all them?'

Sugar begins to toss shoes and boots on top. 'No, Christopher.'

'Got more time for readin' in the new place?'

'I hope so.'

The ingredients for her douche she wraps in a towel and tucks under the slate-grey boots that need new soles and eyelets. There's no point taking the douche bowl now that she has her own bath-tub.

'Good bowl, that.'

'I don't need it, Christopher.'

He watches as she fills the second crate, a long oblong one that looks like an unvarnished coffin. It's ideal for Sugar's dresses — as Rackham no doubt anticipated. One by one, she lays the long garments into it, arranging the layers so that the shapely bodices and bulbous bustles pile up in equal measure. The dark green dress, the one she was wearing on the rainy night she met William, has, she notes, subtle dustings of mildew on the pleats.

The dresses fill two and a half crates; the hats and bonnets account for most of the remaining space. Bending down to cram the hat-boxes closer together, Sugar senses another presence in the doorway.

'So, what's he like, this Mr Hunt of yours?'

Amy has stepped across the threshold, obscuring Christopher behind her skirts. She's only half-dressed, indifferent to her shock of uncombed hair and the dark-areola'd breasts hanging loose inside her chemise. As always, that maternal bosom serves only to emphasise how completely she ignores her son, the unwanted product of her womb.

'No worse than most,' Sugar replies, but the crates lean heavy against the claim. 'Very generous, as you see,' she's forced to add.

'As I see,' says Amy, unsmiling.

Sugar tries to think of a topic of conversation that might interest a prostitute whose specialties are foul language and dripping molten candle-fat onto the genitals of respectable men, but her brains are crammed with what she's learned in bed with William. The analogy of odours as keys of an instrument? The difference between simple and compound perfumes? *Did you know, Amy, that from the odours available to us, we may produce, if we combine them correctly, the smell of almost any flower, except jasmine?*

'So how has everyone been?' sighs Sugar.

'Just as usual,' Amy replies. 'Katy's hangin' on, not dead yet. Me, I keep scum off the streets.'

'Any plans?'

'Plans?'

'For this room.'

'Her Downstairs is after Jennifer Pearce.'

'Jennifer Pearce? From Mrs Wallace's house?'

'What I said.'

Sugar breathes deeply, longing for rescue. Conversations with Amy have never been easy, but this one is exceptional. Sweat is breaking out under her fringe, and she's tempted to plead a dizzy turn and flee downstairs.

'Well,' says Amy suddenly, 'I'd better tart myself up for my own admirers. Today could be the day I meet my Prince, eh?' And she slouches out, knocking Christopher off-balance like a skittle.

Sugar sags where she stands, leaning her palms on the rim of a crate in fatigue.

'You know, Christopher,' she confesses to the boy, 'this isn't easy for me.'

'I'll do it for yer, then,' he says, and walks to her side, immediately laying hold of a spiky wooden lid. 'The man left 'is 'ammer, and the nails is all in.' Keen, he hefts the lid onto its matching crate, almost impaling Sugar's knuckles in the process.

'Yes . . . yes, you do that . . . thank you,' she says, stepping back, sick with inability to touch him, to kiss him, to ruffle his hair or stroke his cheek; sick with shame at the way she backs out towards the door and steps out on the landing – that same spot where, so many times, he has set down the pail of hot water for her. 'Mind your fingers, now . . . !'

And, to the sound of his happy hammering, she retreats below.

Hesitating at the back door of the house of ill repute known as Mrs Castaway's, Sugar gives herself permission to leave forever without saying any more goodbyes. Nothing happens; the hesitation is unbroken. Next, she tries to *force* herself to leave. Again, failure. Force is a language she understands, but only when it comes from without. She turns towards the parlour.

Her mother is ensconced in the usual spot, busy at her usual pursuit: the pasting of paper saints into scrapbooks. Sugar is unsurprised, yet disheartened, to find her at it again, scissors snickering in her bony claws, pot of paste at the ready. Her back is curved, the spine wilting over the table, the crimson bosom sagging, almost touching the low mound of images, a jumble of haloed maidens in shades of engraved grey, or pink and blue.

'No end to my labours,' she sighs to herself, or perhaps as a way of acknowledging Sugar's approach.

Sugar feels her brow spasm in annoyance. She knows only too well the lengths her mother goes to in order to ensure the endlessness of her labours; a small fortune per month is spent on books, journals, prints and holy cards, dispatched from all corners of the globe. Religious publishers from Pennsylvania to Rome are no doubt positive that the world's devoutest Christian is to be found right here in Silver Street, London.

'We-e-ell now,' croons Mrs Castaway, focusing her bloodshot eyes on a fresh Magdalen from the Bible Society of Madrid. 'Your cup rather runneth over, wouldn't you say?'

Sugar ignores the barb. The old woman can't help it, this harping on the soft fortune of the young, contrasted with her own lamentable fate. God himself could fall down on one knee before Mrs Castaway and propose, and she would dismiss it as a pitiful compensation for what she's suffered; Sugar could be burnt to death in a house fire, and Mrs Castaway would probably call her lucky, to have so much valuable property sacrificed just for her.

Sugar takes a long breath, glances at Katy Lester's 'cello case leaning against the empty armchair by the hearth.

'Katy never seems to get up anymore,' she remarks, her voice raised slightly to compete with Christopher's ceaseless banging upstairs.

'She was up yesterday, dear,' murmurs Mrs Castaway, deftly wielding her scissors to create another human-shaped snipsel. 'Played most attractively, I thought.'

'Is she still . . . working . . . ?'

Mrs Castaway lays the snipsel on an already crowded page of her scrapbook, experimenting with where it should go. She has complicated principles determining where the saints can be pasted; overlaps are permissible, but only to disguise incomplete bodies . . . This new weeping beauty could be glued so as to cover another's missing right hand, and then the narrow wedge of space remaining could be filled with . . . where's that tiny wee one, from the French calendar . . . ?

'Mother, is Katy still working?' repeats Sugar, louder this time.

'Oh . . . Forgive me, dear. Yes, yes, of course she is.' Mrs Castaway stirs the glue-pot pensively. 'You know, the closer to death she comes, the more popular she is. I've had to turn callers away, can you imagine? Even extortionate fees don't seem to deter them.' Her eyes go misty, reflecting the perversity of an imperfect world, and her own regret that she's too old to take full advantage of it. 'Sanatoriums could make a fortune, if only they knew.'

The hammering from upstairs suddenly ceases, and silence falls. Nineteen years have passed since Mrs Castaway and Sugar embarked on their life together in the creaking warren of Church Lane; six years have passed since the howling night Mrs Castaway (then in much shabbier garb in the candle-flickering gloom of the old house) tiptoed up to Sugar's bed and told her she needn't shiver anymore: a kind gentleman had come to keep her warm. Ever since then, there has been something of the nightmare about Mrs Castaway, and her humanity has grown obscure. Sugar strains to recall a Mrs Castaway much farther removed in time, a mother less vinegary and more nourishing, a historical figure called simply 'Mother' who tucked her in at night and never mentioned where money came from. And all the while, the Mrs Castaway of here and now stirs her glue-pot, every so often removing the brush and anointing her scrapbook with a gob of adhesive gruel.

'I hear . . .' says Sugar, almost choking, 'I hear from Amy you're considering Jennifer Pearce as my replacement.'

'Nobody could replace you, dear,' the old woman smiles, her teeth flecked with scarlet.

Sugar winces; tries to disguise the wince with a twitch of her nose.

'I didn't think men were to Miss Pearce's taste.'

Mrs Castaway shrugs. 'Men are not to *anyone*'s taste, dear. Still, they rule the world and we must all fall on our knees before them, hmm?'

Sugar's arms have begun to itch, her forearms and wrists especially. Suppressing the temptation to pounce on them and scratch them raw, she tries to steer the conversation back to Jennifer Pearce. 'She's well known in flagellating circles, Mother. It makes me wonder if . . . if you're planning to change the character of the place.'

Mrs Castaway hunches over her handiwork, pushing the shoulder of the latest Magdalen a little closer to the hip of the adjacent saint while the glue is still viscid enough.

'Nothing stays the same forever, dear,' she mutters. 'Old ducks like me and Mrs Wallace, we're . . .' she looks up, eyes wide and theatrical, 'we are hawkers in the marketplace of passion, and we must find whatever niche is not already filled.'

Sugar seizes herself by the forearms, squeezes tight. *Why did you do it?* she thinks. *To your own daughter? Why?* It's a question she's never dared ask. She opens her mouth to speak.

'Wh–what was the arrangement?' she says. 'Between you and M-Mr Hunt, I mean?'

'Come now, Sugar,' chides Mrs Castaway. 'You're young and have your whole life ahead of you. You don't want to bother your pretty head with *business*. Leave that to the men. And to shrivelled old relics like me.'

Is that a glint of supplication in the old woman's shiny pink eyes? A glimmer of fear? Sugar is too despondent, and maddened by the itch, to pursue her further.

'I must go, Mother,' she says.

'Of course, dear, of course. Nothing to hold you here, is there? Onward and upward with Mr Hunt!' And again she bares her crimson-flecked teeth in a mirthless crescent of farewell.

A few minutes later, outside in Regent Street, Sugar tears off her gloves, pushes her tight sleeves up to the elbows and scratches furiously at her forearms until her skin is the texture of grated ginger-root. Only the fear of William Rackham's displeasure inhibits her from drawing blood.

'God damn God,' she whimpers, while smartly-dressed passers-by edge uneasily away from her, 'and all His horrible filthy Creation.'

★   ★   ★

Back in her rooms, her very own rooms in Marylebone, Sugar lies in the bath, almost wholly submerged in a coverlet of aromatic suds. The humid cubicle of air around her is vague with steam, the mustard colour of the walls softened to egg yellow. Dozens of little 'R's, on the bottles and jars and pots all about, twinkle through the lavender-scented mist.

Thirteen, she thinks. *I was thirteen.*

Below the water, her arms sting and prickle, a much preferable sensation to the itching. In one hand she clutches a sponge, bringing it up to her cheeks every time the tears tickle too much.

You understand, Mrs Castaway told her long ago, *that if we are to have a happy and harmonious house here, I can't treat you any differently from my other girls. We are in this together.* In what, Mother?

Sugar shuts her eyes tight and squeezes the sponge against them. Once upon a time this little sponge was alive and swam in the sea. Was it softer then, or hard and fleshy? She knows nothing about sponges, has never been to the sea, has never been outside London. What's to become of her? Will William tire of her and flush her back onto the streets?

He hasn't been to visit her since he installed her in these rooms, days and days ago. Frightfully busy, he said he would be . . . But how busy can he be, not to find time for his Sugar? Maybe he's tired of her already. If so, how long can she cling to this little nest? The rooms are paid for and her allowance is set to come directly from the bank, so there's nothing to fear except William himself. Maybe he'll lack the stomach to evict her? Maybe she can stay here for years provided she keeps very, very quiet . . . Maybe he'll pay a murderer to slit her throat . . .

Sugar laughs despite herself. What time of month is it? Likely as not she's brewing the curse, to be thinking thoughts as daft as these.

How much foam one little bottle of Rackham's Lait de Lavage makes! She must compliment William on it the next time he comes. Will he believe her, though, if she's sincere? How is she to tell him she admires something of his, if she really does admire it? What tone of voice could she use?

'Your bath lotion is a wonderful thing, William,' she says, in the privacy of her misty bower. Her words ring false, false as whores' kisses.

'Your bath lotion is *superb*.' She frowns, scoops a handful of froth from the surface of the water. She attempts to toss the trembling bubbles into the air, but they cling to her palm.

'I *love* your bath lotion,' she croons. But the word *love* rings falser than all the others put together.

For days, Sugar waits for William to come. He doesn't come. Why doesn't he come? How many of a man's waking hours can possibly be swallowed up by an already established, successful concern? Surely it's a simple matter of writing the occasional letter? Surely William doesn't have to oversee every tiny flower and approve its rate of growth?

On the night when she was first given these rooms, she felt as if she'd been allotted a little corner of Paradise. The slate was wiped clean, and she was determined to savour *everything* in her new life – the solitude, the silence, the freedom from filth, the fresh air, her little garden, walks in leafy Priory Close, meals in the best hotels. She would write her novel to a thrilling conclusion while birds sang in the trees.

But, almost at once, the halo began to fade from her luxurious sanctum, and by the fifth day, it's pale indeed. The quiet of this place unnerves her: each morning she wakes, much earlier than she ever did in Silver Street, to the sepulchral stillness of suburbia, invisibly surrounded by neighbours who might as well be dead. Her little garden, by daylight, is a shady, half-subterranean affair, fenced all around by iron spikes. Peeping above the rose-bushes, she has a mole's-eye view of the stony rim of a footpath along which nobody ever seems to walk, whatever the time of day. Oh, *one* morning she did hear voices, deep male voices, and she dashed to the window to listen, but the speakers were from a foreign country.

Every dawn she washes and dresses, then has nothing to do: the books with which William has furnished the bookcases – technical tomes about maceration and enfleurage and distillation, merely to fill up the shelves – mean nothing to her . . . She'll write her novel, of course, when the crates arrive. When *will* they arrive? When William Rackham gives the word. In the meantime, she spends a remarkable amount of her time in the bath.

The opportunity to take her meals in the hotels of Marylebone, so precious to her at first, has fallen far short of Sugar's expectations. For one thing, every time she leaves the house, she fears that William will come visiting at the very moment she sits down to breakfast or luncheon. Besides, the food in the Warwick and the Aldsworth is really nothing special, and they don't have the cakes she likes, only oatcakes, which are no damn use at all. Also, she's convinced the attendants in the Warwick look at her queerly, and whisper amongst themselves when she pretends to be engrossed in her omelette or her kippers. As for the Aldsworth, oh God, the expression on that waiter's face when she asked for extra cream! How was she to know only a whore would ask for extra cream! She can't go back there, no she can't — not unless William himself escorts her . . .

What in God's name is keeping him? Perhaps he tried to visit on the day she went to Mrs Castaway's — an excursion she put off as long as she could, for fear of just that thing. Perhaps, what with meals and going out to the local shops to buy chocolates, spa water, and new bed-sheets, she has missed him half a dozen times already!

Finally, mercifully, on the morning of the sixth day . . . no, William doesn't come, but something else does: the curse. And, damned nuisance though the bleeding is, Sugar feels much better in her spirits: a dark cloud lifts from her prospects and she can see her way forward at last.

All she need do is make it impossible for Rackham to discard her, before he even *begins* to think of doing so. She must weave herself inextricably into the pattern of his life, so that he comes to regard her not as a mere dalliance, but as a friend, as precious as a sibling. Of course, to earn such a place in his life, she must know everything, *everything* about William Rackham; she must know him better than his wife knows him, better than he knows himself.

How to begin? Well, waiting for him in the empty silence of her rooms is emphatically *not* the answer: it merely tempts Fate to sweep her into the gutter. She must act, and act at once!

In the spectral glow of another overcast mid-morning, with a storm predicted, Agnes Rackham stands at her bedroom window, blinking hard. The apparition has vanished. It will return. But for now it's gone.

Not since her childhood visions of her favourite saint, Saint Teresa of Avila, has she felt this way. It all went wrong after that terrible day when Lord Unwin told her *he* was her father now, and there'd be no more Virgin Marys, no more crucifixes, no more rosaries and no more Confessions for her. How fervently she prayed then, for the strength to preserve the flame of her faith against the huffing and puffing of this big bad Protestant wolf. Alas, at ten years old she was poorly equipped to fight like a martyr. Any resistance to her step-father's edicts was crushed by a new nurse from the

Anglican camp, and there was no help from Mother, who seemed wholly under her new husband's evil spell. Agnes's desperate calls to Saint Teresa, which once were intimate conversations, soon sounded like the lonesome whisperings of a child frightened of the dark.

Now, thirteen years later, it looks as though something divine and mysterious is afoot once more. Miracles are in the air.

She wanders through the upper floors of the Rackham house, entering each room except the Ones Into Which She Must Never Go. The servants are all downstairs working, so their rooms are conveniently vacant: Agnes enters them one by one and stands at their tiny windows, looking out into the Rackham grounds from half a dozen vantage points. Letty's window, in particular, has a nice view of the mews behind Chepstow Villas. The apparition doesn't manifest, though.

Dreamily, Agnes returns to her own bedroom. And there, out of her own window, in the side lane not fifty yards away, she sees it again! Yes! Yes! A woman in white, standing sentinel, gazing directly at the Rackham house through the wrought-iron railings. This time, before the apparition has a chance to disappear into the ether, Agnes raises her hand and waves.

For several seconds, the woman in white stands motionless and unresponsive, but Agnes waves on and on, energetically wiggling her hand like a toy rattle on her flimsy wrist. Finally, the woman in white waves back, with a gesture so delicate and hesitant she might never have waved at a human being before. A boom of thunder penetrates the clouds. The woman in white melts away into the trees.

By lunchtime, Agnes's excitement has scarcely abated; extreme joy pulses in her wrists and her temples. The elements outside are wild in sympathy, sending lashings of rain against the windows and whoops of wind down the chimneys, urging her to whirl freely with arms flung wide. Yet she knows she must control herself and be demure, she must act as though the world is just the same today as it was yesterday, for her husband is a man and if there's one thing men despise it's happiness in its raw state. So, chairs scrape and dishes clink as she and William seat themselves in their appointed places at the dining-room table, murmuring thanks for what they are about to receive. Precious little light gets through the storm's watery shimmer and, though Letty has parted the curtains as far as they will go, it isn't enough, and finally a trinity of flaming candles must be set down between the Rackhams to clarify their radically different meals.

'I have a guardian angel, dear,' says Agnes as soon as the servants have finished serving up – before she's even speared her first cube of cold pigeon breast out of its nest of lettuce and artichoke bottoms.

'A what, dear?' William is even more preoccupied than usual, having been (he keeps declaring to anyone in range) up to his ears in work.

'A guardian angel,' affirms Agnes, glowing with pleasure.

William looks up from his own plate, piled high with hot pigeon pie and buttered potato waffles.

'You're referring to Clara?' he guesses, really in no mood for playful feminine effusions when he has the problem of Hopsom & Co. to solve.

'You don't understand, dear,' insists Agnes, leaning forward, radiant, her food quite forgotten in the urgency of sharing her vision. 'I have a *real* guardian angel. A divine spirit. She is watching over our house – over *us* – every instant.'

The corners of William's mouth twitch in a grimace of disappointment which he manfully attempts to convert into a smile. He'd been under the impression Agnes was much improved, after the fiasco on the kitchen floor and two days fast asleep on Curlew's horse dope.

'Well,' he sighs, 'I hope she doesn't come in and steal the new cutlery.'

There is a pause while William cuts his pie and concentrates on conveying it to his mouth without soiling his now luxuriant beard. Thus occupied, he fails to notice that the atmosphere in the room has undergone a chemical change every bit as remarkable as the transition from crushed flower-petals to oily perfume pomade.

'I think she's probably from the Convent of Health,' Agnes declares tremulously, pushing her all-but-undisturbed plate aside, napkin clenched in one white fist.

'The Convent of Health?' William looks up, chewing. In the distorting light of the new silver candelabrum (perhaps *fractionally* too big for their dining table?), his wife's eyes appear to be unequal in size – the right slightly rounder and shinier than the left.

'*You* know:' she says, 'the place I go when I'm asleep.'

'I–I confess I wasn't aware where you've been going,' he says, grinning uneasily, 'when you're asleep.'

'The nuns there are really angels,' Agnes remarks, as if to lay an old misconception to rest. 'I've suspected that for a long time.'

'Aggie . . .' says William, in a gently warning tone. 'Perhaps a different subject now?'

'She waved to me,' persists Agnes, trembling with indignation. 'I waved to her, and she waved back.'

William slaps his knife and fork onto the table and fixes her with his sternest paternal stare: his tolerance is near its limit.

'Does she have wings, this guardian angel?' he enquires sarcastically.

'Of course she has wings,' Agnes hisses back. 'What do you take me for?' But, in his eyes, she can see the answer. 'You don't believe me, do you, William?'

'No, dear,' he sighs, 'I don't believe you.'

The pulse in her temples is clearly visible now, like an insect trapped between translucent flesh and swelling skull.

'You don't believe in anything, do you?' she says, in a low, ugly voice he's never heard from her before.

'I–I beg your pardon, dear?' he stammers.

'You believe in nothing,' she says, glaring at him through the candle-flame, her voice harsher with each successive syllable, all trace of its lilting musicality lost in a snarl of disgust. 'Nothing except William Rackham.' She bares her perfect teeth. 'What a fraud you are, what a fool.'

'I *beg* your pardon, dear!?' He's too astonished to be angry; in truth, he is afraid, for this new voice of hers is as strange and shocking in her rosebud mouth as the growl of a dog, or a Pentecostal torrent of tongues.

'Beg all you like – *fool*,' she spits. 'You make me *sick*.'

He springs to his feet, scattering food and cutlery everywhere. The candelabrum topples with a crash of flame, molten wax and silver, provoking from him a bellow of alarm as he pounces on the candles, dousing them with a smack of his palm.

By the time he's reassured that there isn't going to be an inferno, Agnes is already on the floor, lying not in her usual swoon of decorous recline, but in a twisted rag-doll sprawl of slack limbs and exposed petticoats, as if a crack marksman has just shot her through the spine.

In the shadowy porch of 22 Priory Close, in response to his first pull on the bell, the door swings open and William Rackham is welcomed inside. For a moment he's dazzled, failing to recognise the white-clad woman before him; Sugar's hair hangs newly washed and dark against the snowy silk of her bodice, and her normally pale cheeks are blushing. He has caught her unawares, in fragrant disarray, preparing herself for him.

'Come in, come *in*,' she implores, for the fierce rain at his back is slanted almost horizontal, pelting past him into the hall.

'High time I stopped this foolishness and got a coachman,' he mutters as she ushers him inside. 'This is intolerable . . .' He shies in surprise as she jumps to his aid, cooing nurturingly, laying her hands on his shoulders to help him remove his waterlogged ulster.

'New dress?' he says.

'Yes,' she admits, blushing deeper still. 'I bought it with the money you sent.' Her attempt to hang his coat on the coat-stand fails instantly, as the sodden garment topples the dainty pole. She catches it in her arms as the metal clatters to the floor. 'I didn't mean to be extravagant,' she frets, lifting the coat above her head, and hooking its furry collar over a light fitting. 'It's just that my old clothes haven't come yet.'

Rackham smacks his forehead with the heel of his hand.

'Ach! Forgive me!' he groans. 'I've been up to my ears in work.'

'William, your hand . . .' She grasps it, turning the palm up to reveal scalds and fresh blisters. 'Oooh, how awful for you . . .' And, tenderly, she kisses the burns with her soft dry lips.

'It's nothing,' he says. 'A mishap with some candles. But how could I have left you in this state for so long . . . I'll get those crates sent first thing tomorrow. If you knew what I've had on my mind . . . !'

With a wet thud, his ulster falls again.

'Damn it all!' he explodes. 'I should've bought you a *decent* coat-stand. Damn Jew said it was sturdier than it looked. Flimsy rubbish!' He kicks the recumbent sculpture where it lies, triggering a buzz of vibrating brass.

'No matter, no matter,' Sugar hastily reassures him, scooping the coat off the floor and bearing it into the sitting-room. A fire is blazing in the hearth; the straight-backed chair from the writing-desk makes a good drying frame, she's found.

Rackham follows on, embarrassed that this exquisite creature in white silk should be doing work more suited to a shapeless drudge in calico and black. How lovely she is! He wants to seize hold of her and . . . and . . . well, to be honest, he doesn't want to do anything to her tonight. Rather, he wishes *she* would gather his head to her breast – her fully-clothed, silky white breast – and merely, gently, stroke his hair.

'I'm a poor excuse for a benefactor,' he sighs, as she arranges his coat on the makeshift rack. 'I leave you stranded without fresh clothes, for days. Then I shamble through your door, as though I've just been dredged from the Thames – and within moments I'm making an ass of myself, kicking the place down . . .'

Sugar straightens, looks her Rackham square in the eyes for the first time since his arrival. There's something wrong, she realises now: something weightier than rickety coat-stands or a spate of bad weather. His contorted face, his stooping posture . . . He might almost be the William Rackham she met in The Fireside on that first night, hunched and mistrustful like a recently whipped dog – except that tonight he smells of less easily definable desires.

'Something is troubling you,' she says, in her softest, most respectful voice. 'You aren't a man to concern himself with trifles.'

'Ach, it's nothing, nothing,' he replies, eyes downcast. (How perceptive she is! Is his very soul naked to her gaze?)

'Business?'

He sits heavily in an armchair, blinking dazedly at the glass of brandy hovering before him – exactly what he wanted. He accepts it from her hand, and she glides backwards to the other armchair.

'Business, yes,' he says.

He begins with a heavy heart, sighing deeply in expectation of having to explain the most fundamental principles. But, to his amazement, she needs no such thing; she understands! Within minutes he and Sugar are discussing the Hopsom dilemma – in detail – quite as if she were a business ally.

'But how can you know all this?' he interjects at one point.

'I've made a start on the books you put on my shelves,' she grins. (Yes, indeed she has: screeds of closely-printed tedium, made bearable only by the anticipation of an opportunity like this one.)

Rackham shakes his head in awe. 'Am I . . . *dreaming* you?'

She stretches slightly in her seat and breathes deep, allowing her bosom to swell into view. 'Oh, I'm very real,' she reminds him.

And to the dilemma of Hopsom & Co. they promptly return. Sugar manages her side of the discussion better than she could have hoped, but then everything William knows of perfumery seems to have been cribbed from books and nothing from experience. Anyhow, the underlying principles of commerce are so simple, even an imbecile could understand them: convince your customers you're generous when in fact you're forcing them to pay dear for what you have produced cheap. Conversation with a boring man likewise has its underlying principles. Principle One: humbly apologise for your ignorance, even when you know what he's about to explain. Principle Two: at the point when he grows weary of explaining, appear to grasp everything in an instant.

'I'm not a businessman by nature, I'm more of an artist,' William says, with a stoical sigh. 'But in the end, that may be all to the good. The born businessman is unadventurous, fearful of changing the way things are, if they're ticking along. The born artist is prepared to *dare*.' Softly bleating these words, he strikes her as the last person to dare anything. What's *wrong* with him tonight? At least he's swallowing the brandy . . .

The problem with Hopsom, after all her gentle probings and reassurances, at last comes out in the open. And what a puny little problem it is! The company is a minor manufacturer of toiletries, dwarfed by Rackham's as Rackham's is dwarfed by Pears. Until now, it has not sold lavender in any form, but William was recently approached by Mr Hopsom, with a view to the leasing of some of Rackham's lavender-producing farmland, if there's any to spare. William promised to consider it, but no sooner was Hopsom out the door than he conceived a notion much more radical than the mere leasing of land. Instead, why shouldn't Rackham supply Hopsom with lavender in its fully refined forms – soaps, waters, oils, talcums and so on – at a price much lower than what it would cost Hopsom to produce the same items in his own much smaller factories? Hopsom could then sell them under the Hopsom name. And what, asks Sugar, would be the advantage to Rackham of such an arrangement? Why, it would solve the problem of what to do with crops and manufactures that turn out . . . how shall we say it? . . . less than perfect. Every year an unconscionable amount of harvested lavender is thrown away, which might just as well be refined for what it's worth. Also it seems a waste to discard finished products (soaps and so forth) that are a mite misshapen, or have pock-marks or streaks of undissolved colour.

Not that the lavender produce passed on to Hopsom would *necessarily* be inferior; to the contrary, every effort would be made, as always, to ensure that all crops were perfect, and every manufacture flawless. It might well be that, nine times out of ten, there would be no difference anyone could tell between (for example) the lavender water bearing Hopsom's label and that which bore Rackham's.

Ah, but . . . ah, but . . . What of that one-in-ten eventuality? What if (just for the sake of argument) Hopsom's found itself in receipt of a quantity of substandard perfume, or if a newly-delivered crate of soaps should contain, by an accident of bad luck, a disproportionate number of visibly deformed specimens? What if (to speak plainly) Mr Hopsom should consider himself short-changed, and *complain*? Indeed, what if (driven — just for the sake of argument — by a perverse ingratitude for the generous terms on which his company had been given the goods) he tried to drag Rackham's name through the mud?

'You needn't worry any more, William: I have your answer,' says Sugar.

'There cannot *be* a satisfactory answer,' he moans, accepting his fourth glass of brandy. 'Everything depends on chance . . .'

'Not at all, not at all,' she placates him. 'This Mr Hopsom: do you happen to know if his Christian name is Matthew?'

'Matthew, yes,' says William, frowning with the effort of imagining where, in his cast-off books, she could possibly have gleaned such a fact.

'Known to some as "Horsey" Hopsom?'

'Why . . . yes.'

Sugar chuckles wickedly, and swoops across the room to kneel at his feet.

'Then if Mr Hopsom ever causes you any bother,' she says, propping her thin white arms on one dark trouser-leg, 'I suggest you whisper two short words in his ear.' And, leaning closer still to him, slapping his thigh in a gentle pantomime of rhythmic chastisement, she whispers, 'Amy Howlett.'

William looks into her bright eyes with a mixture of mistrust and wonderment for several seconds, then laughs out loud.

'By God,' he cries. 'This really is the limit!'

'Not at all,' murmurs Sugar, nuzzling her cheek into his lap. 'There are no limits to the heights that can be attained by a man like you . . .'

She moves her palm onto the spot where his sex should, by now, be swelling to erection, but it seems she's misjudged him. The conversation has gone surpassingly well: the Hopsom's problem is solved: and yet . . . and yet Rackham fidgets under her touch, awkward and unready.

'*Dear* William,' she commiserates, falling back, clasping her hands demurely in the lap of her own billowing skirts. 'You are *still* troubled. Yes you are: I can tell. What on earth can be the matter? What terrible thing has upset you so?'

For a full twenty seconds he stares at her, dark-browed and wavering. Has she dared too much? He coughs, to clear his throat for whatever words may come.

'My wife,' he says, 'is a madwoman.'

Sugar cocks her head, in a mute gesture of aghastness, after considering and rejecting such declarations as 'Really?', 'Well, fancy that!' and 'How dreadful!' All her working life, men have been telling her their wives are mad, and still she hasn't hit upon a serviceable way of responding.

'She was a sweet, kind-hearted girl when we first married,' he laments, 'a credit to anyone. She had some odd ways, but who hasn't? I couldn't have known she'd become a candidate for an asylum; that, in my own home, she would . . .' He stops short, closes his eyes in pain. 'There was no happier girl when I first met her. Now she despises me.'

'What a tragedy,' breathes Sugar, venturing, hesitantly, to lay a condoling hand on his knee. It is accepted. 'I imagine she'd love you still, if only she could.'

'The maddening thing . . . I mean, the thing that puzzles me most, is that she changes from day to day. Some days she's as normal as you or I, then suddenly she'll do or say something wholly outrageous.'

'Like . . . ?' Sugar's voice is small and unobtrusive.

'She believes she travels to a Catholic convent in her sleep. She believes she's being watched by angels. They wave to her, she says.'

Sugar lays her hot cheek against his waist, embracing him companionably, hoping the flush will fade before she has to show her face again. Caught spying outside the Rackham house, what else could she have done, when Mrs Rackham waved at her, but wave back?

'Only last week she disgraced herself with a servant on the floor of our kitchen,' William continues miserably. 'The doctor had to come. He thinks *I'm* mad to keep her . . . He has no idea what a darling she used to be! Nowadays, Agnes spends half her life asleep – doped with potions, or simply lazy. I don't know anymore, it's beyond me . . .'

Sugar strokes his knee, regularly and unsensually, the way she might stroke the head of a pet. Inside her pantalettes she feels a trickle of blood, but it appears tonight will not be the night when William Rackham's attitude to the bleeding of women is revealed.

'How long has . . . Agnes been this bad?' she asks.

'Ach! Who knows what she's been hiding in her head since before she knew me! But . . . I'd have to say that her madness was less . . .' (he clenches and unclenches his injured fist, grasping for the right word) '. . . full-flowered, before the child.'

'Oh?' Again, Sugar's voice is weightless, a mouse's tread. 'You have a child?'

'Just one, yes,' William sighs. 'A daughter, unfortunately.'

A sharp twitch of indignation, too instantaneous for her to suppress, passes through Sugar's cheek directly against William's stomach; she hopes his clothing diffuses it. How strange, that she's learnt to listen to all sorts of vile masculine harangues with perfect composure – diatribes against the female sex in general, her body as a cesspool of filth, her cunt as the mouth of Hell – but, every so often, a mild remark about the uselessness of a female child provokes her to fury. Teeth clenched, she holds her man tighter, to exorcise the anger in a vehement show of affection.

'I suppose,' she says, to break the silence that's fallen, 'your wife's illness has lost her all her friends?'

He sinks lower in the armchair, relaxing into her embrace. 'Well you know, that's the odd thing . . . I'd have *thought* so, but apparently it hasn't. The Season's round the corner, and invitations have *poured* in. Amazing, considering what she got up to last time she took part . . .'

'What did she get up to?'

'Oh . . . All sorts of things. Laughed when there was nothing to laugh about, didn't laugh when there was. Shouted nonsense, warned people against invisible dangers. Crawled under a dinner table once, complaining the meat had blood in it. Fainted more times than I can remember. Oh God, the number of times I had to have her carted off . . . !' She feels him shake his head. 'And yet, here she is, forgiven. That's Society for you!'

She rubs her ear against his stomach. He has, by the sound of the gurglings within, eaten nothing: all the quicker will the drink loosen his tongue.

'Have you considered,' she says, 'the possibility that the invitations have poured in on *your* account?'

'*My* account?' He heaves a sigh that lifts her head a full three inches.

'I've never been one for balls and picnics and dinner parties. I'd rather make my own amusement. In any case, I'm monstrously busy this year, and can't think where I'm going to find the time.'

'Yes, but don't you think there'll be people who've been watching your . . . your extraordinary rise? You've become a very great man, William, very swiftly. Great men are wanted everywhere. These invitations . . . well, people can't very well invite you and not your wife, can they?'

William lays his arm down the length of her back, his hand nestling on the swell of her bustle. She's convinced him, she can tell.

'What a simpleton I am . . .' he muses, his voice rich with brandy and tranquillised anxiety. 'Not to have appreciated how things have changed . . .'

'You must be mindful of who your true friends are,' Sugar advises him, as she begins once more to caress the lap of his trousers. 'The richer you become, the more people will stop at nothing to curry favour with you.'

He groans, and guides her head towards his lap.

Afterwards, when his hard-won cockstand has shrivelled to a stub, Sugar presses on, in the hope of getting more out of him.

'How I've yearned for that divine taste,' she gloats, to prevent his bolstered spirits sagging likewise. 'You were gone so long! Didn't you have a thought to spare for your little concubine, stranded here without fresh clothes for days, starving for you?'

'I've been up to my ears . . .' But she laughs and butts in on his apology, kissing his ears with comical rapidity, a flurry of impish kisses to let him know he hasn't hurt her feelings at all. He snortles, ticklish, his double chin visible through his beard as he cringes. 'Being at the helm of a business is more time-consuming than I could have imagined. The Hopsom affair was only one of the things on my plate in the last few days. And the coming weeks are scarcely less busy. Soon I'll have to go to my lavender fields in Mitcham, and sort out why there's—'

'Lavender fields?' she interjects excitedly.

'Yes . . .'

'Where the lavender actually grows?'

'Well, yes, of course . . .'

'Oh, William! How I'd love to see such a sight! Do you know I've never seen anything growing except what's in the parks of London?' She drops onto her haunches, as low to the floor as possible, so he can gaze down on her enraptured face. 'A field full of lavender! To you it may be the most ordinary thing in the world, but for your little Sugar it's like a fairy story! Oh, William, couldn't you take me?'

He squirms, smiling and frowning at the same time. Misgivings struggle to manifest in a brain soggy with alcohol and sensual satiation.

'Nothing would give me more pleasure, sweet thing that you are . . .' he slurs. 'But think of the risk of scandal: you, an unknown young woman, walking alone with me in my fields, for all the workers to see . . .'

'But isn't this place on the other side of England?'

'Mitcham? It's down in Surrey, dear . . .' He grins, to see the undiminished ignorance in her face. 'Quite close enough for gossip.'

'I needn't be alone, then!' she declares eagerly. 'I could be escorted by another man. O-or rather—' she notes the flicker of mistrust in his brow '—*I* could escort someone *else*: a-an *old* man. Yes, yes: I know just the person, a lame old man I could pass off as my grandfather. He's deaf and blind – well, almost. He'd be no trouble. I could just . . . *wheel* him along with us, like a baby in a perambulator.'

Rackham blinks at her in a goggle of incredulity.

'You're not in earnest, surely?'

'I've never been more serious!' she cries. 'Oh, William, *say* you will!'

He lurches to his feet, laughing at his own clumsiness, at the delirious absurdity of a brandy-tinted universe.

'I mustn't fall asleep here,' he mumbles, fastening his trousers. 'Hopsom is coming to see me in the morning . . .'

'*Say* yes, William,' pleads Sugar, helping him tuck his shirt in. 'To me, I mean.'

'I'll have to think about it,' he says, swaying in front of the chair that holds his ulster, still faintly steaming. 'When I'm not so drunk!'

And he hoists his coat by the collar, allowing her to help him wriggle his arms into its obstinate sleeves. The garment is heavy, searingly hot on the outside, humid on the inside, with a peculiar smell; William and Sugar giggle, foreheads together, at the sheer unpleasantness of it.

'I love you!' he laughs, and she embraces him tight, pressing her cheek against his bristly jaw.

Outside, the storm has passed. Night has composed itself over Priory Close, stilling the rain, snuffing the wind. The black sky glitters with stars, the slick streets shine like silver in the lamp-light. The full moon, siren to all lunatics from the rookeries of Shoreditch to the regal bed-chambers of Westminster, winks on the chimneyed horizon.

'Watch your step, dear heart!' calls Sugar from the glowing vestibule of this, his home away from home.

Chepstow Villas, once William's cab has jingled off, is silent as a church-yard, and the Rackham house looms tall as a monument – a grand preten-tious gravestone for an illustrious family that reached the end of its line. William shivers, with cold and with annoyance at the amplified creak of his front gate as he pushes through. He is half-sober now, in a most lugubri-ous mood, dispirited by the cheerless welcome of his own abode. Even the dog that likes to haunt the front gates has retired, and the path through the austerely shorn grounds glows eerie in the moonlight. A glimpse of the empty coach-house, half-hidden and sinister under the trees, reminds him of yet another item on his long list of things to be done.

He rings the doorbell once, but, conceding the lateness of the hour, he fumbles for his key. Feeble light filters through the ornamental window above the architrave – just enough to cast a shadow over his fingers as he bends his head closer to his damned elusive pockets. (Lord Almighty! If his company manufactured clothing instead of perfumes, there'd be some changes made!)

Just as he's found the key and is on the point of inserting it success-fully in the key-hole, the door swings open, and he's greeted by a puffy-eyed Letty, woken no doubt from vertical slumber. Even in the light of the single candle she holds, he can see her left cheek is red and wrinkled from the sleeve of her uniform; no doubt she observes equally well his swollen red nose and sweaty brow.

'Where's Clara?' he says, when she has helped him off with his coat. (Her hands are stronger than Sugar's, yet less effective.)

'Gone to bed, Mr Rackham.'

'Good. You do the same, Letty.' He has one more responsibility to discharge before he goes to bed, and it will be a damn sight easier with Clara out of the way.

'Thank you, Mr Rackham.'

He watches her ascend the stairs, waits for her to be stowed in her attic hutch. Then he follows on behind, straight to Agnes's bedroom.

The chamber, when he enters it, is airless and oppressive – like a sealed glass jar, he thinks. When he first courted Agnes, she ran girlishly across the green lawns of Regent's Park, a flurry of bright skirts in the breeze; now her terrain is this thickly curtained sepulchre. He sniffs warily; were he not already so brandied, he might detect the scent of rubbing alcohol spilled on the carpet by a novice doctor attempting to saturate a cotton swab.

Walking towards the bed, candle held high, William sees his wife's face half-buried in the over-sized, over-plumped pillows. Her lips convulse feebly as she registers his approach; her insubstantial eyelashes flutter.

'Clara?' she whimpers.

'It's me. William.'

Agnes's eyes flip half-open, exposing sightless whites in which her revolving china-blue irises appear and disappear like fish. Plainly, she's doped half-way to fairyland, levitating through the labyrinths of whatever convents or castles she likes to frequent.

'Where's Clara?'

'She's just outside the door,' he lies. How she fears to be alone with him! How she loathes his touch! His pity for her is so strong he yearns to wave a magic wand over her and banish her frailties forever; his resentment is equally strong, so that if he indeed held a wand, he might just as likely bring it crashing down on her head, exploding her pathetic egg-shell skull.

'How are you feeling now, dear?'

She turns her face in his direction; her eyes focus for a second, then close wearily.

'Like a lost bonnet floating along a dark river,' she murmurs. The old music is back in her voice: what a beautiful voice she has, even when it's talking nonsense.

'Do you remember what you said to me?' he says, holding the candle closer, 'before you fell into a faint?'

'No, dear,' she sighs, turning her face away, burrowing nose-first into a warm white depression already filled with her own hair. 'Was it very bad?'

'Yes, it was very bad.'

'I'm sorry, William, so awfully sorry.' Her voice is muffled by her cottony nest. 'Can you ever forgive me?'

'In sickness and in health, Aggie: that's the vow I made.'

For another minute or two he stands there, her apology travelling slowly down his gullet like a shot of brandy, warming his insides by degrees. Then, accepting it as the best outcome he can hope for, he turns, at last, to leave.

'William?'

'Mmm?'

Her face has surfaced again, glistening with tears now, frightened in the candlelight.

'Am I still your little girl?'

He grunts in pain from this wholly unexpected blow to his plexus of nostalgia. Droplets of scalding candle-fat patter onto an already blistered hand as his fists and eyes clench in unison.

'Go to sleep, Precious,' he advises her hoarsely, walking backwards out of the door. 'Tomorrow is a brand-new day.'

FOURTEEN

ne sunny afternoon late in the April of 1875, in a vast rolling field of lavender, a scattered host of workers cease their toil for just a minute. Submerged knee-high in a lake of *Lavandula*, they stand idle with their hoes and slug-buckets, to stare at the beautiful young woman walking past them on the path dividing the acres.

''Oo's that?' they whisper to each other, eyes owlish with curiosity. ''Oo's that?' But no one knows.

The lady wears a lavender dress; her white-gloved hands and bonneted head are like blossoms sprouting from her wrists and neck. The dress is intricately pleated and ruched, like unravelling rope, giving her the appearance of a life-sized corn dolly.

'An' 'oo's that wiv' 'er?'

The woman does not walk alone or unencumbered. She's pushing, with the utmost care along the maze of paths, an indistinct burden in a wheel-chair. It's an ancient, crippled man, well rugged up with blankets and shawls, his head muffled in a scarf, despite the mildness of the weather. And, next to the old man and the woman who wheels him, there walks a third visitor to the fields today: William Rackham, owner of all. He speaks frequently; the old man speaks from time to time; the woman says almost nothing; but the toilers in the field, row upon row, catch only a few words each before the procession moves on.

''Oo d'yer fink she is?' asks a sun-dried wife of her sun-dried husband.

'The old one's daughter, I'd say. Or grand-daughter. Likely the old one's rich. Likely our Curly Bill wants to do business wiv 'im.'

''E'll 'ave to move fast, then. That old crock could cark it any minute.'

'At least 'Opsom 'ad a pair o' legs to walk on.'

And with that they return to work, drifting into separate currents of vegetation.

Yet, further on, more toilers stop and stare. Nothing like this – a lady visitor to the fields – was ever seen in William's father's time; Rackham Senior preferred to keep well-bred females out of the field, for fear their hearts might start bleeding. The last to visit was his own wife, twenty years ago, before the cuckolding.

'Oh but she's beautiful,' sighs one swarthy toiler, squinting after the strange feminine silhouette.

'So would *you* be,' spits a fellow drudge, 'if you never done hard labour.'

'Yarrr!' growls the old man in the wheelchair, his stench of stale clothing and haphazard hygiene much diluted by the fresh air and the acres of damp soil and lovingly tended lavender.

Sugar bows her head down as she continues to wheel him forward, her lips hovering near his scarf-shrouded skull, approximately where one of his ears must be.

'Now, now, Colonel Leek,' she says. 'Remember you're here to enjoy yourself.'

But Colonel Leek is not enjoying himself, or so he would have Sugar believe. Only his lust for the promised reward – six shillings and more whisky in a day than Mrs Leek will let him have in a month – keeps him from outright mutiny. He's certainly not in the least interested in playing the part of anyone's grandfather.

'I need to pee.'

'Do it in your pants,' hisses Sugar sweetly. 'Pretend you're at home.'

'Oh, *so* kind-hearted, you are.' He twists his head, exposing one rheumy malevolent eye and half a mottled, gummy mouth. 'Too good for St Giles, eh, trollop?'

'Six shillings and whisky, remember – *Grandfather*.'

And so they trundle on, with the sun beaming down on them, there in the pampered heartland of Rackham Perfumeries.

William Rackham walks aloof, unimpeachably proper, dressed in his stiff Sunday best despite it being Wednesday. Not for him his father's mole-skin trousers and Wellington boots; a modern perfumery is ruled from the head, and kept in line with the pen. Everything that goes on in these fields, every stoop of a worker's back or pruning of the tiniest twig, is set in motion by his own thoughts and written requirements. Or so he has attempted to convey to his visitors.

He's aware, of course, that the liaison between Sugar and the old man is rather less amicable than she'd claimed, but he has forgiven her. Indeed, had she and Colonel Leek been sharing confidential affections, he might have felt a prick of jealousy. It's better this way: the old man's pneumonic mumbling is so gruff that the field-workers won't understand much of what they chance to overhear, and the fact that Sugar is wheeling him speaks louder than any declarations of kinship.

'Enjoy the sunshine, why don't you,' she admonishes the Colonel as the three of them make their way up the gentle slope of Beehive Hill.

The old man coughs, giving the phlegm in his chest a slight jiggle.

'Sunlight is bad,' he wheezes. 'It's the exact same stuff as breeds maggots in wounded soldiers' legs. And when there's no war on, it fades wallpaper.'

Sugar presses forward, rolling this talking Sisyphus stone farther up the slope, flashing William a smile of reassurance. *Pay him no heed*, her smile says. *You and I know the value of this place – and the significance of this grand day in our lives.*

'It's as I thought: they'll feed on me like parasites, if I let them,' mutters William. 'They think I'll swallow any story they tell me.'

Sugar cocks her head sympathetically, inviting him to explain.

'They wear they've been pruning the older bushes for weeks,' he scoffs. 'Since yesterday afternoon, more likely! You can't see how straggly they look?'

Sugar glances back. To her, the workers appear stragglier and less well cared for than the lavender.

'It all looks magnificent to me,' she says.

'They ought to be putting a damn sight more cuttings in,' he assures her. 'Now's the time when they'll root freely.'

'Hurgh-hurgh-*hurgh*!' coughs the Colonel.

'Your farm is much bigger than I dreamed it would be,' remarks Sugar, to steer the conversation back to flattery. 'There seems no end it.'

'Ah, but,' says Rackham, 'it isn't all mine.' Taking advantage of their elevation, he points downhill, to a long line of white-washed stakes all along one of the paths. '*Those* mark the boundary of another farm. Lavender grows best the more of it there is. The bees don't prefer one man's bush to another's. All in all, some half-dozen perfumeries own a portion of this land; my portion is forty acres.'

'Forty acres!' Sugar has only the vaguest idea how much this is, but appreciates it's an enormous area compared to, say, Golden Square. Indeed, all the streets she's ever lived in, if they were dug out of their polluted foundations by a giant spade, could be dumped in the pillowy centre of this lavender paradise, and discreetly buried in soft brown earth, never to be seen again.

And yet, as William has reminded her several times, this farm is only one tributary of his empire. There are other farms in other places, each devoted to a single bloom; there are even whaling boats on the Atlantic harvesting ambergris and spermaceti for Rackham Perfumeries. Sugar surveys the great lake of lavender before her, and measures it against a pomander of petals such as she might be able to hold in her hand. So much luxury, in such excess! An essence she might purchase in a tiny phial for a considerable sum is so abundant, here at its source, that it's no doubt poured roughly into barrels and the overspills trampled into mud – or so she fancies. The concept is magical and indecent, like a vision of jewellers wading ankle-deep in gems, crunching them underfoot, shovelling them into sacks.

'But really, Colonel,' she implores the old man beneath her, half-teasing, half-impassioned. 'This is all so . . . so *glorious*. Can't you admit, at least, that it makes a nice change from Mrs Leek's?'

'*Ah*? A nice *change*?' The old man fidgets furiously in his squeaking seat, straining to retrieve some salient facts from his encyclopaedic memory for disasters. 'Granville's Combined Orchards, burnt to a cinder, two and a half year ago!' he proclaims in triumph. 'Twelve dead! Lucifer factory in Goeteborg, Sweden, 27th of last month: forty-four burnt to death and nine mortally injured! Cotton plantation in Virginia last Christmas, down to ash in half a day, savages and all!' He pauses, swivels his gaze around to William Rackham, and leers, 'What a bonfire all *this*'d make, eh?'

'Actually, sir,' William replies with lofty condescension, 'it does *indeed* make a splendid bonfire, every year. My fields are divided, you see, according to the age of the plants on them. Some are in their fifth year, exhausted, and will be burnt at the end of October. I can assure you the fire is big enough to make all Mitcham smell of lavender.'

'Oh, how wonderful!' cries Sugar. 'How I should love to be here then!'

William blushes with pride, there on the hillock, his chin pushed out in the direction of his empire. What a miracle he has wrought – he, so recently an effete idler in straitened circumstances – now master of this vast farm with its quaint brown workers moving amongst the lavender like field mice. The sounds of industry belong to him too, plus the smells of a million flowers, plus even the sky immediately above, for if *he* doesn't own these things, who does? Oh, granted, God is still supposed to own everything, but where's the line to be drawn? Only a crackpot would insist on God's ownership of Paddington Station or a mound of cow-dung – why quibble, then, with William Rackham's ownership of this farm, and every-thing above and below it? William recalls the verses of Scripture his father was fond of quoting to the dubious young Henry: 'Be fruitful, and multi-ply, and replenish the earth, and *subdue* it' (Rackham Senior would lay emphasis on this word) 'and have dominion over every thing that moveth upon the earth.'

So vividly does William recall this statement that he feels almost re-instated in the tiny body he occupied at seven years old, on the occasion of his own first visit to this farm, dawdling behind his older brother. Their father, dark-haired and big then, chose the lavender fields as that part of the empire which might appeal most to the boy who would one day inherit.

'And are these ladies and gentlemen p'mitted to take home any of the lavender they harvest, Father?' Clear as a bell across the years comes Henry's childish voice – yes, Henry's, for William would never, even at the age of seven, have asked such a stupid question.

'They don't need to take any home,' Henry Calder Rackham enlight-ened his first-born indulgently. 'They reek of it just by working in it.'

'That is a very pleasant reward, I think.' (What an ass Henry was, always!)

Their father guffawed. 'They won't work for that alone, boy. They must have wages as well.' The expression of incredulity on Henry's face ought to have alerted the old man that he had the wrong son earmarked for heir. But no matter, no matter . . . Time upraises all who are worthy.

'Yaarr!'

Ignoring the bestial grousing of Colonel Leek, William surveys his fields once more before descending Beehive Hill. Everything is identical to how it was when he was a boy – although these workers cannot be the same workers who toiled in Henry Calder Rackham's domain twenty-one years ago, for men and women, too, like enfeebled fifth-year plants, are uprooted and destroyed when they are exhausted.

A wrinkled, thick-set girl carrying on her back a sack of branches passes close by William and his guests, nodding in grim sycophancy.

'You were telling us about the fifth-year plants, Mr Rackham,' comes the voice of Sugar.

'Yes,' he loudly replies, as a second sack-bearer follows the first. '*Some* perfumeries harvest their lavender a sixth year. Not Rackham's.'

'And how soon after planting is the lavender ready to be used, sir?'

'When the plants are in their second year – though they are not at their best until the third.'

'And how much lavender water will be produced, sir?'

'Oh, several thousand gallons.'

'Isn't that an astonishing thought, grandfather?' Sugar asks the old man.

'Eh? Grandfather? *You* don't even know who your grandfather was!'

Sugar cranes her head to confirm that the sack-bearers are out of earshot. 'You're going to get us all into mischief,' she chides Colonel Leek in a feral whisper, jerking the handles of his wheelchair warningly. 'I'd've had less bother from a beggar off the street.'

The old man bares his teeth and shakes his hideous head free of its swaddlings. 'What of it!' he sneers. 'That's what comes of subterfuge. Charades! Fancy dress! Har! Did I ever tell you about Lieutenant Carp, who I served with in the last great war?' (By this he doesn't mean the war against the Ashantees, or even the Indian Mutiny, but the Crimean.) '*There*'s subterfuge for ye! Carp dressed up in a lady's cloak and bonnet, and tried to cross over the enemy lines – the wind blew the cloak up over his head and there he was, hobbling around with his musket dangling between his legs. I've never seen a man shot so many times. Hur!Hur!Hur! Subterfuge!'

This outburst causes a few heads to pop up in the surrounding fields.

'A most diverting anecdote, sir,' says William frigidly.

'Don't mind him, William,' says Sugar. 'He'll be asleep soon. He always sleeps in the afternoon.'

Colonel Leek churns his grizzled jaw in indignation. 'That was years ago, trollop, when I weren't well! I'm better now!'

Sugar bends low over him, one hand digging her thinly-gloved claws into his right shoulder, the other gently caressing his left.

'Whisssky,' she sings into his ear. 'Whisssssky.'

Minutes later, when Colonel Leek is slumped in his chair, snoring, William Rackham and Sugar stand in the shade of an oak, watching the industry from a distance. Sugar is radiant, and not merely from the unaccustomed exercise of pushing the wheelchair; she's deeply happy. All her life, she's considered herself a city creature, and assumed that the countryside (imagined only through monochrome engravings and romantic poetry) had nothing to offer her. This conception she now casts off with joyful abandon. She must make sure this isn't the last time she walks under these grand blue skies and on this soft, verdant earth. Here is air she means to breathe more often.

'Oh, William,' she says, 'will you bring me here again, for the great bonfire?'

'Yes, of course I shall,' he says, for he can recognise the glow of happiness when he sees it, and he knows he is the author of that glow.

'Do you promise?'

'Yes, you have my word.'

Content, she turns to look towards the north-east: there's a swathe of rain far, far away, sprouting a rainbow. William stares at her from behind, his hand shielding his eyes against the sun. His mistress's long skirts rustle gently in the breeze, her shoulder-blades poke through the tight fabric of her dress as she lifts her arm to shield her face. All at once he recalls how her breasts feel against his palms, the bruising sharpness of her hips on his own softer belly, the thrilling touch of her rough, cracked hands on his prick. He recalls the lushness of her hair when she's naked, the tiger textures on her skin like diagrams for his own fingers, showing him where to hold her waist or her arse as he slides inside. He longs to embrace her, wishes he could have his lavender fields empty for half an hour while he lies with Sugar on a verge of grass. What's kept him from going to see her every night? What man worthy of the name wouldn't have that exquisite body next to his as often as possible? Yes, he will, he *must*, go to see her much oftener in future – but not today; he has a lot to do today.

Sugar turns, and there are tears in her eyes.

★　　★　　★

The journey back to London, in the chartered coach-and-four, is purgatorially long, and the rain, so far away when Sugar stood in Rackham's fields, has met them half-way and now beats on the roof. The coach travels slower for the bad weather, and makes mysterious stops in villages and hamlets along the way, where the coachman dismounts and disappears for two, five, ten minutes at a time. Returning, he fiddles with the horses' bridles, combs the excess water from their hair, checks that the old fellow's wheelchair is still safe and snug under the tarpaulin on the roof, performs actions against the undercarriage that make the cabin shake. Haste is not his watchword.

Inside the cabin, Sugar shivers, and grits her teeth to stop them chattering. She's still in her lavender dress and nothing more, not even a shawl. Knowing she'd be wheeling Colonel Leek about today, and keen to make an enchanting impression on William, she did without extra layers of clothing; now she's suffering the lack. The last thing she wants to do is snuggle close to the old man for warmth; he smells vile and, deprived of the support of his wheelchair's arm-rests, he's liable to keel into her lap.

'Collapse of bridge in heavy rain, Hawick, 1867,' he growls into the chilly, darkening space between them. 'Three dead, not including livestock.'

Sugar hugs herself and looks out of the mud-spattered, rain-swept window. The countryside, so colourful and miraculous when she walked at William's side on the lavender farm, has turned grey and godforsaken, like a hundred square miles of Hyde Park gone to seed, without any lights or gay pedestrians. The coach jogs slowly onwards, towards a lost metropolis.

'Urp,' belches Colonel Leek. The unsubtle fragrance of whisky and fermented digestive juices spreads in the bitter air.

A train might have been mercifully swift, not to mention (although William did mention it) a great deal cheaper, but the old man's infirmity would have caused no end of bother at various stations along the way, and he'd still have needed a coach to take him to Charing Cross and again at the Mitcham end, so engaging a coach for the whole journey seemed more sensible. Seemed.

'I give it six months,' Colonel Leek is saying, 'and you'll be out on yer arse.'

'I didn't ask your opinion,' retorts Sugar. (Cunning old blackguard: he's fired an arrow straight into the heart of her anxiety. William Rackham should be sitting here next to her just now, whiling the hours away with lively conversation, warming her hands inside his: why, oh why, didn't he accompany her?)

The Colonel clears his glutinous windpipe for another recitation. 'Fanny Gresham – in 1834, mistress of Anstey the shipping magnate, abode Mayfair; in 1835, discarded, abode Holloway Prison. Jane Hubble, known as Natasha – in 1852, mistress of Lord Finbar, abode Admiralty House; in 1853, corpse, abode Thames estuary . . .'

'Spare me the details, Colonel.'

'Noooobody spared nothing, never!' he barks. 'That's what I've learned in a long life walking this earth.'

'If you were still *walking*, old man, we'd be on a train and back in London by now.'

There is a pause while the insult sinks in.

'Enjoy the scenery, trollop,' he sneers, nodding his gargoyle head towards her streaming window. 'Makes a nice change, eh? *Glo-o-orious.*'

Sugar turns away from him, and hugs herself tighter. William cares for her, yes he does. Said he loves her, even – said it while drunk, admittedly, but not *roaring* drunk. And he allowed her to come to his farm, even though he could easily, once sober, have declared the subject closed. *And* he's promised to let her come again, at the end of October, which is . . . almost seven months in the future.

She tries to take heart from the sheer number of Rackham's employees. He is reconciled to a large amount of money flowing out from his personal fortune every week; it's not as if Sugar's upkeep is an isolated and conspicuous drain on his resources. She must regard herself, not as living out of his pocket, but as part of a grand tapestry of profit and expenditure that's been generations in the making. All she need do is spin out her own stitches in that tapestry, weave herself an inextricable figure in it. Already she's made marvellous progress: just think: a month ago she was a common prostitute! In half a year, who knows . . .

'He's a wind-bag,' snarls Colonel Leek from inside his mulch of scarves, 'and a coward. A nasty piece of work.'

'Who?' says Sugar irritably, wishing she were as snugly wrapped as he, but without the added ingredients.

'Your perfumer.'

'He's no worse than most,' she retorts. 'Kinder-hearted than *you*.'

'Horse-piss,' cackles the old salt. 'The thought of his own fat self at the top of the tree, that's what he loves. He'd kill for advancement, can't you see? He'd fill a dirty puddle with you, to save his shoes.'

'You don't know a thing about him,' she snaps. 'What would someone like *you* understand of his world?'

Provoked to rage, the Colonel rears up so alarmingly that Sugar fears he'll pitch head-first onto the cabin floor. 'I weren't always an old spoony-man, you little bed-rat,' he wheezes. 'I've lived more lives than you'll ever dream of!'

'All right, I'm sorry,' she says hastily. 'Here, drink some more of this.' And she offers him the whisky bottle.

'I've had enough,' he groans, settling back into his mulch of knitwear.

Sugar looks down at the bottle, whose contents are trembling and twinkling in the vibrating gloom. 'You've hardly drunk any.'

'A little goes a long way,' the old man mutters, subdued after his outburst. 'Drink some yerself, it'll stop yer shivering.'

Sugar calls to mind his method of sucking whisky from the neck of the bottle, his toothless mouth closed round the smooth glassy teat. 'No, thank you.'

'I've wiped the end.'

'Ugh,' shudders Sugar helplessly.

'That's right, trollop,' he sneers. 'Don't let anything dirty pass yer lips!'

Sugar utters a sharp moan of annoyance, almost identical to the one she uses for ecstasy, and folds her arms hard against her bosom. Mouth clamped shut to muffle the sound of chattering teeth, she counts to twenty; then, still angry, she counts the months of the year. She met William Rackham in November; now, in April, she is his mistress, with her own rooms and money enough to buy whatever she wishes. April, May, June . . . Why isn't he here with her in this coach? There's nothing she wishes to buy except his enduring passion for her . . .

Colonel Leek begins to snore loudly, a gross embodiment of all the sounds and smells of St Giles. She must never go back there, never. But what if Rackham tires of her? Only a few days ago, he came to visit her (after *not* visiting her for three days) and their union was so hurried he didn't even trouble to undress her. ('I'm expected at my solicitor's in an hour,' he explained. 'You *told* me that Grinling fellow sounded slippery and by God you were right.') And what about the time before that? What a peculiar mood he was in! The way he asked her if she liked the ornaments he'd chosen for her and, having encouraged her to confess she didn't care for the swan on the mantelpiece, jovially snapped its porcelain neck. She laughed along with him, but what the devil was he playing at? Was he granting her greater licence to be candid – or was he letting her know he's a man who'll happily break the neck of anything that has outlived its usefulness?

Her rooms in Marylebone, towards which this coach is ferrying her so painfully slowly, *ought* to glow in her anticipation like a fire-lit haven, but that's not how she envisages them. They are dead rooms, waiting to be inspired by the vivacity of conversation, the heat of coupling. When she's there alone, loitering in the silence, washing her hair over and over, forcing herself to study books without the remotest sensational appeal, she feels surrounded by a gas-lit halo of unease. She can say aloud, as often and as loudly as she pleases, 'This is *mine*,' but she'll hear no reply.

The crates containing her belongings were finally delivered, but she's already thrown most of their contents away – books she'll never read again, pamphlets whose marginal scribbles would enrage William if he chanced upon them. What's the use of keeping these things stowed in her cupboards and wardrobes, attracting silverfish (ugh!) when they might as well be gunpowder waiting to blow up in her face? She worries enough as it is, about William discovering her novel. Each time she leaves the house, she frets he'll come and rummage through all her nooks and drawers. Only when she's nearly sick with hunger does she hurry into the streets, conceding that if she waits any longer for him to visit, she's liable to starve. In the hotels and restaurants where she takes her meals, the attendants serve her wordlessly, as if biding their time before they see her no more.

If only she could remember exactly how many glasses of brandy William had in him when he said he loved her!

'Arghl-grrnugh,' groans Colonel Leek, convulsing in dreams of long ago. 'Come out with it, man! . . . What's the story on my legs? I'll have a limp, yes? . . . need a walking stick, is that it? Arghl . . . Speak, damn you . . . Unff . . . Unff . . . Speak . . .'

In the morning, the rain has passed away and church bells chime. Lying half-uncovered in a tangle of sunlit bed-sheets, bathed in creamy yellow brilliance streaming through the window, Henry Rackham wakes from nightmares of erotic disgrace. God has wrought a perfect new day regardless;

the divine imperative for renewal is proof against whatever evils may have transpired during the hours of darkness. God never loses heart, despite the baseness of Man . . .

Henry disentwines himself from the sheets, which are wet with the same substance that pollutes his night-shirt. He strips naked, shocked as always by the bestiality of the body thus revealed, for he's an exceptionally hairy specimen, and the hair on his body is darker and wirier than the soft blond fleece on his head. It's sexual incontinence that makes all this coarse hair grow, Henry knows. Adam and Eve were hairless in Paradise, and so are the ideal physiques of antiquity and such nudes as Modern Art permits. Were he ever to find himself in a gathering of unclothed men, his own ape-like form would mark him out as a habitual self-abuser, a beast in the making. There is a grain of truth in Darwin's heresy: for, though humankind did not evolve from animals, each human has the potential to devolve into a savage.

The church bells toll on as Henry shambles to his bathroom. Funeral service? Not a wedding, surely, at this early hour. One day, the bells will toll for him . . . Will he, by then, finally be ready?

He sponges himself clean with a cloth dipped in cold water: flesh like his doesn't deserve pampering. His body hair has thickened, over the years, into patterns which, when moistened, lie plastered around his abdomen and thighs like Gothic designs. His penis hangs gross and distended, like a reptile head, and his testicles writhe irritably as he washes them; nothing could bear less resemblance to the compressed, seashell-smooth pudenda of classical statuary.

Bodley and Ashwell have assured him that lewd women can be hairy too — so perhaps it's thanks to his old schoolchums that his dreams are so full of hirsute nymphs. Can he blame Bodley and Ashwell though, for the way Mrs Fox, in his sleeping fantasies, disports herself like a succubus, laughing as she seizes hold of his phallus and guides it between her legs, where it slips through warm wet fur . . . ?

Oh, if only I could grow up! he laments, as, even now, his genitals stir in excitement. *What man of my age still behaves as if pubescence is newly upon him? When, oh when, will First Corinthians 13:11 come true for me? My friends advise me to take Orders without delay, lest I begin 'too old': Lord, if they only knew! I am a little boy trapped inside a monstrous, degraded husk . . .*

Half-dressed now, naked only from the waist up, Henry sits heavily in his chair before the hearth, tired before his day even starts. He longs for someone to bring him a cup of tea and a hot breakfast, but . . . no, he cannot employ a servant. He could easily afford one – his father is more generous than rumour gives him credit for – but no, a servant is out of the question. Think of it: a flesh-and-blood woman in his house, sleeping under the same roof, undressing for bed, bathing naked in a tub . . . ! As if things weren't bad enough already.

'Servants are a boon for every growing boy,' Bodley once told him, in one of those encounters whose sole object was to send the adolescent Henry fleeing under a cloud of his peers' laughter. 'Especially when they come straight from the country. Sun-ripened, clean and fresh.'

Henry's cat comes padding in now, making exotic attempts at conversation as she butts her head against his calves. He has nothing for her, the last of the meat having spoiled.

'Can you not wait?' he mutters, but the innocent animal looks at him as though he's feather-brained.

His own stomach churns noisily. Perhaps a very *old* servant would be safe? But how old would she have to *be*? Fifty? Mightn't the butcher's wife – the one who saves the best scraps for Henry's puss and always has a smile for him – be fifty? And yet he's been known to wonder what she might look like naked. Seventy, then?

He looks down at the fire, at his overzealously-darned socks sheathing his big feet like tubers caked with earth. He gazes at his own bare arms, folded across his chest. His own nipples, framed thus, are of no sensual interest to him –yet identical knobbles of flesh, imagined on a female chest, have the power to drive him to self-pollution. Were his own breasts enlarged with milk he would recoil in disgust – yet, imagined on a woman, those same bladders of flesh become fantastically attractive. And what about the paintings at the Royal Academy exhibitions – the Magdalens and the classical heroines and the martyred saints – he doesn't care who they're supposed to be, as long as their flesh is on show! The way he stares at them, the other gallery visitors must take him for a connoisseur – or perhaps they perceive perfectly well that he's ogling rose-nippled breasts and pearly thighs. And yet, what is he *really* staring at? A layer of pink paint! A layer of dried oil covered with varnish – and he'll stand before it, for minutes at a time, willing a silvery wisp of drapery to slip from between a woman's legs, wishing he could grasp hold of it and tear it out of the way, revealing . . . revealing what? A triangle of canvas? For a triangle of inanimate canvas he is willing to risk his immortal soul! All the so-called-mysteries of the Christian faith, the enigmas beyond human reason, are not so very difficult to understand if one applies oneself, but *this* . . . !

Henry's cat is not to be denied, and begins to cry, having learned that this is the best way to rouse him from concerns not relevant to the feline world. Within fifteen minutes, Henry has been driven from his house, fully dressed, combed and shaved, in search of meat.

On his return, he feels more his own master. The brisk walk and the fresh air have done him good; his clothes have warmed on his body and become part of him, a decorous second skin rather than an ill-fitting disguise. The streets and buildings of Notting Hill were familiar and immutable, reminding him that the real world bears little resemblance to the fluid, shape-shifting locales of his dreams. The bracing impact of stone under his walking feet: that's the truth, not his insubstantial phantasms. Most heartening of all, he has seen the butcher's wife and, thank God, not coveted her. She smiled at him, handed him the cat scraps and some ox tongue for himself, and he didn't imagine her wantonly disrobing to reveal the body of a goddess. She was the butcher's wife: nothing less, nothing more.

'Here, puss,' he says, throwing the animal its breakfast on the kitchen floor. 'Let me think, now.'

Henry ponders while he prepares an omelette, almost from memory, with the merest glance at the ancient copy of Mrs Rundell's *New System of Domestic Cookery* (a gift from Mrs Fox, with the name *Emmeline Fox* inscribed in faded schoolgirl copperplate on the flyleaf and, added in dark indigo ink above the name, in a plainer and more confident hand, *To my valued Friend Henry Rackham, Christmas 1874, from* . . .). He sprinkles the required herbs over the sizzling puddle of whisked egg before it cooks too much, then becomes so absorbed in the curlicued signature of Mrs Fox's younger self that he burns, slightly, the bottom of the omelette before he can fold it. It is still perfectly good. London's destitute would be grateful for far worse.

'It's quite simple, puss,' he explains to his saucer-eyed familiar as he eats. 'The marriage of man and woman produces offspring. It's been going on for thousands of years. It's like plants and flowers growing when the rain falls. A necessary, God-given process; nothing whatsoever to do with fevers, lusts and lubricious dreams.'

Henry's cat looks up at him, unconvinced.

'To a man with a mission, the propagation of humankind shouldn't occupy more than a passing thought.' He forks a wedge of egg into his mouth and chews. 'In any case,' he adds when the mouthful has gone down, 'the one woman I might wish to marry has no wish to marry again.'

Henry's cat cocks its head. 'Miaow?'

With a sigh, he throws a morsel of omelette at her furry feet.

'Hoi! Parson!'

The words, though shouted, are barely audible, sucked in and swallowed up by the dark orifices of the street – the gaping windows, decrepit alleys, broken trapdoors and bottomless pits. A grizzled man of indeterminate age, who has been watching Henry's progress for some time, rises up from a smoky subterranean stairwell like Lazarus from the grave. His filthy gnarled hands grip the rope that hangs in place of the missing handrail; his bloodshot, wolf-browed eyes are narrowed with suspicion. 'Lookin' for anybody in pertickler?'

'Perhaps for you, sir,' answers Henry, summoning all his nerve as he walks closer, for this man is heavily muscled, and already in his shirt-sleeves, so there's little to inhibit fisticuffs. 'But why do you call me "Parson"?'

'You look like one.' The grizzled man draws abreast with Henry, hands on the hips of his mud-coloured trousers. In the darkness of the stairwell behind him, a dog mutters in frustration, claws scrabbling at stone and rotten wood, unable to follow its master up the vertiginous steps to the surface world.

'Well, I'm not a parson,' says Henry, regretfully. 'Forgive my boldness, sir, but *you* have the look of a man who has suffered much. Indeed, of a man who is suffering still. If it's not too much of an imposition, will you tell me your story?'

The man's eyes narrow even tighter, radically rearranging the whiskers of his eyebrows. With one massive, calloused hand he smooths down his hair, which is being blown across his forehead by a foul breeze.

'You ain't a norfer, are ye?' he says.

Henry repeats the strange word to himself silently, straining to divine its meaning.

'I beg your pardon?' he's obliged to ask.

'*Orfer,*' repeats the man. 'A fellow as writes books about poor men that poor men can't read.'

'No, no, nothing of the kind,' Henry hastens to reassure him, and this seems to earn him better favour, for the man steps back. 'What I am is . . . I am a person who knows too little about the poor, as do all of us who aren't poor ourselves. Perhaps you could teach me what, in your opinion, I need to know.'

The man grins, leans his head to one side, and scratches his chin.

'Will you give me money?' he enquires.

Henry sets his jaw, knowing he must be firm on this question if he's ever to be a clergyman, for he'll no doubt be asked it many times.

'Not without first knowing your situation.'

The grizzled man throws back his head and laughs.

'Well, well!' he declares. '*There* you 'ave the plight of the poor man in a nutshell. The likes of *you* gets money gived to you no matter how lazy and wicked you are, and the likes of *us* must press our old trousers, and 'ang curtains on our broken winders, and sing 'ymns while we shines yer shoes, before you'll give us a penny!' And he laughs again, opening his mouth so wide that Henry catches a glimpse of blackened molars within.

'But,' protests Henry, 'haven't you any work?'

The man grows serious at this, and once again his eyes narrow.

'I might 'ave,' he shrugs. ''Ave you?'

This is a challenge Henry has been expecting, and he's determined not to be so easily shamed. 'You take me for someone who's never done a day's hard labour,' he says, 'and you are right. But I can't help the class I was born into, any more than you can. May we not, even so, speak man to man?'

This sets the other scratching his chin again, until it begins to grow quite red.

'You're a queer fish, ain't you?' he mutters.

'Perhaps I am,' says Henry, smiling for the first time since he opened his mouth. 'Now, will you tell me what you think I should know?'

Thus begins Henry's initiation – the surrender of his religious virginity. Thus begins, in earnest, his response to the Call.

For an hour or more the two men stand there, in the squalor of St Giles, while a faint miasma rises towards the sun, and the gutters release their aroma like soup coming to the boil. Other men, women and dogs pass by from time to time; several of these make overtures to join the conversation, but are coarsely rebuffed by the grizzled man.

'You've got me well and truly cranked up now,' he confesses to Henry under his breath, then bawls once more at loitering 'busybodies' to wait their 'own bloody turn' with 'the Parson'.

'But I'm not a parson,' protests Henry each time another gawker is dispatched.

'Listen to me, I'm just gettin' to the guts of it now,' growls the grizzled man, and lectures on. He has a very great deal to say on a large number of topics, but Henry knows that it's not the particulars but the root principles that are important. Much of what this man says can be found, in *précis*, in books and pamphlets, but solutions that appear obvious under Henry's study-lamp at home don't seem to apply here. To a man like Henry, for whom righteousness is a high ideal, it comes as a shock to learn that to men such as this poor wretch, righteousness is worthless, while vice appears not merely attractive but essential to survival. Clearly, anyone who means to fight for the souls of these people won't get far without first understanding this, and Henry is grateful to learn the lesson so early.

'We shall speak again, sir,' he promises, after the man finally runs out of things to say. 'I am indebted to you, for all you've told me. Thank you, sir.' And, tipping his hat, he steps back and takes his leave of his bemused informant.

Walking on, farther down Church Lane, Henry spies a quartet of small boys, huddled conspiratorially near the side door of a drinking-house. Emboldened by his success with the grizzled man, he hails them with the cheery greeting, 'Hello boys! What are you doing?' but their response is disappointing: they disappear like rats.

Next he sees a woman turning into the street from the better parts beyond – a respectable-looking woman in Henry's estimation, wearing a terracotta dress. She negotiates the cobbles carefully, eyes downcast. Gingerly she steps, avoiding the dog filth, but when she spots Henry, she lifts the hems of her skirts higher than he's ever seen hems lifted – revealing not just the toes, but the whole buttoned shank of her boots, and a glimpse of frilly calf as well. She smiles at him, as if to say, 'In a street full of ordure, what's a body to do?'

Henry's first thought is to walk past her as quickly as possible, but then he reminds himself that if he's ever to realise his destiny, he must not ignore opportunities like this one. Filling his chest with breath and squaring his shoulders, he steps forward.

No sooner has he uttered his first words of greeting than Rackham finds himself smothered with kisses.

'Ho!' he laughs, as his ears and cheeks and eyes and throat are grazed, with exuberant speed, by Sugar's moistened lips. 'What have I done to deserve this?'

'You know very well,' she says, pressing her hands tight against his back, straining to make an impression through the layers of his clothing. 'You've changed everything.'

William shakes off his ulster and hangs it on the massive cast-iron coat-stand that was delivered here yesterday. 'You mean, *this*?' he teases, nudging the unyielding framework to remind her how flimsy its discarded predecessor was.

'You know what I mean,' she says, stepping backwards towards the bedroom. She is wearing her green dress, the one she wore when she met him, its mildew painstakingly cleaned off with matchsticks, cotton wool and Rackham's Universal Solvent. 'I'll never forget my day at your lavender farm.'

'Nor shall I,' he says, following her. 'Your Colonel Leek would linger in anyone's memory.'

She flinches in embarrassment. 'Oh William, I'm so sorry: I thought he'd be better behaved – he *did* promise me.' She sits on the edge of the bed, hands folded in her lap, head slightly downcast, so that her abundant fringe falls over her eyes. 'Can you forgive me? I know so few men, that's the problem.'

William sits beside her, laying one of his big hands over hers.

'Ach, he's no worse than some of the hopeless drunkards I have to deal with in my business affairs. The world is full of repugnant old blackguards.'

'He's the nearest thing to a grandfather I ever had,' she reflects ruefully, 'when I was a little girl.' Is this the right moment for winning his sympathy? She glances sideways, to judge if her arrow was wide of the mark, but there's compassion in his face, and the redoubled pressure of his hand on hers lets her know she has reached his heart.

'Your childhood years,' he says, 'must have been Hell on earth.'

She nods and, without having to will it, real tears fall from her eyes. But what if William is one of those men who cannot abide a woman weeping? What does she think she's up to? Something has gone awry inside her breast, where such decisions are made; a valve of self-control has failed, and she feels herself borne on a spillage of unfiltered feeling.

'St Giles has a terrible reputation,' offers William.

'It used to be a lot worse,' she says, 'before they cut it in half with New Oxford Street.' For some reason this strikes her as unbearably funny, and she snorts with laughter, wetting the tip of her nose with snot. What's *wrong* with her? She'll disgust him . . . but no, he's handing her his handkerchief, an eminently pickpocketable square of white silk, monogrammed, for her to blow her nose in.

'Do you . . . do you have any sisters?' he asks, awkwardly. 'Or brothers?'

She shakes her head, burying her face in the soft cloth, regaining her composure. 'Alone,' she says, hoping that her tears have not entirely washed away the subtle brown pigment with which she defines her pale orange eyelashes. 'And you?'

'Me?'

'Do *you* have any sisters?'

'None,' he says, with obvious regret. 'My father married late, and lost his wife early.'

'Lost?'

'She disgraced him, and he cast her off.'

Back in control of herself now, Sugar resists the temptation to pry into the facts of the matter, judging that she'll be granted the answers to a greater number of questions if she probes less boldly.

'How sad,' she says. 'And your wife Agnes: has she a large family?'

'No,' replies William, 'smaller even than mine. Her natural father died when she was a young girl, her mother when she came out of school. Her step-father is a lord: lives abroad, travels a great deal, has married a lady I've never met. As for siblings, Agnes *should* have had three or four sisters, but they all died in childbirth. She herself barely survived.'

'That's why she's sickly, perhaps?'

William's eyes flash with pain, as Agnes's voice, hoarse with demented hatred, yells *You make me sick!* inside his skull: 'Perhaps,' he sighs.

Sugar strokes his hand, insinuates her fingers up his sleeve, pressing her rough flesh against his wrists in a motion she knows arouses him — if he's to be aroused at all.

'I do have one brother, though,' he adds briskly.

'A brother? Really?' she says, as though William must be awfully clever or resourceful to have furnished himself with such a thing. 'What sort of man is he?'

William falls back on the bed, staring up at the ceiling. 'What sort of man?' he echoes, as she lays her head on his chest. 'Now there's a question . . .'

''Ello, sir,' the prostitute calls, in a friendly but offhand manner, as though eager to please but just as content to be refused. 'Want a nice girl — not expensive?'

She is pretty, and in much better condition than the freckled girl who, weeks ago in these same streets, told him her hand was his for a shilling. Yet, to Henry's great relief, his response to this smart little temptress is no different from his response to her shabbier counterpart: he feels pity. The longings that plague him when he walks side by side with Mrs Fox are far from his mind now; he desires only to make a good account of himself, and learn as much from this poor creature as he learned from the grizzled man.

'I wish . . . only to talk with you,' he assures her. 'I am a gentleman.'

'Oh, good, sir,' affirms the woman. 'I don't speak to any man as ain't a gentleman. But let's speak in my 'ouse. If you'll come with me, sir, it ain't very far.' Her speech is common, but not Cockney: possibly she's a ruined maidservant from the country, or some other victim of rural circumstance.

'No, stay,' he cautions her. 'I meant what I said just now: I wish only to talk with you.'

Mistrust, absent from her face while she took him for a partner in crime, now creases her brow.

'Oh, I ain't very good at talkin', sir,' she says, casting a glance over her shoulder. 'I'll not keep you.'

'No, no,' Henry remonstrates, guessing the reason for her reluctance. 'I'll pay you for your time. Whatever is your usual fee, I will pay.'

She cocks her head quizzically then, like a child who has been promised something she's old enough to know is improbable.

'One shillin', please,' she proposes. Without hesitation Henry puts his hand into his waistcoat pocket, produces not one but two shillings, and holds them out to her.

'Come along then, sir,' she says, folding the coins into her small hand. 'I'll take you where we can talk to our 'earts' content.'

'No, no,' protests Henry. 'Here in the street is quite satisfactory.'

She laughs, raucously and without covering her mouth. (Mrs Fox is right: there is no mistaking a fallen woman.) 'Very well, sir. What do you wish to 'ear?'

He draws a deep breath, knowing she thinks him a fool, praying for the grace to transcend foolishness. She has clasped her hands behind her back, the better to show him her body no doubt. She is bosomy, but thin in the waist – very like the women used in advertisements for shoe polish, or his brother's perfumes for that matter. Yet she is nothing to him but an unfortunate in peril of perdition. His heart beats hard in his breast, but only with fear that she'll use her pretty tongue to mock his faith or his sincerity, and leave him stammering in the wake of her scornful departure. Apart from his heartbeat, he is unaware of his body; it might as well be a column of smoke, or a pedestal for his soul.

'You are . . . a prostitute,' he confirms.

'Yes, sir.' She clasps her hands tighter, and stands straighter, like a schoolgirl under interrogation.

'And when did you lose your virtue?'

'When I was sixteen, sir, to me 'usband.'

'To your husband, you say?' he replies, moved by her ignorance of moral science. 'Why, you didn't lose it, then!'

She shakes her head, smiling as before. 'I weren't married to 'im then, sir. We was married in shame, as they say.'

Is she making fun of him? Henry squares his jaw, resolved to demonstrate he knows a thing or two about prostitutes. 'You later left him,' he suggests. 'Or were you cast out?'

'You might say as I was cast out, sir. 'E died.'

'And what is it that keeps you in this life? Would you say it was bad company? Or Society's door being closed to you? Or . . . lust?'

'Lust, definitely, sir,' she replies. 'The lust to eat. If a day goes by an' I ain't 'ad a bite, I crave it, sir. Food, that is, sir.' She shrugs, pouts, and licks her lips. 'Weak, that's me.'

Henry begins to blush: she's no fool, this woman — cleverer than he, perhaps. Is there a future for a clergyman whose wits are duller than those of his parishioners? (Mrs Fox assures him his brain is as sharp as anyone's and that he would make a wonderful vicar, but she is too kind . . .) Surely, for a man with a mind as run-of-the-mill as his to be any use at shepherding a parish, he'd need to be blessed with exceptional purity of spirit, a divine simplicity of . . .

''Ave you finished with me already, sir?'

'Uh . . . no!' With a start, he returns his attention to his prostitute's eyes — eyes which (he notices suddenly) are the same colour as Mrs Fox's, and very nearly the same shape. He clears his throat, and asks: 'Would you leave this life if you had work?'

'*This* is work, sir,' she grins. ''*Ard* work.'

'Well, yes . . .' he agrees, but then, 'No . . .' he disagrees, 'But . . .' He frowns, dumbstruck. That old cynic MacLeish (he now recalls) once spoke of the futility of arguing with the poor. 'More education,' MacLeish declared, 'is precisely what they *don't* need. Already they can outfox philosophers and do circus tricks with logic. They're too clever by half!' But Mrs Fox refuted him, yes she did . . . What was it she said?

The prostitute cocks her head and leans closer to him, in an effort to see through the dreamy sheen in his unfocused eyes. Impishly, she waves her tiny hand at him, as though from a distant shore.

'You're a strange one, ain't you?' she says. 'A ninnocent. I like you.'

Henry feels a fresh rush of blood to his cheeks, much more copious than the last. It throbs across his entire face, even reaching the tips of his ears — what an ass he must look!

'I–I know a man,' he stammers, 'a man who owns a business. A very great concern, that's growing larger as we speak. I . . . I could arrange . . .' (for hasn't William been saying he needs more workers and quickly?) '. . . I'm sure I could arrange for you to be given employment.'

To his dismay, her smile vanishes from her face and, for the first time since they met, she looks as if she despises him. All at once he's afraid of her; afraid like any man of losing the approving sparkle in a woman's eyes; afraid, simply, of letting her go. He yearns to convey to her the glad tidings of God's generosity in times of need, to inspire her with proof of how the grimmest circumstance can be lightened by faith. The desire chokes him, but he knows that words are not enough, especially *his* feeble words. If only he could transmit God's grace through his hands, and galvanise her with a touch!

'What sort of work?' demands the prostitute. 'Factory work?'

'Well . . . yes, I suppose so.'

'Sir,' she declares indignantly. 'I've 'ad work in a factory, and I know that to earn two shillin's like these' (she holds up the coins he has given her) 'I should 'ave to work many long hours, breakin' my back in stink and danger, with never a minute to rest, and 'ardly no sleep.'

'But you wouldn't be damned!' blurts Henry in desperation. No sooner is the word 'damned' past his lips, than he receives his own punishment: the prostitute looks away and irritably thrusts his coins into a slit in her skirts, obviously deciding she's given him as much time as he deserves. Fixing her gaze on the far end of the street, she remarks, 'Parson's tricks, sir, just parson's tricks, all that.' She glances back at him suspiciously. 'You're a parson, ain't you?'

'No, no, I'm not,' he says.

'Don't believe you,' she sniffs.

'No, really, I'm not,' he pleads, recalling Saint Peter and the cock crow.

'Well, you ought to be,' she says, reaching forward to touch, gently, his tightly-knotted necktie, as if her fingertips could conjure it into a clergyman's collar.

'God bless you!' he cries.

There's a moment's pause while his ejaculation hangs in the air. Then the prostitute bends forward, resting her hands on her knees, and begins to giggle. She giggles for half a minute or more.

'You're a character, sir,' she wheezes, shoulders shaking. 'But I must go . . .'

'Wait!' he implores her, his head belatedly crowded with vital questions, questions he could not forgive himself for failing to put to her. 'Do you believe you have a soul?'

'A soul?' she echoes incredulously. 'A ghost inside me, with wings on? Well . . .' She opens her mouth to speak, her lips curved in mockery; then, observing his plaintive expression, she swallows her spite, and softens the blow. 'Anything *you*'ve got,' she sighs, 'I've got too, I'm sure.' She smooths down the front of her dress, her hands sliding over the contours of her belly. 'Now, I must be goin'. Last question, gentlemen, please!'

Henry sways on his feet, horrified to find himself in the grip of Evil. Only a few minutes ago, he was in the Lord's hands: what's become of him now? His self-possession is gone, and he might as well be thrashing in the clammy grip of a dream. One last question his pretty prostitute will answer; one last question, and what shall it be? Aghast, he hears his voice speak:

'Are you . . . are you hairy?'

She squints in puzzlement. 'Hairy, sir?'

'On your body.' He waves his hand vaguely at her bodice and skirts. 'Do you have hair?'

'Hair, sir?' she grins mischievously. 'Why, of *course*, sir: same as you!' And at once she grabs hold of her skirts and gathers them up under her bosom, holding the rucked material with one hand while, with the other, she pulls down the front of her pantalettes, exposing the dark pubic triangle.

Loud laughter sounds from elsewhere in the street as Henry stares for a long instant, shuts his eyes, and turns his back on her. His upbringing makes it almost impossible for him to turn his back on a woman without first politely concluding the conversation, but he manages. Head aflame, he stumbles stiffly down the street, as if her sex is buried deep in his flesh like a sword.

'I only wanted an answer!' he yells hoarsely over his shoulder, as more and more of Church Lane's elusive and subterranean voices join in the laughter without even understanding its cause.

'Jesus, sir!' she calls after him. 'You ought to get *summat* for your extra shillin'!'

'So there you have it,' says William, as Sugar strokes her hands through the thick fur of his chest. 'As different from me as night from day. But not a bad fellow all the same. And who knows? He may yet astound us, and seize his destiny.'

Sugar pauses in her encouragements to William's growing manhood. 'You mean . . . seize Rackham Perfumeries?'

'No, no, that's mine now, forever; no one can take it away,' he says – though his erection, unnerved by the thought, falters and requires reassurance. 'No, I meant Henry may yet seize . . . I don't know, whatever a man of his sort wishes to seize, I suppose . . .' He groans as Sugar mounts him.

This is the safe course, she's found. Through all the years, with all the men, this is what she's learned: a wilted man is an unhappy man, and unhappy men can be dangerous. Sheathe them in a warm hole, and they'll perk up. Whenever the cockstand is uncertain, whenever strong drink has taken its toll, whenever sadness or worry lie heavy on a man's heart, whenever doubt attacks his soul, whenever he glimpses his own nakedness and finds himself ugly or absurd, whenever he sees his manhood and is struck by the morbid fear that this may be the last time it rises from its patch of hair, *then* the only safe course is to cultivate its growth so it can sway unsupported for an instant – just long enough for it to be stowed snugly inside. Thereafter, Nature takes over.

FIFTEEN

pring is here, and everyone who knows Agnes Rackham is amazed at how she's come back from the dead. Such a short while ago she lay like a corpse in her darkened, airless room: now, dressed gaily, she's brightening the house with her angelic singing voice as she prepares to meet the Season.

'Open the curtains, Letty!' she cries, everywhere she goes.

All day she's practising: standing erect, turning demurely, smiling fetchingly, walking without the footsteps showing. There's an art to moving as if on castors, and only an elite few can master it.

'Lay the book on my head, Clara,' she says to her maidservant, 'and stand well back!'

Nor are Agnes's labours confined to the four walls of the Rackham house: she's been making frequent sallies to Oxford and Regent Streets, and returning with candy-striped parcels large and small. The Prince of Wales may still be on the Riviera, but for Agnes Rackham the Party That Lasts A Hundred Days has begun. She feels almost like a Débutante again!

Of course, it's all thanks to her guardian angel. How encouraging it is to know there's one creature in the world who loves her and wishes her well! What a relief to be truly, deeply understood! Her guardian angel appreciates that she has Higher Reasons for seeking success in the Season — no frivolous desire, but a contest of Good against Evil. Evil is what's made her ill and done its utmost to rob her of a place in Society; Evil is what she's banishing from her life now — with the help of her spirit rescuer, and those tiny rosy pills Mrs Gooch has introduced her to. Each pill no bigger than a sequin; each pill more than a match for the pains in her head!

Two dozen kid gloves have arrived yesterday. This will do for a start, though she expects to go through many more, as the silly things aren't washable. ('Honestly, Clara, I don't know why there's such a fuss about Great Advances in Knowledge, when we ladies are constantly having to replace such a simple necessity.') Agnes has a pair of new kids on the glove-stretchers, to break them in, but the thumbs are still impossible to get on even with powder. Ridiculous! Her thumbs haven't thickened, have they? Clara assures her they're as slender as ever.

Gloves are just one of a hundred dilemmas. For example she must decide soon what scent to wear this Season. In past years she avoided all Rackham perfumes, fearing it would offend Good Taste to be a walking endorsement of her father-in-law's business. However, the ladies' journals are lately unanimous in their opinion that the truly refined woman restricts her perfumes to eau de Cologne and lavender water, and as these are the same from one maker to another, mightn't it be all right to use Rackham's? Only *she* would know, after all – making her choice purely a moral one. Also, should she wear her white silk dress on Croquet Day at the Carcajoux? The weather can't be trusted, and her skirts might get muddy and wet, but white would go *so* well, and no one else will be wearing it. Of course she can instruct Mrs Le Quire (her new dressmaker) to add a *port-jupe* to the skirts, but would this solve the problem? Agnes foresees difficulties in attempting, simultaneously, to play croquet and hold her hems suspended on a chain.

Mrs Gooch's visit, and her excellent advice about pills and friendly pharmacists ('That old sourpuss Gosling will only give you a lecture, but the others – if you bat your eyelashes sweetly – are no trouble at all') have made such a difference to the quality of Agnes's life that she's determined to receive, from now on, as many visits from as many ladies as possible. Send out the message for all to hear: Mrs Agnes Rackham is 'in'!

She has thrown away all the calling cards she received during the dark times, the months of illness and pecuniary humiliations. New ones have taken their place – from new people, come to see the new Agnes Rackham.

Today, Mrs Amphlett called. The dear woman, in choosing to visit between four and five o'clock, rather than three and four, treated Agnes not as someone seeking to re-enter Society after an illness, but as a healthy human to whom an ordinary social call was due. How kind of her!

In the flesh, Mrs Amphlett differed remarkably from Agnes's vague recollection of her, glimpsed across a ballroom two years ago. *Then*, Mrs

Amphlett was (not to mince words) buxom and freckle-faced. Today, in Agnes's parlour, she was thin as a reed, with a flawless white complexion. Of course Agnes, mad with curiosity, longed to sweep politeness aside and *ask*, but in the end, Mrs Amphlett volunteered the secrets, namely: (1) a diet of water, raw carrot and mouthfuls of oxtail soup, and (2) Rowlands' Kalydor Lotion, with a little 'finishing off' from a face powder.

'I should never have recognised you!' Agnes complimented her.

'You are too kind.'

'Not at all.'

(In truth, lovely though Mrs Amphlett looked, Agnes was just the *slightest* bit discomposed by the way the dear woman made several references to 'the baby' and 'motherhood', as if under the delusion that this were a fit topic for discussion. Might it perhaps be a little too soon after her confinement for Mrs Amphlett to be back in Society just yet? Agnes did wonder, but laid the thought aside, in a spirit of generosity. An ally in the Season is not to be sniffed at!)

'And *you*, Mrs Rackham; you do look most terribly well. What's *your* secret?'

Agnes merely smiled, having by now learned her lesson not to mention her guardian angel to persons she wouldn't trust with her life.

Now Agnes stands at her bedroom window, wishing that her guardian angel would materialise under the trees, just *there* outside the Rackham gates. Her hand itches to wave. But miracles are not for the asking; they come only when the stern eyes of God droop shut for a moment, and Our Lady takes advantage of His inattention to grant an illicit mercy. God, Agnes has decided, is an Anglican, whereas Our Lady is of the True Faith; the two of Them have an uneasy relationship, unable to agree on anything, except that if They divorce, the Devil will leap gleefully into the breach. So, They tolerate each other, and take care of the world as best They can.

Moving to the mirror, Agnes examines her face. She is almost half-way through her twenties, and the spectre of senescence looms. She must take the utmost care to preserve herself from injury and decay, for there are some things that sleep cannot undo. Each night she travels to the Convent of Health, where her heavenly sisters soothe and tend her, but if she's in too bad a state when she arrives at their ivy-crested gates, they shake their heads and scold her gently. Then she knows that in the morning when she wakes, she'll still be in pain.

She is in pain now. An illusion of falling snow twinkles in front of her right eye, and a pulse beats behind. Could it be that the last little rosy pill she took was disgorged, unnoticed, when she had the mishap with the chicken broth? Perhaps she should take another . . . although the mishap has left a bitter taste in her mouth and she would rather take a sip of Godfrey's Cordial instead.

On her left brow, almost invisible inside the crescent of golden hairs above her eye, is a scar, incurred in a fall when she was a child. That scar is permanent, an indelible flaw. How terrifying is the vulnerability of flesh! She frowns, then hastily unfrowns, for fear of the lines etching themselves permanently into her forehead.

Closing her eyes, she imagines her guardian angel standing behind her. Cool hands, smooth as alabaster, are laid against her temples, massaging tenderly. Spirit fingers penetrate her skin and sink into her skull, insubstantial and yet as satisfying as nails against an itch. They locate the source of the pain, tug on it, and a clump of Evil comes away from Agnes's soul, like a web of pith from an orange. She shivers with pleasure, to feel her naked soul cleansed like this.

She opens her eyes, and is puzzled to find herself on the floor, sprawled supine, staring up at the slowly revolving ceiling and the worried upside-down face of Clara.

'Shall I call for help, ma'am?' the servant enquires.

'Of course not,' says Agnes, blinking hard. 'I'm quite well.'

'That Doctor Harris seemed a nice man,' suggests Clara, referring to the physician who attended Mrs Rackham's previous emergency. 'Not a bit like Doctor Curlew. Shall I . . . ?'

'No, Clara. Help me to my feet.'

'He was ever so concerned about your collapses,' the servant perseveres, as she hauls her mistress up from the floor.

'He was young . . . and handsome, as I recall,' pants Agnes, adjusting to verticality with a giddy sway. 'No doubt you'd enjoy . . . seeing him again. But we mustn't waste his time, must we?'

'I'm only thinking of your health, ma'am,' insists Clara, nettled. 'Mr Rackham has said we're to tell him if you're poorly.'

Agnes's hold on Clara's arm spasms into a claw-grip.

'You're not to tell William of this,' she whispers.

'Mr Rackham said—'

'"Mr Rackham" doesn't have to know everything that goes on,' maintains Agnes, inspired, as if by a tongue of fire, with the means to reassert control over Clara. 'For example, he needn't know where you found the money to buy that corset. It suits you terribly well, but . . . we ladies are entitled to *some* secrets, yes?'

Clara turns pale. 'Yes, ma'am.'

'Now,' sighs Agnes, smoothing the creases from her sleeves, 'be a dear and fetch me the Godfrey's Cordial.'

Intermittent, gentle gusts of wind, blowing through the French windows like the playful teasing of ghostly children, make the pages of Sugar's novel flap. She has long ago put down her pen, and the breezes thrust the fluttering top sheet against the inky-nibbed instrument, creating an aeolian welter of nonsense. Sugar doesn't notice, and continues to squint absent-mindedly into the sunlit foliage of her little garden.

She'd hoped that by moving her escritoire very close to the open windows, close enough to breathe the fresh air of Priory Close and smell the earth below the rose-bush, she would be inspired to write. So far, nothing has come – though at least she's still awake, which is an improvement on what happens whenever she takes the manuscript to bed . . .

Outside on the footpath above her head, where almost no one ever seems to walk, a couple of sparrows are hopping to and fro, gathering scraps for a nest. Wouldn't it be nice if they built their nest in the rose-bush just here? But no, the most interest they take in Sugar's shady patch of untended greenery is to pilfer a twig from it, to house themselves elsewhere.

The wind-blown page flutters again, and this time the pen rolls off, clattering onto the desktop. Instinctively, Sugar jerks forward, but succeeds only in bumping the inkwell so that three or four big droplets of black ink are knocked free of the table, to splash onto the skirts of her jade dress.

'God damn God and all His . . .' she begins angrily, then sighs. This is scarcely the end of the world. She can try to wash the ink out – and if it doesn't go, or if she can't be bothered, well, she can buy a new dress. Another envelope from William's bank arrived this morning, to add to the others in the bottom drawer of her dresser. His generosity hasn't diminished, or perhaps he lacks the imagination to alter the instructions to his banker; whatever the reason, she's accumulating more money than she can spend, even if she were to make a habit of spilling ink on her clothes.

She *must* finish her novel. Nothing like it has ever been published before; it would cause a sensation. If conceited fools like William's school cronies can make a stir with their feeble blasphemies, think of the effect she could have with *this*, the first book to tell the truth about prostitution! The world is ready for the truth; the modern age is here; every year another report appears that examines poverty by means of statistical research rather than romantic claptrap. All that's needed now is a great novel that will capture the imagination of the public – move them, enrage them, thrill them, terrify them, scandalise them. A story that will seize them by the hand and lead them into streets where they've never dared set foot, a tale that throws back the sheets from acts never shown and voices never heard. A tale that fearlessly points the finger at those who are to blame. Until such a novel is published, prostitutes will continue to be smothered under the shroud of The Great Social Evil, while the cause of their misery walks free . . .

Sugar stares down at the ink patterns the wind has made. It's time she replaced them with something more meaningful. All the fallen women of the world are relying on her to tell the truth. 'This story,' she used to say to those of her friends who could read, 'isn't about me, it's about all of us . . .' Now, in her sunlit study in Priory Close, she begins to sweat.

'I'm dying, Shush.' That's what Elizabeth said to her, on the last night she lived – the night before you met Sugar in that stationer's in Greek Street. 'Tomorrow morning I'll be cold meat. They'll clean the room and toss me in the river. Eels'll eat my eyes.'

'They won't toss you in the river. I won't let them.' Elizabeth's grip on her hand was damned strong, for such a wasted bag of bones.

'What do you mean to do?' Elizabeth wheezed mockingly. 'Gather up my mother and father, and all my relations, for a fancy Christian burial, with the vicar telling them how good I was?'

'If that's what you want.'

'Christ Jesus, Sugar, you're such a shameless liar. Don't you never blush?'

'I'm in earnest. If you want a burial, I'll arrange it.'

'Christ Jesus, Christ Jesus . . . what mullock you talk. Is that how you got yourself into the West End? Telling men their cocks are the biggest you ever saw?'

'There's no need to insult me just because you're dying.'

The laughter cleared the air a little, but Elizabeth's hand around her own was still tight as a dog's jaws.

'No one will remember me,' the dying woman said, licking at the sweat rolling down her face. 'Eels'll eat my eyes, and no one will even know I've lived.'

'Nonsense.'

'I was dead already, the first time I opened my legs. "After today, I have no daughter" – that's what my father said.'

'More fool him.'

'A whole life, gone like a piss in an alley.' In the sickly yellow light, and with all the sweat on Elizabeth's cheeks, it was difficult to tell if she was weeping. 'I tried, Shush. I did my best to stay out of God's bad books. Even *after* I was a whore, I did my best, in case I got a second chance. Pick any day from the last twenty years, see what I tried, and you'd have to admit I didn't give up easy.'

'Of course not. Everyone understands that.'

'Nobody's come to see me, you know that? Nobody. Except you.'

'I'm sure they'd all come if they could. They're frightened, that's all.'

'Oh, I'm sure, I'm sure. And that's the biggest cock I ever saw . . .'

'Do you want a drink?'

'No I don't want a drink. Are you going to put me in your book?'

'What book?'

'The book you're writing. *Women Against Men*, wasn't it called?'

'That was years ago. It's had about a dozen titles since then.'

'Are you going to put me in it?'

'Do you want me to?'

'Never mind what I want. Are you going to put me in it?'

'If you want me to.'

'Christ Jesus, Sugar. Don't you never blush?'

Sugar stands up from the writing-desk and walks to the French windows, to shake off the memory of Elizabeth's clammy, grasping hand. Nervously she clenches and unclenches her own, imagining the dying woman's sweat on them still, though she knows it's her own perspiration prickling in the cracks of her leathery palms. She holds up her hands, angles the palms so that they're lit up by the sunlight. Her skin has been fright- ful lately, despite the fact that she's been salving her hands with Rackham's

Crème de Jeunesse nightly. Oh, for a jar of bear's grease such as was always in supply at Mrs Castaway's – but she can't imagine where she could buy bear's grease in Marylebone.

Glancing downwards, she notes that the stains on her dress have expanded and merged into a very big blot indeed; she'd better change into a fresh dress in case William comes. She closes the untidy pages of her manuscript inside its hard covers. The phalanx of crossed-out titles stares up at her; the first few are densely inked, obliterated beyond recall, but the later ones are cancelled perfunctorily with a single line drawn through. *Women Against Men* is still clearly legible, as is its successor, *An Angry Cry from an Unmarked Grave*. The most recent, *The Fall and Rise of Sugar*, is a mere scrawl, tentative and thin. She opens at page one, and reads '*All men are the same . . .*' and the twenty, fifty words that follow, in a single glance. How peculiar, the way a passage that's been read many times can be read so fast, while something new must be read laboriously, word for word. This whole first page plays almost automatically in her mind, like a barrel-organ ground by a monkey.

> *My name is Sugar – or if it isn't, I know no better.*
> *I am what you would call a Fallen Woman, but I assure you I did not fall –*
> *I was pushed. Vile man, eternal Adam, I indict you!*

Sugar bites her lip in embarrassment, so hard she draws blood.

Two hours later, having stowed her novel away in its drawer and read the latest *Illustrated London News* instead, Sugar is in the bath again. Half her life nowadays seems spent in the bath, preparing herself in case William should visit. Not that she regards him as worthy of such fuss, you understand; not that she doesn't despise him, or, if that's too harsh a word, at least strongly disapprove of him . . . It's just that, well, his interest in her is a valuable commodity, and she ought to keep it alive for as long as she can. If she can make his affection last – his love, as he called it – she has a chance – a once-in-a-lifetime chance – to cheat Fate. Under Rackham's wing, anything is possible . . .

Of all the nooks in her Priory Close suite, it's this black-and-mustard bathroom, this glazed little chamber, that she's most at home in. The other rooms are too big, too empty; the ceilings are too far away, the walls and floors too bare. She wishes they were cosy and cluttered with her own furnishings and bric-a-brac, but she's been too timid to buy anything, and she can't imagine what. Only this small bathroom, for all its eerie sheen, feels snug and finished: the ribbon of black wallpaper is perfect for staring into, the wooden floor glows in the light from above, the towels on the bronze rails are soft and plush, and all the little bottles and jars of Rackham produce are cheerful as toys. Most reassuring of all is the humid haze of steam that hangs above her tub, swirling back and forth with the slowness of cloud.

She shouldn't be bathing this often, she knows. It's bad for her skin. That's why her hands are sore and cracking; it's not Crème de Jeunesse or bear's grease she needs, it's to spend less time immersed in hot soapy water! Yet, despite knowing this, every day, sometimes *twice* a day, she fills the tub and allows herself to slide in, because she loves it. Or, if love isn't the right word, then . . . it comforts her. She's awfully disconsolate lately, shedding tears for no apparent reason, suffering fits of anxiety, dreaming of childhood horrors she'd thought she'd forgotten. She, who only recently was the sort of woman who could hear a man say, 'What is there to stop me killing you now?' and disarm him with a wink; *she* seems to be turning into a girl who couldn't endure the sound of a lewd whistle in the street.

'You're going soft,' she says to herself, and her voice, so ugly and unmusical compared to Agnes Rackham's, reverberates in the steamy acoustic of the bathroom. 'You're going soft,' she says again, trying to raise her tone as the words pass through her throat. A lilt, she must try to speak with a lilt. She succeeds only in lisping. 'You sound,' she says, tossing her sponge at her toes, 'like a sodomite.'

Her right hand stings like the devil; squeezing the sponge out has insinuated soap into the cracks of her palms, the tender, almost bleeding fissures in her flesh. In this sense at least, she's undeniably softer than she used to be.

'Oh, William, what a lovely surprise!' she rehearses, trying for the lilt again, then laughs, a harsh sound against the tiles. A fart swims up through the bathwater and breaks the surface with a damp puff of stink.

William, she knows, is unlikely to come today. The Season is at hand, and (as he regretfully explained to her, on his last visit) he's going to be wretchedly busy, pulled from one dinner party to the next, shepherded 'by force' into theatres and opera houses.

'Who'll force you?' she dared to ask. 'Agnes?'

He sighed, already out of bed, reaching for his trousers. 'No, I mustn't blame her. This elaborate game we play, this merry dance we must conform to whether we like it or not . . . its rules are set by grander authorities than my little wife. I blame . . .' (and, apologetic for his hasty leave-taking, he spared a moment to stroke her freshly-washed hair) 'I blame Society!'

In Agnes Rackham's bedroom, on Agnes Rackham's bed, dozens of cards are laid out in the shape (more or less) of a human being.

'Do you know what this is?' asks Agnes of Clara, who has just entered and is contemplating the display with a frown of puzzlement.

Clara looks closer, wondering if her mistress is playing a joke on her, or if she's merely mad as usual.

'It's . . . invitations, ma'am.'

Indeed, the mosaic-like shape with the unnaturally small waist and big head is fashioned entirely from *cartes d'invitation* – all requesting the pleasure of Agnes's company in the Season ahead.

'It's more than that, Clara,' says Agnes, encouraging her servant to develop a latent appreciation of symbolism. Again, the poor menial suspects she's being gulled and, after a long pause, Mrs Rackham puts her out of her misery.

'It's forgiveness, Clara,' she says.

The servant nods, and is relieved to be excused.

Yet, unbeknownst to Clara, Mrs Rackham is quite right, and not mad. To many of the ladies and gentlemen seeking to participate in the Season, the month inaugurated by Fool's Day is one of galling humiliation, as they discover they're among the Unforgiven. The invitations they sent out for dinner parties and other 'occasions' to be held in May have harvested a mound of replies inscribed *Regret Not Able To Attend*, and no reciprocal invitations have come. Thus the lengthening April evenings find men sitting up late by their dying firesides, staring with the stoniness usually reserved for bankruptcy or a wife's infidelity; women shed tears and plot impotent revenges. One can be almost sure, if Lady So-and-So's ball is to be held on May 14th, that not to have received a lace-edged *carte d'invitation* by April 14th is a decree of exile.

Not that social ruin is wrought all at once: few of those who shone in the better constellations one year are utterly cast down the next; more often, in order to identify themselves as fallen, fiendishly complicated calculations must be made in the mathematics of rank. For Agnes Rackham no such calculations are necessary; doors are opening for her everywhere.

It is rather to Henry and Mrs Fox that the April mails have brought no joy. Each received a few invitations – more than none, but less than ever before.

Each of them has laid their invitations away in a drawer, and replied *Regret Not Able To Attend*. In Mrs Fox's case, the reason is ill health: she's no longer in any state to attempt all the standing, promenading, croqueting and so forth that the Season requires. Her well-being has faded so remarkably that strangers notice it at once and murmur: 'Not long for this world.' Friends and relatives are still half-blinded by the after-image of her former vigour, and whisper that Emmeline looks 'under the weather' and 'ought to rest'. They advise her to enjoy the Spring sunshine, as there's no better tonic for pallor. 'And do you think,' they ask her tactfully, 'it's good for you to be spending *quite* so much time in the slums?'

The second Sunday morning in April finds Mrs Fox and Henry Rackham, as always, walking together down an aisle of trees, after church.

'Well,' Henry pronounces stiffly. 'I, for one, am not sorry to be excused from the coming revelry.'

'Nor am I,' says Mrs Fox. 'But that isn't what we're fretting about, is it? We haven't been *excused*; we've been *rejected*. And for what reasons, one wonders? Are we both such Untouchables? Are we *so* far beyond the pale?'

'Evidently so,' frowns Henry, walking slowly and dolefully. He has, as always, failed to notice the tongue in her cheek – one of his most endearing weaknesses, in Emmeline's estimation.

'Ah, Henry,' she says, 'we must face the truth. We have nothing to offer our peers. Just look at you: you could have been the head of a great Concern, but instead you refuse all but a meagre allowance, and live in a cottage the size of a labourer's. No doubt the Best People have decided that if they let *you* in their door, who knows what human refuse will come knocking next?' She observes Henry blushing. Och, why does he blush so? He's worth ten of the 'Best People'!

'Also,' she continues, 'you're a man who can't tolerate God being made to stand aside for gaiety, and . . . well, you must admit that makes you rather a dull prospect at a party.'

He grunts, blushing darker. 'Well, there's a string of dinner parties to which I *was* invited – at my brother's house. I asked to be spared.'

'Oh but Henry, Mrs Rackham thinks the world of you!'

'Yes, but at William's dinner parties I'm always shoved opposite someone I can't abide, and for the rest of the evening I'm condemned to the most tiresome intercouse. This year, I decided: no more. I run into Bodley and Ashwell often enough as it is.'

'*Dear* Henry,' smiles Mrs Fox. 'You could have ignored them. They are jackals; you are a lion. A reticent and gentle sort of lion, I'll admit, but . . .'

'I did *not* ask William not to invite *you*.' Anger is making him walk faster, and she must struggle to keep up with him, her dainty boots, so much smaller than his feet, trotting over the cobbles.

'Ah, well,' she says, lifting her skirts ever-so-slightly to ease her progress. 'I shouldn't imagine an unattractive widow is ever in great demand. Much less one who *works*. And then, if the work is reforming fallen women . . . well!'

'It's charitable work,' declares Henry. 'Plenty of the Best People do charitable work.' Her description of herself as unattractive has made him walk even faster: he must outrun his desire to extol her beauty.

'The Rescue Society *is* a charity, I suppose,' concedes Mrs Fox. 'In the sense that our labour is unpaid.' (As she trots by his side, she fumbles in her sleeve, trying to extract a handkerchief she has stowed there.) 'Though I've met ladies who presumed I *must* be drawing a wage . . . As if no woman would do such work unless she were in desperate want. Nobody quite knows, you see, if Bertie left me well- or badly-off. Ah, rumours, rumours . . . Do let's sit down for a while.'

They've come to a stone bridge, whose bowed walls are low and smooth and clean enough to sit on. Only now does Henry notice that Mrs Fox is breathing laboriously, perspiration twinkling on her pale face.

'I have marched you too fast again, big oaf that I am,' he says.

'Not at all,' she pants, dabbing her temples with her handkerchief. 'It's a fine day for a brisk walk.'

'You look weary.'

'I have a cold, I think.' She smiles, to reassure him. 'A cold, now that the warm weather is here. You see? Contrary as always!' Her breast rises and falls with the rapidity of a bird's but, mindful of the impression she is making, she leaves room for a quick breath between clauses. '*You* look weary too.'

'I haven't been sleeping well.'

'My father has very . . . effective medicines for that,' Mrs Fox declares. 'Or you could try warm milk.'

'I prefer to let Nature take its course.'

'Quite right,' says Mrs Fox, closing her eyes to quell a surge of giddiness. 'Who knows? Tonight you may sleep like a baby.'

Henry nods, hands clasped between his knees. 'God grant.'

They sit for a while longer. Water burbles unseen below them and, in time, another pair of church-goers cross the bridge, gesturing almost imperceptibly in greeting.

'You know, Henry,' says Mrs Fox, when the passers-by have gone. 'My sisters at the Rescue Society have urged me . . . to work less during the Season . . . to enjoy some recreation . . . to take advantage of the coming delights . . .' She squints eastwards, as if she might catch a glimpse of London's squalid rookeries from here. 'And yet, away from the streets, I achieve nothing . . . And every day, one more woman comes to that pass where there's no longer any hope for a good life – only a good death.' She looks to her friend, but his eyes are downcast.

Henry is staring into the chiaroscuro pictures of his imagination. An anonymous woman, unscathed from a thousand carnal acts, has finally reached 'that pass' to which Mrs Fox refers – the fateful copulation when the worm of Death enters her. From that moment on, she is doomed. Hair grows on her body as she degenerates from human to bestial form. On her deathbed, still unrepentant, she is monstrously hirsute, sporting hair not just on her pudendum but also her armpits, arms, legs and chest. Henry imagines a sort of curvaceous ape, raving in agonised delirium on a filthy mattress, witnessed by surgeons aghast under the lanterns they hold in their raised and trembling fists. Those 'wild women' brought back from Borneo – those are probably nothing less than the moribund victims of sexual excess! After all, aren't these island races notorious for their—

'Ah well,' sighs Mrs Fox, pushing herself erect once more and dusting off her bustle with a tiny clothes-brush from her reticule. 'We must have our own private little Season, Henry, just you and I. Its highlights will be conversation, walks, and health-giving sunshine.'

'Nothing could give me more pleasure,' Henry affirms, glad that she's not quite so breathless. But, although the sun is shining strongly on them both, Mrs Fox's face remains most terribly pale, and her mouth is still most indecorously open, as if a physical imperative, in defiance of decorum, has parted her lips.

Sugar looks over her shoulder at her reflection in the mirror, guiding her hands as she buttons up her dress. She wields a pair of 'whore's hooks' — curved, long-handled instruments so nicknamed because they enable a woman to don a lady's dress without the aid of a maidservant.

When the last button, at the very nape of her neck, is fastened, Sugar runs two fingers around the silken lining of the tight collar, freeing the stray hairs trapped there. She has chosen this outmoded slate-grey dress because William has never seen her wear it, and so if he catches a glimpse at a distance, he shan't recognise her. Her hair she has parted, uncharacteristically, down the middle and knotted back in a severe chignon, so that scarcely a wisp of it can be seen under her bonnet.

'This will do,' she decides.

She's tired of waiting for William. Days go by without a visit; then, when he does call on her, he has a mind full of concerns from his secret life — secret from her, that is. All his friends and family know him better than she, and they haven't any use for the knowledge; it's so unfair!

Well, she refuses to remain in the dark. Her destiny advances not one whit while she languishes in her rooms, drying her hair in front of the fire, reading newspapers, reading about excise duty to prepare for conversations that never come, telling herself she isn't hungry, resisting the temptation to fill the bathtub. The more William does without her, out there in a world in which she plays no part, the less inclined he'll be to confide in her. From his cast-off perfume books she can learn about spirituous extract of tuberose, and oil of cassia as a cheap substitute for cinnamon, but she needs to understand so much more about William Rackham than that! More than he's ready to divulge!

So, she has made up her mind: she'll spy on him. Everywhere he goes, she will follow. Whatever he sees, she will see also. Whoever he meets, she'll meet too — if necessarily at a distance. His world will become hers; she'll lap up every drop of knowledge. Then, when at last William finds the time to visit her, and she has his wrinkled brow against her breast, she can astound him with how instinctively she understands his troubles, how unerring is her intuition of his needs. By sharing his life illicitly, she'll earn the privilege of sharing it legitimately.

She pauses, for one last glance in the mirror before leaving the house. She's scarcely recognisable, even to herself.

'Perfect,' she says, and unhooks a parasol from the hideous but sturdy coat-stand. What became of the flimsy one William kicked so angrily? He put it out in the street, and the next day it wasn't there anymore. Did scavengers pounce on it, perhaps? Do such things happen in the decorous streets of Marylebone?

She steps out into the fresh air and casts an eye over her surroundings. Not a soul in sight.

For the next three days and a half — or, as she calculates, fifty-five whole hours of waking existence — Sugar attempts to become William Rackham's shadow.

An unconscionable amount of that time is wasted loitering near his house in Chepstow Villas, waiting for him to emerge. She paces up and down the street and mews on three sides of the Rackham grounds, to keep her toes from going numb and her mind from going off its hinges, and twirls her parasol impatiently. What can William be *doing* in there? He's certainly not playing parlour games with his wife and daughter! Is he writing Rackham correspondence, perhaps? If so, how long can a few letters possibly take, now that the Hopsom affair is out of the way? Rackham Perfumeries is a large concern with a hierarchy of employees; aren't there what-d'you-call-'ems — subordinates, underlings — taking care of more mundane matters? Or is it breakfast that occupies William so long? No wonder he's getting tubby, if he spends half the morning eating. Sugar, by contrast, begins each spying day with a bun or an apple bought from a street-seller on her way here.

Fortunately the weather is mild, on these first few mornings of her surveillance of the Rackham house. The gardener is constantly poking around in the grounds, satisfying himself that the new growth is only in the designated places — another reason why Sugar can't loiter too long in the same spot. She'd hoped that the mild weather would permit William's daughter to come out to play, but the child's nurse keeps her well under wraps. Sugar's not even sure of the child's name; one morning, the gardener yelled 'Hello, Miss Sophie!' while peering up at a window on the first floor

– and was shortly afterwards accosted by a matronly-looking servant, who had a word in his ear, causing him to cringe in apology. Sophie, then – unless Shears's greeting was addressed to the nurse. How humiliating to be acquainted with every vein of William's prick, but not know the name of his daughter! All Sugar's attempts to extract it without appearing to be pumping him have failed; nor can she risk uttering it herself, in case he's withholding it on purpose. So, until the nurse decides that the weather is finally good enough for little girls to be brought forth, Sophie Rackham must remain a rumour.

On the second day, Mrs Rackham herself emerges from the front door and, accompanied by her maid, walks purposefully forth. Sugar is tempted to follow, for Agnes is plainly on her way to town, and her enchanting voice, too far away to be intelligible, sings like Pied Piper flutings on the breeze. But Sugar resolves to stay hidden in her shady bower of trees; it's William she ought to be tailing, and besides, there have been too many moments already when the curtains at one of the Rackhams' windows suddenly parted and Agnes was standing there, staring out at the world – or, more often than not, staring straight at the spot where Sugar happened to be dawdling. It's a good thing Sugar is veiled, and under a parasol for good measure, or Mrs Rackham would surely have committed her face to memory by now.

No, it's William she's waiting for. It's William whose movements and habits she needs to know intimately. And what Sugar learns in these first fifty-five hours of stalking him is that, for all his talk of being an individualist and keeping his duller business rivals guessing, he is a man of habit.

Two p.m. is his hour for catching the city-bound omnibus. On each of the three days, he makes his rendezvous with the great lumbering vehicle and climbs into the cabin, taking his seat facing the sunnier side of the road. Sugar, hurrying on to the steely lip of the omnibus at the last possible instant, climbs up to the roof and takes a seat over William's head. At this quiet time of day, she's spared the indignity of rubbing shoulders with a jostle of bowler-hatted clerks; instead, she shares the hard benches and nippy air with other misfit souls who have reason not to ride below. On the first day, a gaggle of fat mothers with toddling children too restless to risk within the cabin; on the second, an old man with a six-foot-long parcel bound in twine; on the third, another mother and child, four stiffly-dressed sightseers conversing excitedly in a foreign tongue, and one pale young man clutching a dark book in his knobble-wristed hands.

On this third journey, Sugar makes the mistake of folding up her parasol and relaxing against the back of her seat, confident that William will get out at the usual stop, the nearest to his Air Street office. Indeed William does, but not before the pale young man has been captivated by the beauty of the grey-clad woman in the veil and, taking her relaxed pose for a Pre-Raphaelite slump of lassitude, he leaps up gallantly to assist her when she rises to go.

'Allow me,' he begs, his slightly frayed arms offering themselves, his eyes glowing with every kind of yearning imaginable.

Sugar, anxious lest the disembarking William Rackham should turn and look up at them, hesitates on the stair.

'No need, no need,' she whispers, aware that her soft croak will only compound the misunderstanding. 'Thank you.' And the omnibus moves off with her still on it.

Not that it makes much difference. She alights at the next stop, and walks back to the Rackham office, a dreary grey building with an ornamental 'R' on a brass plaque.

William spends the same amount of time there every day, about two hours, doing God knows what. She longs to be a fly on the wall of that inner sanctum, but instead must hang about on the streets, counting hansoms to ease the boredom.

At five o'clock, after consuming the same cake from the same cake-shop and waiting for the worst of the traffic to abate, William heads for home. She wishes he'd decide to go to Priory Close instead (in which event she would follow on behind and contrive to meet him on the footpath, pretending to have been taking a constitutional). But William does not alight prematurely; he stays on the omnibus all the way to Chepstow Villas.

Yet, after William's return to the Rackham house, small rewards do come Sugar's way.

On the first evening, William and Agnes go out for dinner to Lady Bridgelow's and, because the residences are only a dozen houses apart, they set off on foot – with Sugar following at a discreet distance. She notes that the Rackhams, although they advance side by side, are unconnected; not merely disdaining to walk arm-in-arm, but scarcely acknowledging each other's existence. William proceeds with loosely clenched fists, his shoulders squared, as if steeling himself for a formidable challenge.

Hours later, when he and his wife are walking home in the lamp-lit dark, the disjunction between them is even worse; Sugar, grateful for the drizzle that allows her to hide under her parasol, follows close behind.

'Well, that was awfully pleasant,' declares William, awkwardly, 'as always.'

Agnes doesn't reply, but trots mechanically on, her right hand pressed against her temple.

'Do you have a headache, dear?' says William.

'It's nothing,' she replies.

For a minute they walk in silence, then William laughs.

'That Bunce fellow – he's quite a character, isn't he? Constance really does have an extraordinary circle of friends.'

'Yes,' Agnes agrees, as the two of them reach the Rackham gates, and Sugar rustles past them in the gloom. 'It's a pity I detest her so much. Isn't it odd that someone with a title can be so very smarmy and common?'

To this, Sugar is fairly sure, William has no reply.

The following night, the Rackhams stay indoors. Sugar walks the peripheries for as long as she can bear, growing colder and colder, then hails a cab back to Priory Close. The time, she discovers when she gets there, is only half-past eight; she'd imagined it was near midnight. Maybe William will still come and visit her! She haunts her rooms like a disconsolate animal, pacing the soft carpets just as restlessly as she paced the streets, until she surrenders to the comforting embrace of a warm misty bath.

On the third night, however, her decision to sacrifice her idle hours to spying is, at last, richly rewarded. William leaves the house well after dark, alone, and hails a cab. The gods are on Sugar's side, for a second cab trundles close behind, so she suffers not even a moment's anxiety that William may escape her.

'Follow the cab in front,' she instructs her driver, and he tips his hat with a smirk.

The journey ends in Soho, outside a small theatre called The Tewkesbury Palace. William alights, unaware of Sugar alighting twenty feet away from him, and pays his driver, while she pays hers. Then he steps forward into the lamp-lit hurly-burly, glancing quickly around his person for pickpockets, but failing to spot the veiled woman at his rear.

What, thinks Sugar, can William be seeking here? The Tewkesbury is a notorious meeting-place for homosexuals, and here are two well-dressed gentlemen advancing on him with outstretched arms. For a moment her lips curl in bemused disgust: have these florid fellows, now slapping William affectionately on the back, managed to lure him away from her bed? Impossible! No one plays the silent flute better than she does!

Within seconds, however, her misunderstanding is dispelled. These men are Bodley and Ashwell, and the three friends have come here tonight especially to see the Tewkesbury's featured attraction – Unthan, the Pedal Paganini, billed as 'The Only Violinist in the World Without Arms!'

Sugar joins the motley queue of working folk and well-heeled connoisseurs to pay for admission. Although only two bodies separate her from Rackham and his companions, she overhears their conversation only imperfectly through the raucous babble of the crowd.

'. . . if *I* had no arms,' Ashwell is saying, '. . . Impressionist painter!'

'Yes!' cries Bodley. 'Specially made dummy arms! One hand purposefully clutching a paint-brush!'

The three men laugh uproariously, though Sugar fails to see anything witty. Art has never been her strong suit; all those Magdalens and Virgin Marys hoarded by Mrs Castaway put her off. Now, waiting in line to enter a low Soho theatre, she makes a mental note: brush up on Art.

Inside the Tewkesbury, a converted wool hall just about big enough for chamber concerts, but utilised instead for exhibitions of freaks and illusionists, Sugar shuffles amongst the herd of bodies. How horrid they smell! Don't any of them bathe? She can't recall ever noticing before the sheer uncleanness of common people. Rationing her breaths in the oppressive air, she takes her seat one row behind William and his friends.

On stage, a succession of entertainers fritters the time away – whetting audience appetite, with their mediocre songs and surpriseless magic, for the main attraction. Bodley and Ashwell mutter loudly, and share private jokes; William endures passively, as though his companions are children whom he has indulged with an outing.

At last there's a surge of applause and whistling in the theatre, and a stage-hand places a large four-legged stool on the boards, close to the footlights. Moments later, a violin and bow are deposited on a red velvet cushion next to the stool, earning more applause and a few cheers. Finally, Unthan walks on. He's a short man, smartly dressed in the garb of an orchestra musician, complete with tails but devoid of sleeves. His clean-shaven face, obviously not English, is in its structure a little simian, with a monkey's look of alert melancholy. His curly hair has been persuaded to adhere in straight furrows by much oil and combing.

With the profoundest solemnity Unthan takes his seat and begins, with his feet, to remove his shoes and stockings; titters from the audience leave him unmoved. He neatly folds the stockings and places each one into its corresponding shoe, then takes between his naked toes the body of the violin and deftly lifts it up onto his left shoulder, pinning it there with his chin. His left leg he lowers to the floor while the toes of his right move crablike along the violin's neck until they rest on the lower notes of the fingerboard. With no visible difficulty, the contorted Unthan fetches up the bow with his left foot and swings it up to rest on the strings. There's a faint clattering from the orchestra pit, then the ensemble begins to play, softly and sadly, a tune which sounds almost recognisable to all those present — until the Pedal Paganini begins his performance.

Unthan plays execrably, sending a shiver of squeamishness, even outrage, through the theatre. Music is being molested here! Yet there is pity, too, excited by the spectacle of the little cripple sawing away, his face proud and sombre despite its monkeyish shape and the mass of crinkly hair working loose over his wrinkled brow. By the time Unthan has, some twenty minutes later, exhausted his modest repertoire, the audience's mood has shifted, and many patrons — including Sugar — have damp eyes without knowing why. In the echoing decay of the orchestra's final crescendo, Unthan fiddles one last vibrato flourish and, with a jerk of his feet, lets both violin and bow fall into his lap. He utters a startling cry of triumph or agony, then prostrates himself, the last of his hair unravelling. A full three minutes of thunderous applause ensues.

'Ha ha!' hoots Bodley. 'Jolly good!'

Afterwards, Messrs Bodley, Ashwell and Rackham stroll the streets of Soho, drunk as lords. All three are in high spirits, despite the drizzle; Unthan, they agree, was worth the price of admission — an all-too-rare circumstance in a world where, too often, pleasures fail to live up to the claims made for them.

'Well, friends,' declares William. 'After this ape . . . ape . . . apex, all exshperience must be a shtep downwards. I'm going home.'

'My God, Bodley!' exclaims Ashwell. 'Do you hear this?'

'Can't we tempt you with a fuck, Bill?'

'Not with *you*, Philip.'

'A cruel thrust.' The men are slowing to a standstill, allowing Sugar
to move from shadow to shadow, closer and closer, until she's ensconced
in a cul-de-sac barely wide enough for her skirts. Her veil is damp with
breath, her back wet with sweat, as she strains to hear. 'Ach, but it's
spring, Bill,' Bodley says. 'London's *abloom* with cunt. Can't you smell it
on the air?'

Rackham pokes his nose clownishly upwards, and sniffs. 'Horse dung,'
he pronounces authoritatively, as if analysing the constitution of a manufactured fragrance. 'Dog shit. Beer. Cigar shmoke. Soot. Tallow. Rotting
cabbage. Beer – did I shay beer already? Macassar oil, on my own head.
Not an ounce of cunt, sirs; not sho much as a drachm.'

'Oh? That reminds me, Bill,' says Ashwell. 'There's something Bodley
and I've been meaning to mention to you for a while. You recall the night
we saw the Great Flatelli? Afterwards, we consulted *More Sprees In London*,
and there was one girl described in the most glowing terms . . .'

'Sshugar, as I recall, yes?' William, for all his inebriation, sounds
nonchalant.

'Well, the queer thing is, Bodley and I went to her house, but when
we presented ourselves, we were told she wasn't at home.'

'You poor gyps,' mocks William. 'Didn't I warn you that might happen?'

'Yes, I recall you did,' pursues Ashwell. 'However, we tried a second
time, much later that evening . . .'

'—and a *third* time,' interjects Bodley, 'a few weeks later . . .'

'Only to be told that this Sugar girl had been "removed" altogether!
"A rich man has taken her for his mistress," the madam told us.'

Sugar, her breath suddenly intolerably humid inside her veil, fumbles
to pin the gauze back against her bonnet.

'What a shame,' William mock-commiserates. 'Pipped at the post!'

Inch by inch, Sugar leans her face forward, thankful for the rain as it
cools her cheeks and prevents her breath clouding out of the shadowy
passage to betray her.

'Yes, but by whom, one wonders? By whom?'

The men are in her sights now; fortunately they're looking away. William
laughs, and what an impressively natural performance it is! 'No one *I* know,

I'm sure,' he says. 'All the rich men of my acquaintance are pillars of deshency. That's why I reshort to *you* two, for relief!'

'But seriously, Bill . . . if you should hear a whisper . . .'

'. . . About where this girl is to be found . . .'

'If not now, then when her master has tired of her . . .'

'We're still dying to have a bash.'

William laughs again.

'My, my: all this devotion – caused by one li'l entry in *More Shprees in London*. Ah, the power of . . . of advertising!'

'We do hate to miss anything,' admits Bodley.

'The curse of being a modern man,' opines Ashwell.

'Now, friends, goodnight,' says Rackham. 'A most diverting evening thish's been.'

The men shake gloved hands, and half-embrace, whereafter Bodley, being the best whistler of the three, pulls one glove off and shoves his thumb and forefinger into his mouth, to summon a hansom for William.

'Mush obliged,' says William. 'I really muzzbe getting home.'

'Of course, of course. And we really must . . . must what, Ashwell?'

The two comrades are dawdling off into the dark already, leaving Rackham stationed under a lamp-post in expectation of speedy deliverance. Sugar appraises her man from the rear as he stands there. His hands are clasped behind his back, just over the part where, when naked, his unusually protuberant tailbone nestles between his buttocks. He seems taller than she remembered; his elongated shadow, pitch-black against the gas-lit cobbles, is cast straight towards her.

'It's high time *we* were in bed, too,' Bodley is saying – or is it Ashwell? Their bodies are out of sight now, and their voices growing fainter.

'Quite so. Any particular . . . ?'

'I thought Mrs Tremain's.'

'The wine's not so good there.'

'True, but the girls are first-rate.'

'Will they let us bring our own in?'

'Our own girls?'

And they're gone. For a few seconds William stands motionless, his head raised skyward as though he's listening for the approach of a cab. Then, startlingly, he claps one palm against the lamp-post and twirls slowly around it, like an urchin child at play. He chuckles as he walks this narrow circuit, and his free hand swings through the air.

'Abandon hope, you bumblers!' he crows. 'She's gone . . . Shafe from *you* . . . Shafe from *all* of you! No one else will ever touch her . . .' (Round and round the lamp-post still he twirls.) 'No one!'

And, as he laughs again, a hansom rattles into view.

Sugar waits until he has climbed aboard before emerging from her hiding-place; his cheery cry of 'Chepshtow Villas, Notting Hill!' lets her know there's no hurry to follow. He's going home to sleep – and so, at last, can she.

As the clatter of hoofs recedes, she limps into the light. Her muscles, tense as bowstrings for so long, have seized up, and one of her legs is completely numb. The grime of the alley's cramped walls has smirched her skirts on both sides, a glistening sooty brand on the pale material. Yet she is elated. Rackham is hers!

She hobbles along the road, grunting and chortling as the feeling returns to her nerves, longing to sink into her warm bath at home, knowing she'll sleep like a baby tonight. She tries to whistle for a cab, but no sooner does she purse her lips than her mouth widens into a grin and she giggles throatily. Cackling, she hurries towards the thoroughfare.

On her way, she meets a man walking unsteadily in the opposite direction; a massive man, a swell in every sense of the word, whose drunkenness is proclaimed on the breeze. When his downcast eyes see the swirling hems of a woman's dress sweeping over the dark footpath towards him, he raises his face in curiosity. At once his puffy features light up in recognition, though Sugar can't recall ever setting eyes on him before.

'Is it . . . is it not Sugar?' he stammers, rocking on his feet. 'My prodigal siren, where have you been? I beg you, take me to your bed, wherever it is, and cure this cockstand!'

'I'm sorry, sir,' says Sugar, bowing slightly as she hurries past, her eyes fixed on the greater lights. 'I've decided to become à nun.'

SIXTEEN

'etween the bottomless gutter of damnation and the bright road to Paradise,' cries a matronly voice, 'stand we!'

Emmeline Fox cringes, and obscures her grimacing mouth behind her steamy tea-cup. Mrs Borlais is getting carried away again.

'We can but extend our hands – oh, *let* us pray that some desperate soul seizes hold of us!'

All around the meeting hall, the other members of the Rescue Society glance at each other, trying to determine whether their leader is calling them to prayer in the literal sense, or whether this is mere inspirational rhetoric. A dozen sensibly dressed ladies, most of them even less comely than the grey-faced Mrs Fox, reach a silent consensus, and their eyes remain open, their hands unsteepled. Outside the sooty windows of their Jermyn Street headquarters, London's unconverted millions teem, shadowy un-graspables flickering past the glass.

Mrs Nash approaches Mrs Fox, teapot in hand. A simple soul, is Mrs Nash; she's hoping that in this Refreshment Interval between the Discussion and the Going-Forth there's enough time left to pour her fellow Rescuers another cup of tea.

But no: 'Sisters, it's time we were on our way,' declares Mrs Borlais, and she sets the example by waddling out into the vestibule. Among the seated there is a rustle of disinclination, not because they fear the chal-lenge of evangelism but because Mrs Hibbert forgot the biscuits today and had to go out and buy some, which means that most of the Rescuers are only on their first biscuit – some yet to take their first bite. Now their leader beckons them to rise, what can they do? They may be about to wrestle with Vice in the dark cesspools of Shoreditch, but can they be so bold as to walk out into the street eating biscuits? No.

Mrs Borlais senses the wavering of enthusiasm, and takes it to be faint-heartedness.

'I implore you all to remember, Sisters,' she calls, 'that saving a soul from damnation is a thousand times more worthwhile than wresting a body from the claws of a savage beast. If you saved a person from a savage beast, you'd feel the pride of it as long as you lived! Be proud, then, Sisters!'

Mrs Fox is first to stand behind Mrs Borlais, despite having no patience with such vainglorious stuff. In her opinion, the attitude of the Rescuer doesn't matter – whether she's proud or discouraged, zealous or weary. These things are transient. A million Christian people in the past felt pride, a million felt discouragement, and all that's left of them now is their souls, and the souls they were able to save. 'The Rescue, not the Rescuer': this has always been Emmeline's motto, and should have been the motto of the Rescue Society, too, if she were its leader. Not that she ever would be: she was born to be a dissenter within a larger certainty, she knows that.

'Let's be off, then,' she says breezily, to bridge the gap between savage beasts and uneaten biscuits.

They go then, the Rescuers, all eight of them. United, as always, like soldiers in mufti. Yet, less than an hour after the Going-Forth, Emmeline Fox has strayed away from the main group and is in delicate pursuit of a pregnant child in a foul-smelling cul-de-sac.

Sugar, for her part, is sitting in a spic-and-span, brightly lit tea-room in Westbourne Terrace, toying with a cold cup of the house speciality and a nibbled scone, eavesdropping on a servant. The servant sits at one table, eating and drinking merrily, gossiping with a chum; Sugar sits alone at another table, her unfocused eyes fixed on the reflection of the ceiling lamp floating in her tea, her back to the conversation, her ears burning.

Don't be judgemental: this is not the way Sugar usually occupies her Tuesday afternoons; in fact, it's her first time. No, really! William Rackham is in Cardiff, you see, until Thursday, and Agnes Rackham is indisposed. So, rather than being idle, what's the harm in following Clara, Agnes's lady's-maid, on her afternoon off, and seeing what comes of it?

Indeed, it's proved well worthwhile so far. Clara is a wonderfully loquacious creature, at least in the company of an Irish girl she calls (if Sugar hears rightly) 'Shnide' – another lady's-maid, identically dressed. The tea-room is quiet, with only five customers; the ever-improving facilities of Paddington Terminus are bleeding it dry. Fortunately for Sugar, who might have had difficulty eavesdropping in the clinking hustle-bustle of the station, Clara and Shnide are agreed that it's much nicer here, away from all the smelly foreigners and children. Sugar sips very slowly at her tea, occasionally toys with a minuscule mirror-image of Clara and Shnide in her teaspoon, and lets the efflux of gossip and discontent flow into her ears.

This is what she learns: William Rackham is nasty piece of work, a tyrant. His grasp on the workings of his household has metamorphosed from a limp-wristed dabble to an iron fist. Once upon a time he couldn't bear to look you in the face, now he 'stares right through you'. Last week he gave a speech about how other men as wealthy as himself would get themselves grander servants in a flash, but that *he* won't dream of it, for he knows how hard his own girls work to earn their keep. Of course now everyone below stairs is terrified.

But William Rackham isn't the worst of it: no, the brunt of Clara's spite is borne by her own mistress, a sly, two-faced creature who feigns illness and frailty one day, the better to bully her unsuspecting servants with a sudden display of bad temper and outrageous demands the next.

'Last December,' complains Clara, 'I thought she was going to die. Now sometimes I think *I* will.'

Clara is considering, she says, finding a new position with less difficult masters, but she's worried the Rackhams won't write her a good testimonial. 'It would be just like them,' she hisses. 'If I'm good, they won't let me go; if I'm bad, they'll kick me into the gutter.'

'Slaves, that's what we are,' affirms Shnide. 'No better than slaves.'

The conversation moves on to the topic of Clara's and Shnide's men friends; they each have a lover, it transpires. Sugar is taken aback to learn this: she's always forgetting that unattached women seek out male company when they've no need to. Pimps she can understand; rich benefactors, too. But friends? Friends with no money, living in lodging-houses, like Clara's Johnny and Shnide's Alfie? What can the attraction be? Sugar is all ears, but by the time the servants kiss and rise to leave, she's none the wiser. How can these two bundles of spite, this petty pair of gossips, profess 'love' for anybody? (Particularly if that body is a man's gross and dog-smelly one, hairy-faced, oily-headed, dirty-fingernailed . . .)

'Mind what I said,' says Shnide. 'Don't let him walk all over you.'

Who is she referring to? Clara's Johnny? Or William Rackham? Clara simpers as though she feels quite capable now of subjugating either man, or both. *You simpleton!* Sugar feels like shouting at her. *This true love of yours most likely has his cock stuck deep in a trollop! And William will throw you into the street like a rotten apple if you dare to defy him!* Her anger is ferocious, having not existed a moment before; it bursts fully formed out of silent obscurity, like a fire in a shuttered warehouse. She bites her lip as the servants prattle their way out of the door, onto the sunny street; she squeezes her tea-cup in her hands, praying she doesn't shatter it, half-wishing she might.

'Nice cup of tea, was it?' says the tea-room proprietor sarcastically soon after, as Sugar is paying her pittance for the privilege of eavesdropping in comfort for an hour.

Watch your step, hisses Sugar inside her hot skull. *You need all the bloody custom you can get.*

'Yes, thank you,' she replies, and demurely inclines her head, the very picture of a lady.

A couple of hours later, Agnes Rackham is standing at the window of Clara's bedroom – not a place she normally haunts, but nowadays there's no telling when one's guardian angel is going to pop up, and these attic bedrooms make such excellent roosts from which to glimpse her. Squinting through the glass, Agnes examines the sun-dappled trees under which her guardian angel sometimes materialises, on the eastern periphery of the Rackham grounds. There's no one to be seen there – well, no one of conse-quence. Shears is fussing about, tying metal wires around the stems of the flowers to make them grow straight, pulling up weeds and stuffing them into the pockets of his trousers. If only he would go away, perhaps her guardian angel would appear. She's shy of strangers, Agnes has found.

Clara's bedroom smells unpleasantly of perfume. How odd that the girl should be scrupulously odourless while working, but that when she comes finally to bed, she should anoint herself with scent. Agnes leaves the window and bends to sniff the servant's pillow. It stinks of something vulgar: Hopsom's, perhaps, or one of Rackham's cheaper lines. How regrettable that William must put his name to such garbage; in the Future, if his star continues to rise, perhaps he'll produce only the most exquisite and exclusive perfumes – perfumes for princesses.

Agnes sways on her feet. The pain in her head is bad again; if she's not careful, she'll pitch forward and be found sleeping on Clara's bed, her face nestled in that pungent pillow. She straightens, returns to the window. And there, under the sun-dappled trees, barely distinguishable through the incandescent lances of the freshly painted fence, moves the flickering form of her guardian angel. Within moments, it's gone, sucked back into the ether; there's not even time for a wave. But it was there.

Agnes hurries out of Clara's room, breathing deeply. Her heart flutters in her chest, her bosom tingles as if there's a hand pressed hard against each breast, the pain in her head is ebbing deliciously, dwindling to a small lump of coldness behind her left eye, quite bearable; the fist of ice lodged in her skull has melted to the size of a grape.

She descends the stairs – the dreary uncarpeted servants' stairs – to where the proper parts of the house begin. Hurrying to the parlour, she's surprised and delighted all over again by the new wallpaper there, and she takes a seat at the piano. Open before her is the sheet music of 'Crocuses Ahoy!', marked with her own annotations to warn her when the demi-semiquavers are coming. She plays the opening bars, plays them again, plays them over and over. Softly and sweetly, using this piano phrase as accompaniment, she hums a new melody, her own, purely out of her head. The notes she sings, hesitant at first, resolve themselves into a fetching tune. How inventive she is today! Quite the little composer! She resolves to sing this song of hers as long as she can stand it, to send it as far as Heaven, to nag it into the memory of God, to make time pass until someone is summoned to write it down for her, and it's printed up nicely and ferried to the far corners of the earth, for women everywhere to sing. She sings on and on, while the house is discreetly dusted all around her and, in the concealed and subterranean kitchen, a naked duck, limp and faintly steaming, spreads its pimpled legs on a draining board.

Later, when she's tired of composing, Agnes goes to her bedroom and plays with her new hats. She parades them in front of the mirror, holding her head high, smoothing the wrinkles out of her silky hips. Reflected back at her she sees a confident young woman (this word is all the rage in the ladies' journals lately, so it must be safe to use), well-armoured in her shiny bodice; a proud, elegant woman with nothing to be ashamed of.

'I am again a beauty,' she hears herself say.

She picks up the nearest of many hatboxes, lifts its lid and pulls out the mass of crêpe paper. The glass eyes of a stuffed thrush twinkle emerald against the jade felt of the hat on which the bird is fixed. Agnes lifts the treasure from its box by the brim, and tentatively strokes the thrush's feathered shoulder. A year ago she would have been afraid of it, in case it came back to life on her head; now she's merely looking forward to showing it off in public, because it really will look awfully pretty.

'I am not afraid.'

No, Agnes is not afraid – and lately has been proving as much, everywhere. Like a person contriving to pass a vicious dog by hailing it cheerily, she is able to walk into ballrooms and dining-halls that bristle with dangers, and simply sweep past them all. No doubt many of the ladies who call out to her so pleasantly are hiding sharp feminine hatreds with which they'd love to stab her, but Agnes doesn't care. She's the equal of any of them!

Already she has a number of triumphs to her credit, because the Party that Lasts a Hundred Days is well underway, and Agnes Rackham is proving to be one of its unexpected luminaries, all the more fashionable for the slight *frisson* of risk posed to those jaded diversion-seekers who flit towards her light.

'Agnes Rackham? No really, dear: delightful! Yes, who'd have imagined it? But let me tell you about her dinner party! Everything was black and white: I mean everything, *dear. Black tables and chairs, white table-cloth, black candle-holders, white crockery, cutlery painted white, white napkins, black finger-bowls. Even the* food *was black and white, I tell you! There was sole, with blackened skin still on, and the mushrooms were black, and so was the baked pumpkin . . . in white sauce. Alfred was cross, though, that there was no red wine – only white! But he bucked up as the evening went on. Mrs Rackham was so cheerful, she was singing to herself, in the sweetest voice. No one knew how to behave at first – should we just pretend we didn't hear? – but then Mr Cavanagh, the barrister, started singing 'pom pom pom' in a baritone underneath her, like a tuba, and everyone decided it must be all right. And after dinner there were ices – with licorice sauce! By that time we were all feeling ever so unconventional, we were almost wicked, and no one minded a bit. Such a* peculiar *woman, is Mrs Rackham. But oh! such a delightful time we had. I* almost *fainted* with amusement!'

Novelties like the black-and-white dinner party are the hallmark of Agnes's growing fame. Her head is crowded with innovations; the only problem is vetting them to cram the very best into the limited number of scheduled opportunities. The cinnamon-scented candles? The idea for the blindfolds and the parcels? They'll have to wait until the 24th and the 29th respectively . . .

In all things she is the modernest of the modern. The backs of her dresses are perfect curving slopes, their line unbroken by bows and flounces. She's heard a rumour that the days of the cuirass bodice are numbered and that the polonaise is about to return: if and when it does, she's ready! As for hats, she's given all her old ones to Miss Jordan, to do something charitable with. Her new chapeaux are festooned with humming-birds, sparrows and canaries; the grey velvet one (earmarked for an appearance at the Royal Albert Hall on June 12th) features a turtle-dove, which is sure to elicit gasps. (What the gaspers won't realise is that these large fowl actually weigh quite lightly on the head! Something happens to the creatures when they're stuffed, Agnes doesn't know what, but the result of it is that one could easily support half a dozen stuffed doves on one's head, though of course that would be vulgar — a single dove is sufficient.) As for the Prussian blue hat with the pigeon, well . . . her instinctive good taste has caused her to have second thoughts. After much deliberation she's decided to have the pigeon removed and replaced with a blue tit, because . . . well, there's something *common* about pigeons, however expensively they are stuffed.

Ah! Decisions, decisions! But it's not her intrepid judgement alone that's making her shine so brightly this Season: luck is with her also. In no respect is this more obvious than the hair colour that's currently in fashion: her own! She already possesses the blonde tresses that everyone so desperately desires, as well as an excellent store of hair-pieces, allowing her to construct the elaborate styles that are *de rigueur* in the Best People. All her rivals are having terrible trouble obtaining blonde, since most of what's sold to wig factories is dark stuff from French peasant girls.

As for her figure: another stroke of luck! The near-skeletal arms and waist given her by her illness are exactly what the times require; in fact, she's a good few ounces ahead. While other ladies are torturing themselves with starvation diets, she has inherited *la ligne* effortlessly. Is it any wonder, then, that she still doesn't eat much, even now that she's well enough?

Gorging herself when she has the thinnest waist she's ever had would be criminal, and the Queen, God bless her, is a chastening example of what happens to a lady of small stature who overindulges. A segment of fruit and a slice or two of cold meat are quite filling, she's found, especially in conjunction with a dose of that sweet blue tincture recommended by Mrs Gooch. Alone in bed at night, Agnes takes especial pleasure in counting her ribs.

Last week she tried on a dress that she and Clara made on the sewing-machine in December – and its waist and arms were wrinkled and baggy! So, rather than trying to fix it, she's given it up for dead, and started afresh with a proper dressmaker. What extravagance! But there's no longer any question of economy: William is a rich man now, and his allowance to her seems limitless. The disapproving stares and cautioning words of previous years are gone without a trace; he even *suggests* expenditures to her, and smiles benignly whenever she ushers a procession of parcels up the stairs.

He's doing his best, is William, to make amends – Agnes has to admit that. Nothing can ever atone for the pain she's suffered, but . . . Well, there's no doubt he's providing for her now. And he looks really quite presentable with his new beard, and he's dressing smartly.

She's noticed too that he's perfected the knack, essential in the right circles, of behaving as if he made his fortune long ago, rather than being in the midst of making it. Puffing serenely on a cigar, leaning his head back as if contemplating an enquiry from the ether, he radiates the power his wealth confers upon him, but speaks not a word about Rackham Perfumeries, rather about books and paintings and the wars in Europe. (Not that Agnes cares a feather for wars in Europe: let them burn Paris to the ground, and she'll design her *own* dresses!) All sorts of well-connected people, at recent gatherings, seem drawn to William's corner of the room. Imagine that! William Rackham, the overgrown university student, the idler: a success!

As for her own performance in public, she's doing splendidly, better than she could have hoped. She hasn't collapsed once, and there have been no incidents such as occurred in past Seasons, when a perfectly normal remark or action was spitefully misconstrued by others, and she was in disgrace. She's learned a lot from that: she's learned to keep an eye on herself at all times.

Agnes peers into her wardrobe mirror, her favourite because it can be swivelled to any angle and, if she kneels and looks up into it, she can see herself as though from above. Since almost everyone in the world is taller than she, this is invaluable. She kneels now, and looks up, and there she beholds what God or the folk in the Royal Albert Hall's balconies might look upon: a most fetching specimen, a credit to her sex. She opens wide her china-blue eyes, to banish a frown line from her forehead. *Pass*, says a voice from behind the looking-glass.

Prostrated so close to the carpet's complicated Turkish pattern she feels faint again, and staggers to her feet. A few breaths of cool air at the window-sill are all she needs to keep the head-spin at bay.

Which reminds her: how ideal is the itinerary of this year's Season! Why, it might have been devised solely for her! Very few of her assignations are spent cooped up in crowded rooms; instead she's almost always out of doors, in gardens and courtyards and streets and pavilions. The fresh air alone is a tonic, and whenever she feels faint she can seize hold of something solid and pretend to be admiring the view. And when all eyes are raised to watch a fireworks display, no one notices one small pill disappearing between her lips!

She doesn't mind having to attend operas and concerts, for although these confine her indoors they leave her mind free to wander, except during the Intervals. Propped up in her seat next to her husband, she leaves her body unattended, her spirit floating up above, looking down at herself from the chandeliers.

(It's a remarkable view, for others no less than for Agnes. Lately, she's using a novelty fabric in her dresses and gloves that glows in dim light. Thus, when the theatre or the opera house turns dark in anticipation of the tragedy on stage, Agnes Rackham remains visible. The patrons in the balconies observe her white hand raising tiny binoculars to her face, and Mrs Rackham is seen to shed a sympathetic tear, for the binoculars are in fact disguised smelling-salts, and quite pungent when held near the eyes.)

In this fashion, Agnes has sat through Wagner's *Lohengrin* at the Royal Italian Opera, Meyerbeer's *The Huguenots*, and Verdi's *Requiem*, conducted by the alarmingly foreign Signor Verdi himself, at the Royal Albert Hall. She was present and accounted for, too, at Mr Henry Irving's *Hamlet* at the Lyceum, but enjoyed the appetiser, Mrs Compton's *Fish out of Water*, rather more, though she knew better than to mention this to anyone. For variety's sake, and so that she could bring it up in conversation, Agnes also went to see Signor Salvani's *Hamlet*, all in Italian, at the Theatre Royal, and found this to be an altogether superior experience, particularly the sword-play which was conspicuously more vigorous, and the Ophelia who was rather vulgar, and therefore deserved to die more than the English one. (Agnes still shudders at the memory of being confronted, on a visit to an art gallery years ago, with that terrifying painting by Millais: the shock of seeing an innocent young lady of her own age and complexion – though thankfully not blonde – drowned, dead, open-eyed, with a crowd of men standing before her, admiring how well she was 'done'.)

Alone in her bedroom, Agnes crosses herself, then looks around nervously, in case anyone has seen her do it.

'Clara?' she says, experimentally, but Clara is still away, gossiping with Mrs Maxwell's girl Sinead no doubt, or whatever else she can find to occupy her afternoon off.

I must think about getting a maidservant who's closer to me in wit, thinks Agnes, all of a sudden. *Honestly, when I tried to explain the significance of Psycho, she hadn't the foggiest idea what I was talking about.*

(For the benefit of those unlucky souls who missed it: Agnes is recalling here the premier exhibition, at the Lyceum, of 'Psycho', a child-sized mechanical figure which, in the words of the programme, danced and performed tricks 'without the aid of wires or confederates'.)

For Agnes, seeing Psycho has been the highlight of her Season's theatregoing so far. Indeed, so deeply moved was she by the demonstration that she hardly heard the muttered complaints of Bodley and Ashwell from somewhere to the left of her husband. She was utterly convinced that Psycho was independent of the gentleman who stood by him on the stage, and that his life came from an unseen Elsewhere. The conjuring tricks he performed with his noiselessly revolving limbs meant nothing to her in themselves; rather, she was electrified by the realisation that this little mechanical man was *immortal*. Whereas her own soul must be consigned to Limbo should her body happen to be destroyed (in a fire, for instance, such as might break out in this very theatre!) Psycho would endure. Even if he were crushed flat, he could simply be melted down and re-cast, and his animating soul would simply slip back inside. Oh, lucky creature!

Agnes stands at her window now, a handkerchief clasped inside her fist as she scans the grounds' perimeter for signs of her guardian angel. Shears waves to her from the hydrangea beds. Agnes smiles, then casts her eyes down at her fist. She opens it, and the handkerchief blossoms out of her palm, unharmed. Oh, to be like that handkerchief!

Agnes has been thinking a great deal about Death and Resurrection lately. Queer topics to be pondering amidst the hurly-burly of the Season, but she can't help it: it's her philosophical turn of mind. She can be cheerful, and sing enchantingly for guests, but really, is there anything in Life as important as what happens to one's body after Death?

Whisper it not, but Agnes is suspicious of Heaven as conventional religion describes it; she has no wish for any posthumous paradise of wraiths. What she wants is to wake up, corporeal, in the Convent of Health, ready to begin a better life. Almost every night she dreams the same dream, in which she walks through the ivy-laden portcullis of the convent, no longer Agnes Rackham of Chepstow Villas, Notting Hill, but not a ghost either.

How nice it would be to speak of these things with her brother-in-law, Henry. In several of the spiritualist books hidden under her bed, there is mention of a Heaven *on Earth*. Biblical scriptures promise (or so the authors claim) that the virtuous will one day claim their resurrected bodies . . . Surely Henry could tell her more, knowing so much about the Bible and other mystical works! (And besides, she likes him. He's not like most Anglicans she knows; he has an indefinably Catholic sort of air about him. He reminds her, just a little, of the Saints and the Martyrs. William told her once that the reason Henry isn't a clergyman yet is that he doesn't consider himself sufficiently pure and high-minded for it, but she suspects that that's all nonsense, and the real problem is that Anglicanism isn't pure and high-minded enough for Henry.)

'Is Henry invited to this?' she keeps asking William, each time they attend a party.

'No,' William keeps replying, or, 'Damned if I know,' or, 'If he was, I doubt he'll have come.' And sure enough, Henry Rackham is never there.

'What about *here*?' Agnes persists, at public events that are open to all. 'Absolutely *any*one can come to this.'

'Henry detests opera,' William will mutter, grumpy to have yet more of his valuable time wasted by social obligations. Or, 'Henry disapproves of histrionics. Can't say I blame him, either.'

'Chin up, William dear: there's Mrs Abernethy.'

And, determined to make the best of things, Agnes draws a deep breath, clutches her binocular smelling-salts to her bosom, and files in through the glittering vestibule to take her place among . . . well, if not the Upper Ten Thousand, then certainly the Upper Twenty.

Much as Agnes might wish to turn her head, by chance, at one of the Season's events and see Henry Rackham making his way towards her, her wish is never granted. Yet she does have *one* faithful fellow-traveller, if only she knew it: one person who presses through crowds to get close to her, who braves blustery weather to attend the same theatres as she, who pays high prices to sit near her and watch her glow gently under subdued lighting.

Sugar is having her first Season.

Not legitimately, of course; not in the sense that the Best People are having one. But, to the limit of her capabilities, to the fullest extent that money can buy, she is participating. Some doors and thresholds are only for the select few, the haloed gentlefolk with invitations from Mrs So-and-So and Baroness What-Have-You. Whenever the Rackhams pass through one of these, Sugar cannot follow. But when they attend anything less exclusive, particularly in the open air or a large venue that admits a chattering throng, Sugar is sure to be dawdling in the Rackhams' wake, soaking up the atmosphere, revolving slowly in the crowd like flotsam in the slip-stream of a barge.

Anxious to attract as little attention as possible, Sugar has adopted a strict policy of sober dress. Her wardrobe, once so sumptuous in its greens, blues and bronzes, has faded to shades of grey and brown; she walks on the stylish side of mourning. Against such dusky hues, the redness of her hair is a curse rather than a blessing, and her skin appears pale and sickly. Everyone calls her 'madam', and cabbies help her dismount as if she might snap her ankles on the unaccustomed hardness of the street. Only a few days ago, an urchin boy in Piccadilly Circus offered to wipe her wet umbrella dry on his grubby shirt for a ha'penny, and she was so taken aback she gave him sixpence.

It's most peculiar, this respectability; especially since, wherever she follows the Rackhams, she's by no means the only whore in the crowd. Theatres, opera houses, sporting fields and pleasure gardens are favourite haunts of the better-class harlots during the Season, and there's no short-age of stray gentlemen loitering on balconies and behind marquees wish-ing to be rescued from boredom. Amy Howlett used to go once upon a time, before she grew too short-tempered to endure all the waiting.

Face hidden behind a fan, or behind her veil, Sugar plays the game – and enjoys it. Why has she never done this before? Granted, the allowance she gets from Rackham is more than she ever earned at Mrs Castaway's, but she can hardly claim to have been too poor to set foot in a concert hall until now. Yet all those years she shut herself away in her upstairs room, like a prisoner! Oh, all right, yes, she *did* write a novel – or *most* of a novel – but even so, would an outing to the theatre have been so terribly frivolous? How odd to recall that in her book, 'Sugar' solicits a victim in the Haymarket after a performance of *Measure for Measure* – a play Sugar has read and re-read in candle-lit silence but never bothered to cross a few streets to see in the flesh. What can she have been thinking of all this time?

Well, she's making up for it now. Following the Rackhams on their itinerary, she has been to every theatre and opera house in London several times over – or so it seems to her. In the crowded cloakrooms of these gilded palaces she removes her cape or coat, and stares all about her at the authentic ladies doing likewise. Do they notice her staring? And if so, can any of them imagine that she's more accustomed to the company of women dressed only in corsets and pantalettes, powdering the bruises on their naked breasts?

But no, they accept her unquestioningly, these wealthy women, and this pleases Sugar more than she could have thought possible. She'd expected to despise them as she's always despised them but, up close, her hatred fails her. In fact, if truth be told, Sugar feels a thrill, a thrill almost of affection, whenever one of these ladies makes any sort of deferential gesture towards her . . . A smile of courtesy, say, at the hat-stands, a murmur of 'After *you*' in the lavatories, a backwards step conceding her right-of-way on a carpeted staircase . . . Such ephemeral tokens of respect make Sugar tingle with satisfaction.

And what about when she's weaving through crowds of Regent Street shoppers during the three o'clock chaos in pursuit of Agnes Rackham? She's continually brushing against chattering, parcel-carrying ladies, and finding herself showered with apologies. In Billington & Joy, shop-walkers flock around her, begging to assist her, and she must retreat from them in case Agnes should turn around to catch a glimpse of her rival! Smiling behind her veil, Sugar tries to deflect fuss by protesting she's merely the chaperone of a young lady elsewhere in the store.

And by God's hairy bollocks, they seem to believe her!

★   ★   ★

Yes, Sugar is enjoying the Season so far. Its hurly-burly isn't tiring her a bit; in fact, it makes for a nice change. All those lonely, empty days in her rooms at Priory Close have cured her of desire for solitude; the lure of silence, so attractive when she was younger, has faded. Now she's ready for action.

Not that there's much action in some of her assignations with the Rackhams. Plays and concerts can be a trifle on the long side, especially when entirely in Italian and when the seats aren't so soft. Sugar's hindquarters have gone to sleep a number of times during the marathon histrionics of bewhiskered Hamlets and Malvolios, or the heroic trilling of top-heavy matrons. Yet, though her arse may have slept, her attention has remained awake, taking frequent stock of the Rackhams sitting near her.

William's most commonly manifested emotion during the more long-winded spectacles is boredom; he reads his programme, stifles yawns, and allows his eyes to wander from the people in the aisles to the chandeliers above. On more than one occasion he has looked straight at Sugar, blindly ignorant of who she is, seeing her only as a bonnet in the dimness, a nondescript dress amongst surplus finery. Sometimes he snoozes, but mostly he's fidgeting his way through the Season.

Agnes, by contrast, is keenly attentive to every instant of every performance, lifting her opera glasses frequently, smiling when required, and applauding with the nervous rapidity of a cat scratching at a flea. In between times, she sits still, and her face shines pellucid and enigmatic, like a statue of a transfigured saint. Is she enjoying herself? How can Sugar tell? Pleasure is on the inside, and the easiest thing in the world to fake.

Sugar's pleasure is real enough, though. It must be, since no one is watching her and she feels it nonetheless.

Most precious of her discoveries in this, her first Season, is good music. All her life she's been indifferent to music, or hostile to it. Music for her has always been unbearably tainted by poverty, religiosity, drunkenness and disease: the ingratiating warble of beggars, the wheeze of organs ground by monkeys, the tankard-swinging ballads in The Fireside, the sanctimonious toll of church bells. As for Katy Lester's 'cello-playing at Mrs Castaway's all those years – she realises only now how much she loathed it. 'Very beautiful, Katy,' she used to say, whenever the girl had finished playing some lugubrious air or other. What she really should have said was,

'I'm glad you're down here with us rather than upstairs with a man, but can you please stop scraping that damned catgut?'

In this first Season, Sugar is hearing music as if she's never heard the stuff before. Grand, uplifting, inspiring music played by large ensembles on gleaming instruments she can't put a name to. Removed from the forlornness of Mrs Castaway's parlour or the shabbiness of the streets, and marshalled together for no other purpose than to make a joyful noise: this is how it should be. Even the 'cellos look impressive when it isn't Katy Lester playing them; instead of just one scuffed old instrument, pitted by cinders from the hearth, there are eight of them, burnished to a rich lustre, all being bowed with great zest and precision. How strange it is to see a row of men – indeed, a whole orchestra full of men – intent on an activity that's not only innocent but . . . noble. These fellows have nothing on their minds except making music. Can that really be? So many men together, and no evil? She watches them cradle their instruments gently, watches them hastily turn the pages on their music stands in the momentary pauses between blowings or bowings, while above and beyond them the glorious sound goes on and on.

'Bravo!' she cries along with everyone else when it's over. So great is her excitement that she has forgotten what she came here for; standing among a jubilant crowd on her five-shilling balcony, she claps her hands and stares raptly at the performers on stage, not at William and Agnes in their 10s. 6d. arena seats directly beneath her.

This spontaneous display, this abandon, has become part of Sugar's repertoire only gradually. At the very first concert she attended with the Rackhams, she was too shy to open her mouth while all around her were shouting; indeed, she was barely able to applaud. But, finale after finale, she's learned to lose herself, and by now she has a taste for it. The other night, just as the final cymbal clash of *The Huguenots* resonated around the rafters of the Royal Albert Hall, Sugar leapt up from her seat and cheered as loud as anything and, glancing to the left of her, she caught the eye of a bewhiskered old man, similarly moved. In that single instant they understood everything they needed to about each other; they were as intimate as it is possible to be; and they would most likely never see each other again.

'Bravo!' yelled the old gentleman, and she bravoed with him, not daring to look at him again in case their spark of communion should fizzle out.

Of course she knows she's surrounded by people who would, if the truth of her station were obvious, edge away from her in fear of being polluted. She is filth in their midst. Never mind that plenty of these decent ladies resemble prostitutes a good deal more than *she* does; never mind that this throng is full of Mrs So-and-Sos who are garishly dressed, whiffy with scent, scarred with powdered blemishes – still it's *she*, unfailingly demure and freshly washed, who's the secret obscenity here. She might as well be a mound of excrement fashioned into human shape. They smile at her, the Mrs So-and-Sos; they apologise when they brush against her skirts, only because they don't know her. Oh, the bliss of being among people who don't know her!

'Isn't this divine?' enthuses a wrinkly matron in the seat next to Sugar at the Royal Albert Hall. Her eyes are pink from her husband's cigar smoke, her greying hair is supplemented with several not-quite-matching blonde hairpieces. 'All the way from Italy!'

The lady is referring to Signor Verdi on the stage below them, an impish old rogue who is at this moment pointing his stubby baton at the Royal Albert Hall Choral Society, conjuring them to stand, inviting the audience to applaud their efforts to sing his brand-new *Requiem*.

'Yes, divine,' replies Sugar. It's a word that tastes strange on her lips, but not offensive. Signor Verdi has moved her – not just with the tunes of his *Requiem*, but with the dawning understanding that this monumental work of music, this architecture of sounds to rival the Royal Albert Hall itself, was written on smudgy sheets of paper by a single person: an old Italian fellow with hair in his eyes. The rumble of double-basses that reverberated in her abdomen was caused directly by him putting pen to paper, probably late at night as he sat in his shirt-sleeves, Signora Verdi snoring in the next room. It's a kind of male power she hasn't thought about before, a power sublimely uninterested in subjugating her or putting her to use or putting her in prison, a power whose sole aim is to make the air vibrate with pleasure.

So, yes, 'Divine,' she says to the wrinkly matron with the ill-matching hair-pieces, and is rewarded with a smile. Only then, as the applause fades and the more elderly members of the audience stand to leave, does Sugar realise she has forgotten about the Rackhams. Are they still in the building? No sign of them. Perhaps she has missed a highly significant moment, a dumbshow between William and Agnes that would have spoken volumes, had she only witnessed it. Perhaps Agnes did something unforgivable in public.

In time, Sugar decides that being a little distracted in the presence of great music is not such a bad thing. She can't spy on the Rackhams every minute of every day; some things are bound to escape her. And she's awfully dedicated, really: Let there be no music – or bad music – and she'll watch the Rackhams with scarcely a blink, even if on stage there are fierce actors posturing with swords, or metal manikins dancing on invisible strings.

What does she learn, staring down on the Rackhams as they watch these performances? Not much. William is hardly going to leap up from his seat in St James's Hall and shout his deepest fears to all and sundry, while Agnes, despite the outrageous behaviour of which William insists she is capable, refrains from running amok even in the most Gothic of buildings. Nevertheless Sugar is convinced that if she can only share the Rackhams' public life – see what they see, hear what they hear – she's bound to share their private life as well. And there's no telling when something William has seen at one of these concerts or plays will come back to him in their shared bed. Mr Walter Farquhar's *Prometheus in Albion*, for example, at the end of which William was unusually wide-awake and yelling bravo . . . If she can ferret out the poem on which it's based, and profess a love for it, *he* could tell *her* about the play and *she* could introduce *him* to the poem: what a cosy *tête-à-tête* that would make!

At yet another première, she watches William file out of the theatre with Agnes at his side. Is she leaning on his arm? She must be tired or unwell; it can't be affection. *Take her home and put her to bed, William, for God's sake*, Sugar thinks, *then come and see me*. But no sooner have the Rackhams stepped out of the auditorium than they're ushered into the company of smiling strangers, and Sugar spends the night alone.

By far the best and most rewarding spying, which makes her feel as if she's genuinely intimate with the Rackhams, is to be had at open-air events, and the weather this year is unusually good. Even after sundown it's mild, and the nights are lent the illusion of warmth by fairy lanterns, and by the braziers and stoves of street vendors, the glow of pub windows, and swarms of sumptuously dressed ladies everywhere. (Well, not *everywhere*, of course. Church Lane, St Giles, is no doubt as dark and filthy as always. But who'd want to go *there*?)

At the Grand Garden Fête on Muswell Hill, half a crown admits Sugar to the moonlit grounds of the new Alexandra Palace mere seconds after William and Agnes have passed through the gates. (Only vulgar people come during the day.) Thereafter, as long as she doesn't venture too close to the lanterns hung from the trees, she can walk almost directly behind the Rackhams without being recognised.

Sugar has been following William and Agnes for several weeks now. She knows the slope of William's shoulders and the wiggle of his backside like . . . well, like the back of her hand. She knows exactly how much Agnes's hips sway (hardly at all) and how rapidly her bustle bobs up and down (very). In any crowd, especially of pedestrians, Agnes Rackham is likely to be the woman *least* mistakable for a prostitute. Every inch of her diminutive body speaks of containment and untouchability. How beautiful she is! Her skin isn't rough and freckled like Sugar's, but smooth as a newly unwrapped tablet of soap. Her hair is the colour a woman's hair *ought* to be, and fine as embroidery silk. Her shape is so perfect – How can Sugar walk behind her and not feel like a monster? Her own flat chest compared with Agnes's pretty bosom; her own masculine paws, freakishly large compared with Agnes's dainty hands; her own gait – half-man, half-slut – compared with Agnes's graceful locomotion. And, of course, that voice. Even when speaking the most humdrum words ('No thank you, William,' or 'You have some sugar on your moustache'), she sounds as though she's singing softly to herself. Oh, to have a voice like that! Not hoarse and low, but smooth and lilting. How can anyone with such a voice possibly be the burdensome nuisance that William makes her out to be?

Walking behind the Rackhams so often, Sugar has learned to read the signs of their personal disharmony. Their bodies, even when fully clothed, are anathema to each other. And yet they are occasionally, unavoidably, arm in arm. On these occasions William escorts his wife nervously, as if fearful she might fall to bits at his side and cause all eyes to turn on him and the mess he has made on a public footpath. Agnes, for her part, glides irrelative to him, a mechanism that cannot be hurried. Then again, whenever something in the distance attracts her attention – a lady she simply must speak to, for example – she tends to accelerate and pull him along, like a railway car whose mail-hook has accidentally become hitched to the sleeve of a gentleman.

At one juncture in the Grand Garden Fête, a large blue balloon is

floating overhead, high above the marquees, inspiring excited gesticula-
tions from the crowd. Agnes notices nothing. Sugar observes William speaking down to his wife, urging her to look up at the moonlit curiosity. But
though Agnes nods, as if to say, 'That's nice, dear', she doesn't deign to
raise her head. It will take more than a floating blue balloon, it seems, to
win back her approval.

Even more remarkable is the incident at the Sandown Park Races –
another superb opportunity to be the Rackhams' shadow, and in broad
daylight.

Of Sandown Park itself Sugar sees precious little, as it's utterly aswarm
with spectators. Half of London's population, drawn from all classes, seems
to be here (well, excluding the desperately poor, Sugar has to admit . . .
but *besides* them, everybody). There's scarcely an inch of ground not trampled by the surging horde of men, women, children and dogs. Sugar catches
only the most fleeting glimpse of what has ostensibly brought people here:
race-horses and their riders. The stocky old nags and ponies pulling the
carts of refreshments move in ignorance of the fact that somewhere nearby,
equines of a superior caste are prancing or possibly even galloping like the
wind. Every now and then, a cry goes up and Sugar thinks the race has
begun, or been won, but then one knot of the crowd untangles slightly
and the commotion is revealed to be something else: a fainting, an eruption of fisticuffs, a carriage rolling over someone's foot.

But, little though she sees of the races, Sugar does see a lot of the
Rackhams. Agnes, as petite as any jockey, stands well back from the throng
for fear of getting trampled. Poor William! How impotently he flexes his
hands! How beseechingly he looks to the heavens for a loan of some charm
to melt his wife's heart! Maybe he yearns to lift her up onto his shoulders,
like a small child, for a better look . . . Instead, he keeps insinuating his
own bulky body into the crowd, hoping thereby to clear a space for Agnes
to toddle in. Even if she never sees the horses, she might, with his help,
catch a glimpse of the Sultan of Zanzibar, and he's sure she'd like that!

'It's diabolical this year!' William exclaims, in an ingratiating attempt
to voice her own thoughts. But she turns her face away from him, a glint
of terror in her eyes, appalled at his casual invocation of the demonic forces
all around them.

So, the Rackhams remain on the fringes, and Sugar, instead of watching horses race, watches the *pas de deux* of a married couple. The wife

huddling close to her protector, yet shrinking from his touch; the husband stiff with gallantry and annoyance, despairing of finding room in the rudely jostling real world for a creature so fragile. There seems no limit to the repertoire of movements for expressing this subtle discord between them.

After a while, Sugar becomes aware of another dancer on the fringes of the crowd: a pickpocket. At first she takes him for a dandy, a foppish character too timid to risk himself in the thick of the mob, but then she observes the poise with which he hovers behind each person, the almost lascivious pleasure with which he sidles close to them and then withdraws, like a pollinating insect or the world's gentlest rapist. He is, without a doubt, having a sublimely satisfactory day.

It ought not to trouble Sugar in the slightest when the rogue's leisurely progress brings him closer and closer to William and Agnes; after all, they can easily afford to get robbed, and their reactions to such a misfortune can only add to Sugar's store of knowledge. She verifies with a glance that Agnes's soft pink purse is, in accordance with the very latest fashion, hung at the back of her dress, a godsend to thieves. Mrs Rackham is therefore (as they say in the trade) asking for it. So, why shouldn't Sugar simply stand back and enjoy witnessing a true professional at work? This fellow's a damn sight more graceful than the ballet dancers at the Crystal Palace last week . . .

And yet, and yet . . . The pressure of conscience as Sugar watches the tooler's approach is almost unbearable, like a blunt knife held hard to her throat. She must warn Mrs Rackham! How can she not warn Mrs Rackham! How can she just stand here, a mute accomplice to this parasite? Sugar clears her throat, unheard in the hubbub of the crowd, and rehearses what she'll shout to Agnes. Her voice will be all the uglier for shouting. *Who on earth is that common female, bawling so hoarsely at me*, Agnes will think . . .

It's too late; the moment has come and gone. The pickpocket has floated past Mrs Rackham's skirts, pausing for an instant only. In that instant, Sugar knows, he has sliced her purse wide open with a blade as sharp as a surgical scalpel, and scooped out whatever he fancied. William he leaves unmolested; he's got enough watches already, probably.

Queasy with shame, Sugar watches the pickpocket dance his way gently through the crowd, until he's lost to view. Many people are rearing up on their toes now, erect as can be, craning their necks: the race is almost

finished. William makes one last desultory attempt to clear a path for Agnes
and usher her into the front line; his hand hovers awkwardly at her back,
hesitating to touch her. It's then that he notices her purse, hanging limp
like the skin of a burst balloon. He bends and whispers in her ear.

Agnes turns away from the throng of spectators, her face white as
marble. She takes a few steps forward, away from the commotion, and
comes to a halt on a bare patch of ground about ten feet from Sugar, whose
veiled and parasol'd presence she ignores. Her eyes are wide open, staring
fixedly at emptiness, and brimming with tears. A great, ecstatic cheer goes
up behind her; caps are thrown in the air and top hats are waved.

William hurries to Agnes's side, enfolds her shoulders in his comforting arm.

'Come on, tell me, what have you lost?' he implores her, a little gruffly,
patently keen to replace it and have done with this fuss.

'The photograph of my mother,' says Agnes, shivering under his hands.
'The rest doesn't matter.'

'What photograph?' says William, bemused, as if she has just confessed
to carrying a stuffed zebra or a cast-iron cheese press in her reticule.

'The photograph of my mother,' says Agnes, her cheeks shining with
tears. 'In a locket frame. I carry it everywhere.'

William opens his mouth to protest the folly of this, thinks better of
it. After a few seconds he volunteers, 'I'll find the photographer. If he's
an orderly sort of fellow, he may have the original plates . . .'

'Oh, don't be such an *idiot*, William,' says Agnes, closing her swollen
eyes. 'It was a photograph made long before we met. You didn't even *exist*,
then.'

William removes his palms from her shoulders, lays one behind his head,
and looks back at the crowd while he digests Agnes's devastating logic.
The race is over, and already a number of smartly-dressed onlookers are
walking off towards their waiting broughams and cabs. Another occasion
to be seen at has been ticked off the Season's calendar, and the fashionable
ladies, as they disperse, glance surreptitiously at the hems of their dresses
in case the race-course grounds have soiled them.

'Let's go home, dear,' says William.

Agnes stands frozen in her small square of no-man's-land, still weeping.

'Home?' she echoes, as if she can't imagine what fantastical place he
might mean.

'Yes,' says William, leading his little wife towards the exit, past the dawdling woman with the cheap parasol. 'This way.'

And so the Rackhams hail their cab, and Sugar hails hers. So often it has ended like this: so often that by now it's become almost routine. The Rackhams take their leave from some Season event or other, headed for 'home', and Sugar, their shadow, hurries back to her own rooms in Priory Close, gambling that tonight will be the night that William comes. She cannot be forever walking twenty steps behind him, or haunting the perimeters of his house and gardens; sometimes, she must be where he expects her to be, ready to receive him.

So far, her instincts for when to follow and when to dash back to Priory Close haven't been what you'd call unerring. In three weeks, William has come to visit her twice. On one occasion, she was caught completely unprepared, having only just walked in the door, still smelling of the same smoky theatre he himself had come from. (After a moment's hesitation, she decided honesty was the safest policy, and encouraged him to marvel at the coincidence of them both attending the same play. It was quite an agreeable conversation, really, followed by a fuck as passionate as any Rackham has ever spent on her.) On the other occasion, Sugar returned to her rooms to find a handwritten note on the floor of her receiving hall:

Heartbroken, I can no longer wait;
Was I untimely, or You too late?

(For days afterwards, she puzzled over this doggerel, subjecting it to exhaustive exegesis, straining to guess the author's true feelings.)

Now, returning from her day at the races, Sugar lets herself into her unlit love nest, instantly annoyed at the quiet that allows her to hear her own breathing. She has a headache; she tears the ugly bonnet from her head, pulls the combs from her hair, and runs her fingers through. The severe parting in the middle of her scalp has been in place so long that it hurts to disturb it. Sweat has eaten away at the tender flesh behind her ears. Her face, she notes in the hallway mirror, is dusky with grime.

While the bath is filling, Sugar ferrets about for something to eat. She hasn't eaten all day, except for an apple in the morning, a cream bun she devoured in the cab on the way to Sandown Park, and a single bite of sausage at the race-course. That sausage, bought sizzling hot from a stall, was a mistake: it looked just like the bangers she used to love when she lived in Church Lane, when Mr Bing the sausage man used to wheel his steaming cart from door to door, and she and Caroline would haul themselves out of bed and buy the biggest, fattiest, sootiest specimens they could get. But the sausage today didn't taste like Mr Bing's bangers; it tasted like pig offal fried in dirty paraffin. Honestly, who could possibly digest such garbage? She spat it out, and felt bilious for hours.

Now she's hungry. Starving! And there's never anything to eat in these damn rooms of hers! The whole place smells faintly of lavender soap when it should smell of food and wine and love-making. (In her peevish mood, nothing will satisfy her short of William sound asleep in her bed while she devours juicy mouthfuls of hot roast chicken. As for where that chicken is supposed to come from, well . . . if Rackham can arrange for half a dozen Japanese quince trees to be delivered to his garden in Notting Hill, surely he could manage one chicken in Marylebone . . . !)

In the study, on the writing-table where her novel never lies, there sits a fist-sized lump of bread. It's all that's left of the loaf she bought on Friday, at a street stall on the way back from the Crystal Palace. The woman selling it squinted at Sugar in surprise, for her regular clientele was down-and-outs, not ladies in long furry capes.

The bath is filled now. Sugar munches on the stale bread (its shape is awfully peculiar – have mice been at it, perhaps? – best not to think about it) and swallows convulsively to get it down her throat. Is this the life of luxury to which she thought she was graduating when she left Mrs Castaway's? And what about the way William crowed when he was twirling around the lamp-post? 'Safe from all of you' – that's what he said . . . 'No one else will ever touch her' – so why in God's name doesn't he come and touch her himself! Is he fed up with his prize already? And that damned note: *Was I untimely, or You too late?* What did he *mean*?

Sugar takes her bath. As usual, she stays in it for far too long, chiding herself with empty threats, sinking deeper and deeper under the sudsy scum, keeping very still so that the cold water doesn't tickle her. It's late at night before she's out, near midnight before her hair is dry. She sits on her immaculate king-size bed, fragrant and clean, dressed in a snow-white shift.

Come on, you swine, she thinks. *Rescue me.*

SEVENTEEN

andsome and high-minded Henry Rackham, who once upon a time seemed destined to become *the* Rackham of Rackham Perfumeries, and now is merely the brother of that eminent man, stands alone in a turd-strewn street, his rain-dappled topcoat steaming faintly in the afternoon sun, waiting for a prostitute.

No, it's not as bad as it appears: he's waiting for a *particular* prostitute.

No, no, still you misunderstand! He hopes to speak with the woman he met here a few weeks ago, in order to . . . in order to bring their conversation to a more fitting conclusion. Or, as Mrs Fox might put it (she being a champion of plain speaking), to make amends for being such an ass.

Having given the matter much thought, he has decided that his mistake, and therewith his sin, was not that he spoke to this woman in the first place. No, his sin came later. Everything was going so well until he was distracted by fleshly curiosity, and then, provoked by his prurience, she lifted her skirts and . . . well, the rest is branded on his memory, like a dark triangular stigma on the pale flesh of his brain. But he was as much to blame as she, and in any case the question remains: what now? She is a soul in peril, and it would be a mockery of Christ's teaching if no one ever spoke to her but bad men, and she were shunned by decent Christians.

This is why he's standing here in Church Lane, St Giles. His hamper of food he has already given away to urchins (genuinely *hungry* urchins, he tries to reassure himself) and his shoes have already sunk several times into ordure. He has refused the offer of a feeble, ferret-like man to clean his shoes for him; instead, he has knelt in the street and done the job himself, attempting while doing so to engage the ferret-like man in conversation about God. (No success; the man snorted in bemusement and walked off.) Several individuals have called out to him, 'Hoy, parson!' and laughed, melting into dark doorways and windows as soon as he's turned around. So far, no one has attempted to attack or rob him. From such small acorns, ministries may grow.

So, Henry waits on the corner of Church Lane and Arthur Street, sweltering in the sun, squinting at the passers-by. In the short time he has been standing here, four prostitutes – or women he assumes to be such – have spoken to him. They have (respectively) offered him punnets of watercress, directions, a nice shady place to rest, and 'the most reliefsome cuddle in London'. To which his replies have been (respectively) 'No thank you', 'No thank you', 'No thank you', and 'No thank you, God forgive you'. He is waiting for the woman in the terracotta dress. Once he has made good his sin with her, he can begin to consider others.

At last she comes, but looking so different that if it weren't for her heart-shaped face being still vivid in his mind, he would have let her walk by. As it is, he has to lean forward and peer closely to make sure it's really the same person. She has different clothes on, you see, a phenomenon that rather fazes him, for in his mind she had become a symbolic creature, fixed in appearance like a painting hung in church. Nevertheless, pink shawl and shabby blue dress aside, it's she, gingerly negotiating the mucky cobbles as before. Henry clears his throat.

The woman (yes, her pretty upturned nose is unmistakable!) doesn't notice him, or at least feigns not to, until they're almost touching. But then she cocks her head towards his, anoints him with her gaze, and smiles broadly.

''Ello, sir,' she says. 'More questions?'

'Yes,' he replies at once, in a firm voice. 'If you'll permit me.'

'For two shillin's, I'll permit damn near anyfink, sir,' she teases him. 'Anyfink *you* can put to me, anyhow.'

Henry's jaw stiffens. Is she implying he's less manly than other men? Or merely that he's less depraved? And why is her Cockney accent so strong? Last time they spoke, there was a Northern cadence to it . . .

She tugs at his sleeve in amiable reproach, as though already well familiar with his tendency for wool-gathering and determined to stop it getting out of hand. 'But let's not do it in the street this time,' she suggests. 'Let's talk in a nice quiet room.'

'By all means,' agrees Henry at once, and it's her turn to be surprised. A queer expression crosses her face, half-protective, half-fearful – but only for a moment.

'That's us agreed, then,' she says.

He walks at her side, and she leads him along, frequently checking his progress as she might an unreliable dog's. Does she think he's a simpleton? He oughtn't to care what she thinks. God alone will understand why he has accepted her invitation.

'It ain't fancy,' she says, ushering him towards a decaying Georgian house. Henry's impression, at a glance, is of a façade the colour and texture of pork rind; the crumbling stucco might be blisters of mould. But before he can examine it too carefully, she has pulled him across a yard littered with chicken feathers, through a doorway and into a dim vestibule. He, Henry Rackham, would-be pastor of this parish, has crossed the threshold of a whore-house.

There are Turkish carpets underfoot, but they are threadbare, and the floorboards sigh softly beneath them. The walls of the corridor are concave on one side and convex on the other; striped wallpaper bulges and wrinkles like ill-fitting clothing, medallioned with framed prints whose glass is opaque with fug. Radiating from deeper inside the house is a smell of stale humidity, suggestive of . . . suggestive of all manner of things Henry Rackham has never known.

'Plenty of fresh air upstairs,' says the woman at his side, clearly worried he'll leave her yet. If she only knew how salutary it is for him to be confronted with this squalor! On more than one occasion, he's asked Mrs Fox to describe to him what a house of ill repute is really like and, despite her frankness, he's still pictured it through a rosy tint of bacchanalian fantasy. Nothing – not common sense, not conscientious study of reports, not Mrs Fox's word – has been able to banish from his mind the vision of a bawdy-house as a sumptuous grotto of sensual delight. Now, sobered by the smell of truth, he steps into the receiving room: a dismal parlour, a gloomy gallimaufry of exhausted furniture and jaundiced ornamental crockery and military paraphernalia, lit by oil-lamps despite the sunshine straining to penetrate thick curtains the colour of bacon.

Blocking the passage to the staircase sits a ruined old man in a wheelchair, his human features almost entirely obscured by scarves and knitted coverlets.

'Sevenpence for use of the room,' he mumbles, addressing no one in particular. Henry bridles, but his prostitute bats her eyelashes at him apologetically, as if she couldn't have guessed he'd be so ignorant as to imagine she had a room of her own.

'It's only sevenpence, sir,' she whispers. 'To a man like you . . .'

Even as Henry is fetching the coins out of his trouser pocket, the truth is dawning on him: this woman is a convenience of the poor, for the poor. She's not meant for his consumption; possibly no gentleman of his class has ever set foot in this crumbling, malodorous lair. The very clothes on his back are worth more than anything in the room – furniture, crockery, war medals and all.

'I don't have sevenpence, here's a shilling,' he mutters shamefacedly as he hands the coins down. A gnarled claw closes on the money, and a woolly muzzle of scarf sags off the fellow's face, revealing a swollen strawberry of a nose, varicose cheeks and a disgustingly gummy mouth.

'Don't be expecting change,' the old man wheezes, emitting an oral flatus of ulcer and alcohol, and abruptly wheels out of the way, allowing Henry and the prostitute to pass through.

'So,' says Henry, taking a deep breath as they begin to mount the stairs together. 'What's your name?'

'Caroline, sir,' she replies. 'And watch yer step, sir – the ones wiv the nails in are a bit chancy.'

Two shillings buys Henry twenty minutes. Caroline sits on the edge of her bed, having given Henry her solemn promise not to do anything mischievous. Henry remains standing, stationed at the open window. He scarcely looks at Caroline as he asks his questions; instead he appears to be addressing the blackened rooftops and debris-strewn pathways of Church Lane. Every so often, he turns to look at her for half a second, and she smiles. He smiles back, for politeness' sake. His smile, she thinks, is an unexpectedly sweet thing to behold. Her bed, he thinks, is like a manger lined with rags.

In his twenty minutes, Henry learns a good deal about the different kinds of prostitute, and their habitats. Caroline is a 'street girl' who lodges in a house for whose use she (or preferably her customer) pays rent every time she enters. She assures him, though, that the mean and gloomy appearance of this place is entirely due to the 'tight' nature of its owner, Mrs Leek, and that there are other such lodging-houses whose owners take 'a real interest'. In fact, she knows of one house in particular that's owned by the mother of one of its girls. It's 'like a palace, sir' – not that Caroline has ever been there – nor to a palace, neither – but she can imagine it must be true, because the same madam used to run a house in Church Lane, just three doors along from here, that's got a bad sort of people in it now, but when Mrs Castaway was there, you could eat off the floors it was so clean. And the daughter has since become the mistress of a very rich man, but even when she lived here she was always like a princess – not that Caroline has ever seen a princess in the flesh, but she's seen pictures, and this girl Sugar looked no worse. So you see what can be done when the folk in charge takes an interest. Take Caroline's bedroom, now: it's nothing to be proud of, she knows. 'But if it was *you*, sir, workin' 'ere, wiv *'im* downstairs and the place smellin' so bad of damp, would you be fagged polishin' the bedknobs and puttin' posies in a vase? I *don't* fink so.'

Henry enquires about brothels, and learns that they too are 'a mixed bag'. Some are 'prisons, sir, prisons', where bullies and old hags keep the wretched girls ''alf naked and 'alf starved'. Others are owned by 'the importantest people', and the girls 'don't get out of bed except for bishops and kings' (a statement Henry needs to ponder momentarily.) One thing is clear to him: the neat distinctions made by books don't mean much in the real world. There is a hierarchy, yes, but not of categories, rather of individual houses, even individual prostitutes, and the mobility that's possible between one social division and the next is remarkable.

He learns more about Caroline, too, in the twenty minutes his two shillings have bought him. To his dismay, she has nothing but contempt for the virtue she once possessed. Virtue don't pay the rent, she sneers; if those folk who so value virtue in a woman had been prepared to house, feed and clothe her instead of just spectating on her pitiful struggles, she might have remained virtuous much longer.

And Heaven? What's Caroline's opinion of Heaven? Well, she doesn't see herself going there, but nor does she see herself going to Hell, which is only for really 'bad' people. About God and Jesus she has no opinions, but she considers the Devil 'useful' if he really does punish the wicked, and she hopes that the wicked people she's known, particularly the owner of a certain dress-making firm, may suffer dreadful tortures after their deaths, though she has a feeling they'll skip out of it somehow.

'And would you ever consider returning home?' says Henry, when her weariness of so much talking has brought her Northern accent once more to the fore.

'Home? Where's that?' she snaps.

'Yorkshire, I'd say,' says Henry gently.

'You been there?'

'I've visited.'

The bed creaks as she stands up from it. He can tell from her peevish sigh that his twenty minutes are, in her rough innumerate estimation, up.

'I fink they've got all the whores they need in Yorkshire, sir,' she says bitterly.

In parting, they're awkward with each other, each aware that Henry has crossed a boundary, that he has caused pain. Henry is mortified to be leaving her with this shadow of grief on her face: for all that he came here hoping to put the fear of God into her, he can't bear to have caused her the prick of homesickness. She's such a cheerful soul by nature, he can tell; how despicable of him to rob her of her smile! She, for her part, doesn't know how to send him on his way, poor duffer. Kissing him would violate their agreement, but shutting her bedroom door on his earnestly frowning face seems awful harsh.

'Come on, sir, I'll see you down the stairs,' she says, softening.

A minute later, Henry Rackham stands in the alley, staring up at the house he has just left, at the upstairs window through whose filthy glass he has looked with his own eyes. A weight has lifted from his shoulders, a weight so burdensome that to be rid of it makes him almost giddy. Christ Jesus stands by his side here in the alley, and God is looking down from Heaven.

How relieved he feels! If there weren't so much muck on the cobbles just here, he would sink to his knees in grateful prayer. For she — the woman Caroline — touched his hand as he was leaving, and she looked into his face, and he felt no lust for her whatsoever — not for her, not for any of her kind. The love he felt for her, as he returned her smile, was the same love he feels for any man, woman or child in peril; she was a poor thing suspended unawares above the Abyss.

Nothing is impossible now, between him and all the Carolines of this vast metropolis! Let other men seek to win their bodies; he and Mrs Fox will strive to win their souls!

'Forgive me Father, for I have sinned.'

With these words, delivered in a girlish rush, Agnes Rackham makes the leap back into the body which last sat here thirteen years ago. Unconsciously she hunches her shoulders to negate the few inches she's grown, and so put before her eyes exactly that part of the confessional grille she always stared at as a child. The grille is unchanged in every vividly remembered detail: its wooden lattice-work is neither more nor less polished, its curtain of gold-threaded hemp neither more nor less frayed.

'How long is it since your last confession?'

Agnes's heart thuds against her breast (which, in her mind's eye, has become bosomless) as these words pass through the grille; it thuds not because she's alarmed by the question or by the answer she'll have to give, but rather because she hopes so fervently that the voice is the same one that reproved and absolved her all those years before. Is it? Is it? She can't tell from eight short words.

'Thirteen years, Father,' she whispers. Sensational admission!

'Why so long, child?' Her ear is almost touching the screen, and still she can't tell for sure if she knows the voice.

'I was very young, Father,' she explains, her lips almost brushing against the lattice, 'and my father . . . I mean, not *you*, Father . . . and not my *Heavenly* Father . . . and not my—'

'Yes, yes,' the voice hurries her along testily, and with that, Agnes knows beyond any doubt that it's *he*! Father Scanlon himself!

'My *step*-father made us Anglicans,' she sums up excitedly.

'And your step-father is now dead?' surmises Father Scanlon.

'No, Father, he's abroad. But I'm grown up now, and old enough to know my mind.'

'Very well, child. Do you remember how to confess?'

'Oh *yes*, Father,' exclaims Agnes, disappointed that the priest doesn't share her view of the intervening years as mere blinks of an eye. She almost (to show him what's what) launches into the *Confiteor* in Latin, for she rote-learnt it once, but she bites her tongue and plumps for English.

'I confess to Almighty God, to blessed Mary ever Virgin, to blessed Michael the Archangel, to blessed John the Baptist, to the holy Apostles Peter and Paul, to all the Saints and to you, Father, that I have sinned exceedingly in thought, word, and deed, through my fault, through my fault, through my most grievous fault. Therefore I beseech blessed Mary, ever Virgin, blessed Michael the Archangel, blessed John the Baptist, the holy' (here Father Scanlon coughs and sniffs) 'Apostles Peter and Paul, all the Saints, and you, Father, to pray to the Lord God for me.'

A tuneless hum from the other side of the screen invites her to confess. Agnes has come prepared for this moment and removes from her new reticule a leaf of writing-paper onto which she has the previous evening noted all her sins, in order of their appearance in her diaries for the last thirteen years. She clears her throat delicately.

'These are my sins. On the 12th of June, 1862, I gave away a ring that had been given to me by a friend. On the 21st of June of that same year, I told that friend, when she questioned me, that I still had the ring. On the third of October, 1869, at a time when all our roses had a blight, I stole a perfect rose from a neighbour's garden and, later that day, I threw it away, lest someone ask me where I got it. On the 25th of January, 1873, I purposely stepped on an insect that meant me no harm. On the 14th of June 1875 – last week, in fact – while suffering a headache, I spoke harshly to a policeman, saying he was no use at all, and ought to be dismissed.'

'Yes?' the priest prompts her, just as he used to when she was a child.

'That's all, Father,' she assures him.

'All the sins you've committed in thirteen years?'

'Why, yes, Father.'

The priest sighs and shifts audibly in his chair.

'Come, child,' he says. 'There must be more.'

'If there are, Father, I do not know of them.'

Again the priest sighs, louder this time. 'Indiscretions?' he suggests. 'The sin of pride?'

'I may have missed a few incidents,' concedes Agnes. 'Sometimes I've been too sleepy or unwell to keep my diary as I should.'

'Very well then . . .' mutters the priest. 'Restitution, restitution . . . There's very little you can do after such a lapse of time. If you still have the friend whose ring you gave away, tell her you did so and ask her forgiveness. As for the flower . . .' (he groans) 'forget about the flower. As for the insect, you're free to step on as many as you please; they're under your dominion, as the Bible makes clear. If you can find the policeman you insulted, apologise. Now: penance. For the lie and the harsh words, say three *Hail Marys*. And do try to examine your soul more deeply. Very few of us live through thirteen years committing nary a sin.'

'Thank you, Father,' whispers Agnes, folding the leaf of paper tightly in her palm, leaning forward for her absolution.

'*Dominus noster Iesus Christus te absolvat*,' mumbles the old voice, '*et ego auctoritate ipsius te absolvo . . .*' Tears seep out of Agnes's closed eyelids and trickle one after the other down her cheeks. '. . . *ego te absolvo a peccatis tuis, in nomine Patris, et Filii, et Spiritus Sancti. Amen.*'

Agnes Rackham glides out of the confessional lighter than air, and hurriedly takes a seat in the back pews. For her illicit visit here this after-noon she has worn a veil and a plain charcoal-grey dress: a very different outfit from those she's been showing off at Seasonal Occasions to be sure, but then here in Saint Teresa's, Cricklewood, her attitude to being recog-nised is very different too. The back pews, far removed from the regular congregation, far from the altar and the candelabras, are so dark that when Agnes squeezes between them she almost trips on a prayer cushion not replaced in its pouch. Far above her head, the ceiling has been freshly painted sky-blue, and dotted with golden stars whose light is illusory.

Now Agnes sits contented in the gloom, her face in the shadow of an overhanging cornice. The service is about to begin; Father Scanlon has emerged from the back of the confessional and walks towards the pulpit. He lifts the purple stole off his shoulders and hands it to one of the altar-boys in exchange for a different one. He's hardly changed at all! His most important feature – the wart on his brow – is as large as ever.

Enchanted, she watches the preparations for Mass, wishing she could participate, knowing she can't. The fact that she knows no one in the congregation is no guarantee that no one knows her (she's the wife of William Rackham, *the* William Rackham, after all), and she can't afford to provoke gossip. The time isn't ripe for the World to learn of her return to the True Faith.

'*Introibo ad altare Dei*,' announces Father Scanlon, and the ritual begins. Agnes looks on from the shadows, mouthing along with the Latin. In spirit she projects herself into the candle-lit centre of attention; when the priest bows down to kiss the altar, she inclines her own head; his every signing of the Cross she duplicates over her own breast; her mouth waters at the touch of imaginary bread and wine; her wet lips part to let God in.

'*Dominus vobiscum*,' she whispers, in rapturous unison with Father Scanlon. '*Et cum spirito tuo.*'

Afterwards, when the church is empty, Agnes ventures out into the light, in order to be alone with the religious bric-a-brac of her childhood. She dawdles past the seats where she and her mother sat, which, although different people sat in them today, are still identifiable by nicks and blemishes in the wood. All the fixtures are just as they were, except for a new mosaic in the apse depicting Mary's heavenly coronation that's far too bright and gets Her nose wrong. The plaque of the Assumption behind the altar is reassuringly unchanged, with Our Lady floating away from the pudgy, clutching hands of the hideous cherubs swarming around Her feet.

Agnes wonders how long it will be before she's bold enough to snub Anglicanism publicly and reserve a private seat for herself here, in the light near the altar. Not very long, she hopes. Only, she doesn't know whom to ask, and how much it would cost, and whether it's paid for weekly or yearly. That's the sort of thing William would be good for, if she could only trust him.

First things first, though: she must do something to reduce the number of days her mother languishes in Purgatory. Has anyone else pleaded for Violet Unwin since her death? Probably not. On the evidence of her funeral, attended only by Lord Unwin's Anglican cronies, she had no Catholic friends left.

Agnes has always assumed her mother will be in Purgatory a very long time, as punishment for marrying Lord Unwin in the first place, and then for allowing him to rob her and Agnes of their religion. Strong interventions are needed.

Opening her new purse under the light of the altar's candelabra, she removes, from amongst the face-powder shells, smelling salts and button-hooks, a much creased and tarnished Prayer card, on one side of which is printed an engraving of Jesus, and on the other an indulgenced prayer, guaranteed to shave days, weeks or even months off the sentence. Agnes reads the instructions. The requirement that she should just have received communion God will probably waive in the circumstances; in all other respects she's eligible: she's made Confession, she's standing before a crucifix, and she knows by heart the words of the *Our Father, Hail Mary* and *Glory be to the Father for the Pope*. She recites these, slowly and distinctly, and then reads the prayer on the card.

'. . . They have pierced my hands and feet,' she concludes. 'They have numbered all my bones.' Closing her eyes, she waits for the tingling in her palms and soles which always accompanied the reading of this prayer when, as a child, she used it to plead for dimly remembered aunts and favourite historical figures.

To fix an extra wing on her prayer, she walks over to the nave where the votive candles sit, and lights one. The hundred-holed brass tray looks just as it should; the very gobs of melted wax around the holes seem not to have been scraped off since she stood here last.

Agnes next stands under the pulpit, which she never dared do as a child, for the top of it is carved in the shape of a massive eagle, with the Bible resting across its back and spread wings, and its head pointing straight down at the onlooker. Fearlessly, or very nearly fearlessly, Agnes stares up into the bird's dull wooden eyes.

Just then the church bell begins to toll, and Agnes must stare into the eagle's eyes all the harder, for it's at just such a signal that magical creatures come to life. *Cling, Cling, Cling*, goes the bell, but the carved bird doesn't stir, and when the tolling stops, Agnes looks away.

She'd like to visit the crucified Christ behind the pulpit, to verify her recollection that it was the *middle* finger on His left hand that was broken and glued back in place, but she knows time is getting on, and she must go home. William may be wondering what's become of her.

As she walks up the far aisle, she reacquaints herself with the sequence of paintings of Christ's journey to Golgotha hanging high upon the walls. Only, she's passing under them in reverse order, from the Deposition to the Judgement Before Pilate. These dismal images, too, have remained unchanged for thirteen years, retaining all their varnished menace. As a child, she was afraid of these scenes of suffering set against grim, storm-laden skies: she used to shut her eyes against the glistening mark of the birch-whip on the ghastly grey skin, the slender trickles of dark blood from the thorn-pricked forehead, and most especially, the nailing of Christ's right hand. In those days, she only needed to glimpse, by accident, the mallet in mid-swing, for her own hand to spasm into a fist, and she'd have to wrap it protectively in a fold of her skirts.

Today she sees the paintings very differently, for she's since suffered many tortures of her own, and knows there are worse things than an agonising death. Moreover, she understands what she was never able to understand as a child: namely, *why*, if Jesus was magic, did He let Himself be murdered? Now she envies the haloed martyr, for He was a creature, like Psycho and the Mussulman mystics in the Spiritualist books, who could be killed and then return to life intact. (In Christ's case, not *quite* intact, she has to admit, as He had those holes in His feet and hands, but then that would be less of a misfortune for a man than a woman.)

She pauses in the doorway to the vestibule and briefly contemplates, before leaving, the face of Jesus as Pilate condemns him. Yes, there's no mistaking it: the serene, almost smug equanimity of one who knows: 'I cannot be destroyed.' It's exactly the same expression as is on the face of the African chieftain on the burning pyre (– engraving made by an eye-witness, or so the author of *Miracles and Their Mechanisms*, currently under her bed, assures her.) So many people in history have survived death, and here's she, for all her devoted study into the matter, still excluded from that elite! Why? She's not asking for fame – she's not the son of God, after all – no one need even know she's done it, she'd be ever so discreet!

But she mustn't spoil this wonderful day with sorry thoughts. Not when she's had absolution, and mouthed Latin in unison with her childhood priest. She hurries out of the church, looking neither right nor left, resisting the temptation to linger amongst the displays of religious merchandise and compare, as she used to, one painted miniature with another, trying to decide which was the very best Lamb, the very best Virgin, the very best Christ, and so on. She must return to Notting Hill, and have a little rest.

Outside, darkness has fallen. For a moment, she's in a quandary how she'll get home: then she remembers. William's marvellous gift: her very own brougham. She still can't *quite* believe she owns it, but there it stands, waiting outside the stonemason's workshop opposite the church. Its dark-brown horses turn their blinkered heads placidly at her approach, and in the driver's seat, wreathed in smoke from his pipe, sits . . .

'Cheesman?' she calls, but softly, almost to herself, for she's still experimenting with her ownership of him.

'Cheesman!' she calls again, this time loud enough for him to hear. 'Back to the house, please.'

'Very well, Mrs Rackham' is his reply, and within moments she's snug inside the coach, rubbing her shoulders shyly against its upholstery as the horses jerk into motion. What a fine brougham it is! It's grander than Mrs Bridgelow's, and hers cost £180, according to William. A major expenditure, then, but well worth it – and not before time, either, because there isn't much of the Season left.

She has forgiven William for not consulting her; it really is a faultless brougham, and Cheesman could hardly be bettered (he's taller and handsomer than Mrs Bridgelow's coachman, for a start). And it was evidently terribly important to William to keep it a surprise. What a surprise it was indeed, when, a week ago, she mentioned she had an errand in the city and asked him if he knew when the next omnibus was due, and he said, 'Why not take the brougham, my dear?'

'Why, whose brougham?' she naturally enquired.

'Yours and mine, my dear,' he said, and, taking her by the hand, led her to see her birthday gift.

Now the miraculous Cheesman is taking her home – this human birthday present of hers, a man of few words, a discreet fellow on whom she already knows she can rely. Last Sunday he took her to Church – *English* Church – in Notting Hill, and next Sunday he'll do so again, but tonight he's taken her to Mass, and she can tell he'll do *that* again, too. Why, she could probably command him to take her to a Mosque or a Synagogue, and he'd tap the horses' flanks with his folded whip, and they'd be off!

Tomorrow he'll take her to the Royal Opera House, where Madame Adelina Patti is singing *Dinorah*. Everyone will see her (Agnes, that is, not Madame Patti) alighting from her new brougham. *Who's that?* people will whisper, as a Cinderella-like figure emerges from the burnished body of the carriage, white skirts tumbling out like froth . . . Euphoric with anticipation, still tingling from the thrill of Father Scanlon's absolution, and rocked in the bosom of her very own brougham, Agnes dozes, her cheek resting against the tasselled velvet pillow William has given her for just that purpose, as the horses bear her homewards.

That the Rackhams now possess a brougham is no secret from Sugar. She helped William choose it, from a folio of designs, and advised him on what his wife's needs and desires might be.

Yes, thank God, the tide has turned, and Rackham is once again paying her regular visits. He can no longer stand being dragged from one pompous spectacle to another, he says, when he has so much work to do. He has shown his face in all the right places, he's suffered Royal Institution lectures about pterodactyls, he's suffered *Hamlet* in Italian, and now, by Heaven, he's endured enough for the sake of Society.

Lord knows, half of these events he's only attended because he was afraid Agnes might take one of her 'turns', and he'd have to step in. But she seems to have got over whatever was possessing her, she's not fainting or having fits in public anymore, in fact she's behaving perfectly, so he's damned if he's going to chaperone her to every concert, play, garden party, charity banquet, horse race, pleasure garden, flower show and exhibition from now till September. Half a dozen workers at the Mitcham farm were killed on Tuesday, in a poisoning incident wholly unrelated to Rackham Perfumeries, but it meant police enquiries, and where was he at the time? Snoring his head off at the Lyceum, that's where, while a fat Thespian in a cardboard crown pretended to be succumbing to poison. What an abject lesson, if any were needed, in the necessity to draw a line between make-believe and reality! From now on, he'll accompany Agnes only to what's absolutely unavoidable.

Oh, and yes, of course, he's missed Sugar dreadfully. More than he can say.

Sugar glows with happiness, reassured by the fervour of his embrace, the effusion of renewed intimacy between them. She was afraid she'd lost her grip, but no, he's confiding in her more than ever. Her fears were all in vain; she's securely woven into the tapestry of his life.

'Ach, what would I have done without you!' he sighs, as they lie in each other's arms, warm and sated. Sugar pulls the bed-clothes up over his chest, to tuck him in, and as she does so she releases a whiff of their love-making from under the soft sheets, for there's scarcely an inch of her he hasn't reclaimed.

The business with Hopsom has ended well, with Hopsom more or less satisfied and Rackham's reputation intact – thanks, in no small measure, to Sugar's excellent advice. The new Rackham's catalogue is a great success, purged entirely of the old man's crude turns of phrase, and now so much improved by Sugar's elegant suggestions that there's been a notable increase in orders from the gentry. Even a few weeks ago, William was still saying things like 'But this can be of no interest to you' or 'Forgive me: what a subject!'; now, he speaks freely of his business plans and anxieties, and it's plain her opinion is worth gold to him.

'Don't be envious of Pears, dear heart,' she murmurs soothingly to him one night, when, in a flush of melancholy after his passion is spent, he confesses how small he feels in comparison with that industrial colossus. 'They have land and suppliers you don't have, and that's that. Why not turn your thoughts to the things about Pears you *can* compete with, like ... well, like the pretty illustrations on their posters and labels. They're *very* popular, you know: I'll wager half the reason so many people are partial to Pears is the appeal of those pictures.'

'Rackham's *does* use illustrations,' he reminds her, wiping the damp hair on his chest with a handful of bedsheet. 'A fellow in Glasgow paints them, and we have them engraved. Costs a fortune, too.'

'Yes, but fashions change so terribly quickly, William. For instance, the engraving in *The Illustrated London News* just now: with all due respect to your man in Glasgow, the girl's hair is already out of style. She has her frisette gummed to her forehead, instead of hanging soft and free. Women notice these things . . .'

She has her palm cupped over his genitals, can feel his balls moving in their pouch as his manhood comes slowly back to life. He accepts that she's right, she can tell.

'I'll help you with your illustrations, William,' she croons. 'The Rackham woman will be as modern as tomorrow.'

In the days that follow, true to his word, William leaves the hurly-burly of the Season more and more to his wife, and spends the time thus freed with Sugar, or with the affairs of Rackham Perfumeries, or (preferably) both at once. Three times in one week she has him in her bed, including an entire night sleeping side by side! Nor is he in any hurry to leave in the morning; she has bought provisions of shaving soap, razors, cheese, anything he might fancy while he emerges from his nest of slumber.

One particular Friday, though, he has to go to Birmingham, to investigate an insolvent box factory whose asking price is almost too good to be true. And so, on the night that William must spend in a Brummie guesthouse, Sugar accompanies Agnes to the Royal Opera House, to see Meyerbeer's *Dinorah*.

The two of them meet in the foyer – or as nearly as Sugar dares. In the swarming pre-performance crowd, only one body stands between the two women at any given moment, as Sugar hides now behind this person, now that one, peeking over stiff black shoulders and puff sleeves.

Mrs Rackham is dressed all in bone-white and olive green and, if truth be told, looks exceedingly wan. She smiles at anyone who might be watching her, but her eyes are glazed, her grip on her fan is rather tight, and she walks with an ever-so-slight totter.

'Delightful to see you!' she chirps to Mrs This and Mrs That, but her heart clearly isn't in it and, making her excuses after only a few seconds of conversation, she retreats into the crowd. By seven o'clock she's already in her seat for the performance, thus abdicating the chance to display her finery to serried rows of captive onlookers. Instead, she massages her temples with her gloved fingers, and waits.

Two hours later, when it's all over, Agnes applauds feebly while all around her erupt in jubilation. Amid cries of 'Encore!' she squeezes out of her aisle and hurries towards the exit. Sugar follows at once, although she is a *little* worried that the people in her own aisle will conclude that she hasn't enjoyed herself. She has! It was majestic, superb! Can she applaud and cry 'Encore!' while stumbling past people's knees, stepping on their feet in her haste to pursue the fleeing Mrs Rackham? No, that would be too absurd; she'll just have to make a bad impression.

In the entrance-hall, a surprising number of opera-goers have already rendezvoused. These are the jaded élite, the barons and baronesses sleepy with boredom, the monocled critics lighting each other's cigars, the frivolous young things impatient to flit on to other entertainments, the senile dowagers too sore to sit longer. A noisy babble is discussing cabs, the weather, mutual friends; masculine voices can be heard pooh-poohing the performance, comparing it unfavourably with *Dinorahs* seen in other countries in other years; feminine voices are decrying Adelina Patti's dress sense, while epicene ones are just as loudly praising it. Through this throng, Agnes Rackham attempts to make her escape.

'Ah! Agnes!' cries an obese lady in a claret-hued, eye-catchingly horrid satin dress. 'Opinion, please!'

Agnes freezes in her tracks, and turns to face her captor.

'I haven't any opinion,' she protests in an uncharacteristically low and unmusical voice. 'I merely wanted some air . . .'

'Goodness, yes, you *do* look peakish!' exclaims Mrs So-and-So. 'Are you sure you're getting enough to eat, my dear?'

Standing close behind Agnes, Sugar observes a shudder travelling down the buttons of her back. There is a pause, during which the hubbub quietens, perhaps by mere coincidence rather than general curiosity about Mrs Rackham's response.

'You are fat, and ugly, and I've never liked you.' The words ring out distinctly, in a harsh monotone unrecognisable as Agnes's, issuing from somewhere much deeper than her piccolo throat. It's a voice that makes the hairs stand up on the nape of Sugar's neck, and transfixes Mrs So-and-So like the snarl of a savage dog. 'Your husband disgusts me,' Agnes goes on, 'with his slobbering red lips and his old man's teeth. Your concern for me is false and poisonous. Your chin has hairs on it. Fat people shouldn't ever wear satin.' And with that, she turns on her heel and hurries out of the hall, one white-gloved hand pressed hard against her forehead.

Sugar hurries after, passing close by the mortified Mrs So-and-So and her slack-mouthed entourage, who cringe backwards as if the rules of the game are now so topsy-turvy that an attack from a total stranger would be no surprise.

'Excuse me,' wheezes Sugar as she leaves them gawping.

Her haste is justified: Agnes doesn't even stop at the cloakroom, but rushes directly out of the building onto the gas-lit street. The doorman has barely enough time to retract his rubbery neck from the open door before Sugar slips through the space herself, brushing his nose with the velvet shoulder of her dress.

'Pardon me!' they ejaculate simultaneously, to the wind.

Sugar peers into the jostling confusion of Bow Street, a populous glut of hawkers, harlots, foreigners and decent folk. For a moment she fears she's lost Agnes in the kaleidoscope, especially as there's a constant stream of horse-drawn traffic camouflaging one side of the road from the other. But she needn't have worried: Mrs Rackham, lacking the dark green coat and black parapluie she's failed to redeem from the cloakroom, is easy to spot; her white skirts sweep along the dark footpath and weave through the pedestrians. Sugar has only to follow the lightest object, and trust that it's Agnes.

The pursuit lasts less than half a minute; Mrs Rackham ducks sideways out of Bow Street into a narrow alley, the sort that's used by whores and thieves for their convenience – or by gentlemen in need of a piss. Indeed, the instant that Sugar slips inside its murky aperture, she's assailed by the smell of human waste and the sound of furtive footsteps making themselves scarce.

The footsteps are certainly not Agnes's: a short distance into the alley, Mrs Rackham lies sprawled face-down and dead-still, in the muck and the grit. Her skirts glow in the dark like a mound of snow that has miraculously survived the coming of Spring.

'*Damn* . . .' breathes Sugar, paralysed with alarm and indecision. She looks backwards, and verifies that from the point of view of the passers-by in Bow Street five yards behind her, she's in another world, a shadowy limbo; she and Agnes have left the lamp-lit mainstream, which flows on without them, oblivious. Then again, Sugar knows very well that Scotland Yard is not far around the corner, and if there's any place in London where she's liable to be grabbed by a couple of uniformed runners and asked what exactly she knows about this lady lying lifeless at her feet, it's here.

'Agnes?' No response from the motionless body. Mrs Rackham's left foot is twisted at a crazy angle and her right arm is slung wide, as if she fell from a great height.

'Agnes?' Sugar kneels at the body's side. She reaches her hand into the darkness under the soft blonde hair and cups one of Agnes's cheeks in her palm, feeling the warmth of it – the fleshy *heat* of it – smooth and alive like her own naked bosom. She lifts Agnes's face off the cold, gritty cobbles, and her fingers tingle.

'Agnes?' The mouth against Sugar's hand comes to life and murmurs wordlessly against her fingers, seeking, it seems, to suck her thumb. 'Agnes, wake up!'

Mrs Rackham twitches like a cat haunted with dreams, and her limbs flail feebly in the dirt.

'Clara?' she whimpers.

'No,' whispers Sugar, leaning close to Agnes's ear. 'You're not home yet.'

With much assistance, Agnes gets to her knees. In the darkness, it's impossible to tell if the glistening muck on Mrs Rackham's nose, chin and bosom is blood or mud or both.

'Don't look in my face,' commands Sugar gently, clasping Agnes's shoulders and raising her to her feet. 'I will help you, but don't look in my face.'

Moment by moment, the reality of her predicament is seeping into Agnes's reviving brain.

'Dear Heaven, I-I'm . . . *filthy*!' she shudders. 'I'm covered in f-*filth*!' Her tiny hands flutter ineffectually over her bodice and fall into the lap of her soiled skirts. 'H-how can I be seen like this? How am I to get home?' Roused by an instinct for entreaty, she turns her face towards her rescuer's, but Sugar pulls back.

'Don't look in my face,' she says again, squeezing Agnes's shoulders tightly. 'I will help you. Wait here.' And she runs off, back into the lights of Bow Street.

Once more in the mainstream of human traffic, Sugar looks around her, examining each person critically: can anyone in this swirling, chattering swarm supply what she's after? Those coffee-sellers over there, wreathed in the steam of their stall . . . ? No, too shabby, in their burlap caps and stained smocks . . . Those ladies waiting to cross the street, twirling their parasols and preening their furry stoles while the carriages trundle past? No, they're fresh from the Opera House; Agnes might know them; and in any case they would sooner die than . . . That soldier, with his fine black cape? No, he would insist on summoning the authorities . . . That woman over there with the long purple shawl – she's surely a prostitute, and would only make trouble . . .

'Oh! Miss! Excuse me!' calls Sugar, hurrying to accost a matronly woman lugging a basket of over-ripe strawberries. The woman, poor and dowdy, Irish or half-wit by the look of her, nevertheless has one asset (besides her load of squashy fruit): she wears a pale blue mantle, a huge old-fashioned thing that covers her from neck to ankle.

'Mout-waterin' strawberries,' she replies, squinting ingratiatingly.

'Your cloak,' says Sugar, unclasping her purse and scrabbling inside it for the brightest coins. 'Sell it to me. I'll give you ten shillings for it.'

Even as Sugar is extracting the coins, six, seven, eight, the woman begins to cringe away, licking her lips nervously.

'I'm in earnest!' protests Sugar, pulling out more shillings and letting the light catch them in her gloved palms.

'I ain't sayin' you ain't, ma'am,' says the woman, half-curtseying, her bloodshot eyes rolling in confusion. 'But see, ma'am, me clothes ain't for sale. Mout-waterin'—'

'What's *wrong* with you?' cries Sugar in exasperation. Any second now, Agnes could be discovered cowering in the dark by one of the alley's scavenging regulars; she could be having her throat slit by a grunting man in search of necklaces and silver lockets! 'This cloak of yours – it's cheap old cotton – you can buy something better in Petticoat Lane any day of the week!'

'Yes, yes ma'am,' pleads the drudge, clutching her mantle at the throat. 'But tonight I'm awful cold, and under this cloak I've only a shivery t'in dress.'

'For God's *sake*,' hisses Sugar, half-hysterical with impatience as Agnes's head (in her imaginings) is sawn free of her gushing neck by a serrated blade. 'Ten *shillings*! Look at it!' She extends her hand, shoving the shiny new coins almost against the woman's nose.

In another instant the exchange is made. The strawberry-seller takes the money, and Sugar divests her of her cloak, revealing bare arms underneath, a gauzy skirt, and a sagging, bulging bodice much stained with breast-milk. A wince of disgust, too, is then belatedly included in the bargain. Without another word, Sugar walks away, folding the mantle against her own discreet velvety bosom as she retraces her steps to the alley.

Agnes is exactly in the spot where she was left to stand; indeed, she appears not to have moved a muscle, as though petrified by fairytale magic. Obediently, without being reminded, she averts her face as her guardian angel approaches, a tall, almost masculine silhouette with a mysterious pale glow shimmering in front of its torso. The rats which have been circling Agnes's skirts, sniffing at her soft leather shoes, take fright and scurry off into the blackness.

'I've brought you something,' says Sugar, drawing up to Agnes's side. 'Stay still, and I'll wrap it around you.'

Agnes's shoulders quiver as the cloak falls around her. She utters a cry that's little more than a breath, unidentifiable as pleasure, pain or fear. One hand fumbles at her breast, uncertain where to grasp the unfamiliar garment . . . or no! – it's not that at all: she is crossing herself.

'. . . Holy Ghost . . .' she whispers tremulously.

'Now,' declares Sugar, clasping Agnes by the elbows, through the pale fabric of the mantle. 'I am going to tell you what to do. You must walk out of here, and turn right. Are you listening?'

Agnes nods, with a sound remarkably like the erotic whimper Sugar performs when a man's hard prick is nuzzling for entry.

'When you are back on the street, walk a short way, just a hundred paces or so,' continues Sugar, pushing Agnes gently towards the light, step by step. 'Turn right again at the flower-seller's barrow: that's where Cheesman is waiting for you. I'll be watching you to see that you're safe.' Leaning forward over Agnes's shoulder, she steals a glimpse of where the smear of mud and blood glistens, and wipes it off with a dab of her dark sleeve.

'Bless you, bless you,' says Agnes, tottering ahead, yet tilting backward, her internal plumb-line knocked askew. 'William s-says you are a f-fantasy, a trick of my im-m-magination.'

'Never mind what William says.' How Agnes trembles in her grasp! Like a small child . . . Not that Sugar has any experience, outside novels, of what a trembling child feels like. 'Remember, turn right at the flower barrow.'

'This beautiful w-w-white robe,' says Agnes, gaining courage and better balance as she goes on. 'I s'pose he'll say it's a f-fantasy too . . .'

'Don't tell him anything. Let this be our secret.'

'S-secret?' They have reached the mouth of the alley, and still the world streams by, as though they're invisible figments of another dimension.

'Yes,' says Sugar, inspired, in a flash, with just the words she needs. 'You must understand, Agnes: angels aren't permitted to do . . . what I've done for you. I could get into *terrible* trouble.'

'W-with Our Lady?'

'Our . . . ?' What the devil does Agnes mean? Sugar hesitates, until a vision glows in her mind of Mrs Castaway's picture albums, with their lurid host of paste-glazed Madonnas. 'Yes, Our Lady.'

'Oh! Bless you!' At this cry of Agnes's, a passing dandy pauses momentarily in his stride; Mrs Rackham's nose has re-entered the flowing current of Life.

'Walk, Agnes,' commands Sugar, and gives her a gentle shove.

Mrs Rackham toddles into Bow Street, in the correct direction, straight as a machine. She looks neither right not left, despite a sudden commotion elsewhere in Bow Street involving police and gesticulating bystanders; she completes the requisite hundred paces to the cab rank, and turns right just as instructed. Only then does Sugar leave her vantage-point and follow on; by the time she reaches the flower barrow and peeks round the corner, Mrs Rackham has been safely installed in her brougham, Cheesman is climbing up the side, and the horses are snorting in anticipation of the journey.

'Thank God,' says Sugar under her breath, and reels back in sudden weariness. Now for a cab of her own.

The commotion in Bow Street is over, more or less. The dense pack of onlookers is dispersing from the scene of the incident. Two policemen are carrying a stretcher between them, in which sags a human-sized shape snugly wrapped in a white sheet. Carefully, but mindful of the obstruction they're causing to traffic, they load their flaccid burden into a canopied cart, and wave a signal of send-off.

It's not until two hours later, when Sugar has returned to the stillness of her rooms in Priory Close, and she's reclining in her warm bath, staring up at the steam-shrouded ceiling, that the thought comes to her:

That body was the strawberry-seller.

She winces, lifts her head out of the water. Such is the weight of her wet hair that she's almost pulled back under by it, her lathery elbows slipping on the smooth enamel of the tub.

Nonsense, she thinks. *It was a drunkard. A beggar.*

With a jug of fresh water she rinses herself, standing up in the bath. Eddying around her knees, the soapy water is grey with the soot of the city's foul air.

Every bully and bughunter in Bow Street would've seen her take those coins. A half-dressed woman at night, with ten shillings on her . . .

She steps out, wraps her body in her favourite snow-white towel, quite the best thing to be had in Peter Robinson's on her last shopping expedition there. If she goes to bed now, her hair will dry in the wrong shape; she really ought to dry it in front of the fire, brushing it constantly so it achieves the airy fullness that William so much admires. She has all day tomorrow to sleep in; he'll still be *en route* from Birmingham.

Old starvelings drop dead in London every day of the week. Drunkards fall under the wheels of carriages. It wasn't the strawberry-seller. She's snoring in her bed, with ten shillings under her pillow.

Sugar squats naked in front of the hearth, allows her damp mane to tumble down across her face, and begins brushing, brushing, brushing. Necklace-thin rivulets of water trickle down her arms and shoulders, evaporating in the heat from the fire. Outside, a stiff breeze has sprung up, whistling and whooping around the building, blowing innocuous debris against the French windows in the study. The chimney harrumphs; the wooden skeleton of the house, concealed beneath the plaster and wallpaper, creaks.

Finally, something to make her jump out of her skin: a knock at the front door. Extravagant imagination? No: there it is again! William? Who else could it be but William? She springs to her feet, half in panic, half in excitement. Why is he back so soon? What about the box factory? 'I got half-way to Birmingham and thought better of it,' she anticipates him explaining. 'Nothing good can be so cheap.' Jesus, where has she left her night-dress?

On impulse, she runs to the door naked. Why not? He'll be startled and delighted to see her thus, his bold and guileless courtesan, a freshly-unwrapped gift of soft clean flesh, fragrant with Rackham perfume. He'll scarcely be able to contain himself while she dances him playfully back-wards towards the bedroom . . .

She opens the door, unleashing a great gust of biting air onto her instantly goose-pimpled flesh. Outside, waiting in her ink-black porch, there is no one.

EIGHTEEN

enry Rackham pulls a second time on the bell-cord, one hand fingering the calling card he fears he may have to leave instead of being permitted to visit Mrs Fox in person. Can it really be true that in the brief time since he saw her last she's become mortally ill? The brass plaque on her father's door, which once seemed merely informative, is suddenly suggestive of a universe in which sickness and fatality reign supreme: JAMES CURLEW, PHYSICIAN AND SURGEON.

The door is opened by the doctor's elderly housemaid. Henry removes his hat and presses it to his chest, unable even to speak.

'Please come in, Mr Rackham.'

Ushered into the hallway, he catches sight of Doctor Curlew almost disappearing at the top of the stairs, and can barely resist rudely shaking off the servant as she fusses with his coat.

'Doctor!' he cries, yanking his arms clear of the sleeves.

Curlew halts on the top stair, turns and begins to walk back down, silently, with no acknowledgement of his visitor, but rather as if he has forgotten something.

'Sir,' calls Henry. 'How . . . how is Mrs Fox?'

Curlew comes to a stop well above Henry's head.

'It's confirmed: she has consumption,' he remarks emptily. 'What else can I say?'

Henry grasps two struts of the banister in his big hands, and looks up into the doctor's heavy-lidded, red-rimmed eyes.

'Is there nothing . . . ?' he pleads. 'I've read about . . . I think they were called . . . pulmonic wafers?'

The doctor laughs, more to himself than at Henry.

'All rubbish, Rackham. Trinkets and lolly-water. I daresay your prayers might have more practical effect.'

'May I see her?' entreats Henry. 'I'd do my utmost not to tax her . . .'

Curlew resumes his ascent, casting the burden of hospitality carelessly downstairs to his housemaid. 'Yes, yes, by all means,' he says over his shoulder. 'As she'll tell you herself, she feels perfectly well.' And with that, he's gone.

The servant leads Henry through the austere corridors and Spartan drawing-room of the doctor's house – a house which, in marked contrast to his brother William's, is wholly unfeminised. There is no relief from subfusc utilitarianism until he reaches the French windows that open up onto the garden, where Nature has been permitted to embroider the bare earth ever so slightly. Through the immaculately transparent glass, Henry looks out on a sunlit square of clipped lawn bordered with neat evergreen shrubs and, in the middle of it, the most important person in the world save Jesus Christ.

She reclines in a wicker rocking-chair, fully dressed for company, with a tightly-buttoned bodice, boots rather than slippers, and elaborately coiffed hair – more elaborate, in fact, than usual. Nestled in her lap is an upright and open book, into which she gazes intently. She is more beautiful than ever before.

'Mrs Fox?'

'Henry!' she cries delightedly, dropping her book on the grass beside her. 'How very nice to see you! I was going mad with boredom.'

Henry walks out to her, incredulous that Doctor Curlew can so confidently write a death sentence for one who's the very embodiment of life. They don't know everything, these medical men! Couldn't there be some mistake? But Mrs Fox, observing the confusion on his face, mercilessly sets him straight.

'I'm in a bad way, Henry,' she says, smiling. 'That's why I'm sitting still, for once! This morning I've even had my feet up, which is about the limit of what I can submit to with good grace. Do sit down, Henry: the grass is *quite* dry.'

Henry does as he's told, even though she's mistaken and the seat of his trousers instantly begins to dampen.

'Well now,' she carries on, in an odd tone, a mixture of breezy cheer and bitter fatigue. 'What other news do I have for you? You may already have heard that I've been . . . how can I put it? . . . delicately expelled from the Rescue Society. It was decided, by my fellow Rescuers, that I'd grown too feeble to perform my duties. There was one day, you see, when the walk from Liverpool Street Station to a house of ill repute exhausted me, and I had to rest on the front steps while the others went inside. I made myself as useful as I could, by having strong words with the spoony-man, but my sisters plainly felt I'd let them down. So, this Tuesday past, they sent me a letter, suggesting I restrict my efforts to corresponding with Parliamentarians. All the Rescuers wish me the speediest of recoveries, in the most florid of terms. In the meantime, they obviously wish me to be bored to death.'

Unnerved by the ease with which she allows this obscene word to pass through her lips, Henry can scarcely bring himself to press her for more details. 'Has your father,' he ventures, 'discussed with you . . . what exactly it is, or might be, that you . . . ah . . . have?'

'Oh Henry, how you *pussyfoot*, as always!' she chides him affectionately. 'I have consumption. Or so I'm told, and I've no reason to doubt it.' A glow of fervency is ignited in her eyes, the same glow as when she argues points of faith with him on their walks after church. 'Where I *differ* from the general opinion, including my learned father's, is that I know I'm not destined to die – at least not yet. I have, inside me, a sort of . . . how can I describe it? A sort of calendar of my days, put there by God, and on each leaf of that calendar is written what errands and appointments I have in His service. I don't claim to know precisely how many pages there are, nor would I wish to know, but I can feel somehow that the calendar is quite thick still, and certainly not the slim portion of pages everyone supposes. So, I've consumption, have I? Very well, I have consumption. But I shall survive it.'

'Oh, brave spirit!' cries Henry, suddenly on his knees, grasping her hand.

'Oh, nonsense,' she retorts, but locks her cool fingers into his, squeezing gently. 'God means to keep me busy, that's all.'

For a minute they are both silent. Their hands are clasped, channelling naked and inarticulate feelings back and forth between them; that which innocent impulse has joined together, propriety cannot yet put asunder. The garden basks in sunshine, and a large black butterfly appears from beyond the high fences around the garden, fluttering over the shrubs in search of a flower. Mrs Fox withdraws her fingers from Henry's with sufficient grace to make clear that no rejection is implied, and rests her hand on her breast.

'Now tell me, Henry,' she says, inhaling deeply. 'What's new in *your* life?'

'In my life?' He blinks, dazed by the heady indulgence of touching her flesh. 'I . . . ah . . .' But then it all comes back to him, and he finds his tongue. 'Quite a lot is new, I'm pleased to say. I've been' – he blushes, casting his eyes to the grass between his knees – 'conducting researches into the poor and the wretched, with a view to preparing myself, at last, for . . .' He blushes deeper, then grins. 'Well, *you* know what.'

'You've read the Mayhew I lent you, then?'

'Yes, but I've done more than that. I . . . I've also begun, just in these last few weeks, to conduct conversations with the poor and wretched themselves, in the streets where they live.'

'Oh, Henry, have you really?' Her pride in him could scarcely be more evident if he'd told her he met the Queen and saved her from assassins. 'Tell me, tell me, what happened?'

And so, on his knees before her, he tells everything, almost. Full descriptions of the locales and of his meetings with idle men, urchins and the prostitute (he only omits his one lapse into prurience). Emmeline listens intently, her face aglow, her body restless, for she's uncomfortable, shifting about in the chair as if her very bones are chafing against the wicker. While he speaks, he can't help noticing how thin she has grown. Are those her collar-bones he sees beneath the fabric of her dress? What do his ambitions matter, if those are her collar-bones? In his visions of himself as a clergyman Mrs Fox has always been on hand, advising him, inviting him to confess his failings and his sorrows. His ambition is only strong when it wears the armour of her encouragement: stripped of that, it's a soft and vulnerable dream. She must not die!

Uncannily, she chooses this moment to reach out her hand to him and clasp it over his own, saying, 'God grant that we might, in the future, work side by side in this struggle!'

Henry looks into her eyes. Moments before, he was telling her that loose women have no power over him; that in their squalid poverty, he is able to see them as souls and souls only. All true enough, but suddenly he realises, as his hand tingles inside hers, that this high-minded and upright woman, knocked flat on her back by the brutal hand of disease, still inspires in him lusts worthy of the Devil.

'God grant, Mrs Fox,' he whispers hoarsely.

'Church Lane, back entrance of Paradise, fankyerverymuch!'

Having delivered a well-dressed lady to this repugnant quarter of the Old City, the cabman utters a snort of sarcasm; his like-minded horse dumps, as a parting gesture of disdain, a mound of hot turd on the cobbles. Resisting the temptation to tick him off, Sugar keeps her mouth shut and pays the fare, then tiptoes towards Mrs Leek's house with the hems of her skirts lifted. What a morass of filth this street is! – the fresh fall of horse-shit is the least of its hazards. Did it always stink like this, or has she been living too long in a place where nothing smells but rose-bushes and Rackham toiletries?

She knocks at Mrs Leek's door, hears the Colonel's muffled 'Enter!' and lets herself in, as she did so many times during her girlhood. The smell is no better inside, and the view, what with the grisly old man and the ever-increasing clutter of grimy junk in the parlour, no more heartening than the squalor out in the street.

'Ah, the concubine!' crows the Colonel maliciously, without any other greeting. 'Think yerself blessed by good fortune, eh?'

Sugar draws a deep breath as she removes her gloves and stuffs them into her reticule. Already she bitterly regrets bumping into Caroline in New Oxford Street yesterday and promising, in her mad hurry to be released from what threatened to turn into a long conversation, to pay her a visit. What a freakish coincidence, that Caroline should spot her twice in the same year, in a city of several million people – and at just the moment when she was hurrying to Euston Station to spy on the arrival of the Birmingham train! Looking back on it, it would've been better to spend a few more minutes with Caroline in the street, for William wasn't on that damned train anyway, and now there's the risk of him coming back this morning, and knocking at the door of her rooms, while *she* is here, wasting her time in a bawdy-house that smells of old man's piss!

'Is Caroline free, Colonel Leek?' she asks evenly.

Delighted to be the privileged withholder of information, the old man leans back in his wheelchair, and the topmost coils of his scarf fall away from his mouth. He's about to regurgitate something from his festering store of disasters, Sugar can tell.

'Good fortune!' he sneers. 'I'll give you good fortune! Yorkshire woman, name of Hobbert, inherited her father's estate in 1852: squashed by a falling archway three days later. Botanical sketch-maker Edith Clough, chosen out of thousands to accompany Professor Eyde on his expedition to Greenland in 1861: devoured by a big fish at sea. And only November last, Lizzie Sumner, mistress of Lord Price: found in her Marylebone maisonette with her neck—'

'Yes, very tragic, Colonel. But is Caroline free?'

'Give her two minutes,' growls the old man, and sinks once more into his scarves.

Sugar surreptitiously brushes the seat of the nearest chair with her fingertips, then sits. Blessed silence descends, as the Colonel slumps in the thickly-veiled sunlight and Sugar stares at the rust-flecked muskets on the wall, but after thirty seconds the Colonel spoils it.

'How's the perfume potentate, then?'

'You promised not to speak about him to anybody,' she snaps. 'It was part of our agreement.'

'I've said nowt to *this* lot,' he spits, rolling his eyes up towards the rest of the house, that pigeon-warren of rooms he never ascends to, where men perform athletic acts with their young limbs and organs, and three loose women lodge and sleep, and Mrs Leek reads tuppenny books in her den. 'How little trust you have, trollop, in a man's word of honour.'

Sugar stares down at her fingers. The scaling on her flesh is bad at the moment, painful. Maybe she'll ask Caroline if she has any bear's grease.

'He's very well, thank you,' she says. 'Couldn't be better.'

'Slips yer a big cake o' soap every so often, eh?'

Sugar glances up into his inflamed eyes, wondering if this remark was intended to be grossly bawdy. She hadn't thought libidinous acts were of the slightest interest to Colonel Leek.

'He's as generous as I could wish for,' she shrugs.

'Don't spend it all in the one place.'

The dull sound of the back door slamming stumbles through the musty air. A satisfied customer has been discharged into the bright world.

'Sugar!' It's Caroline, appearing at the top of the stairs, dressed only in a shift. At this angle and in this light, the scar from the hat factory is alarmingly livid on her chest. 'Push the Colonel out the way if 'e won't go: 'e's on wheels, aint 'e?'

Colonel Leek, rather than submit to this indignity, wheels clear of the stairs.

'—found with her neck cut almost in two by a silk scarf,' he concludes, as Sugar trots up to her friend.

Having offered Sugar her room's one and only chair, Caroline hesitates to sit on the bed. Sugar understands the problem at once, and offers to help change the sheets.

'There's no clean linen,' says Caroline, 'but we can 'ang this one up for a bit, so's the air can get to it.'

Together they pull the sheet from the bed and try to drape its wettest parts in front of the open window. As soon as they've managed it, the sun shines twice as bright.

'I'm in luck today, eh?' grins Caroline.

Sugar smiles back, embarrassed. In Priory Close, she has a much simpler solution to this problem: every week, when no one's looking, she carries a large parcel of her soiled sheets through the gates of a small park and, shortly afterwards, emerges without it. Then she goes to Peter Robinson's and buys new bed-linen. Well, what's she to do without a washerwoman? A vivid picture of Christopher, his small red arms ringed with soap-suds, flares in her brain . . .

'Are you all right, Shush?'

Sugar composes her face. 'A slight headache,' she says. 'The sun's awfully bright.'

How long have Caroline's window-panes been so appallingly begrimed by soot? Surely they weren't so dirty last time? Did the room always smell this way?

'Beggin' yer pardon, Shush. I ain't done me ablutions yet.'

Caroline carries her ceramic bowl to the far side of the bed, more or less out of sight, as a concession to her guest. She crouches down, and busies herself with her contraceptive ritual: the pouring of the water, the unscrewing of the phials. Sugar feels a chill as she watches her friend unabashedly hike up her rumpled shift, one hand already gripping the plunger with its old rag head, her buttocks plumper than Sugar remembers, dimpled and smeared with semen.

'Ach, it's a bother, ain't it?' mutters Caroline, squatting to her task.

'Mm,' says Sugar, looking away. She herself has not performed this ritual for some time – since moving to Priory Close, in fact. It's not practical, when William stays the whole night, and even when he doesn't stay ... well, she takes long, long baths. Submerged in all that warm, clean water, her legs drifting gently apart underneath a white blanket of aromatic foam, surely she's as thoroughly cleansed as it's possible to be?

'Almost finished,' says Caroline.

'No hurry,' says Sugar, wondering if William is knocking at the door of their love-nest this very minute. She watches the bed-sheet billow placidly in the warm breeze, its glistening shapes already fading to snail-crusts. God, these sheets are filthy! Sugar is stung with guilt, that she discards scarcely used sheets in her local park every week, while Caroline has to toil and sleep on these old rags! *Here are some almost-new sheets for you, Caddie – they only need to be washed* . . . No, it's out of the question.

Caroline walks to the window, carrying her heavy bowl. From the waist up, she disappears behind the billowing sheet, ghost-like.

'Mind yer 'eads,' she murmurs impishly, and sends the slops trickling illicitly down the back of the building.

'I must tell you,' she says a few minutes later, when she's settled on the bare mattress, half-dressed now and combing her hair, 'I must tell you about me newest regular – Well, four times now I've seen 'im. *You*'d like 'im, Shush. Very well spoken 'e is.'

And she begins to tell the story so far of her meetings with the sombre, serious man she's nicknamed 'The Parson'. It's a dirt-common tale, nothing remotely novel in the world of prostitution. Sugar can barely disguise her impatience; she's convinced she knows how this story ends.

'And then he takes you to bed, yes?' she suggests, to hurry Caddie up.

'No!' cries Caroline. 'That's the queer part!' She wiggles her naked feet in suppressed mischief. Dirty feet they are too, thinks Sugar. How can anyone expect ever to make an escape from St Giles with feet as dirty as that?

'Perhaps he's queerer than you think,' she sighs.

'Nah, 'e's no marjery, I can tell!' laughs Caroline. 'I did ask 'im, only last week, if it would be such a terrible thing if 'e took me to bed – just the once – so as 'e could see if 'e liked it, or at least see what the fuss was about for other people.' She squints with the effort of recalling precisely her Parson's reply. 'Standing there at the window 'e was, same as always, never looking at me once, and 'e told me . . . what was it? . . .'e told me that if all men like 'imself gave in to temptation, there would always be poor fallen widows like me, always starvin' children like me own boy was, always wicked landlords and murderers, because the Lord God was not loved enough by those as ought to know better.'

'So what did *you* say?' asks Sugar, her attention wandering over the innumerable taints of poverty in Caroline's room: the skirting-boards too rotten to paint, the walls too buckled to paper, the floorboards too worm-eaten to polish: nothing here could be beautified by anything but fire and a wholly new start.

'I said I didn't see 'ow men like 'imself could stop women like me becoming poor fallen widows, or children from starvin', except by marryin' and pervidin' for 'em.'

'So has he offered to marry and provide for you?'

'Nearly!' laughs Caroline. 'Second time I saw 'im, 'e offered to get me honest work. I asked 'im if it would be factory work, and 'e said yes, and I told 'im factory work wasn't wanted. Well, I thought that was the end of that, but last week 'e was on about it again. Said 'e'd made enquiries, and 'e could get me some work that wasn't in a factory, but in a kind of store. If I was willin', 'e could arrange it with just a word in the right person's ear, and if I doubted the truth of it, the name of the concern was Rackham's Perfumeries, what I must 'ave 'eard of.'

Sugar jerks like a startled cat, but fortunately Caroline has moved to the window, idly stroking the sheet. 'And what did you say then?'

'I said that *any* work 'e could get me would wear me out, wear me to death, for much less than a shillin' a day. I said that for a poor woman, all "honest" work is as near to bein' killed slow as makes no difference.' Abruptly she laughs, and fluffs out her newly combed hair with a few flicks of her hands. 'Ah, Sugar,' she says, spreading her arms wide to indicate her room and all it represents. 'What line of work but *this* pervides the needs of life, for 'ardly no toil, and then enough rest and sleep into the bargain?'

And fine clothes and jewellery, thinks Sugar. *And leatherbound books and silver-framed prints and cab-rides at the wave of a glove and visits to the opera and an Ardent bath and a place of my own.* She looks into Caroline's face and wonders, *What am I doing here? Why am I welcome? Why do you smile at me so?*

'I have to go,' she says. 'Do you want some money?' Well, no, she doesn't say that — not the part about money. She only says, 'I have to go.'

'Oh! What a shame!'

Yes, a shame. Shame. Shame. 'Do you want some money?' Say it: 'Do you want some money?'

'I–I've left my place in an awful mess. I came straight here, you see.'

Say it, you coward. 'Do you want some money?' Five simple words. Stashed in your purse you have far more than Caddie will earn in a month. So say it, you coward . . . you louse . . . you whore!

But Caroline smiles, embraces her friend, and Sugar leaves without giving her anything but a kiss.

In the cab on her way back to Priory Close ('and there's an extra shilling for you if you're quick about it') Sugar stews in her iniquity. The soles of her shoes stink; she longs to wipe them on the lush green grass in the park where she leaves the bed-sheets each week. The parcel's always gone when she next comes — doesn't that mean that poor folk are finding it? Or if it's a park warden who finds it, those sheets will surely be donated to poor folk eventually? Christ, with all the do-gooders that infest London, surely some of them will have this sort of thing in hand? *Coward. Whore.*

When Sugar was poor, she always fancied that if she ever became rich, she'd help all the poor women in her profession, or at least all those she knew personally. Daydreaming in her room at Mrs Castaway's, elbows resting on the pages of her novel, she would imagine calling on one of her old friends, bringing along a supply of warm winter blankets or meat pies. How easy it would be to do such things without the stench of charity! She'd brandish her presents not in the way that a hoity-toity benefactress distributes kindness to inferiors, but rather with robust glee, the way one urchin displays to another an audaciously ill-gotten gain.

But now that she has the wherewithal to fulfil those fantasies, the stench of charity is as real as the horse-shit on her shoes.

Safely back in her own rooms, Sugar prepares for William's return. Then, as the afternoon drags on and he doesn't appear, she loiters into the study and, pricked by self-reproach, pulls her novel out of its hiding-place. Breathing deeply, she deposits the ragged burden on the writing-desk and seats herself behind it.

The light is falling now in such a way that the glass of the French windows is almost a mirror. In amongst the greenery of her garden hovers her own face, perched on an insubstantial body that wafts out of the ground like smoke. The dark leaves of the rose-bushes impose a pattern on the skin of that face; her hair, motionless in reality, swirls and flickers with every gust of wind outside; phantom azaleas shiver in her bosom.

The Fall and Rise of Sugar. So says her story's title, familiar as a scar.

She recalls her visit to the lavender fields in Mitcham. How the lowly Rackham workers ogled her as she walked near! In their eyes she was a lady paying a visit on the toiling poor; there was no sign of recognition, only that peculiar mixture of feline resentment and canine respect. Each one of those workers, as they shrivelled meekly away from the sweep of her skirts, was convinced *she* couldn't possibly know what it's like to lie shivering under a blanket that's too thin for the season, or have shins bloody with flea-bites, or hair infested with lice.

'But I do know these things!' protests Sugar, and indeed the pages that lie before her on the ivory-handled writing-table were conceived in poverty, and are full of it. Wasn't her childhood every bit as hopeless as the child-hood of anyone toiling for Rackham Perfumeries? Granted, her lot is better than theirs *now*, but that's irrelevant: theirs could improve too, if only they were clever enough . . . Yet, on that day in the lavender fields, how hopelessly, how enviously they stared at the fine lady walking beside their employer!

'But I am their voice!' she protests again, and hears, in the intimate acoustic of her silent study, a subtle difference in the way her vowels sound today, compared to how they sounded before the Season. Or were they always as dulcet as this? *Tell us a story, Shush, in that fancy voice of yours,* that's what the girls in Church Lane used to say, half-teasing, half-admiring. *What sort of story?* she'd ask, and they'd always reply, *Something with revenge in it. And bad words. Bad words sound funny when* you *say them, Sugar.* But how many of those girls could read a book? And if she told the lavender workers that she once lived in a London slum, how many of them would believe her, rather than spit on the ground?

No, like all the would-be champions of the poor throughout human history, Sugar must confront a humiliating truth: the downtrodden may yearn to be heard, but if a voice from a more privileged sphere speaks on their behalf, they'll roll their eyes and jeer at the voice's accent.

Sugar chews her lips fretfully. Surely her miserable origins count for *something*? She reminds herself that if William should decide to cast her out of this luxurious nest, she'd be homeless and without income, in direr straits even than the workers in the lavender fields. And yet . . . And yet she can't banish from her mind the wrinkled, ragged men and women bowing to her, shuffling away backwards; the uneasy murmurs of *''Oo's that? 'Oo's that?'* Sugar stares at the reflection in the French windows, the flickering head and shoulders augmented with leaves and flowers. *Who am I?*

My name is Sugar. So says her manuscript, shortly after the introductory tirade against men. She knows all the lines by heart, having re-written and re-read them countless times.

My name is Sugar — or if it isn't, I know no better. I am what you would call a Fallen Woman . . .

Rather than see the embarrassingly pompous sentence: *Vile man, eternal Adam, I indict you!* that lies in wait at the end of the paragraph, she flips the page, then the next, and the next. With sinking spirits, she leafs through the densely-inked pages. She'd expected to meet herself here, because this namesake of hers shares her face and body, right down to the freckles on her breasts. But in the yellowed manuscript she sees only words and punctuation marks; hieroglyphs which, although she remembers watching her own hand write them — even remembers the ink drying on particular blotted letters — have lost their meaning. These melodramatic murders: what do they achieve? All these straw men meeting grisly ends: what flesh-and-blood woman is helped by it?

She could ditch the plot, maybe, and substitute a less lurid one. She could aim to tread a middle ground between this gush of bile, and the polite, expurgated fictions of James Anthony Froude, Felicia Skene, Wilkie Collins and other authors who've timidly suggested that prostitutes, if sufficiently deserving, should perhaps be excused hellfire. With a new century only a generation away, surely the time is ripe for a stronger message than *that*? Look at this stack of papers — her life's work — there must be hundreds of things worth salvaging!

But as she skims the pile, she doubts it. Permeating almost every line, souring every remark, tainting every conviction, is prejudice and ignorance, and something worse: blind hatred for anything fine and pure.

I watched the Fine Ladies parading out of the Opera House. (So wrote the Sugar of three years ago, a mere child of sixteen, cloistered in her upstairs room at Mrs Castaway's, in the grey morning hours after the customers had gone home and everyone else was asleep). *What shams they were! Everything about them was false. False were their pretenses of rapture at the music; false were their greetings to each other; false their accents and their voices.*

How vainly they pretended that they were not Women at all, but some other, higher form of Creature! Their ball-gowns were designed to give the impression that they did not walk on two fleshy legs, but rather glided on a cloud. 'Oh, no,' they seemed to say. 'I do not have legs and a cunt between them, I float on Air. Nor have I breasts, only a delicate curve to give shape to my bodice. If you want anything so gross as breasts, go see the udders of wet-nurses. As for legs, and a cunt between them, if you want those, you will have to go to a Whore. We are Perfect Creatures, Rare Spirits, and we trade only in the noblest and finest things in Life. Namely, Slave Labour of poor seamstresses, Torture of our servants, Contempt for those who scrub our chamber pots clean of our exalted maidenly shit, and an endless round of silly, hollow, meaningless pursuits that have no

There the page ends, and Sugar hasn't the heart to turn it and read further. Instead she shuts the manuscript and rests her elbow on it, chin sunk into her palm. Still fresh in her mind is the night she went to hear the *Requiem* by Signor Verdi. No doubt there were ladies in the audience for whom it was nothing more than an opportunity to flaunt their finery and chatter afterwards, but there were others who emerged from the auditorium in a trance, quite unaware of their bodily selves. Sugar knows: she saw it on their faces! They stood reverent, as if they were still listening to the music; and, when prompted to walk, they walked like sleepers to an adagio rhythm still echoing in their heads. Sugar met the gaze of one such lady, and they both smiled – oh, such a guileless, open-hearted smile! – upon seeing the love of music reflected in each other's eyes.

Years ago, even months ago, if she'd been handed the iconoclast's mallet, she'd gladly have smashed the opera houses to the ground; she'd have sent all the fine ladies fleeing from their burning homes straight into the embrace of poverty. Now she wonders . . . this spiteful vision of pampered ladies growing filthy and haggard in factories and sweater's dens alongside their coarse sisters – what sort of justice does it strike a blow for? Why can't it be the factories that are smashed to the ground, the sweater's dens that are consumed in flames, rather than the opera houses and the fine homes? Why should the people living on a higher plane be dragged down to a lower, rather than those on a lower rising to a higher? Is it really such an unforgivable affectation to forget one's body, one's flesh, as a lady might do, and exist merely for thought and feeling? Is a woman like Agnes really blameworthy for failing to imagine there could exist such a thing as a cloth-wrapped plunger for swabbing a stranger's semen from the . . . the cunny? (The word 'cunt', even in the privacy of her mind, seems unmentionably crude.)

One more time, she opens her precious manuscript, at random, hoping against hope to find something she can be proud of.

'I'll tell you what I mean to do,' I said to the man, as he struggled feebly against his bonds. 'This cock that you are so proud of: I shall make it big and stiff, the way you like it best. Then, when it is at its height, I shall take this strand of sharp steel wire, and tie it around the shaft. Because I am going to give you a little present, yes I am!'

She groans and closes up the pages. No one in the world will ever want to read this stuff, and no one ever shall.

Feeling a wave of self-pity rising inside her, she lets it break, and buries her face in her hands. It's already afternoon, William hasn't come, there are tiny blue birds twittering in her garden, innocent beautiful things that put to shame all the poisonous ugliness in her despicable story . . . Christ, she must be about to have her monthly courses, to be thinking this way. When chirruping blue tits seem like agents of righteous chastisement, it's time to bring out the chauffoirs . . .

The sound of the bell startles her so violently that her elbows jerk forward and send her novel flying. Its pages scatter all over the study, and she pounces on them to gather the mess together again, crawling back and forth across the floor. She barely has enough time to dump the manuscript back in the wardrobe and kick the door shut on it before William lets himself in at the front – for, of course, he has a key.

'William!' she calls, in undisguised relief. 'It's me! I mean, I'm here!'

From the first embrace, in the hallway by the coat-stand, she can tell that her returning Ulysses is not in a lustful mood. Oh, he's very happy to see her and be given a hero's welcome, but there's also a reticence in his stance as she presses her body against his, a subtle evasion of any reunion between Mons Veneris and Mons Pubis. Instantly, Sugar softens her posture, loosens her arms, and strokes his whiskery cheek.

'How dreadfully tired you look!' she observes, in a tone of lavish commiseration such as might be warranted by multiple spear-wounds or at least a very nasty cat-scratch. 'Have you slept at all since I last saw you?'

'Precious little,' admits William. 'The streets around my guest-house were crowded with dipsomaniacs singing at the tops of their voices, all night long. And *last* night, I was worrying over Agnes.'

Sugar smiles and leans her head sideways in empathy, wondering if she should bite on this rare mention of Mrs Rackham – or whether William will bite *her* if she does. While she wonders, she escorts him companionably into . . . which room? The sitting-room, for now. Yes, she's decided: both Agnes and the bedroom can wait until his ruffled spirits have been well and truly smoothed.

'Here,' she says, installing him on the ottoman and pouring him a brandy. 'Something to rinse the taste of Birmingham from your mouth.'

He slumps in gratitude, unbuttons his bulging waistcoat, tugs at his cravat. He hadn't realised, until these attentions were lavished on him, that they're precisely what he's been longing for since his return home yesterday. The arm's-length efficiency of his own housemaids, the uncomprehending indifference of his distracted wife: these were a poor welcome, and have left him hungry for richer fare.

'I'm glad *someone's* pleased to see me,' he says, tilting his head back and licking the brandy on his lips.

'Always, William,' she says, laying the palm of her hand on his perspiring brow. 'But tell me, did you buy the boxing factory?'

He groans and shakes his head.

Sitting beside him on the ottoman, Sugar experiences a perfectly timed visitation from the Muse. 'Let me guess' (she mimics a gruff-voiced, toadying scoundrel of the Northern manufacturing class): "Nowt wrong 'ere, Mr Rackham, that a good engineer and a dollop of mortar wouldn't fix", hmm?'

William hesitates for an instant, then hoots with laughter. 'Precisely.' Her crude stab at a Birmingham accent was closer to Yorkshire, but otherwise she's devilishly accurate. What a superb little machine her brain is! The muscles of his back and neck relax, as the realisation sinks in that he's absolved of explaining his decision about the factory: she understands – as always, she understands.

'Well, the Season's almost over now, thank God,' he mutters, knocking back the last of his brandy. 'The dog days are upon us. No more dinner parties, no more theatre, and just one more wretched Musical Evening . . .'

'I thought you'd excused yourself from everything already . . . ?'

'Well, yes, almost everything.'

'. . . because you believed Agnes was better.'

He stares deep into his glass, frowning.

'She's been fairly good, I must say,' he sighs, 'at least in public. Better than last Season, at any rate. Although she could hardly *fail* to be better . . .' Conscious of how faint this praise is, he strives to brighten his tone. 'She's a highly-strung thing, but I'm sure she's no worse than many.' He winces – he hadn't meant to sound so ungallant.

'But not as good as you hoped she'd be?' suggests Sugar.

He nods equivocally, a loyal husband under duress. 'At least she's stopped prattling about being watched over by a guardian angel . . . Although whenever we go out, she's always casting glances over her shoulder . . .' He slumps further into the ottoman, resting his own shoulder on Sugar's thigh. 'But I've ceased to challenge her; she only gets wound up if I do. *Let* her be chaperoned by ghosts, I say, if that's what's needed to keep her in order . . .'

'And she *is* in order?'

He's silent for a minute, as she strokes his head, and the coals sizzle and adjust their positions in the hearth.

'Sometimes,' he says, 'I ask myself if Agnes is faithful to me. The way she's continually peering into the crowds, hoping, I'd swear, to catch sight of a particular person . . . Have I a rival to contend with, I wonder, on top of everything else?'

Sugar smiles, heavy-hearted, feeling dragged down by the syrupy weight of deception, like a woman wading through deepening waters in fast-swelling skirts and petticoats.

'Mightn't she just be keeping an eye out for her guardian angel?' she suggests scampishly.

'Hmm.' William lounges against her touch, unconvinced. 'I was at a musical evening last week, and in the middle of a Rossini song, Agnes swooned in her chair. It was for an instant only, then she roused and whispered, "Yes, bless you, lift me up – your arms are so strong!" "Whose arms, dear?" I ask her. "Shush, dear, the lady's still singing," she says.'

Sugar feels like laughing, wonders if it's safe to laugh. She laughs. There are no consequences. William's trust in her is, evidently, firmer than ever.

'But how could Agnes be unfaithful to you?' she murmurs. 'Surely she goes nowhere without your knowledge and permission?'

William grunts dubiously. 'Cheesman is sworn to tell me everywhere she goes,' he says. 'And so he does, by God.' His eyes narrow as he reviews his mental ledger of Agnes's excursions, then blink in annoyance when he comes to one circled in red. 'I thought at first that her illicit visits to the Catholic chapel in Cricklewood might be . . . *trysts*. But Cheesman says she enters and leaves alone. What can she possibly get up to while she's sitting in a church service?'

'I don't know; I've never been in a church,' says Sugar. The admission feels raw and risky, a plunge into the dangerous waters of genuine intimacy, an intimacy deeper than genital display.

'Never been . . . ?' gasps William. 'You can't be serious.'

She smiles sadly, wipes a lock of hair off his upturned face.

'Well, I did have a rather unorthodox childhood, you know, William.'

'But . . . damn it, I recall when we discussed Bodley and Ashwell's book – the conversancy you showed with matters of religion . . .'

Sugar shuts her eyes tight, and the interior of her skull is a lurid snake-pit of Magdalens and Marys, darkening into chaos.

'My mother's tutelage, no doubt. Her recitations from the Bible were my bedtime stories, for years and years. And also,' she sighs, 'I've read an awful lot of books, haven't I?'

William reaches up to caress her waist and bosom, with slack and sleepy fingers. When his hand wilts and comes to rest on his own chest, she wonders if he's fallen asleep in her lap. But no: after a minute's silence, his deep voice resonates against her thighs.

'She's inconsistent,' he says, 'that's the problem. Normal one day; mad as a March hare the next. Undependable.'

Sugar ponders the moral arithmetic of this, then plucks up the nerve to ask:

'What would you do if she were . . . dependably mad?'

He hardens his jaw, then, shame-faced, softens it again. 'Ach, she's still growing up, I think; she'll come good with a bit of maturing. She was awfully young when I married her – too young, perhaps. Playing with dolls still . . . and that's what her outbursts tend to be: childish. I recall in April there was a puppet show at the Muswell Hill fête. Mr Punch was wielding his stick, beating the stuffing out of his wife as usual. Agnes became very agitated, grabbed my arm and implored me to snatch Mrs Punch away. "Quick, William!" she said. "You're a rich and important man now: no one would dare stop you." I gave her a smile, but she was in earnest! Still a child, d'you see?'

'And . . . is this childishness the worst of it?' enquires Sugar, remembering Agnes's body sprawled in the alley, the slack limbs soaking up mud. 'Nothing else ails her?'

'Oh, Doctor Curlew thinks she's far too thin, and ought to be sent to a sanatorium and fattened up with beef and buttermilk. "I've seen better-fed women in the workhouse," he says.'

'What do *you* think?' It's a heady thrill, this: probing him for his opinions, not on business matters, but on his private life. And he's opening up to her! With every word, he's opening up to her more!

'I can't deny,' says William, 'that at home Agnes appears to subsist on lettuce and apricots. In other people's houses, though, she eats everything that's put in front of her, like a good little girl.' He shrugs, as if to say: childish again.

'Well,' concludes Sugar, 'this doctor will have to appreciate that "plump" is out of fashion. Agnes isn't the only thin lady in London.'

Thus she invites William to leave the subject, but he's not ready.

'Indeed not, indeed not,' he says, 'but there's another cause for concern. Agnes's monthly issue has dried up.'

An icy chill runs down Sugar's back, and it's all she can do not to stiffen. The thought of William – of *any* man – being so well-acquainted with Agnes's body is an unexpected shock to her.

'How do you know this?'

Again he shrugs against her thigh.

'Doctor Curlew says so.'

Another silence falls, and Sugar fills it with a fantasy of knifing this Doctor Curlew to death in a dark cul-de-sac. He's a suitably shadowy figure, for she's never set eyes on him, but his blood runs as red as that of any of the men in *The Fall and Rise of Sugar*.

William chuckles suddenly. 'Never been in a church . . . !' he marvels, half asleep. 'And I thought I knew everything about you.'

She turns her face aside, astounded to feel warm, tickly tears springing out onto her cheeks. If anything, William's utter ignorance of who she is should provoke her to shrieks of derisive laughter, but instead she's moved by sorrow and pity – pity for him, pity for herself, pity for the pair of them cuddled here together. Oh! What a monster he's caressing . . . ! What terrifying ichor flows through her veins; what hopelessly foul innards she has, poisoned by putrid memories and the bitterness of want! If only she could drive a blade into her heart and let the filth spurt out, let it gush away, hissing, into a crack in the floor, leaving her clean and light. What an innocuous booby William is, with his ruddy cheeks; for all his male arrogance, his philandering instincts, his dog-like cowardice, he's an innocent compared to her. Privilege has kept him soft inside; a benign childhood has protected him from the burrowing maggots of hatred; she can imagine him kneeling at the side of his bed as a boy, praying 'God bless Mama and Papa' under the watchful eye of a kindly nurse.

Oh God, if he only knew what was inside her . . . !

'I have a few surprises left for you,' she says, in her best seductive tone, dabbing her cheeks with her sleeve.

William raises his head from her lap, suddenly wakeful, his bloodshot eyes wide. 'Tell me a secret,' he says, with boyish enthusiasm.

'A secret?'

'Yes, a *dark* secret.'

She laughs, fresh tears springing to her eyes, which she hides in the crook of her arm.

'I don't have any dark secrets,' she protests, 'really I don't. When I said I had a few surprises left for you, I meant—'

'I know what you meant,' he growls affectionately, sliding his arm under her skirts. 'But tell me something I didn't know about you – anything. A thing that no one else in the world knows.'

Sugar is tortured by the yearning to tell him everything, to expose her oldest and deepest scars, to begin with Mrs Castaway's little game, when Sugar was still a toddler, of creeping up to the cot and, with a flourish, pulling the sheets off Sugar's half-frozen body. 'That's what *God* does,' her mother would say, in the same grossly amplified whisper she used for storytelling. 'He *loves* to do that.' 'I'm cold, Mama!' Sugar would cry. And Mrs Castaway would stand in the moonlight, the sheets clutched to her bosom, and she'd cup a hand to her ear. 'I wonder,' she'd say, 'if God heard that. He has trouble hearing female voices, you know . . .'

William is nuzzling his face against her belly, murmuring encouragement to her, waiting to be given his secret.

'I . . . I . . .' she agonises. 'I can shoot water from my sex.'

He stares up at her, startled. 'What?'

She giggles, biting her lip to keep hysteria in check. 'I'll show you. It's
a special talent I have. A useless talent . . .' To his open-mouthed stupefaction, she leaps up, fetches a glass of lukewarm water from the bathroom, and throws herself down on the floor before him. Without any erotic
niceties, she hitches up her skirts, yanks off her pantalettes, and flings her
legs over her head, the sides of her knees almost touching her ears. Her
cunt opens wide like a nestling's mouth, and with an unsteady hand she
sloshes water into it, half a glassful.

'God almighty!' exclaims William as she repositions her feet on the
carpet and, crawling crabwise, sprays a thin jet of water through the air.
It splashes against the ottoman, inches from his trousers.

'Next one will get you,' threatens Sugar wheezily, adjusting her aim,
but she waits until he's ducked aside before squirting the next jet.

'It's not possible!' laughs Rackham.

'Stand still, scaramouch!' she cries, and releases the final spout, the
highest of them all. Then Rackham falls on top of her, pinioning her hands
with his own, one knee lightly pressed against her panting stomach.

'Is it all out now?' he demands, and kisses her on the mouth.

'Yes,' she says. 'You're safe.' Whereupon they realign their bodies, so
that he can settle in between her legs.

'And you?' says Sugar, as she helps him with his clothes. 'Do you have
a secret for me?'

He grins apologetically as his manhood is pulled free of its swaddling.

'What could possibly compare with yours?' he says, and that is the end
of the subject.

Far away, in a squalid bedroom in a damp and grimy house, a prostitute,
surprised by an unexpected visitor, holds out her palm and is given three
shillings.

'More questions, sir?' she winks, but her voice trembles ever-so-slightly:
she can sense from her man's contorted face that he's come for something
different this time.

He walks, rigid as a cripple, to her bed, and sits heavily on the edge.

A square of light from the window shines on the spot directly beside him, leaving him in shadow.

'The woman I love,' he announces, in a low voice hoarse with passion, 'is dying.'

Caroline nods slowly, licking her lips, uncertain how else to respond; ever since the death of her own child, the demise of other human beings has meant less to her than it should.

'That's a shame,' she says, clutching the coins tight in her hand, to prevent them from jingling, as a gesture of respect. 'A – a terrible shame.'

'Listen to me.'

'I–I 'eard you, sir. The woman you love . . .'

'No,' he croaks, staring at the floor, 'listen to me.'

And, as his head sinks towards his chest, his shoulders begin to shake. He clasps his hands together, prayer-style, and squeezes until the flesh goes crimson and white. From his strangled throat come words too soft, and too distorted by sobs, to understand.

Awkwardly, Caroline edges closer to him and, as his weeping grows more convulsive, sits next to him on the bed. The ancient mattress sags, and their bodies meet gently at the hip, but he doesn't seem to notice. She leans forward, unconsciously aping his posture, and listens for all she's worth.

'God damn God,' weeps Henry, giving the obscenity clearer diction, and greater vehemence, as he repeats it. 'God damn God!'

Knowing she's heard him now, he loses what little self-control he had left. Within seconds he's bawling like a donkey in a knacker's yard, his body shuddering, his hands still clasped with such force that the bones beneath must surely snap into splinters.

'Go-o-od da-a-amn Go-o-o-o-od!' Henry continues to roar as, around his back, shyly and fearfully (for who knows what violence a man in despair may do?) Caroline lays one comforting arm.

NINETEEN

'ake up,' hisses a stern voice. 'Remember where you are.'

Sugar rouses with a start, having nodded off in her seat. Blinking in the multi-coloured sunlight beaming through the stained-glass windows, she sits up straight, smooths her dowdy skirts and adjusts her horrid shawl. The ancient wife next to her, her pious duty done, turns her dim eyes once more to the pulpit, where the faraway rector is still busy casting his oratory across the sea of pews.

Sugar glances at the other occupants of the free seats here in the back of the church, worried that they, too, noticed her falling asleep, but they appear oblivious. There's an imbecile boy, growing increasingly cross-eyed in his attempts to scratch his nose with his bottom teeth. Next to him, nearest the escape route to the sunny outdoors, sits a shovel-faced mother with two babes cradled one in each arm, which she jigs slowly and gently to ensure their slumber is uninterrupted.

In truth, much of the congregation is asleep, some with heads slung back and mouths open, others with chins sunk into their stiff, upturned collars, others leaning on the shoulders of relations. Sleep is almost irresistible, what with the hot weather, the tinted sunlight, and the rector's droning voice: a conspiracy of soporifics.

Surreptitiously, Sugar rubs her stiff neck and reminds herself what a fine idea it is to be here. William is away again (just for the day, this time, to Yarmouth), so what better way to spend her Sunday morning than to accompany the Rackham household to church?

Not that there are many Rackhams in evidence. Their contingent has been sadly depleted since the honeymoon days of William's marriage, when

William and Agnes would turn up along with Rackham Senior and all the servants, and clucking ladies of the congregation would hint to the mystified Agnes that she'd soon be bringing a lively family with her.

Yarmouth or no Yarmouth, William rarely attends anymore. Why should he listen to a windbag in a pulpit ranting about intangibles? In the world of Business, nothing is discussed that can't be made real and viable: would that Religion could boast the same! So, usually it's Agnes who attends in his stead, along with whatever servants can be spared. But Agnes isn't here this morning, only her sour-faced maid. (Clara's wide awake, not by virtue of greater piety but because she's seething with resentment at the way Letty, who's trusted to attend the evening service on her own, is in effect given Sundays off. She's likewise envious of Cheesman, who's free to wander around outside the church, smoking cigarettes and reading tombstones. And why doesn't someone poke a parasol into that stupid scullery girl, Janey, to stop her snoring!)

Sugar fidgets in the 'poor pew' of the church, many rows behind a small, barely visible child who may or may not be the daughter of William Rackham. Whoever she is, she moves not a muscle throughout the service, and is almost wholly hidden inside a stiff brown coat and oversized hat. Sugar tries to convince herself there must be something to be learned from the few inches of blonde hair that peep out, but her eyes keep drooping shut. She longs for the next brace of hymns, because even though these require her to sing unfamiliar words to tunes she doesn't know, at least they jog her awake. Pitiless, the sermon saws on and on, a monotone that never reaches a crescendo.

At the far left of the front pew, a handsome but angry-looking man is fidgeting too. He's puffy-eyed and carelessly groomed, an odd sort of character to be at the forefront of the paying congregation. Every now and then, when he disagrees with the rector, he takes a breath so deep that it's visible from the rear of the church, and very nearly audible from there, too.

The rector is vilifying a certain Sir Henry Thompson for heresies whose precise nature Sugar can't guess, having slept through a crucial part of the sermon, but she gathers that Thompson is espousing beliefs of a most foul and depraved kind and, what's worse, winning a large public to his side. The rector suggests accusingly that there might even lurk, within his congregation this very morning, souls already led astray by Sir Henry

Thompson. *Oh God*, prays Sugar, *please make him stop talking*. But by the time her prayer is finally granted, all hope of a truce with God is lost.

After the last hymns are sung, the congregation disperses slowly, many lingering in their seats to peruse their church calendars. The dissolute-looking man from the front row is not one of them; he barges out, striking accidental blows against several persons as he blunders up the aisle. This man, Sugar realises as he passes close by her, must be William's older brother, the 'dull, indecisive' one who's 'been acting damned peculiar lately'.

After Henry, an orderly procession of Notting Hill's smartest and holiest files up the aisle, the men baking stoically in their dark jackets, the ladies decked out in the latest fashion, denying themselves only the glitter of ostentatious jewellery. Straggling in their wake comes the child who may or may not be William's daughter, half-shrouded in the skirts of her matronly chaperone. She has Agnes's china-blue eyes, and William's lack of chin, and the yearning, defeated look of an impounded animal – the self-same look that William had on *his* face, when she first appraised him in the smoky glow of The Fireside. Can a look prove paternity? Hardly conclusive: this child could be anybody's. But for a fraction of an instant, the little girl's eyes and Sugar's meet, and something is communicated. For the first time today in this house of purported divinity, a spark of spirit has leapt through the stagnant air.

It is *you, isn't it? Sophie?* she thinks, but the child is already gone.

As soon as she can safely do so, Sugar leaves her pew and follows the parishioners into the sunny churchyard. The little girl is being hurried – hustled, almost – towards the Rackhams' carriage. Cheesman, loitering beside a marble column with two life-size angels wrapped wantonly round it, discards his cigarette and grinds it underfoot.

With one Rackham whisked away, Sugar seeks out the sole remaining one: brother Henry – and finds she isn't the only woman pursuing him. A wan-faced invalid whom Sugar observed, before the service, being assisted to her pew seat by a servant, is now receiving the same assistance to leave the church. Leaning heavily on a walking stick, she waves to Henry and calls his name, obviously determined to catch up with him.

The effect on William's brother is galvanic. He jerks to attention, doffs his hat to smooth his unwashed hair flat against his head, replaces the hat with care, straightens his tie. Even through the coarse muslin of her veil,

Sugar can see he's wrought a miracle on his face, banishing the anger and the bitter disaffection and replacing it with a mask of pitiful composure.

The invalid, still escorted by a maidservant, moves not as a lame person does (that characteristic three-legged step), but bears down upon her walking stick as if it were a railing at the edge of a vertiginous cliff. She's as pale and thin as a stripped branch, and the left hand which hangs over the servant's arm looks very like a twig; the right, wrapped tightly around the handle of her cane, looks more like a knotted root. In the torrid heat that's giving everyone around her pink or (in the case of some of the more elaborately dressed ladies) red faces, hers is white, with two mottled crimson blushes on her cheeks that flare and fade with each step.

Poor doomed soul, thinks Sugar, for she recognises consumption when she sees it. But no sooner has this droplet of compassion leaked into her veins than she feels a gush of guilt flowing after it: *Why don't you go back to Mrs Castaway's and visit Katy, you coward? She'll be in a worse way than this stranger — if she isn't dead already.*

'Ah! Henry! Were you hoping to escape from me?'

The consumptive has managed to shake the servant from her side and walks alone, striving to make it look easy. The sight of her hunched shoulders and tightly interlocking fingers shocks Henry out of his standstill, and he rushes to her side, almost clipping Sugar across the bosom as he passes.

'Mrs Fox, allow me,' he says, extending his arms like heavy tools he's unused to wielding. Mrs Fox declines the offer with a polite shake of her head.

'No, Henry,' she reassures him, pausing to rest. 'This stick makes me quite steady . . . once I'm out of danger of being jostled.'

Henry glares over Mrs Fox's shoulder, indignant at all the wicked, contemptible people who might jostle her, including (nearest of all) Sugar. His arms, prevented from grasping Mrs Fox's, hang at his sides, useless.

'You shouldn't be putting yourself at such risk,' he protests.

'Risk! Pfff!' scoffs Mrs Fox. 'Ask a destitute prostitute . . . under the Adelphi Arches . . . what risk is . . .'

'I'd rather not,' says Henry. 'And I'd rather you were resting at home.'

But Mrs Fox, now that she's stopped moving, is regaining her breath by sheer force of will, sucking it up, as it were, from the ground through her stick. 'I shall come to church,' she declares, 'as long as I'm able. After all, the church has one great advantage over the Rescue Society – it won't send me a letter telling me not to come anymore.'

'Yes, but you're to rest, your father said.'

'Rest? My father wants me to go travelling!'

'Travelling?' Henry's face contorts with hope and fear and incomprehension. 'Where to?'

'Folkestone Sands,' she sniffs. 'By all accounts an Eden for invalids – or is it a Sheol?'

'Mrs Fox, please!' Henry glances uneasily about him, in case the rector is nearby. There's only an anonymous veiled woman in shabby clothes, turning slowly and hesitantly as if unsure of her bearings.

'Come, Henry, let's walk together,' says Mrs Fox.

Henry is aghast. 'Not all the way . . . ?'

'Yes, all the way – to my father's carriage,' she ribs him. 'Come on, Henry. There are folk who walk five miles to work every morning.'

Henry, provoked beyond endurance, begins to exclaim, 'Not if . . .', but manages to bite his tongue on any mention of fatal illness. 'Not on a Sunday,' he substitutes miserably.

They resume walking, down the old path, the shaded avenue of trees, away from the sunlit congregation, followed by the veiled woman in the shabby clothes. Discreet distance and Mrs Fox's breathlessness make Sugar miss some of what's said; the words are turned to whispers on the breeze, like fluffs of scattered dandelion. But Mrs Fox's shoulder-blades, straining and swivelling under the fabric of her dress, speak loud and clear.

'What does it profit me,' she pants, 'to lie still and alone in my bed, when I could be here in the mild weather, in good company . . .' (a few words go astray) '. . . the chance to sing the Lord's praises . . .' (a few more).

The mention of 'mild' weather sends a chill of pity down Sugar's spine, for she's blinking droplets of sweat from her eyelashes behind her veil. The heat is punishing, and Sugar regrets denying herself – in her pauper's disguise – the luxury of a parasol. What frigid blood must be coursing through this woman's emaciated frame!

'. . . this lovely day . . . indoors I should be cold and miserable . . .'

Henry looks up into the fierce sky, willing the sun to be as mild as she believes it to be.

'... something intrinsically morbid about lying in bed, under white sheets, don't you think?' Mrs Fox presses on.

'Let's talk of something else,' pleads Henry. The graveyard is to their left, the headstones flickering through the trees.

'Well, then ...' pants Mrs Fox. 'What did you think of the sermon?'

Henry looks over his shoulder to make sure that the rector is not on their tail, but he sees only the shabbily dressed woman and, some distance behind her on the path, Doctor Curlew's maid.

'I thought the greater part of it was ... very fine,' he mutters. 'But I could've done without the attack on Sir Henry Thompson.'

'True, Henry, quite true,' gasps Mrs Fox. 'Thompson bravely addresses an evil ...' (several words lost) '... time to admit to ourselves ... very *notion* of burial ... belongs to a smaller world ... than ours has become ...' She stops a moment, sways on her stick, and waves one arm at the graveyard. 'A modest, suburban churchyard like this ... gives no clue to what will happen ... when the population swells ... Have you read ... excellent book ... *What Horror Brews Beneath Our Feet?*'

If there's a reply to this question, Sugar doesn't hear it.

'You ought to, Henry ... you ought to. It will open your eyes. There could be no more eloquent ... favour of cremation. The author describes ... old graveyards of London ... before they were all shut ... noxious vapours ... visible to the naked eye ...'

By now, her speech is painful to hear, and Henry Rackham casts frequent, agitated glances over his shoulder, not at Sugar but at the servant, who he plainly wishes would come and take matters in hand.

'God made us ...' Mrs Fox wheezes, 'from a handful of dust ... so I fail to see ... why some people think Him incapable ... of resurrecting us ... from an urnful ... of ash.'

'Mrs Fox, please don't speak any more.'

'And how substantial ... I should like to know ... do the champions of burial ... think we are ... after six months ... in the soil?'

Mercifully, the servant chooses this moment to bustle past Sugar and take the invalid firmly by the arm.

'Begging your pardon, Mr Rackham,' she says, as Mrs Fox half-collapses against her. He nods and smiles a ghastly smile, a smile of impotence, a smile that acknowledges he's less eligible to take her in his arms than an elderly housemaid.

'Of course, of course,' he says, and stands watching as the two spindly women – whom he could, if required, lift off the ground, one in each hand – totter away together, step by feeble step. Immobile as a pillar, Henry Rackham waits until they're safely installed in the doctor's sombre carriage, then turns back to face the church. Sugar lurches into motion and walks past him, shame-faced behind her veil, for he must surely know she's been spying on his agony.

'Good morning,' she says.

'Morning,' he croaks, his arm jerking a few inches towards his hat, before it falls rudely back towards the ground.

'Oh, but he's a thorn in my flesh!' groans William, mock-despairingly, in Sugar's bed that evening. 'Why did he have to choose *me* as the victim of his intimacies?'

'Perhaps he has no one else,' says Sugar. Then, risking a touch of intimacy herself, she adds: 'And you *are* his brother.'

They're lying with the blanket thrown wide, their hot damp bodies exposed to the cooling air. Despite his concern over Henry, William is in rather a good mood, as confident as a basking lion surrounded by lionesses and a steaming recent kill. His trip to Yarmouth was a resounding success: he and an importer called Grover Pankey got along famously, smoked cigars on the beachfront, and struck a deal to supply Rackham Perfumeries with dirt-cheap ivory pots for the dearer balsams.

During the act (the act of love with Sugar, not the deal with Pankey), William was still full of his achievement, and it lent him a grace she didn't know he could possess. He caressed her breasts with uncommon tenderness, and kissed her navel with the softest touch of his lips, over and over: at that, something inside her opened up, a hard, hidden shell that was hitherto closed to him. He's not the worst man in the world, she thinks; he might even be among the least vicious – and he's grown genuinely fond of her body, treating it like a living thing, rather than (as in the beginning) a void into which he angrily cast his seed.

'I am his brother,' sighs William, 'and it pains me to see him so wretched. But how can I help him? Everything I urge him to do, he rejects as impossible; everything he does instead, provokes me to annoyance. I come back from Yarmouth, in high spirits and pleased as Punch to have missed another of Doctor Crane's boring sermons, and within minutes

Henry's in my parlour, reciting the whole damned thing to me!'

To give Sugar the flavour of what he's had to endure, William sums up the rector's tirade against cremation.

'And what does Henry think?' says Sugar, when his two-minute précis of her own hour-long ordeal is finished.

'Ha! Crippled with indecision, as usual!' cries William. 'His head, he said, is with cremation, but his heart's with burial.'

Sugar represses the impulse to share with William the image that springs into her imagination, of a corpse being carved up by two solemn officials, whereupon one carries the severed head off towards a furnace, and the other bears the bloody heart away on a spade.

'And you?' she prompts.

'I told him I'm a burial man myself, but not for any far-fetched religious reasons. What hoops the pious jump through to make simple things complicated! I've half a mind to write an essay on the subject . . .' Hugging her closer as the sweat on their skins evaporates, he explains that the superiority of burial has nothing to do with religion at all, but with social and economic realities. Grieving friends and relations need to feel that the dead man is going forth from them in the body he had when they last saw him alive; his decay ought to be slow, as slow as the decay of their memories of him. To blast someone to a cinder when, in the minds of his loved ones, he's still large as life, is perverse. And besides, what's to become of all the grave-diggers? Have the cremationists thought of that? And what about the hearse-drivers, the funeral footmen and so forth? Burial generates more industry, and keeps more men gainfully employed, than most folk could imagine. Why, even Rackham Perfumeries would suffer if it were abolished, for there'd no longer be any call for Rackham's scented coffin sachets, nor the cosmetics Rackham's sells to undertakers.

'And what did Agnes make of all this?' enquires Sugar lightly, hoping to find out, without needing to ask, why Mrs Rackham wasn't at church this morning.

'Missed the whole thing, thank God. She's at the seaside.'

'The seaside?'

'Yes, Folkestone Sands.'

Sugar lifts herself up onto one elbow, and pulls the covers gently up over William's chest, trying to decide how brazenly she can pry.

'What's she doing there?'

'Fattening herself up with cake and hokey-pokey, I hope.' He closes his eyes and draws a deep breath. 'Keeping out of trouble.'

'Why? What trouble has she been in?'

But William is not in the mood to tell Sugar about Lady Harrington's ball, and the spectacle of his wife being carried out of a crowded ballroom by two blushing young naval officers, leaving behind her on the burnished floor a long glistening trail of yellow vomit – not to mention a grievously scandalised hostess. He might have told Sugar if the incident had been a simple case of illness, but Agnes, in the minutes leading up to her collapse, said outrageous things to Lady Harrington, ignoring his whispered cautions. Even in the carriage on the way home, she was unrepentant, her speech slurred, her eyes wild and glinting in the dark, as she lolled back and forth on the seat opposite him.

'Lady Harrington will never forgive this, you know,' he'd said, torn between the desire to slap her face so hard that it twirled three hundred and sixty degrees, and the longing to enfold her in his arms and stroke the wet hair off her face.

'Ach, we don't need her,' Agnes sniffed. 'She looks like a duck.'

This made him laugh, despite his mortification; and, in a sense, she was right, and not just about Lady Harrington's appearance. Ever since the ascent of William's fortunes to their current altitude, minor aristocrats – the sort whose own fortunes are ravaged by gambling and drink, and whose estates are covertly crumbling into ruin – have been tripping over themselves to court him.

'That's no excuse,' he chided his wife, 'for insulting one's host.'

'Host, host, host, host,' Agnes coughed wearily, eerily, as the carriage continued to jingle through the dark. 'Holy Ghost . . .'

'William?'

The voice is Sugar's, and she lies naked in the bed next to him, summoning him back to the present.

'Hmm?' he responds, blinking. 'Ah . . . yes. Agnes. She's not in any trouble really, in particular. Feminine frailty.' He reaches for his shirt and, slipping out of the bed, begins to dress. 'I've high hopes for her spell at Folkestone Sands, actually. Sea air is said to cure all sorts of stubborn ailments. And if her illness persists, I may follow the advice of Lady Bridgelow – a friend of mine – and send her abroad.'

'Abroad?' Sugar's hazel eyes are wide. 'But where?'

He pauses for a moment, his underbreeches half pulled up, his prick still wet with their love-making, his swollen scrotum dangling in the heat.

'I'll cross that bridge,' he cautions her gently, 'if and when I come to it.'

Even before the train begins to slacken speed in preparation for its arrival at Folkestone Station, the sharp smell of the sea is already drifting through the carriage windows, and the cries of seagulls can be heard over the staccato racket.

'Ah now, madam, smell *that*,' enthuses the servant, raising the window-blind by its tassel and sniffing deeply at the open window. 'It's a tonic, no doubt about it.'

Mrs Fox closes her book into the lap of her skirt and smiles.

'It smells most agreeable, Laura, I'll give you that. But then, so does roast pork, and that's never yet cured anybody of anything.'

And yet, Mrs Fox can't deny that the sea air is bracing. The salty breeze is opening tiny, hitherto-closed passages between her nose and her head, and the effect is so exhilarating she's unable to read any more of her book. Before slipping it back into the basket by her side, she appraises the title once more: *The Efficacy of Prayer*, by Philip Bodley and Edward Ashwell. What a tiresome book it is! – wholly missing the point that prayer is not some magic spell through which one hopes to achieve ends without effort, but a way of giving thanks, after one has given one's all to a worthwhile labour, for God's companionship at one's side. How like *men* – well, most men – is this finicky cynicism, this Socratic sleight-of-hand; how typical of them to gloat over statistics when outside their windows a million human beings wave in desperate need of rescue.

With a jolt, the rapidity of the steam-chugs decreases, and the grind of brakes announces the train's arrival at the station. Colourful blurs flash past the windows. A whistle blows.

'Folk-stooooone!'

Emmeline sits waiting in her carriage while the other passengers squeeze through the narrow corridor. Sad though she is to admit it, her health is now such that she wouldn't dare insert her feeble body into such a crush of stronger ones. Ruefully she recalls how once, along with her fellow Rescuers, she pushed through a crowd of shouting, foot-stamping onlookers to a street brawl and, finding the brawlers to be husband and wife, pulled them apart with her bare – well, gloved – hands. How amazed those two looked, panting and bloodied – how strangely they regarded each other!

The carriage shudders under the heavy tread of porters on its roof, unloading bags and cases; the furious blasts of steam from the several engines mingle with the chaos of voices. In the crowd, fat cabbies race one another to the wealthiest-looking of the travellers, while porters limp and lurch with enormous suitcases in their hands and beach umbrellas under their arms. Children are everywhere: boys in felt caps and redundant over-coats, girls in miniature replicas of the previous decade's adult fashions. Round and round their mothers and nannies they bumble and dance, made clumsy by baskets, buckets and spades. Emmeline sees one excited lass twirl into the path of a sailor and get bowled to the ground. Yet, instead of howling, the child scrambles to her feet, her joy too robust to be punc-tured by one small mishap. Ah, what a blessing, to be able to fall and get up again! Pricked by envy, Emmeline watches and watches.

When the sea of humanity has washed out of the great portals into the brilliant boulevard beyond, Laura picks up Mrs Fox's suitcase and para-sol, and waddles out onto the platform. Emmeline leans but lightly on her stick as she follows, for she's been resting all the way from London; in fact she feels quite well, and it's only the pitying stares of the railway guards that remind her how naked to the world her illness is.

Her father has reserved rooms in the hotel most nearly adjacent to the sands, and had sent medicines on ahead, to lie in wait for her at her unfa-miliar bedside. As far as Emmeline's nourishment is concerned, Laura has been instructed to eat as often as she fancies – oftener, even – so that Mrs Fox can be tempted to accompany her in a meal, whether it be purchased from a strolling vendor on the sands or from the bill of fare at the hotel's dining-hall. The principal aim, however, is for Mrs Fox to rest as many hours as she can bear, reclining in a quiet spot near the sea. On no account is she to stray into the bathing areas and join those adventurous souls who actu-ally wade in the water. If she grows *intolerably* bored, she may, with Doctor Curlew's blessing, *watch* these daring women springing from their rented bathing-machines fully attired in their swimming-costumes, bound for the sensational shallows. But *she* is to remain among the dry majority, in that safe area where children build their castles out of the reach of the tide.

The dry majority is swelling in number every minute, proliferating in the hot sun. As Laura and Mrs Fox walk along the paved boulevard leading to the sands, they're passed by scores of men and women dressed as if for a day at the races. Some carry collapsible chairs under their arms, others books or even writing-desks. There seems to be one hawker for every ten innocent vacationers. Dray-horses pull bathing-machines towards the ladies' bathing area and, following on behind, a quartet of brass players toot hymns to the rhythm of a shaken coin-cup.

'There's a nice spot,' says Laura when she and Mrs Fox have half-descended the great stone steps that eventually bury themselves in the sand, but Mrs Fox doesn't raise her eyes, being too concerned with her footing and the placing of her stick. The challenge of walking on sand – not easy even for a well person – is beyond her unassisted capabilities, and reluctantly she accepts Laura's arm. Hyperventilating the sea air, she begins to grow light-headed, and perceives the merry-makers and money-makers all around her as though they're figments of a dream, liable to disappear as soon as she blinks, leaving her on an empty beach.

The last few yards to Laura's chosen niche involve several near run-ins with heavily-laden vendors. One of them is selling parasols; another, toy boats; a third, wooden wind-up birds that he loudly claims can fly; and a fourth, slices of plum pudding wrapped in tissue paper, over which he furiously waves one hand, to discourage the audacious seagulls circling overhead.

'This is the place, ma'am,' says Laura, as they walk into the shade of a grassy knoll. Gratefully, Mrs Fox lowers her body to the ground, resting her back against the incline. The horizon tilts giddily, an untrustworthy boundary between a vast blue sky and an aquamarine ocean.

'Leave me alone . . . for a minute,' she gasps, with a fawning smile that promises good behavior.

'Of course, ma'am,' says Laura. 'I'll go fetch us something to eat,' and before Mrs Fox can protest, she's hurrying back towards the hurly-burly.

Later that afternoon, when a large slice of plum cake lies half-buried in the sand beside her skirts, and Laura has been persuaded to go and watch an exhibition of 'Psycho, the Amazing Mechanical Man (Sensation of the London Season!)' at the nearby Folkestone Pavilion, Mrs Fox lies staring up at the azure sky. The sound of children's voices has long ago become indistinguishable from the cries of sea-birds, and all of it is swallowed up by the grand and soothing sound of the waves.

She didn't want to come, no, she didn't want to come, but now that she's here she is content, for it's so much easier here to *think*. The tortuous mazes through which her thoughts have been running lately are left behind in the polluted metropolis. Here, by the great eternal sea, she can, at last, think straight.

A seagull wanders cautiously towards her over the sand, attracted by the wedge of cake, but mistrustful of human wickedness. Emmeline picks up the sticky, gritty slice and gently tosses it at the bird's feet.

'What shall I do about my friend Henry, Mr Seagull?' she murmurs as he begins to peck the cake to pieces. 'Or are you *Mrs* Seagull? Or Miss? I don't suppose such distinctions matter much in your society, do they?'

She shuts her eyes and concentrates on not coughing. Stowed at the bottom of her basket, under Bodley and Ashwell's book, is a crumpled handkerchief glutinous with blood – fragments of her lungs, her father would have her believe, though she'd always imagined lungs to be airy bellows, pale translucent balloons. No matter: the blood is real enough, and she can't afford to lose any more of it.

Tickle by tickle, the temptation to cough ebbs away. But a more serious temptation is not so easily put behind her: her thoughts of Henry. How she wishes he were here by her side! How idyllic it would have been, if she could have whiled away the train journey conversing with him, rather than making small talk with Laura! And how much better it would be if, whenever she felt herself weakening at the knees, it were *he* rather than her father's elderly servant who rushed to embrace her! His strong fingers would slot perfectly into the hollows between her ribs. He'd carry her in his arms if need be. He could lay her down gently on a bed as if she were his cat.

I desire him.

There, it's said, if not aloud. It doesn't need to be said aloud: God hears. And her fleshly desire, while not condemned by God, is (as Saint Paul made perfectly clear in his letter to the Corinthians) nothing to be proud of. Nor does the fact that she and Henry aren't about to commit any indecency mean there's no cause for concern. Who's to say that Matthew 5:28 doesn't apply as much to the widowed as the married, and to females as much as males? In ancient Galilee, the womenfolk would doubtless have been burdened with housework and children, and scarcely at leisure to attend lectures by itinerant prophets; might it not have been the case, then, that from His vantage-point on the mount, Jesus saw only men?

'Whosoever looketh on a woman in lust . . .' If Jesus had seen any women in that crowd, He'd surely have added, 'or on a man'. Which has serious implications for Emmeline, because if it's possible to commit adultery in one's heart, why not fornication as well? Bad Christians are wont to interpret Scripture to excuse their own shortcomings; good Christians ought to do the opposite, reading fearlessly between the lines to catch a glimpse of the admonishing frown of a loving but disappointed Almighty. She's a fornicator, then, in her heart.

For yes, she desires Henry, and not just as a strong pair of hands to catch her when she swoons. She craves the weight of his body on hers; the press of his chest against her bosom; she longs to see him stripped of his dark carapace of clothes, and to discover the secret shape of his hips, first under her palms, then clasped between her legs. There, it's said. The words, unvoiced, glow like miraculous writing on the walls of her heart – that little temple into which God is always looking. Her very soul should be a mirror in which God may see Himself reflected, but now . . . now He's as likely to see the face of Henry Rackham instead. That adorable face . . .

Emmeline opens her eyes and sits up straighter, before she adds idolatry to her sins. The hunchbacked seagull glances up at her, wondering if she has designs on his succulent lump of grub. Satisfied, he resumes his feast.

There's only one sure way to solve this problem, thinks Emmeline, and that's to marry Henry. Fornication, imagined or otherwise, cannot exist between husband and wife. And yet, marrying Henry would be a wicked, selfish misuse of her dearest friend, for Henry doesn't wish to marry: he's said so many times. How much plainer can he make it that he desires nothing more from her than friendship?

'The flesh is selfish,' he told her once, during one of their post-sermon conversations, 'while the spirit is generous. It frightens me to think how easily one can spend an entire lifetime gratifying animal appetites.'

'Oh, I'm sure God won't mind if you spend just a *few* more minutes walking with me in the sunshine,' she replied, playfully, for he was in a grim mood that day, and she hoped to jolly him out of it.

'How I despise my idleness!' he lamented, deaf to her charms. 'I've so little time left!'

'Oh but really, Henry,' she said. 'What a thing for a man of thirty to say! You've a virtual eternity to achieve your ambitions!'

'Eternity!' he echoed mournfully. 'What a grand word! I take it we aren't Reincarnationists, believing ourselves to have as many lifetimes as we please.'

'One lifetime is enough,' she assured him. 'Indeed, in the opinion of some of the wretched creatures I meet in the course of my work, one life-time is intolerably long . . .'

But once Henry was started on this subject, he was loath to stop; the evils of procrastination inspired rhetoric in him worthy of the finest sermons, and boded extremely well for his future as a churchman.

'Yes, time is experienced differently,' he conceded, 'by different people: but God's own clock runs with fearsome precision. When we're children, each minute of our lives is crammed full of achievement; we are born, learn to walk, and speak, and a thousand other things, in a few short years. But what we fail to grasp is that the challenges of maturity are of a different order from the challenges of infancy. Faced with the challenge of building a new church, we may feel just as we did when we built our first sand-castle, but ten years later the first stone may still not be laid.' (How strange, thinks Emmeline, to be recollecting these words while she sits on a sandy beach, watching little boys build sand-castles!) 'And so it is,' Henry concluded, 'with *all* our grand hopes, all our ambitions to achieve what this poor world is crying out for: decades flow by, while we trust in Eternity!'

'Yes, but for goodness' sake, Henry,' she strove to remind him, 'no single Christian can achieve everything. We can only do our best.'

'Precisely!' he cried. 'And I see what's *your* best, and what is mine, and I'm ashamed!'

Basking in the golden sun of Folkestone Sands, Emmeline smiles at the memory of Henry's serious face on that afternoon; his dear face, contorted with the passion of idealism. How she would love to kiss that face, to stroke the wrinkles of earnestness from his brow, to pull him into the here-and-now with an embrace as strong as her enfeebled arms can muster . . .

But to return to the subject at hand: marriage.

If she and Henry *did* marry, why should their friendship suffer any change? Couldn't it remain just as it is now, except that they'd live in the same house? (It would have to be *her* house, though, not his; they couldn't both fit into his!) He could have the bedroom next to hers, if he wouldn't mind clearing the mess out of it (When *is* Mrs Lavers going to come and collect those bags of donated clothes? And will those men from the African Bible Society ever return?) In her current state, having a man about the place would be rather practical – as well as delightful, if that man were Henry. He could bring the coal in, for a start, and help her with her correspondence. And, if she was dog-tired at bedtime, he could carry her up the stairs and, with the utmost gentleness, lay her . . .

She smiles ruefully at the sheer persistence of her ignoble cravings. This illness of hers, whatever it is, has failed to bring her any closer to God, despite all those pretty engravings she's always seeing, of consumptive females lying in haloed beds with angels hovering overhead. Maybe it's not consumption she's got, but some sort of hysterical affliction? To put it bluntly, is she on the road to Bedlam? Instead of floating towards the ethereal portals of Heaven, she seems to be growing ever more gross, like an animal, coughing blood, sprouting pimples on her neck and shoulders, sweating profusely from every pore and, whenever she rouses from a daydream of Henry Rackham, finding herself in need of a good wash between the legs . . .

Disgraceful! And yet, she's never been terribly good at feeling shame. Faced with a choice between self-flagellation and making amends, she'll always choose the more constructive course. So . . . what *if* she and Henry were to cleave together as man and wife? Would that be such a terrible thing? If Henry's fear is that his ministry would be derailed by fatherhood, well then, she's barren, as the childlessness of her marriage to Bertie proved.

How, though, do marriages come to be proposed? What, exactly, is the procedure for crossing the line between courteous nod and nestling together in a warm bed, till death us do part? Poor old Bertie went down on his knee, but he'd been pursuing her since her schooldays. If marriage is the farthest thing from Henry's mind, *he*'s not likely to propose it, is he, and *she* can't very well propose it, can she? Not because it would offend convention (she's so tired of convention!), but because it might offend Henry, and make him think less of her. To lose his respect would be a crueller blow than she could bear, at least in her frail condition just now.

'Then I must wait,' she says aloud. 'Until I'm better.'

At the sound of her voice, the seagull runs off, leaving the last crumbs behind, and Emmeline allows her head to fall back against the grassy knoll, knocking her bonnet askew, so that the pins prick her scalp. All of a sudden her skin is crawling with irritation, and she tears the bonnet from her head. Then she settles back, crooning with relief at how snugly her bare, damp skull fits into the warm hollow behind it.

The decision she's made about Henry spreads through her body like the effects of a medicine or a hearty meal, all the more satisfying because neither medicine nor food has had much effect on her lately. What a superb restorative firm resolve is! The weariness is already draining from her limbs into the sand beneath her.

The seagull, reassured that her squawk was an aberration, walks back and resumes pecking at the sandy cake. He lifts his head while jerking a crumb farther down into his gullet, as though nodding in agreement with her decision. Yes, she must wait until she's better, and then . . . and then take her life into her hands, by offering it to Henry Rackham.

'And will he say yes, Mr Seagull?' she asks, but the seagull spreads its wings and, leaping up from a fluster of sand, flies off towards the sea.

In another part of Folkestone Sands, propped up against another rock, Agnes Rackham yelps in fright as a loudly clicking wooden bird crashes at her feet. She pulls her legs in, crushing the lady's journal she's been reading into her lap, and gathers her skirts tight around her.

Clara, who, unlike her mistress, has not been engrossed in the study of 'The Season: Who Shone Brightest, When, and Where', saw the projectile coming, and merely blinks when it hits the ground. Calmly, without fuss, as if to rub her mistress's nose in her own nervous debility, she reaches over and picks up the bird by one of its plywood-and-paper wings.

'It's only a toy, ma'am,' she says sweetly.

'A toy?' echoes Agnes in wonder as she uncoils.

'Yes, ma'am,' affirms Clara, holding aloft the bird, whose clicking wings have by now wound to a stop, for Agnes's inspection. It's a flimsy construction, with carelessly painted features, animated by a brass key and a tiny metal motor. 'There's a man selling them from a cart. We passed him on the way.'

Agnes turns to look in the direction Clara indicates, but sees only a small boy of six or seven, dressed in a blue cotton seaside suit and a straw boater, capering around the cliff's curve. He skids to a halt in front of the strange lady and the servant who holds his toy in her hands.

'Please miss,' he pipes. 'That's my flying bird.'

'Well, then,' scolds Clara, 'you should take better care where you throw it.'

'I'm sorry, miss,' pleads the little boy, 'but it won't fly straight,' and he nervously scratches at his left calf with his tightly-laced right shoe. The servant is glowering at him, so he prefers to look at the lady with the big blue eyes, who's smiling.

'Ach, poor lad,' says Agnes. 'Don't fret; she won't bite you.' And she motions to Clara to hand her the toy.

Agnes is rather fond of children, actually, as long as they're not babies, and as long as they are someone else's, and as long as they're administered in small doses. Small boys in particular can be charming.

'Does it *really* fly?' she asks this one.

'Well . . .' frowns the lad, reluctant to besmirch the bird's reputation. 'The man who sells 'em made *one* fly very well, and said they all could do the same, but I've one, and my brother has one too, and neither of them flies much. We throw 'em as high as we can, but as a rule they fall imme'atly to the ground. May I go now, ma'am? My Mama thought I should return directly."

'Very good, young sir,' smiles Agnes. 'Honestly spoken. Here is your toy.'

A child made happy: how simple it is! She sends the lad on his way with a benevolent wave, and no sooner has he gone than she turns to Clara and says,

'Go and buy me one of those birds. And a sweetmeat for yourself, if you fancy.'

'Yes ma'am, thank you ma'am,' says the servant, and hurries off on her errand, the bustle of her navy-blue skirt shedding sand with every step.

Agnes waits until Clara's out of sight, then reaches across to the book Clara has left lying on a blanket, curious as to what a servant might read. Ah: it's a novel: *Jane Eyre*. Agnes has read this one herself, from Mudie's, despite Doctor Curlew's injunctions against it. To see this dog-eared volume in Clara's possession gives Agnes a chill, for there's something very wicked about a lady's-maid savouring this horrid tale of a wife driven mad by illness and shut up in a tower by her husband while he attempts to marry another woman. With a twitch of her lips she replaces the book on the blanket.

As she straightens, the pain returns to her head, throbbing behind her left eye. How strange that this evil sensation has the gall to persist, when so many of Mrs Gooch's pink pills have been sent to quash it! All the way from London in the train, she's been swallowing them, while Clara sat dozing. Now she fondles her reticule, tempted to take a swig of laudanum from the little bottle that's pretending to be lavender water. But no, she must save it for when she's absolutely at her wits' end.

Think sweet, light thoughts, she urges herself. Heavy cogitation, she's found, makes the pain worse. If she can clear her head of worry, and let nothing remain inside her brain but cheerful memories and a sense of what the Hindoo mystics call 'Nirvana', she may yet snatch relief from the jaws of wretchedness.

So much in life to be thankful for . . . A highly successful Season . . . A coach and coachman of her own . . . A guardian angel who will risk God's censure to defend her from harm . . . The end, at last, of her terrifying issues of blood . . . A long-overdue reunion with the True Religion of her childhood . . .

As the pain mounts, Agnes tries to picture herself attending Mass, sitting in the candle-lit hush of the old church listening to dear Father Scanlon. It's difficult, with so much distraction from laughing children, the roar of the waves, and the gruff entreaties of vendors, but she manages it, if only for a moment, by wilfully mishearing the gabble of the donkey-ride man as a Latin chant. Then a barrel organ starts up and the spell is broken.

Poor misguided William . . . If he's so concerned about her health, he would have done her more good, instead of sending her to the beach to bake like a biscuit, to ensconce her for a week in church – *her* church, that is. How content she is whenever she's nestled in that cosy sanctuary! And how dreary it is on those alternate Sundays when, to avoid gossip, she must sit among Anglicans and endure a sermon by that insufferable Doctor Crane . . . He's always railing against people she's never heard of, and there's no music in his voice at all, and he sings the hymns quite out of tune – honestly, what sort of nincompoops do they allow to become clergymen these days? It's high time she publicly declared her return to the True Faith. Surely she's wealthy enough now to get away with it? Who'd dare lay a hand on her and say no? Especially now she has a guardian angel looking out for her . . .

She peers along the bright seashore, shielding her eyes with one hand, hoping against hope that amongst the children and the donkeys and the rows of bathing-machines she may spy the tall apparition of her Holy Sister walking towards her. But no. She was foolish to wish for it. It's one thing for her Holy Sister to slip out of the Convent and rendezvous with her in the labyrinths of London, into which even God must have trouble seeing; quite another for Her to visit Agnes on Folkestone Sands, where there's no escaping Heavenly surveillance . . .

Ach, why didn't she bring her diary? She left it at home, for fear of getting it wet or some such nonsense . . . If she had it here with her, she could flip through the pages and be comforted by the marks of her Holy Sister's fingers. For, each night, while Agnes sleeps, her Holy Sister reads her diary, by the light of Her own supernal aura, and leaves faint finger-prints on the pages. (Not that her Holy Sister's fingers are in any way unclean, of course: it's Her inner power that causes it.) (And no, she's *not* imagining it – for sometimes she goes to sleep with the diary closed, and wakes to find it open, or vice versa.)

How long has William arranged to keep her here, anyway? She doesn't even know! The hotel manager knows, but she, the person concerned, is kept in ignorance! She's not the 'strong-minded' sort, but this is a flagrant abuse of the rights of women. Is she expected to sit by the seashore for weeks on end, while her complexion darkens and her supply of medicine dwindles to nothing?

But no: think sweet, light thoughts. How nice it would be to write a letter to her Holy Sister, and post it, and get a letter back. Is it too much to ask that her Holy Sister reveal to her the secret location of the Convent of Health? Yes, she knows it's too much to ask. If she's a good girl, she'll be told in the end. All will be well.

On Agnes's tongue, a sudden bitter taste. She licks her lips, looks down at her hands, which are cradling the little bottle of laudanum. Hastily, in case Clara is near, she replaces it in her reticule. What naughty hands she has, to fetch out the precious liquid while she's busy thinking, and feed it into her mouth so brazenly! How much has she swallowed? It really will be awfully bad if she's lying unconscious on the sand when Clara returns.

With a groan of effort, she stands up and tries to slap the sand off her skirts. How harsh the grains are against her palms – almost as sharp as glass – which is what sand is manufactured into, isn't it, or was William gulling her when he told her that? She examines the soft pale flesh of her hands, half-expecting to see an intricate pattern of bloody grazes, but no, either William was lying, or she's made of tougher stuff than she thought.

A walk, she's decided, will ventilate her head, and keep her awake. All this sitting in the sun is quite sleep-inducing, and has also made her far too hot under the tighter parts of her dress. She trusts that at the very edge of the sea (assuming the recipe of oceans hasn't been changed since last she visited) the air will be damp with spray, like a cool, salty mist: that's just what she needs.

Agnes makes her way to the water and strolls along the brink of the tide, where the sand is wet and dark. Gracefully, as if she's engaged in a courtly dance, she sidesteps each wave of silvery froth as it spills ashore, accustoming herself to the rhythm. But the sea is an awkward dancing partner, and starts to get its movements wrong, and before long the tide comes in too far. A shallow swirl of water surges over her boots, seeping into the thin leather, trickling through the eyelets, dragging at the hems of her skirts. No great calamity . . . There are two big suitcases of dresses and shoes waiting for her in the hotel. And the cold water between her toes is a not unpleasant shock that travels instantly up to her brain, pricking her awake – not that she's asleep, you understand, for how can one sleep while dancing at the edge of the waves?

However, just in case she should trip on a stone half-hidden inside the sand, and drown before she has time to appreciate that she's fallen (for who knows how quickly such things happen?), Agnes starts walking away from the tide, back to . . . back to . . . back to wherever it is she's come from. Her waterlogged skirts weigh heavy, too heavy to carry far. The sensible thing would be to stop here, spread her skirts out on the sand, and walk again when they've dried.

For an instant she shuts her eyes, and in that instant the world turns upside-down, earth and sky changing places. The ground – above her now – whips invisible tendrils around her, gathers her tight against itself, securely woven against its great warm belly so she won't plummet into nothingness. She hangs suspended from the topsy-turvy *terra firma* like a moth on a ceiling, gazing down into a vast formless void of brilliant blue. She goggles, half-blinded, into the face of the deep. If the ground loosed its bonds and let her go, she would fall for all eternity, a rag doll plunging down a bottomless well.

Dizzy and frightened, Agnes turns her head aside, and presses her cheek against the moist ground, nudging her cheekbone into the sand, closing one eye against the light. Slowly, mercifully, the universe begins to revolve again, righting itself, anti-clockwise. And, in the distance, a vision is advancing towards her, a vision of a nun in a black dress and a white coif and veil. With every step this woman takes, the landscape grows greener around her, and the glassy shimmer is diffused to a pastel verdancy. Moss spreads over the sands like a green blush and, leaf by leaf, a forest subtly materialises to cover the sky. The shrieks of seagulls and children grow softer, and metamorphose into the trilling and twittering of thrushes; the immense sound of the ocean is tamed, until all that's left is the faint gurgle of a rural stream. By the time her Holy Sister is close enough to be recognised beyond doubt, Folkestone Sands has disappeared entirely, and in its stead is the far more familiar landscape of her dreams: the tranquil environs of the Convent of Health.

'Oh, Agnes,' declares her Holy Sister in affectionate exasperation. 'Are you here again? What's to become of you!' And she steps back to allow a pair of shadowy figures to approach.

Agnes struggles to speak, but her tongue is a nerveless gobbet of meat in her mouth. She can only groan as she feels strong hands under her shoulders and her knees, the hands of the two sinewy old men who do the fetching and carrying for the nuns at the Convent of Health. They lift her up, as easily as if she were a tiny babe, and lay her gently on a stretcher.

Agnes's response? A regrettable one. She convulses, opens her mouth wide, and unleashes a gush of scalding yellow vomit all over her rescuers.

Clara Tillotson, seeing her name being pencilled into the policeman's notebook, begins to shed tears of indignation and fear.

'She *told* me to leave her,' she pleads. 'She wanted me to buy her one of these.' And she displays, for the officer's inspection, a wire-and-plywood plaything with a brass key in its back.

Mrs Rackham has just been lifted onto a stretcher by two strong men borrowed from the bathing-machine company. A doctor has already laid his palm on her clammy forehead and measured the temperature inside her mouth. Diagnosing bilious headache and possible phthisis, he's judged there's no urgent need for her to go to hospital, but that she must rest inside her hotel room out of the sun.

'Next of kin?' enquires the policeman of Clara as the strongmen carry the unconscious Agnes away.

'William Rackham,' snuffles the servant.

'*The* William Rackham?'

'*I* don't know,' snivels Clara, staring anxiously at the dark stain of vomit left behind on the sand, terrorised by what that stain might mean for her future employment.

'Rackham's Perfumes? "One bottle lasts a year"?'

'I suppose so.' Clara knows nothing of her master's products; her mistress scorns them.

'You're in communication with him, miss?'

Clara blows her nose in her handkerchief. Whatever can he mean? Does he think she can fly through space, reaching Notting Hill in the wink of an eye, to announce the news at William's upstairs window? Nevertheless, she nods.

'Good,' the policeman replies, closing his notebook. 'I'll leave the matter in your hands, then.'

The sky has become overcast, threatening rain. Dawdling infants are being tugged away from sandcastles by their parents; promenading dandies are heading for cover; oddly costumed nereids are emerging from the sea and disappearing into bathing-machines; vendors are trundling their wares back and forth at increasing speed, hoarse from shouting assurances to the retreating multitude that everything is almost for nothing.

Mrs Fox has long ago returned to her hotel, complaining that all this rest is tiring her to death. She's wholly unaware Mrs Rackham is even in Folkestone and, far from having been the Samaritan who found Agnes lying insensible by the water's edge, is fated to return to London without having once glimpsed her.

And Sugar? Was it Sugar, then, whom Agnes saw walking towards her on the topsy-turvy world? No, Sugar is in her rooms in Priory Close, forcing herself to plough on through *The Art of Perfumery*, by G.W. Septimus Piesse. The largest body of water in her immediate vicinity is her undrained bath-tub. There's not an inch of space in her poor brain for Mrs Rackham, crammed as it is with facts about lavender and essential oils. Will it ever benefit her to know that pine-apple oil is nothing more than butyrate of ethyloxide? Is there any point in memorising the recipe of rose cold cream (one pound of almond oil, one pound of rose water, half a drachm of otto of roses, and one ounce of sperm and white wax)? She wonders what kind of man can write about sperm and think only of whales.

'Holy Christ,' she mutters as she catches herself losing consciousness and the book falls shut between her thighs. 'Wake up!'

TWENTY

'o, how *was* the seaside?' enquires Lady Bridgelow, noiselessly replacing her tea-cup in its saucer. 'I didn't go this year: every resort has been invaded by riff-raff. Ah, *thank* you, Rose.'

Rose, the Rackhams' new parlour-maid, is pouring more tea, straight into Mrs Bridgelow's cup from above. The servant's hand is steady as she holds the heavy pot aloft, her wrist ruddy-fleshed against the white cuff, and smelling of carbolic: Lady Bridgelow approves of that.

It's a bright, chilly afternoon early in September, several weeks after William brought home from Folkestone Sands a wife who was thinner and ten times more peculiar than when she was dispatched, and who is, at this very moment, hiding upstairs, resolutely 'not in' to visitors.

To be fair, though, it's not only Agnes Rackham that's queer lately: the weather, having turned warm unseasonably early this year, has been just as unseasonably cold since the end of August, as if to retract an undeserved generosity. Most days, radiant morning sunshine has paled to grey by noon, and nippy breezes hint at what the elements may have in mind. Leaves are falling by the cart-load from the trees, nights are drawing in, and all over England landscape painters are retreating from the overcast countryside in disgust. Those of William's business acquaintances who own orchards have been forced to organise early harvests, for the fruit hangs precariously, virtually falling into the reapers' hands, while even an hour's delay finds it bruised and rotting on the ground. Thank God the lavender's already harvested. Sugar was disappointed not to see it being done, but there are only so many things a man can arrange when he has the Season and a volatile wife to juggle. The bonfire of the fifth-year plants at the end of October – he'll take her to see that, she has his word.

At the Rackham residence in Notting Hill, servants above and below stairs are preparing for an autumn which may, if it pleases, treat England roughly: the thick curtains have been taken out of mothballs; the pantry is chock-full of tinned lobsters, sardines, salmon, turtle and so on; fruits and vegetables have been squirrelled away in the underground store-house; the chimneys have been scoured; Janey has caught an inconvenient disease from cleaning the ovens; Cheesman has inspected the roof and doors of the carriage for possible leaks; and Letty and Rose have removed the summer decorations from the fireplaces and substituted dry logs. Shears, muttering and fussing from dawn to dusk, is best avoided.

Lady Bridgelow, too, has accepted that summer has flown, and has adapted her apparel accordingly, looking a little older – though not *much* older – than her twenty-nine years; she is well rugged up in a serge coat-dress, to ensure that her health remains (as she likes to describe it) 'uninterrupted'. William is tubby with clothing, as well as the extra fat he's accumulated during the Season. His by now thick and square-barbered beard hangs over his cravat, and he wears a woollen waistcoat, heavy tweed trousers, and a tweed coat which he's tried unobtrusively to unbutton but can't wrestle with any more in front of his visitor.

'I can't speak for the other seaside resorts,' he says, in reply to her question. 'But Folkestone has become a circus, from what I saw. It's the fault of the railways, of course.'

'Ah, well, that's modern times,' says Lady Bridgelow philosophically, breaking a sugared biscuit in half. 'Those of us who have our own carriages will simply have to seek out a paradise that the common herd haven't yet discovered.' Whereupon she consumes her sweet morsel with deft rapidity, so as not to let her turn to speak go by. 'I've never been able to understand the lure of the seaside, anyway – except for convalescents.'

'Yes, quite,' says William, handing his empty tea-cup up to Rose.

'How *is* your wife?' commiserates Lady Bridgelow over the rim of her full one.

'Oh, I'm sure it's nothing serious,' he sighs. 'She's caught a chill, I suspect.'

'She's much missed at church,' Lady Bridgelow assures him.

William smiles, pained. It's common knowledge now that Agnes attends Catholic Mass almost every Sunday, and yet he hasn't the heart to forbid it. Deplorable though her apostasy is, and embarrassing though it is for him to sense his neighbours' disapproval, he wants Agnes to be happy, and she's never happier than when she's permitted to ride off to Cricklewood and be a little Papist.

How he'd hoped she would come back from the seaside plumper and more sensible! But she stayed only eight days of the fortnight he paid for and, instead of travelling quietly back to London on the train with Clara, she sent him a postcard complaining that the hotel had Americans in it, and the drinking water was full of organisms, and he must come and fetch her at once. *In the name of all that is Holy, I beg of you, Please!*, she signed the postcard, an otherwise cheerful picture of a donkey with a conical seashell fixed to its head, inscribed *Unicorn, Folkestone Sands*. Mortified at the thought of the postman reading another such missive, William travelled to Folkestone with all speed, only to find there a perfectly composed, apparently contented Agnes who treated him like an unexpected guest whom she was too gracious to turn away.

'How has she been?' he enquired surreptitiously of Clara, as he and the servant stood watching Agnes's absurd suitcases being humped out of the hotel by grunting porters.

'I've no complaints, sir,' Clara replied, with a face on her like someone who's just spent a week in a pillory, pelted ceaselessly with rotten fruit.

On her return home, Agnes lost no time making it clear that the seaside had failed utterly to work its salubrious magic on her, at least not in the way that Doctor Curlew had hoped. No sooner were the souvenirs of Folkestone unpacked than Agnes concocted a new caprice – a foolish ritual which, regrettably, has already become a firm habit. Each morning, before breakfast, she attempts to launch a clockwork flying toy from the sill of her bedroom window. That the clicking automaton falls like a stone, and that its beak has broken off and its left wing is splintered, have failed to discourage Agnes from her ritual. Each morning, after breakfast, Shears finds the thing buried up to its neck in his newly-turned earth, or entangled in a bush, and he delivers it back into the house without a word. (Well may he keep silent! – his protests did him no good at all during the Season, when Mrs Rackham denuded his rose-bushes in order to make a 'red carpet' of flower petals for her dinner guests.)

'Poor woman,' clucks Lady Bridgelow. 'I do pity her so. We who have uninterrupted health ought to be more thankful for our good fortune.

Certainly my husband always urged me to be thankful for it, when he was alive.' At this her eyes glaze over, and she allows her head to sink back against the antimacassar, as if she were gazing at a ghostly vision of her husband. 'Aahh . . . poor Albert,' she sighs, allowing Rose to serve her a slice of ginger cake. 'How lonely it sometimes is without him . . . especially when I know I've so *much* of my life to live yet . . .'

Then with a sudden movement, she's erect once more, clear-eyed and firm-chinned. 'Still, I mustn't pine, must I? I've my son, after all, in whom Albert lives on. Such a wonderful close resemblance, too! You know, I wonder . . . If the poor man were still here . . . and if I bore him a second son tomorrow, would the boy resemble the father just as astoundingly? You know, I suspect *so*! . . . But you must excuse my prattling. I can only plead that *you*'ll be liable to the same foolishness by and by, when you've a son of your own.' She pats her knees as if they are lapdogs to be roused from slumber. 'Well now, I've kept you far too long from your affairs. Please forgive me.'

'No, no,' says William, as she rises to leave. 'It was a pleasure, a pleasure.'

He speaks sincerely: she's always welcome in his parlour, and he's sorry to escort her out of it. She's not a bit like other titled people he's met: for all her lofty connections, there's something appealingly impish about her, which he fancies he sees even in the way she trots down his front steps and contrives, before her coachman can clamber down from his perch, to hop unassisted into her carriage. Once more she waves, as she gathers her skirts into the cabin, and then she's gone.

The most agreeable thing about her, William decides, as he watches her coach trundle down the carriage-way, is how openly she associates with him, even under the eyes of her own exalted set. She's never held it against him that he has what she delicately calls a 'concern'; indeed she often says that the future belongs to industry. He only wishes she wouldn't be so solicitous after Agnes – especially since, to his chagrin, this generosity of heart is not reciprocated.

'I trust her no farther than I can throw her,' Agnes only recently declared, during one of her ever-more-frequent lapses of inhibition. (A drastic insult, this, given the flimsiness of Agnes's arms.) The fact that she denied all knowledge of the remark later, when her fit was past, is neither here nor there.

But Agnes will get better, he's sure she will – almost sure. After all, apart from the usual 'wooden bird' incident this morning, nothing unfortunate has happened today, has it? and it's almost midday . . .

William stands in the receiving hall, pensive now that his visitor has departed and the house is quiet again. Whenever she calls upon him, Lady Bridgelow brings with her a hum of benign normalcy that fades, alas, as soon as she steps out of the door, leaving the air once again volatile with uncertainty. Yes, the place is silent, but what does that silence mean? Is Agnes sewing quietly upstairs, or hatching another outburst? Is she snoozing the sleep of the innocent, or sprawled in a delirious swoon? William listens uneasily, holding his breath at the foot of the stairs.

Within seconds, his questions are unexpectedly answered: from very nearby, as prettily as any man could want, comes the sound of nimble fingers fondling the keys of a piano. Agnes Rackham is musical today! The house brightens at once, becoming a home to all those who dwell in it. William unclenches his fists, and smiles.

Curlew can speak the word 'asylum' as often as he likes: William Rackham doesn't admit defeat so easily! And besides, what about husbandly compassion? William is aware that from October onwards, there'll be an engraving of his likeness stamped on every item of Rackham produce (a fine idea of Sugar's) and, for this purpose, he has chosen a photograph that shows him in a kindly, even fatherly light. What would the ladies who buy Rackham's toiletries think, if they learned that the man responsible for their sweet-smelling indulgences, and who seeks to disseminate his benign face into every household in the land, had condemned his own wife to a mad-house? No, Agnes deserves another chance – in fact, a hundred, a thousand other chances! She's his wife, damn it, to love and to cherish, in sickness and in health.

'Call Cheesman,' he tells Letty, during those precious minutes while the piano melody is still charming, before its obsessive arpeggios start to grate. 'I'm going out.'

Henry Rackham, mere seconds after his paroxysm has passed, and before the bitter reflux of remorse has fully returned him to his senses, lurches in surprise at the sound of his front door being knocked upon. *Who the devil . . . ?* Nobody visits him, nobody! It must be some mistake.

Hastily, he cleans himself and does his best to look decent, though in his hurry he can't find his slippers and, badgered by the persistent knocking, he shambles to the door in socks.

On the footpath near his doorstep, when he opens up, is a baffling vision of female beauty: two fresh-faced young women, twins perhaps, barely out of girlhood, dressed identically in grey with pink bonnets and paletots. They stand behind a hooded carriage resembling a flower-barrow or an outsize perambulator, but with neither flowers nor babies in it.

'Please, sir,' says one. 'We're here on behalf of the freezing, starving women and children of Skye.'

Henry gapes at them uncomprehendingly, as a chilly breeze whips into his house and alerts him, too late, to the unsavoury excess of sweat on his forehead.

'The Isle of Skye, sir,' explains the other girl, in a lilting tone indistinguishable from her sister's. 'In Scotland. Many families have been forced off their land, sir, and are liable to perish this coming winter, which threatens to be a bad one. Have you any clothes you don't need?'

Henry blinks like an idiot, already blushing in the foreknowledge that whatever he says, he's doomed to say with a stammer.

'I–I've given all my u-unwanted clothes to . . . ah . . . a lady who's a-active in a number of charities.' The girls regard him with mild incredulity, as though they're well accustomed to being fobbed off with fictions of this kind but too well-bred to challenge them. 'Mrs Emmeline Fox,' he adds miserably, in case the name might illuminate everything.

'Last winter,' says the first girl, 'the island folk were reduced to eating dulse.'

'Seaweed, sir,' glosses the second, observing his bafflement.

The first girl expands her pretty bosom with a deep breath, and opens her mouth to speak again, but this is as much as Henry can stand.

'Will you accept money?' he asks hoarsely, as his cat ventures onto the scene, butting her head against his ankles, calling attention to his unshod feet.

The twins look at each other as if this proposition has never been made to them before and they're at a perfect loss how they could possibly respond.

'We wouldn't dream of pressing on you, sir . . .' says one, casting her gaze to the footpath, but Henry seizes on this as consent, and rummages in his trouser pockets.

'Here,' he says, pulling out a palmful of coins, along with the pulverised remains of newspaper clippings and forgotten postage stamps. 'Is two shillings enough, do you think?' He winces at the memory of what else this same sum can buy. 'No, take three.' He weeds out the bright shillings from the chaff of farthings, pennies and debris.

'Thank you, sir,' say the girls in unison, as the nearest reaches out her gloved hand. 'We shan't trouble you again, sir.'

'No trouble at all,' he says and, to his great relief, they trundle their barrow away, their bustles bobbing in accord.

Henry shuts the door and returns to his warm front room, the only comfortable room in his house. On the floor by the hearth lies a handkerchief, screwed up into a ball. He knows without unwrapping it – for he threw it down only minutes ago – that it is glutinous with the slime of his own seed.

Heavily, he sits once more in his armchair, cold in his hands and feet, feverish in his head, itchy in his groin; indeed, his whole body is a cumbersome mismatch of flesh, enclosing, in an unwelcome embrace, a soul that's clammy with pollution. To crown his shame, Puss pads into the room and heads straight for the soiled handkerchief, sniffing at it curiously.

'Whoosht,' he scolds, waving one woollen-socked foot at her. 'That's dirty.'

He retrieves the handkerchief from under her nose, and crushes it anew in his fist. The challenge of washing it is too daunting; he's willing to make the effort when it's his night-shirt that's soiled (one of the reasons why he won't employ a washerwoman), but this cheap square of fabric seems hardly worth the humiliation it would cost him to fill his metal tub and stand there scraping at gobs of his tenacious seed with soapy fingernails. What do other self-abusers do? Simply hand their slimy things into the care of female servants, who must surely despise their masters ever after? Or is incontinence a rare event in the lives of stronger-willed men? Miserably ashamed of wasting good cotton when there are so many poor folk shivering for lack of patches on their clothes (in London, never mind the Isle of Skye!), Henry tosses the handkerchief into the fireplace. Landing squarely in the centre of the glowing coals, it sizzles and blackens, then unfurls into bright flames.

Mrs Fox is dying, and he cannot help her. This thought returns to plague him constantly, in his hours of gloomiest despair, in his moments of unthinking light-heartedness, in his sleep and in his waking. Mrs Fox is dying, and he cannot cure her, cannot amuse her, cannot relieve her. All day long she lies on a chaise in her father's garden, or, when the weather is too wild, on the same chaise just inside the windows of the dismal drawing-room, staring out at the barely perceptible impression she's left on the lawn. She's in no pain to speak of, only bored senseless, she assures Henry, in between excruciating bouts of coughing. Does she want any beef tea, he enquires? No, she does *not* want any beef tea; nor would *he*, if he tasted the stuff. What she longs for is to go walking, walking in the sun; but the sun is fugitive, and even when it breaks through the clouds and shines gloriously for a spell, Mrs Fox begs him to be patient while she gathers her breath, and the opportunity passes. In truth, she cannot walk any longer, and he cannot carry her. Once – once only – he shyly suggested a wheelchair, and she refused, with a sharper tongue than she ever revealed to him before. If he weren't so loath to offend her, he could accuse her of the sin of pride.

And yet she looks at him so imploringly, her eyes grown large in her bone-white face, her mouth dry and swollen. Sometimes she falls silent in the middle of a sentence, and gazes at him for a full minute at a stretch, only breathing, a pulse beating in her neck and the bluish veins of her temples. *The power to defeat Death is in your hands*, she seems to be saying, *so why are you letting Him take me?*

'A-are you all right, Mrs Fox?' he then asks, or some such doltish question.

'No, of course I'm not all right, Henry,' she sighs, releasing him from her awful, trusting stare with a blink of her paper-thin eyelids.

On the rare days when she's stronger, she uses that strength to drive him from her side. Yesterday was such a day, with Mrs Fox flushed and restless, her eyes bloodshot, her mood erratic. For an hour she seemed to have fallen asleep, her lips forming words soundlessly, her breast barely moving. Then she came to the surface with a start, raised herself up on her elbows and challenged him:

'Oh Henry, you dear man, haven't you left *yet*? What *is* the good of it, you sitting here all afternoon . . . staring at the palings of my father's back fence . . . You've counted them often enough, surely.' Her tone was an odd and perturbing thing, difficult to read, poised on a knife-edge between companionable teasing and stark anguish.

'I . . . I can stay a little longer,' he replied, staring straight ahead.

'You must keep busy with your own life, Henry,' she urged him, 'and not fritter it away at the side of a dozing woman. I haven't forgotten how much you dread idleness! And I'll be well again one day – but not tomorrow or next week. But I *shall* get better – you believe me, don't you, Henry?'

'God willing . . .' he mumbled.

'But tell me, Henry,' she continued fervidly. 'Your calling . . . What have you done about your calling?'

It was then that he wished he *had* left, before this moment.

'I–I'm having doubts,' he said, superstitiously afraid that she could hear, as clearly as he, the echo of the words *God damn God!* bellowing inside his skull. 'I don't think I'm suited to be a clergyman, after all.'

'Nonsense, Henry,' she cried, seizing hold of his arm to make him look at her face. 'You would make the best . . . the kindest, sincerest, truthfulest, h-handsomest . . .' She giggled sheepishly, expelling a bright tendril of bloody mucus from her nose.

Shocked by the indecorous discharge, he fixed his eyes upon the fence once more, and struggled to make his confession. 'I–I've been . . . My faith has been . . .'

'No, Henry,' she wept, her breath whistling in distress. 'Don't! I don't want to hear it! God is bigger . . . than one small woman's illness. Promise me, Henry . . . promise me . . . promise me you won't give up . . . your mission.'

To which, coward that he was, spineless scoundrel that he was, Godforsaken Godforsaker that he was, he gave the only answer he could give: the answer she wanted to hear.

'Ah, my sweet one . . . I wish we lived together in the same house.'

Sugar's heart leaps as the words vibrate through her breastbone and William nuzzles his whiskery cheek against her bosom. She hadn't thought such a sentiment from a man could ever make her giddy with joy, especially coming from a portly fellow with irksomely ticklish whiskers, but her heart pounds embarrassingly hard, directly against his ear.

'These rooms of mine are very smart and comfortable,' she says, dying for him to contradict her. 'And private.'

He sighs, tracing his forefinger along the tiger-striped patterns of dry skin on her thigh. 'I know, I know . . .' Tenderly, his hand comes to rest in the lush delta between her legs. (He does this sort of thing a lot lately: stroking and petting her flesh even when his own appetite is sated. One day soon, if she can work up the courage, she'll take his hand and instruct him further.) 'And yet,' he laments, 'so often I have matters I dearly wish to discuss with you and, try as I might to clear a path through my responsibilities, I can't get away from the house.'

She fondles his hair, massaging the Macassar oil into the cracked skin of her palm. 'We've discussed everything now, though, haven't we?' she says. 'The shape of the "R" on the new soaps; the bonfire of the fifth-year plants – I'll arrange to bring the Colonel again; what to do about Lemercier's lilac orchards; winkling your father's senile old cronies out of the London office . . .'

All the while, she's thinking, *Tell me how much you love me, tell me.*

'Yes, yes,' he says, 'but there's more that keeps me from your side.' With an irritable groan he removes his head from her bosom, and rubs his face with his hands. 'Ach, it's a curious thing, but I find that managing a business empire, for all its intrigues, is a damn sight less complicated than managing a family.'

Sugar pulls the sheets up to her navel.

'Agnes is bad, then?'

'I wasn't even *thinking* of Agnes,' he murmurs wearily, as though his family is an impossible multitude, each requiring constant unwavering attention.

'The . . . child?' *Come on, give it to me,* she thinks. *Speak the name of your own daughter, why can't you?*

'Yes, there *is* a problem with the child,' William declares. 'A damned inconvenient problem. Beatrice, her nurse, has let it be known that my daughter has, in her *humble* opinion, reached the age where a nursemaid is no longer enough.' He contorts his face into a burlesque of female sycophancy, and whines in imitation of the nurse, '"I haven't the knowledge, Mr Rackham. Miss Sophie needs a governess, Mr Rackham." Of course, the fact that Mrs Barrett has just had a baby, and wants a nursemaid for it, and is blabbering to everyone that money's no object, can have *nothing* to do with Beatrice twitching for my blessing to leave, can it?'

'So . . . How old is Sophie?' asks Sugar, letting the sheets fall from her glistening bosom, to take his mind off her prying tongue.

'Ach, she's only five!' scoffs William. 'No, let me think: six. Yes, six; she had her sixth birthday while Agnes was away at the seaside. Now, Sugar, I ask you: do you think an infant of six needs a professional teacher?'

Sugar's mind conjures up a memory of herself at six, sitting next to her mother's skirts on a stool, her left foot bandaged after a rat bite, studying a ragged copy of a viciously gruesome Gothic novel called *The Monk*, understanding scarcely anything.

'I can't say, William. I received rigorous instruction when I'd barely left my cradle, but I had . . .' (she winces at the memory of reading aloud to Mrs Castaway and being mocked for mispronouncing words she was too young for) 'an exceptional childhood.'

'Hmm.' This answer is not the one William was after, and he changes the subject. 'My brother Henry, too,' he sighs heavily, 'is a constant source of worry to me.'

'Oh?'

'He's taking the decline of a friend very hard.'

'What friend?'

'A very . . .' (he searches for an adjective which, in deference to Mrs Fox's condition, is not too unflattering) '*worthy* woman called Emmeline Fox. She was a leading light in the Rescue Society, before she got consumption.'

Sugar wonders if she should feign ignorance of the Rescue Society, whose representatives visited Silver Street from time to time, and were always made welcome by Mrs Castaway, and even treated to a 'cello performance by Katy Lester – before being subjected to sarcasm and ridicule, and sent away in tears.

'The Rescue Society?' she echoes.

'A body of do-gooders. They reform prostitutes.'

'Really?' Unobtrusively, she retrieves her shift from the floor, and begins to dress. 'With what success?'

'I've no idea,' shrugs William. 'They teach street girls to be . . . I don't know . . . seamstresses and so forth. Lady Bridgelow got her cook's helper through the Society, I believe. The girl's terribly grateful and eager to please, and Lady Bridgelow says you'd never suspect, to look at her.' (Sugar can't dress further, as William is sitting on her pantalettes.) 'I did consider,' he muses, 'when I was looking for a new parlour-maid, getting one through the Rescue Society, but I'm glad I didn't now. Rose is a worth her weight in gold.'

Tentatively, Sugar pushes William, to shift him off her pantalettes, which he does without demur. Emboldened, she decides to take a much bigger risk.

'And your brother,' she enquires, 'is he in this Rescue Society too?'

'No, no,' says William. 'It's for women only.'

'Some similar society, perhaps?'

'No . . . Why do you ask?'

Sugar takes a deep breath, apprehensive not about betraying Caroline's confidence but about falling foul of William's prejudices.

'I have an acquaintance,' she begins carefully, 'who I see from time to time, when I'm . . . buying fruit. She's a prostitute . . .' (Is that a frown on William's face? Has she misjudged his trust in her? Nothing for it now but to push on.) 'The last time we met, she told me a strange and singular story . . .'

And so, Sugar relates Caroline's tale of the pious would-be reformer who pays two shillings for conversation. William listens patiently, until she comes to the part where the fellow offers the prostitute honest employment in the Rackham factories, which provokes a gasp of recognition from him. When she's finished, he shakes his head in amazement.

'Lord God almighty . . . !' he mutters. 'Could it be? Could it be Henry? I suppose it can't be anyone else . . . I distinctly remember him asking if I'd be averse to employing a poor woman without a letter of recommendation . . . Lord almighty . . .' And suddenly he laughs. 'The saucy devil! So he is a man after all!'

Sugar is pricked by remorse, though she's unsure whom – Henry or Caroline – she has betrayed. 'Oh, but he doesn't lay a hand on her,' she hastens to declare.

William snorts, his head tilted in pity at the credulity of women. 'Maybe not on *that* one, you goose,' he says, 'on *that* occasion. But who can say how many other whores he visits?'

Sugar is silent. In the midst of her shame she feels a thrill of pleasure, at hearing him call her 'goose' in such an affectionate, fatherly way.

'Who would have thought it!' William is still muttering and chuckling. 'My pious brother Henry! My holier-than-thou brother Henry! Ha ha! You know, I must admit, I've never liked him so much as at this moment. God bless him!' And he reaches out for Sugar and kisses her gratefully on the cheek – for what, she can't decide.

'You won't . . . mock him, will you?' she entreats, stroking his shoulders uneasily.

'My own brother?' he chides her, with a cryptic smile. 'When he's in the state he is now? Heaven forbid. I'll be the soul of discretion.'

'When are you likely to see him next?' she says, in the hope that the passing of weeks or months may erode the details of her disclosure from his mind.

'Tonight,' says William. 'At dinner.'

That evening, in order to dispel the gloom that Henry customarily brings into the house, William has arranged for the dining-table to be lit with twice the usual number of candles, and festooned with gay flowers. Seen from just outside the door, the effect is (if he does say so himself) invincibly cheery. And, although the dungeon-like segregation of the kitchen is designed not to permit any smells of cooking to escape, William's nose — grown so sensitive over the past few months that he can distinguish between *Lavandula delphinensis* and *Lavandula latifolia* — detects a superlative meal in the making. He'll do his damnedest to banish misery, by God.

Contrary to her custom, Agnes has announced she'll join the brothers for dinner. A disquieting prospect? Not at all, William tells himself: Agnes has always had a soft spot for Henry, and she's in a delightful mood this evening, giggling and singing as she supervises the hanging of the winter curtains.

'I know it's a tall order in the circumstances, but let's not mention Mrs Fox, shall we?' he suggests, as the minutes tick towards Henry's expected arrival.

'I'll pretend the Season's still in full swing, dear,' Agnes winks at him, almost coquettishly, 'and say absolutely nothing about *anything*.'

Only a little late, Henry makes his flustered appearance, and has no sooner been divested of his rain-spattered hat and coat than William claps a fraternal arm around his shoulders and leads him straight to the dining-room. There, Henry is confronted with a vision of Elysian abundance: warmth, illumination, roses everywhere, napkins splayed like peacocks' tails, and a pretty new maid lowering a tureen of golden soup onto the table. Already seated, smiling up at him through a gaudy halo of flowers and silver cutlery, is Mrs Rackham, dressed in colours of peach and cream.

'My apologies,' says Henry. 'I was . . . ah . . .'

'Sit down, Henry, sit *down*,' William gestures magnanimously. 'We're not clock-watchers here.'

'I almost didn't come,' says Henry, blinking in the effulgence.

'Then we're all the gladder that you did,' beams Agnes.

It's not until Henry has been seated in front of the filled wine-glass, gleaming plates, snow-white serviettes, and candelabrum, all of which combine to cast a bright light on his face, that William realises how shabby his brother looks. Henry's hair, urgently in need of barbering, is tucked behind his ears, except for one lock that swings to and fro across his sweaty brow. Neither soap nor oil seem to have been applied for some time. William next takes stock of Henry's clothes, which have a rumpled, baggy look about them, as though he's been crawling around like Nebuchadnezzar, or become a great deal thinner, or both. One of the pins on his shirt-collar, made visible by a skew-whiff cravat, glints irritatingly in the candle-light, making William want to reach over and adjust it. Instead, the dinner begins.

Henry spoons the duckling consommé into his mouth without so much as looking at it, preferring to stare, with bloodshot eyes, into an invisible mirror of torment hanging somewhere to the left of William's shoulder.

'I shouldn't be eating, gorging myself like this,' he remarks, to no one in particular, as he spoons on like an automaton. 'There are folk in Scotland subsisting on seaweed.'

'Oh, but there's really no fat in this soup at all,' Agnes assures him. 'It's ever so well strained.' An awkward silence threatens to ensue, punctured only by the sound of Henry slurping. *Is this*, thinks Agnes, *the real reason why he wasn't invited anywhere during the Season?* 'As for seaweed,' she continues, struck by inspiration, 'we were served some, weren't we William, at Mrs Alderton's, in a sauce? With scallops and swordfish. Most peculiar taste, the nibble I had. I was so glad it was served *à la Russe*, or I'd've had to slip a plateful of it under the table.'

William frowns, suddenly recalling his embarrassment at Mrs Cuthbert's dinner party two years ago, when that lady's dog threw itself under the white damask tablecloth, very near Agnes's place, and began golloping loudly.

'Society is closed to me,' Henry declares lugubriously, as his soup bowl is spirited away by a servant. 'I don't mean balls and dinner parties, I mean *Society — our* society — the community of souls we're all supposed to be a part of. There is nothing I can do for anyone, no part for me to play.'

'Oh dear,' says Agnes, regarding her brother-in-law with wide sympathetic eyes as the main course is carried into the room. 'But weren't you hoping to become a clergyman?'

'Hoping!' cries Henry, in a scathing tone devoid of hope.

'You'd be awfully good at it, I'm sure,' Agnes persists.

Henry's jaw sets rigid, just in time for a sizzling thigh of braised grouse to be forked onto his plate.

'Better than that tiresome Doctor Crane,' Agnes adds. 'Honestly, I don't know why I bother nowadays. He's always warning me against things I haven't the least notion of doing . . .'

And so the evening goes on, forkful by forkful, with Agnes shouldering the greatest burden of conversation (fortified by frequent sips of red wine), while William gazes in growing dismay at the pathetic figure his brother has become.

Over and over, Henry alludes – when he can bestir himself to speak at all – to the gross futility of all endeavour, at least where his own worthless person is concerned. His voice is erratic, dropping to a mumble at times, then swelling with bitter vehemence, or even sarcasm – shockingly unlike him. All the while, his big hands are busy cutting the grouse into smaller and smaller pieces which, to William's annoyance, he then mashes into the vegetables and leaves uneaten.

'You are kinder than I deserve,' he sighs, in response to yet more warm encouragement from his hostess. 'You and . . . and Mrs Fox see me in a very different light from what I know to be true . . .'

Agnes shoots a glance at William, her bright eyes pleading permission to mention the forbidden woman. He writes restraint over and over on his wrinkled brow, but she's unable to read the lines, and immediately exclaims: 'Mrs Fox is quite right, Henry: quite right! You're a man of rare sincerity, in matters of faith: I know it! I've a special intuition about these things; I can see an aura around people's heads – no, don't frown at me, William. It's true! Faith shines out of people like . . . like the haze around a gaslamp. No, William, it's *true*.' She leans across the table towards Henry, her bosom almost touching her uneaten food, her face disconcertingly close to a flaming candelabrum, and engages him mock-conspiratorially. '*Look* at your brother over there, shushing me furiously. He hasn't a God-fearing bone in his—' She stops short, and smiles demurely. 'But honestly, Henry, you mustn't think so ill of yourself. You're more devout than anybody I know.'

Henry squirms in embarrassment. 'Please,' he says, 'I'm sure your food is getting cold.'

Agnes ignores this; she's in her own home and can eat as little as she pleases – which is very little indeed. 'Once upon a time,' she pursues, 'William told me a story. He said that when you were a boy, you heard a sermon which insisted that nowadays, in modern times, God speaks only through the Scriptures, not directly into our ears. William said you were so angry about this sermon that you starved yourself, and denied yourself sleep, just like the prophets of old, only to hear God speak!' She clasps her tiny hands, and smiles, and nods, thus wordlessly letting him know that she has done the same, and felt, as reward, the breath of the divine whisper on the back of her neck.

Henry fixes his brother with a glare of anguish.

'We are all of us foolish when we're young,' offers William, perspiring freely, and wishing something or someone would breeze into the room and cause half of these damn candles to expire at once. 'I myself recall saying, when I was a lad, that only men without an ounce of imagination or feeling could possibly become businessmen . . .'

This manful confession fails to impress Agnes, who has pushed her plates out of her way, and now leans on the tablecloth, the better to continue her heart-to-heart with Henry.

'I like you, Henry,' she says, slurring the words ever-so-slightly. 'I've always liked you. You should have been a Catholic. Have you ever considered becoming a Catholic, Henry?'

Mortified, Henry can do nothing but churn his fruit mousse into a browny-yellow porridge with his spoon.

'A change is as good as a holiday,' Agnes assures him, taking another sip of wine. 'Or even better. I had a holiday not long ago, and I wasn't happy at all . . .'

At this, William grunts in disapproval and, deciding that intervention can be postponed no longer, reaches across the table to shift aside the candelabrum that separates him from his wife.

'Perhaps you've had enough wine, dear?' he suggests, in a firm voice.

'Not at all,' says Agnes, half-fractious, half-winsome. 'That salty grouse has made me thirsty.' And she pecks another sip from the edge of her glass, kissing the red liquid with her rosebud lips.

'We have water on the table, dear, in that decanter,' William reminds her.

'Thank you dear . . .' she says, but she never wavers from staring at

Henry, smiling and nodding as if to say, *Yes, yes, it's all right, I understand everything, you needn't hold back with me.*

'I hear, on the grapevine,' remarks William rather desperately, 'that Doctor Crane is considering buying the house that was formerly lived in by . . . ah . . . what *was* their name?'

Agnes chimes in, not with the missing name, but with another defamation of the minister.

'I do hate to go to church and be scolded, don't you?' she asks Henry, pouting. 'What is one a grown-up for, with all its nasty disenchantments, if not to make up one's own mind?'

And so it goes on, for another five or ten long, long minutes, while mute servants clear away the dishes, leaving only the wine and the three ill-matched Rackhams. Finally Agnes flags, her head slumping down towards the crook of her elbow, her cheek almost brushing the fabric of her sleeve. The progress of her brow towards her forearm is slow but sure.

'Are you falling asleep, my dear?' says William.

'Resting my eyes,' she murmurs.

'Wouldn't you prefer to rest them on a pillow?'

He makes the suggestion with not much hope that the words will reach her; or, if they do, he's half-expecting a peevish rebuff. Instead, she slowly turns her face up to him, her china-blue eyes fluttering closed, and says, 'Ye-e-es . . . I'd like that . . .'

Nonplussed, William pushes his chair back from the table and folds his napkin in his lap.

'Shall I . . . shall I ring for Clara to accompany you?'

Agnes abruptly shores herself up in her seat, blinks once or twice, and bestows upon William a smile of perfect condescension.

'I don't need Clara to put me to bed, silly,' she ribs him, rising unsteadily to her feet. 'What's she to do, carry me up the stairs?' Whereupon, pausing only to say goodnight to her guest, Mrs Rackham steps gracefully back from the table, turns on her heel and, with scarcely a sway, pads out of the room.

'Well, I'll be damned . . .' mutters William, too flabbergasted to bite his tongue on the blasphemy. In the event, his pious brother seems not to have noticed.

'She is dying, Bill,' Henry says, staring hard into space.

'What?' says William, rather taken aback by this suggestion. 'She's a touch the worse for drink, that's all . . .'

'Mrs *Fox*,' says Henry, summoning up, from the depths of his torment, a voice such as might be expected from him in a public debate. 'She's dying. Dying. The life is bleeding out of her, each day, before my very eyes . . . And soon — next week, tomorrow, the day *after* tomorrow, for we cannot know the day or hour, can we? — I shall knock at her father's door, and a servant will tell me she's dead.' Each word is spoken with sour clarity, each word is like a pinch of the fingers extinguishing a feeble flame of hope.

'Steady on, steady on,' sighs William, feeling suddenly exhausted now that Agnes has removed herself from the fray.

'Yes, death will come like a thief in the night, won't he?' Henry sneers, continuing his debate with an invisible apologist. 'That's how Scripture tells us Christ will come, isn't it?' He seizes his wine-glass and downs the contents at a gulp, grimacing scornfully. 'Tales to excite little boys and girls. Trinkets and lolly-water . . .'

William strives, with all his fast-dwindling forbearance, to keep an outburst of exasperation in check.

'You speak as if the poor woman's in the grave already: she's not dead yet!' he says. 'And while she lives, she's a human being, with needs and wishes that may yet be fulfilled.'

'There's nothing—'

'For pity's sake, Henry! Stop reciting this same verse over and over! We are talking of a woman who's . . . preparing to say farewell to this earthly life, and you have been her dearest friend. Are you telling me there's nothing you could do that would make the slightest difference to her feelings?'

This, at last, seems to penetrate Henry's black shell of grief.

'She . . . she stares into my soul, Bill,' he whispers, haunted by the memory. 'Her eyes . . . Her imploring eyes . . . What does she want from me? What does she want?'

'God almighty!' explodes William, able to endure it no longer. 'How can you be so stupid? She wants a fucking!' He rears up from his chair and shoves his face close to Henry's. 'Take her to bed, you fool: she's waiting for you! Marry her tomorrow! Marry her *tonight*, if you can wake a clergyman!' With every second, his excitement increases, inflamed by his brother's look of righteous outrage. 'You miserable prig! Don't you know that fucking is a pleasure, and women feel it too? Your Mrs Fox can't fail to have noticed *that* in her labours for the Rescue Society. Why not let her feel that pleasure just once herself, before she dies!'

With a crash of wine-glasses and a quiver of candle-flames Henry jumps to his feet, his face white with fury, his huge fists clenched.

'You will permit me to leave,' he whispers fiercely.

'Yes, leave!' yells William, with an exaggerated gesture towards the door. 'Go back to your shabby little house and dream that the world is nobler and purer than it really is. But Henry, you're an ass and a hypocrite.' (The words are gushing out of him now, released from years of self-restraint.) 'The man hasn't been born,' he rails, 'who isn't wild to know what's between a woman's legs. All the Patriarchs and Ecclesiastics who sing the praises of chastity and abstinence: chasing cunt, the lot of 'em! And why not? Why indulge in self-abuse when there are women in the world to save us from it? I've had dozens, *hundreds* of whores; if I've a cock-stand, I need only snap my fingers, and within the hour I'm satisfied. And as for *you*, brother, looking as if you couldn't tell a prostitute from a prayer-cushion: *don't* think I don't know what you get up to. *Oh* yes, your . . . your escapades, your so-called "conversations", are the talk of whores all over London!'

With a guttural cry, Henry rushes from the room, flinging the door so wide that it rebounds juddering from the wall. William stumbles out in weary pursuit and, seeing that his brother is already half-way across the tiled floor of the receiving hall, calls after him:

'Forget about being a saint, Henry! Show her you're a man!'

Whereupon, feeling he's said enough, he steps back into the dining-room, and leans his back against the nearest wall, breathing hard. Faintly he can hear an altercation at the front door: Letty pleading with Mr Rackham to let her help him with his coat, and Henry carrying on like a baited bear: then the whole house seems to shake with the impact of the door slamming shut.

'Ah, well,' croaks William (for he has yelled himself hoarse), 'it's all said now. We shall see what we shall see.'

His heart is beating hard – provoked, no doubt, by the sight of his brother's clenched fists and look of fury, a fearsome combination William hasn't had to face since his brother was a child. He shambles to the dining-room table, fetches up a glass and fills it from the almost empty wine bottle. Then, having drunk the restorative potion to the dregs, he makes his way upstairs, mounting the steps with an increasingly resolute tread, heading not for his own bedroom but Agnes's.

By God, he's had enough of other people's prudish quirks and sickly evasions. It's high time, he's decided, to father a son.

In the small hours of the morning, Henry sits in front of his fireplace, feeding into the flames everything he has written for the past ten years or more: all the thoughts and opinions he'd hoped one day to broadcast from the pulpit of his own church.

What a preposterous glut of paper and ink he has amassed, loose leaves and envelopes and journals with spines and notebooks sewn with string, all neatly filled with his blockish, inelegant handwriting, all annotated with symbols in his own private code, signifying such things as *further study needed* or *but is this really true*? or *expand*. The saddest hieroglyph of all, found in the margins of almost every scrap of manuscript from the last three years, is an inverted triangle, suggestive of a fox's head, meaning: *Ask opinion of Mrs Fox*. Page after page, Henry burns the evidence of his vanity.

Puss purrs at his feet, wholly approving of this game, which is making her fur so warm that it almost glows. Coal is pleasant enough, and slow to be consumed, but paper is incomparably better, if a man can only be encouraged to keep it coming.

Henry is busy now with a fat ledger, a cast-off (along with a dozen more such) from his father, during a 'spring cleaning' of the Rackham offices in 1869. 'It pains me to see good paper destroyed,' he remembers telling the old man. 'I can put these to another use.' Vanity! And what's this? *Rejoice, and be Exceeding Glad*, says the inscription on the cover: one of the many titles he daydreamed for his first published collection of sermons. Again, vanity! With a scowl of anguish, he rips the cardboard from the spine, and throws it into the flames.

The heat flares fierce, and he leans back in his chair, closing his eyes until it abates. He is weary, terribly weary, and tempted to sleep. Sleep would come so easefully to him, if only he kept his eyes closed for another few moments. But no, he'll not sleep. Everything must be destroyed.

Before he can resume his task, however, he's jolted almost out of his skin by a knock at the front door. *Who the devil . . . ?* He glances at the clock on the mantelpiece: it's exactly midnight; time for all good folk to be in bed, even zealous lassies galvanised by the plight of the islanders of Skye. Yet the knocking goes on, soft but insistent, luring him out into the unlit hallway. Could this caller be some vile cut-throat, come to kill him and pillage his house for the few antiquated valuables that are in it? Well, come on, then.

Standing at the door in his socks, Henry opens it a crack, and peers out into the dark. There on the footpath near his doorstep, cloaked from head to toe in a voluminous cape and hood, stands Mrs Fox.

'Do let me in, Henry,' she says affably, as if there's nothing odd about the situation, other than that he is being ungentlemanly enough to keep a lady waiting in the cold.

Dumbfounded, he steps backwards, and she slips into the vestibule, pulling the hood off her head. Her hair thus revealed is loose, free of combs and pins, and more abundant than he'd ever thought it was.

'Go back into the warm room, you silly man,' she scolds him gently, walking straight there without waiting on formalities. 'It's raw weather, and you're not dressed.'

Indeed, when he looks down at himself, he can't deny he's in his night-shirt.

'What . . . what brings you here?' he stammers, following her into the light. 'I . . . I can hardly believe . . . I thought . . .'

She stands behind his vacant armchair, her hands laid on the anti-macassar. Her face has lost its ghastly pallor, her cheeks are no longer sunken, her lips are moist and roseate.

'They're all wrong, Henry,' she says, her voice warm and full, wholly cured of its consumptive wheeze. 'All tragically mistaken.'

He stands gaping, his arms hanging paralysed at his sides, the hairs on the nape of his neck all a'prickle. Puss, still curled up by the hearth, looks up at him in languid disdain, as if to say, *Don't put on so!*

'Heaven isn't a vacuum, or a great fog of ether, with ghostly spirits floating all about,' Mrs Fox continues, lifting her hands from his chair to mime, with an impish wiggle of her fingers, the effete flutter of wings. 'It's as real and tangible as the streets of London, full of vigorous endeav-our and the spark of life. I can't *wait* for you to see it — it will open your eyes, Henry, open your eyes.'

He blinks, his breath taken by the reality and tangibility of *her*, the sharply familiar shape of her face and the look on it: that disarming stare, half-innocent, half-argumentative, which has always accompanied her most heretical statements. How often has she made him feel like this: shocked at how blithely she flirts with blasphemy; worried that her views will attract the wrath of the powers that be; but enchanted by the glimpse she shows him of what, all of a sudden, is revealed as the most elementary truth. He moves towards her, as he has moved towards her so many times before – to caution her, restrain her with the frown of his orthodoxy, while at the same time exhilarated by the desire to see things exactly as she does.

'And I was right, Henry,' she goes on, nodding as he approaches. 'The people in Heaven feel nothing except love. The most wonderful . . . endless . . . perfect . . . Love.'

He sits – falls, almost – into his chair, looking up at her face in awe and puzzlement. She unclasps the cloak at her neck, and lets it fall to the floor. Her naked shoulders shine like marble; the undersides of her exquisite breasts brush against the top of his chair as she bends down to kiss him. Her face has never looked like this in his dreams: every eyebrow-hair sharp, the pores on the sides of her nose large as life, the whites of her eyes slightly bloodshot, as if she has been weeping but feels better now. Tenderly she lays her hand on his cheek; purposefully she hooks her fingers under his jaw and guides him towards her lips.

'Mrs Fox . . . for all the world, I wouldn't . . .' he tries to protest, but she can read his mind.

'There's no marriage in Heaven, Henry,' she whispers down to him, leaning further and further over his chair, so that her hair falls onto his chest, and her breath is warm against his brow. 'Mark, chapter twelve, verse twenty-five.'

She's tugging the night-shirt up from his knees, but he grasps her gently by the wrists, to keep her from uncovering his nakedness. Her wrists are strong, with a pulse in them, a heartbeat of blood against his palms.

'Oh Henry,' she sighs, twisting her body around to one side of his chair, resting her buttocks on the arm of it. 'Stop pussyfooting; there's no stopping what has been begun, can't you see that?'

Holding her like this, her wrists still trapped in his hands, he becomes aware of a strange and delicate balance, an equilibrium of will and sinew and desire: his arms are the stronger, and he can bend her however he wishes; he can fold her shut, covering her breasts with her own elbows, or he can spread her arms wide; yet, in the end, the way they move is hers to decide, and the power is hers to wield. He lets her go, and they embrace; for all that he isn't worthy, he lays claim to her as if he is, as if sin has yet to be invented, and they are two animals on the sixth day of Creation.

'They're all jackals, Henry,' she whispers, 'and you are a lion.'

'Mrs Fox . . .' he gasps, suddenly stifling in his night-shirt. The fire in his hearth has made the room so hot there's no need for clothing, and he allows Mrs Fox to make him as naked as herself.

'You know, Henry, it's high time you called me Emmeline,' she murmurs in his ear, as with one sure hand she finds his manhood and guides it into the welcoming place that God has made, it seems, for no other purpose than to receive him. Once joined, they are in perfect agreement how to proceed together; he moving deep inside her, she clinging tighter and tighter, her cheek pressed hard against his, her tongue, cat-like, licking his jaw. 'My love, ye-e-es,' she croons, covering his ears with her hands in case the distant, nagging clang of a fire-engine bell should distract him from the call to rapture. 'Come into me.'

TWENTY-ONE

n a few ticks of the clock, it will be September 29th, in the year of Our Lord 1875. Trapped with no hope of escape in the House of Evil, a fortnight after the twin calamities of Henry Rackham's death and the unspeakable misfortune that befell her own person under the same malignant moon, Agnes sits up in bed and pulls the bell-cord. More blood has flowed: Clara must come at once, to wash her and change the bandages.

The servant responds promptly, and knows what she's wanted for; she carries a metal bowl of steaming water. In it, soap and sponge float like dead sea creatures removed from their natural element.

'There's *more* coming,' whispers Agnes anxiously, but Clara is already pulling back the bedclothes to expose her mistress's swaddled nappy. Hers is not to question why Mrs Rackham behaves as though the common female curse requires the sort of attention one might give to a mortal wound; hers is but to serve.

'This is the sixth day, ma'am,' she says, rolling the blood-stained cloth into a wad. 'It will surely be over tomorrow.'

Agnes sees no justification for such optimism, not with the fabric of the universe torn asunder.

'God willing,' she says, looking away from her stigma in disgust. How sure she'd been that she was cured of this affliction, imagining it to have been a disease of girlhood that passes when one becomes mature: how much joy it must be giving the Devil, to disillusion her!

Agnes looks away while the only part of her body that she has never examined in a mirror is washed and dried. She, who is intimately acquainted with each and every hair in her eyebrows, who keeps every incipient facial freckle under daily surveillance, who could, if required, draw accurate sketches of her chin from a number of angles, has only the vaguest notion of what she calls her 'nethers'. All she knows is that this part of her is, by a deplorable fault of design, not properly closed, and therefore vulnerable to the forces and influences of Evil.

Doctor Curlew is undoubtedly in league with these forces, and can barely conceal his delight at her fall: and just when William had begun to take a dislike to him, too! All through the Season, the doctor's visits were mercifully restricted, but yesterday, William allowed him to stay a full hour, and the two men even retired to the smoking-room and spoke at length — *about what?* In nightmares, Agnes pictures herself fettered in the courtyard of a mad-house, molested by ugly crones and grunting idiots, while Doctor Curlew and William walk slowly out of the gates. She also dreams of bathing in a tub filled with warm, pure water, and falling asleep, and waking to find that she's up to her neck in cold blood, thick and sticky as aspic.

Exhausted, she falls back against her pillow. Clara has gone and she's clean and snug inside the bedclothes. If only sleep would carry her to the Convent of Health! Why has her Holy Sister forsaken her? Not a glimpse, not a fingerprint . . . At Henry's funeral, Agnes looked and looked for her guardian angel to appear, even distantly in the trees beyond the graveyard. But nothing. And, at nights, even when the dream starts promisingly, she never gets farther than the railway station; instead, she waits anxiously inside a train that vibrates ominously but never moves, patrolled by porters who never speak, until it becomes horrifyingly clear that the train is not intended as a vehicle at all, but as a prison.

'Sister, where are you?' cries Agnes in the dark.

'Right nearby, ma'am,' responds Clara through a crack in the bedroom door a few moments later — rather bad-temperedly, if her ears do not deceive her.

'The mail, Mr Rackham, if you please,' says Letty next morning, hesitating to enter the master's study. She holds a silver tray piled high with letters and condolence cards.

'Only the white letters, thank you, Letty,' says William, not rising from his seat behind the desk, and beckoning the servant inside with a single flick of his fingers. 'Take the cards to Mrs Rackham.'

'Yes, Mr Rackham.' Letty separates the business correspondence – the 'wheat', so to speak – from the black-bordered chaff, deposits the harvest on a small clear area of the master's cluttered desk, and leaves the room.

William rubs his face wearily before he tackles what the day has brought; he's red-eyed with lack of sleep, the grief of losing his brother, the sorrow of wounding his wife, and . . . well . . . the ordeal of inconvenience. Nothing, he finds, causes more inconvenience than a death, unless it be a marriage.

Granted, Black Peter Robinson provisioned the household in double-quick time. Barely twenty-four hours after the order was put in, the boxes of crape dresses, mourning bonnets, jackets, shawls *et cetera*, were delivered, sped through the post by those magic words 'immediately for funeral'. But that was the beginning, not the end, of the brouhaha. No sooner were the servants shrouded in black, than they were rushing about shrouding furniture and fixtures, hanging up black curtains, tying black ribbons to bell-pulls and God knows what else. Then the absurdity of choosing a coffin . . . It's one thing to have had fifty kinds of coat-stand to choose from when furnishing Sugar's rooms, but what manner of man would have the appetite, upon the death of his own brother, to peruse five hundred designs of coffin? 'A gentleman with your own high standards, sir, such as we can see from the quality of Rackham's own manufacture, will see the difference immediately, between the Obbligato Oak and the Ex Voto Elm . . .' Vultures! And why must William be the one responsible for this orgy of otiose expenditure? Why couldn't Henry Calder Rackham have organised it? The old man has little enough to do nowadays. But: 'People will be looking to *you*, William. I've been put out to pasture; in the world's eyes, *you're* "Rackham" now.' Wily old blackguard! First tyranny and bullying, now flattery! To what end? – that William Rackham should be the poor devil who must plough through reams of paperwork detailing coffins and coffin mattresses and wreaths and hatbands and God knows how many hundred things else, to be arranged on top of all his other tasks, and in the grip of brotherly grief.

As for the funeral itself . . . ! If there's one thing he *would* gladly have paid an outrageous sum for, that thing would be a miraculous drug to erase the whole lamentable ceremony from his mind. It was a lugubrious sideshow, an empty ritual to no one's benefit, presided over by the insufferable Doctor Crane in the driving rain. What a shuffling herd of sanctimonious hypocrites attended, with MacLeish – a man Henry couldn't stand while he was alive – foremost among them! Honestly, the only person outside the family who had any *bona fide* claim to be there was Mrs Fox, and she was in hospital at the time. Yet there were two dozen mourners at the graveside. Two dozen surplus dullards and pompous make-weights! The whole performance, what with all the coaches-and-fours, pages, feather-men, *et cetera*, will have cost William, when all the accounts are settled, no less than £100. And for what?

Not that he begrudges his brother the money; he would gladly have given Henry three times that sum, to buy a decent house, instead of the shabby fire-trap in which he perished. It's just that . . . God damn it, what good does it do Henry, to be mourned with so much bother? This mania to bedeck every person and every object in black: what's the point of it? The Rackham house is now as gloomy as a church – gloomier! Servants creep about like sacristans . . . the bell is muffled, so he can't even *hear* the damned thing half the time . . . the whole ritual has a Papist flavour. Really, this kind of doleful charade ought to be left to the Romish Church: just the sort of foolishness they'd imagine might bring a man back from the dead!

Remembered with fondness by all who were blessed to know him – the world's loss was Heaven's gain – that's what William composed for Henry's tombstone, with a little help from the stone-mason. The mourners craned their heads to read it – were they thinking brother could have done better credit to brother? Sentiments look different when they're in cold hard print – the coldest, hardest print imaginable.

William gathers the morning's letters into his hands and shuffles the envelopes, noting the names of the senders: Clyburn Glassmakers; R.T. Arburrick, Manuf. of Boxes, Crates &c; Greenham & Bott, Solicitors; Greenham & Bott, Solicitors; Henry Rackham (Snr); The Society for the Advancement of Universal Enlightenment; G. Pankey, Esq.; Tuttle & Son, Professional Salvagers.

This last one William slits open first, and extracts eight folded pages each bearing the letterhead TUTTLE & SON, PROFESSIONAL SALVAGERS. The covering note says:

Esteemed Mr Rackham,
  Herewith a list of the items salvaged from 11 Gorham Place, Notting Hill, on September 21, 1875, following the partial incineration of those

premises. All items not included in this list may be presumed destroyed or else stolen by unscrupulous persons arriving at the site before Tuttle & Son.

CATEGORY 1: WHOLLY OR SUBSTANTIALLY UNDAMAGED
1 Cat (currently held in custody by our selves, <u>please advise</u>)
1 Stove
1 Kitchen cabinet with 4 drawers
Divers kitchen implements, pots, pans &c
Divers kitchen goods, condiments, spices &c . . .

William flicks through the pages, noting odd items here and there:

Divers framed prints, namely,
'A Summer's Day' by Edmund Cole
'The Pious Ragamuffin' by Alfred Wynne Forbes
'No Apparent Title' by Mrs F. Clyde
'The Wise and Foolish Virgins' by John Bramlett, R.A . . . .
Books, 371 in number, mostly on Religious subjects (Full list supplied on request)
World globe, mounted on brass stand (slightly singed) . . .

At the sight of this, William utters a helpless snort of pity and exasperation. A singed world globe! What is he, or anyone else for that matter, to do with a singed world globe? In the turmoil that followed the news of Henry's death, he thought he was showing good sense in calling the salvagers in, to prevent Henry's house being looted by the undeserving poor, but, having averted that disgrace, what now? Where is he to put Henry's worldly goods? If he can't have his flesh-and-blood brother alive, what use is it to possess his stove or his wash-basin?

William tosses the list onto his desk, and rises from his chair to stand at the study window. He peers across the grounds of his property, to the street beyond, where Agnes claims she sees angels walk. Only drab pedestrians walk there now, all of them shorter and less upright than Henry. Ah, the tall and upright Henry! William wonders if he's a hypocrite to be grieving, when his brother annoyed him insufferably while alive? Maybe so, but blood is blood.

They were children together — weren't they? He makes an effort to retrieve memories from their shared childhood, when Henry was too young yet to erect a barrier of piety between them. Very little comes. Vague pictures, like botched photographs, of two boys playing games in plots of pasture that have long ago been transformed into streets, all evidence buried in the foundations.

Of Henry in later years, the memories are not fond. William recalls his brother at university, walking purposefully across the sunlit lawn towards the library, half a dozen books pressed to his breast, affecting not to hear the jovial shouts of William, Bodley and Ashwell as they sprawled picnicking. Then, jumping ahead, he recalls Henry's poky little house, packed to the rafters with the paraphernalia of religion, devoid of cigars, cushions, strong drinks, or anything else that might encourage visitors. He recalls Henry stopping by the Rackham house almost every Sunday, to pass on all the fine and thought-provoking things his brother had missed.

With effort, William travels farther back in time, and sees before him the twelve-year-old Henry reciting, after family prayers, a discourse of his own composition, on the correlation between temporal and spiritual labour. How the servants fidgeted in their hierarchy of seats, not knowing whether (when it was over) they should applaud or keep a respectful silence!

'Very good, very good,' pronounced Henry Rackham Senior. 'What a clever boy I've got, eh?'

William becomes conscious of a pain in his right hand, looks down, and finds he is pressing his fist against the window-ledge, bruising the skin against the wood. In his eyes, tears of childish jealousy. Echoing in his ears, the words of the firemen who assured him that Henry was undone by smoke long before he was taken by the flames.

Wiping his face on his sleeve, he feels a convulsive tickle in his upper chest which threatens to develop into a fit of sobbing, when he's interrupted by another knock at his door.

'Yes, what do you want?' he calls hoarsely.

'Excuse me, sir,' replies Letty, opening the door a slit. 'Lady Bridgelow is here. Is you or Mrs Rackham at home?'

William yanks his watch from his waistcoat pocket to check the time of day, for he's never known Lady Bridgelow to visit outside the hours appointed by convention. Indeed she hasn't: rather, it's his own internal sense of time that's awry. Lord, he has lost *hours* in daydreaming and melancholy reminiscence! He'd thought he was indulging himself for a few minutes only, but he's been doing it all morning, and here he stands, his eyes wet with tears of jealousy for an act of fatherly favouritism eighteen years past! Is this how madmen and hypochondriacs occupy themselves during the long hours of an idle day? Lord Almighty! Sadness has its place, but ultimately someone needs to grasp the nettle of responsibility; *some- one* needs to keep the wheels of life turning.

'Yes, Letty,' he says, after clearing his throat. 'Tell Lady Bridgelow I *am* at home.'

The following week, Agnes Rackham writes:

> *Dear Mrs Fox,*
>
> *Thank you for your letter, to which William has asked me to reply.*
>
> *I am so glad that you have decided to take possession of Henry's effects, as I am sure they should have been sold off in a most shabby fashion otherwise. I have elected to care for Henry's puss until you come out of Hospital. William says that the other things have already been conveyed to your house, and put where ever a space could be found. William says it is rather a small house, and that the men complained of how difficult their task was, but I urge you not to take the complaints of ill-bred workmen to heart.*
>
> *Is it very unpleasant in the Hospital? I was struck down myself with an awful Affliction last week, but it has passed.*
>
> *I am relieved to read that you deplore the fuss of Mourning as much as I do. Isn't it tiresome? I am to be in crape for three months, in black for two, and then in half mourning for another month after that. What about you? I confess I am not sure what rules apply to your case.*
>
> *Do not mistake me, dear Mrs Fox; I had a love for Henry that I had for no other man, and even now I shed tears for him each day, but <u>how I suffer in Mourning!</u> I cannot ring for a simple thing to be done, like the opening of a window or the placing of another log on the fire, without receiving a dismal aparition in black. When I go out in Public, I must appear as an inky creature, and although the Peter Robinson's brochure tries to make the best of things by stating that Spanish lace is very stylish and that black gloves make one's hands look wonderfully small, I remain uncomforted. I am blessed with small hands anyway!*
>
> *Black, Black, all is Black. Every letter must be written on this horrid black- bordered Mourning paper. I seem to be writing on it <u>constantly</u>, for we are getting an endless flow of cartes pour condoler, and William would have me reply to them <u>all</u> on his behalf, saying that I must understand he is in no state to do it. However,*

I am not sure that I do understand: perhaps he merely means that he is too busy. Certainly Henry's cruel fate does not haunt him as it haunts me. I shudder and sometimes let out a cry when ever I think of it. Such a terrible end . . . To fall asleep in front of a fire and be consumed by it. Often enough I have fallen asleep with a fire still burning, but I always had Clara to put it out for me. Perhaps I ought to have given Henry a little servant as a present. But how could I have known?

Black, all is Black, and I am lonely as the day is long. Is it a sin to crave company and distraction at such a sad time? If no one may visit us but kin and close personal friends, what comfort does that offer to such as I, who have hardly any of either? The delightful Acquaintances I have made in this past Season cannot visit me, and I cannot call on them. They will surely forget me now that I am shrouded in Darkness. It's all right for William – his three weeks of mourning are already over, and he can do any thing he pleases, but how am I to endure the months ahead?

Cordially,

Agnes Rackham.

PS: Henry's puss is perfectly contented, and much enamoured of cream, quite as if she never had it until now.

*

Church Lane, St Giles, not a long journey eastwards as the crow flies. Grateful to be given something warm, Sugar curls her hands around the steaming beaker of cocoa, smiling awkwardly at her host. All around the pale glow of her flaxen-yellow dress, the unlit room is drab and dirty grey, and Caroline, returning to her seat on the bed, almost vanishes into the murk. By contrast, given pride of place in the room's only chair, Sugar pictures herself luridly bright, an exotic bird flaunting its finery at the expense of a common butchery-fowl. How she regrets wearing this dress, which looked so modest in her own rooms!

Caroline – tactful soul that she is – has declared how very much she enjoys Sugar's 'fancy rigging', but how *can* she, when she's condemned to wear such dreary unfashionable things? And what about Caddie's grubby bare feet, dangling over the side of the bed? Are they like an animal's, impervious to the elements? Sugar raises the beaker to her lips but doesn't drink from it, preferring to feel its steam on her face and to nurse her palms against the hot earthenware.

'Your 'ands ain't *that* cold, are they?'

Embarrassed, Sugar laughs and takes an unwanted sip of the inferior brew.

'Cold hands, warm heart,' she says, blushing invisibly underneath a layer of Rackham's Poudre Juvenile. She knows very well why she feels so cold: it's that she's grown accustomed to having a generous supply of warmth from morning to night. She thinks nothing nowadays of having a fire blazing in every room, until the windows twinkle with steam and the rich hearth smell has penetrated every nook and cranny. Once a week – twice a week, lately – a man comes to her door with a sack of dry wood, and so distanced is she from penury that she can't even recall what coin she gives him.

''Ow's your Mr 'Unt?' enquires Caroline, rummaging around for a hairbrush.

'Mm? Oh, good. As good as he can be.'

'The Colonel was in a wonderful humour, for days after meetin' 'im.'

'Yes, so I heard from Mrs Leek just now. It's strange; he gave *me* the impression he detested the whole experience.'

''E *would* tell you that,' Caddie sniffs, happy to find an ugly boxwood brush that's furry with old hair. 'Singin', 'e was, as soon as 'e was back.'

The exhibition of Colonel Leek singing is too grotesque for Sugar to imagine, but no matter: she's glad she can use him again. Maybe this time she'll get him drunk *before* he reaches the fields, in case that improves his performance.

Caroline is carrying on with her toilet, examining the face reflected in her dresser mirror.

'I'm gettin' old, Shush,' she remarks off-handedly, almost cheerfully, as she squints to find the natural parting in her hair.

'Happens to us all,' says Sugar. On her lips, it sounds like an arrant lie.

'Yes, but I've been at it longer than you.' And with that, Caroline bows her head low and brushes her hair down over her knees. Through the swaying brunette curtain, she speaks softly.

'You know Katy Lester's dead, don't you?'

'No, I didn't know,' says Sugar, taking a swig of cocoa. A lump of icy shame forms in her stomach even as the warm liquid passes down her gullet. She tries to tell herself that she *has* spared a thought for Kate every day – well, almost every day – since leaving Mrs Castaway's. But thoughts are no substitute for what she was once so well-known for: sitting all night with dying whores, hand in hand, as long as it took. Despite her uneasy intuition, these last months, that Kate's time must be very near, she couldn't bring herself to visit Mrs Castaway's again, and now it's too late. Would she sit all night with Caroline, if Caroline was dying, and there was a chance to lie with William instead? Probably not.

'When did she die?' she enquires, as the guilt grows in her guts.

'Can't say,' says Caroline, still brushing, brushing. 'I lose count of days, when there's more than a few. A long time ago.'

'Who told you?'

'Mrs Leek.'

Sugar feels sweat permeating her tight sleeves and bodice as she strains to think of another question – *any* question; something that would prove, with a few well-chosen words, the depth and the sincerity of her feelings for Kate – but there is nothing she's particularly curious to know. Nothing, except:

'What became of her 'cello?'

''Er what?' Caroline lifts her head and parts her hair, slick from its attentions and the need for a wash.

'A musical instrument Kate used to play,' Sugar explains.

'I expect they burnt it,' says Caroline matter-of-factly. 'They burnt everyfink she ever touched, Mrs Leek said, to clean the 'ouse of disease.'

A whole life gone, like a piss in an alley, weeps a voice in Sugar's head. *Eels'll eat my eyes, and no one will even know I've lived.*

'Any other news of . . . of the old place?' she says.

Caroline is pinning her hair up now, in a rather slapdash fashion, without a mirror. An oily wisp swings loose, provoking Sugar to rude fantasies of seizing her friend by the shoulders and forcing her to begin again.

'Jennifer Pearce is doin' well,' says Caddie. 'Second in command, as Mrs Leek puts it. And there's a new girl – I forget 'er name. But it's a different kind of establishment now. Not so much of the usual, if you get my meanin'. More what you'd call a whippin' den.'

Sugar winces, surprised by how much this bit of news disturbs her. Prostitution is prostitution, whatever the bodies do to one another, surely? Yet the prospect of Mrs Castaway's familiar walls reverberating with screams of pain rather than grunts of pleasure has, for Sugar, the peculiar effect of casting a halo of nostalgia over carnal transactions she once regarded as loathsome. At one stroke, a man paying a woman a few shillings to relieve himself between her legs has acquired a melancholy innocence.

'I didn't think Mother would dare compete with Mrs Sanford in Circus Road,' she says.

'Ah, but ain't you 'eard? Mrs Sanford's givin' up the game. An old flame wants to put 'er out to pasture in 'is country 'ouse. She'll be waited on 'and 'n' foot there, she'll 'ave 'orses, and all she'll 'ave to do is whip 'im with a silk sash, on days when 'is gout's not too bad.'

Sugar smiles, but her heart's not in it; she sees before her a vision of poor little Christopher standing outside her old bedroom, his spindly arms red and soapy from the bucket he's carried up, while inside, a strange woman lashes the bloody back of a squealing fat man on all fours.

'What's . . . what's new in *your* life?' she says.

Caroline peers up at the mottled ceiling for inspiration, and rocks to and fro on the bed.

'Aaahhmm,' she ponders, a faint grin spreading across her lips as she reviews the men she's known recently. 'Well . . . I ain't seen my 'andsome parson for ever such a long time: I 'ope 'e ain't given me up as too wicked for savin'.'

Sugar looks down into the yellow lap of her skirts for a moment, while she decides whether or not to speak. Her knowledge of Henry's demise is burning a hole in her heart; if she could pass it on to Caroline, the burning might stop.

'I'm sorry, Caddie,' she says, once she's made up her mind. 'But you won't be seeing your parson again.'

'Why not?' laughs Caroline. 'Stolen 'im from me, 'ave you?' But she's canny enough to smell the truth coming, and her hands clench in apprehension.

'He's dead, Caddie.'

'Ah, no, fuck me, God *damn* it!' exclaims Caroline, punching her knees. 'Fuck me, fuck me, fuck me.' Coming from her mouth, it's the bitterest cry of pain and regret, a chant of anguish. She falls back on the bed, breathing hard, her fists trembling against the sheets.

After a few seconds, though, she sighs, unclenches her fists, and folds her hands loosely over her stomach. Recovering from nasty shocks in two shakes of a dog's tail is a faculty she's had to hone over years of tragedy.

''Ow do you know 'e's dead?' she says, in a dull tone.

'I . . . knew who he was, that's all,' says Sugar. The violence of Caroline's response to Henry's fate has rather unnerved her; she'd expected curiosity, nothing more.

'So 'oo *was* 'e?'

'Does it really matter, Caddie? Except for his name, you knew him much better than I. I never even met him.'

Caroline sits up, flushed and puffy in the cheeks, but dry-eyed.

''E was a decent man,' she declares.

'I'm sorry to have told you he's dead,' says Sugar. 'I didn't know he meant so much to you.'

Caroline shrugs, self-conscious about being caught with tender feelings for a customer.

'Ach,' she says. 'There ain't nuffink *in* this world but men and women, is there? So you *got* to care about 'em, ain't you, else what you got to care about?' She rises from the bed, and walks over to the window, standing at the sill where Henry used to stand, looking at the rooftops of Church Lane. 'Yes, 'e was a decent man. But I s'pose the vicar already said that at the funeral. Or did they bury 'im under a road with a stake in 'is 'eart? That's what they did to me grandmother's brother, when '*e* did away with 'imself.'

'I don't think it was suicide, Caddie. He fell asleep in his sitting-room, with a lot of papers near the hearth, and the house caught fire. Or maybe he arranged it to appear that way on purpose, to save bother for his family.'

'Not as silly as 'e looked, then.' Caroline leans forward into the window, squints up at the darkening sky. 'Me poor 'andsome li'l baby pastor. 'E meant no 'arm to anyone. Why can't those as mean 'arm, kill themselves, and those as don't, live forever, eh? That's *my* idea of 'Eaven.'

'I have to go,' says Sugar.

'Oh, no, stay a bit longer,' protests Caddie. 'I'm about to light some candles.' She notes Sugar's stiff posture, the hands still clasped around the beaker, the huddle of yellow skirts in the gloom. 'Maybe even light a fire.'

'Please, not for my sake,' says Sugar, eyeing the meagre pile of fuel in the wicker basket. 'It's a waste of wood if . . . if you're going out directly.'

But Caroline is squatting at the hearth already, stocking it with quick and practised hands. 'I've got me customers to fink of,' she says. 'Can't 'ave 'em runnin' away, sayin' the room's too cold, can I? That gets the Colonel paid, but it don't pay me.'

'As long as it's not on my account,' says Sugar, immediately regretting this mercenary turn of phrase, and hoping only that Caroline is too obtuse to notice. Irritable, wishing she'd made her escape sooner, she hides the beaker of cocoa under the chair. (Well, it's gone *cold* now: why should she force herself to drink cold cocoa – cold *nasty* cocoa? Honestly, it tastes like rat poison . . .)

But her humiliation isn't over yet. Caroline's skill in lighting the fire sets a chastening example, reminding Sugar of her own method: to sacrifice great quantities of kindling, handful after handful of delicate dry virgin wood, until sheer attrition sets the larger chocks aflame. Caroline builds a frugal edifice, with tattooed slivers of packing crate and splinters of old furniture, and with a single lucifer makes it crackle and fizz into life. With her back still to Sugar, she resumes their conversation.

'So, what's it like to be old man Rackham's mistress, then?'

Sugar flushes hot red to the roots of her hair. Betrayed! But by whom? The Colonel, probably . . . His vow is worth nothing, the old pig . . .

'How did you find out?'

'I'm not daft, Shush,' says Caroline wryly, still coaxing the flames through the wood. 'You told me you was kept by a rich man; and then my poor parson said 'e could find me work with Rackham's; and today you tell me you knew my parson too . . . And o'course I know one of the Rackhams got burnt to death in 'is house not long ago . . .'

'But how did you know that?' persists Sugar. Caroline's not a reader, and the sky over Church Lane is so palled-over with foulness that the whole of Notting Hill could burn down without anyone here noticing the smoke.

'*Some* misfortunes,' sighs Caroline, 'I can't 'elp but 'ear about.' She points theatrically downwards, through the floor, through the woodwormy honeycomb of Mrs Leek's house to the parlour where the Colonel sits with his newspapers.

'But why do you call my . . . my companion "Old Man Rackham"?'

'Well, 'e's ancient, ain't 'e? Me own mother 'ad some Rackham's perfume, as I recall, for special occasions.' She narrows her eyes at a memory as distant as the moon. '"One bottle lasts a year"!'

'No, no,' says Sugar, (making a mental note to advise William to expunge that vulgar motto from Rackham advertising) 'it's not the father, but the son I'm . . . kept by. The surviving son, that is. He took the reins of the business only this year.'

'And 'ow does 'e treat yer?'

'Well . . .' Sugar gestures at the abundant skirts of her expensive finery. 'As you can see . . .'

'Clothes don't mean nuffink,' shrugs Caroline. ''E might beat you with a poker, or make you lick 'is shoes.'

'No, no,' says Sugar hastily. 'I–I've no complaints.' Nagged all of a sudden by the need to empty her bladder, she yearns to be gone (she'll piss outside, not in here!). But Caroline, God bless her, hasn't finished yet.

'Oh, Shush: what *mighty* good luck!'

Sugar squirms in her seat. 'I wish every woman's luck could be the same.'

'Don't *I* wish it too!' Caroline laughs. 'But a woman needs graces and 'complishments to rope in that sort of fortune. Sluts like me, now . . . we ain't got what it takes to please a gentleman – except on *'ere'* (she pats the bed-sheets) 'for a short spell.' Her eyes go slightly crossed with pleasure, as she realises she's thought of something genuinely clever to say. 'That's the word for it, ain't it Shush: a spell, like a magic spell. If I can catch 'em while their cock's stiff, they're in me power. Me voice sounds to 'em like music, me walk is like an angel on the clouds, me bosom makes 'em fink of their own dear Nurse, and they looks deep into me eyes like they can see Paradise through 'em. But as soon as their cock goes soft . . .' She snorts, miming the end of passion with one limp-wristed hand. 'My, but don't they take offence at me coarse tongue! And me slattern's walk! And me saggy dugs! And when they looks a second time at me face, don't they just see the grubbiest little trollop they ever made the mistake of touchin' without gloves on!' Caroline grins in cheerful defiance, and looks to her friend for the same; instead she's startled to witness Sugar covering her face with her hands and bursting into tears.

'Shush!' she exclaims in bewilderment, rushing to Sugar's side and laying one arm over the girl's convulsing back. 'What's the matter, what've I said?'

'I'm no longer your friend!' sobs Sugar, the words muffled inside her palms. 'I've become a stranger to you, and I hate this place, I hate it. Oh, Caddie, how can you stand to see me? You're poor; I live in luxury. You're trapped; I'm free. You're open-hearted; I'm full of secrets. I'm so full of schemes and plots, nothing interests me if it doesn't concern the Rackhams. Every word I speak I look up and down twice before it leaves my mouth. Nothing I say comes from my heart . . .' Her palms roll into fists and she knuckles her rage into her wet cheeks. 'Even these tears are false. I *choose* to shed them, to make myself feel better. I'm false! False! False to the bone!'

'Enough, girl,' soothes Caroline, gathering Sugar's head and shoulders against her breast. 'Enough. We are what we are. What you can't feel . . . well, it's lost, it's gone, and that's all there is to it. Cryin' don't bring back maidenheads.'

But Sugar weeps on and on. It's the first time since she was a child – a very *young* child, before her mother began to wear red and call herself Mrs Castaway – that she's wept like this on the bosom of a female.

'Oh Caddie,' she snivels. 'You're better than I deserve.'

'But still not good enough, eh?' teases the older woman, poking her sharply in the ribs. 'See? I can read yer thoughts, girl, read 'em right through yer skull. And I 'ave to say, without no lie' – she pauses for effect – 'I've read worse.'

In the darkening room, as the warmth from the fire begins to spread, the two of them keep hold of one another, for as long as it takes Sugar to regain her composure, and Caroline to get a sore back from bending.

'Ugh!' says the older woman in mock-complaint, removing her arm from the younger. 'You've done me back in, you 'ave. Worse than a man that wants it wiv me arse 'n' legs in the air.'

'I–I really must go,' says Sugar, the ache in her bladder returning with a vengeance. 'It's getting late.'

'So it is, so it is. Now, where's me shoes?' Caroline fetches her boots out from under the bed, innocently flashing Sugar a teasing glimpse of a chamber-pot. She slaps the dirt from her feet, and pulls her boots on. 'But one more question,' she says, as she begins to button them up. 'I'm always finkin' to ask you this just after you're away. That time I saw you in that paper shop in Greek Street – remember? And you were buyin' all that writin' paper. 'Undreds 'n' 'undreds 'n' 'undreds of sheets. Now, what was that all about?'

Sugar dabs her eyes, tender from weeping. She could weep all over again, with a touch more provocation. 'Did I never tell you? I'm . . . I *was* . . . writing a book.'

'A book?' echoes Caroline incredulously. 'God's oath? A *real* book, like . . . like . . .' (she looks all around the room, but there's not a book to be seen, save for the tobacco-tin-sized New Testament her parson once gave her, now blocking a mouse-hole in the skirting-board) 'like the ones in bookshops?'

'Yes,' sighs Sugar. 'Like the ones in bookshops.'

'And what 'appened: did you finish it?'

'No.' That's all Sugar has the will to say, but she can see in Caroline's expression that it's not enough. 'But . . .' she improvises, 'I'm going to start a new one soon. A better one, I hope.'

'Will I be in it?'

'I don't know yet,' says Sugar miserably. 'I'm only thinking about it. Caddie, I need to . . . use your pot.'

'Under the bed, my dear.'

'Without you looking at me.' Sugar is blushing again, ashamed this time of feeling ashamed. In their early years together, she and Caroline were like beasts in a degenerate Eden; if ever the need had arisen, they could have lain shoulder to shoulder, naked, and spread their legs for the likes of Bodley and Ashwell. Now, her body is no one's business but her own — and William's.

Caroline gives her an odd look, but lets it pass. Briskly, she shifts from bed to chair, and continues buttoning up her boots while Sugar squats out of sight.

Silence falls, at least in Caroline's room: outside in Church Lane, life creaks and hoots and jabbers on; two men begin to quarrel, shouting in what sounds like a foreign language, and a harsh-voiced woman laughs. Sugar strains and strains to let go, knees and fists trembling, but nothing will come.

'Talk to me,' she pleads.

'What about?'

'Anything.'

Caroline ponders for a second, while outside, someone yells 'Whore!' and the laughter disappears into an unseen stairwell.

'The Colonel wants more than whisky this time,' she says. ''E wants snuff.'

Sugar laughs, and under her yellow canopy of skirt, thank God, a muffled trickle begins. 'I'll get him snuff.'

'It 'as to be *Indian* snuff, 'e says. Dark, sticky stuff just like 'e 'ad in Delhi, durin' the mutiny.'

'If money can buy it, I can get it.' Sugar stands up, tears of relief on her face and, having concealed the evidence, steals around to the other side of the bed.

'You know,' Caroline prattles on, 'I'd *like* to be in a book. Long as it was written by a friend, o'course.'

'Why, Caddie?'

'Well, stands to reason, dunnit: an enemy would make you out to be a right cow—'

'No, I meant why would you like to be in a book?'

'Well . . .' Caroline's eyes glaze over. 'You know I always fancied 'avin' me portrait painted. If I can't 'ave that . . .' She shrugs, suddenly coy. 'It's a crack at immortality, innit?' At the sight of Sugar's face, she emits a raucous hack of laughter. 'Ha! Didn't fink I'd know a word like that, did yer?' She laughs again, then it fades to a sad, sad smile, as the last traces of Henry Rackham's spirit spiral up the chimney. 'Learnt it off a friend o' mine.'

To break the melancholy mood, she winks at Sugar and says, 'Well, I must start work, dear, or the men of this parish'll 'ave nobody to fuck but their wives.'

And with that, the two of them kiss goodbye, and Sugar descends the dismal stairs alone, leaving Caroline to select the finishing touches of her evening attire.

'Watch yer step!' the older woman calls. 'Some of them stairs are rotten!'

'I know!' Sugar calls back, and indeed, she used to know exactly which ones could be trusted and which had had too many heavy men tread on them. Now, she clings to the banister and walks at the edge, tensed to catch herself if the wood gives way.

'The gathering storm,' wheezes Colonel Leek, wheeling out of the shadows below, 'of disaster!'

Safely on firm ground, or what passes for such in the Leeks' mouldering house, Sugar has no inclination to stand listening to the old man's ravings, or to be reacquainted with his unmistakable smell any sooner than she has to be.

'Honestly, Colonel, if this is how you mean to behave on your next visit to the farm . . .' she warns him as she squeezes by, gathering her skirts clear of his oily wheelchair. Far from being chastened, however, he takes umbrage and, with a groan of exertion, begins to follow her across the room. She quickens her retreat, hoping to leave him stranded, but he pursues her all the way down the passage, his elbows scuffing against the narrow walls, his chair's cast-iron framework rattling and squeaking as he wheels himself laboriously along.

'Autumn!' he barks at her heels. 'Autumn brings with it a rash of new calamities! Miss Delvinia Clough, stabbed in the heart by an unapprehended assailant, at Penzance railway station! Three persons in Derry crushed by a collapsing new building! Henry Rackham, brother of the perfumer, burnt to death in his own house! Do *you* expect to escape what's drawing nigh?'

'Yes, you old wretch,' hisses Sugar, annoyed at him for having exposed, unintentionally or not, her mysterious George Hunt as a fiction. 'Yes, I expect to escape this minute!' Whereupon she wrenches open the door and runs out of the house without looking back.

'And this time, you needn't bother to bring that . . . that old man,' says William, when next they meet.

'Oh, but it's no bother,' says Sugar. 'It's all arranged. He'll be a lamb, you can rest assured.'

They are sitting together on the ottoman in the front room in Priory Close, fully clothed, as decorous as you please. William has no time for fornication just now; on the carpet at his feet lie two small, crinkled sheets of wrapping-paper and half a dozen intricately purfled paper borders, and his final decision must be made in time for the next post. Sugar has advised him that the gold-and-olive trimming looks the best, and he's inclined to agree with her, though the blue-and-emerald has a fresh, clean appearance, and would be a damn sight cheaper per thousand wrappers. As for the paper itself, they're agreed that the thinner one hugs the shape of the soap very nicely, and they've experimented with handling it roughly, and found that it only tears under conditions to which no reasonable shopkeeper would subject it. That's *that* decided, then; he need only choose the pattern of the trimming, and to this end he's looking away from the options for a minute, and trusting that his instincts will guide him when he looks again.

'No,' he insists, 'the old man can stay home.'

Sugar sees the glint of steel in his eyes and, for an instant, fears what that glint might mean for her. Is this the beginning of a chill between them? Surely not – only a minute ago he was telling her, with a crooked smile, that she's become his 'right-hand man'. So: if it's merely the Colonel that's in disgrace, what other men does she know who'd come to Mitcham with her, to lend her a whiff of respectability in the eyes of the workers?

In a flash, she reviews all the males she's known in her life: a dark void where her father ought to be; a couple of giant, angry-faced landlords who made her mother cry (in the very early days before her mother expunged tears from her repertoire); the 'kind gentleman' who came to keep her warm on the night of her deflowering; and all the men since, an indistinct procession of half-naked flesh, like a carnival freak composed not of two conjoined bodies, but hundreds. She recalls a one-legged customer, for the way his stump banged against her knee; she recalls the thin lips of a man who almost strangled her, before Amy came to the rescue; she recalls a slope-headed idiot with breasts bigger than hers; she recalls shoulders thick with hair and eyes opaque with cataracts; she recalls pricks the size of beans and pricks the size of cucumbers, pricks with purple heads, pricks bent in the middle, pricks distinguished by birthmarks and welts and tattoos and the scars of attempted self-castration. In *The Fall and Rise of Sugar*, there are pieces of many men she's known, all butchered with the knife of revenge. Dear Heaven, hasn't she known any male she doesn't loathe?

'I—I must admit,' she says, as she dismisses a fantasy of herself arm-in-arm with little Christopher, 'I'm having trouble thinking of a suitable companion.'

'Don't bother to bring *any*, my dear,' Rackham mutters, returning his attention to the paper trimmings at his feet.

'Oh but William,' she protests, scarcely able to believe her ears. 'Mightn't that cause a scandal?'

He grunts irritably, his mind once more preoccupied with gold-and-olive versus blue-and-emerald.

'I won't be held to ransom by petty minds, damn it. Let a few farmhands whisper, if they want to! They'll be out on their ear if they dare do more than whisper . . . God almighty, I'm the head of a great concern and I've just buried my brother: I've more serious matters to lose sleep over than the gossip of inferiors.' And, with a decisive forward lurch, he snatches up the olive-and-gold. 'Hang the expense,' he declares. 'I like it, and what I like my customers will like too.'

Dizzy-headed with delight, Sugar embraces him, and he kisses her brow indulgently.

'The letter, we must write the letter,' he reminds her, before she gets too frolicsome.

She fetches paper and pen for him, and he dashes off the letter to the printer. Then, with ten minutes to spare before the last post, he stands in the vestibule and allows her to help him into his coat.

'You're a treasure,' he says, the words clear despite the envelope clenched between his teeth. 'Indispensable, that's the only word for you.'

And, hastily buttoned up and dusted down, he's gone.

Scarcely has the door shut behind him than Sugar springs into motion, released from her shackles of demure behaviour. Squealing in triumph, she dances from room to room, pirouetting till her skirts twirl and her hair lifts from her shoulders. Yes! At last: she can walk at his side, and damn what the world thinks! That's what he said, isn't it? Their liaison can't be held to ransom by petty minds – he won't stand for it! Joyous, joyous day!

Her exhilaration is marred only by the thought that she must pay another visit to Church Lane, to inform the Leeks of the change of plan. Or must she? Inspired, she fetches a fresh sheet of writing-paper, sits at the escritoire and, trembling with nerves, dips her pen in the inkwell.

Dear Mrs Leek
My outing this Friday has been cancelled, so I shan't be coming for the Colonel.
(That's all she can think of for a long while. Then:)
There is no need to return the Money I gave you.
Yours faithfully,
*   Sugar.*

For a further ten or fifteen minutes, well beyond the deadline for the next post, Sugar deliberates about a P.S., along the lines of *Give Caroline my love*, but not quite so effusive. There are, in English, only so many alternatives to 'love'. Sugar considers them all, but in the end, the chances of Mrs Leek being willing to convey an affectionate emotion to anyone, let alone one of her lodgers, seem remote. So, as the sun sets, and squally weather besieges Priory Close, Sugar resolves to save her love until she next sees Caroline in person, and seals the letter in its envelope, to be posted when the skies have cleared.

'At the ready!' shouts William Rackham to the fidgeting torch-bearers. 'Very well: start the bonfire!'

All around the towering pyre, batons tipped with flaming tallow are lowered onto the gnarled branches and grey leaves, and within half a minute the smell of lavender is mingling with that of burning wood. The men are all smiles, waving smoke away from their eyes: the privilege of wielding the power to start this destruction flatters their meagre pride and, just for the afternoon, lends a shine to their miserable existence working in these fields for ninepence a day plus free lemonade.

'This lot'll need a damn sight more torchin', I reckon,' says one, wielding his flaming baton like a sword, and indeed the fire shows signs that, unassisted, it might die out rather than engulf the mountain of uprooted plants. A haze of smoke begins to rise into the heavens, adding obscurity to the lowering clouds.

'A hallmark of Rackham's high standards,' announces William to Sugar. 'The bushes are slow to catch fire because they're not quite exhausted: they've life in them yet. But Rackham's doesn't try to wrangle a sixth harvest out of plants that aren't robust any longer.'

Sugar looks at him, unsure how to respond. He's addressing her as if she might yet be the daughter or granddaughter of an elderly investor, wheeling an invisible Colonel Leek around the fields. There's a distance between them, not the arm-in-arm intimacy she'd imagined.

'I once witnessed,' declares William loudly, over the babble of voices and crackle of burning wood, 'a bonfire of plants which had been allowed to stand six seasons: it went up, whoosh!, like a pile of dry bracken. The oil distilled from that last harvest would have been third-class, I assure you.'

Sugar nods, keeps silent, stares at the growing flames. Shivering from the cold wind that blows on her back, and wincing at the heat thrown into her face, she wonders if she's as well-suited to country life as she once fancied she might be. All around the perimeter of the fire, men are reapplying their torches, discussing the progress of the flames. Their accents are opaque to her; she wonders if she's grown too refined lately to understand them, or if they really are as thick as all that.

They are aliens to her, these workers; dressed in their uniform of rudely-cobbled shoes, rough brown trousers and collarless cotton shirts, they are like a common breed of creature, a hardy herd of bipeds troubled neither by the chill wind nor the hot flames.

Sugar is grateful they're so engrossed in their bonfire, as it means they're taking less notice of her, and she yearns to be excused scrutiny today. Her own choice of clothes is dark and sober, unlike the lavender plumage that drew all eyes to her on her first visit here. If she can't be hanging on William's arm, then anonymity is what she craves.

Waves of smoke, teeming with the livid tadpoles of sparks and cinders, are billowing up into the darkening sky; the men are cheering and laughing at the incandescent fruit of their labours. But, as the fumes of lavender grow more powerful, there grows in Sugar a fear that she might be overcome – a very reasonable fear, given her physical state, which is underslept, underfed, and in the grip of a chill she blames on the visit to Caroline's unheated bedroom. Is it better to breathe deeply, getting as much fresh air as possible along with the fumes, or is it better to hold one's breath? She tries both, and decides to breathe as normally as she can manage. If only she'd eaten something before coming here! But she was too giddy, even then, with anticipation.

'I'm not likely,' says William to her suddenly, very near to her flushed face, 'to call on you for some time.' His voice is no longer that of the master of ceremonies, but of the man who lies against her naked body in the afterglow of love-making.

Sugar's beclouded mind strains to interpret his words. 'I suppose,' she says, 'it's a busy time of year.'

William waves at the men to step back from the bonfire, as it has no further need for their encouragement. The fumes evidently aren't having anything like the effect on him that they're having on her.

'Yes, but it's not that,' he says, speaking out of the corner of his mouth, as he surveys the men's retreat. 'There are affairs at home . . . Nothing is ever resolved satisfactorily . . . It's a hornets' nest, I tell you . . . God, what a household . . . !'

Sugar concentrates with effort, thick-headed with perfume.

'Sophie's nurse?' she guesses, aiming for a sympathetic tone, but sounding (she feels) merely bilious.

'You deduce rightly – as always,' he says, daring to stand closer to her now. 'Yes, Beatrice Cleave has handed in her notice, bless her fat heart. She's still convinced Sophie needs a governess, she's champing at the bit to move to Mrs Barrett's, and I'm sure she's not at all pleased to be in a house that's in mourning, either.'

'And is a governess so very difficult to find?' says Sugar, her heart beginning to beat heavily.

'Well-nigh impossible,' he scowls. 'I have my work cut out for me, you can be sure, for the foreseeable future. Bad governesses are legion, and there's no way of weeding them out. Offer a pitiful wage, and only the most wretched specimens apply; offer a handsome reward, and every member of the female sex is galvanised by greed. Tuesday evening my advertisement was in *The Times*, and I've had forty letters already.'

'But can't Agnes be the one who chooses a governess?' ventures Sugar.

'No.'

'No?'

'No.'

Sugar sways dizzily on her feet, her heart pounding so much that she feels her rib-cage shudder, and hears herself say in a weak voice:

'William?'

'Yes?'

'Do you *truly* regret we can't live together?'

'With all my heart,' he replies at once, in a tone not so much sentimental as wearily annoyed, as though the impediments to their perfect union were irksome trade restrictions or senseless laws. 'If I could wave a magic wand . . . !'

'William?' Her breath wheezes, her tongue feels swollen with lavender, the earth on which she stands is slowly beginning to revolve, like a giant piece of flotsam on an ocean too vast and dark to see. 'I–I believe I have your solution, and . . . and *our* solution. Let *me* be your daughter's governess. I've all the necessary skills, I think, except music, wh-which I could learn from books, I'm sure. Sophie could do worse, couldn't she, than learning reading, writing, arithmetic a-and manners from me?'

William's face is distorted in the firelight, his eyes reddened by the conflagration; his flame-yellow teeth are bared, in amazement – or outrage. Desperately, Sugar pleads on:

'I–I could live in whatever quarters Sophie's nurse has now . . . No matter if they're plain; I should be happy, m-merely to be near to you . . .'

Her voice gives out on the final word, a feeble bleat, and she stands swaying, gasping in expectancy. Slowly, oh how slowly! he turns to answer her. Dear Heaven, his lips are curled in disgust . . . !

'You cannot possibly be—' he begins to say, only to be interrupted by a gruff rustic voice:

'Mr Rarck'm, sir! May Oi speak wi'ye?'

William turns to deal with the intrusion, and Sugar can stand no longer. A sickly hot flush shoots up through her whole body and, as the inside of her skull is flooded in darkness, she faints to the ground. She doesn't even feel the blow of impact; only – strangely enough – the cool blades of grass pricking the flesh of her face.

Then, after a measureless lapse, she has the distant sensation of being lifted up and carried, but to where, or by whom, she cannot tell.

PART 4

The Bosom of the Family

TWENTY-TWO

ll through the long night, a thousand gallons of rain distilled indiscriminately from the effluvia of London's streets and the sweet exhalations of faraway lakes are tossed down upon the house in Chepstow Villas. One bedroom window glimmers in the darkness like a ship's beacon, and whenever the torrent intensifies, this lonely light wavers, as though the house is floating off its foundations. At dawn, however, the Rackham residence is unmoved, the dark clouds are exhausted, and a pale new sky is allowed to venture through. The storm, for now, is over.

Still the house and its grounds are steeped in the glimmering residue of the deluge. The carriage-way streams, its fine black gravel floating, grain by grain, towards the gates. Around the house proper, bright water spouts from drainpipes and leaks down the outer walls, washing over windows already as immaculate as they can be. In the garden, every leaf glistens in the glow of sunrise, and every branch hangs low; a spade which was driven securely into the earth the day before leans to one side and topples.

In the subterranean kitchen, a bleary-eyed Janey mops at the puddles which, during the night, have trickled in through the grimy steam-vents, the scullery window and the stairwell. She stokes up the coppers with fresh coal, so the floors will dry and her fingers will thaw by the time she has to do anything complicated with them. Though she can't see the daylight yet, she hears, by and by, the birds begin to sing.

If Sugar were standing in the lane just off Pembridge Crescent, in that bowered spot where she waved to Mrs Rackham months ago, she would see Agnes standing at the bedroom window already, gazing out at the world through the sparkling glass. For Agnes slept most of yesterday's daylight hours away, and has been wakeful through the hours of darkness since, waiting for the sun to follow her example. At the North Pole (if she's to trust what books tell her) it's day all the time, never night, which certainly would be agreeable. But what she can't quite understand is: does that mean that Time itself stands still there? And if it doesn't, does one's numerical age, at least, never increase? She wonders which would be preferable: never changing because *nothing* ever changes, or growing hoary while remaining twenty-three forever. A conundrum to exercise the brain.

Wary of risking a headache at the very start of the day, Agnes lays the North Pole aside and instead moves through her dim and silent house, descending the stairs and padding through the passage-ways, until she reaches the warmth and brightness of the already industrious kitchen. The servants there are not surprised to see her, for she pays a visit every morning lately; they know she hasn't come to complain, so they carry on with their work. Amid a haze of delicious steam, the new kitchenmaid, What's-her-name, is removing a fresh batch of Vienna bread from the oven; Cook is forking sheep's tongues out of their bowl of marinade, selecting only those whose shape and size are likely to meet with the master's approval.

Agnes passes straight through to the scullery, where Janey is scrubbing out the wooden sink, having already finished with the stone one. The girl stands on tiptoe, her rump gyrating with effort; in her endeavour to keep the noise of her grunts and umphhs as soft as she can, she doesn't notice Mrs Rackham's approach.

'Where's Puss?'

Janey jerks as if something has poked her, but recovers quickly.

''E's be'ind the copper, ma'am,' she says, pointing her swollen red hand. Why, you wonder, does she refer to Henry's cat as 'he'? Because Henry's cat, despite the reputation that went before him, is male. On the morning of his arrival in the Rackham kitchen, Cook lifted him up by the tail to check his sex — something that poor Henry Rackham evidently never did.

Agnes kneels on the spotless stone floor in front of the largest of the boilers.

'I can't see him,' she says, peering into the shadows.

Janey is prepared for this: she fetches a dish into which the kitchen-maid has doled a few rabbit and chicken hearts, necks and kidneys, and sets it down near the copper. Puss emerges at once, blinking sleepily.

'Darling Puss,' says Agnes, stroking his back, smooth as a muff and as hot as bread from the oven.

'Don't eat that,' she advises him, when he sniffs at the dark clammy meat. 'It's dirty. Janey, fetch some cream.'

The girl obeys, and Agnes continues to stroke the cat's back, pushing him down on his belly, inches short of the bowl, in a slow rhythm of teasing restraint.

'Your new mistress is coming today,' she says. 'Yes she is. You're a heart-breaker, aren't you? But I'll give you up, yes I will. I'll be brave, and content myself with memories of you. You little charmer, you.' And she strokes him away from his offal one more time.

'Ah!' she sings in delight, as Janey returns with a china bowl. 'Here's your lovely, clean, white cream. Show me what you do with *that*.'

On her last morning in Priory Close, Sugar sits shivering at her writing-desk, staring through the rain-specked French windows at her little garden. The imminence of leaving it behind renders it, all of a sudden, inexpressibly precious, even though she's done nothing to take care of it while living here: the soil has been scattered out of its orderly bed by weeks of heavy rain, the azaleas hang brown and rotten on their stalks, and a slimy heap of fallen leaves is banked up against the window-glass. Ah, but it's *my* garden, she thinks, knowing she's being ridiculous.

Indeed there's scarcely an inch of these rooms of hers that doesn't inspire some nostalgia, some pang of loss, in spite of all the dissatisfaction and anxiety she's endured here. All those lonely hours pacing the floor, and now she's sorry to leave! Madness.

Sugar shivers continually. She doused the fires too long ago, for the sake of not delaying William when he comes, and her rooms have grown cold. They seem colder still for being stripped of ornaments and decorations, and the pallid autumn light, mingling uneasily with the gas-lamps, worsens the denuded look of the walls. Sugar's hands are chilled white, her bloodless wrists poking out of inky sleeves; she blows on her knuckles, and her breath is lukewarm and damp. All in black she sits, her mourning bonnet already fastened, her gloves ready in her lap. Everything she wishes to take along with her is already, at William's request, gathered in the front room for easy portage; the rest he'll no doubt dispose of somehow. Anything even slightly soiled – sheets, towels, clothing, no matter how expensive – she has already thrown out into the streets, for deserving scavengers to find. (The rain will have soaked everything, but with a bit of patience, some poor devil can surely redeem them.)

In the discussion she and William had about the removal, no mention was made of the bed, though Sugar imagines her new quarters will be very small indeed. Will there be enough leg-room, she wonders, for her and William to do all they're accustomed to doing? At the thought of her naked feet bursting out through the windows of a tiny steepled attic, *Alice in Wonderland*-style, she sniggers in suppressed hysteria.

What in God's name has she volunteered for? In a few hours, she'll be solely responsible for Sophie Rackham – *What on earth is she going to do with her?* She's an imposter, a fraud so outrageously transparent that . . . that even a child could see through it! Axioms, dictums and golden rules are what's wanted in a teacher, but when Sugar racks her brains for some, what does she find?

An occasion, five years ago perhaps, when her mother was called to her bedside shortly after the departure of a customer endowed like a horse. Having inspected the damage, Mrs Castaway decided that her daughter's torn flesh would heal without stitches and, even as she was shutting up the medicine chest, gave this excellent advice for avoiding 'bloodshed down below':

'Just remember: everything hurts more if you resist.'

'They say,' says Mrs Agnes Rackham to Mrs Emmeline Fox, 'that your recovery is nothing short of miraculous.'

Mrs Fox murmurs thanks as she accepts cocoa and a slice of cake from Rose. 'Miracles are rare,' she gently but firmly reminds her host, 'and God tends to save them for when nothing else will do. I prefer to think I was simply nursed back to health.'

But Agnes is having none of it. Here before her sits a woman whom she last saw limping painfully through the grounds of the church like a grotesque *memento mori*, causing an illicit susurrus of disgust and pity. Now, Mrs Fox looks in remarkable fettle, especially around the face; the skull that was so ghoulishly intent on disclosing itself is snugly clothed in flesh, the eye-sockets are no longer hollow. Indeed she looks almost pretty! And, let's not forget, she walked in without the aid of a stick, carrying herself with that confidence (as unmistakable as it is mysterious) that there is at one's disposal enough breath and strength to last the whole day.

'You've been in the Convent of Health, haven't you?' whispers Agnes.

'No, Saint Bartholomew's Hospital,' Mrs Fox replies. 'You wrote to me there, as I'm sure you recall . . . ?' But Emmeline isn't sure at all, because to be frank she's finding Mrs Rackham's wits a little on the scattered side today. For example, there are suitcases in the hall, and a mound of hat-boxes and furled umbrellas and so forth, clearly indicating that a member of the household is about to leave, but when tactfully questioned about this, Mrs Rackham appeared not to hear.

'Perhaps I came at an inconvenient time?' Emmeline fishes again. 'Those suitcases in the hall . . .'

'Not at all,' says Agnes. 'We have hours yet.'

'Hours before what?'

But Mrs Rackham has the same response to crude explicitness as she has to more delicate probing.

'Hours before we might be interrupted,' she assures her guest, 'by anything that doesn't concern us.'

Rose offers the silver plate, and Mrs Rackham picks a slice of cake from the extreme left-hand side where, according to prior arrangement, the thinnest specimens are always laid. The slice in her fingers, a survivor of many abortive hot-knifings in the kitchen below, is so slender that the parlour lamp-light shines right through the fruit.

'Come now, Mrs Fox,' she simpers, nibbling her moist little rasher. 'Are you saying you were snatched from the jaws of . . . You-Know-What, by nothing more extraordinary than good nursing?'

Emmeline is beginning to wonder if, during the long months of her indisposition, the rules of casual intercourse have radically changed: what a strange little *tête-à-tête* this is! Still, she'll give as good as she gets.

'I never went about declaring I had consumption. Other people said I had it, and I didn't contradict them. There are more important things to lock horns over, don't you think?'

'Henry told us he most definitely saw you on your deathbed,' says Mrs Rackham, undaunted.

Mrs Fox blinks incredulously, and for a moment seems in danger of some sort of outburst. Then she leans her head back against her chair and lets her big grey eyes grow moist.

'Henry saw me at my worst, it's true,' she sighs. 'Perhaps it would have been better for him if I'd disappeared for a while, and come back when it was all over.' Staring over the railing of tragedy into that misty valley of the recent past where Henry can still be spied, Emmeline fails to notice Agnes nodding childishly, electrified by this apparent admission of super-natural powers. 'I *did* tell him, though, that I'd get better. I remember telling him about what I call the calendar of my days, that God has put inside me. I don't know exactly how many pages it has, but I can feel there are many more left than people thought.'

By this point, Agnes is nearly squirming with excitement. Oh, to have such a magic calendar inside herself, and be able to verify (contrary to the estimate of that horrid newspaper article she simply can't erase from her mind) that she has more than 21,917 days on the earth! Does she dare demand the secret, here and now, in her parlour on a chilly mid-morning at the beginning of November? No, she must tread softly, she can tell: Mrs Fox has that cryptic look about her, that Agnes recognises from portraits of mystics and death-survivors throughout the ages. Why, in a book hidden under her embroidery, *The Illustrated Proofs of Spiritualism*, there's an engrav-ing, done directly from a photograph, of an American Redskin gentleman sporting a 'necklace' of poisonous snakes, and his face bears an uncanny resemblance to Mrs Fox's!

'But do tell me,' says Agnes, 'what have you brought in your parcel?'

With an effort, Mrs Fox retrieves herself from her reverie, and fetches up the heavy paper package that's been leaning against the leg of her chair.

'Books,' she says, removing a pristine-looking volume and handing it over to Mrs Rackham. One by one she proffers them: slim treatises with such titles as *Christian Piety in Daily Intercourse*, *The Bone Men's Folly*, and *Carlylism and Christian Doctrine: Friends or Foes?*

'My goodness,' says Agnes, trying to sound grateful despite her disap-pointment, for these books don't appear to promise anything she wants to know. 'This is awfully generous of you . . .'

'If you turn to the fly-leaves,' explains Mrs Fox, 'you'll see that generos-ity has nothing to do with it. These books belong to your husband – or at least, they're *inscribed* to him, as gifts from Henry. I can't imagine how they came to be back among Henry's things, but I thought I should return them.'

An awkward moment ensues, and Agnes decides she's learned as much as she's likely to learn during this particular visit.

'Well,' she says brightly, 'shall we go down to the kitchen now, and see what we may find waiting for you there?'

More than two hours after Sugar first considers the possibility that William has thought better of the whole idea, and an hour after she's wept copious tears of dread and self-pity, convinced she'll never see him again, the Rackham carriage jingles to a stop in front of the building, and William knocks for her.

'Unavoidable delay,' he declares laconically.

After this, he doesn't speak another word, preferring to supervise his coachman in the loading of luggage onto the roof of the brougham. Sugar, neither instructed to wait nor invited to leave, loiters in the hallway, as stiff as the coat-stand, while Cheesman lumbers in and out, a smirk on his face. Out of the corner of her eye, as she pulls on her tight black gloves, she can see him lifting one of her suitcases onto his broad shoulders, and fancies she can hear him sniffing for incriminating smells. If so, he sniffs in vain, for the rooms have a strangely sterile air.

When the loading is finished, William gestures for her to leave, and she follows him out into the street.

'Mind your step, miss,' advises the cheerful Cheesman as, moments later, she clambers into the Rackham carriage, assisted ever-so-fleetingly by his hands on her rear end. She turns to stare daggers at him, but he's gone.

'I'm so glad to see you,' whispers Sugar to her rescuer, settling her rustling excess of black skirts on the seat opposite him.

For answer William lays one index finger against his lips, and raises his bushy eyebrows towards the spot above their heads where Cheesman is taking up the reins.

'Save it,' he cautions her softly, ''till later.'

The great front door of the Rackham house opens a crack, then opens wider as the servant sees her master and the new governess. The hinges squeak, because this door was installed only last week: a massive show-piece of ornamental inlays and an elaborately carved 'R'.

'Letty,' announces William Rackham augustly. 'This is Miss Sugar.'

The servant curtsies – 'How d'you do, miss' – but receives no reply.

'Welcome to the Rackham house,' proclaims the man himself. 'I hope, no, I *trust*, you'll be happy here.'

Sugar crosses the threshold into the hall, and is immediately surrounded by the trappings of wealth. Above her head hangs a colossal chandelier, lit up by the sunshine beaming in through the windows. Vases of flowers so enormous and so liberally supplemented by green foliage that they resemble shrubs, stand on polished tables on either side of the great stairwell. On the walls, wherever a few square feet are not otherwise occupied, hang paintings of rural idylls in fine frames. Near the archway of the corridor leading to the dining-room and parlour, a grandfather clock swings its golden pendulum, its tock clearly audible – as are Sugar's hesitant foot-steps on the polished tile floor. Her eyes follow the spiral of mahogany banisters up to the L-shaped landing; somewhere up there, she knows, is *her* room, on the same level, thrillingly, as the Rackhams'.

'What a beautiful house,' she says, too overwhelmed to know if she means it. Her employer is gesturing in welcome; housemaids are scurry-ing all about; her predecessor's luggage is stacked up in the hall; all this fuss is caused by *her*, and makes her feel like the heroine of a novel by Samuel Richardson or those Bell sisters, whose name isn't Bell at all but what is it? Her brain resounds with Bell, Bell, Bell . . . the true name escapes her . . .

'Miss Sugar?'

'Yes, yes, forgive me,' she says, jerking into motion again. 'I was merely admiring . . .'

'Allow me to show you your room,' says William. 'Letty, Cheesman will help you carry the luggage in.'

Together they ascend the staircase, their hands sliding along a polished banister each, a decorous space between their bodies, the tread of their feet muffled by the carpeted steps. Sugar remembers the many ascents she and William made on the stairs at Mrs Castaway's; remembers especially the very first, when William was an idler in reduced circumstances, a miser-able cringing creature with a fierce desire to see the whole universe flung to its knees before him. She glances sideways as they mount the stairs now: is this bearded gentleman really the same person as her baby-faced George W. Hunt, who, less than a year ago, begged her to let him be 'debased'?

'There is nothing I won't submit to,' she assured him then, 'with the utmost pleasure.'

'This is your room,' declares William when, having led her along the landing, he ushers her through a door already set ajar.

It's even smaller than she'd expected, and plainer. Tucked under the single window, a narrow wooden bed, neatly made up with a quilt and flannel blankets. A pale-yellow birchwood chest of drawers with white china handles and a hinged mirror perched on top. One stool and one comfortable-looking armchair. A tiny table. For any more furniture than this, there simply isn't the space. Picture-hooks dot the faded blue wallpaper like squashed insects; an ugly ceramic vase stands empty by the hearth. On the bare floorboards, not entirely covering them, lies a large rug, tolerably well-made, but no Persian splendour like the ones downstairs.

'Beatrice has lived very modestly,' admits William, closing the door behind them. 'I don't necessarily mean *you* to do the same — though you'll appreciate there are limits to what a governess can be seen to possess.'

Just kiss me, she thinks, offering him her hand — which, after an eye's-blink of hesitation, he takes and squeezes, as he might a business associate's.

'I can live as modestly as anyone,' she tells him, drawing solace from the memory — the very *recent* memory — of his trembling fingers clasped on her naked hips.

There's a knock on the door, and William extracts his hand, to let the servants in — whereupon, without another word, he strides out of the room. In comes Letty, staggering lopsidedly through the door with Sugar's heavy Gladstone bag, which contains, among other things, the manuscript of her novel. At the sight of the servant pulled askew by this distended luggage, Sugar rushes over and tries to take the burden from her.

'Ooh, it's all right, miss, *really* it is,' the girl cries, flustered by what's evidently a shocking breach of decorum. Sugar steps back, confused: if she's so superior in rank to the household servants, where does she get her deep-seated notion that governesses are lowly and despised? From novels, she supposes — but aren't novels truth dressed up in fancy clothes?

The clomp of a big man's boots and the grunt of a big man's exertion can be heard coming up the stairs, and Letty hurries out of the room to make way for Cheesman. He lumbers in with a suitcase hugged to his chest.

'Just say where you want it, miss,' he grins, 'and I'll put it there.'

Sugar casts a glance over her tiny room, which already seems cluttered up by the presence of one bag.

'On the bed,' she gestures, aware that of all responses this is the most likely to tickle Cheesman's bawdy imagination, but . . . well, there's really nowhere else for the suitcase to go, if she's to have space to unpack it.

'Best place, I grant yer, miss.'

Sugar appraises him as he staggers past and deposits her case, with exaggerated gentleness, on the bed. He's tall, and seems taller for his knee-length, brass-buttoned greatcoat, his wiry frame, and his long fingers. He has a long, pock-marked face with a saddle-hump of a chin, tough wayward eyebrows, curly dark hair subjugated by oil and comb, and a mouthful of straight white teeth, clearly his proudest and (given his origins) most unusual possession. Despite the thick greatcoat, his male arrogance pokes out from him like an invisible goad, for women to blunder against. Even as he turns to face her, one eyebrow cockily raised, and says 'Will 'at be all, miss?' she's already made up her mind how she'll handle him.

'All for the moment.' Her tone is prim, but her face and body are artfully arranged to suggest that she might, in spite of herself, desire him: it's an intricate pose, first learned from a whore called Lizzie and perfected in mirrors: a combination of fear, disdain and helpless arousal which men of his sort are convinced they inspire wherever they go.

The twinkle-eyed smirk on Cheesman's face as he's leaving reassures her she's chosen wisely. She can't hope to erase what he already knows; to him, she'll always be William's whore, never Sophie's governess, so he may as well cherish the delusion that one day he'll add her to his roll-call of conquests. All she need do is maintain the delicate balance between repulsion and attraction, and he'll be charmed enough not to wish her harm, without ever going so far as to risk his position.

Good, she thinks, suppressing a flutter of panic, *that's Cheesman taken care of* – as if each member of the Rackham household is nothing more than a problem to be solved.

She walks across to the bed and, leaning her palms on the suitcase, peers through the window. Nothing much to be seen out there: an empty, rain-sodden swathe of the Rackham grounds . . . but then, she doesn't need to spy anymore, does she? No! All her labours have been repaid, all her careful cultivation of William rewarded, and here she is, ensconced in the Rackham household, with the blessing of both William and Agnes! There's really no reason for her guts to be churning . . .

'Miss Sugar?'

She flinches, but it's only what's-her-name – Letty – at the door again.

Such a good-natured face Letty has – a friendly face. She'll have no trouble with Letty, no, she'll . . .

'Miss Sugar, Mr Rackham invites you to tea.'

Ten minutes later, Miss Sugar is stiffly seated amongst the dense bric-a-brac of the parlour, with a tea-cup in her hand and a servant dressed in the same mourning garb as herself hovering around with a tray of cake, while William Rackham holds forth on the history of Notting Hill. Yes, the history of Notting Hill. On and on he speechifies, like Doctor Crane in his pulpit, the words pouring out with mechanical relentlessness – *which* families were first to build in Chepstow Villas, *how much* Portobello Farm was sold for, *when* precisely Kensington Gravel Pits Gate changed its name to Notting Hill Gate, and so on.

'And you'll be interested to know there's a free library, opened only last year, in High Street. How many parishes can boast *that*?'

Sugar listens as attentively as she can, but her brain is beginning to revolve like a cauliflower in fast-boiling water. The air of unreality is bad enough while the parlour-maid is in the room with them, but, to Sugar's bewilderment, William fails to drop the façade when Rose retreats, and carries right on lecturing.

'. . . from sheep to shop-keepers in two generations!'

He pauses for effect and, not knowing what else to do, Sugar smiles. Would calling him 'William' summon him back from wherever he's hiding, or would that land her in trouble?

'Those suitcases in the hall . . .' she begins.

'Beatrice Cleave's,' he says, lowering his voice, at last, to a more intimate tone.

'I'm keeping her waiting, then?' Another small flutter of panic must be suppressed, at the thought of the woman she has come here to supplant – a woman who, in Sugar's imagination, has metamorphosed from nonentity to fearsomely competent matron – and a canny judge of frauds to boot.

'Let her wait,' sniffs William, glancing up at the ceiling resentfully. 'Her timing in leaving my employ could scarcely have been more inconvenient; I'm sure she can twiddle her thumbs for a few more minutes while you drink your tea.'

'Mmm.' Sugar brings the tea to her lips, though it's too hot to drink.

William rises from his armchair and begins to pace back and forth, stroking the pockets of his waistcoat. 'Beatrice will tell you all you need to know about my daughter,' he says, 'and more, I don't doubt. If she begins to drive you mad, mention trains, that's my advice – she has one to catch.'

'And Agnes?'

William stops dead, hands arrested in mid-stroke.

'What *about* Agnes?' he says, narrowing his eyes.

'Will Agnes be . . . ah . . . looking in on us?' It seems to Sugar a perfectly reasonable question – might not Mrs Rackham have a stipulation or two regarding the upbringing of her own daughter? But William is amazed.

'Us?' he echoes.

'Me and Beatrice, and . . . Sophie.'

'I don't think so,' he says, as if the conversation has veered into the realm of miracles. 'No.'

Sugar nods, though she doesn't understand, and sips the scalding tea as quickly as she can, in between bites of cake. A raisin falls from the fragment she holds in her fingers and instantly disappears in the dark pattern of the carpet. A clock, discreet up till now, begins to tick loudly.

After some deliberation, William clears his throat and addresses her with *sotto voce* seriousness. 'There's something I'd hoped wouldn't need saying. I'd hoped it would be obvious, or else that I could trust Beatrice to tell you. But in the event that neither—'

At that instant, however, their privacy is interrupted by Letty, who ventures through the door and, realising she's not welcome, immediately begins to twitch and tremble with the tics of obeisance.

'What *is* it, Letty?' snaps William, glaring her half to death.

'Begging your pardon, sir, it's Shears, sir. Wanting to speak with you, sir. He's found something in the garden, sir, of Mrs Rackham's.'

'Lord almighty, Letty!' growls William. 'Shears knows what to do with that damn bird . . .'

'It's something *else*, sir,' she cringes.

William clenches his fists; it seems quite possible he'll fly into a rage and chase the servant from the room. But then, all of a sudden, his shoulders slump, he breathes deep, and turns to face his guest.

'Please excuse me, Miss Sugar,' he says – and is gone.

Left behind among the bric-a-brac, Sugar sits still as a vase, straining

her ears to hear what's amiss. She doesn't dare leave her seat, but angles
her head, dog-like, for any words that might leak into the parlour from the
hallway, the source of the fuss.

'What the devil are these?' William is demanding impatiently, his reso-
nant baritone rendered harsh by the acoustics. The gardener's answering
voice is unclear – a tenor grumble, disdaining to compete with the volume
of his questioner's outcry. '*What?* Buried!?' exclaims William. 'Well, who
buried them?' (Another muted response, this time from a duet of Shears
and Letty). 'Fetch Clara!' commands William. 'Ach, look at this floor . . . !'

Several minutes pass before the voice of Clara, indistinct in word but
unmistakably humiliated in tone, is added to the medley. Her muffled
account becomes more quavery the more she's interrupted. '"Clean slate"?'
William challenges her. 'What d'you mean, "clean slate"?' The girl's reply,
whatever it is, fails to impress him, and he blasphemes. Eventually, the
voice of Shears is heard again, just as Clara begins to weep, or sneeze, or
both. 'No, no, no,' groans William, irritably dismissing the gardener's
suggestion. 'She'll want them back soon enough. Put them somewhere
safe and dry . . .' (More murmurs ensue.) '*I* don't know, anywhere out of
the way of visitors! Must I make *every* damn decision in this world?'
Whereupon he leaves the matter in their hands and, with an emphatic
tread that Sugar can feel through the floorboards, returns to the parlour.

'Trouble, my love?' she yearns to say when he steps back into the room,
but he looks so unlike the man whose lips have kissed her belly that she
doesn't dare, and merely looks up at him questioningly.

'Agnes's diaries . . .' William explains, shaking his head in disbelief.
'A dozen or more. Agnes . . . *buried* them in the garden. Or obliged Clara
to bury them for her . . .' His eyes glaze over as he pictures the act –
the servant in her mourning dress, huffing and puffing with a spade; the
hole; the wet black earth closing over the cloth-bound journals. 'Can you
imagine?'

Sugar frowns sympathetically, hoping that's what's wanted. 'Why would
she do such a thing?'

William collapses into his armchair, staring at his knees.

'She told Clara she's . . . "finished with the past"! "Starting afresh"!
"Clean slate"!' Before Sugar's eyes, his incredulity is turning to distress;
he shakes his head again, and on the lines of his brow is written, for anyone
to read: *Is there another husband in England who endures what I endure?*

If they were in Priory Close now, she would take him in her arms and stroke the back of his head; she'd pull him to her breast and remind him that there can be such a thing as a woman who does only what her man requires: nothing less, nothing else. But here in the Rackham parlour, with the loudly ticking clock and the framed horticultural prints and the embroidered doilies and the Persian carpet in which a raisin is lost . . .

'I believe there was something you wanted to tell me?' she says. 'Before we were interrupted?'

He passes a hand across his mouth and composes himself, without the benefit of her comforting arms.

'Yes,' he says, leaning as close to her as decorum will permit. 'What I wanted to say to you is this: It would be best if . . . for the next little while . . . indeed, until I tell you different . . .' He's squeezing one hand inside the other, praying for inspiration to reveal a truth without having to strip it naked. 'It would be best if Sophie were taken care of in such a way that Agnes was . . . ah . . . troubled as little as possible. In fact, if you can ensure that whenever Agnes is up and about . . . that is, *in* . . .' (he gestures vaguely at the house in general) 'she . . . that is, Agnes . . . is . . . ah . . . free to go about her business without . . .'

Sugar can stand it no longer. 'You mean,' she clarifies, 'that Agnes is not to set eyes on Sophie.'

'Precisely.' His relief is patent, but almost immediately marred by fresh embarrassment; he'd like to redeem his wife, it seems, from the stigma of unreason. 'I'm not saying that if Agnes catches a *glimpse* of you and Sophie walking down the stairs it's the end of the world, or that you're expected to keep my daughter prisoner in the nursery, but . . .'

'Discretion,' she sums up, groping her way back into his confidence, willing him to draw comfort from her decisive tone and her mild-eyed, dispassionate gaze.

'Precisely.' He leans back against the chair and breathes like a man whose tooth has been pulled with less pain and bloodshed than he'd feared.

'Now, it's time,' he says, when the clock's ticking becomes intrusive once more, 'that the reins of power were handed over, don't you think?'

In the bedroom of Sophie Rackham, an atmosphere of austere severity prevails. Except for the child-sized bed tucked in one dim corner, it might be a cell within a nunnery – a nunnery founded by an order that long ago forswore all pastimes but prayer and silent contemplation. No picture hangs on the wall, no ornament or plaything is anywhere in evidence; in fact, not a speck of dust – much less a toy – mars the perfection of the darkly polished surfaces. A dozen or so books stand stock-straight in a bookcase the height and breadth of a coffin, each tome looking uncompromisingly difficult.

'I am Sophie's nurse,' says Beatrice Cleave, in a tone that demands congratulation – or commiseration. 'Six years I've been here.'

Hysteria tickles Sugar's brain, tempting her to reply: '*Enchantée!* I am William Rackham's mistress, and I've been here forty-five minutes.' But she swallows hard, and says, 'Miss Sugar.'

'I have been both a wet- and a dry-nurse to this child,' says the amply bosomed but otherwise starchy-looking Beatrice, 'and I've seen the fortunes of this family rise and fall and rise again.'

Sugar can't think what to reply to this, other than to reassure Beatrice that if her milk has dried up for good, she can always get a job at Mrs Gill's house in Jermyn Street, which specialises in large-breasted whores.

'Time flies,' she says, looking around a little more.

This bedroom is, despite first impressions, exactly the same dimensions as her own bedroom next door; it only appears bigger, because there's so little in it. Sophie sits perched on a large, straight-backed chair, a miserable waxen poppet dressed up in the sombre-est, tightest, Sundayest clothes Sugar has ever seen, like a figure in a Temperance Society diorama. She has not been introduced. She is merely the subject under discussion. She gazes at the floor or, for variety, at her shoes.

'You will find,' says Beatrice, 'that in the main Sophie is a well-meaning child. There's no malice in her, although she'd rather stand gaping at the window than do most anything else. You will also find, I hope, that she isn't stupid, although her mind is very easily jolted off its rails.'

Sugar casts a glance at Sophie to see how she takes these criticisms, but the little girl is still studying the wax on the floorboards.

'There's times,' Beatrice continues, 'when she behaves like a baby, and her reason deserts her. Not a pretty sight. At such times, she requires firm handling, if she's not to become just like . . .' Beatrice stops short, even though she's about to flit the Rackham household forever. 'Just like a Bedlamite.'

Sugar nods politely, hoping her face isn't betraying her growing dislike of the woman with the hard black bosom, thin lips and unexpectedly well-educated speech. The Beatrice she'd imagined, when William first mentioned his daughter's nurse, was a different breed altogether – a stouter version of Caroline perhaps, all smiles and provincial heritage, or else a doting, cuddly Cockney, much given to sentimental excess. Sugar even feared a last-minute orgy of weeping and embraces, with a frantic Sophie clutching the skirts of her roly-poly protectress amid lamentations of 'My babe!' and so forth.

Instead, here are three figures dressed in mourning keeping resolutely to their places in a chilly room, and the closest Beatrice gets to holding Sophie Rackham is with her sidelong glance, like a ventriloquist willing a relinquished doll to stay put and not keel over. Rosy-cheeked nurses voluptuous with natural love? Another romantic preconception it seems, got from reading too many novels, doomed to wither in the face of harsh reality.

'She wets the bed, you know,' says Beatrice. 'Every night.' And she raises one eyebrow, a stoical invitation for Sugar to appreciate the sheer scale of bother this must have caused during these six years past.

'How . . . unfortunate,' says Sugar, again glancing at Sophie. The child seems lost beyond recall in the enchanted world of her shoe-buckles.

'In summer it's not so hard to deal with,' says Beatrice. 'In winter, it's a nightmare. If you'll come with me, I'll show you the best place for drying bed-sheets indoors.'

'Mm, yes, I'd be grateful,' says Sugar, suddenly gripped by the strangest desire to slap Beatrice Cleave across the face, over and over, with a piss-soaked slipper.

'It's a small mercy,' Beatrice carries on, 'but at least Sophie is not one of those children who hate water. If anything, she's overly fond of being washed. Which puts me in mind . . .' Her eyes gleam inquisitively as she examines Sugar's skinny build. 'I expect you and Mr Rackham have discussed exactly which tasks you'll be answerable for? *I* have been nurse *and* teacher and goodness knows what else, these past six years, and thought nothing of it, but I can understand that you, being a governess, may not be willing to do . . . certain things.'

Sugar opens her mouth, but finds her tongue momentarily useless; she hadn't imagined, nor did William warn her, that Sophie would have any needs whatsoever beyond tutelage.

'I . . . we agreed . . . W— Mr Rackham and I,' she stammers, 'that I'll care for Sophie in all respects.'

Beatrice raises her eyebrow again, her gaze steady despite the rain of invisible blows she's receiving from the urine-soaked slipper.

'You can always insist on a nursery-maid being hired,' she says, in a tone that suggests this would be a most excellent idea, and that Mr Rackham is deplorably remiss not to have arranged it already. 'There's money pouring into this house, Miss Sugar – *pouring* in. A new front door was installed only last week, did you know?'

Sugar shakes her head and, as Beatrice launches into a nuisance-by-nuisance, screw-by-screw account of the door's investiture, she begins seriously to consider how to raise the subject of trains without appearing daft.

'I'm sure Sophie won't be any trouble,' she says, in Beatrice's pause for breath after a pair of 'swindling' carpenters have (according to the nurse's reckoning) been paid for one oblong of carved wood much the same sum as would employ a nursery-maid for a year. 'I'm sure you've reared her so well that nothing remains but for me to . . . ah . . . carry on your good work.'

Beatrice frowns, momentarily dumbstruck, praise having succeeded where the invisible slipper failed. But, before Sugar can follow through with a pointed allusion to long journeys and precious time, the nurse recovers.

'Come and I'll show you where Sophie's wet bedding can be hung,' she says. Whereupon, as she and Sugar move towards the door, she addresses her first words directly to the child: 'Stay here, Sophie.' The black-shrouded manikin, still perched motionless on the high-backed chair, merely blinks her big blue Agnes eyes, and doesn't even dare turn her head to watch them go.

All the way downstairs, Beatrice speaks of Sophie – or rather, of Sophie's clumsiness, Sophie's deficiencies in posture, Sophie's forgetfulness, the unreasoning prejudice Sophie has against certain perfectly suitable items of clothing, and the great importance of not weakening in one's stand on Sophie and broccoli. As they walk through the sumptuously decorated corridors below stairs, Beatrice shares with the new governess an inventory of what Sophie can be granted if she's good, and what she can be denied if she's 'not so good'. This inventory is so exhaustive that it isn't finished – only interrupted – by their arrival in a claustrophobic storeroom adjacent to the kitchen.

'It was built as a wine cellar,' explains Beatrice, as they're enveloped in warmth and the pleasant smell of evaporated linen-soap, 'but then Mr Rackham ran out of wine, and hadn't the means to replace it.' She casts Sugar a meaningful glance. 'This was a few years ago, of course – before *the change* came over him.'

Sugar nods, oddly perturbed by the knowledge that *she* was that change. Beatrice is removing a cotton bed-sheet from a long copper pipe which, for no divinable purpose, connects one wall with the other.

'Then he got a craze for photo-graphy,' she goes on, folding the rectangle of linen against her breast, 'and for a while it was what you call a "dark-room". But then he had an accident with some poison, and the smell never went no matter how much the floors were sluiced out, and then a man came and said it was the fault of damp, and so this boiler pipe was passed through . . .' She halts in mid-explication, her eyes narrowing. 'Hello, what's this?'

On the floor, in one shadowy corner, lies a heap of what appears to be garbage. It proves, on closer inspection, to be wet and muddy papers, in the form of notebooks or diaries.

'I must have a word with whoever's responsible,' she sniffs. 'This room is not a cesspit.'

'Ah, but you have a train to catch,' blurts Sugar. 'Don't you? Please, leave the matter in my hands.' And, like an answered prayer, a nearby grandfather clock goes *bong, bong, bong* and *bong* again.

When Beatrice Cleave is finally gone, and her belongings have been removed from the hallway, and the servants are no longer standing at the windows watching the carriage dwindle out of sight, Sugar returns, alone, to the bedroom where Sophie was told to 'stay'. What else can she do?

She'd expected William to seek her out after the nurse's departure and give her a more fulsome welcome, but he's melted away, and she can hardly go poking her nose into all the rooms of the house in search of him, can she? No. With every carpeted stair she mounts, she appreciates ever more sharply that her brief hour of grace is over. She's not a visitor here anymore, but . . . a governess.

Even as she opens the bedroom door, she's preparing for a dismal sight, a sight to sink her heart and send a shiver down her spine: the sight of Sophie Rackham sitting bolt upright on that stiff-backed chair, like an eerie museum specimen not quite killed by taxidermy, rigid with fear and mistrust, her huge eyes staring straight into Sugar's soul, and expecting . . . what?

But this, when Sugar enters, is not the sight that greets her. Little Sophie, although she most assuredly did stay where she was told, has found the long wait far *too* long, and fallen asleep in her seat. Her posture, so maligned by Beatrice, is indisputably poor just now, as she lies slumped and skew-whiff, her head lolling against one shoulder, her skirts rucked and wrinkled, one arm lying limp in her lap and the other dangling in space. A wisp of her blonde hair flutters as she breathes and, clearly evident on the black material of her tightly-buttoned bodice, there's a patch that's blacker than the rest, from drool.

Sugar approaches softly, and kneels, so that her face is level with the slumbering child's. In sleep, with cheeks puffy and lower lip protruding, it's obvious that Sophie's face has failed to replicate Agnes's beauty; as soon as those big china-blue eyes are shut, there's nothing of the mother left, only William's chin and brow and nose. How sad, that unless the Rackham fortune intervenes, spinsterhood can already, at the age of six, be foretold in this girl's flesh and bones! Her torso, too, is William's, puppy-ish enough now, but carrying the seeds of stockiness. *Why not let her sleep?* suggests a tempting voice of cowardice and compassion. *Let her sleep for ever.* But Sugar, knowing she must wake her, kneels and waits, wishing that the proximity of her breath would somehow be enough to do the job.

'Sophie?' she whispers.

With a wet snortle, the child begins to convulse into consciousness and, for one priceless instant, the universe offers Sugar a gift: the chance to be the first thing that a newly-woken spirit encounters, before there's any time for fear or prejudice. Sophie is blinking in confusion, too befuddled to recognise whose face is hovering near – a far less fundamental concern, for someone freshly yanked out of the womb of dreams, than how this world compares to the one she's left. What's it like, this waking life? No sooner has it dawned on the girl that she's most likely committed some terrible sin, and can expect to be punished, than Sugar reaches out a hand and lays it gently on her shoulder, saying,

'It's all right, Sophie. You fell asleep, that's all.'

Stiff and sore, Sophie allows herself to be helped off the chair, and Sugar decides, then and there, that being a governess is not going to be as hard as she feared. Flushed with relief, she makes her first mistake.

'We've met before,' she says. 'Do you remember?'

Sophie, striving with all her might to compose herself into that strange new animal, a pupil, looks perplexed. Here's the inaugural question from her governess, and it's a puzzler – maybe even a trick, to catch her out!

'No, Miss,' she admits. Her voice is Agnes's exactly, but softer and less finely modulated – still musical, but more a mournful little bell than an oboe d'amore.

'In church,' Sugar prompts her. 'I looked at you, and you looked back.' (Even as she says it, it does sound rather a flimsy experience.)

Sophie bites her bottom lip. A hundred times her nurse has told her she ought to pay more attention in church, and here's the retribution!

'Don't 'member, Miss.' Words spoken in infant despair, in the shadow of a dunce's cap.

'No matter, no matter,' says Sugar, and raises herself off her knees. Only when they're both standing up straight does the scale of things become disconcertingly obvious: Sophie's head scarcely reaches her waist.

'Well now,' Sugar presses on, making her second mistake, 'I'm so glad Beatrice is gone, aren't you?' Her tone, she hopes, is playfully conspiratorial, like one child to another, to leave no doubt where her sympathies lie.

Sophie looks up at her – such a distance between their faces! – and pleads, 'I don't know, Miss.' Her brow is creased with anxiety; her tiny hands are clasped tight in front of her skirts, and this queer new world, now that she's fully awake, is a dangerous place after all.

What to do? What to do? Bailing up, from the well of books she's read, whatever she can find on the subject of children, Sugar asks, 'Do you have a doll?' An inane question, she reckons, but it lights an unexpected spark in Sophie's eyes.

'In the nursery, Miss.'

'The nursery?' Sugar is reminded with a jolt that she hasn't been there. The very place where she'll be teaching Sophie, and she's yet to see it! Granted, in Beatrice's lecture on the proper maintenance of the Rackham child, the nursery *was* frequently referred to, but somehow Beatrice ended up leaving the house without having gone so far as to show the governess 'what I expect you'll be calling the school-room now'. Maybe she would have, if only Sugar hadn't mentioned trains and sent her scurrying.

'Take me there, then,' she says, offering, after a moment's hesitation, her hand. Will it be accepted? To her great relief, Sophie takes hold.

At the first touch of the child's warm fingers, Sugar feels something she would never have guessed she *could* feel: the thrill of flesh against unfamiliar flesh. She, who has been fingered by a thousand strangers, and grown insensible to all but the crudest probings, now experiences a tingle, almost a shock, of tactile initiation; and with that shock comes shyness. How gross her own fingers are in comparison with Sophie's! Is the child disgusted by the cracked and horny surface of Sugar's skin? How snugly or loosely should their hands clasp? And who will decide when they let go?

'Lead the way,' she says, as they step out.

Once again, the Rackham house seems deserted, less a home than a hushed emporium of clocks, mirrors, lights, paintings, and a dozen different wallpapers. The nursery is tucked away in the tail of the landing's L-shape, and on the way to it Sugar and Sophie pass several closed doors.

'That's Father's thinking room,' whispers Sophie, unasked.

'And the next one?'

'I don't know, Miss.'

'And what about the first door, back there?'

'That's where Mother lives.'

The nursery, when they step inside it, is quite a heartening sight, at least by contrast with Sophie's bedroom. It's a fair size, with a larger than average window, an assortment of cabinets and trunks, a writing desk, and some toys – indeed, more toys than Sugar ever possessed. Over here are some painted wooden animals for a Noah's ark (the ark itself not in evidence), over there is a crudely-fashioned but generously proportioned doll's house with a few bits of dolls' furniture in it. In the far corner, a rocking horse with a hand-knitted 'saddle', and a stack of gaily-coloured baskets filled with knick-knacks too small to identify. A dull green writing-slate, unsullied by chalk, stands ready on four wooden legs, purchased specially for this new chapter in Sophie Rackham's life.

'And your doll?'

Sophie opens a trunk, and fetches out a flaccid rag-doll with a dark brown head, a grinning nigger on whose threadbare cotton chest is embroidered the word 'Twinings'. He could hardly be more hideous, but Sophie handles him tenderly, with a hint of sadness, as if conceding that he's ever-so-slightly less alive than she'd like to think he is.

'My grandpapa gave him to me,' she explains. 'He's supposed to sit on top of an elephant, but the tea weren't empty yet.'

Sugar ponders this for a second or two, then lets it go.

'Why do you keep him in a trunk?' she asks. 'Wouldn't you like to take him to bed?'

'Nurse says I'm not to have a smelly old doll in my good clean room, Miss,' Sophie replies, a note of grievance creeping into her stoicism. 'And when he's in here, she don't like to look at his black face.'

This is the opportunity Sugar has been waiting for, to redeem herself.

'But it must be very gloomy and dreadful inside that trunk,' she protests. 'And surely he must get lonely!'

Sophie's eyes have grown larger even than normal; she's teetering on the brink of trust. 'I don't know, Miss,' she says.

Again Sugar kneels, on the pretext of examining the doll more closely, but really to allow Sophie to read her face. 'We'll find a better use for this trunk,' she says, helpfully tucking one of the doll's dangling legs into the crook of Sophie's arm. 'Now, what's your doll's name?'

Another puzzler. 'I don't know, Miss. My grandpapa never said.'

'So what do you call him?'

'I don't call him any name, Miss.' Sophie chews her lip, in case such rudeness, even to a creature made of biscuit and rag, warrants a scolding.

'I think you should give him a name,' declares Sugar. 'A handsome English name. And he may live in *your* room from now on.'

For just a few seconds longer, Sophie looks doubtful, but when the extraordinary new governess nods her head in reassurance, she draws a deep breath and cries,

'Thank you, Miss!'

In joy, she's not so plain after all.

A few dozen streets away, while Sophie is introducing Miss Sugar, item by item, to the wonders of her nursery, Emmeline Fox is sitting half-way up her stairs, taking a rest before continuing. She's done rather a lot today, for a woman still not wholly well, and it's a kind of bliss to sit here, one's head nuzzled in the carpeted hollow of a stair, breathing in silence.

Is there still a wheeze in her windpipe? Perhaps a slight one. But she has definitely, as Mrs Rackham put it, escaped the jaws of You-Know-What. How sweet it is, and how tiresome too, to feel the ache of exhaustion in one's legs, the hard edge of a stair against one's shoulder-blades, the pulse of her heart in the veins of one's temples. She has been given this body, this poor vehicle of bone and sinew, for a while longer; pray God she uses it well.

The visit to Mrs Rackham was awfully tiring, especially the walk home, carrying the cat (a solid creature, no featherweight!) in its wicker basket through the streets of Notting Hill. No doubt her decision to do without a cab, or even her servant Sarah, will keep the gossips prattling – all the more so, if any of them should learn the truth, that Sarah has gone back to prostitution, her 'ailing grandfather' having landed himself calamitously in debt at horse races throughout the Season.

Another girl, likewise from the Rescue Society's stable of rehabilitated strumpets, is supposed to be starting next Wednesday, but Emmeline wants to tidy the house a little before then, so as not to discourage the girl at the outset of a respectable career. So, that's what she's doing now: getting things in order. Well, not *right* now, of course; right now she's sitting halfway up the stairs, watching the passing of ghostly pedestrians through the frosted glass of the front door below.

The delivery of Henry's worldly goods, especially since it was effected while she was in Saint Bartholomew's and unable to supervise the workmen, has pushed this little house of hers over a line – the line, to be frank, between clutter and chaos. There's not a room where there's enough free space remaining for one to . . . well, swing a cat, as they say. Certainly Puss has, since his arrival, been most intrigued and confused, roaming up and down the stairs, in one door and out the other, reacquainting himself with his master's furniture and his master's contraptions, all stacked and crammed in unfamiliar places. Of particular concern to him is the bewildering phenomenon of Henry's bed, which stands upright against the wall of the sitting-room, its mattress slumped drunkenly against the iron framework, no use to man or beast. At least half a dozen times since Emmeline released him into her house, he has attempted to draw this to her attention, in the clear hope that she'll put it right.

Emmeline has to admit that her house looks more like a Cheapside junk shop now. In the kitchen, there are two of everything: two stoves, two crockery cupboards, two ice-pails, two stock-pots, two kettles, two bain-maries, and so on and so on – even two spice racks, Henry's selection almost identical to hers. All very unfortunate, given that she's no better at cooking than she ever was, and even less inclined to improve.

Throughout the house, chairs and stools are stacked two- and three-high, some precariously, others inextricably, but by far the greatest source of muddle is the superabundance of books: Henry's volumes added to her own. In every room, and in the passages as well, great piles of them, some stacked logically, sandcastle-style, from large up to small, others stacked the other way round, tempting gravity and the caressing snout of Henry's cat. Nor can she blame the men from the salvage company for the haphazard stacking: it was *she* who removed these books from their boxes, only to see what had survived the fire, and what hadn't. Her skills in the storage of physical objects, however, leave a lot to be desired, and already there have been several spills. The never-particularly-stable tower of New Testaments, which the man from the Bible Dissemination Society never did come back for, has sprawled all over the landing, and some unlucky exemplars have even fallen through the banisters onto the floor below.

Somewhat neater-looking, but more disheartening, are the bags of clothing. Not Emmeline's usual store of uncollected donations – the woollen gloves and darned socks and carefully mended bedding destined for the destitute of London and beyond – but Henry's clothes. Three bags full, lying unopened in her bedroom, tied with string and stamped *Tuttle & Son*.

Puss is dawdling around her skirts, miaowing, doing his best to butt her legs through the voluminous barrier of her skirts. Before he goes so far as to crawl underneath, Emmeline gets to her feet. How tired she is! It's only afternoon, but she yearns to sleep. Not a doze, either, but a long, dark sleep to separate one day from the next. Impiously, she wishes God would relax the rules just this once and allow night to fall a few hours prematurely. The imbalance could be made up next day, couldn't it, with a few extra hours of light?

Stiff – so stiff that she almost wants her walking stick again – Emmeline shuffles to the kitchen, assuming that Puss, having taken the measure of the place, is now ready for some food.

'Is that what you want, Puss?' she asks, as he hesitates on the kitchen threshold, sniffing at the dirty bristles of a broom.

What to give him? Now that she's installed him in her home, she's going to have to put some serious thought into how to persuade him to stay. An inspection of her cupboards and cool-chests confirms that, as well as having no cream, she has no raw meat, for she hasn't been cooking lately, preferring to take her meals in restaurants (yes, deplorable, she knows: all those gaunt-cheeked families eking out their sustenance from scraps of mutton and crusts of bread, and here's she, dining like a courtesan! But without Sarah's help she just hasn't been up to the challenge of cooking, and anyway, the stove that's connected to the flue is the one that's now out of reach.) Rather a shame she can't take Puss with her to a restaurant, and order his dish along with hers . . . precisely the kind of common-sense solution that people can always be relied upon to reject out of hand. Ah! how English society hates pragmatism! Not the sort of pragmatism that gets factories built, but the sort that makes the life of its citizens more agreeable! Something to be discussed with Henry, when next she . . .

With a sigh, she opens another cupboard and extracts a hunk of Leicester cheese, her own staple when the maid's away. Puss yowls encouragingly.

'I don't suppose cats eat cheese?' she says, tossing a small piece between his paws, but he pounces on the morsel and devours it with great relish. Another preconception disproved; she learns something new each day. Leaning against the superfluous oven, she feeds Puss the cheese, fragment by fragment, until he's had enough, or is too thirsty to go on. She leads him to a dish of water, which he contemplates without enthusiasm; tomorrow she'll buy him some milk.

She ought to eat something herself; she's had nothing today except bread, some cheese, tea, and Mrs Rackham's fruit-cake. Her normal appetites have yet to be restored, and she still hasn't recovered from the unpleasant discovery, on her return from hospital, of a box marked 'PERISHABLES' whose contents, after a brief sojourn at the warehouse of Tuttle & Son and then a rather longer one here, were perished indeed.

She leans across a jumble of copper saucepans to open another cupboard, where she thinks she might have left a tin of biscuits. Instead, she finds another cache of books. A few minutes later, or maybe fifteen, having leafed through Mrs Rundell's *New System of Domestic Cookery*, and stared a while at the inscription on its flyleaf, *To my valued Friend Henry Rackham, Christmas 1874*, she climbs the stairs, step by painful step.

On the landing, very near the door to her bedroom, she spies two small dark-brown objects which appear from a distance to be cigars, but which prove at closer quarters to be faeces, and very smelly too. Emmeline closes her eyes and feels tears leak out; she cannot, cannot, *cannot* walk up and down the stairs again. Instead, she fetches a handkerchief from her bedside, from a box full of them, belonging to those days not so long ago, when she could be seized, at any time of day or night, with an irresistible desire to cough blood. Gingerly, she wraps the cat's mess in the soft cotton, folding it round and round until it's a kind of pomander. Parceled thus, it can surely wait till morning.

In her shambles of a bedroom, she begins to undress, then, when she's half-unbuttoned, suddenly realises why she can't locate her night-dress. After a rather too vigorous attempt this morning to scrub an old blood-stain from it, she was obliged to mend a rip in the fabric, and – Lord help her sieve-like memory – she's left it downstairs, slung over the back of a chair. *Cannot, cannot, cannot.* Just this once, she'll have to sleep in her under-things.

She struggles out of her dress and petticoat, clumsy-fingered with fatigue, but, once reduced to her chemise and pantalettes, becomes belatedly aware that she's clammy with sweat, plagued by itches in her armpits, groin, and the cleft of her behind. Swaying on her feet, she briefly considers praying for the strength to go downstairs and dispose of the cat dung, fetch her night-dress, and boil some water for a wash, but decides that this would be an unworthy claim on God's attention. Instead, she strips off her remaining clothing and, with a gasp of relief, crawls naked and feverish between the sheets.

Only the very wicked or the very sick, she thinks, *go to bed in the daytime.* Tomorrow she must conserve her energies better, and not overtax this body which she so very nearly lost.

The sheets are heavenly against her flesh, sweet numbness is spreading through her limbs, and although the sanction of nightfall is still a long way off, she feels herself drifting into sleep, only vaguely aware of a gentle commotion next to her in the bed which, only when she wakes next morning, she will discover to be Puss, by then nestled, in a state of perfect contentment, at her feet.

TWENTY-THREE

ugar's bed, just right for the woman who slept in it previously, is too small for her. During her long first night in the Rackham house, during a sleep that's tainted by the fitful barking of a distant dog, Sugar dreams all sorts of queer things. A while before dawn, she tosses one time too many, and a gangly naked leg swings out from under the sheets, dangling in the chill air, before bumping against the flank of her suitcase. In Sugar's dream, this is translated into the callused fingers of a man, seizing her calf, crawling up her flesh towards her groin.

'You needn't shiver any more,' says Mrs Castaway. 'A kind gentleman has come to keep you warm.'

Sugar tries to curl into a ball, bumps her ankle on an unfamiliar bedpost, and wakes.

For a few moments she's quite lost in her new room, this dark little chamber high above the ground, having grown so used to the spacious ground-floor quarters in Priory Close, always gently illuminated by the street-light. She could almost be back in her old bedroom at Mrs Castaway's, except that *that* was a good deal bigger than this. Also, there's a peculiar smell under the bed, an earthy, damp smell, that reminds her of the rot in the first house she ever lived in — the hovel in Church Lane.

Sugar leans over the edge of the bed and scrabbles underneath, and her fingers brush against the filthy pile of Agnes's diaries. Ah yes, now she remembers. No sooner did the front door shut on Beatrice Cleave yester-day than she crept back down to the store-room and snatched the diaries while the snatching was good. Then, having stashed them under her bed, she hurried to attend to Sophie.

Ah, Sophie.

Sugar fumbles for a lucifer and lights two candles on her ugly yellow dresser, and rubs the sleep out of her eyes. *I am a governess*, she tells herself, as the world flickers into focus. Immediately she's conscious of a gripe in her innards, then a sharp stab of pain. She's eaten almost nothing for days, nor moved her bowels. Anxiety has frozen her. Now, she's thawing out, and her belly is full of noises.

The clock says half past five. How long has she slept? Quite a while; she went to bed last night almost immediately after the child did, at the infant hour of seven. She expected William to come and join her then, and was determined to stay awake – she even considered giving her clitoris some attention to prepare herself – but within minutes of laying her head on the strange-smelling pillow she was gone. If William did come to see her – and there's no evidence that he did – he must have left her sleeping.

In her memory, Sugar retrieves the events of yesterday in reverse order from Sophie's bedtime – Sophie falling asleep, right before her eyes, as though obeying a command. Or perhaps only pretending? Sugar, too, knows how to fake unconsciousness, if there's something to be gained from it . . .

She's a little actress, I warn you, was one of Beatrice's parting wisdoms. *She'll wrap you round her finger, if she's given half a chance.*

Sugar recalls the gently breathing face of Sophie on the pillow, the crisp sheets and blankets only half-way up Sophie's stiff white night-gown, for Sugar was too shy to tuck them up to the child's neck.

What came before that? Hearing Sophie's prayers. A litany of God-blesses. Who and what did Sophie pray for? Sugar can't remember. The thought that she'll surely hear the same prayers again this evening is at once reassuring and perturbing.

But what happened *before* the prayers? Oh, yes, bathing Sophie in a tub next to her bed. The child did it all herself, really, except for the towel draped over her tiny wet shoulders. Sugar looked away, bashful, and, when the laundry-maid came to collect Miss Rackham's washing, blenched as if caught in a naughty act.

And before then? Ah yes, the business with the Gregory powder. Beatrice had stressed the absolute necessity of administering a nightly dose – indeed, her last words to Sugar before leaving the house were 'Remember the Gregory powder!' – but the look of revulsion on the child's face as the vile spoonful approached her lips made Sugar lower the spoon at once.

'Would you rather not, Sophie?'

'Nurse says I'll be sorry without it, Miss.'

'Well,' Sugar responded, 'let me know if you're sorry, and I'll give it to you then.' And, to the child's relief, she tapped the horrid concoction of rhubarb, magnesia and ginger back into the tin.

There were no formal lessons yesterday, because Sugar was trying to find out what Sophie had learned in life so far. This turned out to be a great deal, and Sophie grew quite exhausted recalling and reciting it all. Bible stories and moral homilies made up the bulk, but there was also a fair amount of what Beatrice Cleave described as 'general knowledge', such as which countries belong to England, and which ought to but don't. There were nursery rhymes, little poems about the importance of being virtuous, and Sophie's topic of greatest erudition, the elephants in India.

'Their ears are smaller,' stated the child, after many other revelations.

'Smaller than what?' Sugar enquired.

'I don't know, Miss,' confessed Sophie after a dumbfounded pause. 'Nurse knows.'

Throughout the afternoon, as fact piled upon fiction in an ever greater muddle, Sugar repeatedly smiled and said, 'Very good, Sophie.' She didn't know what else to say, and it seemed the right thing to be telling the child anyway. Judging by Sophie's response – an ever-brighter glow of pride and relief – the words 'good' and 'Sophie' had all-too-rarely been coupled in the same sentence. Sugar spooned them into the child's mouth like an illicit gift of bon-bons, enough to make her gloriously sick.

So much for yesterday. Today, Sophie's formal education must begin. *Dressing the lamb before the kill*, as Mrs Castaway once put it, when Sugar dared to ask what, exactly, education is.

In the early morning gloom, by candle-light, Sugar opens the book handed to her, like a sacred chalice, by Beatrice. 'Purchased by Mr Rackham himself, this was,' the nurse said. 'Everything Sophie should know is in it.' *Historical and Miscellaneous Questions for the Use of Young People* is its title, and very thick and densely printed it is too. The author's name, Richmal Mangnall, sounds like the growl of a dog refusing to surrender a ball from its mouth.

Sugar examines the first question, concerning the ancient monarchies that were founded after the Deluge, but gets stuck because she isn't sure how to pronounce 'Chaldean' and is loath to start Sophie's tuition off on the wrong foot. She reads further and, by the time she gets to 'What were the Amphictyonies or Amphictyonic confederations?', she's fairly certain that some of this material is not yet within the scope of Sophie's brain. She decides to skip a few thousand years — or, say rather, a dozen pages — and begin after the birth of Jesus, whom Sophie at least has heard of.

That's settled, then. Sugar lays Mangnall's *Questions* to one side and fetches Agnes's diaries out from their hiding-place. To her surprise, they are (she notices now) locked, each grimy volume banded shut with a hasp and a tiny brass padlock. Specks of soil fall into her lap as she strains to tear one of them open, but its dainty fastening proves stronger than it looks. Eventually, pricked by conscience, Sugar forces the lock by thrusting the point of a knife into it until the mechanism yields.

At random, the pages fall open, to reveal Agnes in 1869, as follows:

I am gripped by terror today — I feel <u>certain</u> there is a great trial in store for me, greater even than I have endured yet . . . Just this minute Clara has come in to tell me that Doctor Curlew is on his way, to "help me out of my misery". Whatever can he mean? I know that the last time he was here I complained bitterly, and I <u>may</u> have said that after so many months of Illness I wished for nothing but Death, but I didn't mean it! His black bag frightens me — it has knives in it, & leeches. I have begged Clara to stop him doing me any mischief if I should swoon, but she doesn't appear to listen, and prattles that everyone is very worried about 'the baby' — how very late it is, & that it must come soon. Whose baby can this be? I wish William would keep me better informed about whom he invites to this house . . .

A barb of pain burrows down through Sugar's guts. With a groan she perches on the chamber-pot and doubles over, her loose hair piling up in the lap of her night-gown, her forehead resting on her knees, prickling with sweat. She balls her fists, but nothing comes, and the spasm passes.

Back in bed, she takes up Agnes's diary again, and flicks to the entry she saw before, expecting to learn, on the page following, how Sophie arrived into the world. But the very next entry after the one describing Agnes's unenlightened labour begins thus:

Have just returned from Mrs Hotten's house, where I had my first dinner "out" since regaining my Health. Either the Hottens are most peculiar people, or manners have flipped Topsey-Turvey during my time of Illness. Mr Hotten put his napkin on his chest, and I was expected to eat my melon with a __spoon__. There were no asparagus tongs, and one of my potatoes had a "bone" in it. Everyone talked cease-lessly about the Barings, and made jokes about the cost of a Peerage. Mrs Hotten laughed with her mouth open. All evening I was either a'ghast or else bored. I shan't go again. When will Mrs Cecil reply to my invitation, I wonder?

And so on, and so on. Sugar flips through the pages: more and more of the same. Where is William? Where is Sophie? Their names don't appear. Agnes goes to parties, presumably with her husband at her side; she returns home, presumably to her infant daughter.

At Mrs Amphlett's, I saw Mrs Forge, Mrs Tippett, Mrs Lott, Mrs Potter, Mrs Ousby ... Such roll-calls fill the pages, stitched together with a tireless embroidery of *I, I, I, I, I, I, I, I.*

Sugar prises open another couple of diaries. She reads a few lines here and there, but is daunted by the enormity of the task ahead. Twenty diaries, hundreds of pages, all cluttered with Agnes's wearyingly tiny script. And instead of revelations that could be of some use to her should she bump into Mrs Rackham on the stairs today, there are only complaints about inferior china, dreary weather, and dust on the banisters. Only a few weeks ago, Sugar would have been very excited if she could have retrieved, from a pillar-box or a garbage-heap, just one letter written by Agnes Rackham; she would have pored over each line, wringing out maximum insight. Now, Agnes's entire life lies here before her, in a mound of grubby diaries, and she doesn't know where to start.

Eventually, she decides there's only one way to do it: begin at the begin-ning. Breaking each of the diaries open, she sorts them according to date until she has the earliest one in her hands.

The inaugural page of this first diary, the smallest and most delicate of all the volumes, consists of several false starts, written in a neat if some-what slanted hand. The date, 21 April, 1861, is rendered with especial care.

> *Dear Diary,*
> *I do hope we shall be good friends. Lucy keeps a Diary and she says it is a very fine & amusing thing to do. Lucy is my best friend, she ~~lives~~ ~~lived~~ lives in the house next-door to where I ~~live~~ ~~lived~~*

Agnes's second attempt is directly underneath the first, equally neat, showing her determination not to be discouraged by one failure.

28 April, 1861
Dear Diary,
I do hope we shall be good friends. I think you will find I am as Faithful a
little girl as ever lived. In May I shall be Ten Years Old. When I was younger
I was very happy, tho' we lived in a smaller house than we do now. Then my dear
Papa was taken from us, and Mama said I ort not to be without a Father, and

The two entries following this are not quite as neat, as if Agnes wrote
them in a rush – hoping, perhaps, that sheer momentum might carry them
over the obstacles that derailed the others.

Dear Diary,
How do you do? My name is Agnes Pigott, or should I say that _was_ my name,
but now

Dear Diary,
I

The next entry, undated and obviously scribbled in furious haste, fills
a double page overleaf.

My dearest, most beloved Saint Teresa,
Is it such a great Sin to hate my father if he is not my True father? I hate
him so, I hate him until my teeth bite holes in my lips. He is an evil man and has
cast a Spell over Mama to make her forget our dear Papa and she looks at him like
a dog waiting for meat. She cannot see what I see – the cruelity in his eyes and his
smile which is not a smile. I dont know what is to become of us because he has
forbiden us to go to Church – the True Church – and instead he has taken us to
his church and it is a shameless frord. Hardly anyone is properly dressed and every-
thing is so common, they even have a Book Of Common Prayer. I dont suppose,
dear Saint Teresa, that You have ever seen inside one of these places. There is only
emptyness where Our Lady ort to be standing, and there is nothing to take home
except a beging letter about the Clock-Tower Fund. ~~My father~~ ~~My new father~~
Lord Unwin says everything is the same as my old Church except that they are
speaking the Queens English, but he does not understand (or perhaps he pretends
not to) that if even _one_ small word of a Spell is left out or pernounced wrong it
doesnt work _at all_, as in "Columbine's Enchanted Forest" when Columbine forgets

to say 'zabda hanifah' and she loses her wings. Lord Unwin hates the Church and Our Lady and all the Saints, he says "No more of that jibrish in this house" and by jibrish he means You, Saint Teresa.

Why do You not speak to me any more? Are the walls of this unhappy new house a shield against Your voice? I cannot believe he is stronger than You. If You cannot speak to me aloud, perhaps You could wisper to me when Miss Pitt takes me out walking, or perhaps You could cause Your answer to appear on this page by the morning (or the next page if there is no room left.) I shall leave the pen in the ink, but please do not spill as Miss Pitt (my new governess) is very strict.

Oh yes, You need to know what my questions are, they are, Where has my own dear Papa gone and when am I to see him again? And, How much longer is this evil man to have Mama and me in his power? He says I am to go to a School for Young Ladies as soon as can be aranged. I am very frightened of this as it will mean leaving Mama, and I have heard that schooling is a thing that takes many years. Also I dont wish to be a Young Lady because they are not permited to play with hoops any more and must get married instead.

The remainder of the diary consists of blank pages, creamy and secretive. Sugar feels another barb of pain burrowing through her guts, and sits on the chamber-pot again. Foulness sputters out of her, scalding her as it goes. She hugs herself, shivering, biting her lips so she won't exclaim blasphemies or obscenities. Instead, in between cramps, she breathes deeply and deliberately. *I am a governess.*

A little while later, at half past six, Rose brings her a cup of tea. Sugar is fully dressed by then, her unruly abundant hair wound into a tight chignon, her body sheathed in black. The room is tidied, the diaries invisible – stashed under the bed, wrapped in the same shabby old dress she used as a disguise on her visit to the Rackhams' church. God knows why she kept that dress – she needs no disguises now! But she did, and it's come in useful after all.

'Morning, Miss Sugar,' says Rose, her nose wrinkling only momentarily at the diarrhoea stench still flavouring the air. 'I–I didn't know what biscuit you might like.' And she proffers a plate containing three different ones.

'Thank you, Rose,' says Sugar, moved almost to tears by how friendly the servant is being. Either Rose hasn't read any novels, or she's under strict injunctions from her master to be amiable. 'That's very kind of you.

I wonder if you could advise me on opening this window? I've tried, and can't manage it.'

'It's painted shut, Miss, from the outside.' Rose inclines her head apologetically. (The whole house is afflicted with minor inconveniences following the recent orgy of improvements.) 'I'll ask Mr Rackham to ask the gardener to climb up and fix it for you, Miss.'

'No need, no need.' Sugar is determined not to cause William the slightest bother, lest he feel that a governess from a more conventional source would have been less troublesome. When he comes up to see her, let it be because he desires her, not because he must face the consequences of hurried renovations. Nodding encouragingly at Rose, Sugar takes a sip of lukewarm tea and a bite of biscuit.

'Qwor!' her stomach exclaims, as the servant turns to leave.

Minutes later, in a bedroom virtually identical to her own, Sugar wakes Sophie, and finds her drenched with urine. The little girl, confused and squinting in the lamp-light, is trapped in a swaddle of night-gown and bed-sheet clinging to her wet flesh, as though a pitcherful of piss has been poured on her body from knee to chest.

'Uh . . . Goodness me, Sophie,' says Sugar, after biting her tongue on several coarser responses.

'I'm sorry, Miss,' says the child. 'I'm bad.' Her tone is matter-of-fact, not cringing or pitiful; she might be reciting a titbit of general knowledge that escaped her memory the day before.

The metal tub of warm water is already stationed by the bed, deposited there by whoever does the work of little Christopher in the Rackham household. Sugar helps Sophie out of bed, assists her to remove her night-gown in such a way as not to rub her face in her own pee. The rest, the child does herself. Her stocky body and spindly arms disappear under a frothy lather of Rackham's Bath Soap (still *Supreme in its Bubble Production Far Beyond the Capacities of Other Soaps!*, until such time as Sugar's suggested rephrasing is adopted.)

'Very good, Sophie,' she says, looking away. The hairs on the nape of her neck tingle as she notices a pair of eyes glinting in the darkness: Sophie's doll, slumped louchely on top of the dresser, its chin buried in its chest, its painted teeth grinning. Sugar and the manikin stare at each other until the bathwater has gone quiet, then she turns back to Sophie. The child is

standing ready to be dried, her shoulder-blades quaking with cold, and
Sugar wraps a towel around them; but, as she does so, she catches a glimpse
of the smooth infantile vulva between Sophie's legs, the firm, clearly
defined sex glistening with water – and helplessly imagines a swollen,
mauve-headed prick shoving its way inside.

'I'm sorry, Miss,' says Sophie when she hears her governess grunt in
distress.

'You've done nothing wrong, dear,' says Sugar, looking away towards
the window as the child finishes drying. The sun appears to be on the rise,
or at least the night is receding, and in Sugar's lap, a very small petticoat
lies ready.

At half past eight, after they've eaten the bowls of porridge Rose has
brought up to them, Sugar escorts Sophie to what used to be, until yesterday, the nursery. They tiptoe past dark, closed doors behind which are
hidden the personal effects, and possibly the bodies as well, of William and
Agnes Rackham respectively. Quiet as mice or burglars, they proceed to
the end of the landing and let themselves into the unlit room where slate
and rocking horse stand at the ready.

A servant has stoked a fire in the hearth, raising the temperature of
the air to a bearable chill. While Sugar lights the lamps, Sophie walks
directly to the writing desk and sits down, her tightly-shod feet dangling
a few inches short of the floor.

'Dictation first, I think,' says Sugar, as her intestines continue to make
loud noises. 'A few words at random, just to see how well you can write
when you're still half asleep!'

The humour is lost on Sophie; she appears to regard this as a genuine
attempt to catch her out when she's least prepared. Still, she lays a blank
sheet of paper on the writing-desk before her, and sits attentively, waiting for the first humiliation.

'Cat,' declares Miss Sugar.

Face bowed to the page, Sophie inscribes the word, her tiny hand gripping the pen awkwardly, her big eyes gleaming as she strives to make the
inky calligraphy perfect and beautiful.

'Dog.'

A fresh dip in the ink. A wince of disappointment as a dark blob disfigures
the initial 'd' – this was the intended trap, no doubt! A second attempt.

'Master.'

Again the child writes the letters, painstakingly but (as far as Sugar can judge upside-down) with no apparent uncertainty about spelling. Which of them is being made a fool of here?

'Mistress – no . . . ah . . . Girl.'

Virgin, suggests a phantom prompter in Sugar's head, a sly devil with the voice of Mrs Castaway. *Virgin.*

'Ah . . .' (she looks around for inspiration) 'window.'

Kept intact especially for you, sir.

'Door.'

Whore.

The sun is shining brighter now, lightening the shadows of the schoolroom, warming the stale air. Sugar dabs her damp forehead with the black fabric of her sleeve. She hadn't thought dictation could be such hard work.

All morning, Sophie Rackham does as she is told. She writes, she reads aloud, she listens to an Aesop fable and regurgitates the moral. Her first formal history lesson is a model of compliance; Miss Sugar recites the facts five or six times, and Sophie repeats them until she has them engraved, or at least pencilled, on her memory. Thus does Sophie learn that in the first century, London was founded by the Romans, Jerusalem was destroyed by Titus, and Rome was burnt in the reign of Nero. Memorisation of these bare facts is a mere ten minutes' work, mostly spent correcting Sophie's tendency to pronounce the Holy City 'Juice'lem'. However, the remainder of the morning flies by, as Sugar lays Mangnall's book aside and attempts to answer Sophie's questions arising from her lesson, such as: Where was London before the Romans found it; Why didn't Titus care for Juice'lem; and How could Rome catch fire if it was raining? Then, as soon as she's mopped up these enigmas (in the case of Titus, with an improvisation of pure fiction), Sugar tackles the more fundamental questions, like What is a century and how does a person know he's living in one; and Are there elephants in London.

'Have *you* seen any elephants there?' teases Sugar.

'I've never been, Miss,' says the child.

At midday, when Sophie is scheduled to adjourn her lessons and play for a couple of hours, Sugar is free to do the same. The ritual, common in other households, of a child being brought downstairs, immaculately dressed and on its best behaviour, to eat lunch or dinner with its parents, is unknown in the Rackham house.

The bright morning sunshine has been replaced by rain. Rose brings them their portion of the lunch that's being served down below (to whom? Sugar wonders) and disappears again. Lessons aren't due to resume until two, and Sugar is longing for the respite, if only for the opportunity to remedy her physical discomforts – numb, half-frozen feet, armpits clammy with sweat, a sore and itchy arsehole. While she eats her carrot pudding, she searches her vocabulary for an alternative to 'arsehole' – not 'anus', which still sounds coarse, but some elusive word that's wholly innocuous and refined, that could be spoken in elegant company. No success. She'll have to purify her words and thoughts, though, if she's to be a fit governess. However little interest William may have shown in his daughter until now, he certainly won't want her learning coarse language.

'Be good, Sophie,' she says, as she prepares to shut the child in the nursery – the school-room, rather.

'*Be Good, sweet maid, and let who will be clever,*' recites Sophie, playfully seizing her chance to complete the poem, like a catechism. '*Do Noble things, not dream them all day long; And so make Life, Death, and that vast For-ever, One glad, sweet Song.*'

'Very good, Sophie,' says Sugar, and closes the door.

Back in her own room, the chamber-pot has been emptied and cleaned, and lavender essence has been sprayed in the air. The bed is made with fresh sheets and pillow-cases, and Sugar's hair-brush, pin-box, buttonhook and so forth have been tidied into a neat pattern on the blanket. The swaddle of diaries under the bed hasn't been disturbed, thank God. A decanter of water has been placed on the dresser, as well as a clean glass and a folded slip of paper.

Sugar snatches up the note, thinking it must surely be from William. It's from Rose, and says, *Shears will see to the window – Rose.*

She undresses, washes the parts that need washing, and puts on the burgundy-coloured dressing-gown with the quilted breast that William particularly likes. She sits on the bed, her feet wrapped in a blanket, and waits. Tempting though it is to read Agnes's diaries, she can't risk it, because when William comes – as he surely must – he may not knock before entering, and what would she say then? Even if he did knock, the diaries are dirty, and cleaning the soil off her hands would take time . . .

The clock ticks. The rain patters against the window, desists for a while, then returns. Her toes thaw one by one. William doesn't come. Sugar calls to mind the frantic way he grips her when he's fucking her from behind, his hands bearing down on her shoulders as if in the wild hope of collapsing their two bodies into one – as if, with a sudden, fantastical contraction of flesh, she might be concertina'd into his groin, or he disappear completely into hers.

At ten minutes to two, she gets dressed again, buttoning herself into her black governess garb and hanging her burgundy gown back in the wardrobe. She has remembered, to her relief, that it's Wednesday – William's day for checking what proportion of the goods he's ordered during the previous week has in fact turned up at the docks. By now, he'll be in Air Street, frowning over dispatch notices, already formulating letters in his head that she'll help him write when his annoyance has cooled. It's a dreary task, but it must be done.

The remainder of the day passes quickly. Sophie, Sugar discovers, loves to be read to. So, in amongst more rote-learning from Mangnall's *Questions*, and more disentanglement of confusions arising from that venerable book, Sugar reads aloud from Aesop, acting out the animals in different voices. At one point, after a particularly spirited duck-quack, she glances across at Sophie and thinks she detects a twitch of the lips that might be a hastily suppressed smile. Certainly the child's eyes are wide and bright, and she barely breathes for fear of missing a single word.

'*Whisssss*-kers,' says Sugar, gaining courage.

Shortly before four, there's a grinding and a jingling in the grounds below, and Sugar and Sophie go to the window to see the carriage emerging from the coach-house. Mrs Rackham, it seems, is going out to take her tea at another lady's 'At Home', or perhaps intending to flit to several such. Darkness is already descending, and the weather is drizzly, but when Agnes hurries out of the parlour onto the carriage-way she is resplendent in pink, and her matching parasol looks luminous in the twilight. Cheesman gathers her into the cabin, and she's borne away.

'I should prob'ly get sick,' says Sophie, nose pressed against the window-pane, 'if I had a ride in that.'

At seven, after a roast dinner and another hour or two spent in her bedroom waiting for William, Sugar returns to Sophie to discharge the last of her responsibilities. She can't help thinking it's futile to bathe Sophie at bedtime when, in all likelihood, it will need to be done again in the morning, but Sophie seems used to it and Sugar is loath to unravel established routines so soon. So, she goes through the ritual, and wraps the sweet-smelling child in her plain white night-dress.

'God bless Papa and Mama,' says Sophie, kneeling at the side of her bed, her tiny hands arranged in a steeple on the coverlet. 'God bless Nurse.' So incantatory is her tone that it hardly seems to matter that of this triumvirate, two have scant involvement in Sophie's life and the third has abandoned her to suckle a new baby called Barrett. Father, Mother and Nurse are folkloric fixtures like Father, Son and Holy Ghost, or Great Huge Bear, Middle Bear and Little Small Wee Bear.

'. . . and I am grateful that I am a little girl in England with a home and a bed, and God bless the little black children in Africa, who have no beds, and God bless all the little yellow children in China, who are made to eat rats . . .'

Sugar's eyes, focused on Sophie's pale bare feet poking out from the hem of her night-dress, slowly cross. Whatever qualms she may have about embellishing, with sentimental and unhistorical anecdotes, the decision by Constantine the Great to stop the persecution of the Christians, she's clearly doing no more than following in Beatrice Cleave's footsteps. A great deal of rubbish has already been deposited in Sophie's skull, and there's more to follow.

'Shall I . . . shall I read you a bedtime story?' says Sugar, as she's tucking Sophie in, pulling the sheets up to the child's chin.

'Thank you, Miss.'

But by the time Sugar has fetched a book, it's too late.

In her own bed that night, after she's finally given up waiting for William, Sugar lays out a selection of Agnes's diaries before her on the blanket, one nestled in her lap, several others within easy reach. If she should hear William at her door, she's decided what she'll do: blow out the bedside candle and, under cover of darkness, toss the diaries back under the bed. Then, if he's in the state she expects he'll be in, he's scarcely likely to notice, even by the light of a rekindled candle, that her hands are grubby. She'll wipe them at her leisure, when his face is safely nuzzled between her breasts.

Agnes's next attempt at keeping her memoirs after the tirade against her step-father and his fiendish plan to have her schooled, is dated 2 September 1861, on the maiden page of a fresh volume grandly inscribed *Abbots Langley School for Girls*. The misery she'd expected to suffer if she were sent to such a place is nowhere in evidence; for, not only does she render the name of the school with a proud flourish, but she also decorates the page margins with elaborate watercolour reproductions of the school's hollyhock laurel emblem and its motto, *Comme Il Faut*.

Addressing herself once more to 'Dear Diary' rather than 'Saint Teresa' or some other supernatural correspondent, the ten-year-old Agnes thus commences an unbroken record of her six years at school.

Well, here am I in Abbots Langley (near Hampstead). Miss Warkworth & Miss Barr (the headmistresses) say that no girl is permited to leave here until 'finished', but do not be alarmed, dear Diary, for by this they mean Clever & Beautiful. I have been thinking deeply on this and have decided that it would be a good thing if I was Clever & Beautiful because then I should marry well, to an Officer of the True Faith. I should describe my Papa to him and he would say, "Why, I have seen the very man fighting in distant lands!" and directly after we were married he would go on a Quest to find him. Mama & I should live together in his house, waiting for him and Papa to return.

I do not know how Miss Warkworth & Miss Barr & the other mistresses mean to 'finish' me, but I have seen some of the older girls who have been at Abbots Langley for years, & they look most pleased with themselves & are some of them very Tall & Graceful. In evening dress I am sure they would look just like Ladies in paintings with a fine Officer by their side.

I have been instaled in my room, which I must share with two other girls. (There are, I think, thirty all-together. I was very worried about this before I came, for I knew I should have to live with strange girls who might be cruel & was almost sick with dread at the thought of being at their mercy. But the two girls in my room are not so bad after all. One is named Letitia (I think that is how it is spelt) and though she is a little older than me & says she comes of better family, she has been made so teribly ugly by a Disease that she lacks the spirit to put on airs. The other girl has wept & snifled since her arrival but said nothing.

At Dinner some other girls (whom I first took for school-mistresses, they looked so old — I suppose they are almost finished) tried to make me reveal who my Father was & I would not tell them, because I feared they would make fun of

Papa. But then another spoke up, "I know who her father is — He is Lord Unwin", & that struck them all very quiet! Perhaps I betrayed Papa a little by not speaking up for him as my <u>True</u> father, but dont you think I should be glad of what small benifit I recieve from being now the step-daughter of Lord Unwin? Whether it is wrong or not, I am greatful for whatever helps me suffer less, for I hate to suffer. Every scratch and gash upon my heart is there yet, not the <u>slightest</u> bit healed, making me fear that the next injury will be my last. If only I could be spared any more wounds, I should arrive safe into Marriage, and after that I should be free of all care. Wish me luck!

(I can speak freely to <u>you</u>, dear Diary, for it is only the letters I send by the Post that I must give up unsealed to Miss Barr.)

I have more to tell, but Miss Wick (of whom more to-morrow) has just called by, warning us that we must put out the lights. And so, dear Diary, I must put you under lock and key, & ask you not to worry over me <u>yet</u>, for it seems I may survive my education after all!

Your loving Friend,
Agnes.

Sugar reads another twenty or thirty pages before succumbing to exhaustion — and, to be honest, the odourless, deadly gas of boredom. Agnes's promise that there should be 'more to-morrow' of Miss Wick is faithfully kept, and indeed Miss Wick, and all the other Misses whom Agnes lacks the literary talent to bring to life, rear their featureless heads not just tomorrow, but tomorrow and tomorrow and tomorrow.

In her final minutes of wakefulness, Sugar wishes she could float through the Rackham house like a ghost and see its inhabitants *now*, as they really are. She wishes she could pass through the heavy wooden door of William's study and see what he's up to; wishes she could peer into his very brain and winkle out his reasons for avoiding her. She wishes she could see Agnes, the real flesh-and-blood Agnes whom she has touched and smelled, doing whatever it is that Agnes does in her room at night . . . Even the sight of Mrs Rackham sleeping would, Sugar's sure, reveal more than these ancient soil-stained reminiscences!

Lastly, she imagines floating into Sophie's room, and murmuring in the child's ear the gentle suggestion that she hop out of bed and use the pot one more time. No supernatural fantasy, this: she *could*, if she chose, make it come true. How happy Sophie would be, waking next morning in a dry bed! Sugar breathes deeply, gathering her nerve to throw the warm bed-clothes aside and hurry barefoot through the dark to Sophie's room. A minute or two of discomfort is all she'll have to endure to complete this mission of mercy — yes! She's up, she's tiptoeing along the landing, candle in hand!

But, like those childhood dreams she can still recall, when she'd be convinced she was leaving her bed to use the pot, only to discover, as soon as she let go, that she was wetting herself inside a humid cocoon of bedding, the mission of mercy occurs in her sleep only, and its happy ending is trapped like a moth in her snoring head.

Next morning, in the cold light of dawn, while the wind whoops and fleers and a chatter of sleet harasses the eastern windows of the Rackham house, Sugar tiptoes up to Sophie's bed, pulls back the covers, and finds the child steeped in urine as usual.

'I'm sorry, Miss.'

What to reply? 'Well, we've no other sheets, and it's raining outside, and I'll soon be entertaining visitors who won't appreciate your dirty smell in their noses — so what do *you* suggest we do, hmm, my little sorry poppet?' The words echo in Sugar's memory, tempting her to speak them aloud, with that same teasing, affectionately bitter tone Mrs Castaway used fifteen years ago. How quickly they spring to the tip of Sugar's tongue! She bites them back in horror.

'Nothing to be sorry about, Sophie. Let's get you clean.'

Sophie wrestles with her night-dress, whose sodden fabric sucks at her flesh inch by inch, plastered to the contours of her ribs. Sugar comes to the rescue, tugging the horrid thing free of Sophie's arms and rolling it into a wad, disguising with a cough her sharp intake of breath as the acid urine stings the cracks in her palms and fingers. She can't help noticing, when the naked child steps from her sour-smelling bed into the tub, that Sophie's vulva is an angry red.

'Wash well, Sophie,' she advises airily, looking away into the shadows, but there's no escape from the memory of her own inflamed genitals, exam-ined in a cracked mirror in Church Lane, the moment the fat old man with the hairy hands finally left her alone. *I have a clever middle finger, yes I have!* was what he'd told her, as he poked and prodded between her legs. *A most frolicsome little fellow! He loves to play with little girls, and make them happier than they've ever been!*

'Finished, Miss,' says Sophie, her legs trembling with cold, her lamp-lit shoulders smouldering with steam.

Sugar wraps the towel around Sophie's shoulders, half-lifts her out of the tub, and helps her dry everywhere, dabbing at the clefts. Then, just before the pantalettes go on, she sprinkles some Rackham's Snow Dust between Sophie's legs, and pats the talc gently onto the sore flesh. The smell of lavender flavours the air between them; the child's sex has been powdered pale as a whore's face, with a thin red mouth, only to disappear inside white cotton in a faint puff of talcum.

After Sugar has buttoned Sophie into an ill-fitting blue dress and straightened her white pinafore, she pulls the bed-sheet from the mattress (lined with a waxed undersheet, just like her own bed at Mrs Castaway's!) and pushes it into the bathwater to soak. Is there a reason, she wonders, why the bed-sheet must be washed immediately and hung to dry in that nasty little room downstairs, while Sophie's night-dress and indeed all the other laundry in the house is taken care of in the normal way by the servants? Was there perhaps, once upon a time, a complaint from the laundry-maid that a daily load of soiled linen was an intolerable imposition? Or was this ritual Beatrice Cleave's idea, with no purpose but to remind Sophie how much bother she caused her long-suffering nurse?

'I wonder what would happen,' muses Sugar as she sploshes up to her elbows in the tepid yellowish water, 'if we put this sheet with the other things to be washed.' She scoops the tangle of heavy linen up and begins to wring it, waiting for Sophie's response.

'It's too full of dirtiness, Miss,' says the child, solemn in her rôle of introducing a newcomer to the unchallengeable realities of the Rackham domain. 'My bad smell would be spread into the good parts of the house, onto the nice clean beds, ev'ywhere.'

'Did your Nurse tell you that?'

Sophie hesitates; the day's interrogations have evidently begun, and she must be careful to answer correctly.

'No, Miss. It's . . . common knowledge.'

Sugar lets the matter drop, wrings the sheet as dry as she can. She leaves Sophie to comb her hair, and carries the wad of damp linen out of the room, to follow in Beatrice Cleave's footsteps one more time.

The landing is still quite gloomy, but the receiving-hall below is thinly covered with milky daylight, and the sun's overspill extends half-way up the stairs, making the second part of Sugar's descent more confident than the first. What would William think, if he met her hurrying through his house like this, carrying a wad of wet whiffy linen before her? A vain conjecture, since she meets no one. Although she knows the nether regions of the Rackham house must be a hive of industry at this hour, none of it is audible, and she feels like the only soul haunting its luxurious passage-ways. The silence is such that she hears the carpet underfoot, the barely perceptible squirm of its dense-woven pile as she walks upon it.

The odd little store-room with the copper pipe spanned between its walls is warm as an oven half an hour after a cake has been removed. All trace of mud and mucky water has been scrupulously cleaned from the corner where Agnes's diaries lay in those few hours before Sugar snatched them; and, contrary to her fears, there is, in the diaries' place, no stern notice to the effect that theft will be punished with instant dismissal.

Sugar hangs the bed-sheet over the copper pipe. Only now does she notice that the talcum powder trapped in the cracks of her palms has mingled with bathwater, delineating the freakish convolutions of her skin with a network of creamy lines. Clots and smears of this perfumed slime also cling to the bed-sheet, resembling thick male seed.

William, where are you? she thinks.

The morning is spent on the Roman Empire and dictation, with two fairy stories as a treat. Sugar recites them from a slim cloth-covered book whose spine is frayed and whose pages are much-thumbed. *Illustrated and with Revised Morals*, proclaims the title page, along with a hand-written inscription:

Dear Sophie, A good friend of mine has scolded me for giving you the Bible last Christmas, saying you are too young for it yet. I hope you will enjoy this little book almost *as much. Fond wishes from your tiresome Uncle Henry.*

'Do you remember your Uncle Henry?' enquires Sugar lightly, in between exotic enchantments and supernatural rescues.

'They put him in the ground,' says Sophie, after a few moments' wrinkle-browed thought.

Sugar reads on. Fairy stories are a novelty for her; Mrs Castaway didn't approve of them, because they encourage the belief that everything turns out exactly as it should, whereas 'You'll find out soon enough, child, that nothing ever does.' Mrs Castaway preferred to nurture the infant Sugar on folk tales (the nastier the better), selected episodes from the Old Testament (Sugar can still list each of Job's trials), and true-life accounts: indeed, anything with a full complement of undeserved suffering and apparently motiveless deeds.

At midday, when Rose brings Sugar and Sophie their share of luncheon, she brings a message too. Mrs Rackham is entertaining visitors downstairs, and wishes to show them – the visitors, that is – the house. Mr Rackham therefore requests that Mrs Rackham be left wholly undisturbed in this objective. *Wholly* undisturbed, you understand. 'And if you fancy, there's more galantine, and I'll bring up the cake shortly,' adds Rose, to sweeten the bitterness of their imprisonment.

Silence settles over governess and pupil when the servant has left. True to the pattern of this November, the morning sun fades away and the room dims, its windows rattling in the wind. The slap of raindrops sharpens into the clatter of hailstones.

'Well, these visitors are much the poorer,' says Sugar at last, 'for not seeing your lovely nursery – your lovely school-room, I should say. It's the cheerfulest room in the house, and your toys are very interesting.'

There is another pause.

'Mother hasn't seen me since my birthday,' says Sophie, staring at the pistachio kernel on her plate, wondering if, under this strange new post-Beatrice regime, she may go unpunished for refusing to eat this bit of her galantine.

'When was your birthday?' enquires the governess.

'I don't know, Miss. Nurse knows.'

'I'll ask your father.'

Sophie looks at Sugar wide-eyed, impressed at the easy familiarity the governess seems to have with the exalted and shadowy figures of the adult world.

Sugar picks up the Mangnall and opens it at random. '. . . commonly called the "Complutensian Polyglot", from Complutum, the Latin name for Alcala,' is what her eyes light upon. Instantly she resolves to tell Sophie a story from The Bible instead, embellished with her own character glosses and evocations of Galilean fashions of dress, followed perhaps by a little more Aesop.

'What happened on your birthday?' she asks Sophie, in an even tone, as she leafs backwards and forwards through the Bible. 'Did you do something wicked?'

Sophie gives the question some thought, her frowning, slightly pudgy face flickering with silvery-grey light from the hail-spattered window. 'I don't 'member, Miss,' she says at last.

Sugar hums amiably, as if to say, 'No matter'. She's decided against *Job*, considers doing *Esther* until she sees how thick it is with murder and the purification of virgins, and then gets ensnarled in *Nehemiah*, whose endless lists are even more boring than Agnes Unwin's. She looks around the room for inspiration, and spots the painted wooden animals jostled in a corner.

'The story,' she declares, closing the book, 'of Noah's flood.'

That evening, after Sophie has been laid to rest, Sugar returns to her own room for the long night. William is in the house, she knows, and Agnes has gone out visiting: ideal conditions for him to pay a visit on his paramour. Secreted here in a dingy, box-like little chamber with ugly wallpaper disfigured by pictureless picture-hooks, she disports herself on the bed, her breasts perfumed under the quilted fabric of her burgundy dressing-gown.

An hour passes, boredom begins to set in, and Sugar pulls Agnes's diaries out from under the bed. The rain batters against the window. Perhaps it's just as well that Shears has not yet climbed up and broken the paint-seal, for that wind-swept water looks as though it would love to get in.

Back in Abbots Langley, in a revamped cloister stocked to the ceiling with adolescent girls, Agnes Unwin's education goes on and on. As far as Sugar can tell (reading between the lines of Agnes's breathless but soporific account) hard study is no longer much on the menu, supplanted by an increasing stress on ladylike 'accomplishments'. On such subjects as Geography or English Agnes has nothing to say, but she records her elation at receiving praise for her needlepoint, or the misery of going for walks in the school grounds accompanied by a teacher of German or French and having to do conjugations on demand. As the years pass, Agnes never achieves more than mediocrity in any academic pursuit, earning many a 'P' (for 'Pretty well') in her copybook, but Music and Dancing are an almost effortless joy to her. One of the few vividly evoked pictures in

Agnes's narrative is of being seated at one of the music room's pianos with her best friend Laetitia two octaves to the left of her, playing at the tap of a baton the same tune that four other girls at two other pianos are playing likewise. Her poor spelling never attracts anything harsher than a tut-tut of reproof, while in Arithmetic, she's often spared penalty for mistakes, as long as the calligraphy of the sums is perfectly formed.

Although Agnes misses not a single day of her journal, Sugar is unable to show the same diligence, and skips pages here and there. Where's her reward for risking being caught red-handed – grubby-handed – by William, should he burst in and find her reading his wife's stolen diaries? And dear God, how much of this school-room froth can she swallow? Where is the real Agnes in all this? Where is the flesh and blood woman who lives farther down the landing, that strange and troubled creature who is William's wife and Sophie's mother? The Agnes in these diaries is a mere fairytale contrivance, as far-fetched as Snow White.

A knock at her door makes her jerk violently, sending the diary flying off her lap. In a couple of frenzied seconds she's retrieved it and shoved it under her bed, wiped her hands on the rug, and licked her lips three times to give them a glisten.

'Yes?' she says.

Her door swings open, and there stands William, fully dressed, immaculately groomed, much as a business associate might expect to see him standing in the doorway of an office. On his face, nothing readable.

'Come in, sir,' she bids him, doing her best to modulate her tone halfway between solemn deference and seductive purr.

He walks inside, and shuts the door behind him.

'I've been fearsomely busy,' he says. 'Christmas is almost upon us.'

The absurdity of this statement, combined with her own tightly-screwed nerves, brings her to the edge of hilarity.

'I'm at your service . . .' she says, squeezing one sharp-nailed fist behind her back, using the pain to remind her that whatever she may be about to do with William – discuss the finer points of Rackham merchandising, pull him to her breast – it won't be improved by shrieks of hysterical laughter.

'I think I have it under control,' he says. 'The orders for bottled perfumes are even worse than I feared, but the toiletries are thriving.'

Sugar squeezes her fist so hard that her vision blurs with tears.

'How are you getting on?' William enquires, his tone simultaneously breezy and glum. 'Tell the truth, now: you rue the day you came, I shouldn't wonder.'

'Not at all,' she protests, blinking. 'Sophie is a well-behaved little thing, and a willing pupil.'

His face darkens subtly; this is not a topic he relishes.

'You have a weary look — especially under your eyes,' he says.

With effort, she shows him a fresher and livelier face, but it's not necessary: he wasn't complaining, only expressing concern. And what a relief, that he remembers what her eyes *ought* to look like!

'Shall I hire a nursery-maid for you?' he offers. His voice is a queer mixture, as subtle a blend of elements as any perfume: there's disappointment, as though he too had cherished a dream that as soon as she crossed the threshold into his house they'd embark on a life of uninterrupted carnal bliss; there's sheepishness, as if he knows he's to blame for what's happened instead; there's contrition, for any nuisance she's endured in his daughter's company; there's dread, at the prospect of finding an additional servant when he has a thousand other things to do; there's pity, at the sight of her lying in Beatrice Cleave's utilitarian little bed; there's affection, as if he wishes he could restore the sparkle to her eyes with a single caress; and, yes, there's desire. A sentence of eight words only, and it's suffused with all these nuances, evaporating like the notes that make up the octave of a well-crafted bouquet.

'No, thank you,' says Sugar. 'There's no need, really there isn't. I haven't slept very well yet, it's true, but I'm sure it's the new bed. I do miss our old one in Priory Close: it was such a pleasure to sleep in, wasn't it?'

He inclines his head — not quite a nod; a gesture of concession. It's all Sugar requires; at once, she steps forward and embraces him, clasping her palms well down his back, lifting one thigh to nuzzle between his trouser-legs.

'I've missed *you*, too,' she says, laying her cheek against his shoulder. The odour of masculine desire is faintly perceptible, escaping from the almost hermetic seal of his shirtcollar. His prick hardens against the soft pressure of her thigh.

'There's nothing I can do,' he says hoarsely, 'about the dimensions of this room.'

'Of course not, my love, I wasn't complaining,' she coos in his ear. 'I'll get used to this little bed soon enough. It wants only to be . . .' (she shifts one hand to his groin, and traces the shape of his erection with her finger-tips) 'christened.'

She walks him a few steps backward, sits down on the edge of the bed, and frees his cock from his trousers, taking it immediately in her mouth. For a few moments he stands silent as a statue, then begins to groan and – thank God – stroke her hair with clumsy but unmistakable tenderness. *I have him still*, she thinks.

When he begins to thrust, she lies back on the mattress and pulls her dressing-gown up over her bosom. With a muffled cry he falls inside her; and, contrary to her fears, her cunt gives him a welcome more lubricious than she could have organised with half an hour of preparation.

'Yes, my love, spend, spend,' she whispers, as he pushes to a climax. She wraps her legs and arms tightly around him, peppering his neck with kisses, some of which are artfully calculated, some heartfelt, but how many of each, she has no way of knowing. 'You are my man,' she assures him, as the cleft between her buttocks runs warm and wet.

A few minutes later, lacking a source of washing water, she is cleaning his groin with a handtowel dipped in a drinking glass.

'Remember the first time?' she murmurs mischievously.

He tries to grin, but it turns into a mortified wince. 'What a disgrace I was then,' he sighs, staring up at the ceiling.

'Oh, I knew you were a great man in the making,' she soothes him, as the rain finally stops and silence settles around the Rackham house. Dried and dressed, William lies in her arms, though there's barely room for the two of them on the bed.

'This business of mine . . .' he muses regretfully. 'Rackham Perfumeries, I mean . . . I lose hours, days, entire weeks of my life to it.'

'It's your father's fault,' says Sugar, echoing an old complaint of his as though it were an impetuous outburst of her own. 'If he'd built the company on more well-reasoned foundations . . .'

'Exactly so. But it means I spend an eternity unearthing his mistakes and shoring up his . . . his . . .'

'Flimsy architecture.'

'Exactly. And all the while neglecting' (he reaches up to stroke her face, and one of his legs falls off the side of the narrow mattress) 'the pleasures of life.'

'That's why I'm here,' she says. 'To remind you.' She wonders if this is the moment to ask him if she's permitted to knock at the door of *his* room, rather than waiting for him to knock at hers, but the crunching of gravel on the carriage-way outside, under wheels and hoofs, alerts them both to Agnes's return.

'She's better lately, isn't she?' asks Sugar, as William rises to his feet.

'Lord knows. Yes, conceivably.' He smooths his hair back over his scalp, preparing to leave.

'When is Sophie's birthday?' asks Sugar, loath to let him go without learning one small thing about this strange household she has come to, this warren of secret rooms whose inhabitants so rarely seem to recognise each other's existence.

He frowns, consulting a mental inventory already over-full with burdensome particulars. 'August the . . . August the something.'

'Oh, that's not so bad, then,' says Sugar.

'How so?'

'Sophie told me Agnes has kept away from her since her birthday.'

William regards her with the oddest look, a mixture of annoyance, shame, and a sadness deeper than she'd ever imagined could reside in him.

'By "birthday",' he says, 'Sophie means the day of her birth. The day she was born.' He opens Sugar's door, impatient lest his wife should, on this night of all nights, be quicker than usual in dismounting from the carriage. 'In this house,' he sums up wearily, 'Agnes is childless.'

And with that, he steps out onto the landing, makes a stern hand gesture as if to say 'Stay!' and shuts her in.

Many hours later, when Sugar has been lying awake, in the dark, for as long as she can bear, and the Rackham house has grown so still she's sure everyone in it is shut into one room or other, she gets up out of bed and lights a candle. Barefoot, carrying the waxy flame in her hand, she pads out onto the landing. So tiny she feels, tiptoeing through the gloom of this grand and cryptic residence, but her shadow, as she passes the doors forbidden to her, is huge.

Silent as a wolf or a fairytale ghost, she slips into Sophie's bedroom, and creeps up to the little girl's bedside. William's daughter sleeps deeply, her eyelids quivering infinitesimally with the strain of keeping those enormous Agnes eyes veiled with skin. She breathes through her mouth, occasionally moving her lips as if responding to a dreamed or remembered stimulus.

'Wake up, Sophie,' whispers Sugar. 'Wake up.'

Sophie's eyes flutter open; her china-blue irises revolve in delirium, like those of a baby doped into a coma by Godfrey's Cordial or Street's Infant Quietness or some other brand of laudanum. Sugar pulls the chamber-pot out from under the bed.

'Jump out for a minute,' says Sugar, sliding her hand down the warm, dry back of Sophie's night-dress and pulling her heavy little body upright. 'Just for a minute.'

Sophie struggles to obey, inept, her eyes wild with confusion at the extremity of the darkness.

Sugar takes hold of the smooth infant hands inside her own cracked and peeling palms, and lifts them into space. 'Trust me,' she whispers.

TWENTY-FOUR

adness! Sheer madness!

Half the problem with this house, if you ask the servants, is that the Rackhams have a wicked habit of staying up when they should be sleeping, and sleeping when they should be awake.

Take this very instant, for example. Clara tiptoes along the landing, candle in hand, at half past midnight, a time when long-suffering servants ought surely to be able to rest their heads on their pillows, secure in the knowledge that their masters and mistresses will cause no more trouble till the morning. But what's this? Clara confirms, by bending to squint into the key-hole of each of the bedrooms in turn, that *not a single Rackham is asleep*.

Madness, if you ask Clara. Just because William Rackham has increased her yearly wage by ten shillings, does he expect her to kiss his shoes in gratitude for the privilege of working here? Ten shillings is all very well, but how much is a good night's sleep worth? She's lost plenty of those! Take tonight, for example! Doors opening and shutting, noises she simply must investigate, for who can tell what Mrs Rackham will do next? Ten shillings per year . . . What's *that* to a man whose face is engraved on placards in the omnibus? Why, she has half a mind to tell him she wants a shilling for every hour his mad wife keeps her awake! What's the wretched woman up to now? Something daft, no doubt. And tomorrow, while the faithful lady's-maid is expected to stand at the ready, dead on her feet, Mrs Rackham will likely as not be lying in bed, snoring the day away, drooling onto her sunlit pillow.

As for the Rackham child, she ought to be put down at seven p.m. and *stay* put down till seven next morning. The new governess – Miss Sugar – clearly has no idea how to deal with children . . . What foolishness is she up to? Clara peers through the key-hole of Sophie Rackham's bedroom, and sees – madness! – candle-light swaying this way and that, and the shadow of Miss Sugar enveloping the child's. Interfering with her, Clara shouldn't wonder. From the moment the woman set foot in the house, Clara could smell it on her: the stink of badness. This self-styled governess, with her highly suspect walk and her slut's mouth – where on earth did Rackham find her? The Rescue Society, maybe. One of Emmeline Fox's 'success stories', come to fiddle with little Sophie in the middle of the night.

And Rackham himself? What's *he* doing awake? Clara peers through his key-hole, and has an unimpeded view of the great man's desk, with the great man busily scribbling. Can't he wait till morning to persuade more people to buy his perfumes? Or are these scribbles the novel he always used to tell his wife he was busy conceiving? *William is going to publish a novel, Clara*, Mrs Rackham would say, at least once a month during the lean years. *The best novel in the world. Soon we shan't need to put up with his father's bullying anymore.*

Clara moves on to Agnes's door, and bends to peek. Mrs Rackham has all the lights on, and is decked out in a magenta gown. Lunacy! At least she hadn't the nerve to summon her lady's-maid to help her dress . . . But why is she pacing to and fro? And what is that book she holds aloft like a hymnal? It looks like an accounts ledger – not that Mrs Rackham can add twelve and twelve, poor simpleton.

Clara would like to spy longer, but Agnes suddenly stops pacing and stares directly at the key-hole, as if she's noticed a glimmer of Clara's eye on the other side. Acute hearing? Animal cunning? The sixth sense of the mad? Clara doesn't know quite what it is, but she's learned to be wary of it. Holding her breath, she hurries back to bed on tiptoe.

Agnes Rackham stands tall – as tall as a person of her height can stand – and raises her eyes to the ceiling. There's a spider on it, climbing over the ridges of the plaster rosette. Agnes isn't afraid of spiders, at least not thin wispy ones, and has no desire to have him removed. Freshly inspired by a pamphlet sent to her all the way from America – *The Divine Enthreadedness of All Things*, by Ambrosius M. Lawes – she knows that this little spider is a soul just like herself, albeit of a lower order.

Moreover, she feels unusually well just now. The bilious headache that ruined her day is gone, and the interior of her skull feels fresh and purified. She really must learn to act faster when her stomach tells her she oughtn't to have eaten her dinner – out with it at once! A moment of unpleasantness, and she's a new woman!

Accordingly, she has tonight begun a new diary – no, *not* a diary – that was a slip of the tongue, or a slip of the mind. No, she's already promised herself she shan't be writing any more diaries. Such tiresome things they are, full of complaints and grievances, which are better buried in case prying eyes should find them.

No, what she's writing now is something much greater and more profound. This past Season, for all its triumphs, was the last Season she'll ever take part in. A different destiny has grown to fruition inside her, and she must acknowledge its calling. For years she has moved as a fashionable lady among other fashionable ladies, denying her deeper nature. For years she has devoured every book of arcane knowledge she could find, and told herself she was merely doing it out of curiosity – now the time has come to declare the Truth.

She holds her new diary – no, *not* diary – up to the light. What is she to call it? It's a big, handsome thing, the size of a ledger, but without lines or columns. On its virgin first page, she has written, in her best Gothic calligraphy, *The Illuminated Thoughts & Preturnatural Reflections of Agnes Pigott*. For short, she'll call it . . . 'The Book'.

She walks back and forth in her bedroom, re-reading that first page-full of words which, for the sake of ceremony, she refrained from penning until the stroke of midnight. Now it's a quarter to one, and here it is: inscribed for posterity, the inky 'o's still glistening!

> Lesson 1. <u>God and oneself</u>
> *God is a Trinity. But what all-too-few people know is that we are <u>all</u> Trinities. We have firstly our First body, (which I shall call our Father Body), being the body we inhabit from day to day. We have secondly our Second body, (which I shall call our Sun Body. This body is kept safe for us, by the Angels of Paradise, in Secret Places all over the world, waiting for the Resurrection. Thirdly we have our Third, or Spirit body, which I shall call our Holy Ghost Body, also known as the soul).*
> Lesson 2. <u>The mistake often made</u>

Most of the suffering in this World comes from ignorance of our Second body.
We make the mistake of thinking that when our First body is gone, we must spend
the rest of Eternity as a Ghost. Not so! All the great & reliable authorities,
including Saint John the Divine, Mr Uriah Nobbs, &c, are agreed that the Afterlife
will be conducted upon this Earth, and the Saved will be given new bodies for the
occasion.
   Lesson 3.

Agnes paces her bedroom, trying to decide on a sufficiently powerful
Lesson 3. She considers writing about the Convent of Health and her own
guardian angel, but rejects this as too personal. Everything she writes from
now on must have universal appeal, illuminating essential truths.
Discussing the particulars of her own situation would make 'The Book'
too much like a diary – and diaries are dead thoughts, lost yesterdays,
vanity. Words for the grave.
   Which is why she doesn't regret burying her diaries one little bit, and
why they can be eaten by worms, for all she cares! From this night onward,
all her words are immortal!

Safely back in bed after putting Sophie on the pot, Sugar opens another of
Agnes Unwin's diaries and balances it in her lap. She lifts one thigh slightly
to catch the candle-light, then begins to read.
   It's 1865 in Abbots Langley, and Agnes considers herself a Lady at last.
By Sugar's standards, she hasn't yet done a single grown-up thing or thought
a single grown-up thought, but in Agnes's view she is nearly 'finished'.
The elegant mademoiselles of the ladies' journals, once her idols, are now
rivals. She informs her diary, in case her diary didn't already know, exactly
how she wears her hair (swept back from the ears, two thick ringlets on
each side, 'sealed' with a small chignon at the nape of the neck). She wears
copies of the latest French fashions, constructed in needlework class.
Although no mention is made of anything so gross as flesh, she's presumably near enough full-grown to fill the dresses she so lovingly sketches.
   Her curriculum, now that she's thirteen, is even flimsier than when
she was nine; everything has been reduced to the essentials: Dancing, Music,
French and German. These last two are a stumbling block for Sugar: she
has little French and no German, Mrs Castaway having been of the opinion that men are partial to a bit of French on a girl's tongue, but that

German sounds like old clergymen vomiting. So, whenever Agnes starts a diary entry with *Bonjour, mon cher journal,* or *Liebes Tagebuch,* Sugar yawns, and flicks ahead.

Little Miss Unwin is learning the gavotte, the cachuca and the minuet but, despite the romantic purpose of such dances, seems wholly ignorant of the male sex. Her experience of courtship, aside from secretive and short-lived infatuations with schoolmistresses and other girls, amounts to nil. The hope she once had, of marrying a soldier who would set off in search of her real father, has been discreetly permitted to die; now her imaginary husband is a dashing nobleman with a winter residence in the south of France. Another fantasy, to be sure, but this one doesn't come out of thin air:

Eugenie was taken away from school today, in tears. She is to be married next month, to her secret correspondent from Switserland! In the circumstances, I thought it would be mean to remind her about my water-colour brushes. Perhaps she will post them.

Sugar snorts aloud, a helpless exclamation of contempt. How sweet it would be to cure Agnes's selfishness with a stinging slap to the cheek! But then she remembers the time she helped Agnes in the Bow Street alley, when Mrs Rackham was nothing more than a bloodied and frightened child, trembling in Sugar's arms, pleading to be taken home.

In all the excitement, Eugenie has also forgotten her Scrapbook of kittens, writes the fourteen-year-old Miss Unwin. *Some of the little darlings are not even paisted in yet! I do declare, if this Swiss banker loves Eugenie half as much as he says, he had better make sure she gets her Scrapbook back!*

Now at last Sugar understands: this muddle-headed, minuetting adolescent *is* a lady, as fully adult as she'll ever be. Yes, and all the ladies Sugar has ever seen, all those patrician damsels dismounting imperiously from their carriages, or promenading under parasols in Hyde Park, or parading in to the opera: they are children. Essentially unchanged from when they played with dolls and coloured pencils, they grow taller and gain a few 'accomplishments' until, at fifteen or sixteen, still accustomed to being made to sit in a corner for failing to conjugate a verb or refusing to eat their pudding, they go home to their suitors. And who are they, these suitors? Self-assured young men who've already travelled the world, fathered illegitimate children and survived the pox. Bored with young men's pleasures, they turn their attention to the enterprise of marriage and, casting their eye over the new season's bloom of elaborately dressed children, they pick themselves a little wife.

Laetitia has lately begun to <u>smell</u>, poor thing, writes Agnes on the final page of yet another journal. *What a misfortune, to be first ugly and now smelly! But I am far too well-bred to tell her so. God bless Education, for it teaches us to spare the feelings of our fellow creatures. If all the girls in the World were sent to Abbots Langley, what a World this would be! — with ne'er a cross word spoken, and everyone knowing precisely how to behave. Is there any "mal du monde" that Education cannot cure? Je ne crois pas!*

With an incredulous shake of her head, Sugar closes the volume and picks up the next in chronological sequence.

Liebes Tagebuch, it announces on its opening page. *Ich hatte einen <u>zehr ermudenden</u> tag. Welche Erleichterung zu dir zusprechen . . .*

Sugar lets the pages flutter shut, and blows out the candle.

Enough, for a while, of the yellowed pages of the past. Life in the present goes on, and before we know it 1876 will be upon us.

Leaving aside Clara's opinion that the Rackham residence is no better than Bedlam, the days of November pass peacefully. Sunrise and sunset follow each other at the scheduled intervals, and the house in Chepstow Villas fails to echo with screams or altercations. The mourning period for Henry Rackham is at an end, and everyone dresses cheerfully once more. Meals are cooked and judged a success; servants beaver at their tasks without requiring chastisement or dismissal. William spends his days plotting a bumper Christmas for Rackham Perfumeries, a Christmas that will show his business rivals how much the runty firm of his father's day has grown. Agnes continues to commit her wisdom to 'The Book' and has not the slightest inclination to dig up her diaries, no, none, despite the pitiful vision of them swelling up with wetness in the cold dirty ground. She has received a visit from Mrs Vickery and, instead of gossiping as usual, astonished her with an account of Mr Allan Kardec's excellent book, *The Gospel as Explained by Spirits*.

As for Sugar, her fears of being unequal to the task of teaching Sophie have faded. She'd imagined tantrums and cruel insolence — the sort of thing that happens in novels, where the poor governess is reduced to sobs of humiliation — but once again, novels are proved wrong, and her pupil is as diligent and placable as any teacher could hope for. Indeed, Sophie seems to regard her with awe, if only for her miraculous power to cure bedwetting. Each morning, Sophie wakes in a dry, warm bed, blinking in disbelief at the wonder of it. What an extraordinary person Miss Sugar must be, to understand the Roman Empire *and* be able to control the flow of another person's naughty wee-wee in the night!

Sugar is proud of her success, prouder than she's been of anything else she can remember. The urine rash has faded entirely, leaving a pale pink bud between Sophie's chubby thighs. This is how it should be. This is how everything should be.

Sugar basks in the child's admiration, and gives her ten new words to spell each afternoon. She's even been so bold as to write William a note, signed 'Miss Sugar', in which, rather than beseeching him to visit her bed, she primly requested the purchase of more books for the school-room. The act of inserting that letter under the door of his study felt, in its own way, every bit as roguish as her parlour trick with the squirting quim.

To Sugar's surprise, her audacity is rewarded within thirty-six hours. On yet another rainy morning, she and Sophie enter the school-room, both half-asleep, and find a mysterious parcel perched on top of the writing-desk.

'Ah!' says Sugar as she unwraps the brown paper. 'These are the books I asked Wi— uh . . . your father to get.'

Sophie is wide-eyed, impressed not just by the immaculate new volumes but by this clear evidence of Miss Sugar's intimacy with the enigma that is her father.

'Are they . . . presents?' she asks.

'Not at all,' declares Sugar. 'They are highly necessary items for your learning.' And she lets Sophie see the spoils: a history book with engravings on every page, a country-by-country guide to the British Empire, a compendium of things to do with paper, glue and string, and a smart, slim volume of poems by Edward Lear.

'These are modern books, up-to-date books,' enthuses Sugar. 'Because you're a modern person, living today, don't you see?'

Sophie's eyes threaten to revolve in confusion, at this amazing notion that History is on the move, like a vehicle in which a six-year-old girl may ride. She's always imagined History as a cobwebbed edifice, to whose colossal pedestal the insignificant speck of Sophie Rackham adheres like dirt.

By midday, Sophie has already memorised some of the verses of Mr Lear, a writer who is still alive – indeed, who wrote these words after Sophie Rackham was born!

'The Owl and the Pussy-Cat went to sea
In a beautiful pea-green boat.
They took some honey, and plenty of money
Wrapped up in a five-pound note.
The Owl looked into the stars above,
And sang to a small cigar,
'O lovely Pussy, O Pussy, my love,
What a beautiful Pussy you are, you are,
What a beautiful Pussy you are!'

And Sophie does a quick curtsy, a rare gesture of jaunty exuberance.

'Not *quite* right, Sophie,' says Sugar, smiling. 'Let's read it again, shall we?' Her smile hides a secret: this is not patience for its own sake, but a blow of revenge against her mother. Sugar has never forgotten the day in Church Lane when, as a child of seven, she made the mistake of reciting, once too often in Mrs Castaway's hearing, a favourite nursery rhyme.

'No, my poppet,' Mrs Castaway said, in the gentle tone she reserved for threats. 'We've had enough of that now, haven't we?' This was always her mother's final word on any matter, and so the nursery rhyme was dead, dead as a cockroach stamped underfoot.

'It's time,' announced Mrs Castaway, 'you learned some *grown-up* poetry.' Standing at the bookcase, she ran her fingers – already red-nailed by then – along the spines. '*Not* Wordsworth and such,' she murmured, 'for then you might get a taste for mountains and rivers, mightn't you, and we shan't ever live anywhere near *those* . . .' With a smile, she extracted two volumes, weighing them in her hands. 'Here, child. Try Pope. No, better still: try Rochester.'

Sugar took the dusty book away with her into a corner, and how earnestly she studied it! But she found that with every line she read, she entirely forgot what little she'd understood of the last one, leaving only an odour of male superiority clinging to her brain.

'Is there any other poetry you like, Mother?' she ventured to ask when, shamed by her own stupidity, she handed back the volume.

'I never said I liked poetry, did I?' rejoined Mrs Castaway sourly, replacing the Rochester in the bookshelf with a hard shove, so that the book hit the wall behind. 'Hateful stuff.'

How charmingly sweet you sing, Sugar now recites to Sophie, in her sincerest, most encouraging voice. *Oh, let us be married; too long we have tarried: But what shall we do for a ring?* Can you repeat that after me, Sophie, and practise it until I return?'

Sophie and Sugar smile at each other. The child is imagining owls and pussycats. The governess is imagining Mrs Castaway perched on a dunce's stool, her red-nailed hands trembling in impotent fury as a roomful of little girls circle her, reciting the same nursery rhyme for the thousandth time.

'Let me hear it as I walk out,' says Sugar, at the nursery door.

Ensconced in her bedroom during the midday interval, whiling away the hours until Sophie's lessons resume, Sugar applies herself to Agnes's diaries. She finds that Miss Unwin's schooldays are, at long last, drawing to a close.

Thank God for that! She's read so many thousands of words, waded through a silky, satiny, cottony tide of make-believe gowns and gauzy friendships and woolly thoughts, in the hope that she'll turn a page and *there*, suddenly, William's tormented wife will stand starkly revealed. Instead, these schoolgirl journals have been like a novel whose cover trumpets gruesome deeds and mad passions, but which proves dull as an invalid's omelette.

In her final days at Abbots Langley, the fifteen-year-old Agnes remains frivolously sane, and the final entry written on the last morning, dated May 3rd 1867, is a model of convention. She even composes a poem in honour of her school — seven stanzas so limp with feminine rhymes as to be almost boneless.

For none can thwart the Future onward rushing! she concludes, though the Future in her poem has long since stopped moving, stunned in its tracks by deadly sedatives of sentimentality.

Valedictory ode dispensed with, Agnes turns to the challenge of finding a keepsake of Abbots Langley to take home with her.

The other girls, I'm afraid to say, have purloined every <u>concievable</u> trifle. Linen-clips, chalks, sheets of music, hair-pins fallen from Miss Wick's head, honour cards: all have been gathered up. I even detected a shortage of spoons at the dinner table today.

On the next double page, the signatures of Abbots Langley's twenty-four girls are committed, in blotchy rows, to the yellowed paper. Overleaf, Agnes continues:

As you see, I asked them all to sign, and so they did, even Emily, whose sins against me in Calisthenics I have decided to forgive. Dear Diary, I shall not have such friends again! How I wept when I had all their names before me! The paper was quite *wet when the tears were fresh-fallen, as you may see from the blurrs on the ink.*

How various are the Hopes of we parting young Ladies! Some will soon be Married, but that is not for me, for Mama is ill and I must help her get Well. Some, with slimmer Prospects, are going to be governesses: may they find generous masters and agreable pupils! Of the ones who have failed to become Ladies (eg, Emily) I cannot imagine what will become.

Dear Diary, I had hoped to write so much more, but the day is almost gone, and I must rise early for my journey to-morrow. What a sorry Farewell this is! and what a muddle I am in! I shall write to you next from Home!

Your loving friend,

Agnes.

With these words, the volume ends.

The next, in a script so minuscule and clotted it's like hemming stitch, begins:

My Mama is dead, and I am soon to follow. Lord have mercy upon us. Spare my Mama from Thy wrath, from the rigour of Thy justice, from eternal flames. Thou who forgavest Magdalen, I beseech Thee. But no One hears. My prayers turn to sweat on the cieling and drip down again. Mama bled until she was empty; He (her "husband") stood by and did nothing. Now my Mama has been removed, to a grave in a cemetery where no one knows her. Day by day, our house becomes more infested with Demons. They chuckle in the rafters. They wisper behind the skirting-boards. They wait to have their way with me. He waits to have his way with me.

Sugar rummages through the stack of diaries and checks the opening pages, in case an intervening volume has escaped her notice. But no. One week it's callisthenics and hollyhocks, the next it's a smear of dried blood in the shape of a crucifix. Nor is this blood from a pinprick on the thumb, solemnising a schoolgirl pledge; this is thicker matter, incorporating a stiff clot at the point of the crucifix where Christ's head might be.

Here you see my own blood, Agnes explains underneath. *Blood from deep within me, flowing from a hidden wound. Whatever killed my Mama, now kills me. But why? Why, when I am Innocent?*

Sugar turns the page, and there's more, much more: a welter of ink so thick as to turn the paper purple.

> *In the Dark of my sleep, the iron curls of the bed-frame become soft, and pout up like lips, to recieve the droplets of my blood through the honeycomb of the matress. Under the bed, demons as grey as mushrooms wait until the blood trickles down to them, then they suck and become pink. They suck until they are red and almost bursting. How tasty this one is, they cry! So much tastier than her mother! Give us more of this divine juice!*
>
> *There can be no Rescue in this house where even the Rosary is forbidden. At His command, all who might help me are locked out. On the window of my bedroom is the cloud of steam Our Lady's nose made as She pressed against it, and the marks of Her fingers.*
>
> *How I long to lie down! But I will not give them my blood! I shall walk on, round and round my room, writing this in the crook of my arm. Their demon mouths will suck at nothing. When I can walk no longer I shall crawl into the fireplace, and give them such a bitter, ashen broth to feed on!*

A brave declaration, but evidently Agnes weakened and went to bed after all. The next day's entry begins:

> *I wake in a bed of blood, and yet I live.*

Another tirade follows, though less fervid than the first. Despite frequent recourse to words like 'doom' and 'the end', Agnes is niggled by the suspicion that Death has rather missed His moment.

> *A sumpcious dinner was served just now, with everyone urging me to join in. Mama is dead, and my own life ebbes away, and they expect me to dine on snipe and quail! I had a single ortolan on buttered toast, and a few mouthfuls of dessert, then begged to be excused.*

Each day that follows, Agnes has greater difficulty maintaining the high pitch of her despair. Normalcy nibbles at the edges of her madness, infecting it with mundane thoughts. Lord Unwin, for all that she styles him Satan's accomplice, takes her to a concert of 'Mendelshon' at the Crystal Palace one Saturday afternoon. Agnes's terror of expiring in a pool of blood proves unfounded, and she 'almost forgets' her fatal affliction for the duration of the 'really quite beautiful' concert. When, on the fifth day, the bleeding ceases altogether, Agnes concludes that a compassionate angel must have interceded on her behalf. Her handwriting grows bigger, the demons in the rafters become pigeons and, within a few entries, she's complaining that Cook put too much pepper in the kedgeree.

Thus does Agnes Unwin survive her passage to adulthood. Everyone, from her step-father to the man who delivers the woodfowl, compliments her on how she has blossomed into a lady, but no one informs her she has become a woman.

'And when his prick comes out all bloody, you say, "Oh, sir, you have taken my maidenhood!" And weep a little, if you can.'

So speaks the long-forgotten voice of Sadie, a prostitute at Mrs Castaway's in the Church Lane days, instructing Sugar how to make the most of the curse while she's still young.

'What if he doesn't believe me?'

'Of course he'll believe you. You're shaved smooth as a baby, and you've nothing on your chest — what's to betray you?'

'What if he's seen me before?'

'No chance. For deflowerings, Mrs Castaway does her soliciting outside London. Madams all over England spread the word, put a whisper in ears that are waiting to hear. He'll be a merchant or a clergyman, this fellow, and he'll *towk lahhk thaahht*.'

'What if I bleed before he even comes into me?'

'Do I have to teach you every little thing? Just keep yourself clean as a whistle! If he's slow to start, bid him look at something amusing outside your window, and give yourself a quick wipe while his face is turned.'

'Nothing outside my window is amusing.'

To which Sadie's response was a raised eyebrow, as if to say, *I can see why your mother calls you ungrateful.*

Sugar closes Agnes's diary, irritated by the need to blow her nose. Watery snot dampens her handkerchief, along with the tears on her cheeks. It's November the 30th, 1875, and Sadie's been dead for years, murdered not long after she left Mrs Castaway's for Mrs Watt's.

'Gone to a better place' was Mrs Castaway's arch comment when she got the news. 'She did say she would, didn't she?'

Sugar drops her sodden handkerchief to the floor and wipes her face on her sleeve, then wipes her forearm on the bed. This black dress she's wearing hasn't been washed since she came to the Rackham house. She, who until recently wore a different gown every day of the week, now wears the same weeds day in, day out. The fringe of her hair has grown long; she ought to have it cut, but for the moment combs and pins keep it under control.

Her little room is as modest as it was when she first arrived. Aside from a few toiletries – old gifts from William – she's imposed nothing of her own. The prints and knick-knacks from Priory Close, as well as her favourite clothes, are still packed up in her suitcases, which in turn are stacked on top of the wardrobe. There are other clothes too, boxes full, whose whereabouts she doesn't even know; William has them 'in storage' somewhere.

'You need only ask,' he assured her, in that distant part of her life, little more than a month ago, when she was his mistress in rooms that smelled of perfumed baths and fresh sweat.

Sugar stands to look out of her window. The rain has eased off, and the well-manicured bushes and hedges of the Rackham grounds glisten spinach-green and silver. Shears the gardener is patrolling the faraway fences, checking that his *Hedera helix* is fanning out nicely against the lattice-work, for there have been too many nosy folk peering at the house lately. It's five to two in the afternoon, almost time for a governess to return to her pupil. What the master of the Rackham house is up to, and who he's thinking of, God knows.

Sugar scrutinises her face in the mirror, applies a little powder to her nose and peels a fleck of dry skin off her lower lip. She has run out of Rackham's Crème de Jeunesse, and doesn't know how to ask for more, short of adding it to a list of books for Sophie.

On the landing, as she walks towards the school-room, she pauses first outside William's door, then Agnes's, and peeks furtively through the key-holes. William's study is flooded with afternoon sunlight, but vacant; he must be out in the world at large, bending it to his will. Agnes's bedroom is dark; Mrs Rackham's day is either already over, or has not yet begun.

On impulse, Sugar peeks through the nursery key-hole, in case the child should be revealed, vignetted in an act of misbehaviour. But no. Sophie sits on the floor next to her writing-desk, tidying up the carpet's tufted edges with her stubby fingers, staring down contentedly at the faded Turkish patterns.

'Small guitar, small guitar, small guitar . . .' she murmurs, to brand the words indelibly on her brain.

'God bless Papa,' says Sophie that evening, her hands clasped over the coverlet, casting a steepled shadow in the candlelight. 'God bless Mama. And God bless Miss Sugar.'

Sugar shyly reaches out to stroke the back of the child's hair, but the candle-flame enlarges the shadow of her hand grotesquely, and she withdraws with a jerk.

'Are you cold, Sophie?' she asks, when the child lies shivering in the crisp sheets.

'N-not very m-much, M-miss.'

'I'll speak to Rose about getting you another blanket. Your bedding is quite wrong for this time of year.'

Sophie looks up at her in wonder: to the great inventory of things Miss Sugar understands, must now be added the precise relation between bed-linen and the seasons.

Half past eight. The Rackham house is muffled in darkness, quiet and orderly. Even Clara would be satisfied, if she weren't already resting in her room, nose stuck in a periodical called *The Servant*. Mrs Rackham is downstairs in the parlour, re-reading a novel called *Lady Antonie's Abduction* – not strictly a book of arcane philosophy, she'll admit, but a rattling good read nonetheless, especially when one has a headache. William is in Plymouth – or Portsmouth – something-mouth, anyway. Overnight excursions of this kind – ever-more-frequent – are essential, my dear, if the Rackham name is to be spread far and wide.

The key-holes on the landing, should Clara feel inclined to inspect them, reveal nothing that would annoy her. All the rooms are dark except the governess's, whose light is demure and static. That's how Clara prefers the inhabitants of the Rackham house: asleep, like Miss Sophie, or reading in bed, like Miss Sugar.

Sugar rubs her eyes, determined to finish another of Agnes's diaries. If nothing else, the task will keep her awake until midnight, when she'll put Sophie on the pot as usual. The child needs less and less prompting each time; before long, a whisper from the doorway will do it, and soon after that, perhaps just the memory of a whisper. The history of the world and the function of the universe may take a little longer for Sophie to grasp, but Sugar is determined to get her house-trained before the year is out.

In the diaries, Agnes Unwin has just turned sixteen.

How proud Mama should have been of me, she reflects wistfully. *Although I suppose she looks down upon me from Limbo — if she can recognise me from the top of my head, at such a distance.* Exactly what Mrs Unwin might be proud of in her daughter is left unspecified, though Agnes has become (if she does say so herself) very beautiful.

Whenever I am tempted to despair, she declares, *by the cruelty of Fate and my loneliness in this God-forsaken house, I count my blessings. Principle among which, my hair and eyes . . .*

Grief and menarche have made of Miss Unwin a most peculiar little creature, demented and conventional by turns. When not bleeding, she divides attention more or less equally among clothes, garden parties, balls, shoes, hats, and secret rituals for maintaining a spotless Catholic soul while going through the motions of Anglican observance. She shuns the sun, avoids all but the feeblest exercise, eats like a bird, and seems in good health, mostly.

Each time she's struck down by her 'affliction' — which comes at erratic intervals — she regards it as a life-threatening illness caused by evil spirits. The day before the bleeding starts, she'll be complaining that there was *indisputably* a finger-mark on the inside of the soup tureen at the Grimshaws; the day after, she bids farewell to all earthly affairs and devotes her few remaining hours to fasting and prayer. Demons creep out from wherever they have been hiding, hungry for her blood. Agnes, terrified they'll crawl into bed with her, keeps herself awake with smelling-salts ('*I think I may have sniffed too deeply and too often last night, as I began to imagine I had twenty fingers and a third eye*'). She refuses to allow her servants to dispose of the soiled napkins, for fear the demons will scavenge them; instead she burns the bloodied wads of cotton in the fireplace, causing an almighty stench which Lord Unwin is forever summoning chimneysweeps to investigate.

Lord Unwin, for all Agnes's efforts to malign him, fails to live up to his reputation for monstrosity; indeed, to Sugar he appears an innocuous enough step-father. He doesn't beat her; he doesn't starve her (she does that for herself, while he cajoles her 'most cruelly' to put some meat on her bones); he chaperones her to concerts and dinner parties. An indulgent if not attentive guardian, he funds his step-daughter's most wanton extravagances without objection.

On one matter only he will not bend: Agnes is to attend Anglican worship. And not only that: she's to attend as the sole representative of the Unwins, for he himself is disinclined to put in an appearance. 'Faith is a woman's province, Aggie dear,' he tells her, and she must go and suffer horrid songs that aren't even in Latin.

I mouth the words, but don't sing them, she assures her diary, like one prostitute assuring another that she'll suck but not swallow.

Aside from this weekly humiliation, and the curse that attacks her innards every few months, Agnes's sense of herself as the miraculous survivor of a million horrific onslaughts seems rather at odds with reality. She is constantly being invited to garden parties, balls and picnics by the all the right people, and having an 'immensely pleasant' time there. By her own account, she has at least half a dozen suitors, whom Lord Unwin neither encourages nor opposes, so she maintains a coy flirtation with all of them. None of these suitors, as far as Sugar can tell from the scanty descriptions, is a professional man: rosy-cheeked aristocrats all.

Elton is sweet, and manly too, says Agnes at one point. *He took off his coat and rolled up his sleeves, in order to punt our little Boat. He did frown terribly, but we went <u>almost</u> in a straight line, and when we chose our spot, he helped us all back onto the bank.*

To read one of these accounts is to have read them all. It's a high-born world, a world in which ambitious merchants who arrange meetings with sweaty dock-workers in Yarmouth, or argue over the cost of burlap, simply don't exist. That is to say, a world in which men such as William Rackham are inconceivable.

From downstairs, in the world of November 30th, 1875, comes the muted toll of the doorbell, then:

'Willi-a-a-am, you blackguard, show yourself!'

This bellowing male voice, bursting the silence of the Rackham household, makes Sugar jump.

'Coward! Poltroon! Draw your sword and come out of hiding!'

A different, but equally loud, male voice. There are intruders downstairs! Sugar slips out of bed and kneels at her bedroom door, opening it a crack to peer through. She can see nothing except the silhouetted bars of the landing's balustrade, and the gaudy glow of the chandelier. Still, the voices are more distinct: Philip Bodley and Edward Ashwell, uproariously drunk.

'What d'you mean, he's in Yarmouth? Hiding under his bed, more like! Avoiding his old friends! We demand shatish . . . shatisfaction!'

For another thirty seconds or so, Rose's flustered pleas are intermingled

with Bodley and Ashwell's jovial blustering, then – to everyone's surprise
– Mrs Rackham arrives on the scene.

'Do let Rose take your coats, gentlemen,' she says sweetly, her breathy
lilt amplified by the acoustics of the receiving hall. 'I'll try to entertain
you as best I can, not being my husband.'

A remarkable invitation, given how fastidiously Agnes has avoided
Bodley and Ashwell in the past. It certainly has the effect of quietening
the two men, reducing them to snorts and mumbles.

'I hear,' says Agnes, 'that you have another book about to . . . ah . . .
issue forth?'

'Tuesday next, Mrs Rackham. Our best yet!'

'How very gratifying for you, I'm sure. What's it called?'

'Oh, um . . . its title is p'raps not fit for the ears of a lady . . .'

'Nonsense, gentlemen. I'm not quite the fragile flower William thinks
I am.'

'Well . . .' (self-conscious clearing of throats) '*The War with the Great
Social Evil – Who is Winning?*' (inebriated snigger).

'How interesting,' coos Agnes, 'that it should be possible for you to
have so many books published, and none of them novels, but merely your
own opinions! You really must tell me how you manage it. Is there a particular publisher who likes to help you? You know, I've become awfully
interested in this subject lately . . .'

The voices grow more muffled; Agnes is leading the men towards her
parlour.

'The subject of . . . the Great Social Evil?' enquires Ashwell incredulously.

'No no no,' trills Agnes coquettishly, as she passes under the stairs,
'the subject of *publication* . . .'

And they are gone.

For a couple more minutes Sugar kneels at her bedroom door, but the
house is quiet again, and cold air is draughting through the crack, bringing gooseflesh to her barely covered arms and chest. Scarcely able to believe
what she's just witnessed, Sugar returns to bed and takes up Agnes Unwin's
diaries where she left them.

She reads on, with one ear cocked for further developments down below,
breathing shallowly in case one of the men should raise his voice. She tries
to be disciplined and read every word, but her patience with Agnes's exhaustive cataloguing of balls and dressmakers has snapped, or perhaps the

presence of Bodley and Ashwell downstairs has spoiled her concentration. Whatever the reason, she skims, looking for tell-tale signs of something more interesting: the clotty, minuscule handwriting of madness, for instance.

Pages rustle over one another, full of words, empty of meaning, and the months flutter by. It's not until July 1868 that Agnes Unwin first mentions William Rackham. Ah, but what a mention it is!

I have today been introduced to the most extraordinary person, the seventeen-year-old writes. *Part barbarian, part oracle, part swell!*

Yes, much to Sugar's bafflement, here is William, the dashing young dandy, fresh from continental travels, flamboyant and full of mystery. Tall, too! (Although, to a woman as tiny as Agnes, perhaps all men are tall). Still, whatever William's true height in inches, he stands out signally from those pea-brained sons of the peerage to whom Agnes is more accustomed.

This vigorous young Rackham moves in Miss Unwin's circle with presumptuous nerve, apparently fearless, despite his dubious credentials, of being snubbed. He has the knack of strolling through a crowd and disarranging it so that it regroups in half-reluctant crescents around him, whereupon he pushes (by means of superior wit) the other males to the periphery, leaving a preponderance of young females for him to entertain with tales of France and Morocco. It's from within this covey of ladies that Agnes prefers, at first, to experience him, to prevent his fierce aura shining exclusively on her blushing face. But, in a turn of events that Agnes bemoans as *tellement gênant!*, Rackham selects her out of all her set, and finds ways of getting her alone. Lest her dear diary accuse her of complicity in this, Agnes emphatically denies any, complaining that whenever William Rackham is about, her companions abruptly move off without her, and there he'll be, grinning like the cat that got the cream!

While claiming his attentions to be 'most worrisome', Agnes describes her pursuer thus:

> *He is robust but yet he has a fine-boned face and hands, and abundant curly hair of gold. His eyes have an insouicant sparkle to them, and he looks at everyone too directly, though he affects not to be aware of this. He dresses as few men Nowadays dare to dress, in check trousers, canary-yellow waistcoat, hunting caps, and suchlike. I have only seen him once in sober Blacks (and a handsome figure he cuts too!) but when I asked him why he does not wear them more often, he replied, "Black is for*

*Sundays, Funerals and dull men. What have I to fear from dressing as I do? That
I might be refused admission to Churches, Funerals, or the company of dull men?
Why then, I will go about in deerstalker and dressing-gown!"*

*His father is a man of Business — this he does not conceal. "It is my father's
affair how he makes his way in the world, and mine how I make mine." I cannot
determine to my satisfaction from what source he derives his income: perhaps it is
from his Writings. He is certainly ineligible to appear very high on my list of
Suitors.*

This half-hearted attempt to be severe fails to impress Sugar, for not
only does she already know how the story ends, but also she can't help
noticing that the half-dozen barely differentiated suitors of earlier months
have all but vanished from the diary, and more ink is expended on William
Rackham than ever was spilt for any of them. Before long, Agnes is record-
ing entire conversations from hello to adieu, rushing to transcribe them
immediately afterwards so that none of the man's sagacious pronouncements will be lost or misquoted. By Autumn 1868, those entries in which
William features have grown so vivid they read like episodes from a novel:

*"Let us have done with this small talk," he said suddenly, extending a fore-
finger to either side of my open fan, and clapping it shut right in front of my nose.
I was frightened, but he was smiling. "In ten years," he said, " Will either of us
remember any of it?"*

*I was all a'blush, but my wits did not desert me. "I do not presume we shall
have each others aqcaintance in ten years," I said.*

*Hereupon he clapped his hand to his breast, as though I had shot him through
the heart. Loath to offend him, I hastened to add — "In any case, I confess I've nothing but small talk to offer you: it is all I have been taught. I am untravelled, and a
most uninteresting and shallow little thing, compared to you."*

*I hoped to flatter him with this speech, but he took it <u>very</u> seriously, and insisted,
"Oh, but you are more interesting and less shallow than any young lady I know!
There are desires deep within you, which no one can imagine — no one but me. You
move as one young lady among other young ladies, but you are not <u>really</u> one of them.
You are different, and whats more, <u>I can tell that you know it</u>."*

*"Mr Rackham!" — was all I could say — he had made me blush so. Whereupon
he did a most peculiar thing, namely he reached forward, took the edges of my fan
once more, and spread it open, so that my face was hidden from him. I heard his voice
explain it thus:*

"Now, I see that I was wrong to shine my light into the secrets of your soul: it has frightened you, and I would not frighten you for all the world. Let us return, then, to small talk. Look over there, Agnes, at the Garnett girls, and the hats they are wearing. I saw you coveting those hats earlier this afternoon — yes I did, theres no use denying it. Well, covet them no longer! I was in Paris not two weeks ago, and everyone there agrees that the moment for those hats has passed."

This encounter is a turning-point in Agnes's feelings for William Rackham; hereafter, she ponders his every word like a devoted disciple. No remark of his, however lighthearted, can be without deeper significance and, when he deigns to be wise, he is wiser than anyone she's ever met. Knowledgeable about a host of religions, he sums up their shortcomings with *such* a fine phrase — something about there being 'more in Heaven and Earth than is dreamt of by their philosophy'. (Ah, if only she hadn't eaten dinner before writing her diary, she might have recalled it exact!) He attends Anglican worship when he attends any, but he's of the heretical opinion that English religion has been in a shambles ever since Henry VIII — a conviction Agnes naturally shares. He's expert in the identification of flowers, can predict the weather, knows the stuffs from which women's garments are made, and is a personal friend of several artists regularly exhibiting at the Royal Academy. What a man! Only the precise sources of his income remain difficult to map, but, as Agnes puts it:

He is an Author, a Scholar, a Man of Science, and cleverer than any Statesman. Why should he not be undecided which path to follow, when he may yet follow them all? I feel my heart thump in my breast when I draw near to him, and am enfeebled when we part. Though I am sure I should repel him if he dared lay his hands upon me, I half wish that he would do it, and sometimes in idle moments after he has left me I fancy I can feel his arms clasped around me. Each morning I wake wishing that the first thing I saw was his face, and when I go to bed at night, the first face I see in my dreams is his. Am I going mad?

Downstairs, an almighty crash. Glassware or china — gruff exclamations of surprise — the smack of a door against a wall, sending a jolt right through the house.

'Out with you! Out of my sight!' screams Agnes.

In an instant, Sugar is kneeling at her door again, face pressed to the crack. Shadows and light are gyrating below the landing, as a scuffle spills

out into the receiving hall. So violently was the parlour door flung open
that the chandelier in the hall still sways gently under the ceiling.

'Mrs Rackham!' protests one of the men. 'There's no need . . .'

A loud clatter and an alarming *spoinggg*: the hat-stand being thrown
across the floor. 'Don't tell *me* what there's a need for, you fat drunken
dog!' Agnes cries. 'You are useless and . . . and ridiculous, the pair of you!'

'My dear Mrs Rackham . . .'

'Nothing is dear to you except filth! Muck-sniffers! Sewer-rats! Your hair
smells like rotten banana! Your skulls are full of slime! Get out of my house!'

'Yesh, yesh . . .' mutters one of the men.

'Our coats, Bodley . . .' his companion reminds him, as a harsh influx
of icy air barges into the house.

'Coats!' cries Agnes witheringly. 'Your fat oily skins will keep you warm!
That, and your prostitutes!'

'Ah, Rose – there you are!' says Ashwell, in a stab at genial good grace.
'I think your mistress may be . . . ah . . . having one of her turns . . .'

'I am *not* having "one of my turns"!' rages Agnes. 'I'm merely trying
to rid my house of some garbage before I step in it! No, don't touch them,
Rose: if you knew where they have been . . . !'

Bodley, the drunker of the two, can bear the provocation no longer.
'*If* I may shay so, Mrs Rackham,' he declaims, 'your a-ashitude is half
the reason why proshtishushion is shpreading so . . . so muchly! If
inshtead of inshulting us, you took the chubble to read our researches
on the shubject . . .'

'You conceited fool – you think I don't even know what prostitutes
are!' shrieks Agnes, discordant harmonics of her voice seeming to ring out
from every metal and glass surface in the house. 'Well, I *do*! They are sly,
common women who will stoop to kiss your ugly faces for money! Hah!
Why don't you kiss each *other* for *nothing*, you apes!'

And with that, Bodley and Ashwell flee, the front door slams, Agnes
utters one last throaty cry of frustration, and there's a muffled thud of
flesh on the hall floor.

After a few moments' silence, Rose's voice pipes up, thin and anxious.
'Miss Tillotson! Miss Tillotson!'

Still on her hands and knees, Sugar scuttles backwards from the crack
in her door, and jumps into bed like a good girl.

★   ★   ★

'A night like this . . .' (pant) 'is worth ten shillings alone,' complains a voice on the stairs.

'Watch her fingers,' whines another.

With no master in the house to carry the insensible Agnes upstairs, the task is being shouldered by Rose, Letty and Clara. They take a long time over it, too, puffing and grunting, but eventually the procession passes Sugar's room and, soon afterwards, silence is restored.

Sugar waits as long as she can bear for everyone to be asleep. Enthralling though this fiasco has been, it must not undo her good work with Sophie. Off to bed, everyone, and let a poor governess come out to play!

Sugar checks the time. A quarter to midnight – surely the last of the servants must be in the Land of Nod by now. They have to rise again early in the morning: they ought to keep that in mind, if they know what's good for them. Clara especially, with her sullen mouth and her glittering suspicious eyes – she should give those a rest until tomorrow, the poisonous little shrew. Lay her nasty pock-marked cheek on her pillow and let the world turn without her for a few hours . . .

Ten minutes to twelve. Sugar tiptoes along the frigid landing towards Sophie's bedroom. All the hearths in the house have cooled, and the warmth has ceased to rise; the rafters creak in the wind and there's a pattering of hail on the roof. Sugar slips inside Sophie's room like a ghost, but finds the child already sitting erect in bed, eyes wide in the candle-light.

'Bad dream, Sophie?' enquires Sugar gently, taming the unstable shadows by settling the candle on top of the dresser, right next to the nigger doll, which, she notes, has been swaddled in a white knitted scarf.

'My Mama,' announces Sophie, in a queer didactic tone, 'has fits, Miss. She's awful rude, and she shouts, and then she falls over.'

'It's all right, Sophie,' says Sugar, knowing it's not all right, but unable to come up with a better reassurance. 'Have you . . . done your doings yet?' The euphemism, her own coinage, sounds prissy on her lips – those lips which until recently exhorted William to fill her cunt with spunk.

Sophie clambers out of her bed and squats obediently on the pot. Euphemisms are all she knows; and, if Sugar can manage it, they're all she ever *will* know.

'Nurse told me,' quotes Sophie as a puppyish squirt of piss hisses onto the porcelain, 'that my Mama will end her days in a mad-house.' A moment later she adds (just in case her governess's encyclopaedic knowledge is missing this one lurid titbit): 'A house where they keep mad people, Miss.'

Ugly old tattle-tale, die and rot in Hell, thinks Sugar. 'What an unkind remark for your Nurse to make,' she says.

'But Mama *will* have to go there, won't she, Miss?' persists the child as she's helped back into bed.

Sugar sighs. 'Sophie, the middle of the night, when we should all be sleeping, is not the time to worry about such things.'

'What time is it, Miss?' asks the child, wide awake.

Sugar glances at the clock on the mantel.

'A minute to midnight.' She tucks the blanket up to Sophie's neck. The room is so cold her hands are trembling. Yet the child's eyes are imploring her not to go.

'I have to get back into my own bed now, Sophie.'

'Yes, Miss. Is it tomorrow yet?'

Sugar checks, considers lying. 'Not quite yet,' she admits. 'Here, let me show you the clock.' She fetches the heavy time-piece from the mantel; it's steel-grey, pitted, and shaped like a jelly-mould, a most unsightly thing. She cradles it in her hands and lets Sophie watch the seconds ticking away under its jaundiced glass face. The wind howls outside, overriding the mechanism of the time-piece.

'*Now* it's tomorrow,' Sophie declares, relieved, as if an unpleasant disagreement has been settled to universal satisfaction.

'Not only that, little one,' says Sugar, suddenly remembering the date. 'It's December. The last month of the year, the one that brings us Winter and Christmas. And when December is over, what comes then, Sophie?'

Sugar waits, willing to accept either 'January' or '1876'. The house creaks in the heavy rain, infiltrated by all sorts of mysterious noises louder than the soft breaths of a child. When it's clear no answer is going to come, she blows out the candle.

TWENTY-FIVE

'ut we've discussed everyone except *you*, William,' says Lady Bridgelow, as they stroll side by side on the glistening footpath. 'Your life is becoming shrouded in mystery, and I am *so* curious!'

William chuckles, momentarily relishing his status as enigma. But he wouldn't wish to keep Constance (as Lady Bridgelow insists he should refer to her) uninformed for long. She is, after all, his best friend – well, certainly of those with whom he can nowadays be seen in public.

The morning drizzle has cleared up, making way for a Sunday afternoon of exceptional mildness. Pale though the sun is, there's real warmth in it, as it lights up the tiles of Notting Hill's rooftops and brings a corona of brilliance to the church spire. William is glad he came out today; with weather like this, his resolution to be seen in church more regularly promises to be quite painless.

'Did you find a governess for your daughter?' enquires Lady Bridgelow.

'Yes, yes, I did, thank you.'

'Because I know of an excellent girl available very soon – frightfully clever, placid as a lamb, father just gone bankrupt . . .'

'No, no, I'm sure the one I've employed is perfectly adequate.'

Lady Bridgelow frowns slightly at this reminder of yet another unknown quantity in her friend's life.

'She's not a Rescue Society girl, is she?'

William feels his cheeks and neck growing pink, and is grateful for his ever-more-plenteous beard and high collar.

'Certainly not: what makes you think that?'

Lady Bridgelow casts a backwards glance over the ermine stole wrapped

around her neck, as though absolute privacy is required for what she's
about to divulge.

'Well, you've heard that Mrs Fox has returned to her old . . . *profession*,
haven't you? And working harder than ever, I'm told. Striving to convince
ladies with *any* sort of servant problem at all, that one of these . . . reformed
specimens is the solution. She knows better than to approach *me*; I had a
Rescue Society girl in my kitchen, and was obliged to dismiss her after
four months.'

'Oh?' Stability has finally returned to William's own household, at
considerable cost in money and brain-racking; he hates the thought of
anything going awry. 'What went wrong?'

'Nothing I can mention in polite company,' smirks Lady Bridgelow,
miming, with a subtle sweep of her kid-gloved fingers through the air in
front of her silky abdomen, a swollen arc.

'Am *I* polite company, Constance?'

She smiles. 'You are . . . *sui generis*, William. I feel I could discuss *any*
subject with you.'

'Oh, I hope you could.'

Emboldened, she presses on: 'Such a shame you couldn't attend the
launch of Philip and Edward's new book. Did you know I was one of only
five ladies there? Or *four* ladies, actually: Mrs Burnand was fetched out of
the hall by her *furious* husband, in front of everyone!'

William gives her a grin, but is a little pained, wondering if he was
justified in taking umbrage at the heavy-handed way his old friends
scrawled the injunction '*sans femme*' on his own invitation.

'Well, Bodley and Ashwell's book *is* close to the bone,' he sighs. 'And
I'm not wholly convinced by their statistics. If there were as many prostitutes in London as they claim, we'd be tripping over them . . .'

'Yes, yes, but let me tell you: Mrs Fox was there at the launch. She
stood up from the crowd and commended the authors for helping to bring
the problem to wider public notice – then scolded them for insufficient
seriousness! "There is nothing to laugh about when a woman falls!" she
said – and of course, everyone roared.'

'Poor Mrs Fox. "Forgive her, Lord, for she knows not what she
says" . . .'

Lady Bridgelow chuckles, a surprisingly earthy sound. 'Ah, but one
mustn't be unkind about other people's indiscretions, must one?' she says.

'I was speaking with Philip and Edward afterwards, and they mentioned how very concerned they are about your poor Agnes . . .'

William stiffens as he walks.

'Their concern's appreciated,' he says, 'but happily unnecessary. Agnes has quite recovered.'

'Not in church with us this morning, though . . . ?' murmurs Lady Bridgelow.

'No.'

'But possibly attending Catholic Mass in Cricklewood?'

'Possibly.' William knows very well she is. His wife's belief that she and her coachman share 'a little secret' is a pitiable delusion. 'She'll grow out of it, I trust.'

Lady Bridgelow heaves a deep, elegiac sigh, and her eyes mist over. 'Aahh, trust,' she echoes sadly, hinting at the slings and arrows she's had to endure in her life so far. Melancholy suits her face, lending her that faraway look that's come into vogue lately. However, she can't be glum for long, and bounces back with:

'Do you have anything extra-ordinary planned for Christmas?'

'Just the usual, I'm afraid,' says William. 'I really am a very boring fellow nowadays. I sleep, I eat breakfast, I conquer another part of the British Empire with my manufactures, I have dinner, and I go to bed. Honestly, I can't imagine why anyone besides my banker should take the slightest bit of interest in me . . .'

'Oh but no, you must make room for me, too, William,' she demurs. 'Every great businessman needs a female friend. Especially if what he manufactures is of such value to females, hmm?'

William struggles to keep his face composed, almost irresistibly tempted to beam. It hadn't occurred to him that Lady Bridgelow would ever use Rackham's. The new catalogues and placards must be having the desired effect . . .

'As for me,' says Lady Bridgelow, 'I've achieved something of a coup for my next party, haven't I? Both Lord *and* Lady Unwin, together in the same country, at the same dinner table!'

'Yes, how did you manage it?'

'If truth be told, sheer swiftness! I popped the question before anyone else had recovered from the surprise of Lord Unwin's return. I certainly can't claim *my* charms brought him back here; I think his wife decided they should celebrate Christmas in England *en famille*, and ordered him to put in an appearance – or else.'

William has trouble imagining Lord Unwin being coerced in this way. 'I'd have thought it would take more than that.'

'Ah well, you must remember his current wife is not the submissive creature Agnes's mother was. And, of course, he has children of his own now. That is, of his own blood.'

William responds with an empty hum; he's never met the current Lady Unwin. Not that the Rackhams haven't been invited to her house several times, but these invitations, in Agnes's view, might as well have issued from Beelzebub, and she invariably responded with a *Regret Not Able To Attend*.

('I'm sure she means you well, dear,' William would counsel her, but Agnes has never forgiven her step-father's remarriage. The *least* he could have done was mourn, for the rest of his life, the saintly Violet Pigott, who 'sacrificed her soul' to please him! Instead, the hoary beast rushed to marry this . . . this *thing*.)

'I must admit,' says William, 'I'm apprehensive about meeting the old man after all this time. When I petitioned him for Agnes's hand, I may've led him to expect that she'd be kept in grander style than . . . Well, *you* know the story of my fortunes, Constance. I always wondered if he thought badly of me . . .'

'Oh no, he's an old pussycat,' Lady Bridgelow affirms, as they approach the corner of Chepstow Villas. 'He and my poor Albert were friends, you know, and he did his best to dissuade Albert from all those imprudent . . . Well, *you* know the story of *my* fortunes, too. And when Albert died, Lord Unwin wrote me the *sweetest* letter. Not an unkind word in it. And Albert did some foolish, foolish things, I assure you! He wasn't clever like *you* . . .'

Lady Bridgelow suddenly hushes in mid-flow: she and William no longer have the footpath to themselves. A tall scrawny woman in a plain black dress, with gangly arms and red hair that badly needs cutting, is advancing with a roly-poly child at her side.

'How do you do, Miss Sugar,' William hails her, cool but cordial.

'Very well, thank you, sir,' replies the scrawny woman. Her lips, deplorably, are flaked with dead skin, although she has comely enough eyes. Her demeanour is as dejected as one expects from a governess.

'A rather brighter day today,' remarks William, 'than some we've had lately.'

'Yes,' agrees the governess, 'to be sure.' She reaches awkwardly for her pupil's hand, and grasps it. 'I . . . I took Sophie out of doors because she's so very pale . . .'

'A lady can never be too pale nowadays,' says Lady Bridgelow. 'Rosy complexions seem to be a thing of the past, don't they, William?'

Neither she nor William lower their attention to Sophie's level. Their gazes and their words pass through the air in a straight line to Miss Sugar, well above the child's head.

'I am finding Sophie,' says the governess, transparently at a loss for any sophisticated conversation, 'a most obedient and . . . um . . . hard-working little girl.'

'How very agreeable for you,' says Lady Bridgelow.

'Very good, Sophie,' condescends William, meeting his daughter's wide blue eyes for the merest instant before moving on.

Back at the house, in the suffocating warmth of the nursery, Sugar can barely control herself. Her body wants to tremble – to shake – with indignation, on her own behalf, and Sophie's. All her sinews and nerves are tingling with the undischarged desire to propel her body through the air, a whirling fury of claws and feet to tear that smug little bitch apart.

'Who was that lady, Sophie?' she asks evenly, after a very deep breath.

Sophie is playing with the wooden animals of her toy Noah's ark – still her favourite Sunday activity, despite the permission Miss Sugar has given her to do whatever she pleases on the Sabbath. She shows no sign of anguish at how shabbily she's just been treated by her father and his companion; her cheeks are a little flushed, true, but the unaccustomed exercise and the blazing fire accounts for that.

'I don't know, Miss.'

'How often does she visit your father?'

Sophie looks up from shepherding the giraffes, her brow knotting in bafflement. A historical question about the succession of Mesopotamian monarchs would be an easier challenge than this.

'But you've seen her before?' pursues Sugar, her voice tightening.

Sophie ponders for a while. 'Sometimes I hear the servants 'nounce her,' she says.

Sugar lapses into a sulk. For the first time in months, she itches for pen and paper, to write a fiction of revenge like the ones in her novel.

Only this time, the victim wouldn't be a man, but a horrid little pug-dog of a woman, bound with twine at her wrists and ankles.

"Have pity! Have pity!" she yammered, as she felt a sharp object probing the tightly-clenched hole between her buttocks — a cold, leathery protuberance bristling with hair.

"What's that? What's that?" she cried in terror.

"Don't you recognise it? It's the snout of a stoat," replied Sugar, twisting the sharp head of the ermine stole in her fist. "The poor creature is sure to be happier up your arse than around your neck . . . "

'Did you hear,' pipes up Sophie, 'what my father said, Miss? He said I am a good girl.'

Sugar is jolted from her fantasy of revenge, and is confused to see a happy smile on the child's face, a sheen of pride in her eyes.

'He didn't say that,' she snaps, before she can stop herself.

Sophie's look of contentment evaporates, and her brow creases — a change that serves only to emphasise her resemblance to William. She turns her head away, taking refuge in the less dangerous world of her playthings. Held erect in her tiny hand, Noah begins to ascend the gangplank of the Ark with slow, dignified hops.

'But my dear Rackham, if you'll forgive me saying so: you are still evading the subject.'

'Am I?' says William. It's Monday morning, and he's entertaining a guest in his smoking-room. Cigars are already lit, and William uncorks the port-bottle with a *thwipp*. 'Perhaps we aren't agreed,' he says, 'on what the subject *is*. I am asking you for advice on how to hasten my wife's progress back to full health, here in her own home. *You* seem intent on cataloguing the merits and demerits of mad-houses from Aberdeen to Aberystwyth.'

Doctor Curlew grunts. His effusion of information was only natural, provoked by Rackham's pretence to know something about lunatic asylums that *he* doesn't. In fact, Doctor Curlew has probably spent more time in mad-houses than any sane man; as a young physician, in the years before he decided that surgery was not his *forte*, he performed many operations on asylum inmates, and learned a great deal besides scalpelling techniques. He knows the good asylums from the bad; knows which of them are nothing but glorified prisons, or boarding-houses with medical pretensions —

or, at the other end of the scale, first-class hospitals devoted to the increase of knowledge and the full recovery of the patient. He has observed many times that hysterical ladies, so degraded as to be no use to man or beast, may effect miraculous recoveries once removed from the circle of indulgent fuss-pots on whom their illness feeds.

Knowing all this, Doctor Curlew can predict with authority that, in her own house, Agnes Rackham is doomed. What hope for recovery has she, when she not only has a permissive husband, but is pampered by obsequious and gullible servants?

'There's no virtue, Rackham,' he says, 'in keeping a sick person at home. No one blames a man for sending his wife to a hospital when she breaks a leg or gets smallpox. *This* is no different, I tell you.'

William sips unhappily at his port. 'I do wonder,' he muses, 'if there isn't something *physically* the matter with her . . .'

'I've investigated her inside out. There's nothing wrong that won't correct itself if she's properly handled.'

'Sometimes, when she's behaving very badly, just before she collapses, I could swear one eye is bigger than the other . . .'

'Humphh. I imagine she's having trouble looking you straight in the face. I'm sure any woman would, during such a performance.'

Abruptly, the fuggy silence of the smoking-room is penetrated by the pure tones of a piano, fingered most fetchingly in the parlour nearby. After a fluent prelude, Agnes begins to sing, serene and joyful as a bird. The look of wistful sentimentality that softens William's features makes Curlew want to groan with frustration.

'Rackham,' he argues, 'you really must rid yourself of this fond notion that your wife is a well person who suffers occasional bouts of illness, rather than a sick person who occasionally has a good day. Tell me: if one of the machines that bottle your perfumes was running amok, breaking all the glass and spraying scent everywhere, and it was doing it time after time, and then, just as you summoned a fellow to repair it, it seemed to cure itself, would you assume the fault was gone, and no repairs were necessary?'

'Human beings are not machines.'

An odd philosophy, Curlew refrains from remarking, *for an industrialist*. 'Well,' he sighs, to the accompaniment of Agnes's angelic trills, 'if you won't consider an asylum, there are some immediate measures I urge you to take. First, stop her going to Mass. Being a Catholic is no crime, but your wife was an Anglican when she married you and an Anglican she should still be. If her faith in the Roman Church were anything more than a delusion, she'd be trying to convert you, not pleasuring herself with secret excursions to Cricklewood. Secondly, it's high time Agnes admitted she's a mother. This absurd pantomime of avoidance has gone on far too long. If you won't consider what's best for Agnes, think of your daughter, now that she's old enough to ask questions. Being deprived of a mother's love can't be doing her any good, don't you see?'

William nods slowly. Unpalatable though the truth may be, there's no gainsaying the superior wisdom of a man who knows his profession. A mother cannot deny her offspring forever without some harm coming of it: that's a fact.

'It seems like only a few months ago she was a babe in arms,' he mutters in Agnes's defence, calling to mind his occasional glimpses of the infant Sophie swaddled in Beatrice's embrace. But the child has grown like a weed, and he has to concede that yesterday, when he met Sugar and Sophie in the street, he was taken aback by his daughter's look of watchful intelligence.

'I don't wish to distress Agnes unnecessarily,' he says.

'With what's at stake here, Rackham,' pronounces the doctor, 'a modicum of your wife's distress may prove a cheap price to pay.'

William grimaces assent; the negotiations are concluded, both parties having conceded some ground while appearing to stand firm. Breathing easier, the host offers his guest more port.

'Now tell me, Doctor,' he says. 'How is *your* daughter?'

Emmeline Fox stoops to pick up the cat turds at the top of the stairs with her fingers. The droppings are *quite* dry, after all, and she can wash her hands as soon as she's disposed of Puss's mess. Honestly, the fuss some people make about dirt. They should be obliged to live for a day in a Shoreditch slum, where slime drips down the walls and children are disfigured by rat bites . . . !

Emmeline squats to her task, her loose hair falling over her face – the more shit she picks up, the more she finds. Puss really has been very naughty. If he doesn't mend his ways soon, she'll have to banish him from her bed and make him sleep out of doors.

'Do you hear that, Puss?' she says, as if the casual inspection of her thoughts is another of his bad habits. He doesn't deign to reply.

She tosses the turds into a cardboard box that used to contain stationery, and now contains about a fortnight's worth of cat droppings. The whole caboodle will be tipped into a hole in the garden, as soon as she buys a spade, which she certainly will do this morning, and never mind the stares of the ironmonger.

She descends the dusty stairs in her bare feet; indeed, she's altogether naked. The convention of dressing for bed has ceased to make sense to her and, despite the approach of winter, she doesn't miss her night-gowns at all. She scarcely feels the cold; her extremities can be bone white and she'll be unaware of suffering. What do the fortunate know of cold, anyway, snug in their well-heated houses?

Not that her own house is terribly well-heated just now. She's forgotten to bring the coal in, and all the hearths need cleaning. It really is high time she replaced Sarah; three months without a servant is taking its toll. There are plenty of good girls to be had through the Rescue Society; she need only tidy the place a little so as not to make too bad an impression.

Emmeline washes with a flannel (she had a proper bath only yesterday) and dons her work clothes – that is, the smart but practical dress she wears when visiting the poor. Her stomach growls, reminding her not to leave the house without eating, as she too often does.

In the kitchen, she squeezes between Henry's stove and her own, to fetch the bread from the cupboard overhead. The loaf still has the knife stuck in it, which is just as well, since she's mislaid a lot of cutlery lately. There's no butter, but there's a bounteous supply of tinned meat and fish, a wonderful boon for the independent woman. She considers the Belgravian Ox Tongues, but plumps for salmon. Fish oil, she's read, is good for the brain.

Henry's cat comes padding in, making ingratiating noises and butting his head against Emmeline's skirt.

'Wait, wait,' she scolds him, as she rummages for a clean cup to make herself a hot drink. Then she remembers she has no milk, and without milk she dislikes both tea and cocoa. No matter; soon enough, Mrs Nash will pour her a nice cup of tea at the meeting hall.

'Here, you shameless thing,' she says, emptying the remainder of the salmon directly onto the kitchen floor. 'Always taking advantage of me

. . . Why don't you go out and get some honest work, hmm? I ought to call you Spoony-Puss.'

Henry's cat cocks its head. 'Miaow?'

Emmeline must hurry now; she slept later than she thought, having stayed awake most of the night writing dozens of replicas of the same letter urging the governors of local schools not to forsake the children hiding in the rookeries. If she doesn't leave soon, she'll miss the tea and biscuits.

Where is her bonnet? Oh yes: it's hung on Henry's bed-frame, which still stands upright against the wall of the sitting-room. (She did find a home for the mattress, courtesy of Mrs Emerson's recent appeal for bedding, but the iron frame was judged too heavy.) With a couple of hat-pins, and a ribbon tied under her chin, Emmeline transforms herself into Mrs Fox, ready for the fray.

Just as she's about to open her front door, a letter whispers through the slit, and falls at her feet. She stuffs it into her purse, and dashes.

Comfortably seated at the Rescue Society's meeting hall, cup of tea at her elbow, Mrs Fox opens the envelope. A single sheet, obsessively folded into a tiny square, falls onto the table. Mrs Fox smooths it out before her, and squints at its Lilliputian script.

Time is fast running out, it says. *I know that you are a good and kind person, despite your Father's dark Allegiences. (I too had an evil father, so I sympathise) I know that you have already claimed your Second Body. People say that you are not pretty and that your Complexion is bad but they do not look beneath at the beauty of your Soul. How radiant that Soul must be, knowing its fleshly home is Immortal! As for me, my earth-born flesh is showing dreadful signs of decay, and I cannot bear the thought of being trapped in it for much longer. I happen to know that my Second Body is waiting for me at the Convent of Health. Please, please, please divulge to me where the Convent is. I am ready to go, but I fear my Guardian Angel expects me to be patient and wait until the Bitter End. You are my only hope. Please grant me the Secret Knowledge I crave.*

In the name of the regard we held in common for Henry, I beseech you,

Agnes R.

Mrs Fox folds the letter back into its envelope. All around her, the refreshments are being cleared away and her sisters are putting on their coats and gloves. Mrs Rackham's plea will have to wait, in favour of lost souls nearer to hand.

★   ★   ★

That evening, resting on her bed with Puss purring against her thigh, Mrs Fox re-reads the letter.

She's in irritable spirits; her afternoon with the Rescue Society has not been a success. The streets of Shoreditch are rich veins of Godless destitution, true, but devilishly difficult to penetrate: the residents are hostile, and most doors slam shut at the approach of a Rescuer. There was one whore who consented to speak to Mrs Fox, but she was in a state of inebriation so severe that serious discussion was impossible.

'You'd make a good whore yerself!' the giggling trollop assured her. 'I c'n tell! You ain't wearin' a corset, are yer? I c'n see yer teats!'

Mrs Fox tried to explain that she'd been very ill, and had found it difficult to breathe when constrained by a stiff carapace; and that, in any case, modesty has nothing to do with corsets, for decent women existed long before such garments were invented . . . But the whore was having none of it.

'You ain't 'ad children, by the looks of yer,' she chortled, tickling Emmeline under the swell of her bosom. 'Men *like* that.'

Now Emmeline slumps on her bed, footsore, grimy, with particles of soot gritting on her tongue, and (*bother!*) still no milk for cocoa. And if that weren't bad enough, here, again, is this letter in which Agnes Rackham begs her for the secret of physical immortality.

How to reply?

With the truth, of course, however unwanted it may be. Emmeline fetches pen and paper, and scrawls the following:

> *Dear Mrs Rackham,*
>
> *I am sorry to tell you that you are mistaken. None of us can hope to be immortal unless it be in the spirit through Christ (see Romans 6: 7–10; I Corinthians 15:22 and most particularly 15:50). If I can help you in <u>any</u> other way, I will do it gladly.*
>
> *Yours sincerely,*
>
> *E. Fox*

She folds this note into an envelope, seals it and, almost in the same motion, tears it to shreds. The vision of Mrs Rackham receiving the letter in an ecstasy of anticipation, only to find a rebuttal and a few Scriptural references, is too pitiful.

Perhaps sending a book would be more use? It would obviate the need for a personal rebuff, and might be more effective in dispelling the miasma of Mrs Rackham's delusion. Emmeline leaps off the bed and begins to fossick in the dusty, furry piles of books that litter her house, searching for *The Ruined Temple*, an autobiography written by an evangelist with a wasting disease, which she lent to Henry when he was making such a fuss about her own decline. It was a slim volume, with a distinctive spine, but she cannot, for the life of her, find it, and the dust she raises provokes her to a frenzy of sneezing.

But what's this? A thick pamphlet she can't recall ever seeing before. On its reverse, commendations from such authorities as 'A. E., of Bloomsbury': *For lovers of pleasure, this is nothing less than the bible!* On the front, in embossed black print: *More Sprees in London – Hints for Men About Town, with advice for greenhorns.* She opens the book, and finds it inscribed on the flyleaf *to Henry, from Philip & Edward*, with an additional note: *Your future parish? Good luck!*

Emmeline winces in pain at Bodley and Ashwell's cruel prank and, to her own astonishment, hot tears spring to her eyes, falling onto the pamphlet. Through a haze of weeping, she flips through the pages, some of which are dog-eared, presumably to mark particular prostitutes whom Bodley and Ashwell were keen to sample.

Mrs Fox leans her head back, embarrassed at her incontinence of snivelling. She'll study this horrid little book in detail later; it may, for all the grief it's causing her now, prove to be a blessing in disguise. She must regard it . . . yes, that's it: she must regard it as an invaluable inventory of the women whom she'll do her utmost to find and rescue. Yes, some good will come of this after all!

'Your cup of tea, Miss.'

Sugar jerks awake from troubled dreams, blinking in the half-light. She looks up: a figure she doesn't recognise is looming over her bed, holding a tea-cup in one hand, and a burning lamp in the other, for the day has barely begun. As she hauls herself up onto her elbows, disentangling her arms from the bed-clothes, she senses a weight on her legs, and finds an open diary nestled face-down on her left thigh.

Damn! She can only hope the servant takes it to be a schoolbook, or a diary of Miss Sugar's own, rather than stolen property.

'Uh . . . thank you . . . Rose,' she croaks, her throat parched, her vision blurred. 'What . . . uh . . .'

'Half past six, Miss, on a fine Tuesday morning.'

'Fine?' Sugar cranes her head towards the dark window in which Rose's lamp is reflected in a halo of frost.

'I mean only to say, Miss, that it's stopped snowing.'

'Ah, yes . . .' Sugar rubs her eyes. 'I'm sure I'd sleep all day if it weren't for you. ' Instantly she regrets this limp gesture of ingratiation, which only makes her seem a slattern. *Keep your mouth shut until you've woken up,* she cautions herself.

When Rose and her lamp have made their exit, the first feeble glimmerings of dawn edge into Sugar's room. If she squints hard, she can discern strange white shapes suspended outside her window, like ghosts hovering absolutely immobile, twenty feet above the ground. A rustling gust of wind, and the ghosts begin to disintegrate at the edges, their white extremities falling out of sight. Snow in the trees, powdery and evanescent.

Shivering, Sugar takes a swig of tea from the absurdly dainty cup. How strange she still finds it, this ritual of being served tea at the crack of dawn by a servant, instead of waking at ten or eleven with the sun beaming on her face. In an instant, she's transported back in time – not to Priory Close, but farther still – to the top floor of Mrs Castaway's, with the pigeons cooing in the rafters, the sun mercilessly golden, and little Christopher knocking for the dirty linen.

You should have taken Christopher with you, a reproachful voice hisses in her sluggish brain. *Mrs Castaway's is no place for a child.*

She bites her biscuit, spilling a flurry of crumbs on the breast of her night-gown. *He's a boy child,* she tells herself. *He'll grow into a man like all the rest of them. And the world is made for men.*

She drains her tea, a mere swallow's worth, barely enough to wet her dry tongue. Why is she so tired? What happened yesterday? The last thing she can remember, before falling into a long, confused dream in which a woman shrieked and wailed in a howling wind, is Agnes Unwin's announcement that she's engaged to marry William Rackham.

The diary has fallen shut in Sugar's lap. She opens it again, thumbs its soil-stained pages, finds the part where she lost consciousness.

I am Engaged to Marry a man, writes Agnes, *and I scarcely know Who he is. How terrifying! Of course I am awfully well <u>aqcuainted</u> with him – so well that I could write a book of all the clever things he says. But Who is he <u>really</u>, this*

William Rackham, and what does he want of me that he doesnt have already? O, I pray I dont bore him! He smiles & calls me his odd little sprite — but am I singular enough for a man of his disposition?

When I think of marrying, it is like thinking of diving into dark waters. But do dark waters become any clearer if one stares into them for years & years before diving? (Oh dear: perhaps I oughtnt to have used this comparison, since I am not a swimmer!)

But I mustnt fret. All things are possible for two persons in love. And it will be unutterably sweet not to be Agnes <u>Unwin</u> anymore! I can hardly wait!!!

'My Mama didn't go to bed at *all*,' complains Sophie, befuddled and whimpery, as Sugar helps her into her clothes. 'She was outside in the garden, shouting, all night, Miss.'

'Perhaps you dreamed it, Sophie,' suggests Sugar uneasily. The sheer effort of facing the day, of getting dressed and groomed by seven o'clock so that she can help Sophie do the same, has pushed her nightmare into the past; the tormented wailing has been muffled to a murmur. Now, when she tries to recall it, the woman's voice is no longer solitary, but accompanied by others, male and female. Oh yes, and there's a vague impression of a ruckus on the stairs.

'Nurse says that weeping and making a fuss fools no one,' Sophie remarks out of the blue, pouting like an imbecile as Sugar brushes her hair, teetering in her tight little shoes each time the comb snags her scalp. She's not quite awake yet, that's plain.

'We all must do our best, Sophie,' says Sugar, 'to be brave.'

At half past nine, shortly after the day's lessons have begun, the lonely privacy of the school-room is interrupted by a knock on the door. Normally, once the breakfast dishes have been removed, no one disturbs them until lunch, but here is Letty appearing in the doorway, empty-handed and solemn.

'Mr Rackham would like to see you, Miss Sugar,' she says.

'See . . . me?' Sugar blinks uncomprehendingly.

'In his study, Miss.' Letty's face is benign, but not very rewarding to read; if there are any woman-to-woman confidences written on it, they're written too faintly for Sugar to decipher.

Sophie looks up from her writing-desk, waiting to learn what turn the world will take next. With a nod and a hand gesture, Sugar signals for work to continue on the naming and drawing of musical instruments, having just convinced Sophie that her sketch of the violin with the droopy neck can stay, rather than be ripped out of her copy-book and portrayed afresh. Sophie bows down to her task again, pressing her ruler onto a half-drawn violoncello as if it's twitching to slither from her grasp.

'I'll be back soon,' says Sugar. But, as she follows Letty out of the room, her confidence in the promise suddenly wavers. *He wants me gone*, she thinks. *He's found someone with French and German, who plays the piano.* Then, lurching from unwarranted dread to unwarranted excitement, she thinks: *No, he wants to kiss my throat and lift my skirts and fuck me. He's had a cockstand since he woke up this morning, and can contain himself no longer.*

The carpets all along the landing are wet under her feet, and smell of soap and wet fabric; Letty, having discharged her summons, rolls her sleeves up and returns to her bucket and sponge, leaving the governess to face the master alone. The water in Letty's bucket is pink.

Heart beating hard in her breast, Sugar knocks at the door of William's study, his *sanctum sanctorum*, which, in all the weeks she has been in his house, she has never entered.

'Enter,' he calls from within, and she obeys.

Sugar's first thought when she sees him at his desk, clouded in smoke, leaning wearily forward, elbows pushing aside two molehills of correspondence, is that he resembles a man who has spent the night in drunken debauchery. His eyes are red and puffy, his hair is plastered with moisture, his beard and moustache are uncombed. He rises from his chair to greet her, and she notes dark speckles of water on his waistcoat, spilt from the rude splashing he's given his face.

'William, you look . . . so terribly tired! Surely you're working too hard!'

He crosses the room – his shoes and trouser-legs are smeared with dirt – and, seizing her shoulders so abruptly it makes her flinch, he pulls her against his chest. Even as she responds to his embrace, wrapping her long thin arms around him and pressing her cheek against his, she's tempted to rebuff him as a good governess should; all sorts of daft remonstrances spring to her mind: *Unhand me, sir! Oh! Mercy! I shall swoon!*, and so forth.

'What's wrong, my love?' she whispers into his hair, hugging him tight, straining to let him feel the sharp edges of her hips through the layers of

clothing that rustle between them. 'Tell me your cares.' Scarcely less hack-
neyed phrases, she knows, but what else can she say? All she wants is for
this untidy room, with its confusion of papers and tobacco-stained wallpaper and carpets the colour of beef stew, to melt away, and for the two
of them to be magically transported back to Priory Close, where soft warm
sheets would wrap themselves around their naked bodies and William would
gaze at her in wonder and say . . .

'Ugh, this is a rotten, hopeless business.'

She catches her breath as he squeezes her even harder. 'The . . .
perfume business?' she prompts him, knowing full well he means something else.

'Agnes,' he groans. 'She has me at my wits' end.'

The likelihood of William's wits being nearer their end than those of
his poor wife seems small, but there's no doubting his distress.

'What has she done?'

'She was out in the snow last night, in her night-gown! Digging up her
diaries — or trying to. Now she's convinced they've been eaten by worms.
I ordered the cursed things kept safe; no one seems to have any idea where
they are.'

Sugar makes an inarticulate sound of sympathetic puzzlement.

'And she's wounded herself!' exclaims William, shuddering in Sugar's
arms. 'It's horrible! She's gashed both her feet with a spade. Never dug a
hole in her life, poor baby. And with no shoes on! Ach!' He shudders again,
violently, at the thought of those dainty naked feet being penetrated, in
one clumsy thrust, by the blunt wedge of metal. Sugar shudders too — the
first helpless spasm they've shared that's genuinely mutual.

'How is she? What did you do?' she cries, and William breaks away
from their embrace, covering his face with his hands.

'I fetched Doctor Curlew here, of course. Thank God he didn't refuse
. . . though he'll have his pound of flesh from me for this . . . Amazing how
a man can be in his overcoat and night-shirt, stitching a screaming woman's
flesh, and still look smug! Well he can look smug all he likes; Agnes is staying here! Am I to condemn my wife to a living Hell because she can't use
a spade? I'm not a beast yet!'

'William, you're beside yourself!' Sugar cautions him, though her own
voice trembles with disquiet. 'You've done all you can for now; once you've
slept, you'll be able to think with a clearer head.'

He paces away from her, nodding and rubbing his hands.

'Yes, yes,' he says, frowning with the effort of banishing illogic from his brain. 'I have a hold of myself now.' He focuses on her with a strange stare, his eyes agleam. 'Can you imagine who could possibly have taken those damn diaries?'

'M-mightn't Sophie's old nurse have taken them with her? Weren't they dug up just before she left?'

William shakes his head, about to object that Beatrice Cleave regarded Agnes with barely concealed disdain; then it occurs to him that this is precisely why she might have relished the chance to cause trouble.

'I'll write to Mrs Barrett, and get her room searched,' he declares.

'No, no, my love,' says Sugar, alarmed by how easily her soiled and ill-gotten secrets could, if his suspicion turned to her, be hauled out from under her little bed. 'If she did it for mischief, she'll have thrown them in the nearest river. And besides, is a pile of old diaries what Agnes needs just now? Surely she needs rest and tender care?'

He paces back to his desk, opening and shutting his hands nervously. 'Rest and tender care. Yes, damn it. If only she could sleep until her injuries have healed! I'll get something from a doctor – not Curlew, damn him – a pill or a potion . . . Clara can make sure she's given it religiously, every night . . . No excuses. No excuses, d'you hear!'

His voice has warped from acquiescence to rage in the course of a few seconds. Sugar rushes to his side and lays her rough palm against his contorted face.

'William, please: your anguish is blinding you to who I am. I'm your Sugar, don't you see? I'm the woman who has listened to your woes, advised you, helped you write letters you dreaded writing . . . How many times have I proved there's nothing I won't do for you?' She snatches his slack hand and guides it to her bosom, then down to her belly, a gesture she hopes will rouse his desire, but which he condones with dumb bemusement, as if she's using him to make the sign of the cross.

'William,' she pleads. 'Remember Hopsom's? The long nights we spent . . . ?'

Finally his expression softens. His overheated skull, it seems, is filling with the cool balm of remembered intimacy: the way she helped him sail through a stormy patch in Rackham Perfumeries' growth when bad counsel might have sunk him.

'My angel,' he sighs, contrite. To Sugar's great relief, he leans forward and kisses her full on the mouth; his tongue is dry and tastes of brandy and dyspepsia, but at least he's kissing her. Taking courage, she strokes his hair, his shoulders, his back, breathing quicker, almost wanting him, wanting him to want her.

'Oh, by the way,' he says, breaking free of her again. 'I have something to show you.' His prick is bulging up through his trousers, but it's not that; no, he isn't quite ready for that. Instead, he rummages in the chaos of papers on his desk and pulls out a folded copy of *The Times*.

'I don't suppose you've seen this?' he says, rapidly leafing through it – past the news, past the weddings and engagements, until he's found the page he wants to show her. There, prominently placed in the midst of small advertisements for blood purifiers and homœopaths, is a large announcement featuring an engraving of William Rackham's face circled by a wreath of holly.

A Merry Christmas Season,
Anticipating A Most Happy New Year
FROM
RACKHAM'S
PURVEYORS OF FINE PERFUMES AND TOILETRIES

Sugar reads the greeting several times over, racking her brains for compliments. How strange it feels to be shown one of William's ideas as a *fait accompli*, without having been consulted beforehand!

'Very striking,' she says. 'And well-worded. Yes, awfully good.'

'It's a way of getting my Christmas greeting in the newspaper well in advance,' he explains, 'before my rivals put theirs in, you see?'

'Mm,' she says. 'They'll be wishing they'd thought of it, won't they?' Flaring in Sugar's imagination, over and over, is the sickening picture of Agnes thrusting a filthy spade downwards in the dark, and the blade gashing into the pale flesh of her feet.

'No doubt they'll be wise to me *next* Christmas,' William is saying. 'But this year, the advantage is mine.'

'You'll think of something even cleverer next year,' Sugar assures him. 'I'll help you.'

They kiss again, and this time he seems ready to proceed. She slides her hand inside his trousers, and his cock is stiffening even as she gropes for it.

'When are you going to put me out of my misery?' she purrs into his ear, managing to modulate a tremor of hysteria into a trill of lust. Yet, when she lifts her leg to climb onto him, she's surprised to feel how wet her sex is. William is behaving like a brute, it's true, but he's deranged by worry, and his heart's in the right place, she's sure, and – thank God – he still desires her. If she can only fuck him now, and hear his helpless groan of surrender as he spends, everything can still be all right.

Her pantalettes are around her ankles, she's lowering her arse into his lap, she gasps with relief as the head of his prick nudges into her – when suddenly there's a sharp rap at the door. Without a moment's hesitation she catapults off his body, yanking up her drawers even as she regains her balance. William is busy likewise. Their mutuality, their synchronicity, as they straighten their clothing and rearrange their bodies into decorous poses, is as instinctive and fluent as any act of eroticism.

'Enter!' says Rackham hoarsely.

It's Letty again, looking embarrassed this time – not because of her master and the governess, whose interrupted discussion is plainly a model of propriety, but because of the onerous burden of the message she has to deliver.

'It's . . . Mrs Rackham, sir,' she cringes. 'She wants you, sir.'

'Wants me?'

'Yes, sir. As a matter of urgency, sir.'

William stares across the room with his heavy-lidded, bloodshot eyes, reluctant to concede the hardness of his luck.

'Very well, Letty,' he says. 'I'll be there directly.'

The servant retreats, and William steps out from behind his desk, fingering his tie and the collars of his shirt.

'How flattering,' he murmurs sardonically to Sugar as he trudges past her, 'to be wanted by so many women at once.'

Agnes's bedroom, so often darkened in the daylight hours, is ominously bright, its curtains parted to admit the maximum amount of sun. Mrs Rackham should be doped insensible, but she's fully conscious, sitting bolt upright in bed, a spotless fresh night-gown buttoned up to her chin, with a big bulge half-way down the bed, where her heavily bandaged feet are

THE CRIMSON PETAL AND THE WHITE 592

shrouded under the sheets. Her face is calm, although there are a few scratches on her cheek from her scuffle with her husband, Shears and Rose in their attempts to drag her back into the house. Her improbably blue eyes are rimmed with red. All these things William notices the instant he walks into her room. These things, and the fact that Clara is standing sentinel by the bed-head, a guard of honour at her mistress's side.

'All right, Clara,' says William, 'you may go.'

The servant curtsies negligibly, a mere twitch of the torso.

'Mrs Rackham says I am to stay, sir.'

'She's my maid, William,' Agnes reminds him. 'I think I'm entitled to *one* person in my house who has my best interests at heart.'

William squares his shoulders. 'Agnes . . .' he begins to warn, then thinks better of it. 'What would you like to discuss?'

Agnes takes a long, deep breath. 'I have just suffered a most humiliating rebuff,' she says, 'from my own coachman.'

'Cheesman?'

'I believe we have only one coachman, William, unless you have others squirrelled away for your own amusement.'

Was that a smirk on Clara's face? Damn her impudence, the snotty little minx. He'll see her on the street yet, for this . . .

'Has Cheesman been impertinent to you, my dear?' enquires William with the utmost *politesse*.

'He's as well-bred as a creature of his sort can be,' demurs Mrs Rackham. 'My humiliation is *your* doing.'

'My doing?'

'Cheesman says that he's been forbidden to take me to church.'

'It's Tuesday, my d—'

'*My* church,' snaps Agnes. 'In Cricklewood.'

William shuts his eyes for a moment, the better to imagine Clara banished into destitution, or spontaneously combusting on the spot.

'Well . . .' he sighs, 'it's actually on Doctor Curlew's orders, my dear.'

Agnes repeats the words, giving each one the fastidiously disdainful attention it deserves. 'Doctor. Curlew's. Orders.'

'Yes,' says William, marvelling at how it can be, that he, William Rackham, a man who has no difficulty turning aside the wrath of a loutish dock-worker, should so lose his nerve when faced with the displeasure of his elfin wife. How did the sweet nature with which she once delighted him turn so bitter? 'Doctor Curlew feels that it's not good for your health to be pursuing . . . ah . . . to be of a faith other than . . . ah . . .'

'I need a miracle, William,' she says, speaking very distinctly, as though to an exceptionally slow-witted child. 'A miracle of healing. I need to pray in a church which God recognises, and which Our Lady and Her angels are known to visit. Do you recall ever witnessing a miracle in *your* church, William?'

Clara's hands, until now folded behind her back, move to her front – an innocuous fidget which nonetheless strikes William as a gesture of mockery.

'I . . .' (he gropes for a rueful quip to steer the conversation into less turbulent waters) 'I probably wasn't paying enough attention, I must confess.'

'Confess?' hisses Agnes, her eyes opening to their widest circumference. 'Yes, I agree you must confess. But you never will, will you?'

'Agnes . . .' Once more he braces himself for a quarrel; once more he resists the goad. 'Can't we discuss this after you're better? Whether your church is Catholic or Anglican, you're in no fit state to visit either of them now. Your poor feet need rest and cosseting.' A shrewd line of reasoning suddenly occurs to him: 'And after all, how would you feel, Agnes, being carried into church like a piece of heavy baggage, with everyone watching?'

This appeal to Agnes's social sensibilities evaporates in the air, blasted by a look of indignation. 'I shouldn't feel like a piece of baggage,' she quavers. 'I should feel . . . divine. Anyway, I'm not heavy: how *dare* you say so.'

William realises that his wife, for all her apparent composure, is in the grip of delirium. Arguing further with her is futile, and will only prolong Clara's entertainment.

'Agnes,' he declares gruffly, 'I . . . I will not allow it. You'd be a laughing stock, and me along with you. You're to remain at home, until—'

With a cry of anguish, she casts the bed-sheets aside, and crawls along the mattress to the foot of the bed, with the scurrying agility of an urchin. She grips the brass curlicues of the bed-frame, and wails to him, tears springing onto her cheeks.

'You promised me! To love, cherish and honour me! "I don't care a fig for what the world thinks," you said. "Those other girls are dull to the bone," you said. "My odd little sprite," you used to call me! "What our society fears, it calls eccentric" – that was another of your fine sayings. "The future can only be interesting if *we* have the courage to be interesting – and that means putting the world's nose out of joint!" '

William stands slack-jawed with astonishment. He'd thought the night he's just endured was the bizarrest ordeal of his life, but *this* . . . this is worse. To have his youthful pretensions, his callowest pronouncements, resurrected from oblivion, and flung back at him from his wife's mouth!

'I . . . I'm looking after you as best I can,' he pleads. 'You're ill, and I want to take care of you.'

'Take care of me?' she exclaims. 'When have you ever taken care of me? Look! Look! What do you propose to do about *this*?'

She throws herself back on her rear, lifts her night-dress, and frantically starts unwrapping the bandages from her feet.

'Agnes! No!' He lurches over to her, and seizes her wrists, but her hands continue to squirm and writhe near her ankles. Tentacles of bloodstained bandage unfurl from her feet, and there's a glimpse of bruised blue flesh, and a sticky occlusion of crimson. He also can't help glimpsing, between the stick-thin legs that Agnes has so unthinkingly uncovered, the blonde wisps of her sex.

'Please, Agnes,' he whispers, striving to remind her, with furious nods of his brow, the mute witness of Clara behind them. 'Not in front of a servant . . . !'

She laughs hysterically, a terrible, bestial sound.

'My body is turning into . . . raw meat,' she cries, in outrage and disbelief, 'my soul is almost lost, and you are concerned about the *servants*?' She struggles desperately against his restraining grip, while her feet churn into the bed-clothes and blood begins to smear the snowy linen. Her bosom presses against his arm; he's reminded of the fullness of her breasts compared to Sugar's, the cherubic compactness of her body, how fervently he once anticipated the blessed day when he could have it in his arms at last . . .

Abruptly Agnes stops fighting him. They are shoulder to shoulder, almost nose to nose. Panting and red-faced, spittle on her chin, she fixes him with a stare of righteous disgust.

'You are hurting me,' she says softly. 'Go play with someone else.'

He releases her wrists, and she crawls to the head of the bed, trailing ribbons of tainted bandage. In the wink of an eye, she's back under the

covers, her head on the pillow, her cheek resting on one palm. She sighs
stoically, like a child being pestered after bedtime.

'I . . .' he stammers, but no words come. He turns to Clara, imploring
her, with a gesture of impotence, not to misuse the power this incident
has delivered into her hands.

She nods, inscrutable.

'I'll attend to her, Mr Rackham,' she assures him, and with that, it
appears he's dismissed.

Numb with wretchedness, William shambles back to his study. There's no
one to receive him there, Sugar having evidently returned to the school-
room when she could wait for him no longer. Well, so be it. He sniffs the
air. Cigar smoke. Burning coal from the hearth. Sugar's sex.

He stands in front of the flickering hearth, leans his forehead against
the wall, opens his trousers, and abuses himself, moaning in distress. Within
a few seconds, his seed is spurting out, falling directly onto the sizzling
coals. His belly is fat; the hairs on it are prematurely grey; what a ridiculous creature he is; no wonder he is despised. Orgasm over, his penis shrivels
to a slimy scrag, and he stows it away.

Shoulders slumped, he turns and, at the sight of his paper-strewn desk,
his heart sinks further. So much to do, and his life is falling apart at the
seams! He sits heavily in his chair, and covers his face in his hands.

Steady, steady. Nothing will be gained if he loses his grip now.

Hardly conscious of what he is doing, he slides open the capacious
bottom drawer of his bureau, where he keeps the correspondence that's
been answered but which he feels unable to discard. In amongst it is other
flotsam – *More Sprees in London*, for example, and . . . this. He pulls it out,
with trembling fingers.

It's a much-thumbed photograph of Agnes – Agnes Unwin, as she was
then – taken by him at a summer picnic on the banks of the Thames. A
fine photograph, and quite well printed too, given his inexperience in the
darkroom at the time. What he particularly likes is the way Agnes (on his
instruction) kept absolutely still, thus ensuring that her serenely lovely
face was captured in sharp detail, while her companions – sons of the
aristocracy, idiots all – fiddled with their trouser-cuffs and gossiped
amongst themselves, thus condemning their faces to a blur of anonymity.
This fellow here, with the carnation in his buttonhole, is possibly that

jackass Elton Fitzherbert, but the others are grey, murky phantoms, serving only to highlight William Rackham's radiant beloved. Countless times he's stared at this photograph, reminding himself that it captures an incontestable truth, a history that cannot be rewritten.

Unaware that he's weeping, he continues to scrabble through the papers in his bottom drawer. Somewhere here, unless he's very much mistaken, he still has a perfumed letter Agnes wrote to him, mere days before their marriage. In it, she tells him how she adores him, how each day that she must wait before she's his wife is an agony of delicious anticipation – or words to that effect. He rummages and rummages, through handbills of forgotten theatre performances, invitations to art galleries, unread letters from his brother quoting Scripture, threats from creditors long repaid. But the scented proof of Agnes's passion for him . . . this eludes him. Is it really possible that all trace of her devotion has vanished? He bends his face down and sniffs. Old paper; the soil on his shoes; Sugar's sex.

Losing heart, he pulls a crumpled sheet of paper from the very bottom of the drawer, just in case it's the one. Instead, he finds it to be written in his own hand, an abandoned draft of a letter from a few years ago, to Henry Rackham Senior:

Dear Father,

In the fluster occasioned by the birth of my daughter and the emergency medical attentions required by my wife subsequently, I have naturally had little time to devote to the Responsibilities which await me. Of course I intend to embrace these with my customary enthusiasm as soon as the first opportunity arises; in the meantime, however, I am the unhappy recipient of a letter from our Solicitors . . .

With a grunt of pain, William crushes the page in his fist, and casts it to one side. Christ, he's twice the man he was then! How can Fate be so cruel as to rob him of Agnes's admiration, when he was once a weak-chinned groveller, and is now the master of a great concern? Is there no justice?

Stung to action, he hunches over his desk, lays a fresh sheet before him, and dips pen in ink. William Rackham, head of Rackham Perfumeries, doesn't wallow in self-pity: he gets on with his work. Yes: his work! What was he attending to, before . . . ? Ah yes: the Woolworth question . . .

To Henry Rackham, Snr., he writes, knuckling his brow to summon forth the details that were so clear to him twelve hours ago, when the night-mare had yet to begin.

It has come to my attention that, in 1842, Rackham Perfumeries leased to a certain Thomas Woolworth a large tract of arable land in Patcham, Sussex, the concern having been judged (by yourself, I presume) too bothersome to cultivate. I have found but slender documentation of this transaction, and trust that more exists. I there-fore request that you convey to me whatever papers may relate to this matter or any other Rackham matter, for that matter, which you may hitherto have withheld . . .

William frowns at the unfortunate cluster of *matter*s in this last sentence. It's the sort of thing Sugar could help him with, if she were here; but she, too, has slipped from his grasp.

TWENTY-SIX

'Christmas,' declares Sugar, and pauses.

Sophie hunches over her copy-book, in the grey light of early morning, and inscribes the exotic word at the top of a fresh page. Even upside-down, and from the corner of her eye, Sugar can see that the 't' is missing.

'Holly.'

More scratching of Sophie's pen. Correct this time.

'Tinsel.'

Sophie looks to the glittering silver and red barbs on the mantel for inspiration, then dips her pen in the inkwell and commits her guess to paper: 'tintsel'. Sugar resolves to make light of this error, combining humour with an educative purpose: *The poor little 't' from your Christmas has gone wandering, Sophie, and blundered into the tinsel . . .*

'Mistletoe.' She regrets this one as soon as it's off her tongue: poor Sophie's frown deepens as she must relinquish her last hope of a perfect score. Also, the word unexpectedly brings to Sugar's mind a vision of Agnes's accident: once again, the spade slices through the white flesh, and blood spurts.

'Misseltow,' writes Sophie.

'Snow,' says Sugar, to give her an easy one. Sophie looks up at the window and, yes, it's true. Her governess must have eyes in the back of her head.

Sugar smiles, content. This Christmas that she's soon to spend with the Rackhams is, in a sense, her first, for Mrs Castaway's was never the most festive of places. The notion that there will soon be a day that's guaranteed to be special regardless of what Fate brings is a novelty, and the more she tries to caution herself that December 25th will be a day like any other, the more expectant she grows.

There's something different about the Rackham house lately, something more than can be explained by its garnish of holly, tinsel and ornamental bells. The fact that William still loves her is a tremendous comfort, and the thought that they will face the future together, collaborators and confidantes, helps her resist the poisonous murmur of foreboding. But it's not even William's love that fuels her hopes; she detects a change in spirit, all through the household. Everyone is friendlier and more familiar. Sugar no longer feels as if she's haunting two rooms of a large and mysterious house, hurrying past closed doors for fear of provoking the evil spirits inside. Now, with Christmas coming, she goes everywhere with Sophie in hand, and is welcomed as part of the proceedings. Servants smile, William nods in passing, and no one need mention what's understood: that Mrs Rackham is safe upstairs, snoozing the days away in a chloral stupor.

'Hello, little Sophie!' says Rose, as the child proudly produces yet another basket of freshly-made paper streamers. 'Aren't you a clever girl?'

Sophie beams. She'd never expected so much admiration in her life, and all for cutting strips of coloured paper and gluing them together in chains, exactly as her governess has instructed her! Perhaps the business of making one's way in the world is not as arduous and thankless as Nurse led her to believe . . .

'Where shall we hang these, Letty?' calls Rose to her upstairs counterpart, and the servants do their best to pretend there's still an urgent need for more streamers, despite the fact that they're hung everywhere, including the banisters, the smoking-room (pray God those men are careful with their cigars!), the scullery (they're limp with moisture already, but Janey was awfully pleased a thought was spared for her), the piano, and that odd little room which used to smell faintly of linen and evaporated urine, but is now empty. Only a matter of time, then, before the stables and Shears's glasshouses are approached.

The holly man visited yesterday, and was relieved of three large bundles, two more than the Rackham house took from him last year. ('Rich pickin's 'ere, ducks,' he winked at a young mistletoe seller he met in the carriageway on his way out.) And indeed, the Rackham house is sparing no expense to expunge the memory of Christmas 1874, which was 'celebrated' – if that word will stoop to being so misused – under a cloud. This year, let everyone be assured – from lords and ladies to the lowliest scullery maid – that William Rackham's festive provisions are the equal of any man's! So: Holly? Three bags full! Comestibles? The kitchen groans with them! Streamers? Let the child make all she wants!

When she's not making streamers, little Sophie loves to make Christmas cards. Sugar bought her some expensive ones from a hawker whom William permitted, after some hesitation, to cross the Rackham threshold and lay out his wares in the parlour for the servants to peruse. Apart from the usual depictions of firelit domestic bliss and charity to the ragged poor, there were comical scenes of frogs dancing with cockroaches, and pompous squires being bitten on the arse by reindeer – a great favourite with the kitchenmaids, who expressed regret at not being able to afford them. Sugar bought the dearest cards on show: the ones with moveable parts and trick panels, in the hope of inspiring Sophie to similar inventions.

And so it has come to pass. Sophie, to judge by her delight, has never possessed a toy more luxurious and fascinating than the Christmas card in the shape of an austere-looking Georgian house which, when the paper tab is pulled, parts its curtains to reveal a colourful family enjoying a banquet. Lacking the word 'genius', she describes as 'master-clever' the person who conceived this extraordinary thing, and she frequently consults the card and pulls its tab, to be reminded how sublimely it works. Her own efforts to draw, paint and assemble Christmas cards are crude, but she perseveres, and makes a succession of cardboard houses with tiny celebrating families hidden inside them. Each one is better than the last, and she gives them away to whoever will accept them.

'Why, thank you, Sophie,' says the Cook. 'I shall send this to my sister in Croydon.'

Or, 'Thank you, Sophie,' says Rose, 'This is sure to bring a smile to my mother's lips.'

Even William is glad to receive them, for, despite his unusual dearth of relations, he has no shortage of business associates and employees who'll be charmed by such a gesture, especially if it appears unique.

'Another one!' he says in mock astonishment when Sugar escorts Sophie up to his study to deliver the latest card. 'You're turning into an industry all by yourself, aren't you?' And he winks at Sugar, though quite what this wink is supposed to mean she can't guess.

After these brief encounters with her father, which are always terminated by William's inability to think of a second sentence, Sophie is liable to be fragile-tempered, passing from excited babble to fractious whimpers in a trice; but, overall, Sugar has decided it's good for Sophie to be noticed by the man who made her.

'My father is rich, Miss,' the child announces one afternoon, just before making a start on the history, so far, of Australia. 'His money is kept in the bank, and it's growing bigger every day.'

More regurgitated wisdom from Beatrice Cleave, no doubt.

'There are a great many men richer than your father, dear,' Sugar gently suggests.

'He'll beat them all, Miss.'

Sugar sighs, imagining herself and William sitting under a giant parasol on the summit of Whetstone Hill, sipping lemonade, gazing drowsily down on the fields of ripe lavender. 'If he's wise,' she says, 'he'll be satisfied with what he has, and enjoy his life without having to work so hard.'

Sophie swallows this gobbet of moralism, but is clearly not going to be able to digest it. She's already concluded that the reason why her own father is so very unlike the doting Papas in Hans Christian Andersen's fairy tales is that he is under strict orders from the Almighty to conquer the world.

'Where's *your* Papa, Miss?' she enquires.

In Hell, my poppet. Mrs Castaway's reply, once upon a time.

'I don't know, Sophie.' Sugar strains to recall anything more about her father than her mother's hatred of him. But in the story as Mrs Castaway told it, the man who, with a single jerk of his pelvis, transformed her from a respectable woman into a pariah, didn't wait to find out what happened next. 'I think he's dead.'

'Did he have an accident, Miss, or go to a war?' Males tend to get shot, or burn down in their houses: Sophie appreciates that.

'I don't know, Sophie. I never met him.'

Sophie cocks her head sympathetically. Such a thing could easily happen, if a father were sufficiently busy.

'And where's your Mama, Miss?'

A chill goes down Sugar's spine. 'She's . . . at home. In *her* house.'

'All alone?' Sophie, coached in these matters by her sentimental story-books, sounds at once concerned and hopeful.

'No,' says Sugar, wishing the child would drop this thread. 'She has . . . visitors.'

Sophie casts a resolute glance at the scissors, paste and art materials that have been laid aside until Australia is dealt with.

'The next card I make will be for her, Miss,' she promises.

Sugar smiles as best she can, and turns away before Sophie sees the angry tears glimmering in her eyes. She leafs through the history book, backwards and forwards through its pages, passing Australia several times.

While she stalls, she wonders if she should tell Sophie the truth. Not about her mother's house of whoredom, of course, but about Christmas. About how the festival was never celebrated in the Castaway confines; how Sugar was seven before she understood that there was a communal *occasion* that made street musicians play particular tunes near the end of what she didn't know was called December. Yes, seven years old she was, when she finally plucked up the courage to ask her mother what Christmas was all about, and Mrs Castaway replied (once only, after which the subject was forever forbidden): 'It's the day Jesus Christ died for our sins. Evidently unsuc*cess*fully, since we're still paying for them.'

'Miss?'

Sugar is roused from a dream; she has the history book gripped tight in her hands, and the topmost pages have begun to tear under the pressure of her nails.

'I'm sorry, Sophie,' she says, hastily letting go. 'I think I've eaten something that's disagreed with me. Or perhaps . . .' (she observes the child's perturbed expression, and is ashamed to have caused it) 'Perhaps I'm simply too excited by the coming of Christmas. Because, you know,' (she draws a deep breath, and brightens her tone as much as she can without squeaking) 'Christmas is the happiest time of the year!'

'My dear Lady Bridgelow,' blurts Bodley, 'although we all know that in a few days from now, a huge fuss will be made over the *spurious* birthday of a Jewish peasant, this wonderful party of yours is the *true* high point of the December calendar.'

He turns to the other guests, and they reward him with a few nervous titters. *So* amusing, that Philip Bodley, but he does say some outrageous things! And without his more sober associate, Edward Ashwell, to restrain him, he's an even looser cannon! But it's all right: Lady Bridgelow has steered him towards Fergus Mcleod, who's more than a match for him – how effortlessly she keeps her *soirées* on the rails!

William stands well back from Bodley, wondering how the fellow can have the bad manners to arrive at a dinner party already drunk. Constance is handling the situation with effortless good grace, but even so . . . William turns on his heel, and notes that a servant is busy dampening the fire, to compensate for the fact that the number of bodies in the room is raising the temperature. How extraordinary that the girl should know to do this, without needing to be told! It's the little things about Constance that are the most impressive – the way her household hums like a well-oiled machine. God, she could teach his own servants a thing or two . . . They're well-meaning, most of them, but they lack a firm mistress . . .

This party of Lady Bridgelow's is a small affair of twelve persons only, most of whom William met for the first time in the Season just past, or never before. As usual, though, Constance has assembled an interesting mixture. She specialises in people who are slightly divorced from the staid old world but not quite beyond the pale: 'the occupants of the Age-To-Come', as she likes to call them.

There's Jessie Sharpleton, fresh from Zanzibar, skin the colour of cinnamon and brain full of lurid tales of heathen barbarity. Also in attendance are Edwin and Rachel Mumford, the dog-breeders; Clarence Ferry, the author of *Her Regrettable Lapse*, a two-act play currently doing well; and Alice and Victoria Barbauld, two sisters who come in very useful at dinner parties for their decorative faces and their skill at playing short, tuneful airs on the violin and oboe. (As Lady Bridgelow often says, it's *so* difficult to find 'musical' people who aren't a bore: the tuneful kind tend not to know when to stop, and the stopping kind tend not to be terribly tuneful.) The presence of Philip Bodley might have been awkward for William, given the rift that Agnes has caused between them but, thank God, Bodley is deep in conversation with Fergus Macleod, a High Court judge well known for his expertise in sedition, libel and treason, and is pumping him for all he's worth.

It's an amusing and convivial party, and the smell of the approaching food, being trundled through the corridors towards the dining-room, is mouth-watering. Still William isn't quite at his ease. He'd set off from home full of hope for Agnes's recovery (she looks so angelic in her slumbers, and when he's moved to kiss her cheek she murmurs affectionate pleas for indulgence . . . Surely what a woman says in her sleep is closer to the truth than what she says in wakeful anger!) But here at Lady Bridgelow's party, whenever the existence of his wife impinges on the conversation, people look at him with pity. How is this possible? He'd thought Agnes was so popular this Season! Granted, there were a few sticky moments, but overall her performance was excellent – wasn't it?

'The biggest exhibition of mechanical toys in the world, you say?' he rejoins, struggling to keep up with Edwin Mumford's account of the Season's greatest triumphs. 'I never heard about this!'

'It was advertised in all the newspapers.'

'How odd that it escaped me . . . Are you sure you don't mean the show at the Theatre Royal, that little mechanical man, what was its name – Psycho?'

'Psycho was a glorified hoodwink, a puppet for children,' sniffs Mumford. 'This was more like the Great Exhibition, except solely for automata!'

William shakes his head in disbelief that he could have missed such a marvellous event.

'Perhaps, Mr Rackham,' Rachel Mumford chips in, 'your poor wife's illness distracted you at the time.'

The butler announces that dinner is served. In a daze, William takes his seat, and chooses the rhubarb and ham soup, even though there's a consommé he might have liked better. But he's too confused to make such decisions. As the meal gets underway, and the dining table proliferates with bowls of broth, he's already chewing on something more substantial: the notion that his peers, far from blaming him for his wife's wretched state, might actually be waiting for him to hold up his palm and say 'Enough'.

He glances discreetly at each of the guests as they spoon their soup: they're perfectly at ease, a paradigm of civilised fellowship. *He* could be perfectly at ease too, he could take his place within their paradigm – if only he didn't see before him the spectre of Agnes, at just such a dinner party two years ago, accusing the hostess of serving a chicken that was still alive.

Sunk in reverie while he eats whatever's put in front of him, William recalls the early days of his marriage, recalls his wedding day, even recalls the drafting of the marriage contract with Lord Unwin. His recollection of Lord Unwin is particularly vivid – but that's hardly surprising, since Lord and Lady Unwin are, at this moment, sitting diagonally opposite him at the dinner table.

'Ah yes!' chuckles Lord Unwin, when Lady Bridgelow remarks how much his estate has expanded. 'I try to keep it within reasonable bounds, but my neighbours keep selling me more damn land, and so the damn place grows and grows – like my stomach!'

Indeed he's a fat man now, bulging into old age, and his former vulpine expression has disappeared under jowls swollen by Continental pastries and cheeks reddened by liquor and sunshine.

'What's this? Sirloin? How can you do this to me, Constance? I sh'll'ave to be wheeled out of here in a barrow!'

Nevertheless, he betrays no difficulty consuming his steak, the sorbet *à l'Imperiale*, a hunk of roast hare (he declines the offer of vegetables with an apologetic pat to his gravid belly), a second helping of roast hare ('Hell! If it's going spare!'), a quivering mound of jelly, some savoury forcemeats, a bowl of pears and cream and, to the exasperation of his wife, a handful of crystallised fruits and nuts from a bowl near the door.

Then he leaves the ladies to their own devices and limps with the men into the smoking-room, where a crystal decanter of port and six glasses stand ready.

'Ah, Rackham!' he exclaims. (Before dinner, he was too jealously monopolised by the Mumfords to do more than exchange pleasantries with his son-in-law; now they have a second chance.) 'When I said it's been years since I last saw your face, I was lying: I see your face everywhere I go! Even in the apothecaries of Venice I find your phiz, stamped on little pots and bottles!'

William inclines his head solemnly, unsure if he's being mocked or praised. (Still, that Bagnini fellow in Milan would seem to be as efficient a distributor as he claims to be . . .)

'It's really quite a rum thing,' continues Lord Unwin, 'to be standing in a shop in a foreign country, pick up a cake of soap, and observe, "Ah: so William Rackham has grown a beard!" Don't you think that's a rum thing, William?'

'The wonders of the modern world, sir: I can be making a foolish exhibition of myself in Venice and Paris, while doing the same here.'

'Ha ha!' shouts Lord Unwin. 'Jolly good!' And he pokes his cigar into the proffered flame of his son-in-law's lucifer, enveloping his face in smoke. He's only five-foot-eleven, William notes; six feet at the very most. The fearsome aristocrat whom he petitioned for Agnes's hand impressed him, at the time, as being nearer to six-and-a-half.

'Of course, in the provinces,' Clarence Ferry scoffs on the other side of the room, 'they haven't a hope of *spelling* it, let alone understanding it.'

'But they enjoy it, do they?' suggests Edwin Mumford wearily, his roving eye catching William's, in the hope of rescue.

'Oh yes, in their own *way*.'

Much later in the evening, when most of the other guests have reeled home, and the smoking-room is thick with alcohol-scented mist, Lord Unwin cuts short his anecdotes of Continental adventure and, as the inebriated are wont to do, turns abruptly serious.

'See here now, Bill,' he says, creaking forward in his chair. 'I've heard how Agnes is going, and it's no surprise to me, I can tell you. She always had bats in her belfry, even as a child. I could count the sensible things she ever said on the fingers of one hand. D'you understand me?'

'I daresay,' says William. In his mind there glows a memory of Agnes as she was only a few hours ago, her hair fluffed out on her pillow, her lips swollen with stupefaction, her eyelids fluttering, as she kicked her legs under the bed-sheets and murmured 'Too hot . . . too hot . . .'

'You know,' the old man confides, 'when you asked me for her hand, I did rather think you'd end up with less than you bargained for . . . I should've warned you, man-to-man, but . . . well, I s'pose I hoped that giving birth might put her right. But it didn't, did it?'

'No,' concedes William glumly. If there's one thing that did his wife's mind no good at all, it was giving birth to Sophie.

'But listen, Bill,' advises Lord Unwin, his eyes narrowing. 'Don't let her cause any more trouble. This may surprise you, but news of her exploits has been known to cross the Channel. Yes! I've heard about her screaming fits as far abroad as Tunisia, would you believe? Tunisia! And as for her bright ideas as a hostess, well, they may be terrifically novel here, but to a level-headed Frenchwoman they don't seem so witty I can tell you. And that "blood-in-the-wine-glasses" fiasco: everyone talks about that! It's practically a legend!'

William squirms, sucking so hard on his cigar it makes him cough. How unforgiving is the spread of ill fame! This incident to which Lord Unwin refers happened so very long ago . . . in the Season of 1873, perhaps, or even 1872! How unfair the world is, that a man can spend a fortune advertising his perfumes in Sweden, and a month afterwards, no Swede appears to have heard of him, while the momentary indiscretion of a hapless woman behind closed doors on a certain evening in 1872 travels effortlessly across seas and national borders, and remains on everyone's lips for years!

'Believe me, Bill,' says Lord Unwin, 'I don't mean to tell you what to do with your own wife. She's *your* business. But let me tell you one more story . . .' He drains the rest of his port and leans even closer to William than before.

'I've a little place in Paris,' he mutters, 'and my neighbours are damn nosy. They'd heard I was Agnes's father, but they didn't know I wasn't her *natural* father. So, when they found out I had a couple more children with Prunella, they took me aside and asked me if they were "all right". I said, "What d'you *mean*, 'all right' – 'f'course they're all right." They said, "So they show no signs?" I said, "Signs of *what*?".' The pitch of Lord Unwin's voice rises as he re-lives his exasperation. 'They think I father mad children, Bill! Now is it right that I, and my children, should be suspected of . . . of *bad blood*, only because John Pigott's feeble-minded daughter is still at large? No-o-o . . .' He slumps, the veins in his nose livid. 'If she won't improve, Bill, put her away. It's better for all of us.'

The clock strikes half past ten. The room is empty, apart from William and his father-in-law. Lady Bridgelow's butler pads in, bends to the old man and says,

'Begging your pardon, sir, but milady has asked me to convey to you that your wife has fallen asleep.'

Lord Unwin winks heavily at William, and digs his liver-spotted hands into the upholstery of his chair, preparing to haul himself up.

'Women, eh?' he grunts.

A most perturbing encounter, this, and one which William ponders for days afterwards. However, in the end, the thing that brings him closest to a decision regarding Agnes's fate is not the advice of his friends, nor the urgings of Doctor Curlew, nor even the corrosive words poured into his ear by Lord Unwin. No, it's something utterly unexpected, which ought not have the slightest authority to sway him, but does: the tree-carving talents of an anonymous field-worker in his own employ.

On December 22nd, William pays a visit to his farm in Mitcham, to oversee the installation of a lavender press which, come next summer, will eliminate, from one stage of refinement at least, the need for human labour. He's long been dissatisfied with the practice of employing barefooted boys to tread down the lavender as it's loaded for distillation; apart from qualms of hygiene, he's not convinced the lads are as cheap or efficient as his father thinks, for they're always hobbling away from their work, complaining of bee-stings. Machinery, William is certain, will prove superior in the long run, and he surveys the new press proudly, although there's not yet any lavender to test it with.

'Splendid, splendid,' he compliments the steward, while peering into a cast-iron cavity whose function is frankly mysterious to him.

'The best, sir,' the steward assures him. 'The very best.'

All of Mitcham, indeed most of Surrey, lies deep in snow, and William takes the opportunity to stroll unaccompanied though his fields, savouring the immaculate whiteness under which next year's harvest lies dormant. Incredible, how once upon a time his future was invested in abstruse poems and unpublishable essays, instead of this vast and comforting tract of land, this irreducible, fertile, solid-underfoot foundation. He tramps towards the line of trees which serves as a windbreak for his lavender, his galoshes sinking deep into the snow. By the time he reaches it, he's sweating liberally inside his sealskin coat and fur-lined gloves. He leans against the nearest tree bough, puffing clouds of steam into the chill air.

Only after he's been standing there for a minute or two, catching his breath, does he glance sideways at the trunk that supports him, and notice the inscription crudely carved in the snow-flocked bark:

HELP I AM STUK
UP THIS TREE
AGNES R

He reads and re-reads the words, flabbergasted. He has no wish to find out which of his hirelings is such an idler as to have spent valuable time carving this joke. All he can think about is that his wife's insanity is common knowledge of the most shop-soiled kind. Even farm-hands discuss it amongst themselves. He might just as well be a cuckold, with all the sniggering that surrounds him!

A breeze agitates the crêpery-papery vestiges of the tree's foliage, and William, knowing he's being absurd, but unable to resist, peers up into the branches, in case Agnes may be up there after all.

In the Rackham house, there's an embarrassing surplus of angels, far too many to fit onto the Christmas tree. Sugar, Rose and Sophie have been pottering around downstairs, looking for spots not already festooned with decorations. Loath to admit defeat, they've fastened their fragile-winged fairies onto the unlikeliest surfaces: window-sills, clocks, the new hat-stand, the frames of prints, the antlers of a stuffed doe-head, the lid of the piano, the antimacassars of seldom-used chairs.

Now it's the morning of Christmas Eve, and time for the finishing touches. Outside, the snow whirls and flusters, an eerily silent storm. The mail has just been delivered and, through the fogged and frosted parlour window, the hunched figure of the postman can still be glimpsed disappearing into the milky gloom.

Indoors, the hearths blaze and crackle, so that the Christmas tree has had to be moved to the opposite side of the parlour, for fear of floating sparks igniting it. Sugar, Rose and Sophie crouch around the X-shaped wooden base, their skirts wrapped modestly around their ankles, as they replace the decorations that have fallen off. Rose is singing to herself,

'*Christmas is coming,*
The goose is getting fat
Please put a penny
In the old man's hat . . .'

There's scarcely a clump of pine-needles that doesn't sag with coloured thread, silver balls and matchwood sculptures, but the *coup de grâce* is yet to come: Rose is an avid reader of the ladies' journals, and has been inspired by a 'tip' for gilding an indoor tree with the ultimate Yuletide illusion. Following a simple recipe, she's filled some empty Rackham perfume spray-bottles with a water-and-honey mixture, described as *a harmless and effective 'glue' to hold a snowy sprinkling of flour*. Armed with a bottle each, Rose, Sugar and Sophie now spray this sticky fluid onto the tree's extremities.

'Oh dear,' laughs Rose nervously. 'We ought to've done this before we dressed the tree.'

'We shall have to sprinkle the flour very carefully,' agrees Sugar, 'if we're not to make a dreadful mess.' All this talk of *we* is delicious; she could kiss Rose for starting it!

'I'll know better next year,' says Rose. She's just observed Miss Rackham spraying water and honey directly onto the carpet, and wonders if she has the authority to forbid the child from participating in the flour-sprinkling. Flattered though she is that Miss Sugar is willing to work side by side with a housemaid, there's always the risk that a trifling mistake will suddenly sour their relations.

'Stand back, Sophie,' says Sugar, 'and be our adviser.'

The two women take turns to shake flour into each other's cupped palms, which they then allow to fall, as neatly as they can manage, onto the sticky branches. Sugar's head is light with the triumph of it: to be a member of the Rackham household, virtually one of the family, sharing a rueful smile with Rose as they commit this foolishness together. No act between herself and another woman has ever felt so intimate, and Sugar has done many things. Rose trusts her; she trusts Rose; with their eyes alone they've made a pact to see this business through to its completion; they sprinkle flour into each other's hands, and hope it will remain their little secret.

'We must be mad,' frets Rose, as the sifted powder begins to drift into the air and make them sneeze.

Sugar holds out her hands, in whose dry flesh every crack and flake is clearly delineated with flour. But nothing needs be said; every woman has her imperfections, and Rose, now that Sugar sees her up close, is ever-so-slightly cross-eyed. They are equals, then.

'If you haven't got a penny
A ha'penny will do
If you haven't got a ha'penny,
Well, God Bless You!'

Another few sprinkles, and the deed is done. The flour has made an unholy mess, but that portion of it which adhered to the branches resembles snow quite as remarkably as the ladies' journal promised, and the spills can be swept up in no time at all. This, Rose makes clear, is no task for a governess.

While she sweeps, Rose sings 'The Twelve Days of Christmas', limiting herself to repetitions of the first day. Her voice is a crude and quavery thing compared to Agnes's, but the sound of singing really does lend good cheer, and no other voices are going to be raised. Sophie and Sugar regard each other shyly, each hankering to hum along.

'On the first day of Christmas, my true love gave to me . . .'

Without warning, William walks into the parlour, a sheet of paper in his hand, a preoccupied expression on his face. He stops short, as if he'd meant to step into a different room altogether but took a wrong turn in the corridor. The Christmas tree, by now a rococo edifice of baubles, flour and folderol, seems barely to register on his consciousness, and if he notices that the two grown women are powdered up to their elbows, he doesn't let on.

'Ah . . . splendid,' he says, and promptly retreats. Still dangling from his slack hand is a letter which, if Doctor Curlew's handwriting were only ten times larger, might have been readable from across the room — not that Sugar could have made much sense of a message consisting simply of: *As we discussed, I have made arrangements for December 28th. You won't regret this, believe me.*

Rose heaves a sigh of relief. The master has had his chance to be angry, and hasn't taken it. She bends to her dustpan and brush, and resumes singing.

Once the spilled flour has been swept up, Rose, Sugar and Sophie replace the gaily-wrapped gifts under the tree. So many boxes and packages, tied with red ribbon or silver string — what, oh what, can be in them all? The only package whose contents Sugar knows for sure, is Sophie's present to her father; the rest are mysteries. As she helps to arrange them attractively, stowing the smaller ones amongst the larger, the shapeless parcels on top of the sturdy cartons, she affects to be uninterested in the tiny labels inscribed with the recipients' names. The few that she manages to catch sight of give her no satisfaction (Harriet? Who the devil is Harriet?), and with Rose and Sophie watching she can't very well go probing, can she?

Please God, she thinks. *Let there be something for me.*

Upstairs, William opens the door of his wife's bedroom as noiselessly as he can, and slips inside. Although he has persuaded Clara to leave the house for a few hours, he turns the key in the lock, just in case her vixenish instinct should lure her unexpectedly back.

Within the four walls of Agnes's room, there's no evidence of the festive season. Indeed, there's very little evidence of anything whatsoever, as all the clutter of Agnes's pastimes – indeed, any object that might obstruct Clara's nursing – has been consigned to storage, leaving scrupulously dusted vacancy in its place. As for the walls, they were bare even before this piti- ful affair, for Agnes has never had an easy rapport with pictures. The last print to grace her bedroom was banished when a ladies' journal decreed that ponies were vulgar; the one before had to be removed when Agnes complained that it was dripping ectoplasm.

Now Agnes lies sleeping, insensible to everything, even the extraordi- nary performance of the snowstorm just outside her window, even the approach of her husband. William gently lifts a chair, deposits it near the head of the bed, and lowers himself onto the seat. The air stinks of narcotic syrup, beef tea, mulled egg, and soap – Rackham's Carnation Cream, if he's not mistaken. A great deal of soapy water is sloshed about in this room lately; Clara, rather than risk a mishap – a fall, a drowning – in a tub, washes her mistress in bed, then simply exchanges the sodden linen for dry. He knows this, because she's told him so, only to refuse his offer of a second lady's-maid with a sniff of injured stoicism.

Agnes's feet are healing slowly, he's given to understand. There may, according to Doctor Curlew, be lasting damage to the left one, causing her to limp. Or perhaps she'll walk as gracefully as she ever did. It's difficult to predict, until she's up and about again.

'Soon,' he murmurs near her sleeping head, 'you'll be in a place where you'll get better. We don't know what to do with you anymore, do we, Agnes? You've led us a merry dance, yes you have.'

A wisp of flaxen hair is tickling her nose, making it twitch. He combs it aside with his fingertips.

''Ank you,' she responds, from the depths of her anaesthesia.

Her lips have lost their natural pinkness; they're as dry and pale as Sugar's, but glisten with medicinal salve. Her breath smells stale, which disturbs him more than anything: she always had such sweet breath! Can what Curlew says really be true, that women a damn sight more degenerate than Agnes have walked out of Labaube Sanatorium restored to the peach of health?

'You *want* to be good, don't you?' he whispers into Agnes's ear, smoothing her hair against her delicate scalp. 'I know you do.'

'Far . . . farther . . . Scanlon . . .' she whispers in return.

He lifts the sheets off her shoulders, and folds them down to the foot of the bed. The necessity for Agnes to be forced . . . no, persuaded, to eat a more robust diet is all too obvious; her arms and legs are terribly wasted. How cruel a dilemma, that when she's responsible for herself, she starves on purpose, whereas when she's rendered helpless, she achieves the same effect unconsciously! Whatever his qualms are about the treatment she'll receive at the hands of strange doctors and nurses, he has to admit that Clara and her porridge-spoon are not equal to the challenge.

Agnes's feet are snugly bandaged, two soft hoofs of white cotton. Her hands are bandaged too, tied with a bow at the wrists, to keep her from interfering with her dressings in her sleep.

'Ye-e-es,' she says, stretching to greet the cooler air.

Gingerly, William strokes the line of her hip, which is now as sharp as Sugar's. It doesn't suit her: she needs to be more rounded there. What looks striking on a tall woman can look worryingly gaunt on a tiny one.

'I never meant to hurt you, on that first night,' he assures her, stroking her tenderly. 'I was . . . made hasty by urgency. The urgency of love.'

She snuffles amiably, and when he hoists his body onto the bed next to her, she emits a muted, musical 'Oo'.

'And I thought,' he continues, his own voice trembling with emotion, 'that once we . . . once we were underway, you'd begin to like it.'

'Umf . . . lift me up . . . strong men that you are . . .'

He hugs her close, from behind, cuddling her bony limbs, her soft breasts.

'You like it now, though, don't you?' he asks her earnestly.

'Mind . . . you don't let me fall . . .'

'Don't be afraid, my dear heart,' he whispers directly into her ear. 'I'm going to . . . embrace you now. You won't mind that, will you? It won't hurt. You'll let me know if I'm hurting you, won't you? I wouldn't hurt you for all the world.'

The noise she utters as he enters her is a strange, lubricious sound, pitched half-way between a gasp and a croon of compliance. He lays his whiskery cheek against her neck.

'Spiders . . .' she shudders.

He moves slowly, more slowly than he's ever moved inside a woman in his life. The snow against the window turns into sleet, pattering against the glass, casting a marbled shimmer on the bare walls. When his moment of rapture comes, he suppresses, with great effort, his urge to thrust, instead keeping absolutely still while the sperm issues from him in one smooth, uncontracted flow.

'. . . Num . . . numbered all my bones . . .' mumbles Agnes, as William allows himself a solitary groan of ecstasy.

A minute later, he is standing by her bed once more, wiping her clean with a handkerchief.

'Clara?' she whimpers peevishly, one bandaged hand pawing the air for the bedclothes. 'Cold . . . !' (He's opened the window a crack, just in case the servant's nose is as sharp in sense as it is in shape.)

'Won't be long, dear,' he says, bending to wipe her again. Suddenly, to his dismay, she starts peeing: an amber-yellow, foul-smelling trickle onto the white bed-sheets.

'Dirty . . . dirty . . .' she complains, her distant, dozy voice tinged now with fear and disgust.

'It's . . . it's all right, Agnes,' he assures her, pulling the sheets over her. 'Clara will be back very soon. She'll attend to you.'

But Agnes is squirming under the bedclothes, groaning and tossing her head. 'How am I to get home?' she cries, as her unseeing, demented eyes flash open and she licks her jellied lips. 'Help me!'

Sick with grief and regret, William turns from her, shuts the window, and hurries from the bedroom.

'Next time I wake,' reflects Sophie that evening as she's being tucked into bed, 'it will be Christmas.'

With a forefinger, Sugar taps the child lightly, mock-sternly, on the nose.

'If you don't go to sleep soon,' she says, 'Christmas will come at midnight, and you won't know *what*'s what.'

Oh, how sweet it is, to have won so much of Sophie's trust that she can raise a hand to her in playful rebuke, without causing a flinch. She pulls the blankets up; Sophie's chin is still a little damp, and Sugar's hands still warm and pink, from the bathwater.

'And you know what happens, don't you,' Sugar teases, 'to little girls who are still awake at midnight on Christmas morning?'

'What happens?' Sophie's apprehensive now, that she might stay awake despite her best efforts to sleep.

Sugar hadn't expected this; her threat was empty rhetoric. She delves into her imagination and, within an instant, is opening her mouth to say this: *A horrible ogre bursts into your room, seizes you by the legs, and tears you in two bloody pieces like a raw chicken.*

'A horr—' she begins, her voice rough with malicious glee, before she manages to clamp shut her mouth. Her stomach abruptly revolves inside her, her face flushes blood-red. It has taken her nineteen years to reach this understanding, that she is Mrs Castaway's daughter — that the brain which nestles in her skull, and the heart which beats in her breast, are replicas of those same organs festering in her mother.

'N-nothing happens,' she stammers, stroking Sophie's shoulder with a shaky hand. 'Nothing at all. And you'll be asleep before you know it, little one, if only you close your eyes.'

So saying, she extinguishes Sophie's light and, still burning with the shame of what she almost did, retires to her own room.

In Agnes Unwin's diary, on the morning of her wedding, the seventeen-year-old girl appears in high if somewhat frenzied spirits. Certainly, as far as Sugar can tell, Agnes's fears and doubts about giving herself to William Rackham have fallen — or been pushed — away. Only the ceremony now fills her with trepidation — but trepidation of a thrilled and puppyish kind:

> *Oh, why is it, dear Diary, that although there have been a million Weddings in the history of the world, and thus a million opportunities to learn how to make their course run smooth, my Wedding has turned into such a mad scramble! Here I am with only four hours left before the Great Event, half dressed in my Wedding gown, and my hair not even done! Where is that girl? What can she be doing that is more important than my hair, on this Day Of Days! And she has put the orange blossoms on my veil too soon, and they are drying out! She had better find fresh ones, or I shall be cross!!*
>
> *But I must stop writing now, in case in my haste to record every precious event, I break a finger-nail, or spill ink all over myself. Imagine that, dear Diary: ink-stained at the Altar!*

Until to-morrow then — or (if I can snatch a moment) perhaps even
tonight! —
by which time I shall be,
no longer Agnes Unwin,
but Forever yours,
Agnes Rackham!!!

Sugar turns the page, and finds it blank. She turns another: blank again.
She riffles through the remainder, and just when she's convinced that Agnes
must have begun a fresh diary to chronicle her married life, she spots a
few more entries — undated, clotted, fearsomely small.

Riddle: I eat less than ever I did before I came to this wretched house, yet I grow fat.
Explanation: I am fed by force in my sleep.

And, on the page following:

Now I know that it is true. Demon sits on my breast, spooning gruel into my mouth. I turn
my head, his spoon follows. His vat of gruel is as big as an ice pail. Open wide, he says, or we
shall be here all night.

More blank pages, then, finally:

The old men lift the stretcher on which I lie, & carry me through the sun-lit trees to the Hidden
Path. I hear the train which delivered me hooting & moving off on its return journey. One of
the Nuns, She who has taken me especially under Her wing, is waiting at the Gates, Her hands
clapsed under Her chin. Oh Agnes dear, She says, Are you here again? What is to become of
you! But then She smiles.

I am carried into the Convent, into a warm cell at its very heart, which glows in colours
from the stained glass windows. I am lifted off my stretcher & on to a sort of high bed — like
a pedestal with a matress on top. The awful pains in my swollen stomach, the giddy biliusness
I have been suffering each day, return with a vengeance. It is as if the demon inside me fears the
Holy Sister's healing powers, & seeks to take firmer hold.

My Holy Sister leans over me; She is many different colours in the light of the stained
glass, Her face is buttercup yellow, Her breast is red, Her hands are blue. She places them
gently on my belly, and inside me the demon squerms. I feel it pushing and lungeing in rage and
terror, but my Sister has a way of causing my belly to open up without injury, permitting the
demon to spring out. I glimpse the vile creature only for an instant: it is naked and black, it is
made of blood & slime glued together; but immediately upon being brought out into the light,
it turns to vapour in my Holy Sister's hands.

Falling back in exzaustion, I see my belly shrinking.
'There now', my Holy Sister says to me with a smile. 'It is over.'

Sugar flips to the end of the volume, hoping for more; there isn't any.
But . . . but there must be! Her curiosity is aroused, she's gripped by
Agnes's narrative as she never was before, and besides, she's arrived at the
period she most fervently wishes to know about: the early days of William
and Agnes's marriage. Breathing shallowly in anticipation, she fetches, from
the pile stacked against her thigh, the next diary in chronological sequence.
She's seen it before. It reveals nothing. She finds the next one.
  It begins:

"Season"-al Reflections, by Agnes Rackham
  *Ladies, I ask you: Can there be any greater annoyance, than hat pins which
are too blunt to penetrate a perfectly ordinary hat? Of course, when I say "ordinary", I don't mean to imply that my hats are not "extra-ordinary" in the sense of*

Sugar stops reading and lays the diary down, confused and disappointed.
Ought she press on? No, she simply hasn't the stomach for more of this
stuff, especially on the night before Christmas. Besides, it's late: a quarter
to twelve. Overcome suddenly by that peculiar breed of tiredness which
waits for a clock's permission before it strikes, she can barely summon the
energy to stow the diaries back under her bed; only the thought of Rose
discovering her snoring under a mound of them in the morning prods her
to action. Secret safely concealed, Sugar has one last piss in the pot, slips
inside the sheets, and blows out the candle.
  In the pitch dark, she lies listening, her face turned towards the window
her eyes cannot yet descry. Is it snowing still? That would explain how
little street noise she can hear. Or are there no revellers? In Silver Street,
Christmas Eve was always a noisy affair, with street musicians competing
for festive generosity, a cacophony of accordions, barrel-organs, fiddles,
pipes, drums – all woven together in a web of unintelligible chatter and
uproarious laughter, a web that was spun to the top floors of the tallest
houses. No hope of sleeping amid such a hubbub – not that anyone at Mrs
Castaway's was trying to sleep, busy instead with organ-grinding of an
unmusical kind.
  Here in Notting Hill, the sounds are fainter and more cryptic. Are
those human voices, or the snortings of a horse in the stable? Is that a

fragment of a minstrel's tune being blown across the grounds from Chepstow Villas, or the squeak of a gate, much nearer by? The wind whimpers under the eaves, fluting across the chimney tops; the rafters creak. Or is that the creaking of a bed, inside the house? And is that whimpering Agnes's, as she tosses in her poisoned sleep?

You ought to help her. Go help her. Why don't you help her? nags Sugar's conscience, or whatever she's to call that unruly spirit whose sole delight is to pester her when she craves rest. *They're keeping her doped because she says things they don't care to hear. How can you let them do it? You promised you would help her.*

This is a low blow, a promise scavenged from the meeting in Bow Street, when Agnes collapsed in the mud, and her guardian angel came to her rescue.

What happened was . . . I promised to help her get home, no more, she protests.
Didn't you say, 'I'll be watching you to see that you're safe'?
I meant, only to the end of the street.
Ooooh, you are a slippery, cowardly slut, aren't you?

The wind is blowing harder now, cooing and lowing all around the house. A shaft of whiteness plummets through the gloom past Sugar's window. Agnes in a white night-gown? No, a quantity of snow dislodged from the roof-tiles.

Why should I care what happens to Agnes? she sulks, turning her face into her pillow. *She's spoilt, and addle-brained, and a bad mother, and . . . and she'd spit on a prostitute in the street, if spitting were fashionable.*

Her mischievous opponent doesn't deign to answer; it knows she's remembering the tremble of Agnes's shoulders beneath her hands, there in the alley, as she whispered into the poor woman's ear: 'Let this be our secret.'

I'm in William's house. I could get into terrible trouble.

The unruly spirit is silenced by this – or so she imagines, for a minute or two. Then, *What about Christopher?*, it harangues her.

Sugar balls her fists inside the bedclothes and digs her brow into the pillow. *Christopher can take care of himself. Am I supposed to rescue everyone in this damned world?*

Oh, poor baby, is the mocking rejoinder. *Poor cowardly slut. Poor whore, poor-whore, poor-hoor, pooor-hoooor . . .*

Outside in the windswept streets of Notting Hill, someone blows a horn and someone else raises a joyous cheer, but Sugar doesn't hear them; she's narrowly escaped learning what really happens on Christmas Eve, to little girls who stay awake too long.

TWENTY-SEVEN

'erry Christmas! Merry Christmas, one and all!'

Thus blusters Henry Calder Rackham upon entering his son's house, as if he were Old Father Christmas himself, or at the very least Charles Dickens bellowing from a rostrum.

'Merry Christmas to *you*, Father,' William responds, embarrassed already, not just because of his father's jovial effusion, but also because of the difficulty the maid is having divesting the old man of his coat. Like Lord Unwin, Henry Calder Rackham appears to have made an abrupt transition from portliness to fat, during the same passage of time in which William has transformed himself from an effete good-for-nothing into a captain of industry.

'Ah, that *smell*,' rhapsodises the elder Rackham. 'I can tell already this visit will prove my undoing!' And with that, he allows himself to be ushered into his son's parlour, where he receives a warm welcome from the servants. 'Hrrmph! Haven't seen *you* before!' he says to the new ones, and 'Ah!: *you're* – No, don't tell me!' he says to the old ones, but they take it in good part, and within minutes he's the ring-leader, commandeering the rituals of fun and sentiment. 'Where are the crackers? Where are the crackers?' he demands, rubbing his hands, and lo! the crackers are fetched forth.

The progress of Time, which had rather slowed down since the opening of the gifts this morning, speeds up once more, as William's father devotes himself single-mindedly to the playing of parlour games. 'Splendid! Splendid! Whatever next?' he cries, as William watches in bemusement, unable to reconcile the festive buffoon with the stubborn old tyrant who made this house such a miserable place for so long.

Odd twinge of embarrassment notwithstanding, William feels quite tolerant of – even grateful for – his father's vulgarity today; it serves to keep the Christmas spirit buoyant whenever this terrible business with Agnes might have dragged it down. Everyone here is acutely aware (well, everyone except the likes of Janey) that the mistress of the house lies senseless upstairs, and that the master is sick at heart. He's done his best not to mope, but every so often the pity of Agnes's plight attacks him with a vengeance, and a pall of silence threatens to descend over the celebrations. You'd think a bevy of women could keep a house humming amiably for a day! But no: a male is needed, and William is tired of being that male.

All right, it's true that the gardener put in an appearance this morning, which lifted William's burden for a while, but a damn short while it was. Ten minutes, and Shears had already fled what he plainly regarded as a rampant superabundance of femaleness, for the safety of his outhouse. Cheesman would've been more use, but he's gone altogether – visiting his mother, a likely story.

So, with a parlour full of the fairer sex, all constrained by good manners to carouse as demurely as possible, the coming of Henry Calder Rackham – a roly-poly old man full of good-natured bombast – offers nothing less than William's rescue. Bluster on, old man! This is just what's required, to while away the long hours till dinner.

Mind you, the day has gone very well so far. Rather better, to be honest, than in previous years, when Agnes (beautiful though she invariably looked) was apt to sour the frivolity with damn queer remarks – remarks intended, he could only presume, to lift Christmas up from its nadir of commercialism and restore its proper religious significance.

'Have you ever wondered why we don't celebrate Childermas anymore?' she enquired one year, her gift from William lying half-unwrapped and forgotten in her lap.

'Childermas, dear?'

'Yes: the day that King Herod slaughtered the Innocents.'

This year, thank God, such conversations have not arisen. And, regrettable though the circumstances may be, the absence of Agnes from the festivities has made possible one happy benefit: the presence of her daughter downstairs. Yes, after years of strictly segregated Christmases, with Sophie being smuggled her presents and lukewarm portions of Christmas dinner in the nursery while the rest of the family fussed around the mistress downstairs, the child finally has her chance. Which is a jolly good thing, William thinks, and not before time! She's a pleasant little creature, with a most winsome smile, and far too big now to be treated like a baby. Besides, despite his willingness, in years gone by, to play along with Agnes's notion of Christmas as a ritual for grown-ups, he's always secretly thought there's something melancholy about a Christmas tree without a child frolicking in front of it.

Last year, the opening of the presents was blighted by all manner of restraints – odious economies, the dark cloud of Henry Calder Rackham's mistrust of his son, Agnes's haughty contempt for anything that smacked of cheapness or make-do, and the servants' fidgetings of unrest and ingratitude.

This year, the same ceremony, conducted with all the household on their knees in front of the Christmas tree in an ever-burgeoning froth of coloured paper, has proved highly satisfactory. Freed from the shackles of his debt, William decided to be a fountain of generosity. (To the dubious Lady Bridgelow, when she warned him of the perils of spoiling one's servants, he replied: 'You have too little faith in human nature, Constance!') Thus, while Lady Bridgelow has no doubt upheld convention and given her female servants a parcel containing the fabrics for making a new uniform, *his* female servants received a parcel containing their new uniform ready-made (honestly, why oblige the poor biddies to sew their own clothes, when ready-made is the way of the future?). Not only this, but each servant received extra parcels which, instead of containing the sort of mundane objects they might have expected – kitchen implements for the cook, a new scrubbing brush for the scullery maid, and so forth – contained out-and-out luxuries. God Almighty, he's a rich man now: does he *really* need to solicit a sour and grudging 'thank-you-sir' for the derisory gift of a soup-ladle or a wash-pail, when he can sit back and enjoy an expression of genuine, unfeigned pleasure?

So, this morning, each girl got (to her considerable astonishment) a box of chocolate bon-bons, a pair of kid gloves, a bronze-plated button-hook, and a delicate Oriental fan. The gloves were, he feels, an especially inspired gesture; they demonstrate that William Rackham is a master who appreciates that his servants are not mere household fixtures and drudges, but women who might wish to enjoy some sort of life on their afternoons off, in the world *out there*.

It was damned interesting observing each girl's essential nature asserting itself once the first flush of surprise had faded. Clara promptly restored the suspicious glint to her eye, the obstinate set to her mouth, and requested leave to attend to Mrs Rackham. Rose stacked her gifts carefully at her side, and resumed her vigilance of the party, in case anything should go wrong. Poor Janey continued to fondle and stare at her gifts, overwhelmed by their exoticism and by the implication that a dogsbody like her could possibly make use of them. Letty, ever the placid simpleton, hugged her treasures in the lap of her skirt and looked around in wonder, as if it had only just become clear to her that she needn't worry her head about anything anymore, ever. The new kitchenmaid, Harriet, and the laundrymaid, whose Irish name he can neither spell nor pronounce, both betrayed a sly impatience to indulge in their windfalls, an eagerness to gobble chocolates or go gallivanting down the street with their kid gloves on. By contrast, Cook (not a girl anymore, admittedly) made a show of good-humoured incomprehension, as if to say, 'Mercy! What could a person of my age and station possibly do with such things?' But she was flattered, he could tell . . . her sex made sure of that.

Sugar was a trickier challenge. How to reward her for all she's done, without arousing the suspicions of the others? For a time he considered the possibility of celebrating a second, clandestine Christmas alone with her in her bedroom, but as the day drew near he decided this would entail too great a risk – not of detection, but of his responsibilities crowding in on him, claiming every spare moment.

No, better to honour her publicly. But with what? By all means, for appearances' sake, she should get her own kid gloves, bon-bons, buttonhook and fan, but what more could he give her that wouldn't set the others' tongues wagging, while doing justice to her unique qualities? This morning, in front of the Christmas tree, with all the household looking on, he was proud to see the wisdom of his choice thoroughly confirmed.

Sugar, when Letty handed her the mysterious box, was surprised enough by how big and heavy it was, but when she removed its red wrapping-paper and hefted its contents into the light, her eyes widened further still, and her mouth fell open. *Ah*, thought William, *a response like that can't be faked!* Straining to keep his own face impassive, he watched her gape, speechless, at the leather-bound volumes of Shakespeare, each manufactured to the highest standards – the tragedies a dark maroon tooled with gold, the comedies a rich umber tooled with black, and the histories pure black tooled with silver. The other servants stared too, of course – the illiterate ones in bafflement, the readers in something closer to envy. But not *quite* envy – for what joy would they get from a set of Shakespeare, if it were theirs? And what more sensible, what more *defensible* gift could there be, than books for a governess to share with her pupil?

Sugar, of course, knew better. Choked with emotion, she could barely speak her thanks.

As for what to give Sophie . . . now *that* was an even thornier problem. After much soul-searching, William decided that this year, the convention of presenting Sophie with a gift 'from Mama' should be suspended. In previous years, Beatrice Cleave took care of this little subterfuge, at Christmases and birthdays, and the child was none the wiser. This year, several things conspired against it: his disinclination to burden Sugar further, Doctor Curlew's stern disapproval of the custom, Agnes's absence from the celebrations, and an uneasy sense that Sophie has surely grown too old to believe such a threadbare lie.

So: no gift 'from Mama'. Doctor Curlew has assured him there'll come a time when Agnes, cured of her delusions, will give her daughter something far more precious than any gaudy parcel. Maybe so, maybe so . . . but this morning, William made sure that Sophie wasn't starved of gaudy parcels.

In recognition of how much she's grown, he gave her gloves of her own, delicate pigskin miniatures to make her feel like a little lady. A turtle-shell hair-brush, too, he gave her, and a whale-bone hairclip, an ivory-handled mirror, and a chamois purse to put them in.

All these things she received with evident wonderment and pleasure. Her greatest amazement, however, came when she unwrapped the largest parcel under the tree, and found it to contain a surpassingly beautiful doll. Everyone in the room gasped and cooed to see it: a sumptuous French construction dressed as if for the theatre, with an alabaster-pale bisque head and an elaborately curled mohair wig topped with an ostrich-plush hat. In one hand it held a blue fan; in the other, nothing. Its satin gown (lower-cut in the bodice than any English doll's) ballooned out below the wasp waist, a rosy pink hemmed with white plush. Most unusually of all, the doll was mounted, by means of firmly glued shoe-soles, on a wheeled trolley, allowing it to be trundled back and forth across the floor.

'By gad,' William's father ruefully exclaimed, 'this is a class above the cheap nigger doll I got her a few years ago, ain't it?'

But Henry Calder Rackham had a surprise up his sleeve – or rather, under his chair, and he produced a cylinder wrapped in plain brown paper and string (which William had taken to be a bottle of wine) and handed it to Sophie, as soon as her wits were recovered from the shock of her father's generosity.

'There, dear,' the old man said. 'I think you'll find *this* is a superior thing to a lump of old rag from a tea-chest . . .' And he leaned back in satisfaction as Sophie unwrapped . . . a steely-grey spyglass.

Once again, there were gasps and murmurs among the servants, of wonderment and incredulity. What could this thing be? A bottle jack? A kaleidoscope? A fancy receptacle for knitting-needles? William knew at once, but was privately of the opinion that a spyglass is hardly the thing to give to a young miss. And, as the awed Sophie turned the apparatus over in her hands, he also noted that the metal was somewhat pitted and scratched.

'This ain't a toy, Sophie,' the old man said. 'It's a precision instrument, entrusted to me by an explorer I once met. Let me show you how it works!' And, crawling on his knees, he traversed the ribbon-strewn carpet to Sophie's side, and demonstrated the telescope's function. Within seconds she was swivelling the thing to and fro, her expression flickering between radiant joy and frustration as she focused on deliriously vague wallpaper and monstrous disembodied eyes.

And William himself? What did *he* get? He struggles to remember . . . Ah yes: a lace coverlet for a cigar-box, embroidered by Sophie (unless her governess helped her, in which case Sugar's skills as a seamstress leave a lot to be desired!) with a facsimile of his own face, copied directly from a Rackham soap-wrapper. Oh, and also: a quantity of middling-quality cigars, courtesy of his father. That, Lord help him, was the sum total of his Christmas bounty! Pitiful, but such is the fate of a man with a pack of servants, one small female child, a brother gone to an early grave, a mother cast out in disgrace, a father without a generous bone in his body, two old chums whom he has offended, and a wife who cannot be trusted while she's awake. What other man in England is in such a predicament? God willing, it won't last forever.

'Musical chairs!' exclaims Henry Calder Rackham, clapping his hands with a fleshy *whup-whup-whup*. 'Who's for musical chairs?'

★   ★   ★

Some distance from the Rackhams, in a modest house stacked to the ceilings with rubbish and surplus furniture, Emmeline Fox sits eating fruit
mince while her cat purrs at her naked feet.

Before you jump to conclusions: it's only her feet that are naked today;
the rest of her is fully, unimpeachably dressed – indeed, she still wears her
bonnet, for she's been out and about. A visit to her father, to give him his
Christmas present – a pointless exercise, since he celebrates nothing and
desires nothing, but he's her father, and she's his daughter, so there it is.
Every year they give each other a book, destined to remain unread, and
wish each other a merry Christmas, though Doctor Curlew doesn't believe
in Christ, and Emmeline doesn't believe that her Saviour was born on the
25th of December. Such are the silly compromises we make, to preserve
peace with those of our own blood.

Since returning from her father's house, she hasn't bothered to take
anything off except her boots, which were pinching her toes. Once upon a
time it was a mystery to her, how the dirt-poor could go barefoot in all
weathers and appear to mind so little – indeed, how the tireless efforts of
Mrs Timperley to collect shoes from the more fortunate and distribute
them among the unshod never seemed to reduce the number of bare feet
in London by even a single pair. Now she knows: feet that have grown used
to nakedness are no longer happy in shoes. One might as well press shoes
upon a cat.

'Do you fancy a pair of smart black boots, Puss?' she asks her companion, tickling his furry cheek. 'Just like in the story?'

They're sitting together in the spot she likes best – half-way up the
stairs. Christmas Day is half over, and her beloved Henry is three months
dead. Three months by the calendar, three blinks of God's eye, three eter-
nities within the veiled confines of Emmeline's house, where no one but
she is permitted to enter anymore. *Three French hens, Four collie birds, Five
gold rings* . . . improbable proofs of true love, extolled in ebullient singing
voices from the house next door. How is it she can hear these folk so clearly
today? She's never heard them before . . . A high-pitched female voice and,
underpinning it perfectly, the sonorous baritone of a male . . .

Three months since Henry walked the earth, three months since he
was buried inside it. The longer he's gone, the more she thinks of him;
and the more she thinks of him, the more those thoughts swell with feeling. Compared to him, all other men are selfish and sly; compared to

Henry's upright and muscular form, the shapes of other men appear cringing and grotesque. How it hurts her – like a claw squeezing her tender heart in a callous grip – to imagine him liquefying in the grave, his dear face mingling with the clay, his skull, once the home of so much passion and sincerity, an empty shell for worms to squirm in. She knows she's a fool to indulge such gross phantasms, to torture herself so, when she ought to be anticipating the joyful day she and Henry are reunited . . . But will the Second Coming occur in her lifetime? She very much doubts it. A thousand years may pass before she sees his face again.

Last Christmas Day, they walked the streets, side by side, and discussed the Gospels while everyone else was indoors playing parlour games. Henry had just read . . . what had he just read? He was always in a state of just having read something, bursting to share it with her before it passed out of his mind . . . Oh yes, an essay by a scholar of Greek, settling once and for all (said Henry) the centuries-old dispute over the meaning of Matthew I, verse 25. The Catholics were wrong beyond a shadow of a doubt; the new scholarship confirmed that when Saint Matthew said 'till' he *meant* 'till'; and Henry wished the newspapers would have the moral backbone to advertise these momentous findings, instead of filling their pages with lurid accounts of murders and endorsements for hair-dye.

And she? How did she respond to his earnest idealism? Why, the way she always did! By arguing with him, poor man. She said the dispute would never be settled, as no one who believed that a virgin could bear a child was going to take a blind bit of notice of a Greek scholar, and anyway, it didn't matter to *her*, because when it came to the Gospels, she much preferred Mark and John, sensible men who had better things to do than discuss the fettle of Mary's private parts.

'But you do believe, though, don't you,' Henry said, with that adorable frown of worry on his forehead, 'that our Saviour was conceived out of the Holy Ghost?'

In response to which, she'd brazenly changed the subject, as she so often did. 'For me,' she asserted, 'the real story doesn't begin until later, in the River Jordan.'

Lord! How Henry knit his brow at such moments! How earnestly he laboured to reassure himself she wasn't a blasphemer against the faith that had brought them together. Did she enjoy teasing him? Yes, she must have enjoyed it. So many sunny afternoons she sent him on his way home perplexed, when she ought to have kissed him, thrown her arms around him, pressed her cheek against his, told him she worshipped him . . .

She wipes her face on her sleeve, and trusts that God will understand.

'Now?' enquires her cat, butting his furry head against her naked ankle. She hasn't fed him since this morning, and the closed curtains downstairs are glowing amber from a sun poised to disappear in twilight.

'Do you eat fruit mince, Puss?' she asks, offering him a gooey spoonful from the big glass jar in her lap. He sniffs it, even touches it with his nose, but . . . no.

'Pity,' she murmurs. 'There's rather a lot of it.'

It's Mrs Borlais's surplus fruit mince; each member of the Rescue Society got a jar of it, on the understanding that it would fill Christmas tarts. No doubt her fellow Rescuers took up the challenge, either with their own hands or via their servants, but Emmeline's pie-making days are lost in the mists of her marriage to Bertie. The raw mixture is very tasty, though. She spoons it from the jar into her mouth, dollop after dollop, knowing it will most likely make her sick or give her the runs, but relishing its spicy sweetness.

Her father will soon be sitting down to Christmas dinner with his doctor friends. For politeness' sake, and perhaps because he has some inkling of her domestic circumstances of late, he did invite her repeatedly to join them, but she declined. And so she ought! The last time she attended a dinner with her father's friends, she shamed him terribly by lecturing them on the reasons why prostitutes shun doctors, and then urging them to donate their services *gratis* to desperate women once a week. If she'd accompanied him today, she would no doubt have muttered 'Pleased to make your acquaintance' a couple of times, suffered small talk for ten minutes or so, then reverted to type. She knows herself too well.

The food would've been awfully convenient, though. Just think of it all, steaming and sizzling on silver dishes, course after course . . . Not that she condones the gluttony to which the privileged classes fall prey in this once-holy festival; not that she fails to appreciate the terrible chasm between those who stuff their bloated bellies with a mountain of meat and those who stand shivering in line for a dish of watery soup. Her appetites are modest: sit her down at a Christmas banquet, and she'd have a slice of chicken or turkey and some roast vegetables, then nothing else until the pudding. A gourmand she most certainly is not. It's only that hot meals – especially roast ones – are such a colossal bother to prepare for oneself.

'Poor Puss,' she croons, stroking him from head to tail. 'You'd be very happy with a couple of nice juicy turtle-doves, wouldn't you? Or a partridge in a pear tree? Let's see what I can find for you.'

She rummages in the kitchen, but there's nothing. The unwashed chopping-board has a sheen of fish oil on it that keeps him occupied for two minutes, but the leftover portion of ham hash she can't find anywhere is, she suddenly recalls, inside her own stomach. Henry once said: 'It's frightening to think how easily one can spend an entire lifetime gratifying animal appetites.' *She*, perhaps, will spend the rest of her life remembering all the things Henry said.

'Now!' her cat chastises her, and she's forced to concede that good intentions are no substitute for action; so, she fetches her boots for another foray outdoors. Christmas or no Christmas, there will undoubtedly be meat for sale somewhere, if she's willing to descend through the strata of society to find it. Decent folk may have shut their shops in honour of the infant Jesus, but the poor have hungry mouths to feed, and every day is the same to them. Emmeline buttons up her boots and slaps dust from the hem of her skirt, sending Puss skittering under a stockpile of chairs. She fetches her purse and checks how much money she has left. Plenty.

Mrs Rackham's letter is still stowed in the bottom of her purse, getting rather mulched now amongst the coins and biscuit-crumbs. Will she reply, after what her father said this morning? She doubts it.

She wonders if she has betrayed Mrs Rackham, by discussing her case with the very man whom she so vehemently mistrusts. In her own defence, she can only plead that she did her best not to betray the wretched woman's confidence, by soliciting her father's professional opinion on the delusions of insane females generally.

Naturally he demanded at once, 'Why do you want to know?' Blunt and undiplomatic as ever! But she could hardly expect him to beat about the bush, when she wholly lacks that facility herself.

'Oh, curiosity merely,' she replied, aiming for, and probably missing by a mile, the insouciant manner of other women she's met. 'I don't like to be ignorant.'

'And what do you want to know in *particular*?'

Still she kept Mrs Rackham's secret. 'Well . . . for example: what is the best way to convince a madwoman that an opinion she holds is mad?'

'You can't convince her,' he shot back.

'Oh.' In earlier times, that might have been the end of the conversation, but her father is less brusque these days, since he almost lost her. The stimulus of her illness has brought his love for her (which Emmeline has never doubted) closer to the surface of his skin, like a blush of infection, and he's not quite managed to regain his chill composure since.

'There's nothing gained by it, my dear,' he explained this morning. 'What's the use of a person with a diseased mind being induced to say, "Yes, I admit I suffer from delusions?" An hour later she'll only insist the opposite. It's her diseased brain *itself* that must be cured, so that she's no longer *capable* of suffering delusions. Consider the man with a broken arm: whether he denies or admits it's broken makes no difference to the treatment required.'

'How good, then, are the chances of a cure?'

'Pretty decent if the woman's of mature age, and was tolerably level-headed until – for example – the grief of a tragic loss attacked her senses. If she's been entertaining delusions since early girlhood, slim, I'd say.'

'I see,' she said. 'I think my curiosity is satisfied. Thank you.'

Her disappointment with the efficacy of science must have pricked him, because he added, 'One day, I expect pharmaceutics will offer a cure for even the severest mental illnesses. A vaccination, if you like. We'll see all manner of wonders in the next century, I'm quite convinced.'

'Small comfort to those now suffering.'

'Ah,' he smiled, 'now that's where you're wrong, my girl. The intractably insane are intractable precisely because it suits them to be so. They don't wish to be rescued! In which respect – if you'll forgive me saying so – they're very like your fallen women.'

'Pax, father,' she warned him. 'I ought to be going. Thank you for the gift. Merry Christmas.'

But, worried that they would part on a sour note, he made a last gesture of appeasement.

'Please tell me, Emmeline: why these questions? I might have something better to offer you if I knew a little more . . .'

She hesitated, and thought carefully before speaking – though as always, not carefully enough.

'A lady has written to me, begging for the secret of eternal life. Eternal physical life, that is. She seems convinced that I know the location of a place where her . . . ah . . . immortal body is being kept waiting for her.'

'It's very kind of you,' her father said then, in a low and confidential tone, 'to be concerned for Mrs Rackham. I can only assure you that she will soon be in the very best of hands.'

'Now!' howls Puss, digging his claws into her skirts.

'Yes, yes, I'm going,' Emmeline responds.

Night has fallen on the Rackham house and, as far as William is concerned, Christmas is still ticking along as agreeably as possible, in the circumstances.

His father's call for a game of musical chairs causes a moment of awkwardness when the aroused volunteers suddenly remember that no one can play the piano – at least, no one present in their midst. However, Sugar saves the day – God bless her – with her devilish clever suggestion to use a music box instead. Sighs of relief all round, and the machine works a treat! William selects Clara to raise and lower its lid, on the assumption that this activity will suit her better than jostling for seats with her fellow servants – and he's right. Why, is that a *grin* he sees twitching on her lips, when Letty almost falls? She certainly has a knack, whenever she flips the box shut, for cutting a musical note clean in half, foiling the quickest listener. The one player who gets a seat every time, despite his stiff joints, is Henry Calder Rackham, for he doesn't mind whose hips he brushes against, or how rudely.

The old man is also a dab hand at Snapdragon, the next game on the agenda. When the lights are extinguished and the bowl of brandy is lit, three generations of Rackhams stand ready to plunge their hands into the flames. Henry Calder Rackham is first, his short wrinkled fingers darting into the flickering spirit in the blink of an eye, and almost as quickly tossing the raisin into his mouth.

'Don't be frightened, little one,' he urges his grand-daughter. 'You won't get hurt if you're quick enough.'

But Sophie hesitates, staring in fascination at the big shallow dish of blue flame, and William, fearing the spirit might burn itself out while she dithers, plucks out a raisin of his own.

'Go on, Sophie dear,' he commands her gently, as Rackham Senior seizes the opportunity to snap up another raisin.

Sophie jerks into obedience, squealing with fear and excitement as she snatches a raisin from the flames. Furtively she examines the tiny fruit between her fingers and, finding no flames on its dark wrinkled flesh, transfers it cautiously into her mouth, while the older Rackhams go after the rest.

The next game is dinner, and William's father tackles it with the same gusto. As course follows course, he eats as much as Lord Unwin did at Lady Bridgelow's party, allowing for the differences in the fare. (The Rackhams' cook is no enthusiast for what she calls 'recipes learned from savages', but what she does turn her hand to is delicious, and Henry Calder Rackham is its ideal consumer.) Turkey, quails, roast beef, oyster patties, mince pies, Christmas pudding, port jelly, apple hedgehog – all these are put before him, and all vanish inside his chuckling frame.

Small wonder, then, that when the time comes for after-dinner amusements, and he sits beside the magic lantern to feed the painted slides into the brass slot, he takes advantage of the dark and the fact that everyone's attention is directed elsewhere, to unbutton his waistcoat and trousers.

'*A little flower-girl am I,*' he recites breathily, for Sophie's benefit, from the subtitles as the image glows on the parlour wall: a plump-cheeked poppet in rags, posed on a fake London street corner lovingly beautified by the tiny paintbrushes of the magic lantern company's workers.

'*I'll sell you pretty posies*
Of buttercups and daffodils
Nothing so rich as roses.'

The child dies, of course, in the eighth slide. Already angelic when she was hawking her daffodils, she appears only marginally more radiant when a pair of sweet seraphs catch her swooning body and point her towards Heaven.

William, more accustomed to the pornographic slide shows put on by Bodley and Ashwell, is rather bored, but hides it, for his father has gone to the bother of buying three sets, and has already apologised *sotto voce* beforehand ('So few of these damned things are suitable for children, y'know: they've nearly all got murder and infidelity in 'em.')

A second magic lantern story, about heroism during a shipwreck, follows close upon the first, and is well received by all the family, despite the fact that it has no parts for females in it. The third and last, a woeful tale of a young watercress-seller who dies trying to save her dipsomaniac father, reduces Letty and Janey to helpless sobs, and ends with the word 'TEMPERANCE!' glowing on the parlour wall – a slightly irksome conclusion to the proceedings, since William and his father are by now looking forward to a strong drink.

'Good night, little Sophie,' says William, as Rose rekindles the lamps and the magic lantern is extinguished. For an instant Sugar hesitates, uncomprehending, then realises with a jolt that the Christmas celebrations have come to an end – for child and governess, at least.

'Yes, goodnight, little Sophie,' says Henry Calder Rackham, spreading an unused table napkin over his lap. 'Run up to your fine new toys now – before a thief comes and steals 'em!'

Sugar casts a glance around the parlour, and notices that the presents have already been removed, every scrap of wrapping-paper cleaned away, even the tiniest curls of stray tinsel picked up from the carpets. Apart from Rose, who's uncorking the liquor, the servants have melted back into the recesses of the Rackham house, each to her own function. The male Rackhams are slumped, heavy-lidded, in their chairs, tired out from administering so much pleasure.

Lingering momentarily in the threshold of the room, with Sophie's hand clasped in hers, Sugar looks over to Rose, and succeeds in catching her eye, but the servant is unresponsive; she lowers her head to concentrate on the unveiling of a tray of rum slices. Whatever intimacy she and Sugar have shared, whatever foolhardy acts they enjoyed together, a line has now been drawn between them.

'Good night,' says Sugar, too quietly to be heard, and she escorts Sophie out to the stairs, and up into the silent parts of the house, where their gifts await them, leaning against their bedroom doors in the dark.

Putting Sophie to bed is out of the question; the child is too excited, and there are miraculous new toys to play with. While Sugar looks on, unsure how to behave, Sophie kneels on the floor, face to face with the French doll, and wheels the creature gently back and forth. In the dim yellowish light of her bedroom, it looks more mysterious than it did downstairs in the parlour; more mysterious, and yet also more realistic, like a real lady who's just emerged from a ball or a theatre, venturing across the carpeted street in search of her private carriage.

'Now *where* can that fellow be?' murmurs Sophie in an affected, help-less voice, turning the doll three hundred and sixty degrees. 'I *told* him to wait for me here . . .'

She picks up the spyglass, extends it to its full length, lifts it to her right eye.

'I'll find him with *this*,' she declares, in a more boyish, confident tone. 'Even if he's far, far away.' And she inspects the environs, focusing on likely prospects – a knot in the wood of the skirting-board, a dangling curtain-sash, the blurry skirts of her governess.

Suddenly serious, she looks up at Sugar and says,

'Do you think I could be an explorer, Miss?'

'An explorer?'

'When I'm older, Miss.'

'I . . . I don't see why not.' Sugar wishes Sophie would make a mention – indeed, make just a *small* fuss – of the little book that's lying neglected on the floor, inscribed on its flyleaf *To Sophie, from Miss Sugar, Christmas 1875.*

'It mightn't be permitted, Miss,' reflects the child, wrinkling her brow. 'A lady explorer.'

'These are modern times, Sophie dear,' sighs Sugar. 'Women can do all sorts of things nowadays.'

Sophie's forehead wrinkles deeper still, as the irreconcilable faiths of her nurse and her governess collide in her over-taxed brain. 'Perhaps,' she muses, 'I could explore places the gentlemen explorers don't wish to explore.'

A noise drifts up from somewhere outside the house: a procession of strangers is tramping up the Rackham path, singing 'We wish you a Merry Christmas', their rough voices indistinct in the gusty night. Sophie walks over to the window, stands on tiptoe, and tries to peer down into the dark, but sees nothing.

'*More* people,' she declares, in a fanciful 'well-I-never!' tone, like a fairy-tale hostess who has invited half a dozen guests, only to be deluged by a thousand. Sugar realises the child is deliriously tired and ought to be steered towards sleep after all.

'Come, Sophie,' she says. 'Time for bed. Your bath can wait until tomor-row. And I'm sure you will need a whole fresh day to get properly acquainted with all your gifts.'

Sophie totters away from the window and surrenders herself into Sugar's hands. Though she doesn't resist the undressing, she's less helpful than usual, and stares dumbly ahead of her while her clothes are stripped off her unbending limbs. There's an odd, haunted expression on her face, a hint of wounded affront in her naked body as Sugar prods her gently to raise her arms for the night-gown.

'Now bring us some figgy pudding
Now bring us some figgy pudding
And a cup of good cheer . . .' the carol-singers are chanting below.

'There's no use anyone waking my Mama now, is there, Miss?' Sophie blurts out. 'She has missed everything.'

Sugar pulls back the bed-sheets, removes the warming-pan Letty has nestled there, and pats the hot spot.

'We won't go until we've got some,
We won't go until we've got some . . .'

'She's not very well, Sophie,' Sugar says.

'I think she'll die soon,' decides Sophie, as she climbs into bed. 'And then they'll put her in the ground.'

Downstairs, a door slams, and the voices are silent – presumably satisfied. Sugar, trying not to show the nauseous chill that the child's words have injected into her blood, tucks Sophie up and straightens her pillow. Mindful of first impressions in the morning to come, she gathers up the gifts and arranges them carefully on top of the dresser, standing the queenly French doll next to the slumped form of the grinning nigger manikin. Sophie's new purse, hair-brush, hairclip and mirror she lays in a row, punctuated with the spyglass stood on its end. Finally, she displays, upright, the book.

Alice's Adventures in Wonderland, it says. But Sophie has already fallen down the rabbit-hole of unconsciousness, into an uneasy wonderland of her own.

Rap-rap.

'Miss Sugar?'

Rap-rap-rap.

'Miss Sugar?'

Rap-rap-rap-*rap*.

'Miss Sugar!'

She sits bolt upright in her bed, gasping in terror and confusion as the brute who has 'come to keep her warm' is whisked off her childish body and she's left alone once more – older, bigger, elsewhere, in the dark.

'Wh-who is it?' she calls into the blackness.

'Clara, Miss.'

Sugar rubs her eyes with the rough heels of her palms, thinking that if she blinks hard enough, she'll see sunlight. 'Have . . . have I slept too long?'

'Please, Miss Sugar, Mr Rackham says I'm to come in.'

The door swings open, and the servant steps inside, lamp held high, uniform rumpled, head haloed with unbrushed hair. Clara's face, normally inscrutable or smug, is distorted by wavering shadows and a look of naked fear.

'I'm to make sure no one's come into your bedroom, Miss.'

Sugar blinks dumbly, through the orange fuzz of her own disordered hair. She motions consent for Clara to reconnoitre the geography of her tiny room, and the girl immediately hoists her lamp towards the four corners, here, there, here, there, sending the light and shadow veering dramatically. In her solemn thoroughness she looks like a Papist officiating a censer ritual.

'F'give me, Miss,' she mumbles, opening Sugar's wardrobe a crack.

'Is Sophie all right?' says Sugar, having by now lit her own bedside lamp. The time, she notes, is 3 a.m.

Clara doesn't reply, except with an extravagant curtsy, so low as to be fit for a queen. Only at the last possible instant does Sugar realise it's not a curtsy at all, but that the servant is preparing to look under the bed.

'Let me help you!' she says hastily, and dangles over the side, her mass of uncombed hair tumbling to the floor. Supported on one elbow, she sweeps her other arm into the shadowy space under her bed, thwacking the diaries against one another to emphasise their status as non-human debris.

'Apologies, Miss,' mutters Clara, and hurries from the room.

As soon as she's gone, Sugar jumps out of bed and gets dressed. The house, she hears now, is in a state of whispery, flustery commotion. Doors are opening and shutting, and, through the crack in her door, she can see lights grow brighter in sudden increments. Hurry, hurry: her hair is impossible, she ought to've had it cut weeks ago, but who's to cut it? All trace of the original frizzed fringe is gone, and only the use of a dozen pins and a cluster of clasps keeps the mess under control. Where are her shoes? Why is her bodice so difficult to button up? Her chemise must be rucked under-neath . . .

'Darkroom!' shouts William from somewhere below. 'Are you deaf?'

A female voice, unidentifiable and small, pleads that *all* the rooms are dark.

'No! No!' cries William, clearly in a state of great agitation. 'The room that used to be . . . Ach, it was before your time!' And his heavy tread thumps down the hallway.

Sugar is presentable now, more or less, and rushes out onto the land-ing, candle in hand. Her first port of call is Sophie's room, but when she ventures inside, she finds the child sleeping deeply, or at least affecting to.

Only when Sugar is walking back along the landing does she notice how very peculiar and unusual it is, to see the door of Agnes's bedroom ajar. She runs downstairs, following the noise of voices.

'Oh, Mr Rackham, and on a night like this!' cries Rose, the words reverberating queerly through the maze of passages leading to the rear of the house.

The rendezvous-point is the kitchen, in whose mausoleum frigidity a glum, sleepy-headed company has gathered. By no means the entire house-hold: Cook has been left to snore upstairs, and the newer, less trustworthy servants, curious though they naturally are about the commotion, have been told to settle back under the covers and mind their own affairs. But fully dressed and shivering down here are William, Letty, Rose and Clara. Oh yes, and there stands Janey in the doorway of the scullery, in tears, humil-iated by her failure to produce Mrs Rackham from out of the ice-chest or the meat larder, despite Miss Tillotson's angry expectation that she should.

Letty hugs herself, her mulish teeth clenched to stop them chattering. The white bib of her uniform glistens with moisture: she's braved the elements once already, to bang on the door of Shears's little bungalow. But Shears is too drunk to be roused, and Cheesman has evidently been charmed by his 'mother' into staying the night, so once again William Rackham is the only male on hand to deal with the crisis.

He greets Sugar's arrival with an unwelcoming scowl; his face looks ghastly in the light reflected off the chopping-table and the stone floor, both of which still shimmer from the liberal sponging they were given only a few hours ago.

'She's out *there*, sir,' pleads Rose, her voice shaking with the urgency of what she dare not say to her master: that he is wasting precious time – perhaps even condemning his wife to death – by failing to move the search out of doors.

'What about the cellar?' William demands. 'Letty, you were in and out of there in a flash.'

'It was *empty*, Mr Rackham,' the girl insists, her indignant whine ringing in the copper pans hung around the walls.

William runs his hands through his hair, and stares up at the windows, whose inky-black panes are spattered with sleet and garlanded with snow. This cannot be happening to him!

'Rose, fetch the storm-lanterns,' he croaks, after an excruciating silence. 'We must search the grounds.' His eyes grow suddenly bright, as if a flame has belatedly kindled behind them – or a fever. 'Put warm coats on, all of you! And gloves!'

A cursory inspection of the grounds confirms the worst: a trail of footsteps in the snow leading from the front door to the gate, and the gate swung wide open. The street-lamps of Chepstow Villas glow feeble in the drizzly gloom, each illuminating nothing more than a drab sphere of air suspended fifteen feet off the ground. The road is pitch black, with a hint, in the murk beyond, of unlit buildings and convoluted passageways. A woman in sombre clothing could quickly be lost in such a darkness.

'Is she in white, d'you know?' asks William of Clara, when the company of searchers is ready to set off from the house. She regards him as if he's an imbecile, as if he has just enquired which of Mrs Rackham's ball gowns she has chosen to wear on this momentous occasion.

'I mean, is she in her night-dress, God help her!' he snaps.

'I don't know, sir,' Clara replies, scowling as she represses the desire to tell him that if Mrs Rackham has frozen to death, it probably happened while Clara was being forced to search for her in broom-cupboards and under the governess's bed.

Stiff-limbed in a bulky overcoat, William blunders forward in a haze of his own breath and, in his footsteps, two women follow. Since only three functioning storm-lanterns have been found, those three have been divided amongst William, Clara, and Rose. Letty and Janey are in such a state of agitation that they're useless anyway, and had better go back to bed, while Miss Sugar oughtn't to have troubled herself to get up in the first place.

Sugar stands at the front door and watches them go. Even as they pass through the Rackham gate and strike off in different directions, a hansom cab rattles by, raising the possibility that, despite the extreme lateness of the hour, Agnes may have hailed one, and be miles away by now, lost in a vast and intricate city, stumbling through unknown streets of unlit houses full of unknown people. Drunken laughter issues from the cab as it rolls past, a reminder that death from exposure is only one of several dangers awaiting a defenceless female in the world at large.

It occurs to Sugar, as she stands shivering on the porch, that the interior of the Rackham house is unguarded; assuming the other servants stay in bed as they're told, there's no one to observe her opening prohibited doors, no one to stop her poking about wherever she chooses. Loath to let such a golden opportunity go by, she pictures herself standing at William's study-desk perusing some secret document or other. Yes; she should hurry upstairs and make this lantern-slide fantasy come true . . . But no; her will is lacking; she's so weary of stealth; there is nothing more she wants to discover; she wishes only to be a member of the family, absolved of suspicion, cosily welcome, forever.

Suddenly, quite out of the blue – well, out of the black – she's assailed by the thought that Agnes is close by. The certainty of it infuses her brain like a religious belief, a Damascene conversion. What idiots William and the others are, following a will-o'-the-wisp of tracks made by carol singers too careless to shut the Rackham gate! Of *course* Agnes isn't out there in the streets, she's *here*, hiding near the house – *very* near!

Sugar rushes indoors to fetch a lamp, and emerges a couple of minutes later with a rather flimsy, puny type, better suited for lighting a few yards of carpeted passage between one bedroom and the next. Gingerly she carries it out into the wind and the wet, holding her palm above the open bulb to shield the trembling flame. Sleet stings her cheeks, sharp little spits of it so cold they feel hot, like fiery cinders in the wind. She must surely be mad, yet she cannot turn back until she has found Agnes.

Where to look first, in this deadly serious game of hide and seek? She tramps onto the carriage-way, her boots going *krift, krift, krift* in the gravelly snow. *No, no*, says a voice in her head, as she makes her way along the flank of the Rackham house, past the bay windows of the parlour and the dining-room – *No, not here; you're not even 'warm'. Move farther away from the house: yes: farther into the dark. Warmer, yes, warmer!*

She ventures into unfamiliar parts of the Rackham grounds, beyond the vegetable glass-houses whose snow-covered carapaces gleam like marble sarcophagi in the dark. Every few steps, in her efforts to keep the lamp sheltered, she's distracted from her footing and almost stumbles, here on a garden tool, there on a coal-sack, but she reaches the stables without having fallen.

Very hot, the voice in her head commends her.

The coach-house doors are shut but not padlocked; so strong is the instinct that brought her here, that she presumes this fact before her eyes confirm it. She undoes the latch, tugs the doors open a crack and lifts her lamp into the aperture.

'Agnes?'

No answer, except the burning of intuition in her breast. She opens the coach-house doors a little wider, and slips inside. The Rackhams' carriage stands immobile in the gloom, larger and taller than she remembered, oddly disquieting in its burnished, steel-studded bulk. A puddle of chains and leather straps drools from its prow.

Sugar walks up to the cabin window and lifts her lamp to the dark glass. Something pale stirs within.

'Agnes?'

'My . . . Holy Sister . . .'

Sugar opens the door, and finds Agnes huddled on the floor of the cabin, her knees drawn up against her chin. That chin is speckled with vomit, and Agnes's eyes are heavy-lidded, blinking too feebly to expose more than a slit of milky white. In her frigid lethargy, she's passed beyond shivering, but at least she's not deathly blue: her lips, smeared with lubricant, are still rosebud-pink. Thank God she's wearing more than just her night-dress – not enough to keep her warm, but enough to discourage the cold from piercing her heart. A magenta dressing-gown, of thick silk in an oriental style, partly covers the white cotton night-dress, though the front has been buttoned clumsily, with most of the buttons in the wrong holes. Agnes's feet are bandaged up to the ankles, and additionally shod in loose knitted slippers, the wool sodden with melted snow and prickly with fragments of leaf and twig.

'Please,' says Agnes, barely able to lift her head off her knees. 'Tell me it's my time.'

'Your time?'

'To go . . . to the Convent with you.' And she licks at her lips, trying ineffectually to dislodge, with her listless tongue, a small glob of vomit stuck in the mouth-salve.

'N-not yet,' says Sugar, doing her best, in spite of her revulsion, to speak with the authority of an angel.

'They're poisoning me,' whimpers Agnes. Her face nods down again, and damp strands of fine blonde hair slither off her shoulders, one by one. 'Clara's in league with them. She gives me bread and milk . . . soaked in poison.'

'Come out of here, Agnes,' says Sugar, reaching into the cabin to stroke Agnes's arm, as if she were a wounded pet. 'Can you walk?'

But Agnes appears not to have heard. 'They're fattening me up for sacrifice,' she continues, in an anxious, high-pitched whisper. 'A slow sacrifice . . . to last a lifetime. Each day, a different demon will come to eat my flesh.'

'Nonsense, Agnes,' says Sugar. 'You'll get well.'

Agnes swivels her head towards the light. Through a veil of hair, one eye blinks wide, bloodshot-blue.

'You've seen my feet?' she says, with sudden, angry clarity. 'Bruised fruit. And bruised fruit doesn't get well again.'

'Don't be afraid, Agnes,' says Sugar, though in truth she is very afraid herself, that the glare of Agnes's eye and the sharpness of Agnes's torment will cause her own nerve to crack. She takes a deep breath, as discreetly as an angel might, and declares, in a seductive voice she hopes is serenely trustworthy, 'All will be well, I promise. Everything will turn out for the best.'

But the assurance fails to impress Agnes, despite its fairytale flavour; it only reminds her of more nastiness.

'Worms have eaten my diaries,' she moans. 'My precious memories of Mama and Papa . . .'

'Worms haven't eaten your diaries, Agnes. They're safe with me.' Sugar leans into the cabin to stroke Agnes's arm again. 'Even the Abbots Langley ones,' she soothes, 'with all their French dictation and Callisthenics. All safe.'

Agnes raises her head high, and utters a cry of relief. Her pale throat trembles with the breath of that cry, and her hair slithers back over her shoulders, revealing tears on her cheeks.

'Take me,' she begs. 'Please take me, before *they* do.'

'Not yet, Agnes. The time isn't yet.' Sugar has set the lamp on the ground, and is hoisting herself gently and slowly into the cabin. 'Soon I'll help you get away from here. Soon, I promise. But first you must get warm, in your nice soft bed, and rest.'

She lays an arm around Agnes's back, then smoothly slides her fingers into Agnes's armpits, which are hot and damp with fever.

'Come,' she says, and raises Mrs Rackham up off the floor.

The walk back to the house is not quite the nightmare Sugar feared. True, they must make their way across the grounds without any light, because she can't support Agnes and carry a lantern at the same time. But the sleet and wind have eased off, leaving the air quiet and apprehensive under gravid snow-clouds. Also, Agnes is no dead weight: she has rallied somewhat, and limps and lurches alongside Sugar without complaint – like a drunken strumpet. And, now that the objective is the single monumental structure of the house, whose downstairs windows helpfully glow with lamp-light, the going is easier than when Sugar was groping into the inky unknown.

'William will be angry with me,' Agnes frets, as they walk along the carriage-way, their four feet going *krift*, *krift*, *krift* and *fro*, *fro*, *fro*.

'He isn't here,' says Sugar. 'Nor is Clara.'

Agnes looks at her rescuer in wonder, imagining William and Clara being rolled aside like the two halves of the Red Sea, their startled limbs waving impotently as the irresistible force of magic pushes them out of the picture. Then she stops in her tracks, and casts a critical glance over the house across whose threshold her guardian angel is about to lead her.

'You know, I've never liked this place,' she remarks, in a distant, reflective tone, as snow-flakes begin once more to flutter down from above, twinkling on her head and shoulders. 'It smells . . . It smells of people trying terribly hard to be happy, without the slightest success.'

TWENTY-EIGHT

ut now, my dear Children — for that is how I think of you, blessed readers of my Book throughout the world — I have taught you all the Lessons I know. And yet I hear your voices, from as far away as Africa and America, and as far removed as the Centuries to come, clammering Tell Us, Tell Us, Tell Us _Your_ Story!

Oh, Ye of little understanding! Have I not told you that the details of my own case are of no consequence? Have I not told you that this Book is no Diary? And still you hanker to know about _me_!

Very well, then. I will tell you a story. I suppose, if you have read _all_ my Lessons and pondered them, you have earned that much. And perhaps a book looks better if it is not quite so thin — though I believe there is more substance in this little volume of mine than in the thickest tomes written by unenlighted souls. But let that pass. I will tell you the story of when I witnessed a thing that none of us is permit-ted to see until the Resurrection — but I saw it, because I was naughty!

It happened on one of the occasions I was transported to the Convent of Health for healing. I had arrived in a dreadful state, but after an hour or two of my Holy Sister's sweet attentions, I was much improved, and madly curious to explore the other cells of the Convent, which I was forbidden to do. But I felt so well I was bored. Curiosity, which is the desparaging name that men give to womens' thirst for Knowledge, has always been my greatest flaw, I admit. And so, dear readers, I left the confine of my cell.

I moved stealthily, as Wrongdoers do, and looked into the key-hole of the next chamber. What a surprise! I had always presumed that only _our_ sex could be offered Sanctuary at the Convent of Health, but there was Henry, my brother in law! (I didnt mind in the least, for Henry was the decentest man in the world!) But I _swear_ *that I should never have looked through the key-hole if I had known he wouldnt be wearing any clothes! However — in a glimpse I had seen him. One of the blessed Sisters was at his side, tending to his burns. I looked away at once.*

In the hallway behind me I suddenly heard footsteps, but, rather than run back into my own cell, I took fright and hastened on ahead. I ran directly to the Most Forbidden Room, the one with a golden A fixed upon it, and passed inside!

How can I pretend to be contrite for my sin of disobedience? I could say a thousand Hail Marys, and still smile in bliss at the memory. There I stood, dazzled with wonder at the Apparition in the middle of the room. A giant column of flame, for which I could detect no source: it seemed to issue from empty air a little distance off the floor, and taper to nothingness far above. I estimate — though I was never much good at calculations — that it was fully twenty feet high, and four feet wide. The flame was bright orange, gave off no heat and no smoke. At its heart, suspended inside it like a bird floating on the wind, was the unclothed body of a girl. I could not see her face, for she was floating with her back to me, but her flesh was so fair and free of blemish that I guessed her to be perhaps thirteen. The flame was so transparent that I could see her breathe, and knew thereby that she was alive, but sleeping. The flame did not harm her at all, it merely bore her aloft and made her hair swirl gently, all about her neck and shoulders. I nerved myself to extend one hand towards the glow, guessing that it must be something like the flame that issues from burning brandy. But it was more peculiar even than that — I was able to put my fingers quite inside it, for it was cool as water — indeed it felt <u>just</u> like water running over my hand. I do not know why this should have startled me more than getting burned, but I cried out in surprise and snatched my hand away. The great flame was disturbed by the motion, and wobled irregularly, and to my very great alarm the girls body began to turn!

I was too awestruck to move an inch, until the floating body had turned entirely around, and I could see that it was — my own!

Yes, dear readers, this was my Second Body, my Sun Body — utterly perfect — every mark that Suffering ever inflicted upon me, gone. So eager was I to see its flawless state, that I leaned my face right into the flame, a most delicious sensation.

I was most especially delighted with my bosom, so small and smooth, my lower parts, free of gross hair, and of course my face, with all the cares erased. I must say, I was relieved she was asleep, as I dont think I should have had the courage to look myself in the eyes.

Overcome at last with fear — or satisfaction — I left the room and ran back to my cell as fast as my feet could carry me!

Sugar turns the page, but this ecstatic episode was evidently as much of *The Illuminated Thoughts & Preturnatural Reflections of Agnes Pigott* as Agnes managed to write before arriving at her fateful decision to dig her old diaries back out of the ground.

'Well, what do you think?' says William, for he's perched on the rim of his desk, and Sugar stands in front of him in his study, holding the open ledger.

'I–I don't know,' she says, still trying to guess what his summons here this morning might have in store for her. Both she and William are mortally tired, and surely have better things to do with their fagged brains than dissect Agnes's ravings. 'She . . . she tells a story quite well, doesn't she?'

William stares at her in bafflement, his eyes smarting pink. Even as he opens his mouth to speak, his stomach emits a growl, for he's given the servants – those of them who were disturbed in the night – leave to sleep late.

'Are you making a joke?' he says.

Sugar closes the ledger and hugs it to her breast. 'No . . . No, of course not, but . . . This account, it's . . . it's a dream, isn't it? A record of a dream . . .'

William grimaces irritably. 'And the rest of it? The earlier part? The . . .' (he quotes the word with exaggerated distaste) 'lessons?'

Sugar shuts her eyes and breathes deep, plagued by a temptation to laugh, or to tell William to leave his damned wife alone.

'Well . . . you know I'm not the most religious of people,' she sighs, 'so I really can't judge—'

'*Madness!*' he explodes, slamming the palm of his hand against the desk. 'Complete lunacy! Can't you see that!'

She flinches, takes an instinctive step backwards. Has he ever spoken so harshly to her before? She wonders if she should burst into tears, and plead 'You f-frightened me' in a tremulous voice so that he'll enfold her penitently in his arms. A quick glance at those arms, and the fists at the ends of them, dissuades her.

'Look – look at these!' he rages, pointing to a precarious stack of books and pamphlets on his desk, all of whose covers are concealed under curious hand-made jackets of wallpaper or cloth. He snatches up the topmost, yanks it open to its title page, and loudly, jeeringly recites: '*From Matter to Spirit: The Result of Ten Years' Experience in Spirit Manifestations, with Advice for Neophytes*, by Celia E. De Foy!' He flings it from his hand like an unsalvageably soiled handkerchief, and snatches up another. '*A Finger in the Wound of Christ: Probings into Scriptural Arcana* by Dr Tibet!' He flings that away also. 'I searched Agnes's bedroom, to remove anything she might use to cause herself a mischief. And what did I find? Two dozen of these vile objects, hidden inside Agnes's sewing-baskets! Solicited from as far afield as America, or stolen — yes *stolen* — from a spiritualist lending library in Southampton Row! Books that no sane man would publish, and no sane woman would read!'

Sugar blinks dumbly, unable to appreciate the point of this tirade, but shaken by its vehemence. The stack of books and pamphlets, as if likewise unnerved, suddenly collapses, spilling across William's desk. One tract falls onto the carpet, a hymnal-sized little thing snugly clad in lace.

'William — what do you want of me?' she asks, straining to keep her voice innocent of exasperation. 'You've called me in here, while Sophie sits idle in the school-room, to look at these things of Agnes's you've . . . confiscated. I agree that they're proof of . . . of a severely muddled mind. But how can I help you?'

William runs a hand through his hair, then grabs a handful of it and squeezes it hard against his skull, a fretful gesture she last saw him exhibiting during his dispute with the jute merchants of Dundee.

'Clara has told me,' he groans, 'that she absolutely refuses to give Agnes any more . . . medicine.'

Sugar bites her tongue on several replies, none of them very respectful to men who wish to keep their wives doped to the gills; she breathes deep, and manages to say instead: 'Is that such a calamity, William? Agnes was walking fairly well, I thought, when I escorted her back to the house. The worst of the danger is probably past, don't you think?'

'An incident such as last night's, and you suggest the danger is *past*?'

'I meant, to the healing of the wounds in her feet.'

William lowers his gaze. Only now does Sugar detect a furtiveness in his bearing, a dog-like shame she hasn't observed in him since he first lifted her skirts at Mrs Castaway's and entreated her to submit to what other whores had refused. What does he want of her now?

'Even so,' he mumbles, 'Clara — a servant in *my* employ — has openly defied me. I instructed her to give Agnes that medicine until . . . until further notice, and she refuses to do it.'

Sugar feels her face beginning to contort with reproach, and hastily smooths it as best she can. 'Clara is Agnes's maid, William,' she reminds him. 'You must ask yourself, how can she possibly fulfil that function if Agnes doesn't trust her?'

'A very good question,' remarks William, with a portentous nod, as if it's only too clear to him how untenable Clara's employment has become. 'She has *also* refused, point-blank, to lock Agnes's door.'

'While she's attending to Agnes?'

'No, after.'

Sugar tries to insert this wedge of information into her mind, but it's just a little too big to fit through the aperture. 'You mean, you want – uh, the plan is . . . for Agnes to be kept a . . .' (she swallows hard) 'locked up in her bedroom?'

Face burning, William turns away from her; he waves one arm indignantly towards the window, his stiff fore-finger stabbing the air. 'Are we to be fetching her out of the coach-house, or from God knows where else, every night of the week?'

Sugar hugs the ledger tighter to her breast; she wishes she could put it down, but feels she'd be unwise to take her eyes off William even for an instant. What does he *really* want? What act of extravagant submission would deflate the anger from his pumped-up frame? Does he need to batter her with his fists, before exerting his remorse between her legs?

'Agnes seems . . . very placid just now, don't you think?' she suggests gently. 'When I brought her in from the cold, all she talked about was how much she was looking forward to a warm bath and a cup of tea. "Home is home," she said.'

He glowers at her in stark mistrust. A hundred lies he's swallowed; lies about the superior size of his prick to other men's, the erotic potency of his chest hair, the inevitability of Rackham's one day being the foremost manufacturer of toiletries in England; but this – this he cannot believe.

For a moment she fears he'll seize her by the shoulders to shake the truth out of her, but then he slumps back against the desk, and wipes his face with his hands.

'How did you know where to find her, anyway?' he enquires, in a calmer tone. It's a question he didn't get around to asking hours ago, when he arrived back at the house at dawn, soaked to the skin, wild with worry, only to discover his wife tucked up and dozy in her bed. ('My goodness, William, what a state you are in' was Agnes's sole comment before letting her eyelids droop shut again.)

'I . . . I heard her calling,' Sugar replies. How much longer does William intend to keep her here? Sophie is waiting in the school-room, rather distractible and peevish today, craving the familiar routine of lessons, yet resisting it . . . There'll be trouble – tears, at the very least – if normality isn't restored soon . . .

'It's . . . *exceedingly* important,' declares William, 'that she doesn't run away in the next few days.'

Sugar's self-control cannot bear the weight any longer, and she snaps. 'William, why are you telling me this? I thought you wanted me to have nothing to do with Agnes. Am I to be her warden now? Is she to sit in a corner of the school-room while I teach Sophie, to make sure she behaves?' Even as the words slip out of her lips, she regrets them; a man requires constant, tireless flattery to keep him from turning nasty; one careless remark can make his fragile forbearance shrivel. If a girl's going to be sharp-tongued, she's better off making a career of it, like Amy Howlett.

'Oh, William, please forgive me,' she implores, covering her face with her hands. 'I'm so very tired. And so are you, I'm sure.'

At last he crosses the floor to embrace her: a hard clinch. Agnes's ledger falls to the floor; their cheeks collide, bone against bone. Each of them squeezes harder as the other responds in kind, until they're quite breathless. Downstairs, the doorbell rings.

'Who's that?' gasps Sugar.

'Oh, tradesmen and spongers,' he replies, 'turning up for their Christmas boxes. They'll have to come back later, when Rose is ready to face the world.'

'You're sure . . . ?' she asks, as the ringing persists.

'Yes, yes,' he retorts irritably. 'Agnes is being watched by Clara just now – watched as close as I'm watching you.'

'But I thought you said you gave all the servants leave to—'

'All except Clara, of course! If the little minx won't do what's needful for Agnes to sleep, and won't lock her up either, the least she can do is stay in the room with her!' The callousness of his own words provokes a twitch of mortification in him, and he adds: 'But can't you see that this is no way for a household to be run!'

'I'm sorry, William,' she says, stroking his shoulders. 'I can only play my part as well as I'm able.'

To her relief, this does the trick. He holds her tight, uttering little grunts of distress, until the tension begins to leave his body, and he's ready to confess.

'I need . . .' he whispers urgently, conspiratorially, into her ear, 'your advice. I have a decision to make. The most difficult decision of my life.'

'Yes, my love?'

He squeezes her waist, clears his throat, and then the words come rushing out, almost in a gabble. 'Agnes is mad, she's been mad for years, and the situation is unmanageable, and the long and short of it is . . . well, I believe she ought to be put away.'

'Away?'

'In an asylum.'

'Oh.' She resumes stroking his shoulders, but he's so prickly with guilt that her momentary pause has already struck him like a slap to the face.

'She can be *cured* there,' he argues with the passion of unconviction. 'They have doctors and nurses in constant attendance. She'll come home a new woman.'

'So . . . when have you arranged . . . ?'

'I've put this off years too long! The twenty-eighth, God damn it! Doctor Curlew has offered to . . . uh . . . escort Agnes to the place. Labaube Sanatorium, it's called.' In a strangely cloying tone, he adds: 'In Wiltshire.' – as though mention of the locality ought to be enough to banish any doubt of the asylum's salubrious credentials.

'Then your decision is already made,' says Sugar. 'What advice did you hope to get from me?'

'I need to know . . .' He groans, nuzzles his face into her neck. 'I need to know . . . that it's . . . that I'm not a . . .' She feels his brow furrow against her skin, feels the twitch of his jaw push through her clothing. 'I need to know that I'm not a monster!' he cries, racked by a spasm of anguish.

With the lightest, tenderest touch, Sugar strokes his hair and cossets his head with kisses. 'There now,' she croons. 'You have done your best, my love. Your *very* best: always, since you first met her, I'm sure. You . . . you are a *good* man.'

He utters a loud groan, of misery and relief. This is what he wanted

from her from the beginning; this is why he summoned her out of the
nursery. Sugar holds him tight as he sags against her, and her heart fills
with shame; she knows that no degradation to which she has ever consented,
no abasement she's ever pretended to enjoy, can compare in lowness to
this.

'What if Clara tells Agnes of your plans?' It's a loathsome question,
but she must ask it, and she's so steeped in perfidy already, does it really
make any difference? There's a bilious taste of conspiracy on her tongue
– the poisonous, lip-licking saliva of a Lady Macbeth.

'She doesn't know,' William mutters into her hair. 'I haven't informed
her.'

'But what if, come the twenty-eighth—?'

He breaks their embrace, and begins immediately to pace back and
forth, his eyes glassy, his shoulders hunched, his hands wringing each other
in agitation.

'I'm giving Clara a few days off,' he says. 'I owe her Lord knows how
many free afternoons, not to mention some good nights' sleep.' He looks
to the window, and blinks hard. 'And – and I shall be gone too, on the
twenty-eighth. God forgive me, Sugar, I can't bear to be here when Agnes
is taken. So, I'll . . . I'll attend to some business. I'm leaving tomorrow
morning. There's a man in Somerset who claims he's invented a method of
enfleurage that requires no alcohol. He's been sending me letters for
months, inviting me to come and see the proof for myself. Most likely he's
a fraud, but . . . Ach, I'll give him an hour of my time. And when I return
. . . Well . . . by then it will be December twenty-ninth.'

Sugar's imagination glows with two vivid pictures, side by side. In one,
William is being led into the luridly lit lair of a leering mountebank,
surrounded by beakers bubbling and frothing. In the other, Agnes is arm-
in-arm with Doctor Curlew, the man her diary describes as Satan's lackey,
the Demon Inquisitor and the Leech Master; captor and captive are walking like father and bride towards a waiting carriage . . .

'But . . . what if Agnes should *resist* the doctor?'

William wrings his hands all the more nervously. 'It would've been so
much better,' he laments, 'if Clara hadn't been difficult about the
laudanum. Agnes is wide awake and on the alert now. She tastes everything that's given to her with the tip of her tongue, like a cat . . .' And he
casts a glance at the ceiling, recriminating whatever baneful power may

lurk in the skies above, for sowing such mischief. 'But Curlew will have men with him. Four strong men.'

'Four?' The vision of Agnes's wasted little body set upon by five hulking strangers makes Sugar's flesh creep.

William stops pacing and looks at her directly, his tortured bloodshot eyes imploring her to indulge just one more little outrage, to bestow upon him, with her silence, with her complaisance, just one more illicit blessing.

'Should there be any unpleasantness,' he maintains, fumbling for a handkerchief to dab the sweat on his brow, 'the extra men will only ensure that the event proceeds with . . . dignity.'

'Of course,' Sugar hears herself say. Downstairs, the doorbell rings, and rings again.

'God damn it!' William barks. 'When I told Rose she could sleep, I didn't mean all day!'

A couple of minutes later, when Sugar returns to the school-room, all is not well. She knew it wouldn't be, and it isn't.

Sophie has left her desk, and now stands on a foot-stool facing the window, immobile, apparently unaware of her governess re-entering the room. She peers through her spyglass at the world outside – a world which consists of nothing very spectacular, just a leaden grey sky and a few flickering hints of pedestrians and vehicles through the camouflage of Shears's ivy on the Rackham palisades. To a girl with a spyglass, however, even these indistinct phenomena can be engrossing, if she has nothing better to do; for who knows how long her governess – despite solemn announcements about how much needs to be learned before the new year – means to leave her like this?

So, Sophie has turned her back on the promises of grown-ups, and is conducting her own investigations. Several odd-looking men have come through the gate this morning, rung the doorbell, and gone away again. Rose seems not to be doing any work today at all! The gardener came out and smoked one of those funny white snippets that are not cigars; then he left the Rackham premises and disappeared up the road, walking extremely slowly and gingerly. Cheesman has returned from his Mama, walking in the same peculiar manner as Shears – indeed, the two men narrowly avoided each other at the front gate. The kitchen servant with the ugly red arms hasn't been out yet, to empty her buckets. There was no proper breakfast this morning – no porridge or cocoa – only bread-and-butter, water, and Christmas pudding. And what a muddle over the gifts! First Miss Sugar said the Christmas gifts should stay in the bedroom, so as not to be a distraction to the lessons, then she changed her mind – why? Which is right – the gifts in the bedroom, or the gifts in the school-room? And what about Australia? Miss Sugar was going to make a start on New South Wales, but nothing has come of it.

All in all, the universe is in a state of confusion. Sophie adjusts the lens of her spyglass, sets her mouth, and continues her surveillance. The universe may right itself any moment – or explode into chaos.

The moment she walks into the room, Sugar can sense these dissatisfactions emanating from the little girl, even though Sophie's back is turned; a child's disquiet is as potent as a damp fart. But Sugar smells something else too: a *real* smell, pungent and alarming. Christ, something is burning here!

She crosses over to the fireplace, and there, smouldering on the livid bed of coal, lies Sophie's nigger doll, its legs already reduced to ash, its tunic shrivelled like over-crisped bacon, its teeth still grinning white as sluggish flames lick around its sizzling black head.

'Sophie!' cries Sugar accusingly, too exhausted to soften the sharpness of her tone; the effort of being well behaved with William has leeched every last ounce of tact from her. 'What have you done!'

Sophie stiffens, lowers the spyglass, and turns slowly on her stool. Her face is disfigured by apprehension and guilt, but in her pout there's defiance too.

'I'm burning the nigger doll, Miss,' she says. Then, in anticipation of her governess making an appeal to her childish credulity, she adds: 'He's not alive, Miss. He's just old rag and biscuit.'

Sugar looks down at the disintegrating little carcass, and is torn between the urge to snatch it up in her hands, and the urge to prod the horrid thing with a poker so it stops smouldering and burns properly. She turns back to Sophie and opens her mouth to speak, but she catches sight of the beautiful French *poupée* standing witness on the other side of the room, towering over Noah's ark with its plumed hat, its smug impassive face oriented directly towards the fireplace, and the words die in her throat.

'He came from a tea chest, Miss,' Sophie continues. 'And there was s'posed to be an elephant under him, Miss, that's missing, and that's why he won't stand up, and anyway he's black and proper dolls aren't black, are they, Miss? And he was all dirty and stained, Miss, from the time he got blood spilt on him.'

The room is growing hazy with smoke, and both child and governess are rubbing their eyes, irritable, near tears.

'But Sophie, to throw him on the fire like this . . .' Sugar begins, but she can't go on; the word 'wicked' just won't come. It burns in her mind, branded there by Mrs Castaway: *Wicked is what we can't help being, little one. The word was invented to describe us. Men love to wallow in sin; we are the sin they wallow in.*

'You ought to have asked me,' she mutters, grasping the poker at last; they'll start coughing soon, and if the smoke seeps out into the rest of the house there'll be trouble.

Sophie watches the familiar contours of her doll being stirred into fiery oblivion. 'He was mine, though, wasn't he, Miss?' she says, her bottom lip trembling, her eyes blinking and shiny. 'To do with as I pleased?'

'Yes, Sophie,' sighs Sugar, as the flames grow brighter and the grinning head slowly rolls over into the body's ash. 'He was.' She knows she ought to put this incident behind her without delay, and return to the lesson, but a riposte comes to her in a belated flash, and she's too weak to resist it.

'A *poor* child might have wanted him,' she says, poking the ashes with rough emphasis. 'A wretched poor child that hasn't *any* dolls to play with.'

At once, Sophie erupts into a fit of weeping so loud it makes the hair on Sugar's neck stand on end. The child jumps off her stool and collapses straight onto her rump, screaming and screaming, helpless in a puddle of petticoat. Her face, within moments, is a swollen lump of red meat, slimy with tears, snot and saliva.

Sugar stands watching, buffeted by the ferocity of the little girl's grief. She sways on her feet, wishing this were only a dream, and she could escape it simply by turning over in bed. She wishes she had the courage to embrace Sophie, now when she's at her ugliest and most detestable, and that such an embrace could soothe all the hurt and the despicable notions from the child's convulsing body. But she hasn't the courage; that bawling red face is frightening as well as repulsive; and if there's one thing that would shatter Sugar's nerve today, it would be a shove of rebuff from Sophie. So, she stands silent, her ears ringing, her teeth clenched hard inside her jaw.

After several minutes, the door of the school-room opens – presumably after an unheard knock – and Clara pokes her sharp snout in.

'Can I be of assistance, Miss Sugar?' she calls over the din.

'I doubt it, Clara,' says Sugar, even as Sophie's wailing abruptly reduces in volume. 'Too much excitement at Christmas, I think . . .'

Sophie's hullabaloo ebbs to a hacking sob, and Clara's face hardens into a white mask of indignation and disapproval – how *dare* this beastly child, for the flimsiest of reasons, cause such a noise.

'Tell Mama I'm sorry!' snivels Sophie.

Clara shoots Sugar a glance that seems to say *Is it you who's putting such stupid thoughts in her head?*, then hurries back to her mistress. The door clicks shut, and the school-room is once more full of smoke-haze and sniffling.

'Please get up now, Sophie,' says Sugar, praying that the child will obey without further fuss. And she does.

The long remainder of the second day of Christmas, the day of inexplicable turtle-doves and invisible preparations for journeys, passes like a dream that has, in its inscrutable wisdom, decided to stop short of being a nightmare, sinking instead into a state of benign confusion.

Following her tantrum, Sophie becomes calm and tractable. She devotes her attention to New South Wales and the names of different breeds of sheep; she memorises the oceans between her house in England and the continent of Australia. She remarks that Australia looks like a brooch pinned onto the Indian and Pacific Oceans; Sugar suggests that it more closely resembles the head of a Scotch terrier, with a spiked collar. Sophie confesses she has never seen a terrier. A lesson for the future.

Normal function returns to the Rackham house as its servants rise from their beds and resume their work. Lunch is delivered to the school-room – hot slices of roast beef, turnip and potato, served at one o'clock sharp – and although the dessert is Christmas pudding again, instead of something reassuringly normal like suet or rice, at least it's hot this time, with custard and a neat sprinkle of cinnamon. Clearly, the universe is edging back from the brink of dissolution.

Rose is back to normal, too, answering the doorbell, which rings persistently, as those oddly dressed men who were disappointed before return for another crack at their Christmas boxes. Each time, Sophie and Sugar go to the window to look, and each time the child says, 'Who's that, please, Miss?' humbly trying to make amends for her earlier misdeeds.

'I don't know, Sophie,' says Sugar about each man. The impression is forming, from these confessions of ignorance, that Miss Sugar may know a great deal about ancient history and the geography of far-flung lands, but when it comes to the affairs of the Rackham house, she's almost completely in the dark.

'Once my lessons are over, this evening,' announces Sophie, during a lull in the afternoon when her governess's head nods bosomwards with weariness.'I shall read my new book, Miss. I have looked at the pictures, and they have made me . . . very curious.'

She looks up at her governess's face, hoping to see approval radiating from it. She sees only a wan smile on dry, flaking lips, and eyes that have tiny red lines scratched across the whites. Will those lines heal themselves, or are they etched there forever? And is it wicked to look at a storybook's illustrations before reading the tale? What else can she offer Miss Sugar, to make everything all right again?

'Australia is a very interesting country, Miss.'

Alone in bed that night, Sugar lies awake, plagued by an anxiety that she may, on top of everything else, be unable to sleep. That would be the finish of her, the absolute finish. With a muffled curse, she shuts her eyes tight, but they spring perversely open, staring up into the darkness. There's a natural order to sleeping and waking, and she has sinned against it, and it's having its revenge.

And what if William should come to her, for one last debauch of reassurance before he leaves in the morning? Or perhaps he'll ask her, with that beaten-cur expression on his face, if she wouldn't mind forcing a dose of laudanum down Agnes's throat? Or perhaps he'll simply want to bury his face in his loving Sugar's bosom? For the first time in many, many months, Sugar feels disgust at the thought of William Rackham's touch.

She lies awake for what feels like an hour or more, then lights a lamp and fetches a diary from under the bed. She reads a page, two pages, two and a half pages, but the Agnes Rackham revealed in them is an intolerable irritation, a vain and useless creature whom the world would not miss for an instant if she were removed.

So what will you do when the good doctor comes with his four merry men? Sugar asks herself. *Take Sophie for a stroll in the garden while Agnes is manhandled, screaming for rescue, into a black carriage?*

In the diary, Agnes is two years married, complaining about her husband. He does nothing all day, she alleges, except write articles for *The Cornhill* that *The Cornhill* doesn't publish, and letters to *The Times* that *The Times* doesn't print. He's not nearly as interesting in his own house as he was in hers. And his chin is not nearly as firm as his brother's, she's noticed, nor his shoulders as broad – in fact, his brother Henry is the handsomer man altogether, and frightfully sincere with it, if only he wouldn't dress like a provincial haberdasher . . .

Sugar gives up. She stows the diary back under the bed, extinguishes the light, and tries once more to sleep. Her eyes ache and itch – what has she done to deserve . . . ? Ah yes. Uneasy lies the head that conspires in the betrayal of a defenceless woman . . .

And William? Is *he* sleeping now? He deserves to toss and sweat in torment, yet she hopes he's snoring peacefully. Perhaps then, when he wakes fully rested in the morning, he'll recant his plans for Agnes. Unlikely, unlikely. Sugar knows from experience the face and the embrace of a man who's passed the point of no return.

All will be well, I promise. Everything will turn out for the best.

That's what she promised Agnes. But mightn't everything turn out for the best if Agnes goes to the asylum? Her wits are addled, without a doubt – couldn't they be . . . *un*-addled, with expert care? This vision that's haunting Sugar, of a woman in chains, wailing piteously in a dungeon lined with straw – sheer fantasy, from cheap novels! It'll be a clean, friendly place, this Labaube, with doctors and nurses in constant attendance. And it's in Wiltshire . . . And who's to say the poor deluded Mrs Rackham won't fancy she's in the Convent of Health, and that the nurses are nuns?

Soon I will help you get away from here. Soon, I promise.

That's what she said to Agnes, as she offered the terrified woman an arm to clutch. Ah, but what are promises in a whore's mouth? Nothing more than saliva to lubricate compliance. Sugar rubs her eyes in the gloom, loathing herself. She's a fraud, a failure, she invents facts about Australia . . . and dear Heaven, the ghastly smile of that nigger doll, as the flames licked around its head . . . !

A new woman, she counsels herself. *Agnes will come home a new woman.* That's what William said, and mightn't it be true? Agnes will be cured in the sanatorium; she'll kiss the cheeks of the nurses as she's leaving, and shake the doctors' hands with a tear in her eye. Then she'll come home, and acknowledge Sophie as her own daughter . . .

This thought, conceived as a reassurance, has quite the opposite effect – it sends a sick chill through her body. In the final waking moments before her soul lurches into sleep, Sugar knows, at last, what she must do.

It is the evening of the twenty-seventh of December, and William Rackham sits nursing a glass of whisky in a public house in Frome, Somerset, wishing he could be transported into the day after tomorrow.

He has travelled so far, and engaged in so many diversions (who'd have thought a tour of the town's old wool mill would fail so utterly to fascinate him!), and yet there are still thirteen, fourteen hours left to fill, before Doctor Curlew is due to arrive at Chepstow Villas . . . *Anything* could happen in that time – not least his own nervous disintegration . . . And with Clara absent from the house, and only Rose and that idiot Letty to keep an eye on things, there's an appalling risk of Agnes escaping . . . that is, of exposing herself to harm . . .

If only he could make contact with his household here and now, to confirm Agnes's safety. Only last week, he read an article in *Hogg's Review*, about a device very soon to be produced in America, a contrivance of magnets and diaphragms, which converts the human voice into electrical vibrations, thus making possible the transmission of speech across vast distances. If only this mechanism were in general use already! Imagine: he could speak a few words into a wire, receive the answer, 'Yes, she's here and sleeping,' and be spared this misery of uncertainty.

On the other hand, perhaps it's all tosh, this wonderful voice-telegraph, a tall story to fill space in a journal lacking worthier submissions. After all, think of what brought him here to Frome! The fellow with the new method of enfleurage was a fraud, of course, and not even an interesting fraud. William had expected at least to be entertained with bubbling gases, malodorous perfumes and hushed cries of 'Behold!', but was instead invited to study the scribbled notebooks of a mere university student angling for a benefactor to fund his researches. God preserve us from fuddle-headed young men who want money for building cloud-castles!

'But I don't understand,' William told the fellow, barely able to keep his temper. 'If the process works, why can't you demonstrate it in action?

On a smaller, cruder scale, with a few blossoms in a pie-dish?'

To which the young man's response was to gesture helplessly at the meanness of his lodgings – implying that in such pauperish circumstances, even the most modest miracles are impossible. Balderdash! But let the fellow stew in his self-pity; there's no chance of disabusing him of it anyway. William promised to keep the fellow in mind, wished him well with his studies, and fled.

After this dismal encounter, and a desultory tour of the town's attractions, he returned to his lodging-house, and loitered for a while in his room. Reclining on a strange, too-soft bed, he tried to read a treatise on the subject of civets and the practical obstacles, from a perfumer's point of view, to breeding them in northern climes, but he found it well-nigh impossible to take in, and wished he'd brought a novel with him instead.

Moreover, the lodging-house has had a most demoralising effect upon him. Its proprietress required the name 'Rackham' to be spelled out for her when she was committing it to the register, and looked him square in the face without any notion that she might have seen that visage before. And sure enough, in the bathroom, all the soaps were Pears'. Not one of them bore the impression of the ornamental 'R'. Perched on the edge of that ugly blue-veined bathtub, William could have wept.

It's all clear to him now. All these months since he took hold of the Rackham reins, he's been pulled along by an engine of optimism; each month has seen his fortunes grow, and in those heady late-night conversations with Sugar in Priory Close, he was encouraged to believe that the future would fall open to him in submission, that the rise of Rackham's to the pinnacle of fame was an historical inevitability. Only now does he glimpse the truth, winking at him from the mists of the future. He'll build up his heirless empire, grow old and, in his senescence, watch it crumble. He will be Ozymandias, and the despair will be all his, as the edifice of his business turns into a colossal wreck – or (worse) is snaffled up by one of his rivals. Either way, in a century or two, the name Rackham will have ceased to mean anything. And the seed of that humiliation lies here, in a soap dish in Frome, Somerset.

Unable to endure his own wretchedness, he fled his lodging-house and sought out a tavern – *this* tavern, The Jolly Shepherdess, in which he now sits nursing his glass of whisky. Far from being the convivial sanctuary he'd hoped for, it's melancholy and dim, with a sickly caramel-coloured wooden floor and a bar reinforced in fake marble. There's a blazing fire, but this is the beginning and end of its resemblance to The Fireside; an elderly, rheumy-eyed dog crouches near the hearth, whimpering and frowning in its half-sleep each time a cinder jumps. The human patrons are certainly not the lively provincials whose chatter he hoped would distract his mind; they drink quietly, alone or in huddles of three, occasionally lifting their torpid chins to ask for a refill. Two ugly matrons are busy with obscure chores behind the bar – too busy, evidently, to show the newcomer to a table. So, William chose his own, in a shadowy enclave near the lavatory door.

The clock above the bar has stopped at midnight – God knows which midnight, how long ago – expired from the strain of chiming the maximum hour once too often. William pulls out his watch to measure how many hours he has to wait before he can go to bed with some chance of sleeping, and is promptly accosted by a disreputable-looking fellow offering to sell him a gold watch to replace his silver one. When William shows no interest, the fellow leers and says,

'Missis fond of rings or necklaces, sir?'

William balls his fists on either side of his whisky glass, and threatens the fellow with police. This has the desired effect, though William finds his hands are trembling even after the man has scurried off. Frowning, he downs the rest of his drink and signals for another.

In any event, only a few minutes elapse before he's accosted afresh – not by a thief this time, but a bore. The fellow – a lugubrious, beetle-browed creature in a tweed overcoat – asks William if they haven't met somewhere in the past – a horse auction, maybe, or a sale of old furniture – and hints heavily that if William should lack anything in those departments, it would be well worth his while to speak up. William is silent. In his mind, a seventeen-year-old Agnes is dashing across a sunlit expanse of lush green grass, in the grounds of her step-father's estate, chasing a wobbling hoop, her white skirts swirling. 'Oh dear, I must grow up now, mustn't I?' was what she panted afterwards, alluding to her impending entry into the ranks of married ladies. Ah God! The translucent flush on her face as she said it! And what did he reply?

'What's *your* line, then?'

'Huh? What?' he grunts, as the vision of his bride-to-be vanishes.

The boring man is leaning across the table at him, revealing, at close quarters, a subtle dusting of scurf in his liberally oiled hair. 'What line of business,' he says, 'are you in?'

William opens his mouth to tell the truth, but suddenly fears that the man will take him for a liar; that the man will poke his greasy nose into one of Frome's shops tomorrow and confirm that no such thing as Rackham produce exists.

'I'm a writer,' says William. 'A critic, for the better monthly reviews.'

'Is there good money in that, then?'

William sighs. 'It keeps the wolf from the door.'

'What's the name, then?'

'Hunt. George W. Hunt.'

The man nods, discarding the name into a bottomless pit without an instant's hesitation. 'Mine's Wray. William Wray. Remember that name, if you ever need a horse.' And he's away.

William casts a furtive glance around the pub, dreading more unwanted company, but it seems he's experienced the gamut of the tavern's nuisances. Only now does he notice that, apart from the barmaids and the execrable oil-painting of the shepherdess above the front door, there's not a female face in the place. The barmaids are as ugly as sin, and the painted shepherdess has crossed eyes − not the artist's intention, surely? − and a vulgar toothy smile. Ach, Agnes's mouth is so small and perfect, her smile a rosebud blush on her peachy skin . . . although the last time he kissed her full on the mouth, five years ago or more, her lips were cold against his, like segments of chilled orange . . .

He raises his glass, to order more whisky. He's never been much of a spirits man, but the ale here is of a quality that would provoke the likes of Bodley and Ashwell to spit it out with a *pshaw* of contempt. Besides, if he can only calm the churning of his mind with the opiate of strong drink, he can then retire to his lodgings and, despite the early hour, fall blissfully asleep. A crashing headache in the morning would be a small price to pay for a night of dreamless unconsciousness.

After two more whiskies, he judges that the alcohol has worked its magic on his brain, and that now's the time to be going. The clock above the bar still stands at twelve, and his watch is too much bother to extract from his waistcoat, but he feels sure that if he laid his head on a pillow now, he wouldn't regret it. He rises . . . and is suddenly convinced of the necessity of vomiting and urinating as soon as he possibly can. He lurches towards the lavatory, decides that the anonymity of an alley would be preferable, and stumbles out of The Jolly Shepherdess into the dark streets of Frome.

Within seconds he has found a narrow alley that already smells of human waste: an ideal niche for what he needs to do. Swaying with nausea, he fumbles his penis free and pisses into the muck; regrettably, he's not quite finished squirting and dribbling when the sickness overcomes him, and he must pitch forward and release a gush of vomit from his mouth.

'Oh, deary, deary,' cries a female voice.

Still spewing, he looks up, and through the glimmering veil of his watering eyes he can see a woman walking towards him – a young woman with dark hair, no bonnet, a slate-grey dress striped with black.

'You poor man,' she says, advancing on him, her hips swaying from side to side.

William waves dismissively at her, still retching, appalled at the rapidity with which scavengers gather round a vulnerable man.

'You need a soft bed to lie down in, you poor baby,' she coos, close enough now for him to see the mask of her face powder and the beauty spot inked on her bony cheek.

Again he sweeps his arm, furiously, through the foul-smelling air.

'Leave me alone!' he bawls, whereupon – thank goodness for small mercies – she retreats.

But thirty seconds later, several pairs of strong hairy hands seize William Rackham by the shoulders and coat pockets and, when he tries to shrug them off, a savage blow to the head sends him plummeting into the abyss.

'All change!'

Shuddering to a stop, a train swings its doors open and spills its human contents into the tumult of Paddington Station. The hissing of steam funnels is overwhelmed almost at once by the greater din of voices, as those of the crowd who wish to retrieve their baggage from the top of the train struggle not to be borne away by the jostling multitude who wish only to be gone.

The thick of the crowd is composed of all categories of human: it swirls with the bright and bulky skirts of its women, set off against the funereal shades of the men, though there are many children too, buffeted in the lurch of bags and baggage. How pretty children can be, if they're nicely dressed and well-cared for! What a pity they make such a racket, when they're badly behaved! Look: there's one bawling already, ignoring the entreaties of its Mama. Child! – listen to your Mama, you little imp; she knows what's best for you, and you must be brave, pick up your fallen basket, and walk!

The woman who stands watching this scene, thinking these thoughts, appears to be one of London's myriad unfortunates – poorly clad, companionless, and lame. She wears a rumpled dress of dark blue cotton with a grey apron front – a style no fashionable female has worn for ten years or more – a threadbare bonnet that looks ecru but began life as white, and a pale-blue cloak so roughened by age that it resembles the sheep's-fleece from which it was spun. She turns her back on the commotion, and joins the queue at the ticket window.

'I should like to go to Lostwithiel,' she tells the man at the counter when it's her turn to speak. The man at the counter looks her up and down.

'No third class compartments on the Penzance line,' he cautions her.

She produces a crisp new bank-note from a slit in her shabby dress. 'I shall be travelling second class.' And she smiles shyly, really quite excited by the adventure of such a novelty.

For a moment, the man at the window hesitates, wondering if he should call the police, to investigate how a woman in such embarrassed apparel came by a bank-note. But there are other folk in the queue, and there is something winsome about this poor starveling's face, as if, given an easier life, she might have blossomed into the sweetest little wife a man ever had, instead of being obliged to live by her wits. And anyway, who's to judge that a woman in a shabby dress cannot be the legitimate owner of a bank-note? It takes all sorts, after all, to make the world. Only last week, he served a woman in a frock-coat and trousers.

'Return?' he enquires.

The woman hesitates, then smiles again. 'Yes, why not? One never knows . . .'

The man chews his top lip as he prepares the ticket with his fountain pen.

'Seventeen past seven, platform seven,' he says. 'Change at Bodmin.'

The shabby woman takes the slip of paper in her tiny hands and limps away. She looks around, half-forgetting that she's alone, half-expecting her lady's-maid to be coming up behind her, trundling a suitcase of clothes. Then she remembers she'll never need a maid again; these poor rags she wears are her last vestments in this life, and serve no purpose but to cover her nakedness while she conveys her old body to its final destination.

One deep breath to summon courage, and she begins to weave through the crowd, moving carefully in case someone steps on her feet. She hasn't got very far before her progress is blocked by a matronly woman. They do a little *pas de deux*, the way two ladies meeting in a narrow doorway might, and then both come to a halt. The older woman's face oozes compassion.

'Can I help you, dear?'

'I don't think so,' says Agnes. She has been specifically instructed to ignore entreaties from strangers.

'New to London?'

Agnes doesn't reply. Her recollection of her send-off this morning may be a little vague, given how dark and early was the hour when her Holy Sister's whisper roused her from her sleep, but if there's one thing she recalls with complete clarity, it's her Holy Sister's command that Agnes must reveal nothing to any person on her journey, however kindly that person may appear.

'I have a Christian lodging-house for ladies who are new to London,' continues the matronly stranger. 'Forgive me if I presume, but might you have been recently widowed . . . ?'

Again Agnes does not reply.

'Abandoned . . . ?'

Agnes shakes her head. A shake of the head is permissible, or so she hopes. Having obeyed her Holy Sister in every detail through all the trials of her escape – the shocking news of her impending betrayal; the donning of her disguise; the insertion of her sore feet into shoes; the stealthy progress downstairs, like a common thief in her own house; the dignified, wordless parting at the front door, nothing more than a single wave of her hand as she limped into the snowy gloom – yes, all these things she has faced every bit as bravely as her Holy Sister exhorted her to; it would be a tragedy if she weakened and sinned against Her now.

'You look half-starved, dear,' remarks the stubborn Samaritan. 'Our house has food aplenty, three meals a day, and a roaring fire. And you don't need money; you can earn your keep with needlework or whatever you're good at.'

Agnes, very much affronted by this suggestion that her physical form would be improved by the gluttony that has bloated the bulbous creature who accosts her, raises herself to her full height. With withering politeness, she says, 'You are very kind, madam, but mistaken. I desire nothing from you, except that you step aside. I have a train to catch.' The woman's face drops, its look of compassion vanishing into ugly creases, but she steps aside, and Agnes hurries on, steeling herself to walk as gracefully as if she were crossing a ballroom. The pain is dreadful, but she has her pride.

On platform seven, the station-master is ushering passengers into the Penzance train, gripping the clapper of his bell and pointing with the handle. 'All aboard!' he cries, and yawns.

Agnes enters her appointed carriage, wholly unassisted, and finds a place to sit. The seats are wooden, just like in church, without the sumptuously padded upholstery she's accustomed to, but everything's quite clean and not at all the stable-on-wheels she always imagined a second class carriage would be. Her fellow passengers are an old man with a beard, a young mother with a babe-in-arms (sleeping, fortunately!) and a sulky-looking boy with a bruised cheek and a satchel. Agnes, mindful of her Holy Sister's instruction, settles in her own spot by the window and closes her eyes at once, to discourage anyone making conversation with her.

In truth, she's suddenly so fatigued she doubts if she could summon the strength to speak; her feet throb from their punishment – the long walk through Notting Hill before she was rescued, at dawn, by a cab; the long wait for Paddington Station to open for business; the humiliation of being told to move along by a policeman; and being propositioned by a man delirious with drink. All these ordeals she has withstood, and now she's paying the price. Her head aches terribly, in the usual spot behind her right eye. Thank God this is the last day she will ever have to suffer it.

'Any person not intending to travel on the train, please disembark now!'

The station-master's voice barely penetrates the beating of blood in her head; but she doesn't need to hear him, having heard him so many times in her dreams. Instead, it's her Holy Sister's voice that echoes in her feverish skull, whispering, 'Remember, when you arrive at your destination and leave the train, speak to no one. Walk until you are deep in the countryside. Knock at a farmhouse or a church, and say you are looking for the convent. Don't call it the Convent of Health, for it will not be known by that name. Simply insist that you be shown to the convent. Accept nothing less, tell no one who you are, and don't take "no" for an answer. Promise me, Agnes, promise me.'

The train hisses and shudders, and rolls into motion. Agnes opens one eye – the one that doesn't feel as if it's about to burst – and peeks through the window, hoping against hope that her guardian angel may be there on the platform, to acknowledge, with a solemn nod, what a brave girl Agnes has been. But no, she's busy elsewhere, saving souls and tending bodies. Agnes will see her soon enough, at the end of the line.

PART 5

The World at Large

TWENTY-NINE

Basking in the warmth of Heaven, she floats weightless and naked, far far above the factory chimneys and church spires of the world, in the upper reaches of a sultry sky. It's an intoxicatingly fragrant atmosphere, surging and eddying with huge, gentle waves of wind and pillowy clouds – nothing like the motionless, transparent oblivion she'd always imagined Paradise would be. It's more like a breathable ocean, and she treads the heavy air, narrowing the distance between her body and that of her man who's flying beside her. When she's close enough, she spreads her thighs, wraps her arms and legs around him, and opens her lips to receive the incarnation of his love.

'Yes, oh yes,' she whispers, and embraces the small of his back to take more of him inside; she kisses him tenderly; their sexes are cleaved together; they are one flesh. A swirl of cloud folds around their conjoined bodies like a blanket as they drift through the balmy waves of eternity, borne along, like swimmers, by rhythmic currents and their own urgent thrusts.

'Who would ever have thought it could be like this?' she says.

'Don't talk now,' he sighs, as he shifts his hands down from her shoulder-blades to the cheeks of her behind. 'You're always talking.'

She laughs, knowing it's true. The pressure of his chest against her bosom is at once comforting and arousing; her nipples are swollen, her birth passage sucks and swallows in its hunger for his seed. On a great flank of cloud they roll and wreathe, until her passion rushes through her body like a fire and she thrashes her head from side to side, gasping with joy . . .

'Emmeline!'

Despite her convulsions of ecstasy, she still has the presence of mind to recognise that the voice comes not from Henry, whose inarticulate breath heaves hot in her hair, but from another, unseen source.

'Emmeline, are you there!'

How peculiar, she thinks, as the clouds unfurl and she pitches backwards through the sky, plummeting towards earth. *If it's God calling, surely He knows perfectly well I'm here?*

'Emmeline, can you hear me!'

She lands in her bed – a remarkably soft landing, given the dizzying speed of her descent – and sits up, panting, while the racket at her front door continues.

'Emmeline!'

Lord save her, it's her father. She leaps out of bed, sending Puss tumbling onto his back, all four paws flailing. She looks around the bedroom for something to cover her nakedness, but all she can find is Henry's coat and shirt, which – along with several other items of Henry's clothing from the *Tuttle & Son* sack – she's been taking into bed with her lately, for consolation. She throws the warm, rumpled coat over her shoulders like a cape, ties the arms of the shirt around her midriff for an apron, and runs downstairs.

'Yes, I'm here, Father,' she calls through the oblong barrier of wood and frosted glass. 'I – I'm sorry I didn't hear, I was . . . working.' The sunlight is quite strong; she guesses it must be eleven o'clock at least – far too late to admit to having been asleep.

'Emmeline, forgive me for disturbing you,' her father says, 'but it's an urgent matter.'

'I . . . I'm sorry, Father, but I can't let you in.' What's wrong with the man! She doesn't receive visitors anymore – surely that's understood between them! 'Couldn't I come and see you a little later this morning? Or afternoon?'

The distorted shape of his head, crowned with the dark top hat, looms closer to the glass. 'Emmeline . . . !' His tone suggests he's not at all pleased to be a public spectacle, hammering at his daughter's door in plain view of passers-by. 'A woman's life may depend on it.'

Emmeline considers this for a moment. Melodrama, she knows, is not in her father's nature, so a woman's life probably *is* at risk.

'Uh . . . please, if you could wait a few minutes, I . . . I'll come out . . .'

She rushes back upstairs and dresses faster than she ever has before – donning pantalettes, camisole, dress, coatee, stockings, garters, shoes, gloves and bonnet in much the same time that Lady Bridgelow might deliberate over the placement of a single hairpin.

'I'm ready, Father,' she pants at the front door, 'to walk with you.' His silhouette steps back, and she slips out of her house, locking its dusty chaos securely behind her, taking a deep breath of the fresh, cold air. She feels her father's eyes upon her as she turns the key, but he refrains from comment.

'There!' she says brightly. 'We're on our way.'

She turns to face him; he's immaculate, as always, but his frown tells her that she, regrettably, is not. He's a handsome and dignified old fellow, yes he is, although his face is lined with care. So much illness in the world, and only an old man with a satchel to combat it . . . If there was one thing in that pitiful letter from Mrs Rackham that convinced Emmeline the poor woman's mind had snapped like a collarbone, it was the reference to Doctor Curlew's evil nature; in Emmeline's eyes, her father is the archetype of benevolence, a mender of bones and a dresser of wounds, whereas the best *she* can do, in emulation of his philanthropic example, is write letters to politicians and argue with prostitutes.

All this she thinks in an instant, as he towers over her on the footpath outside her house; then she sees the twitch of impatience in his bearing, and the nervous way he looks up and down the street, and she appreciates that something is very badly amiss.

'What is it, Father? What's wrong?'

He motions for them to start walking along the footpath, away from an apparition a few doors down – a nosy old gossip garnished with stuffed blue tits and fox-fur.

'Emmeline,' he declares, as they proceed apace, leaving their pursuer straggling behind, 'what I'm telling you is a secret, but it can't remain a secret much longer: Mrs Rackham is missing. She was to've been taken to a sanatorium yesterday morning. I arrived at her house to escort her – and she was gone. Vanished.'

Emmeline, although listening attentively, is also looking for clues in the sky and in the behaviour of other pedestrians as to what time of day it might be. 'Visiting a friend, perhaps?' she suggests.

'Out of the question.'

'Why? Hasn't she any friends?' The sky is darkening: it can't be twilight yet, surely? No: those are rainclouds up there, gathering to discharge their burden.

'I think you fail to grasp the situation. She fled her house in the middle of the night, in a state of utter derangement. All her clothing – every dress, jacket, coat and blouse – is accounted for, except one pair of shoes and some articles of underwear; in other words, she took to the streets near-naked. Quite possibly she has frozen to death.'

Emmeline knows she ought to be dumbstruck with sympathy, but her instinct for argument gets the better of her. 'Taking to the streets near-naked in winter,' she remarks, 'is something many women do without dying of it, Father.'

Again he casts a glance over each shoulder, to be satisfied that the motley scattering of street-sweepers, errand-boys, pampered dogs and ladies is out of earshot. 'Emmeline, I'll come straight to the point. In Mrs Rackham's letter to you, she mentioned a place she badly wished to go. Did she give any hint where she might imagine this place was? Geographically speaking?'

Emmeline hardly knows whether to be amused or mortified. 'Well, you know, father, she was rather relying on *me* to tell *her*.'

'And what did you advise?'

'I never replied,' says Emmeline. 'You dissuaded me.'

Doctor Curlew nods, obviously disappointed. 'God help her,' he mutters, as a dray-horse and carriage jingle past, disgorging a long trail of tumbling turds.

'I didn't know Mrs Rackham was so far gone,' says Emmeline. 'In her head, I mean.'

Curlew checks the current whereabouts of the street-sweeper, but the fellow hasn't budged, having set his sights on a different, more generous-looking couple approaching a different pile of ordure.

'She ran away on Christmas night, too,' he explains. 'Half the Rackham household was out in the sleet and snow, searching for her until dawn. Eventually she was found hiding in the coach-house, by Miss Sugar, the governess.'

Emmeline's ears prick up at the name: unusual though it is, she could swear she's seen it in print only recently. But where?

'What a lamentable business – I had no idea!' she says. 'But what about her husband, William – hasn't *he* any suspicion where his wife might be?'

Doctor Curlew shakes his head.

'Our champion of industry,' he says, with weary sardonicism, 'has only this morning been fetched home from a hospital in Somerset. He was attacked by bughunters in Frome.'

Emmeline snorts most indecorously. 'Attacked by . . . what?'

'Bughunters. Robbers who wait outside public houses, preying on helpless drunkards. Really, Emmeline, you've spent so long in the Rescue Society among London's low-life, and never heard the term?'

'I've heard other terms *you* may not have heard, Father,' she retorts. 'But how is Mr Rackham?'

Doctor Curlew sighs irritably. 'He's minus one silver watch, one overcoat, and a quantity of money; also he's black and blue, with concussion, fogged vision, and a couple of broken fingers. One of the ruffians jumped on his right hand, it seems. He's damned lucky to have escaped a knifing.'

Emmeline sees the butcher's shop up ahead, a place where she's lately become quite well-known. If she'd remembered to bring her purse, she could have bought Puss some breakfast. Perhaps the butcher will give her credit . . .

'It sounds like a matter for the police,' she says, slowing her pace, wondering how much longer her father means to walk with her before he accepts she's of no use to him and leaves her to her own devices. If only she can have a few friendly words with the butcher, in private . . .

'Rackham won't hear of it. The poor fool is afraid of scandal.'

'But surely, if his wife's been missing for two days . . .'

'Yes, yes, of course he'll have to call the police, and soon. But in his mind they are the last resort.'

Emmeline dawdles to a standstill in front of a window crowded with upside-down lamb and piglet carcasses, the yawning slits of whose abdomens are adorned with strings of sausages.

'Which means, I suppose,' she says, 'that *I* was the next-to-last?'

Doctor Curlew stares hard at the woman by his side, this carelessly dressed, indifferently groomed, scrawny package of flesh and bone which, thirty years ago, he created. She's grown tall since then, and not very beautiful – a less than felicitous combination of his own long face and his wife's knobbly, irregular skull. In a flash he recalls the date of her birth and her mother's death – bloody events that occurred in the same bed, on the same night – and suddenly appreciates that despite her ill health Emmeline has reached a far greater age than her own mother ever did. Her mother died rosy-cheeked and uncomprehending, without these worry-wrinkles on her brow, these crow's-feet at the corners of her eyes, that expression of weary wisdom and stoically endured grief.

He bows his head as the heavens open and heavy drops of rain begin to spatter down on the pair of them.

'Pax, daughter,' he sighs.

'The police,' says William. 'I shall have t-t-to tell the p-police.' And he winces in exasperation at this cursed stutter his cracked skull has inflicted on his tongue. As if his share of calamity weren't generous enough already!

He and Sugar are in his study, quite late in the evening of the 30th of December. If the servants wish to gossip, they'll no doubt feel free, but there's no impropriety here, damn it: the governess is merely lend-ing her services after-hours as a secretary, while the master's injuries render him unfit to write his own correspondence. Lord Almighty, why can't he make use of the only properly literate woman in his household without a busybody like Clara suspecting him of debauches? Let her poke her sticky nose in here if she dares, and she'll find no goings-on but the rustling of papers!

'What d'you think, hmm?' he challenges Sugar, from across the room. (He's stretched out on an ottoman, his head wreathed in bandages, his puffy, purplish face embroidered with black designs of dry blood, his right hand noosed in a sling, while Sugar sits erect at his desk, pen poised over an as-yet-undictated letter.) 'You're damn silent.'

Sugar considers carefully before responding. She's found him awfully peevish since his return from Somerset; the knock on the head hasn't done him any good. Her initial elation at being trusted with his correspondence, at being installed in his very own chair at the polished walnut helm of Rackham Perfumeries, has been spoilt by his frighteningly volatile moods. Even the thrill of receiving his blessing to forge the Rackham signature, after she and William agreed this would be preferable to the infantile botch he made of his name left-handed, was not quite so thrilling once she was scolded for taking too long over it.

'Police? You know best, William,' she says. 'Although I must admit I can't see how Agnes could have got very far. A woman hobbling on injured feet, without even a dress on, if we're to believe Clara . . .'

'It's been th-three days!' he exclaims, as if this proves, or refutes, everything.

Sugar picks through various courses of action she could recommend, but unfortunately most of them carry some risk, great or small, of Agnes being found.

'Well . . .' she suggests, 'instead of hordes of bobbies, and notices in the newspapers, could you perhaps engage a detective?' (She knows nothing about detectives beyond what she's read in *The Moonstone*, but she hopes the bumbling Seagraves outnumber the clever Cuffs.)

'Damned if I do, damned if I don't!' William cries, his left hand reaching for a handful of hair to squeeze, and finding only bandage.

'I–I'm sorry, my love?'

'If I th-throw Agnes's predicament into the public domain, her disgrace will be unim-m-*mag*inable. Her name – and mine – will be ridiculed from here to . . . to . . . Tunisia! But if I'm discreet, and another day passes, and sh-she's in deadly danger . . . !'

'But what danger can she be in?' argues Sugar in her mildest, most reasonable tone. 'If she succumbed to the cold on the night she ran away, she . . . well, she can't come to any more harm now, and all that remains is to find her body. And if she's alive, that can only mean someone has taken her in. Which means she'll remain safe for a little while longer while discreet investi—'

'She's my w-w-*wife*, damn it!' he yells. 'My *wife*!'

Sugar bows her head at once, hoping his fury dies down before the servants or Sophie get wind of it. The page of Rackham stationery under her hands says 'Dear Mr Woolworth' and nothing more; a droplet of ink has fallen unnoticed off her pen and stained the letterhead.

'Can't you appreciate A-Agnes may be in urgent need of *rescue*?' William rails, waving his good hand accusingly at the world outside.

'But William, as I've just said . . .'

'It's not a simple ch-choice between her being dead or alive – th-there is a fate w-w-*worse* than death!'

Sugar raises her head, incredulous.

'Don't play the in-innocent with me!' he rages. 'Even as we speak, some f-foul old hag like your Mrs Castaway may be in-in-*installing* her in a f-filthy bawdy-house!'

Sugar bites her lip, and turns away from him, facing the tobacco-stained wallpaper. She breathes regularly and doesn't wipe the tears off her cheeks, but lets them trickle down her chin and into the collar of her dress.

'I'm sure,' she says, when she can trust her voice not to betray her, 'that Agnes is too frail and unwell to . . . to be made use of as you fear.'

'Haven't you read *More Sprees in L-London*?' he demands, quick as a whiplash. 'There's a n-nice little trade in dying girls – or have you forgotten!' And he utters a sharp groan of disgust, as though the eggshell of his innocence has only just this minute been smashed, allowing the offensive stink of human depravity to invade his nostrils.

Sugar sits silent, waiting for him to speak again, but his tantrum appears to have passed, his shoulders have slumped, and after a few minutes she begins to wonder if he's slipped into a doze.

'William?' she says meekly. 'Shall we reply to Mr Woolworth now?'

Farewell then, 1875.

If there are any rituals of celebration, in the Rackham house, on the 31st of December, they are conducted in secret, and emphatically do not involve the master. Other households all over the metropolis – indeed, throughout the civilised world – may be abuzz with New Year expectancy, but in the house in Chepstow Villas the commencement of a fresh calendar is of pale significance compared to the event everyone is waiting for. Life hangs suspended between two eras: the time before Mrs Rackham's disappearance, and the time – whenever that may come – when her fate is discovered, and the house can exhale its painfully bated breath.

On the first day of January, 1876, the servants busy themselves with their tasks as though it's a day like any other. Baking-pans are greased for loaves that may or may not be required; linen is ironed and added to stacks of superfluous bedding; a quantity of duck flesh which has sprouted maggots has had to be given to Shears for compost, but otherwise efficiency rules. Even Clara walks purposefully up and down the stairs, and in and out of Mrs Rackham's bedroom, warning the other servants, with one scowl from her sour face, that they'd better refrain from asking why.

By contrast, no one could accuse the governess of being surplus to requirements; the first half of New Year's Day finds her fully occupied with her new routine: lessons with Miss Sophie in the morning, a hasty lunch, and then two hours of work for the master in his study.

Sugar and William get down to business without niceties or preambles. The cogs of industry pause for no man or woman; there's no use pleading that one's fingers are broken or that one's head hurts or that one's wife is missing; accounts must be paid, errant suppliers must be pursued, the failure of Rackham's Millefleur Sachets must be unflinchingly confronted.

Sugar writes letters to a number of So-and-So Esquires, gently counsels William to amend the often belligerent and wounded tone of his dictation, and does her best to ensure the letters don't ramble into incoherence. Almost without thinking she translates phrases like 'L-let him chew on that, the scoundrel!' as 'Yours, ever', and corrects his arithmetic whenever his patience with numbers is exhausted. Already today he has indulged in one furious outburst against a lampblack manufacturer in West Ham, and now slumps on the ottoman, snoring stertorously through his swollen, blood-clogged nose.

'William?' says Sugar softly, but he doesn't hear, and she's learned that rousing him with a loud voice makes him very cross indeed, whereas if she lets him sleep he tends to absolve her with a mild reproach.

To help time pass until William's discomforts wake him, or until she must return to Sophie, Sugar reads *The Illustrated London News*, turning the pages in silence. She's aware that the police have by now been alerted to Agnes's disappearance, but William's request for utmost discretion has evidently been honoured, for the newspaper makes no mention of Mrs Rackham. Instead, the sensational news of the day is what's dubbed (as if already legendary) The Great Northern Railway Disaster. An engraving, 'based upon a sketch hastily made by a survivor of the accident', depicts a squad of burly men in thick coats congregating around an overturned carriage of *The Flying Scotsman*. The engraver's lack of skill, or perhaps his surfeit of delicacy, makes the rescuers look like postmen offloading sacks of mail, and conveys nothing of the true horror of the event. Thirteen persons dead, twenty-four severely injured, in a dreadful collision at Abbots Ripton, north of Peterborough. A signal frozen into the 'Off' position signal is blamed. A calamity to make Colonel Leek's juices surge!

Sugar thinks of Agnes, of course; pictures her being extracted, broken and disembowelled, from the wreckage. Is it conceivable that Agnes took so long to make the journey from Notting Hill to the city, and that she would then have boarded this Edinburgh-bound train? Sugar is at a disadvantage, having no idea what destination Agnes chose once she arrived – *if* she arrived – at Paddington Station; 'Read the boards, and the right name will reveal itself to you' was the only advice the 'Holy Sister' gave – the only advice she *could* give, given Sugar's ignorance of railways and where they go. What if Agnes was charmed by the ecclesiastical ring of 'Abbots Ripton', and made up her mind to alight there?

Printed underneath the article is a footnote entitled 'The Safety of Rail Travel':

> *In 1873, 17,246 persons met with violent deaths, averaging 750 per million. Of these 1,290 were due to railways, 990 to mining, and 6,070 to other mechanical causes; 3,232 were drowned, 1,519 were killed by horses or conveyances, and 1,132 by machinery of various kinds; the rest by falls, burns, suffocation, and other events to which we are liable daily.*

While William snores and groans in uneasy dreams, Sugar pictures Agnes falling down a mine-shaft, Agnes floating face-down in a filthy pond, Agnes being scooped screaming into a threshing-machine, Agnes disappearing under the trampling hooves and grinding wheels of a horse and carriage, Agnes pitching headlong off a cliff, Agnes writhing in agony as her body is consumed by flames. Perhaps she would've been better off in Labaube Sanatorium, after all . . .

But no. Agnes wasn't on that train, nor has she suffered any of these gruesome fates. She has done exactly what her Holy Sister told her to. By the evening of the 28th, she was already far out of harm's way, safely housed in a pastoral sanctuary. Imagine a simple farmer toiling in his field, doing . . . doing whatever it is that farmers do in their fields. He spies a strange woman coming through the corn, or wheat, or whatever; a shabbily dressed, limping woman on the point of collapse. What does she seek? The convent, she says, and swoons at his feet. The farmer carries her to his house, where his wife is stirring a pot of soup . . .

'Nff! Nff!' moans William, fighting off phantasmagoric attackers with his free hand.

Sugar imagines an alternative story for Agnes: a bewildered Mrs Rackham stumbles out of a rural railway station, by the light of the moon, into a sinister village square, and is instantly set upon by a gang of ruffians, who rob her of the money Sugar gave her, then rip the clothes from her body, wrench her legs apart, and . . .

The clock chimes two. It's time for Sophie Rackham's afternoon lessons. 'Excuse me, William,' she murmurs, and his whole body jerks.

As the days pass, and the new year that dare not speak its name ventures uneasily forward, it seems the only member of the Rackham household to remain unaffected by Agnes's absence is Sophie. No doubt the child has feelings on the matter, hidden somewhere within her compact, tightly-buttoned frame, but in her articulate responses she betrays nothing more than curiosity.

'Has my Mama still run away?' she asks each morning, with somewhat blurry grammar and an unreadable expression to match.

'Yes, Sophie,' her governess replies, catechism-style, whereafter the day's work begins.

In a topsy-turvy contrast that's not lost on Sugar, Sophie's behaviour is the very epitome of studious calm, patience and maturity, while William Rackham sulks and stammers and bawls, and falls asleep in mid-task, like a querulous infant. Sophie applies herself to the study of Australia with the earnestness of one who might expect to live there shortly, and she memorises the prejudices of ancient English monarchs as though this is quite the most useful information a six-year-old girl could arm herself with.

Even in play, she seems determined to atone for her sinful excesses at Christmas. The gorgeous French doll, which might have expected a busy schedule of social activities, is made to spend a great deal of its time standing in a corner, meditating upon its own vanity, while Sophie sits quietly at her desk drawing with her crayons, producing sketch after sketch depicting a brown-skinned menial mounted on an elephant, each more lovingly rendered than the last.

She's working her way through *Alice's Adventures in Wonderland* too, a chapter at a time, re-reading each episode over and over until she has either memorised it or understood it, whichever comes first. It's quite the strangest tale she's ever read, but there must be a reason why her governess has given it to her, and the more she reads it, the more accustomed she grows to its terrors, until the animals seem *almost* as friendly as Mr Lear's. Judging from the illustrations in the later parts she hasn't read yet, the story may be heading for a violent end, but she'll find out when she gets there, and the final three words are 'happy summer days', which can't be too bad. Some of the drawings in it she likes very much, like the one of Alice swimming with the Mouse (the only time her face looks carefree), and also the one which has the power to make her laugh out loud every time she sees it, of the uncommonly fat man spinning through the air. It must surely have been executed by a wizard, that drawing – a pattern of inky lines that works as a magic spell, acting directly upon her belly to call forth a hiccup of laughter no matter how hard she tries to resist. As for the part where Alice says 'Who in the world am I? Ah, *that's* the great puzzle!', Sophie must take a deep breath whenever she re-reads it, so alarmed is she by this quotation from her most secret thoughts.

'I'm so glad you're enjoying your Christmas book, Sophie,' says Miss Sugar, catching her at it once again.

'Very much, Miss,' Sophie assures her.

'You are being a very good girl, doing all this reading and sketching while I help your father.'

Sophie blushes and bows her head. The desire to be good is not what impels her to draw her poor nigger doll riding on an elephant, nor is it why she reads Alice's adventures and mouths 'EAT ME' and 'DRINK ME' when no one is listening. She does these things because she is powerless to do otherwise; a mysterious voice, which she doubts is God's, urges her to do them.

'Is it New Zealand's turn yet, Miss?' she enquires hopefully.

On the eighth day of Agnes's absence, Sugar notes that Sophie doesn't bother to ask if her Mama has still run away. A week, it seems, is the maximum time that the child believes a person could possibly remain missing before being discovered. No game of hide and seek could be drawn out to such length, no naughty deed could escape punishment so long. Mrs Agnes Rackham has gone to live in a different house, and that's that.

'Is Papa's hand still sore?' Sophie asks instead, when she and Sugar have finished eating their lunch and Sugar is about to leave for the study.

'Yes, Sophie.'

'He should kiss it and then hold it like *this*,' the child says, demonstrating the manoeuvre with her own right hand and left armpit. 'That's what *I* do.' And she gives Sugar an odd suppliant look, as if hoping that her governess will dutifully pass this remedy on to her grateful father.

★   ★   ★

Sugar does no such thing, of course, when she reports for work in William's study. His visible injuries may be healing quickly, but his temper is worse than ever, and his stutter — to his utter fury — shows no sign of diminishing. Quaint advice from his daughter is not what he wants to hear.

With third and fourth posts still to be delivered, a daunting pile of correspondence has already accumulated, but precious little work gets done today, for William digresses constantly, bemoaning the treachery and disloyalty of his business associates. He also reminisces about Agnes — one moment asserting that the house is a mere shell without her, and that he'd give anything to hear her sweet voice singing in the parlour; the next that he has endured seven long years of suffering, and is surely entitled to an answer now.

'What answer, my love?' says Sugar.

'Do I have a w-w-wife, or don't I?' he groans. 'Seven years I-I've been a-a-asking myself that q-question. You cannot know the torment, of w-w-wishing only to be a husband, and being taken f-for everything else under the sun: an ogre, a f-fraud, a f-fool, a gaoler, a w-well-dressed prop to be s-seen w-with in the S-S-Season — God *damn* this s-stutter!'

'It's worse when you excite yourself, William. When you're calm, it's hardly there at all.' Is this too arrant a lie? No, he appears to have swallowed it.

Stutter aside, Rackham is definitely on the mend. His sling hangs unused around his neck, and he no longer slumps snoring on the ottoman, but regularly lurches to his feet, to pace the floor. His vision is almost back to normal, and each time he wipes his liberally perspiring face with his handkerchief, more flakes of dried blood are dislodged, revealing pink new flesh underneath.

'Shall we return to business, my love?' Sugar suggests, and he grunts assent. For a few short minutes he's composed, humming indulgently as she reads back the letters, nodding his approval of the figures, but then some unfortunate turn of phrase offends him, and the flimsy casing of his temper bursts again.

'Tell the b-blackguard to hang himself with his own f-f-flax!' he exclaims, and, ten minutes later, about a different merchant: 'The dirty s-s-swine: he won't get away with this!' To such outbursts, Sugar has learned to respond with a long, tactful pause, before suggesting a more emollient wording.

But if William's reaction to business correspondents is immoderate, it's the soul of rationality compared to his reaction to visiting cards left by women of Agnes's acquaintance.

'Mrs Gooch? She has a l-lot to answer for! There's more gin and opium swilling in her fat hide than in h-half a dozen Ch-Cheapside sluts put together. What does the ugly cow w-want, to invite Agnes to one of her s-séances?'

'It's a simple calling card, William,' says Sugar. 'Left as a courtesy.'

'God damn the w-woman! If she's s-so clairvoyant, sh-she should know better than to come s-sniffing around here!'

Sugar waits. There are several other calling cards on the silver tray Rose has brought in. 'Would you rather,' she suggests, 'I made no mention of mail that doesn't concern Rackham Perfumeries?'

'No!' he yells. 'I w-want to know everything! Tell me everything, d'you hear!'

Ten days after Agnes's disappearance, when the sun peeps through the clouds, Sugar decides to take Sophie out into the garden for her afternoon lessons.

It's not a very pretty or comfortable garden just now – full of discoloured snow, slush and mud, and only the hardiest plants growing – but it makes a change from the house, whose interior is stormy with bad temper and apprehension, from the empyrean thunderbolts of the master to the draughty squalls below stairs.

Now that hopes are fading for Mrs Rackham's safety, the servants have exchanged one anxiety for another: instead of worrying about the brouhaha the mistress will cause when she's fetched home, they've become infected with the fear of their own dismissal. For, if Mrs Rackham doesn't come home, the Rackham household will have too many servants. Clara will be the first casualty, but she may not be the only one; Mr Rackham is in a constant foul temper and makes threats and accusations of incompetence to any girl who fails to anticipate his whims. Letty has been in tears several times already, and the excitable new kitchenmaid, after being provoked to retort '*I* 'ain't got yer blessed wife!', was ordered to pack her bags yesterday, only to be reprieved hours later with a gruff retraction.

All in all, it's an unhappy household, pregnant with foreboding. So, out into the grounds Miss Sugar and Miss Rackham go, well rugged up in serge winter-wear, fur-lined boots, and gloves. There's a whole world beyond the Rackham walls, if only one dresses warmly.

First they visit the stable, where Sugar endures an insolent stare from Cheesman in exchange for Sophie's shy smile as she strokes the flank of a horse.

'Don't let that governess of yours get up to any naughty tricks, will you Miss Sophie!' calls Cheesman jovially as they leave.

Next they visit the greenhouses, under the watchful eye of Shears, who won't let them touch anything. Inside the glass receptacles, obscured by a fog of condensation, unseasonal vegetables are being nurtured – the first fruits of Shears's grand plan to have 'everything, all year round'.

'What are you learning today, Miss Sophie?' says the gardener, nodding towards the history book her governess hugs to her breast.

'Henry the Eighth,' replies the child.

'Very good, very good,' says Shears, who sees no point in schooling except to read instructions on bottles of poison. 'Never know when he might come in handy.'

Social calls over and done with, Sugar and Sophie cross over to the perimeter of the Rackham grounds, and begin to make the rounds of its fences, exactly as Sugar used to do when she was spying on the house, except on a different side of the metal railings. Seeing the house now, without being obliged to squint through a barrier of wrought-iron, Sugar reminds herself that she once ached to know what lay inside those walls, and now she knows. Cheesman can be as insolent as he likes: she's come further than she could ever have dreamed, and she'll go further yet.

As they walk, Sugar relates the story of Henry VIII, as sensationally as she can, and with not the slightest qualm about embellishing. Indeed, she must discipline herself not to reproduce *too* much of the protagonists' conversation, for fear of straining Sophie's seemingly limitless credulity. The history of this dangerous king, with its simple plot and six complementary episodes, so much resembles a fairy-tale that Catherine of Aragon, Anne Boleyn and Anne of Cleves could almost be the Three Little Pigs or the Three Bears.

'If Henry the Eighth wanted a son so badly, Miss,' asks Sophie, 'why didn't he marry a lady who already had one?'

'Because the son must be his own.'

'But wouldn't any lady's son belong to him, Miss, as soon as he married her?'

'Yes, but to be a true heir, the son must be of the king's own blood.'

'Is that what babies are made of, Miss?' enquires Sophie, there at the perimeter of the Rackham grounds, on the eighth of January 1876, at half past two in the afternoon. 'Blood?'

Sugar opens her mouth to speak, then shuts it again.

One squirt of slime from the man, one fishy egg in the woman, and behold: they shall call his name Emmanuel, prompts Mrs Castaway helpfully.

Sugar passes a hand across her forehead. 'Uh . . . no, dear, babies aren't made of blood.'

'How are they made, then, Miss?'

For a moment Sugar considers wild fabrications involving elves and fairies. Discounting these, she next remembers God, but the notion of God being responsible for conjuring individual infants into being, when He shows so little interest in their subsequent welfare, seems even more absurd. 'Well, Sophie,' she says, 'the way it happens is . . . uh . . . babies are grown.'

'Like plants?' says Sophie, peering over the lawn at the coffin-like glass-houses and cucumber-frames littering Shears's domain.

'Yes, a little like plants, I suppose.'

'Is that why Uncle Henry was put in the ground, Miss, when he was dead? To grow babies?'

'No, no, Sophie dear,' says Sugar hastily, astonished at the child's ability to uncork the genies of death, birth and generation all at once. 'Babies are grown in . . . they are grown in . . .'

It's no use. No words will come, and even if they did, they'd mean nothing to the child. Sugar considers reaching down and touching Sophie on the belly; recoils from the thought.

'In *here*,' she says, laying one gloved palm on her own stomach. Sophie stares dumbly at the ten splayed fingers for a few seconds before asking the inevitable question.

'How, Miss?'

'If I had a husband,' says Sugar, proceeding with caution, 'he could . . . plant a seed in me, and I might grow a child.'

'Where do the husbands get the seeds, Miss?'

'They make them. They're clever that way. Henry the Eighth wasn't quite so clever, it seems.' And with that, the conversation is steered back into the tranquil waters of Tudor history – or so Sugar thinks.

But, hours later, when Sophie has been bathed and powdered and put into bed, and Sugar is tucking the blanket up to her chin and playfully arranging the halo of wispy blond hair on the pillow all around her sleepy head, there is one more thing to be fathomed before the extinguishing of the light.

'I came out of Mama, then.'

Sugar stiffens. 'Yes,' she says warily.

'And Mama came out of . . .'

'*Her* Mama,' concedes Sugar.

'And her Mama came out of her Mama, and her Mama came out of her Mama, and her Mama came out of her Mama . . .' The child is on the verge of sleep, repeating the words like nonsense verse.

'Yes, Sophie. All the way back through history.'

Without knowing why, Sugar suddenly longs to crawl into bed with Sophie, to hug her tight and be hugged in return, to kiss Sophie's face and hair, then clasp the child's head against her bosom and rock her gently until they're both asleep.

'All the way back to Adam and Eve?' says Sophie.

'Yes.'

'And who was Eve's mother?'

Sugar is too tired, at this stage of the evening, to think of solutions to religious enigmas, especially since she knows William is waiting for her in his study, with another stockpile of Rackham correspondence and irritable outbursts. 'Eve didn't have a mother,' she sighs.

Sophie doesn't reply. Either she's fallen asleep, or this explanation strikes her as quite credible, given what she's learned of the world so far.

'Tell me,' challenges William without warning, when Sugar is half-way through the scribing of a letter to Grover Pankey, concerning the brittleness of ivory. 'Did you and A-Agnes ever become . . . intimate?'

Sugar lifts her face, and carefully lays the fully-loaded pen on the blotter. 'Intimate?'

'Yes, intimate,' says Rackham. 'The police detectives, w-when they spoke with the servants, were particularly interested in s-s-special f-friendships.'

'Police? Here in the house? When was this?' Even as she asks, she recalls Sophie standing at the school-room window with her spyglass, commenting on the departure of yet more 'tradespersons' belatedly soliciting Christmas charity. 'no one spoke to *me*.'

'No,' says William, turning his face away from her. 'I th-thought it was best they left you alone, because you w-were occupied with Sophie, and in-in case you might – for w-whatever reason – already be known to the police.'

Sugar stares across the desk at him. He's done his pacing for the evening, and has, for the last hour, been stretched out on the ottoman. All she can see is his turban of bandage, his by-now rather grubby sling, and his fore-shortened legs, which he keeps crossing and uncrossing. It's difficult to believe that she ever was his lover, that she should have spent so many hours and nights in Priory Close bathing and perfuming her body espe-cially for him.

'A-Agnes f-formed some damn peculiar attachments w-w-with w-women she barely knew. W-we've f-found out she wrote to Emmeline F-Fox begging her for the ad-address of Heaven.'

'I didn't know your wife at all,' says Sugar evenly.

'When the police in-interviewed Clara, she said A-Agnes insisted that the person who f-fetched her back from the coach-house was her guardian angel, always at her s-side, her only f-friend in all the world.'

A chill of nauseous guilt travels down Sugar's spine, simultaneous with an almost uncontrollable urge to giggle – a combination which, despite her long experience of abnormal physical sensations, she has to admit she's never felt before.

'The whole affair took five minutes at most,' she tells William. 'I heard her calling, I found her in the coach-house, and I escorted her back into the house. I didn't say who I was, and she didn't ask.'

'Yet she trusted you?'

'I suppose she had no reason to mistrust me,' says Sugar, 'never having met me.'

William turns and looks directly into her eyes. She holds his gaze, unblinking, innocent, calling upon the same reserves that have in the past allowed her to persuade dangerous customers that she's more useful to them alive and yielding, than strangled and unco-operative.

The clock strikes half past the hour of ten, and William sags back against the ottoman.

'I mustn't keep you,' he sighs.

Next day, having hurried to William's study shortly after lunch as usual, Sugar finds the room empty.

'William?' she calls softly, as though he might spring, like a jack-in-the-box, from a cigar-case or a filing cabinet. But no: she's alone.

She takes her seat at the helm of Rackham Perfumeries and waits for a few minutes, tidying stacks of paper, browsing through *The Times*. A new steamer is offering passage to America and back in twenty-five days, including visits to New York and Niagara Falls, leaving from Liverpool every Thursday. Sol Aurine produces the golden tint so much admired for five shillings and sixpence. An article called 'A Multitude of Mishaps' collects together the week's explosions, fires and other calamities for the benefit of Colonel Leek. There's a civil war in Spain, and another in Herzegovina. France is in a delicate new state. Sugar finds herself wondering what a republican victory in the elections might mean to the French perfume industry.

Also on the desk is a small stack of unopened correspondence. Should she make a start on it before William has the chance to complicate matters with his bad temper? She could read what his business associates have to say, plan the appropriate response, and then, when William arrives, pretend to open the letters afresh, loudly slitting a different side of the envelope with the paper knife . . .

The clock ticks. After five minutes of idleness, she toys with the possibility of summoning a servant to the study and enquiring after William's whereabouts, but she can't quite muster the audacity to pull the bell-cord. Instead she leaves the study and goes downstairs, something she rarely does without Sophie in tow. Discoloured patches of the carpet appear under her shoes; she hadn't noticed them until now. Stains of Agnes's blood. No, not stains: the vigorously scrubbed *absence* of stains, leaving a blush of cleanness on surfaces otherwise subtly tarnished.

Tiptoeing, Sugar pokes her face into each of the rooms until she finds Rose — a rather startled and guilty-looking Rose, caught in the act of reading a tuppenny storybook by the parlour fire, with her feet on the coal-chest. In an instant, the easy familiarity they shared at Christmas shrivels like lace in a flame, and they are governess and housemaid.

'Mr Rackham had no appointments today, as far as I'm aware,' says Sugar primly. 'I don't suppose you know . . . ?'

'Mr Rackham was fetched early this morning, Miss Sugar,' says Rose, 'by police.'

'By . . . police,' echoes Sugar, like a half-wit.

'Yes Miss Sugar,' says Rose, clutching her book against her bosom, its

lurid front cover obscured in favour of the back which, instead of a swooning slave-girl proclaims the wonders of Beecham's Pills. 'They came for him
at about nine o'clock.'

'I see,' says Sugar. 'I don't suppose you know why, Rose?'

Rose licks her lips nervously. 'Please don't tell anyone I said so, Miss,
but I think Mrs Rackham has been found.'

William Rackham signals, with nods of his head and inarticulate grunts,
that the two police officers who've caught him can safely let him go. He
is ready, once more, to stand on his own two feet; his moment of giddiness has passed, and he no longer needs to be supported under the armpits.

'If you can manage it, sir,' advises the mortuary attendant, 'concentrate your attention on the parts that are least corrupted.'

William steps forward, looking all around him, confirming that he is
in Hell — an echoing, hissing, phosphorescent factory chamber whose
apparent purpose is to manufacture the dead. Breathing the vile atmosphere — a vinegary, camphoric concoction kept at glacial temperature —
more shallowly than he did when he was first brought in, he forces his
chin to dip lower, and looks down at the naked corpse on the slab.

The body is Agnes's height, extremely thin, and female: that much he
can swear to. A recent dousing of fresh water from the mortuary attendant's hose has given it a glassy sheen; it glistens and sparkles under the
mercilessly bright lights overhead.

The face . . . the face is slack-jawed and half-rotten, an approximation
of humanity, like a raw chicken carved into the shape of a face, an appalling
culinary prank that was left uncooked. Three holes yawn in it: a mouth
without lips or tongue, and two eye-sockets empty of eyes; each orifice is
half-full of water and shimmers with reflected light. William imagines
Agnes floating under the sea, imagines fish swimming up to her open eyes
and nibbling tentatively at the plum-like flesh of her china-blue irises —
and he sways on his feet, to gruff cries of 'Steady, steady!' on either side
of him.

Attempting to take the attendant's advice, William searches for some
part of the body that's in tolerably good condition. This woman's — or
girl's — hair is darkened from its sousing, and matted; if he could see it
dried and neatly combed, he'd be able to tell its true colour . . . Her breasts
are quite full, like Agnes's, but the space between them has suffered a deep

injury against submarine rock, ploughing the flesh apart, exposing the sternum, altering the contours of the bosom. There seems no part of the carcass on which he can rest his eyes without being revolted by the unveiling of bloody bone through chafed flesh, or a luridly pigmented blight on what ought to be alabaster perfection. On the gnawed hands, a few of the fingers are more complete than others, but there's no wedding ring – a fact which the police inspector has already warned him means nothing, since every corpse dredged out of the Thames is bare of jewels by the time it reaches Pitchcott Mortuary, however gaudy it may have been when it first fell in.

William's eyes blur; his skull feels as though it will burst. What do these people want of him? What answer are they waiting for? Faced with a body so disfigured, would any other husband be able to do better? Are there men who could identify their wives from three square inches of unblemished flesh – an uncorrupted curve of shoulder, the precise shape of her ankle? If so, these wives must surely have offered their husbands more opportunities for intimate acquaintance than Agnes ever offered him! Perhaps, if it were Sugar here on this slab . . .

'We understand, sir, if . . .' begins the police inspector, and William groans in panic: the moment of truth has come, and he mustn't be found wanting! One last time he surveys the corpse, and this time he focuses on the triangle of pubic hair and the mount of Venus from which it sprouts, a small haven of peachy flesh and delicate fleece which has escaped miraculously undamaged. He closes his eyes tight, and conjures forth the vision of Agnes on her wedding night, the only other occasion on which she lay exposed to his gaze in quite this pose.

'This is sh-she,' he announces hoarsely. 'This is my wife.'

The words, although his own voice has uttered them, deal him a ferocious blow: he reels as the fabric of his present and his past is wrenched asunder. The features of the woman on the slab swim out of focus, then sharpen fantastically, like a photograph emerging from developing fluid, until she *is* Agnes, and he cannot bear what has become of her. His Agnes, dead! His exquisite, angel-voiced bride, blighted, reduced to butcher's refuse on a slab. If she had died seven years ago when he was courting her, on that same sunny afternoon when he bade her sit perfectly still for his camera and she looked at him as if to say, *Yes, I am yours*; and if she had fallen into the Thames an hour later, and he had searched desperately for her all the seven years since, diving and diving in the same stretch of river;

and if he had only just now pulled her lifeless body from the water, he could not have been more distressed than he is now.

Convulsed with sobs and stammering blasphemies, he allows the steady arms of other men to escort him from the mortuary, a widower.

THIRTY

SECOND TRAGEDY BEFALLS RACKHAMS

MRS. AGNES RACKHAM, wife of the Perfume Manufacturer whose products bear that name, was found drowned in the Thames on Friday. Although convalescing from rheumatic fever, she had made the journey from her Notting Hill residence to attend a concert at the Music School in Lambeth Palace, and a misunderstanding resulted in her being separated from her companions. Strong winds, slippery conditions on Lambeth Pier and Mrs. Rackham's delicate health were the reasons given by the police for the fatal accident. This tragedy comes only four months after Henry Rackham, Mrs. Rackham's brother-in-law, lost his life in a house fire. A funeral service will be held for Mrs. Rackham at her parish church of St. Mark's, Notting Hill, on Thursday at eleven o'clock.

Sugar hunches over the chamber-pot, stares down into its glossy porcelain interior, and inserts three fingers in her mouth. It takes a lot to make her gag, and her fingernails are scratching her gullet before she's rewarded with a retch. But nothing substantial comes, only saliva.

Damn! For the last week, or even longer — let's say, ever since Agnes's disappearance — she's been sick most mornings, obliged to excuse herself from the school-room when the lessons are scarcely underway, to vomit up her breakfast. (Small wonder, what with her dread of Agnes being apprehended, her fears for her own part in the affair being discovered, the hazards of William's terrible moods, and the sheer fatigue caused by working-hours that start at dawn and end at midnight!) Today she's worried that if she doesn't get her vomit over with now, in privacy, it will demand satisfaction of her later, in public, where she has nowhere to hide.

She looks up at the clock; the funeral coaches are due to arrive any minute; her breakfast is determined to stay just where it is. She rises to her feet, and is dismayed to note that the heavy crape of her mourning-dress is already wrinkled. The horrid stuff creases at the slightest oppor-tunity, the bodice is so tight it pinches her ribs when she breathes, and the double-stitched seam where the bodice joins the skirts is chafing her hips. Could the seamstresses at Peter Robinson's have made a mistake? The box in which these clothes were dispatched has her measurements pencilled on the lid, exactly as she stated them on the order slip William had her complete, but the garments are a poor fit.

Sugar has never been to a funeral before, though she's read about them. In her former life, dead prostitutes simply disappeared, without fuss or ceremony; one day there'd be a corpse lying in a darkened room, the next day there'd be sunlight beaming in on an empty mattress, and bed-linen hanging out on the ropes between the houses. Where did the bodies go? Sugar was never told. Oh, there *was* that time when poor little Sarah McTigue was sold to a student doctor, but that wouldn't have happened very often, surely? Maybe all the dead whores were clandes-tinely dumped in the Thames. One thing was certain: they didn't have funerals.

'Must Sophie go?' she dared to ask William when he first gave the command. 'Isn't it unusual for a child—'

'I don't care if I put the world's n-nose out of joint!' he retorted, colour-ing up at once. 'A-Agnes was a Rackham. There are damn f-few of us left, and we should all be there to m-mourn her.'

'Could she perhaps go to the church service, but not to the graveyard?'

'All of it, all of it. A-Agnes was m-my wife, and Sophie is m-my daugh-ter. They say f-females at a f-funeral bring a risk of w-weeping. What's wrong with w-weeping at a f-funeral? Someone has died, for God's sake! Now stop p-paltering and write your m-measurements on this slip . . .'

Sugar breathes shallowly, biliously, in her tight dress. For the dozenth time, she unfolds the torn-out newspaper page and re-reads the announcement of Agnes's death. Every word of it is engraved on her memory, but still there's something eerily authoritative about the actual print; the lies are stamped indelibly into the very fibres of the paper. Thousands of replications of this tragic little story, about the convalescing lady undone by her love of musical divertissements, have spilled from the printing presses and been disseminated into thousands of households. The pen is indeed mightier than the sword; it has killed Agnes Rackham and consigned her to History.

To prevent herself re-reading Agnes's death notice yet again, Sugar picks up one of her splendid volumes of Shakespeare. Truth to tell, she's barely peeked in them since receiving them, having been so preoccupied with children's schoolbooks and stolen diaries. It's high time she exercised the more . . . *literary* muscles of her brain.

She flips through the pages, searching for *Titus Andronicus*, which she used to think was unjustly underestimated – in fact, she recalls defending its gory frenzy for the benefit of a certain George W. Hunt when she first met him in The Fireside. Having found *Titus* now, she can't make head nor tail of it; she must have been mad. William did tell her, on that first night, that she would come around to *King Lear* in the end – and he was right. She flips through the pages, reading no more than a word here and there, pausing only to look at the illustrations. What's happened to her intellect? Has caring for Sophie softened her brain? She who once regarded the million words of *Clarissa* as a banquet, and would devour the latest book by Elizabeth Eiloart or Matilda Houston in a single sitting . . . Here she is, staring stupidly at an engraving of Lady Macbeth standing poised to jump off a parapet, as if this leather-bound compendium of literature were nothing more than a picture book for infants.

From outside the window comes the sound of horses' hoofs and a crunching of gravel: the funeral coaches have arrived. She ought to return to the school-room immediately, and show herself ready and able to chaperone Miss Rackham, but she looks through the window-pane first, leaning as close as she can short of pressing her nose to the glass. No doubt Sophie is doing the same.

There are two coaches-and-fours visible below. One of the horses is directly under her bedroom window, fidgeting and snorting. In a more mischievous past she might have thrown a missile down on its nodding, befeathered head, or even aimed for the sable top hats of the coachmen perched behind. She can make out at least six sombre officiaries taking turns to poke their heads out of the coaches' curtained windows. Every detail is monochrome: men, horses and harness, woodwork, wheels and upholstery, even the carriage-way gravel from which the last snow has melted: all black. Thoughtlessly Sugar wipes at the breath-clouded window-pane with her sleeve, then desists when she realises two things with a jolt: that crape is not waterproof, but leaves a grey smear on wet glass; and that the men down below may think she's waving to them.

She steps back from the window, shoves the chamber-pot back under the bed, snatches her gloves out of the Peter Robinson's box, and hurries to rejoin Sophie.

Sophie is at the window of the school-room, peering down at the horses and carriages with her spyglass. The French doll stands in the corner, its pink ball gown and bare arms more or less hidden under a makeshift cape of black tissue-paper, its plumed hat crudely disguised under a shawl fashioned from a black handkerchief. Sophie's own mourning-clothes are not so flimsy; they encase her diminutive body like a black cocoon.

'They have come for us, Miss,' she says, without turning.

'I'm a little frightened, Sophie,' says Sugar, her black-gloved hand hovering in the air near Sophie's shoulder, hesitating to stroke it. 'Are you a little frightened, too?' Ever since being told of her mama's death, the child has neither wept nor misbehaved, instead exhibiting a stoicism too breezy to be true. Surely one cannot lose one's mother and feel nothing?

'Nurse told me all about funerals, Miss,' says Sophie, pivoting on her heel to face her governess. She lowers the spyglass and collapses its ridged metal skin, with an oiled click, to the shortest length. 'We shan't have to do anything, only watch.'

Sugar bends to re-tie the ribbon of Sophie's bonnet, hoping that the gentleness with which her fingers brush against Sophie's throat will reassure the child that she need only give a sign – the merest sign – of distress, and Miss Sugar will give her all the sympathy and affection she craves. But the over-gentle tying of a ribbon communicates no such thing: it only makes a knot that's too loose, as though the governess is too clumsy and weak-fingered to dress a child properly.

'What a sad beginning this is to the year!' sighs Sugar, but Sophie doesn't nibble at the hook.

'Yes, Miss,' she says, in deference to the greater authority of her guardian.

A pit four feet wide, six feet long and six feet deep has been dug in the dark, moist earth, and it is around this neat cavity that the throng of Agnes Rackham's acquaintance is gathered. They stand shoulder to shoulder, or very nearly, allowing for the minimum proper distance between one body and another. Doctor Crane stands at the grave's head, conducting the proceedings in his trumpustuous voice. He's already delivered a long sermon in the church beforehand; now it appears he's going to deliver it all over again, for the benefit of the additional mourners who've turned up for this stage of Mrs Rackham's send-off.

The slender and petite coffin, swathed in black velvet and garlanded with white blossoms, has been carried to the graveside by the undertaker's assistants (the pallbearers being no more than an escort of honour) and now lies waiting on the rector's word. It has a pregnant aura about it, as though it might burst open at any moment to discharge a living person, or the corpse of someone other than the deceased, or even a spill of potatoes. Such are the macabre fancies of quite a few of the mourners – not just those two who have reason to doubt that the casket contains Agnes Rackham.

('It was she? You're sure?' Sugar asked William as soon as he returned from Pitchcott Mortuary.

'I . . . yes, I'm sh-sh-sure,' he replied, eyes glassy, sweat twinkling in his beard. 'As sh-sh-sh . . . as certain as I c-can be.'

'What was she wearing?' Anything, please, but a shabby dark-blue dress with a grey apron front, and a pale-blue cloak . . .

'Sh-she was n-naked.'

'But was she *found* naked?'

'God almighty, d'you th-think I w-would ask such a question? Ach, if you could have seen w-w-what I have s-seen today . . . !'

'What have you seen, William? What have you seen?'

But he only shuddered, and screwed his eyes tight, and left the state of Agnes's body to Sugar's imagination. 'Oh God, I pray th-this is the end of it!'

Whereupon she stepped forward and embraced him, inhaling the vile odour with which his clothing was permeated. She stroked his clammy back, murmured assurances in his ear, saying yes, yes, this was indeed the end of it, and it *was* Agnes he saw, and thousands of people are drowned every year, more lives are lost that way than from almost any other cause, it said so in the newspaper only a week ago, and think of the weather on the night Agnes ran away, and her perilously delicate state. On and on she prattled, until his sobbing and shuddering subsided, and he was still.)

Now he stands erect and solemn, a waxwork at the graveside, his face the instantly identifiable emblem of Rackham Perfumeries set atop the dark column of his mourning-suit. His facial injuries are disguised under a film of Rackham cosmetics expertly applied by Sugar, and his right hand – the only part of him that cannot be clothed according to strict convention – is sheathed in a loose black mitten and supported in a black sling. Underneath the tight circumference of his hat, his head throbs to a dolorous rhythm.

Unlike Henry's funeral, which was conducted in the rain, Agnes's ceremony is blessed with a clear sky, a lukewarm sun and a mild breeze. Two birds chirrup in the bare trees above, discussing the progress of Winter and the possibility that they will live to see Spring. The mourners fail to interest them; this jostling assembly of black creatures may have the attentive, hungry look of crows, and some of them are even festooned with feathers, but they've congregated in the wrong place, the silly things: there's no food here, not a crumb.

Just for curiosity's sake, though, who has come today? What human beings have made the journey from their comfortable nests to witness Agnes Rackham being committed to the earth?

Well, Lord Unwin of course – although what he would have done had he not happened to be vacationing in England, and had instead been in his more accustomed haunts of Italy or Tunisia, is anyone's guess. Nevertheless, he's here, and his beautiful wife too, although she and Mrs Rackham regrettably never met.

Henry Calder Rackham is the patriarch on William's side, a less distinguished looking specimen than Agnes's step-father, true, but not bad for his age. Poor man: the prospects of a grandson have grown dimmer the older he's become; first he had two sons, one determined to be a bachelor clergyman and the other determined to be a bachelor profligate; then one son was dead and the other married to a woman whose child-bearing efforts stopped short of a male; now even she is gone. Well may he look glum.

Who else has come? Well, moving on to the other sex: Lady Bridgelow, as well as a great many ladies of Agnes's acquaintance, among them Mrs

Canham, Mrs Battersleigh, Mrs Amphlett, Mrs Maxwell, Mrs Fitzhugh, Mrs Gooch, Mrs Marr – and is that Mrs Abernethy over there? Oh dear, one really *should* know. It *looks* like Mrs Abernethy, but wasn't Mrs Abernethy supposed to have moved to India? Only after this ceremony is concluded will it be possible to clear up these little mysteries.

And that child? Who is that child, standing in front of her whey-faced scarecrow of a governess? Sophie Rackham, is it? Some of the ladies gathered here today were aware that Mrs Rackham had a daughter, others not. They stare at the little girl inquisitively, noting the similarity to the father's bone structure, though she has her mother's eyes.

What a curious funeral this is! So many women, and hardly any men! Did Mrs Rackham have no male relations? No brothers, cousins, nephews? Apparently not. There are rumoured to be several living uncles, but they're . . . well, they're Catholics, and not of the decently discreet sort, but firebrands and crackpots.

What about Doctor Curlew, Mrs Rackham's physician? Mightn't one expect him to be here? Ah, but he's in Antwerp, adding his views to a symposium on myxœdema. That's his daughter, Mrs Emmeline Fox, standing inconspicuously at the back of the crowd. Another widow! My goodness, have you ever been to a funeral before that had so many widows and widowers in attendance! Even Lady Unwin isn't the *original* Lady Unwin, you know – no, even Agnes Rackham's mother wasn't that – there was *another*, a *third*, that is to say a *first*, Lady Unwin, who died almost the instant she was married, and then, within a matter of weeks, Lord Unwin met Violet Pigott, you know, who was herself a widow – are you keeping up? Really, it was all rather a scandal, best left forgotten in the mists of history, especially on a solemn occasion such as the one for which we're gathered here today, at which gossip is unseemly, and besides, Violet Pigott was twirling her parasol at Lord Unwin when his poor wife's body was barely cold, and who knows what errors of judgement a newly widowed man may make in the madness of his grief?

Anyway, all that's in the past, and we won't speak of it any more, especially as none of us is acquainted with the full facts, not even Mrs Fitzhugh, whose older sister knew the first Lady Unwin *intimately*. She's the one wearing the black feather boa, and will certainly be attending Mrs Barr's party tomorrow afternoon, an informal affair for ladies only.

But where were we? Ah yes, Mrs Fox. She's looking well, isn't she? Half a year ago, there was every expectation that she should attend no more funerals except her own; and here she is, proving you never can tell. Were she and Mrs Rackham particularly well acquainted, though? The two of them never appeared in public together, as far as anyone can recall. Perhaps she's here as a representative of her father? She looks regretful, but – dare one say it? – ever-so-slightly disapproving. She's a staunch advocate of cremation, did you know? Doctor Crane can't abide her; she stood up during one of his sermons once and said, 'I'm sorry, sir, but that isn't true!' Can you imagine that? I wish I had been there . . .

Anyway, here she is, keeping her counsel while Doctor Crane speaks. She's dry-eyed and dignified – indeed, all the ladies are dry-eyed and dignified, a credit to the occasion. Mrs Gooch ventures a snivel at one point, but perceives herself to be alone in it, and instantly desists.

And the men? How are they bearing up? William Rackham's expression is one of pained bewilderment; no doubt his wife's death is a wound whose true severity has yet to register upon him. Lord Unwin's grief is so well controlled that it almost resembles boredom. Henry Calder Rackham stands still and melancholy, his attention never wavering from the rector, his chest expanding with a deep, silent sigh each time a pause in the oration is broken by a fresh salvo.

Doctor Crane's monologue appears to be reaching its climax: he's just made a tantalising reference to 'ashes and dust', which must surely mean the coffin will very soon be lowered into the hole. Ashes and dust, he reminds his congregation, are our only material remains, but compared to our spiritual remains they mean nothing. In the harsh glare of physical death, our soul stands revealed as the original essence from which a small, almost insignificant particle – the body – has been shed. Mrs Rackham's corporeal form is no loss to her, for she lives on, not only in the memory of her character and deeds, to which all those gathered here can no doubt attest, but, more importantly, in the bosom of her heavenly Father.

Remembered with fondness by all who were blessed to know her – the world's loss was Heaven's gain, reads the inscription on the tombstone, almost identical to the one on Henry's stone nearby, for how can a man in the throes of bereavement compose clever new words? Did they expect a metaphysical poem from him, in the style of Herbert? Is there anyone here who could have done better, in his shoes? Death is too obscene for pretty verses.

William stares at the coffin as the undertaker's assistants lift it onto the ropes. His jaw is rigid as he resists the temptation to dab the sweat on his brow, for fear that the patina of Rackham's Foundation Cream and Rackham's Peach Blush will come off on his handkerchief, unveiling the scabs and bruises. The time has come: the slender, lustrously varnished box is finally lowered into the grave, and Doctor Crane intones his age-old incantation to help it on its way. William is not comforted; 'ashes to ashes, dust to dust' is all very fine as graveside oratory, but from a brutally scientific point of view, ash is the stuff of cremation, not burial. The corpse inside this casket is already well advanced in its metamorphosis, as William knows from having seen it on the mortuary slab, but its end product will not be ash; it will be a liquid, or at most an unguent.

Indeed, in William's mind, the corpse has already deteriorated from what he saw last week and, as the coffin descends smoothly into the pit, he pictures the lacerated and putrid flesh wobbling like jelly within. He swallows hard, to suppress a groan of horror. How strange, the way he can't believe that anything solid of Agnes remains, whereas his brother Henry – who has lain in the ground for months and must therefore, logic-ally, be in a far worse state – he pictures mummified, firm as a log. Even in the grave, his brother puts up a wooden resistance to corruption, a stiff integrity, whereas (in William's imaginings) Agnes's volatility, her typic-ally female instability, condemns her to alchemical dissolution.

He looks away; he can't bear it. Tears sting his eyes; is there anyone here today who doesn't secretly believe he drove his wife to suicide? They despise him, all these women, all these gossipy 'intimates'; in their hearts, they blame him; who can he turn to? He cannot look to Sugar, for she stands with Sophie, and he can't face the thought of what's to be done with Agnes's child now that all hope of her having a mother is gone. Instead, in desper-ation, he looks to Lady Bridgelow, and is amazed – and deeply moved – to see that her eyes, too, are shining. *You brave, brave man*, she is saying. Not aloud, of course, but in every other way possible. He shuts his eyes tight, and sways on his feet, and listens to the sound of soil falling on soil.

Eventually there's a gentle tug on his arm. He opens his eyes, half-expecting to see a female face, but it's one of the officiaries.

'This way, if you please, sir.'

William gapes, uncomprehending.

The officiary points to the world beyond the churchyard with a black-gloved hand. 'The carriages are waiting for you, sir.'

'Yes . . . I . . . ah . . .' he stammers, then claps shut his mouth. All day, he has dreaded having to speak, to account for himself and stutter out the reasons why Agnes is not alive and well. Suddenly he appreciates he's not required to say anything. He is excused. There are no questions. It's time to go home.

Next day, Clara Tillotson is dismissed. Or, to put it more diplomatically, she is sent on her way with Rackham's blessing, to find employment in a household whose master is not a widower.

'In the changed circumstances': that's the phrase William used, when breaking the news to her. Of course, it was hardly news, and she knew very well what was coming, so why couldn't she have spared him the nuisance and simply disappeared overnight, taking her wasp waist and her sharp little snout with her? Ah yes: because she needed a letter of recommendation. Couldn't he have left one out in the hall for her, dangling by a ribbon from the hat-stand? No, of course he couldn't. Much as he despises the girl, he was obliged to endure one more encounter with her.

Mind you, on her final day of employment in the Rackham house, Clara's demeanour undergoes a remarkable transformation; she's as sweet as a flower-seller and as servile as a shoeblack. Why, she almost smiled! Early in the morning, she has exercised that skill so highly valued in a lady's-maid: packing clothes and other belongings into a suitcase so that they'll emerge at their destination uncreased and undamaged. The sum total of her possessions fills fewer cases than Agnes took to Folkestone Sands; to be precise, one trunk, one small tartan suitcase, and a hat-box.

Rackham doesn't see her off; in fact, when the cab arrives to fetch her, not one member of the household can spare a minute to come and wave her goodbye. Only Cheesman is on hand, helpful and cheerful, lifting her cases for her, loudly assuring her that today is the first day of a new life, laying his sinewy paw against the small of her back as she steps into the coach. Caught between conflicting desires to weep against his chest and spit in his face, Clara does nothing, allows him to flick the hem of her skirt out of harm's way as he shuts the cabin door, and sits stony-faced as the vehicle jerks into motion.

In her reticule, in her lap, nestles William Rackham's letter of recommendation, which she hasn't yet read. The etiquette of applications for employment is such that there's a subtle but distinct advantage in handing

over a sealed, virgin envelope, thus suggesting one's supreme confidence
that it can contain nothing less than the highest praise. Once Clara is
settled at her sister's place, she'll have plenty of leisure to steam the envelope open – at which time she'll discover that Rackham describes her as
being of average intelligence, admirably loyal to her mistress if less than
ideally so to her master, a canny and competent lady's-maid whose lack of
a sweet temperament need not be an obstacle to loyal service to a compat-
ible employer. Then Clara will blaze with fury, and lament her lost chance
to tell that pompous, vulgar bully Rackham precisely what she thinks of
him, and her sister will tactfully agree, knowing in her heart that Clara
wouldn't have dared utter a peep, in case Rackham snatched the letter
back again and tore her future to pieces on the doorstep.

'A pox on that house!' Clara will cry. 'I hope everyone in it dies and
rots in Hell!'

Yes, that's what she'll say later. But for now, she bites her lower lip,
counts the trees as her cab trundles past Kensington Gardens, and wonders
if the ghost of Mrs Rackham will haunt her for stealing a few small items
of jewellery. What would a ghost care about a few bracelets and earrings,
especially ones she scarcely ever wore and which she probably wouldn't even
have missed while she was alive? If there's any justice in the world, nothing will come of this theft, except a little much-needed money. Ah, but the
dead are rumoured to be vengeful . . . Clara hopes that Mrs Rackham, wherever she may be, remembers the long years during which her lady's-maid
was her only ally against her detestable husband, and that she can find it
in her ethereal heart to say, 'Well done, good and faithful servant.'

It's unseasonably mild weather, and the sun shines as brightly as anyone
could want, the day that Sugar turns twenty.

Despite the fact that January 19th is by rights the heart of Winter, the
last vestiges of slush have been swept off the streets, birds sing in the
trees, and high above Sugar's head the sky is lavender-blue and the clouds
eggshell-white, like a colour plate in a children's story-book. Beneath her
feet the grass of the public garden is wet, but not with snow or rain, only
melted frost, scarcely enough to dampen her boots. The only firm evidence
of the season is the long tongue of opaque ice that hangs from the mouth
of a stone dragon perched on the rim of the garden's empty fountain, but
even this icicle glimmers and perspires, slowly yielding to a great thaw.

On a day just like this, thinks Sugar, *I was born.*

Sophie looks up at the stone dragon, then up at her governess, wordlessly requesting permission to examine the monster closer. Sugar nods assent and, with some difficulty (for her mourning-clothes are extremely tight and stiff) Sophie clambers up onto the fountain's edge, steadied by her governess's hands. The child finds her balance, one mittened hand pressed to the dragon's bone-grey flank. Not very elegant, these old woolly mittens of hers, but the tiny pigskin gloves her father gave her at Christmas never did fit, and when Miss Sugar tried to put them on a glove-stretcher for grown-ups, one of them burst.

Sophie leans her face right under the dragon's stone jaws, and shyly extends her pink tongue towards the glistening spike of ice.

'Don't do that, Sophie! It's dirty.'

The child pulls back as sharply as if she's been smacked.

'I'll tell you what to do instead: why not break it off?' Dismayed by how easy it is to frighten a child, Sugar is keen to restore Sophie's cheerful spirits. 'Go on: give it a whack!'

Hesitantly Sophie extends her mitt and pats the great gob of ice, to no effect. Then, after more encouragement from her governess, she fetches it a biff, and it snaps off. A feeble trickle of ochre-stained water gurgles out of the exposed iron spout.

'There you are, Sophie!' says Sugar. 'You've got it started.'

Under the watchful eye of her governess, Sophie walks the imaginary tightrope of the fountain's rim. The full skirts of her mourning-dress make it hard for her to see her own feet, but she advances slowly and solemnly, her arms extended, wing-like, for balance.

Is it permissible, according to the rules of mourning, for a bereaved daughter to be taken out in public mere days after the funeral? Sugar hasn't the faintest idea, but who's to reprimand her if it isn't? The Rackham servants don't say boo to a goose, and William has secluded himself so absolutely in his study – a grief-stricken widower for all the world to see, or rather not see – that he's hardly in a position to know what she gets up to when she's not with him.

And if he should discover the truth, what of it? Must she and Sophie skulk in a darkened house, stifling in an atmosphere where laughter is forbidden and black the order of the day from breakfast to bedtime? No! She refuses to creep around under a pall! Sophie's lessons will be conducted

out of doors as often as possible, in the public parks and gardens of Notting
Hill. The poor child has spent quite enough of her life hidden away like
a squalid secret.

'Time for your History rhymes, little one,' Sugar announces, and
Sophie's face lights up. If there's one thing she likes better than play, it's
work. She looks down at the ground, preparing to leap off the fountain-
edge; it's just a few inches farther than she can easily manage in her stiff
clothes. What to do?

All of a sudden, Sugar rushes forward, scoops the child into her arms
and swings her to the ground in one dizzying, playful swoop. It's over in
a couple of seconds at most, the space of a single breath, but in that long
moment Sugar feels more physical joy than she's felt in a lifetime of
embraces. The soles of Sophie's dangling feet brush the wet grass, and she
lands; Sugar releases her, gasping. Thank God, thank God, the child looks
tickled pink: clearly this act has her blessing to happen again sometime.

Lately, Sugar has been confounded, even disturbed, by how intensely
physical her feelings for Sophie have become. What began, on her arrival
in the Rackham house, as a determination to do her hapless pupil no harm,
has seeped from her head into her bloodstream and now pumps around her
body, transmuted into a different impulse entirely: the desire to infuse
Sophie with happiness.

On this nineteenth day of January, standing in a public park on the
morning of her twentieth birthday, her whole body still tingling from
Sophie's embrace, Sugar imagines the two of them in bed together wearing identical white night-gowns, Sophie fast asleep, her cheek nestled in
the hollow between Sugar's breasts – a vision that would have been ridiculous a year ago, not least because she had so little bosom to speak of. But
her bosom feels bigger nowadays, as though an over-long adolescence has
finally ended, and she's now a woman.

Sophie begins to tramp slowly round the fountain, in a heavy-footed,
ceremonial rhythm, and recites her rhymes:

'William the First made the Domesday Book,
William Rufus was shot by a brook,
Henry the First rendered Aesop's fables,
But to crown his daughter he was unable.'

'Very good, Sophie,' says Sugar, stepping back. 'Practise by yourself,
and come to me if you get stuck.'

Sophie continues to march and chant, adding her own instinctive melody to the words, so that the poem becomes a song. Her arms, stiff with crape, beat time against her sides.

'*Stephen and Maude waged civil war,*
Until the end of 1154.
Henry, called Plantagenet,
Had troubles with children and Thomas B'cket.'

Sugar walks away from the fountain and takes a seat on a cast-iron bench about twenty feet farther on. The sound of the chant fills her with pride, for these rhymes are Sugar's own invention; she devised them as a mnemonic for Sophie, who in her History lessons was finding it difficult to tell one scheming, bloodthirsty king of England apart from another, especially since so many of them are called William and Henry. These little verses, paltry though they are, represent Sugar's first literary scribbles since she pronounced her novel dead. Ach, yes, she knows it's pitiable, but they've ignited in her a candle-flame of hope that she may yet be a writer. And why *not* write for children? Catch them young, and you shape their souls . . . Did she ever seriously believe that any grown-up person would read her novel, throw off the chains of prejudice, and share her righteous anger? Anger against what, anyway? She can barely recall . . .

'*Coeur de Lion was abroad all the time,*
Died of an arrow in 1199.
John was qua'lsome, murd'rous and mean,
But the Charter was signed in 1216.'

Sugar leans back on her seat, stretching out her legs and wriggling the toes inside her boots to discourage them from freezing; all the rest of her is warm. She lets the focus of her eyes grow hazy, so that Sophie tramps past as a black blur every time she rounds the fountain.

'*Good* girl . . .' she murmurs, too softly for Sophie to hear. How delicious it is to hear one's own words, doggerel or not, sung by another human being . . .

'*Henry the Third reigned second longest,*
But his mind and health were not the strongest.
Edward Longshanks was almost wed,
Which might have saved the Scots bloodshed.'

'Why, it's little Sophie Rackham!' cries an unfamiliar woman's voice, and Sugar is roused to seek out the person that goes with it. There, at the gate of the park, stands Emmeline Fox, waving madly. How odd, to see a respectable woman waving so hard! And, as she waves, her ample bosom swings loosely inside her bodice, suggesting she hasn't a corset on. Sugar is no expert when it comes to the finer details of respectability, but she does wonder if these things can be quite *comme il faut* . . .

'Miss Sugar, unless I'm mistaken?' says Mrs Fox, already crossing the distance between them.

'Y-yes,' says Sugar, rising from the bench. 'And you are Mrs Fox, I believe.'

'Yes, indeed I am. Pleased to make your acquaintance.'

'O-oh, and I'm pleased to make yours,' responds Sugar, two or three seconds later than she should. Mrs Fox, having strolled into arm's reach, seems content to loiter there; if she's noticed Sugar's unease, she takes no notice of it. Instead, she nods towards Sophie, who, after a momentary pause, has resumed her marching and singing.

'A novel approach to History. I might have disliked the discipline less myself, had I been given such rhymes.'

'I wrote them for her,' blurts Sugar.

Unnervingly, Mrs Fox looks her straight in the face, eyes slightly narrowed. 'Well, clever *you*,' she says, with a strange smile.

Sugar feels sweat prickling and trickling in the black armpits of her dress. What the devil is wrong with this woman? Are her wits cracked, or is it mischief?

'I . . . I find that some of the books given to children are deadly,' says Sugar, ransacking her brains for appropriate conversation. 'They kill the desire to learn. But Sophie has a few good ones now, up-to-date ones that W— were bought by Mr Rackham, at my request. Although I must say' (a breath of relief cools the perspiration on her brow, as she's suddenly inspired by a memory) 'that Sophie is still very fond of a book of fairy stories given her one Christmas, by her uncle Henry, who I believe was a dear friend of yours.'

Mrs Fox blinks and goes a little paler, as though she's just been slapped, or kissed. 'Yes,' she says. 'He was.'

'On the flyleaf,' Sugar presses on, 'he signed himself *Your tiresome Uncle Henry.*'

Mrs Fox shakes her head and sighs, as though hearing a rumour made vicious by its passage from gossip to gossip. 'He wasn't in the least tiresome.

He was the dearest man.' And she sits heavily on the bench, without warning or formality.

Sugar sits down beside her, rather excited by the way the conversation is going – for she seems, after a shaky start, to have won the upper hand. After only a moment's hesitation, she decides to kill two birds with one stone: show off her intimate knowledge of Sophie Rackham's books, in case Mrs Fox should have any doubts as to her credentials as a governess – and pry.

'Tell me, Mrs Fox, if it wouldn't be prying: am I right to suppose that *you* were the "good friend" Henry Rackham referred to in his inscription? The friend who scolded him for giving Sophie a Bible when she was only three years old?'

Mrs Fox laughs sadly, but her eyes are bright, and they gaze at Sugar unwaveringly. 'Yes, I did feel that three was a little young for *Deuteronomy* and *Lamentations*,' she says. 'And as for Lot's daughters and Onan and all that business, well . . . a child deserves a few years of innocence, wouldn't you agree?'

'Oh yes,' says Sugar, a trifle hazy on the particulars but in full agreement with the sentiment. Then, in case her ignorance has shown on her face, she assures Mrs Fox: 'I do read to Sophie from the Bible, though. The thrilling stories: Noah and the Flood, the Prodigal Son, Daniel in the lion's den . . .'

'But not Sodom and Gomorrah,' says Mrs Fox, leaning closer, never blinking.

'No.'

'Quite right,' says Mrs Fox. 'I walk the streets of our very own Sodom several days a week. It corrupts children as gladly as it corrupts anyone else.'

What a strange person Mrs Fox is, with her long ugly face and her searching eyes! Is she safe? Why does she stare so? Sugar suddenly wishes Sophie were sitting here between them, to keep the conversation sweet.

'Sophie can join us, if you like, since you've known her so long. I'll call her, shall I?'

'No, don't,' Mrs Fox replies at once, in a not unfriendly but remarkably firm tone. 'Sophie and I aren't nearly as well acquainted as you suppose. When Henry and I used to visit the Rackham house, she was never in evidence; one would scarcely have guessed she existed. I only used to see her at church, and then only at services not attended by Mrs Rackham. The co-incidence – or whatever is the *opposite* of co-incidence, I perhaps should say – grew very curious after a while.'

'I'm not sure I understand what you mean.'

'I mean, Miss Sugar, that it was plain Mrs Rackham was no lover of children. Or, to speak even plainer, that she appeared not to acknowledge the existence of her own daughter.'

'It's not for me to judge what went on in Mrs Rackham's head,' says Sugar. 'I saw little of her; she was already unwell when I came into the household. But . . .' (Mrs Fox's raised eyebrow is an intimidating thing: it suggests that any governess professing ignorance of the facts must be either stupid or lying) 'But I do believe you are right.'

'And what about you, Miss Sugar?' says Mrs Fox, laying her hands on her knees and leaning forward, in an attitude of getting down to business. '*You* like children, I trust?'

'Oh, yes. I am certainly very fond of Sophie.'

'Yes, that's easily seen. Is she the first pupil you've had?'

'No,' replies Sugar, her face composed, her mind spinning like a catherine wheel. 'Before Sophie I took care of a little boy. Called Christopher. In Dundee.' (William's long-running battle with the jute merchants has branded plenty of names and facts about Dundee on her memory, should she be challenged to quote them; God forgive her for claiming to have done anything for Christopher, when, far from nurturing the poor child, she's left him in the lion's den . . .)

'Dundee?' echoes Mrs Fox. 'What an awfully long way for you to come. Although you don't sound like a Scotchwoman – more like a Londoner, I'd say.'

'I've lived in quite a few places.'

'Yes, I'm sure you have.'

There follows an awkward pause, during which Sugar wonders what on earth became of the upper hand she thought she had. The only way to regain it, she decides, is to go on the offensive.

'I'm so pleased you decided to go out walking on the same morning as Sophie and me,' she says. 'I believe you were recently in very poor health?'

Mrs Fox tips her head to one side and smiles wearily. 'Very poor, very poor,' she concedes, in a sing-song tone. 'But I'm sure I suffered less than those who watched me suffer. They were convinced I'd die, you see, whereas

I knew I wouldn't. Now here I am' – she waves an open hand, as if signalling an invisible queue of people to pass ahead of her – 'witnessing a pressing crowd of unfortunates blunder to their graves.'

But you don't understand: Agnes is alive! thinks Sugar, indignant. 'A crowd?' she demurs. 'I admit it's awful, two members of the same family, but really . . . !'

'Oh no, I didn't mean the Rackhams,' says Mrs Fox. 'Oh dear now, I do apologise. I thought you would know that I work for the Rescue Society.'

'The Rescue Society? I confess I've never heard of it.'

Mrs Fox laughs, an odd throaty sound. 'Ah, Miss Sugar, how crestfallen, how *mortified*, some of my colleagues would be to hear you say that! However, I shall tell you: we are an organisation of ladies that reforms, or at least *tries* to reform, prostitutes.' Again the mercilessly direct stare. 'Forgive me if that word offends you.'

'No, no, not at all,' says Sugar, though she feels the heat of a blush on her cheeks. 'Please go on; I should like to know more.'

Mrs Fox looks theatrically to heaven, and declares (wryly or in earnest, Sugar cannot tell), 'Ah! the voice of our sex's future!' She leans still closer to Sugar on the bench, inspired it seems to even greater intimacy. 'I pray a time will come, when all educated women will be anxious to discuss this subject, without hypocrisy or evasion.'

'I-I hope so too,' stammers Sugar, longing for Sophie to come to her aid, even if it's with a wail of distress following a fall. But Sophie is still marching around the fountain, by no means finished with the kings of England.

'. . . *Wat Tyler's mob and Wycliffe's Scripture,*
We find in the reign of the second Richard.'

'Prostitution is certainly a terrible problem,' says Sugar, keeping her face turned towards Sophie. 'But can you – can your Rescue Society – really hope ever to stamp it out?'

'Not in *my* lifetime,' replies Mrs Fox, 'but perhaps in *hers*.'

Sugar is tempted to laugh at the absurdity of the notion, but then she sees Sophie stamping into view, singing,

'*Henry the Fourth slept with his crown*
While Arundel put the lollies down,'

and suddenly catches such a strong whiff of innocence that she's half-convinced Mrs Fox's dream might yet come to pass.

'The greatest obstacle,' Mrs Fox declares, 'is the persistence of lies.

Principally the foul and cowardly lie, that the root of prostitution is women's wickedness. I've heard this a thousand times, even from the mouths of prostitutes themselves!'

'What *is* the root, then? Is it *men*'s wickedness?'

Mrs Fox's grey complexion is growing rosier by the second; she's warming to her topic. 'Only insofar as men make the laws that determine what a woman may and may not do. And laws are not merely a matter of what's in the statute books! The sermon of a clergyman who has no love in his heart, *that* is law; the way our sex is demeaned and made trivial in newspapers, in novels, even on the labels of the tiniest items of household produce, *that* is law. And, most of all, *poverty* is law. If a man falls on hard times, a five-pound note and a new suit of clothes can restore him to respectability, but if a woman falls . . .!' She puffs with exasperation, cheeks flushed, quite worked up now. Her bosom swells and subsides in rapid respiration, nipples showing with every breath. 'A woman is expected to remain in the gutter. You know, Miss Sugar, I've never yet met a prostitute who would not have preferred to be something else. If only she *could.*'

'But how,' says Sugar, quailing once more under that stare, and blushing from her hairline to her collar, 'does your Society go about . . . uh . . . rescuing a prostitute?'

'We visit the brothels, the houses of ill repute, the streets . . . the parks . . . wherever prostitutes are found, and we warn them – if we're given the chance – of the fate that awaits them.'

Sugar nods attentively, rather glad, in retrospect, that she never stirred from her bed on those mornings when the Rescue Society used to call on Mrs Castaway's.

'We offer them refuge, though sadly we've precious few houses available for this purpose,' continues Mrs Fox. 'If only this country's half-empty churches could be used more sensibly! But no matter, we do what we can with the beds available . . . And what do we do then? Well, if the girls have a trade, we do our utmost to restore them to it, with letters of recommendation. I've written many such. If they have no trade, we see to it they're taught a useful skill, like needlework or cooking. There are servants in some of the best households who got there by way of the Rescue Society.'

'Goodness.'

Mrs Fox sighs. 'Of course, it says very little for our society – English society, I mean — that the best we can offer a young woman is respectable servitude. But we can only address one evil at a time. And the urgency is great. Each day, prostitutes are dying.'

'But what *of*?' enquires Sugar, provoked to curiosity, even though she knows the answers already.

'Disease, childbirth, murder, suicide,' Mrs Fox replies, enunciating each with due care. '"Too late": that's the wretched phrase that haunts our efforts. I visited a house of prostitution only yesterday, a place known as Mrs Castaway's, looking for a particular girl I'd read about in a vile publication called *More Sprees In London*. I found that the girl was long gone, and that Mrs Castaway had died.'

Sugar's guts turn to stone; only the cast-iron seat of the bench stops her body emptying its heavy innards onto the ground beneath.

'Died?' she whispers.

'Died,' confirms Mrs Fox, her big grey eyes sensitive to every tiny flicker of reaction in her quarry.

'Died . . . of what?'

'The new madam didn't tell me. Our conversation was cut short by the door slamming in my face.'

Sugar cannot endure Mrs Fox's gaze anymore. She lowers her head, giddy and sick, and stares into the crumpled blackness of her own lap. What to do? What to say? If life were one of Rose's tuppenny Gem Pocket books, she could stab Mrs Fox through the heart with a dagger, and enlist Sophie's help in burying the corpse; or she could fall at Mrs Fox's feet and beg her not to divulge her secret. Instead, she continues to stare into her lap, breathing shallowly, until she becomes aware of something bubbling in her nostrils, and, wiping her nose, finds her glove slicked with bright-red blood.

A white handkerchief appears in front of her eyes, held in Mrs Fox's own rather dingy and wrinkled glove. Bewildered, Sugar takes it, and blows her nose. At once she feels deliriously giddy, and sways where she sits, and the handkerchief is transformed, with miraculously suddenness, from a soft warm square of white cotton to a sopping-wet rag of chilly crimson.

'No, lean back,' comes Mrs Fox's voice, as Sugar slumps forward. 'It's better when you lean back.' And she lays a firm, gentle hand on Sugar's breast and pushes, until Sugar's head is tilted as far back as it will go, dangling in space, her shoulder-blades pressed painfully hard against the iron bench, her face blinking up into the blue of the sky. Blood is filling her head, trickling into her gullet, tickling her windpipe.

'Try to breathe normally, or you'll faint,' says Mrs Fox, when Sugar begins to pant and gasp. 'Trust me; I know.'

Sugar does as she's told, and continues to stare up into the sky, her left hand pressed, with the handkerchief, to her nose, her right – incredibly – enfolded inside Mrs Fox's. Hard, bony fingers give her a reassuring squeeze through the two layers of goatskin that separate their naked flesh.

'Miss Sugar, forgive me,' says the voice at her side. 'I see now that you must have been very fond of your old madam. In my arrogance, I failed to imagine that possibility. In fact, I failed to imagine all sorts of things.'

Sugar's head is tilted so far back now that she sees pedestrians walking along Pembridge Square past the park, upside down. A topsy-turvy mother suspended from the ceiling of the world pulls a topsy-turvy little boy along, scolding him for staring at the lady with the blood on her face.

'Sophie,' murmurs Sugar anxiously. 'I don't hear Sophie anymore.'

'She's all right,' Mrs Fox assures her. 'She's fallen asleep against the fountain.'

Sugar blinks. Tears tickle her ears and dampen the hair at her temples. She licks her bloodied lips, working up the courage to ask her fate.

'Miss Sugar, please forgive me,' says Mrs Fox. 'I'm a coward. If I'd been brave enough, I would have spared you this game of cat-and-mouse, and told you at once what person I took you to be. And if by chance I was mistaken, you'd have discounted me as a madwoman, and that would have been the end of it.'

Sugar lifts her head, cautiously, still clutching the blood-soaked handkerchief to her nose. 'So . . . what *is* the end of it? And who do you take me to be?'

Mrs Fox is facing away, peering across the park at the sleeping form of Sophie. Her profile is strong-jawed and quite attractive, although Sugar can't help noticing that there's a bright cinnamon smear of earwax stuck in a curlicue of her ear. 'I take you to be,' says Mrs Fox, 'a young woman who has found her calling, and means to be true to it, whatever her former means of livelihood may have been. That's as much as the Rescue Society can hope for the girls it puts into good homes, and many of them, sadly, return to the streets. You won't return to the streets, will you, Miss Sugar?'

'I would sooner die.'

'I'm sure that won't be necessary,' says Mrs Fox, looking, all of a sudden, profoundly tired. 'God is not as bloodthirsty as all that.'

'Oh! Your handkerchief . . .' cries Sugar, reminded of the ruined scrap of gory cloth dangling from her fist.

'I have a big box of them at home,' sighs Mrs Fox, rising to her feet. 'The legacy of my failing to die of consumption. Goodbye, Miss Sugar. No doubt we'll meet again.' She has already begun to walk away.

'I . . . I hope so,' responds Sugar, at a loss for what else to say.

'Of course we shall,' says Mrs Fox, turning once to wave, much more decorously than she did before. 'It's a small world.'

When Mrs Fox has gone, Sugar wipes her face, conscious that there's dried blood on her cheeks and lips and chin. She tries to sponge up some wetness from the grass, with little success, as the sun has evaporated the melted frost. The blood-stained handkerchief reminds her of something she's done her best not to think about these last few weeks: the fact that not a drop of menstrual blood has issued from her for several months now.

She gets to her feet, and sways, still dizzy. *She's dead*, she thinks. *Damn her; she's dead.*

She tries to picture Mrs Castaway dead, but it's impossible. Her mother always looked like a corpse, reanimated and painted luridly for some obscene or sacrilegious purpose. How could death alter her? The best Sugar can do is to tip the picture sideways, changing Mrs Castaway's orientation from vertical to horizontal. Her pink eyes are open; her hand is extended, palm-up, for coins. '*Come, sir,*' she says, ready to usher another gentleman to the girl of his dreams.

'Sophie,' she whispers, having crossed over to the fountain. 'Sophie, wake up.'

The child, slumped like a rag-doll, head lolling on one shoulder, jerks awake at once, eyes rolling in astonishment that she could have been caught napping. Sugar gets her own apology in first:

'Forgive me, Sophie, I was talking to that lady for much too long.' It must be nearly midday, Sugar reckons; they'd better hurry back to the house, or William may be angry to be deprived of his secretary, or his lover, or his nursemaid, or whatever combination of the three he needs today. 'Now tell me, little one, how far did you get with your kings of England?'

Sophie opens her mouth to answer, then her eyes grow wide.

'Did someone hit you, Miss?'

Sugar's hands flutter nervously to her face. 'N-no, Sophie. My nose started bleeding, that's all.'

Sophie is quite excited by this revelation. 'That's happened to me too, Miss!' she says, in a tone suggesting that such an occurrence is a thrilling, ghoulish adventure.

'Really, dear?' says Sugar, straining to recall, through the fog of her own anxious preoccupations, the incident Sophie's referring to. 'When?'

'It was before,' says the child, after a moment's reflection.

'Before what?'

Sophie accepts her governess's hand to help her to her feet; the arse-end of her bulky black dress is damp, creased, and plastered with fragments of soil, twig and grass.

'Before my Papa bought you for me, Miss,' she says, and Sugar's hand, poised to slap the dirt off Sophie' backside, freezes in mid-air.

THIRTY-ONE

here are too many people! Millions too many! And they will not keep still! Lord, make them stop pushing and jostling for just one minute, freeze them like a *tableau vivant*, so that she can get by!

Sugar cowers in the doorway of Lamplough's Pharmacy in Regent Street, waiting for a parting in the sea of humanity that doesn't come. The relentless grinding din of traffic, the shouts of street vendors, the swirling babble of pedestrians, snorting horses, barking dogs: these are sounds that were familiar once upon a time, but no longer. A few months of seclusion have made her a stranger.

How is it possible that for years she walked these streets lost in thought, daydreaming her novel, and was never once knocked down and trampled underfoot? How is it possible that there exist so many human beings squashed together in the same place, so many lives running concurrently with her own? These chattering women in dresses of licorice-stripe and purple, these swaggering swells, these Jews and Orientals, these tottering sandwichboard-men, these winking shop-keepers, these jaunty sailors and dour office workers, these beggars and prostitutes – every one of them lays claim to a share of Destiny every bit as generous as hers. There's only so much juice to be extracted from the world, and a ravenous multitude is brawling and scuffling to get it.

And the smells! Her habituation to the Rackham house and the tidy streets of Notting Hill has made her lily-livered: now her breath catches, her eyes water, from being forced to take in the overbearing stench of perfume and horse dung, freshly-baked cakes and old meat, burnt mutton-fat and

chocolate, roast chestnuts and dog piss. The Rackham house, despite belonging to a perfumer, smells of nothing much, except cigar-smoke in the study
and porridge in the school-room. Even its flower vases – enormous, preten-
tious copies of classical urns – stand empty now that the memorial bouquets
from Agnes's well-wishers have gone the way of all flesh.

Misreading Sugar's mind, a pretty young flower-seller fetches a bouquet
of shabby pink roses out of her rickety cart and waves the offering in
Sugar's direction. The fact that she owns a trolley, and is bothering to
make overtures to a female, probably means she really *is* a flower-seller and
not a whore, but Sugar is unnerved all the same, and pricked into action.
One deep gulp of breath, and she steps into the human stream, joining
the rush of advancing bodies.

She purposely avoids seeing anyone's face and hopes the crowd will
return the favour. (If she weren't so afraid of being knocked sprawling,
she'd lower her black veil.) Every shop she passes, every narrow lane, may
at any moment spew out someone who once knew her, someone who may
point the finger and raucously hail the return of Sugar to her old stamping grounds.

Already she can't help noticing the regulars: there, outside Lockhart's
Cocoa Rooms, stands Hugh Banton the organ grinder – has *he* seen *her*?
Yes he has, the old dog! But he gives no sign of recognising his 'Little
Toothsome' as she passes him by. And there!: shambling straight towards
her: it's Nadir, the sandwichboard-man – but he passes her by without a
second glance, clearly judging that a lady in crape is not about to attend
the exhibition, 'for the first time in England!', of a live Gorilla-ape.

Loitering in shop doorways and cab ranks are prostitutes Sugar knows
only by sight, not by name. They regard her with listless indifference: she
is a creature as alien to them as the monster advertised on Nadir's sandwich-
board, but not nearly as interesting. The only thing about the black-clad
newcomer that holds their attention for longer than an eye's-blink is her
stilted gait.

Ah, if only they knew why Sugar is limping today! She's limping
because, last night before going to bed, she lay on her back, lifted her legs
as though preparing to be arse-fucked, and poured a tea-cupful of tepid
water, sulphate of zinc and borax directly into her vagina. Then she swaddled herself in an improvised nappy and went to sleep, hoping that the
chemicals, despite being rather stale after sitting unused in her suitcase

for so long, still had some vim left in them. This morning, unrewarded by a miscarriage, she woke to find her vulva and inner thighs flame red, and so sore she could barely dress herself, let alone Sophie. At nine, clenching her jaw with the effort of appearing normal, she presented herself at William's study and asked his permission, as nonchalantly as she could manage, for her first day off.

'What for?' he asked her – not in suspicion; more as if he couldn't imagine what desires she could have that were not met within the confines of his house.

'I need a new pair of boots, a world globe for Sophie, several other things . . .'

'Who'll take care of the child while you're gone?'

'She's quite self-reliant and trustworthy, I've found. And Rose will look in on her. And I'll be back by five.'

William looked rather put out, pointedly shuffling the letters on his desk, which he'd opened and read, but to which his bandaged fingers still didn't permit him to reply. 'That Brinsmead fellow has written back to me about the ambergris; he wants my answer by the third post.'

'You gain nothing by jumping to his will,' she said, feigning umbrage on his behalf. 'Who does he think he is, William? Which of you has the greater standing? A few days' wait will remind him you're doing *him* a favour, not he you.'

To her relief, this did the trick, and within minutes she was walking out the front door, white-faced with determination not to limp until she was safely in the omnibus.

The pain is not quite so bad now; perhaps the Rackham's Crème de Jeunesse she slathered on her groin is helping. What it fails to do for faces (despite the label's immoderate claims), perhaps it does, uncelebrated, for unmentionable parts. At all costs she must heal soon, or she'll have to refuse William when he wants her for a more carnal purpose than writing his correspondence.

Sugar limps into Silver Street, praying no one calls her name. The prostitutes here are a cruder sort than the ones on Regent Street, scavengers of men who can't afford the more expensive fare in The Stretch. Their face-paint is lurid, a mask of deathly white and blood red; they could be pantomime witches dolled up to scare children. How long has it been since her own face was dusted so? She distinctly remembers the powder's floury taste, the way it would permeate the air each time she dabbed the puff into the pot . . . but nowadays she's clean-scrubbed, with skin the texture of a well-peeled orange. Her daily observances in front of the looking-glass no longer include preening her eyelashes, painting her cheeks, plucking wayward hairs from her eyebrows, inspecting her tongue, and removing flakes of imperfection from her pouting lips; nowadays, she cursorily confirms that she looks tired and worried, then pins up her hair and starts work.

Mrs Castaway's house is in sight now, but Sugar hangs back, waiting for the coast to be clear. Stationed only a few yards from the doorstep is a man who witnessed her returning from The Fireside many times with her customers. He's a sheet-music seller, and at this moment he's performing a clumsy, lurching dance while playing his accordion, grimacing like a lunatic as he stamps on the cobble-stones.

'*Gorilla Quadrille!*' he rasps by way of explanation when he's finished, and snatches aloft a copy of the music. (From where Sugar stands, the illustration on the front remarkably resembles the Rackham figurehead.) Three young swells amble up to the music seller, applaud, and encourage him to repeat his performance, but he shrugs evasively; he doesn't dance for the fun of it.

'Any ladies of your hacquaintance play the piano, guvnors?' he whines. 'My music costs next to nuffing.'

'Here's a shilling,' laughs the swellest of the swells, shoving the coin into the music seller's coat pocket with a jab of his slender fingers. 'And you may keep your grubby sheets of paper — Just do your dance for us again.'

The music seller cringes over his instrument, and acts the gorilla one more time, his teeth bared in an obsequious grin. Sugar watches until the swells have had their fun and swan off in search of other titillations; when they do, the music seller dashes in the opposite direction to spend his shilling, and Sugar is free to approach her former home.

Heart in her throat, she steps up to Mrs Castaway's door, and raises her hand to grasp the old iron door-knocker and tap out the code: *Sugar here, unaccompanied*. But the familiar cast-iron Cerberus has been removed, and its screw-holes neatly filled with sawdust and shellac. There's no bell, either, so Sugar is obliged to knock her gloved knuckles against the hard lacquered wood.

The waiting is awful, and the scrape of the latch is worse. She keeps her eyes low, expecting to see Christopher, but when the door swings open, the space where the boy's pink face ought to be is occupied by the crotch of a man's smartly-tailored trousers. Hastily looking up, past the stylish waistcoat and the silken cravat, Sugar opens her mouth to explain herself, only to be struck speechless by the realisation that this man's face is in fact a woman's. Oh, granted, the hair is cut short, oiled, and combed close to the scalp, but there's no mistaking the physiognomy.

Amelia Crozier – for it is she – appraises her visitor's confusion with a feline smirk. 'I think,' she suggests, 'you have mistaken your way.' With every word she speaks, a furling haze of cigarette smoke leaks out through her lips and nostrils.

'No . . . no . . . I . . .' Sugar falters. 'I was wondering what became of the little boy who used to answer the door.'

Miss Crozier raises one dark, fastidiously plucked eyebrow. 'No little boys ever come here,' she says. 'Only big boys.'

From inside – presumably the parlour – Jennifer Pearce's voice rings out. 'Little boys is it he wants? Give him Mrs Talbot's address!'

Miss Crozier turns her back on Sugar, serenely rude. The fine-clipped hair in the nape of her neck resembles greased duck's-down.

'It's not a man here, my dear!' she calls. 'It's a lady in black.'

'Oh, it's *not* the Rescue Society, I trust,' exclaims Miss Pearce, mock-exasperated, from within. 'Please, *spare* us.'

Sensing that the two Sapphists can, and will, keep up this sport as long as it amuses them, Sugar decides it's time to identify herself, loath as she is to lose the halo of virtue they've so unhesitatingly ascribed to her.

'My name is Sugar,' she announces loudly, reclaiming Miss Crozier's attention. 'I lived here once. My m—'

'Why, Sugar!' exclaims Amelia, her face lighting up with a wholly feminine animation. 'I would *never* have guessed! You look nothing like you did when I saw you last!'

'Nor do you,' counters Sugar with a strained smile.

'Ah, yes,' grins Miss Crozier, running her hands over the tailored contours of her suit. 'Clothes *do* make the man – or woman – don't they? But come in, dear, come *in*. Someone was asking for you only a couple of days ago. You see, your fame endures!'

Stiffly, Sugar steps over the threshold and is escorted into Mrs Castaway's parlour, or rather, the parlour that once was Mrs Castaway's.

Jennifer Pearce has transformed it from an old woman's cluttered grotesquerie into a showpiece of fashionable bareness, worthy of an expensive ladies' journal from across the English Channel.

'Welcome, welcome!'

With Mrs Castaway's desk gone, and the old woman's jumbled display of Magdalen pictures removed from the freshly-papered pale pink walls, the room appears much bigger. In place of the pictures, there's nothing, except for two rice-paper fans painted with oriental designs. A spiky green houseplant has pride of place next to the sofa on which Jennifer Pearce reclines, and a delicate *chiffonier* of honey-coloured wood presumably serves (in the absence of any other suitable receptacle) as the repository of money. Amelia Crozier's interrupted cigarette lies on a silver cigar stand with a waist-high stem, emitting a slender cord of smoke that shivers when the door is slammed shut.

'Do sit down, dear,' sings Jennifer Pearce, swinging her legs off the sofa in a flurry of satiny skirts. She scrutinises Sugar from tip to toe, and pats the couch. 'See? I've cleared a nice warm spot for you.'

'I'll stand, thank you,' says Sugar. The ribald mockery to which these women would subject her if she let on that she's too sore to sit doesn't bear thinking about.

'The better to see all the changes we've made, hmm?' says Jennifer Pearce, leaning back on the sofa again.

It's obvious to Sugar by now that Jennifer has promoted herself from being the luminary whore of the Castaway house to being its procuress. Everything about her suggests the status of madam, from her elaborate dress that looks as if it couldn't be removed without at least an hour's notice, to her languidly supercilious expression. Perhaps the most telling proof is her hands: the fingers are thorny with jewel-encrusted rings. Pornography may describe the penis as a sword, staff or truncheon, but there's nothing like a fistful of spiky jewellery to make a man's fragile flesh shrink in fear.

'May I have a word with Amy?' says Sugar.

Miss Pearce locks her fingers together, with a soft clicking of rings. 'Alas: like Mrs Castaway, no longer with us.' Then, when she observes the look of shock on Sugar's face, she smiles, and unhurriedly corrects the misunderstanding. 'Oh no, my dear, I don't mean in the same *way* that Mrs Castaway is no longer with us. I mean, she's gone to a better place.'

Amelia laughs – a horrid nasal whinny. 'However you put it, Jen, it still sounds like death.'

Jennifer Pearce pouts gentle censure at her companion, and continues: 'Amy came to feel that our house had become rather too . . . *specialised* for her talents. So, she took those talents elsewhere. The name of the place escapes me . . .' (she sighs) 'There are *so* many houses nowadays, it's a job keeping up with them all.'

Suddenly her expression sharpens, and she leans forward on the sofa, with a whispering of many-layered skirts. 'To be frank with you, Sugar, Amy's departure, and the fact that *I* am no longer working on what one might call the factory floor, leaves us two girls down. Girls who enjoy giving men the punishment they deserve. I don't suppose *you* are looking for a new home?'

'I have one, thank you,' says Sugar evenly. 'I came here to . . . to ask about my . . . about Mrs Castaway. How did she die?'

Jennifer Pearce settles back into her seat once more, and her eyelids droop half-shut.

'In her sleep, dear.'

Sugar waits for more, but none is forthcoming. Amelia Crozier picks up her cigarette from the tray, judges it too short to be elegant, and drops it down the hollow stem of the stand. The room is so quiet that the sound of the papery stub hitting the metal base is audible.

'Did . . . did she leave anything for me? A letter, a message?'

'No,' says Jennifer Pearce casually. 'Nothing.'

Another silence falls. Amelia extracts, from a pocket in the lining of her jacket, a silver cigarette case, her elegant wrist brushing the swell of bosom beneath her waistcoat.

'And . . . what happened to her?' Sugar asks. 'After she was found, I mean.'

Jennifer Pearce's eyes glaze over, as though she's being interrogated about events that happened before she was born, or even before the advent of recorded history. 'Undertakers took her away,' she says doubtfully. 'Isn't that right, my love?'

'I think so,' says Amelia, and applies a lucifer-flame to the tip of a fresh cigarette. 'Rookes, Brookes, some name like that . . .'

Sugar looks from one face to the other, and understands there's no point asking any more questions.

'I must go,' she says, her fingers tightening on her handbag with its burthen of medicinal poisons.

'So sorry we couldn't help you,' says the sleepy-eyed madam who, in the next edition of *More Sprees in London*, will doubtless be listed as 'Mrs Pearce'. 'And do spread the good word about us, won't you, if you meet any girls who are looking for a change.'

All the way to Regent Circus, Sugar tells herself what to do next. It's most important that she doesn't leave the city without buying some new boots, and a world globe, and whatever other items may convince William she spent her day purposefully. Yet the idea of walking into a shop and conversing with a shop-keeper about the shape of her feet seems as fantastic as jumping over the moon. She glances at signs and hoardings, and occasionally pauses in front of a window display, trying to imagine how a Venetian glass manufacturer or a professor of music or a hair doctor could help her get home from her shopping trip with something to show.

Other pedestrians bear down on her constantly, weaving around her, making a play of *almost* bumping into her and exclaiming 'Oh! I beg your pardon!' when they plainly mean 'Can't you decide if you're going into this stationers or not!' Her eyes swim with tears; she'd counted on being able to use the toilet in Mrs Castaway's, and now she burns for relief.

'Ooh! Watch your step!' says a fat old woman, also in mourning, but grumpy with it. She looks a little like Mrs Castaway. A little.

Sugar dawdles in front of a suitcase-maker's shop. In its window, a travelling case is exhibited, clasped wide open by means of invisible wires, to show off its luxuriously quilted interior. Nestled inside it like a huge pearl, signifying that the ownership of such a superb suitcase makes the world one's oyster, sits . . . a world globe. All she need do is walk into this shop and ask if they'd consider selling the globe; they can easily buy another, for a fraction of what she's willing to pay for this one; the entire transaction ought to be over in five minutes, or five seconds if they say no. She balls her fists and cranes her chin forward; the soles of her boots seem glued to the footpath; it's no use. She walks on.

She reaches Oxford Street just as the Bayswater-bound omnibus pulls away. Even if she were prepared to treat the onlookers of Regent Circus to the bizarre spectacle of a woman in mourning running after an omnibus, she's far too sore to run. She ought to have bought the globe; or else, she should not have loitered like an imbecile in front of cigar importers and court dressmakers. Everything she does will be wrong today; she's doomed to make one bad decision after another. What has she achieved since leaving the Rackham house? Nothing, only buying the medicines in Lamplough's, and it's too late for all that, too late. And while she's away from the house, William will be maddened with suspicion, and he'll search her room, and find Agnes's diaries . . . and oh God: her novel. Yes, at this moment, William is probably sitting on her bed, his jaw stiff with rage as he reads the manuscript, a hundred pages written in the same hand that drafts his tactful replies to business associates, but here describing the desperate entreaties of doomed men as a vengeful whore called Sugar cuts their balls off.

Amy tells me you're writing a novel, dear.

I wouldn't believe everything Amy tells you, Mother.

You know no one in the world will ever read it, don't you, blossom?

It amuses me, Mother.

Good. A girl needs amusement. Toddle upstairs now, and put in a happy ending for me, won't you?

The pain in Sugar's bladder has grown unbearable. She crosses the Circus because she has a notion there's a public lavatory on the other side; when she gets there, she discovers it's a men's urinal. She looks back towards Oxford Street, and observes another omnibus trotting past. Between her legs, the Crème de Jeunesse has turned disgustingly slimy and her flesh throbs in pain, as if she's been abused by a party of men who refuse to stop and refuse to leave and refuse to pay. *Oh, don't snivel so,* hisses Mrs Castaway. *You don't know what suffering is.*

Sugar stands in the street, weeping and sobbing and shaking. A hundred passers-by avoid her, regarding her with pity and disapproval, letting her know with their expressions that she's chosen a most inconvenient spot for this performance; All Souls' Church is nearby, or she could have availed herself of a park, or even a disused graveyard, if she'd been prepared to walk half a mile.

Finally, a man approaches her — an uncommonly fat, clownish-looking man, with a bulbous nose, furzy white hair, and fearsome great eyebrows like crushed mice. He edges towards her shyly, wringing his hands.

'There, there,' he says. 'It's not as bad as all that, is it?'

To which Sugar's response is a helpless, snot-nosed giggle that rapidly develops, despite her efforts to control it, into paroxysmal sobs of laughter.

'That's my girl,' says the old man, squinting benignly. 'That's what I like to hear.' And he waddles back into the crowd, nodding to himself.

The head of Rackham Perfumeries, muddle-headed from his afternoon nap, stands in his parlour staring at the piano, wondering if he'll ever hear it played again. He lifts its melancholy lid and strokes the keys with his good hand, his fingertips brushing the same ivory surfaces that Agnes's finger-tips were the last to touch: intimacy of a kind. But his touch is too heavy: one of the keys triggers the hidden hammer and strikes a solitary resound-ing note, and he stands back, embarrassed, in case a servant comes and investigates.

He walks over to the window and pulls the sash, parting the curtains as wide as they can go. It's raining: how dismal. Sugar is out there some-where, without an umbrella he shouldn't wonder. Better she'd stayed at home and helped with the correspondence; the second post has been deliv-ered, and it appears Woolworth has indisputable proof that Henry Calder Rackham never paid the £500 that was owing, thus putting William at one corner of a damn awkward triangle.

A vision of the naked woman on the mortuary slab flickers in his brain. Agnes, in other words. She's resting peacefully now, he trusts. The rain intensifies, pelting down, turning into hail, tittering against the French windows, sighing into the grass.

He fumbles to light a cigar. His broken fingers are healing slowly; one of them has set a little crooked, but it's a deformity only he and Sugar are likely to notice.

Obscure noises emanate from elsewhere in the house, not recognisable as footsteps and voices, scarcely audible above the downpour. Will he ever write that article for *Punch*, about rain making servants skittish? Probably not: during this last year he hasn't written a single word that was not directly related to his business. Anything philosophical or playful has been postponed into oblivion. He's gained an empire, but what has he lost?

A slight dizziness prompts him to take a seat in the nearest armchair. Is it the concussion? No, he's hungry. Rose didn't disturb his sleep at lunch; he need only ring for her and she'll bring him something. She could fetch *The Times* from his study, too; he's only glanced at it so far, to verify that the news of the day concerns a gorilla, and not Agnes Rackham being found alive.

Foolishness. He'll know that his head has fully recovered from its battering when such daft fantasies cease to plague him. Agnes is gone forever; she exists only in his memories; there isn't even a photograph of them together, more's the pity, except for the wedding portraits taken by that blackguard of an Italian, in which Agnes's face is a blur. Panzetta, that was the fellow's name, and he had the impudence to charge a fortune too . . .

He reclines in the armchair, and stares out into the rain. Through the shimmering veil of years he glimpses Agnes caught in a summer shower, hurrying under the shelter of a pavilion, her pink dress and white hat emphasising the healthy flush of her rain-flecked cheeks. He remembers running at her side, and being light-headed with pleasure to have shared this moment with her, to have been the man – out of all her suitors – who saw her like this, a radiantly beautiful girl on the very brink of ripeness, flushed rosy-pink, skin twinkling with rain, panting like a deer.

She never once snubbed him, he recalls now. Never once! Not even when she was surrounded by her other suitors, rich well-connected fellows all, whose lips were wont to curl at the very sight of a manufacturer's son. But they hadn't a chance with Agnes, these effeminate boobies. Agnes appeared only intermittently aware of their presence, as if she might at any moment wander off and leave them stranded, like pets someone had unwisely left in her care.

But she never wandered off from the company of William Rackham. He wasn't boring: that was the difference. All those other fellows liked nothing better than to hear the sound of their own voices; he preferred the sound of hers. Nor was it solely the music of that voice that charmed him; she was less stupid than the other girls he knew. Oh, granted, she was ignorant about the usual topics girls are ignorant about (broadly, anything of consequence), but he could tell she had an unusual and original mind. Most strikingly, she had an instinct for metaphysics that her flimsy education had left entirely uncultivated; she truly did 'see a World in a grain of sand, and a Heaven in a wild flower.'

Recalling these things in his parlour as the rain begins to ease and his head droops back onto one of Agnes's embroidered antimacassars, William suddenly sneezes. This, too, reminds him of his radiant Agnes Unwin – in particular, how irritatingly, delightfully, superstitious she was. When he asked why she always exclaimed the words 'God bless you!' so promptly – and *loudly* – whenever anyone sneezed, she explained that during that momentary convulsion, the invisible demons that fly all about us may seize their chance to enter. Only if a considerate bystander blesses us in the name of God, when we're too busy crying 'Achoo' to bless ourselves, can we be sure we haven't been invaded.

'Well, I see I owe you my life, then,' he commended her.

'You're laughing at me,' she retorted mildly. 'But God *should* bless people. It's what He's supposed to be for, isn't it?'

'Oh, Miss Unwin, you must be careful. People will accuse you of taking God's name in vain.'

'They already do! But . . .' (a charming smile played on her lips) 'they only say so because of the demons inside them.'

'From all the unblessed sneezes.'

'Precisely.'

At which William laughed out loud: damn it, this girl was funny! It only required a special sort of man to perceive her gently mischievous brand of wit. Each time he met her, she came out with more of it, always delivered in a teasing, solemn tone before breaking out into a smile behind her fan; and on the feathery foundations of their banter, they built their engagement.

He desired her, of course. He dreamed of her, lost seed over her. And yet in his heart of hearts, or loin of loins, he had no urgent designs upon her; there was, after all, a whole class of women provided especially for *that* purpose. When he imagined Agnes and himself married, his vision was scarcely physical at all; he pictured the two of them lying asleep in each other's arms in an enormous white raft of a bed.

When they were newly engaged, she confided to him how afraid she was of losing her figure – by which he took her to mean, through childbirth. Immediately he decided he would take precautions, and spare her this burden. 'Children?' he declared, relishing the thought of flouting yet another convention, for in those days he cared not a button for the petty expectations of fathers and other busybodies. 'Too many of them in the world already! People have children because they want immortality, but they're fooling themselves, because the little monsters are something *else*, not oneself. If people want immortality, they should claim it on their own behalf!'

He'd consulted her face then, fearful that his resolve to win enduring fame through his writings might impress her as vainglorious, but she looked deeply pleased.

In dreams, both waking and sleeping, he would imagine himself and Agnes together, not just as newlyweds, but in their mature years, when their reputation would have achieved its zenith.

'There go the Rackhams,' envious onlookers would say, as they strolled through St James's Park. '*He* has just published another book.'

'Yes, and *she* has just returned from Paris, where I'm told she had thirty dresses made for her, by five different dress-makers!'

A typical day, in this future of theirs, would begin with him lounging in a wicker chair in his sunlit courtyard, checking the proofs of his latest publication, and dealing with correspondence from his readers (the admirers would get a cordial reply, the detractors would be instantly destroyed with his cigar-tip). And he'd have no shortage of detractors, for his fearless opinions would ruffle many feathers! On the lawn beside him, a pile of ash would smoulder, of all the bores who needn't have bothered to send him their complaints. Agnes would come gliding across the grass at around noon, resplendent in lilac, and scold him serenely for making the gardener's life a trial.

Slumped in his parlour now, in January 1876, a man bereaved, William winces in pain at these recollected dreams. What a fool he was! How little he understood himself! How little he understood Agnes! How tragically he underestimated the ruthlessness with which his father would humiliate them both during the tenderest years of their marriage! From the outset, every portent was already pointing towards Pitchcott Mortuary, and the wretched woman on that slab!

As he lapses once more into a doze, he sees Agnes before him, as she was on their wedding night. He lifts her night-dress: she is quite the most beautiful thing he has ever seen. Yet she is rigid with fear, and gooseflesh forms on her perfect skin. So many months he's spent praising the beauty of her eyes, to her obvious delight; but much as he'd like to spend two hundred years adoring each breast, and thirty thousand on all the rest, he yearns for a more spontaneous union, a mutual celebration of their love. Should he quote poetry to her? Call her his America, his new-found-land? Shyness and unease dry his tongue; the look of dumb horror on his wife's face obliges him to continue in silence. With only his own laboured breath for company, he presses on, hoping she might, by some magical process of communion, or emotional osmosis, be inspired to share in his ecstasy; that the eruption of his passion might be followed by a warm balm of mutual relief.

'William?'

He jerks awake, confused. Sugar is standing before him in the parlour, her mourning-clothes shining wet, her bonnet dripping rain-water, her face apologetic.

'I didn't achieve anything,' she confesses. 'Please don't be annoyed with me.'

He straightens up in his seat, rubbing his eyes with the fingers of his good hand. There's a crick in his neck, his head aches and, swaddled inside his trousers, his prick is slackening in its sticky, humid nest of pubic hair.

'No matter,' he groans. 'You need only tell me w-what you want, and I can arrange it for you.'

Three days later, during the writing of a letter to Henry Calder Rackham, which Sugar has been instructed, after some hesitation, to begin 'Dear Father', William suddenly enquires,

'Can you use a sewing-m-machine?'

She looks up. She'd thought she was ready for anything today: her sore privates have cleared up enough for her to contemplate the act of love, provided it's done gently; her stomach has just this morning ceased convulsing from the effects of the wormwood and tansy tincture, and she's giving her poor body a much-needed rest before trying, as a last-ditch resort, the pennyroyal and brewer's yeast.

'I'm sorry,' she says. 'I've never handled one.'

He nods, disappointed. 'Can you sew the usual w-way?'

Sugar lays the pen on the blotter, and tries to judge from his face how kindly he might take to a joke. 'Skill with a needle and thread,' she says, 'was never the greatest of my talents.'

He doesn't smile, but nods again. 'It wouldn't be possible, then, for you to a-alter a dress of A-Agnes's, so that it fit you?'

'I don't think so,' she says, much alarmed. 'Even if I were a seamstress, I . . . well, our shapes . . . they're very different . . . uh, weren't they?'

'Pity,' he says, and leaves her to stew in her unease for several minutes. What the devil is he getting at? Does he suspect her of something? He was away in the city yesterday, for the first time since the funeral, and in the evening made no mention of where he'd been . . . To the police, perhaps?

At last he rouses himself from his reverie and, in a clear and authoritative tone, with scarcely any stammer, declares: 'I have arranged for us all to go on a l-little outing together.'

'Us . . . all?'

'You, me and Sophie.'

'Oh.'

'On Thursday, we'll go to the city, and have our photographs taken. You'll have to wear your m-mourning-clothes on the way there, but please take along with you a cheerful and pretty dress, and another for Sophie. There's a changing room at the photographer's, I've checked.'

'Oh.' She waits for an explanation, but he's already turned his head as if the subject is closed. She lifts the pen from the maculated blotter. 'Is there any particular dress you'd like me to wear?'

'One that's as attractive as possible,' William replies, 'w-while still looking completely respectable.'

'Where is Papa taking us, Miss?' says Sophie on the morning of the big day.

'I've told you already: to a photographer's studio,' sighs Sugar, trying not to let her displeasure at the child's excitement show.

'Is it a big place, Miss?'

Oh, be quiet: you're just babbling for the sake of it. 'I don't know, Sophie, I've never been there.'

'May I wear my new whale-bone hair clip, Miss?'

'Certainly, dear.'

'And shall I take my shammy bag, Miss?'

The mere sound of you, little precious, suggests Mrs Castaway, *is becoming tedious in the extreme.* 'I . . . Yes, I don't see why not.'

Decked out in mourning, with a change of clothing packed in a tartan travelling case that once belonged to Mrs Rackham, Sugar and Sophie venture out into the carriage-way, where the coach and horse stand waiting for them.

'Where's Papa?' says Sophie, as Cheesman lifts her into the cabin.

'Putting his toys away, I expect, Miss Sophie,' winks the coachman.

Sugar climbs hurriedly in, while Cheesman is busy with the case and before he has a chance to lay his hands on her.

'Mind how you go, Miss Sugar!' he says, delivering the words like the concluding line of a bawdy song.

William emerges from the front door, fastening a dark-grey overcoat over his favourite brown jacket. Once all the buttons are done up, it will take a sharp-eyed pedestrian indeed to spot that he's not in strict mourning.

'Let's be off, Cheesman!' he calls, when he's climbed into the cabin with his daughter and Miss Sugar – and, to his daughter's delight, his word instantaneously becomes fact: the horses begin to trot, and the carriage rolls along the gravel, up the path towards the big wide world. The adventure is beginning: this is page one.

Inside, the three passengers examine each other as best they can while affecting not to be staring: a tricky feat, given that they are seated with knees almost touching, the male on one seat, the two females opposite.

William notes how wan and ill-at-ease Sugar appears, how there are pale blue circles under her eyes, how her sensuous mouth twitches with a nervous half-smile, how unflattering her mourning dress is. Never mind: at the photographers it will cease to matter.

Sugar appreciates that William has, in appearance at least, fully recovered from his injuries. A couple of white scars line his forehead and cheek, and his gloves are slightly oversized, but otherwise he looks as good as new – better even, because he's lost his paunch during his convalescence, and his face is thinner too, giving him cheekbones where he had none before. Really, it was unfair of her to compare his face to the caricature on the 'Gorilla Quadrille'; he may not be the handsome fellow his brother was, but he does have a touch of distinction now, courtesy of his suffering. His temper and his stammer are likewise improving, and he's still sharing his correspondence with her, despite the fact that his fingers have healed sufficiently for him to manage the task alone. So . . . So there really is no reason to loathe and fear him, is there?

Sophie's corporeal form sits still and behaves impeccably, because that's what children *ought* to do, but in truth she's beside herself with excitement. Here she is, inside the family carriage for the first time, going to the city for the first time, in the company of her father, with whom she's never gone out before. The challenge of absorbing all these things is so great she scarcely knows where to begin. Her father's face impresses her as old and wise, like the face on the Rackham labels, but when he turns towards the window or licks his red lips, he looks like a younger person with a beard stuck on. In the street, gentlemen and ladies stroll, each one of them different, adding up to hundreds and hundreds. A horse and carriage passes on the other side of the road, a polished wooden and metal cabin full of mysterious strangers, pulled by an animal with hoofs. Yet Sophie understands that the two carriages, at the moment of passing, are like mirror-images of each other; to those mysterious strangers, *she* is the dark mystery, and *they* are the Sophies. Does her father understand this? Does Miss Sugar?

'You've grown so big,' remarks William, out of the blue. 'You've sh-shot up in no time at all. How have you m-managed it, hmm?'

Sophie keeps her eyes on her father's knees: this question is like the ones in *Alice's Adventures in Wonderland*: impossible to answer.

'Has Miss Sugar been keeping you busy?'

'Yes, Papa.'

'Good, good.'

Again he is calling her good, just like he did on that day when the lady with the face like the Cheshire Cat was at his side!

'Sophie likes nothing better than learning,' remarks Miss Sugar.

'Very good,' says William, clasping and unclasping his hands in his lap. 'Can you tell me w-where the Bay of Biscay is, Sophie?'

Sophie freezes. The one and only necessary fact of life, and she hasn't been prepared for it!

'We haven't done Spain yet,' explains her governess. 'Sophie has been learning all about the colonies.'

'Very good, very good,' says William, returning his attention to the window. A building they're passing is adorned with a large painted design advertising Pears' soap, causing him to frown.

The photographers' studio is on the top floor of an address in Conduit Street, not so very far away, as the crow flies, from the house of Mrs Castaway. The bronze plaque says *Tovey & Scholefield (A.R.S.A.)*, *Photographers and Artists*. Half-way up the gloomy stairs hangs a framed photographic portrait of a callow, cupid-lipped soldier, much retouched, cradling his rifle like a bouquet of flowers. *Perished in Kabul; IMMORTAL in the memory of those who loved him*, explains the inscription, before adding, at a discreet remove, *INQUIRE WITHIN*.

Within, the Rackhams are met by a tall, mustachioed individual dressed in a frock-coat. 'Good day, sir, madam,' he says.

He and William have plainly met before, and Sugar is left to guess who is Scholefield and who is Tovey – this man who resembles an impresario, or the bird-boned, shirt-sleeved fellow who can be seen, through a crack in the reception-room door, pouring a colourless fluid from a small bottle into a larger one. The walls are crowded with framed photographs of men, women and children, singly and in family assortments, all without fault or blemish, and also one really enormous painting of a plump lady dressed in Regency finery, complete with hounds and a basket overflowing with still-life debris. In one corner, superimposed on the tail-plumes of a dead pheasant, glows the signature *E. H. Scholefield, 1859.*

'Look, Sophie,' says Sugar. 'This picture was painted by this very gentleman who stands before us.'

'Indeed it was,' says Scholefield. 'But I forsook my first love – and abundant commissions from ladies just like this one – to champion the Art of photography. For it was my belief that every new Art, if it's to *be* an Art, needs a measure of ... Artistic midwifery.' A second too late, he remembers he's delivering his spiel to a person of the weaker sex. 'If you'll forgive the phrase.'

Without delay, Sugar and Sophie are shown into a small room with a wash-basin, two full-length mirrors, and an ornamental queensware water-closet. The walls bristle with clothes-hooks and hat-pegs. A single, barred window looks out on the rooftop that connects Tovey & Scholefield's establishment with the dermatologist's next door.

The travelling case is opened up and its sumptuously coloured, silky, pillowy cargo is pulled into the light. Sugar helps Sophie out of her mourning and into her prettiest blue dress with the gold brocade buttons. Her hair is re-brushed and the whalebone clip slid into place.

'Turn your back, now, Sophie,' says Miss Sugar.

Sophie obeys, but wherever she looks there's a mirror, reflecting back and forth in an endless rebound. Disturbed at the prospect of seeing Miss Sugar in her underwear, Sophie gazes into her Mama's travelling case. A crumpled handbill advertising *Psycho, the Sensation of the London Season, exhibited exclusively at the Folkestone Pavilion!* gives her something to ponder while the body of her governess is disrobed all around her. Over and over she reads the price, the times of exhibition, the disclaimer about ladies of a nervous disposition, while catching unwilling half-glimpses of Miss Sugar's underwear, the swell of pink flesh above the neckline of her chemise, naked arms wrestling with a flaccid construction of dark green silk.

Sophie lifts the handbill up to her nose, sniffing it in case it smells of the sea. She fancies it does, but maybe it's only her imagination.

Tovey and Scholefield's studio proper, when Sugar and Sophie emerge into it, is not very large – no bigger, perhaps, than the Rackhams' dining-room – but it makes ingenious use of three of its walls, dressing them up as backdrops for every conceivable requirement. One wall is a *trompe-l'œil* landscape for men to pose in front of – forests, mountains, a brooding sky and, as an optional extra, moveable classical pillars. Another wall functions as the rear of a sitting-room, papered in the latest style. The third wall is subdivided into three different backdrops side by side; on the extreme left, a floor-to-ceiling library bookcase from whose shelves the posing client can select a leather-bound volume and pretend to be reading it – as long as he doesn't stand too far to the right, for then he'll step across the 'library' boundary and find himself framed in front of a cottage window decorated with lace curtains. This country idyll is likewise a very narrow slice of life, scarcely an inch wider than the diameter of an old-style crinoline, and gives way to another scene, that of an infant's nursery papered with robins and crescent moons.

It's in front of this nursery backdrop – evidently the least often used – that most of the studio's props are to be found: not just the rocking-horse, toy locomotive, miniature writing-desk and high-backed stool that belong to the nursery, but a jumble of other accessories to the other backdrops, like a mountaineer's walking-staff (for Artists and Philosophers), a large *papier-mâché* vase glued to a plywood pedestal, various clocks hung on brass stands, two rifles, an enormous ring of keys suspended by a chain around the neck of a bust of Shakespeare, bundles of ostrich feathers, footstools of various sizes, the façade of a grandfather clock, and many other less easily identifiable things. To Sophie's horrified fascination, there's even a stuffed, soulful-eyed spaniel which can be made to sit without demur at any master's feet.

Out of the corner of her eye, Sugar observes William appraising her and Sophie. He looks slightly ill-at-ease, as if fretting that unforeseen complications may spoil the day's business, but he doesn't look disappointed with the outfits; and if he recognises that she's wearing the same dress she wore when he first met her, he betrays no sign. The hitherto elusive Tovey takes his place behind the camera stilts and casts the hulking mechanism's thick black cape over his head and shoulders. Thus he remains shrouded for the remainder of the Rackhams' visit, his buttocks occasionally swinging, wagtail-like, under the light-proof fabric, his feet as deliberately placed as the legs of his tripod.

The exposures are made in a matter of minutes. Scholefield has dissuaded William from his original intention to have only one picture made; four can be accomplished in a single sitting, and needn't be paid for or enlarged unless they give complete satisfaction.

So, William stands in front of the painted skyline and gazes into what Scholefield describes as 'the distance', a point which, in the confines of the studio, can be no further than the ventilation grille. Scholefield raises one fist, slowly, and rhapsodises: 'On the horizon, bursting through the clouds: the sun!' Rackham peers instinctively, and Tovey seizes the moment.

Next, William is persuaded to stand in front of the bookcase, holding a copy of *Rudimentary Optics* splayed open in his hands. 'Ah yes, *that* notorious chapter!' remarks Scholefield, peeking at the text as he gently pushes the book a little closer to the customer's face. 'Who would think that a tome as dry as this could contain such saucy revelations!' William's glassy expression becomes suddenly keen as he begins to read in earnest, and, again, Tovey doesn't hesitate to act.

'Ach, my little joke,' says Scholefield, hanging his head in mock penitence. His manner is growing more flamboyant the longer he has his customers in his command; he might almost be tippling whisky from a hipflask, or taking furtive sniffs of nitrous oxide.

Sitting on the sidelines with Sophie awaiting her turn, Sugar wonders if there's another room to this studio, a secret chamber furnished for pornography. When Tovey and Scholefield are left to themselves at the end of a working day, is it only respectably-clad gentlemen and ladies they develop, or do they also pull naked prostitutes from the malodorous darkroom fluids, and peg them up to dry? What could be more Artistic, after all, than a set of card-sized photographs sold in a package labelled 'For the Use of Artists Only'?

'And now, your charming little girl,' announces Scholefield, and with balletic efficiency he clears away the props from in front of the fake nursery, until only the toys remain. After an instant's hesitation, he removes the locomotive; then, after deliberating slightly longer, he judges that Mr Rackham is not the sort of father who would adore to see his child perched side-saddle on a rocking horse, so he removes that as well. He leads Sophie to a spindly table and shows her how to pose next to it, surveys the scene with a nimble step backwards, and then leaps forward again, to remove the superfluous stool.

'I shall now summon an elephant down from the sky,' he declares, raising his hands portentously, 'and balance it on the tip of my nose!'

Sophie does not raise her chin or open her eyes any wider; she only thinks of the part in *Alice's Adventures* where the Cat says, 'We're all mad here.' Is London full of mad photographers and sandwichboard-men who look like the playing-card courtiers of the Queen of Hearts?

'Elephants having failed to come,' says Scholefield, noting that Tovey has not yet made an exposure, 'I shall, in disappointment, screw off my own head.'

This alarming promise, accompanied by a stylised gesture towards its consummation, succeeds only in putting a frown on Sophie's face.

'The gentleman wants you to lift your chin, Sophie dear,' says Sugar softly, 'and keep your eyes open without blinking.'

Sophie does as she's told, and Mr Tovey gets what he wants at once.

For the group photograph, William, Sugar and Sophie are posed in the simulacrum of the perfect sitting-room: Mr Rackham stands in the centre, Miss Rackham stands in front of him and slightly to the left, her head reaching his watch-chain, and the unnamed lady sits on an elegant chair to the right. Together they form a pyramid, more or less, with Mr Rackham's head at its apex, and the skirts of Miss Rackham and the lady combining at the base.

'Ideal, ideal,' says Scholefield.

Sugar sits motionless, her hands demurely folded in her lap, her shoulders ramrod straight, and stares unblinking at Scholefield's raised finger. The hooded creature that is Tovey and his contraption has its eye open now; hidden chemicals are reacting, at this very instant, to the influx of light and a deepening impression of three carefully arranged human beings. She's aware of William breathing shallowly above her head. He still hasn't told her why they're doing this; she'd assumed he would have told her by now, but he hasn't. Dare she ask him, or is it one of those subjects that are liable to provoke him to a rage? How strange that an occasion which ought to fill her with hope for their shared future — a family portrait that installs her in the place of his wife — should arouse such foreboding in her.

What use can he possibly have in mind for this portrait? He can't display it, so what does he mean to do with it? Moon over it in private? Give it to her as a gift? What in God's name is she doing here, and why does she feel worse than if she were being made to submit to naked indignities for the Use of Artists only?

'I think,' says Scholefield, 'we have quite finished, don't you, Mr Tovey?' To which his partner replies with a grunt.

Many hours later, back in Notting Hill, when night has fallen and all the excitement is over, the members of the Rackham household retire to bed, each to their own. All the lights in the house are extinguished, even the one in William's study.

William snores gently on his pillow, already dreaming. The largest of Pears' soap factories is ablaze, and he is watching the firemen labour hopelessly to save it. Permeating the dream is the extraordinary odour of burning soap, a smell he's never smelled in real life, and which, for all its unmistakable uniqueness in the dream, he'll forget the instant he wakes.

His daughter is fast asleep too, exhausted from her adventures and the distress of being scolded by Miss Sugar for being fractious and her after-dinner mishap in which she sicked up not just her beef stew but the cake and cocoa she had at Lockhart's Cocoa Rooms as well. The world is an awfully strange place, bigger and more crowded than she could ever have imagined, and full of phenomena even her governess quite clearly doesn't understand, but her father said she is a good girl, and the Bay of Biscay is in Spain, should he ever ask again. Tomorrow is another day, and she'll learn her lessons so well that Miss Sugar won't be in the least cross.

Sugar lies awake, chamber-pot clutched in her arms, spewing a vile mixture of pennyroyal and brewer's yeast. Yet, even in the midst of a spasm, when her mouth and nostrils are burning with poison, her physical misery is trifling compared to the sting of the words with which William sent her away from his study tonight: *Mind your own business! If it were any affair of yours, don't you think I would have told you? Who do you think you are?*

She crawls into bed, clutching her belly, afraid to whimper in case the noise should travel through the walls. Her stomach muscles are sore from convulsing; there can't be anything left in there. Except . . .

For the first time since falling pregnant, Sugar imagines the baby as . . . a baby. Up until now, she's avoided seeing it so. It started as nothing more than a substanceless anxiety, an absence of menstruation; then it became a worm in the bud, a parasite which she hoped might be induced to pass out of her. Even when it clung on, she didn't imagine it as a living creature clinging for dear life; it was a mysterious object, growing and yet inert, a clump of fleshy matter inexplicably expanding in her guts. Now, as she lies in the godforsaken midnight, clutching her abdomen in her hands, she suddenly realises her hands are laid upon a life: she is harbouring a human being.

What is it like, this baby? Has it a face? Yes, of course it must have a face. Is it a he or a she? Does it have any inkling how Sugar has mothered it so far? Is it contorted with fear, its skin scalded with sulphate of zinc and borax, its mouth gasping for clean nourishment amidst the poisons that swirl in Sugar's innards? Does it regret the day it was born, even though that day has yet to come?

Sugar removes her palms from her belly, and lays them on her feverish forehead. She must resist these thoughts. This baby – this creature – this tenacious clump of flesh – cannot be permitted to live. Her own life is at stake; if William finds out she's in the family way it will be the end, the end of everything. *You won't go back on the streets, will you, Miss Sugar?* That's what Mrs Fox said to her. And *I would sooner die* is what she promised in reply.

Sugar covers herself with a sheet in preparation for sleep; the nausea is ebbing and she's able to drink a sip of water to rinse the pennyroyal and gall from her tongue. Her abdomen is still sore from ribcage to groin, as though she's subjected rarely-used muscles to a regime of punishing exercise. She lays one palm on her belly; there's a heartbeat there. Her own heartbeat, of course; it's the same as the one in her breast and temples. The thing inside her probably hasn't a heart yet. Has it?

Scholefield and Tovey are awake too; in fact, despite the lateness of the hour, they haven't even left their premises in Conduit Street. Among other activities, they've been working on the Rackham pictures, attempting to produce miracles.

'The head's come out too small,' mutters Tovey, squinting at a glistening female face that has just materialised in the gloom. 'Don't you think the head's too small?'

'Yes,' says Scholefield, 'but it's useless for the purpose anyway. It's too bright; she looks as if she has a lamp burning inside her skull.'

'Wouldn't it be simpler to photograph the three of them again, out of doors, in bright sunlight?'

'Yes, my love, it would be simpler,' sighs Scholefield, 'but out of the question.'

They labour on, into the small hours of the morning. This commission of Rackham's is a much more difficult challenge than the usual business of superimposing a boy's face onto the body of a soldier, to give grieving parents an almost-authentic record of their missing son's military eminence. This Rackham assignment involves all but insuperable incompatibilities: a face from a photograph taken in brilliant sunlight, by an amateur whose opinion of his own skills is grossly inflated, must be rephotographed, enlarged to several times its size, and imposed on the shoulders of a woman done in the studio by professionals.

By three o'clock, they have the best result that they can manage, given the raw materials. Rackham will simply have to be satisfied with this, or, if he isn't, he can pay for the straightforward images of himself and his daughter, and forfeit the imperfect composite.

The photographers take themselves to bed in a little room adjoining the studio; it's far too late now for them to catch a cab back to their house in Clerkenwell. Suspended from a wire in the darkroom hangs their day's work: a fine photograph of William Rackham gazing into the Romantic eternity of a mountain summit, a fine photograph of William Rackham engrossed in the study of a book, a fine photograph of Sophie Rackham daydreaming in her nursery, and a most peculiar photograph of the Rackham family all together, with Agnes Rackham's head transplanted from a summer long ago, abnormally radiant, like one of those mysterious figures purported by spiritualists to be ghosts captured on the gelatin emulsion of film, which were never visible to the naked eye.

THIRTY-TWO

ophie Rackham stands perched on a stool by the window and wiggles her bottom slightly, to test if the stool wobbles. It does, a little. Carefully, because she can't see below her skirt, she shifts her feet for balance, until she's secure.

I am going to grow bigger than my Mama, she thinks, not defiantly, nor competitively, but because she has fathomed that her body is different in nature from her mother's, and not destined to be petite. It's as if she was fed a morsel of Alice's Wonderland cake when she was a baby, and instead of shooting up to the ceiling in seconds, she is expanding the tiniest amount each minute of her life, an expansion that won't stop until she's very big indeed — as big as Miss Sugar, or her father.

Soon, she won't need this stool to look out at the world. Soon, Miss Sugar — or *someone* — will have to arrange for her to get new shoes, new underwear, new everything, because she's growing so big that almost none of her clothes fit her comfortably. Perhaps she'll be taken into the city again, where there exist whole shops devoted to the selling of a single object, and each day they manage to sell one, because of the marvellous abundance of people endlessly surging through the streets.

Sophie lifts her spyglass, curling her fingers around the ridges of its telescoped design. She extends it to its full length of fourteen inches and peers out at Chepstow Villas. Pedestrians are few; nothing much is happening. Not like in the city.

Behind her, the handle of the school-room door squeaks. Can this be Miss Sugar returning already, even though she's only just gone to help Papa with his letters? Sophie can't turn too quickly in case she falls off the stool;

if her spyglass shattered she would suffer seven hundred and seventy-seven years of bad luck, she's decided.

'Hello, Sophie,' says a deep male voice.

Sophie is amazed to see her father standing in the doorway. The last time he visited her here, Beatrice was still her nurse, and Mama was at the sea-side. She wonders whether curtsying would make a good impression on him, but a wobble of the stool dissuades her.

'Hello, Papa.'

He closes the door behind him, crosses the room and waits for her to step down onto the carpet. Nothing remotely like this has ever happened before. She blinks in his shadow, looking up at his frowning, smiling bearded face.

'I have something for you,' he says, his hands hidden behind his back.

Sophie's thrill of anticipation is tempered with fear; she can't help wondering if her father has come to tell her she's to be removed to a home for naughty girls, the way her nurse used to threaten he might.

'Here, then.' He hands her a picture-frame the size of a large book. Enclosed behind the glass is the photograph of her taken by the man who claimed to be able to balance elephants on his nose. The Sophie Rackham captured by him is noble and colourless, all greys and blacks, like a statue, but awfully dignified and grown-up looking. The fake backdrop has turned into a real room, and the young lady's eyes are beautiful and lifelike, with tiny lights glowing inside them. What a beautiful picture! If it had colours, it would be a painting.

'Thank you, Papa,' she says.

Her father smiles down at her, his lips forming the smile-shape jerkily, as though he's unaccustomed to using the stiff muscles involved. Without speaking, he reveals another framed photograph from behind his back: a picture of himself this time, standing in front of the painted mountains and sky, gazing into the future.

'What do you think?' he asks her.

Sophie can barely believe her ears. Her father has never asked her what she thinks before, about anything. How is it possible that the universe could permit this? He is old and she is young, he is big and she is small, he is male and she is female, he is her father and she is only his daughter.

'It's very good, isn't it, Papa?' she says. She wants to tell him how real the illusion is, of him standing in front of those mountains, but she doesn't trust herself not to get tongue-tied and betrayed by her puny vocabulary. Nevertheless, he seems to guess what she's thinking.

'Queer, isn't it, the way w-we know that this photograph was made in an upstairs room in a crowded street, and yet here am I, standing in the w-wilds of Nature. But that's what we must all do, Sophie: present ourselves in the best light. That's w-what A-A-Art is for. And History too.' His stutter is getting worse as his ability to condescend to her level of discourse reaches the end of its rope. He's about to leave, she can tell.

'What about the other picture, Papa?' she can't help asking as he takes a step backward. 'The one of us all?'

'It . . . it wasn't a success,' he says, with a pained look. 'P-Perhaps we'll go back one day, and try another. But I can't p-promise.'

And, without further conversation or parting words, he turns on his heel and walks stiltedly out of the room.

Sophie stares at the closed door, and hugs her portrait to her chest. She can scarcely wait to show Miss Sugar.

Late that night, when Sophie has long been asleep and even the servants are going to bed, Sugar and William are still discussing business by lamplight in the master's study. It's a never-exhausted subject, whose intricacy continues to deepen even when they're too tired to speak of it anymore. A year ago, if someone had asked Sugar what the running of a perfumery might involve, she'd have replied: Grow some flowers, get them harvested, mix them up in a potage, add the essence to bottles of water or cakes of soap, affix a paper label to the results, and trundle it to shops by the cartload. Now, such abstruse questions as whether that swindler Crawley can be trusted to estimate the cost of converting beam engines from twelve to sixteen horsepower, or whether it's worth sinking more money into wooing the port authorities at Hull, can easily swallow up twenty minutes each, before the first item of unanswered correspondence is even lifted off the pile. Sugar has come to think that *all* professions are like this: simple to outsiders, inextricably complex to those within. Even whores, after all, can prattle about their trade for hours.

William is in a strange mood tonight. Not his usual bad-tempered self; more reasonable, and yet melancholy with it. The challenges of business, to which his response in the early days of his directorship was rash enthusiasm, and more recently pugnacious defiance, seem suddenly to have sapped his spirit. 'Useless', 'profitless', 'futile': these are words he resorts to frequently, with a heavy sigh, burdening Sugar with the task of re-inflating his confidence. 'Do you really think so?' he says, when she reassures him that Rackham's star is still on the rise. 'What a little optimist you are.'

Sugar, knowing she ought to be grateful he isn't angry with her, is perversely tempted to snap at him. After what she's endured with Sophie today, she has grievances of her own, and is in no mood to be his encouraging angel. When will someone reassure *her* that everything is going to be all right?

I'm carrying your child, William, she's tempted to tell him. *A boy, I'm sure. The heir you want so badly, for Rackham Perfumeries. No one need know it's yours, except we two. You could say you got me from the Rescue Society, not knowing I was already with child. You could say I'm a good governess to Sophie and you can't bring yourself to condemn me for sins committed in my former life. You've always said you don't give a damn what other people think. And in years to come, when your son has taken after you, and tongues have stopped wagging, we could be married. It's a gift from Fate, don't you see?*

'I think you should leave things as they are,' she advises, pulling herself back to the realities of beam engines. 'In order to recoup your investment, you'd have to see ten years of good harvests and no expansion from your competitors. The risks are too great.'

This reminder of his rivals darkens William's mood even further.

'Ach, they'll leave me flapping my arms in the wind from their coat-tails, Sugar,' he says, half-heartedly miming the motion from where he sits slumped on the ottoman. 'The twentieth century belongs to Pears and Yardley, I can feel it in my bones.'

Sugar chews her lower lip and suppresses an irritable sigh. If only she could set him to work drawing pictures of Australian kangaroos, or give him simpler sums to do! Would he reward her with a big smile then?

'Let's worry about the rest of our own century first, William,' she suggests. 'It's what we're living in, after all.' To signal the importance of dealing with the correspondence item by item, in the order that it comes, she takes the next envelope off the pile and recites the sender's name. 'Philip Bodley.'

'Leave that,' groans William, allowing himself to slide further towards horizontal. 'It's nothing to do with you. With Rackham's, I mean.'

'It's not trouble, though, is it?' she murmurs sympathetically, trying to let him know with her voice that he can share his most secret woes with her, and she'll fortify him, like the best wife in the world.

'Trouble or not, it doesn't concern you,' he points out, not belligerently, but with mournful resignation. 'Remember I do have *some* sort of life beyond this desk, my love.'

She takes the endearment at face value, or does her best to. After all, he's alluding to how indispensable she is to his business, isn't he? She picks up the next envelope.

'Finnegan & Co, Tynemouth.'

He covers his face with his palms.

'Tell me the worst,' he groans.

She reads the letter aloud, pausing only when William's snorts of annoyance and mutters of scepticism prevent him from hearing the words. Then, while he's digesting the missive, she sits silent behind his desk, breathing shallowly, feeling the ominous distension against her tender stomach, feeling the gorge of aggrieved pride inching upwards.

'Sophie was impossible this afternoon,' she finally blurts.

William, preoccupied with the Solomonic challenge of deciding whether bone-idle dockhands are truly to blame for the delays in unloading shipments at Tynemouth or whether his supplier is lying to him again, blinks uncomprehendingly.

'Sophie? Impossible?'

Sugar takes a deep breath, and the seams of her dress press in on her swollen bosom and belly. In a flash, she recalls Sophie's excitement following the visit her father paid on her; her preening pride in the photograph; her babbly happiness and scatter-brained inattentiveness that gradually gave way, as the afternoon wore on, to tearful frustration at getting sums wrong and failing to memorise the names of flowers; her poor appetite at dinner-time and hungry fretfulness at bedtime; her general air of having been pumped full of a foreign substance she couldn't digest.

'She claims you told her we're all going to go back to the photographers again, very soon,' says Sugar.

'I . . . I said no such thing,' objects William, frowning as he comes to the conclusion that life is a morass of misconstruance and treachery: even one's own child, as soon as one makes a generous gesture, calls trouble down upon one's head!

'She insists that you promised,' says Sugar.

'Well, she's m-mistaken.'

Sugar rubs her tired eyes. The flesh of her fingers is so rough, and the flesh of her eyelids so tender, she feels she could do herself an injury.

'I think,' she says, 'that if you mean to pay more attention to Sophie, it might be better to do it while I'm present.'

William rears up on his elbows and glowers at her, incredulous. First Sophie and now Sugar! How fertile with complications and inconvenience females can be!

'Are you telling me,' he enquires tersely, 'w-when and under w-what circumstances I sh-should see my own daughter?'

Sugar tips her head in submission, softens her tone as much as she can. 'Oh no, William, please don't think that. You're doing wonderfully well, and I admire you for it.' Still he glowers; dear Christ, what else can she say? Should she keep her mouth shut now, or is there anything useful she can do with it? *My my, you've learned a dictionary full of words, haven't you, dear?* Mrs Castaway taunts her from the past. *And only two of them will do you the slightest bit of good in this life: 'Yes', and 'Money'.*

Sugar takes another deep breath. 'Agnes's requirements made things *so* difficult for you,' she commiserates, 'for *so* many years, and now it's awkward, I know. And Sophie really is terribly grateful for any interest you show in her, and so am I. I only wonder if it might be possible for you . . . for *us* . . . to be together a little more often. As a . . . as a family. So to speak.'

She swallows hard, fearful that she's gone too far. But wasn't it *he* who wanted a photograph of the three of them together? What was that picture leading to, if not to this?

'I'm doing all I p-possibly can,' he warns her, 'to keep this w-wretched household functioning.'

His self-pity tempts her to shoot back a volley of her own, but she manages to resist; he's clenching his fists, his knuckles are white, his face is white, she ought to have known better, their future is about to shatter like a glass flung against a wall, God let her find the right words and she'll never ask for anything more. With a rustle of skirts she slips from behind the desk and kneels at his side, laying her hand solicitously over his.

'Oh, William, *please* let's not call this household wretched. You have achieved great things this year, *magnificent* things.' Heart thumping, she slides her arm around his neck, but thank God, he doesn't push her aside or explode into a rage. 'Of course what befell Agnes was a tragedy,' she presses on, stroking his shoulder, 'but it was a mercy too, in a way, wasn't it? All that worry and . . . and scandal, for all those years, and now at last you're free of it.' He is slackening; first one of his hands, then the other, settles on her waist. What a narrow escape she's had! 'And Rackham's is having such a *superb* year,' she goes on. 'Half the problems we're facing are caused by its growth, we mustn't forget that. And it's a *happy* household you have here, honestly it is. All the servants are very friendly to me, William, and I can assure you, from what I've overheard, they're quite contented, and they think the world of you . . .'

He gazes up into her face, confused, sorrowful, needy, like a masterless dog. She kisses him on the mouth, strokes the insides of his thighs, nuzzles her knobbly wrist against his soft genital bulge.

'Remember what I told you when we first met, my love,' she whispers. 'I will do anything you ask of me. *Anything.*'

Gently, he restrains her arm as she begins to gather up her skirts.

'It's late,' he sighs. 'We should be in bed.'

She takes hold of his hand and guides it through the warm cottony layers towards her naked flesh. 'My opinion exactly.' If he can only feel what's between her legs for one second, she'll have him. More than any other incitement, it's a woman's juices he finds irresistible.

'No, I'm serious,' he says. 'Look at the time.'

Obediently, she consults the clock, and while her head is turned, he wriggles away from her embrace. It's half past eleven. At Mrs Castaway's, half past eleven was the peak of evening trade. Even in Priory Close, William would sometimes visit her as late as midnight, bringing life and noise into her quiescent rooms as he barged in from the street, his over-coat dappled with rain, his voice rich with desire. So closely attuned were they then, that she could tell by the way he embraced her exactly which orifice he would plump for.

'Oh, Lord, I'm tired,' he groans, as the grandfather clock tolls the half-hour. 'No more correspondence, please. Back into the breach tomorrow, eh?'

Sugar kisses him on the forehead.

'Whatever you say, William,' she says.

Next morning, Sugar prepares Sophie as usual. She helps her dress, break-fasts with her, installs her at her writing-desk in the school-room. Mere minutes into the lesson, an upsurge of nausea prompts Sugar to hurry out the door, taking deep breaths of an atmosphere that is suddenly stiflingly suffused with the flavour of oversweet porridge and chloral. She pauses on the landing, so dizzy she doubts she can reach her bedroom before vomiting, but then the constitution of the air seems to change, and the urgency passes.

She stands poised at the top of the staircase. The stairs are quite still, although the walls and ceiling continue to revolve slowly. An optical illusion. The light is dim this morning, and the traces of Agnes's blood wholly invisible. How many steps has this staircase? Many, many. The receiving hall is far, far below. Sugar stands poised. Her hands are laid one over the other, cradling the curve of her belly. She forces herself to remove them. The house breathes in and out. It wants to help her; it knows the trouble she's in; it knows what's best for her. She steps forward, then notices she's cradling her belly again. She spreads her arms wide, like wings, and the blood in her head pumps so hard that the gas-lights pulse in sympathy. She closes her eyes, and lets herself fall.

'Mr Rackham! Mr Rackham!' (*Bam, bam, bam,* on his study door.) 'Mr Rackham! Mr Rackham!' (*Bam, bam, bam!*)

William bounds out from behind his desk, and opens up so abruptly that Letty almost raps her knuckles against his heaving chest.

'Oh, Mr Rackham!' she squeaks frantically. 'Miss Sugar's fallen downstairs!'

He pushes past her, strides across the landing and looks down the long, long swath of carpeted steps. The body of Sugar lies sprawled far below, a tangle of black skirts, white underclothing, loose red hair and splayed limbs. She's motionless as a doll.

With one hand sliding on the banister to prevent a similar accident befalling him, William leaps down the stairs two and three at a time.

A short while later, Sugar's plunge through unconsciousness ends with a gentle slap to her cheek. She's lying on her own bed, with William standing over her. The last thing she can remember is flying through space, ecstatic with terror.

'How did I get here?'

William's face, though careworn, is not angry. In fact, she detects a faint glow of loving concern for her – or of exertion.

'Rose and I carried you,' he says.

Sugar looks around for Rose, but no, she's alone with her lover . . . her employer . . . whatever he is to her now.

'I lost my footing,' she pleads.

'W-we're an accident-prone household, to be sure,' he jokes mirthlessly.

Sugar tries to lift herself up on her elbows, but is made helpless by a stab of pain like a knife through her ribs. She cranes her head forward, chin on breastbone, and notices two things: her hair has come loose from its pins, untidy masses of it falling all around her face; and her skirts are rucked up, exposing her underwear.

'The servants,' she frets. 'Did they see me disordered like this?'

William laughs despite himself. 'You do w-worry about some queer things, Sugar.'

She laughs too, and tears spring to her eyes. It's such a relief to hear him speak her name. She pictures him as he might have been a few minutes ago, carrying her upstairs in his arms – then reminds herself that he didn't manage it alone, and that the ascent was most probably blundering and undignified.

'I'm so sorry, William. I . . . I lost . . .'

'Doctor Curlew is on his way.'

Sugar feels a chill at the thought of Doctor Curlew, whom she knows only from Agnes's diaries, hurrying towards her. She imagines him gliding along the street, supernaturally fast, his eyes glowing like candles, his taloned hands disguised in gloves, his black bag teeming with maggots. Robbed of Mrs Rackham, his intended prey, he'll make do with torturing Sugar instead.

'I-is that necessary?' she says. 'Look: I'm all right.' She lifts her arms and legs and wriggles them slightly, panting with pain, to which William's response is a glare of pity and distaste, as if she were a giant cockroach, or raving mad.

'Don't move from this bed,' he commands her, an edge of steel in his voice.

Sugar lies waiting, breathing shallowly to keep on the right side of the pain. What damage has she done in one moment of insanity? Her right ankle is stiff and sore, and she can feel her heart's pulse beating in it; her ribcage feels broken, as if splinters of sharp white bone are needling the soft red membranes of her organs. And for what? Has she ever *known* a woman who induced a miscarriage by falling downstairs? It's another fiction, a fairytale that whores tell each other . . . Harriet Paley miscarried after being beaten black and blue, but that was different: William's hardly likely to punch and kick her in the belly, is he? (Although he does sometimes get a look in his eye that makes her wonder if he's considering it . . .)

There's a knock at her door, the knob turns, and a tall man walks into her bedroom.

'Miss Sugar is it?' he says, in an affable, businesslike tone. 'I'm Doctor Curlew: please allow me . . .'

Holding his bag before him like a diplomatic gift, he steps towards her, with scuffed leather shoes that are not cloven, eyes that do not glow, and wisps of grey in his beard. Far from resembling the Devil, he much resembles Emmeline Fox, though the long face looks handsomer on him than it does on her.

'Do you recall,' he asks respectfully as he kneels at her bedside, 'how far you fell, and what part of your person took the brunt?'

'No, I don't recall,' she says, recalling the uncanny, attenuated second when her spirit floated free of her body, suspended in the air, while a lifeless dummy of flesh and cloth began to tumble down the steps. 'It all happened so suddenly.'

Doctor Curlew opens his bag and removes a sharp metallic instrument, which proves to be a buttonhook. 'Please allow me, Miss,' he murmurs, and she nods permission.

With callused but gentle hands, Doctor Curlew proceeds to examine his patient, manifestly uninterested in anything except the state of her bones beneath the flesh. He removes or rolls up her clothing one item at a time, and replaces each in turn, except for her right boot. When he pulls down her pantalettes and lays his palms on her naked belly, Sugar blushes crimson, but he merely prods her with his thumbs, satisfies himself that she's not in pain there, and digresses to her hips, instructing her, in a dispassionate tone, to attempt various movements.

'You are fortunate,' he pronounces at last. 'It's not uncommon for people to break their arms or even their necks falling off a chair. *You* have fallen down a staircase, and all you have to show for it is two cracked ribs that will heal themselves in time, and a number of bruises of which you may not be aware yet, but soon will be. You also have a sprained, but not broken,

ankle. By tomorrow morning it will have swollen to the size of my fist . . .'
(he holds up his loosely curled fist for her appraisal) 'and I don't expect
you'll be able to move it then as you can still move it now. Don't let this
alarm you.'

Curlew reaches into his bag, withdraws a large roll of thick white bandage, and plucks off the paper-clip that holds it snug.

'I am going to bind your ankle tightly with this bandage,' he explains,
as he lifts her leg off the bed and onto his knee, ignoring her gasps. 'I must
ask you *not* to remove the binding, no matter how tempted you may be.
It will grow tighter as your injury swells, and you may imagine it's about
to burst. I assure you that's impossible.'

When he's finished with her leg, Doctor Curlew pulls down her dress
as if it were a blanket or a shroud.

'Don't do anything foolish,' he says as he rises, 'keep to your bed as
much as possible, and you'll make a good recovery.'

'But . . . but I have duties to perform,' protests Sugar feebly, hoisting
herself up.

He looks down at her, a twinkle in his dark eyes, as though entertaining a suspicion that the duties for which William Rackham has engaged
her can all be performed horizontally.

'I'll arrange,' he reassures her solemnly, 'for you to be equipped with
a crutch.'

'Thank you. Thank you so much.'

'No bother at all.'

And, with a click of his satchel, the man who's identified, in the diaries
hidden under Sugar's bed, as the Demon Inquisitor, the Leech Master,
Belial, and the Usher of Maggots, bids her a polite good day and, pausing
only to waggle one finger in a gesture of *remember: keep out of mischief*, leaves
her in peace.

Exactly as Doctor Curlew predicted, Sugar wakes up on the morning after
her fall grievously tempted to remove the binding from her foot. She does
so at once, and feels much better.

Before long, however, her liberated foot swells to half the size again of
the uninjured one, and she's unable to rest it on the floor without severe
pain, let alone walk on it. Limping is all but impossible, and hopping is
out of the question for, quite apart from the indignity, the exertion makes

her bruises hurt more. Dragging her body around the room by sheer force of will, she has to admit she can't possibly be a governess to Sophie in this state.

Before her fear can grow into a panic, it's quelled by the arrival of a gift from her master, delivered to her door by Rose: a dark-lacquered pine-wood crutch. Whether William already owned it or has purchased it especially for her she dares not ask. But she hobbles back and forth, three-legged, and marvels how a simple tool can change the world, making light of dark prospects and turning calamity into inconvenience. A staff of wood with a crossbar, and she's upright again! A miracle. Shortly after lunch, having missed only half a day of Sophie's lessons, she emerges from her room with her books under one arm and the crutch under the other, ready to discharge her duties.

She knows Sophie well enough by now not to be surprised to find her sitting at her writing-table in the school-room, as patiently as if it were four minutes and not four hours since Rose delivered her there. The mark of Rose's grooming is unmistakable: a certain way of brushing and pinning the hair, different from Sugar's, that makes Sophie look more like Agnes. On the table before her is arranged the sole evidence of her morning's idle-ness: drawings of houses, half a dozen of them, in blue pencil with red windows and grey smoke. Sophie covers them with her palms, as if caught in an act of mischief, as if she ought instead to have been deeply immersed in the Moorish Wars.

'I'm sorry, Miss.'

'Nothing to be sorry about, Sophie,' sighs Sugar, slumping on her crutch in disappointment. Mad though it was to hope for, she would have preferred to be received with a yelp of relief and an outburst of childish kisses. 'Here, Sophie,' she says, twitching one shoulder, 'take these books from under my arm. I'm afraid I shall drop them any moment.'

Sophie leaps up from her seat to obey, without showing any sign of having noticed her governess's disability. She reaches up to extract the books clamped in Sugar's armpit, and her fingers bumble against Sugar's bosom as she does so, grazing the nipple through the fabric. Sugar adjusts her centre of gravity and gasps at the pain in her foot.

'Thank you,' she says.

Back in her place, Sophie waits for guidance. Her determination to pretend there's nothing different about her governess today is obvious;

when Sugar sways on her crutch and clumsily lowers herself into a chair, the child averts her eyes in order not to witness the inelegant spectacle.

'For goodness' sake, Sophie,' cried Sugar, 'aren't you a *little* curious to know what's happened to me?'

'Yes, Miss.'

'Well then, if you *are* curious, why don't you ask?'

'I . . .' Sophie frowns, and looks down into her lap. It's as though she's been tricked by a cleverer opponent, manoeuvred into a trap of logic in the name of education. 'Rose told me you fell down the stairs, Miss, and that I mustn't stare . . .'

Sugar shuts her eyes tight, and tries to summon what she'll need to get through the afternoon. *Please hold me, Sophie*, she thinks. *Please hold me.*

But what she says is: 'The doctor says I'll be better in no time.'

'Yes, Miss.'

Sugar peers across at the drawings on Sophie's writing-table. Each of the emblematic houses has depictions of three human figures drawn alongside it: one small, two big. Even from Sugar's upside-down perspective, the man in the dark suit and top hat is unmistakably William, and the puppet-sized girl with too few fingers is Sophie. But who is the female parent? The drawing has a heart-shaped face and blue eyes like Agnes, but is tall, as tall as William, and the lines of her abundant hair are sketched in red. For an instant Sugar is thrilled, then she notices that Sophie hasn't a yellow colouring-pencil on the table, only red, blue and grey. Also, who's to say that all grown-ups aren't the same height to her?

'All right then,' Miss Sugar declares, clasping her hands together. 'Arithmetic.'

That afternoon, William Rackham answers his own correspondence. He answers it in a painstaking, rather clumsy hand: but he manages. By folding his crooked ring finger over his middle one, he keeps its tip from smudging the ink, and by holding the pen almost vertical between his thumb and forefinger, he can achieve quite a bit of fluency.

I have read your letter, he writes. *And now I'm damn well replying to it*, he thinks. The direct connection between his brain and his pen has been restored, however torturously.

But never mind the discomfort. What a blessing it is to be independent – and what a relief to be able to tell that blackguard Pankey exactly what's what, without Sugar taking all the sting out of his words. Some people *deserve* to be stung! Grover Pankey especially! If Rackham Perfumeries is to survive into the next century and beyond, it will need a strong hand at the helm now – a hand that doesn't stand for nonsense. How dare Pankey suggest that ivory is bound to crack when it's carved as thin as Rackham's pots require?

Perhaps you have lately engaged the services of a lower class of elephant, he scrawls. *The pots you showed me in Yarmouth were sturdy enough. I suggest you return to that pedigree of beast.*

Yours . . .

Ah well, perhaps not 'yours' much longer. But there's more than one ivory merchant in the world, Mr Grover Hanky-Pankey!

William signs his name, and frowns. The signature looks wrong, a childish approximation of his old one, inferior even to Sugar's sleepiest forgery. Well, what of it? The way he signed his name before he took control of Rackham Perfumeries was different from the way he signed it after, and the signature on letters he wrote as a schoolboy bore little relation to the signature on his wedding certificate. Life goes on. Change, as the Prime Minister himself has said, is constant.

He seals the letter, and is gripped by the urge to post it at once, to hurry out to Portobello Road and slip it into the nearest pillar-box, in case Sugar should come unexpectedly into the room and spy the letter lying here. The fresh air would do him good, anyhow. Ever since the hullabaloo yesterday he's been restless, searching for a good reason to leave the gloom of his house, to walk down a public street with a spring in his step. Should he stay or should he go?

For a little while longer he delays, and the satisfaction of tearing into Pankey evaporates like essence of tuberose flying off a handkerchief. He reflects on the long, hard journey he has made since taking the reins of this perfumery. Again the vision of William Rackham the author and critic returns to haunt him, and he feels a pang of regret for the man who never was, the man whose pen was feared and admired and who set fire to boring correspondents with the tip of his cigar. That man had perfectly formed fingers, long golden hair, a radiant wife, a keen nose not for tainted jasmine but for the great Art and Literature of the future. Instead, here he is, a widower, a stammerer, grunting with the effort of penning his own signature on letters to merchants he loathes. The bonds he once enjoyed with his family, friends and fellow travellers: all altered beyond recognition. Altered beyond rescue? If he doesn't make amends now while he still has the chance, a once-intimate relationship will sour into estrangement or even hostility.

So, he swallows his pride, leaves the house, commandeers Cheesman for a ride into the city, and travels direct to Torrington Mews, Bloomsbury, in the hope of catching Mr Philip Bodley at home.

Five hours later, William Rackham is a happy man. Yes, for the first time since Agnes's death, or even – yes, why not admit it? – long before, he is a truly happy man. The passage of a mere five hours has ferried him from the brink of despond to the shore of contentment.

He's strolling along a narrow street in Soho, after sundown, slightly drunk, accosted from all sides by pedlars, urchins and whores wanting his money for grubby goods not worth tuppence. Their leering, gap-toothed faces and gesticulating sleeves ought to fill him with anxiety, given how recently he was beaten half to death by just such ruffians in the dark streets of Frome. But no, he's unafraid of being attacked; he is fearless, for he has his friends with him. Yes, not just Bodley, but Ashwell as well! There's really nothing, nothing in this world, quite as comforting as the company of men whom one has known since boyhood.

'We're founding our own publishing house, Bill,' says Ashwell, his head swivelling in curiosity as he's passed by a hawker wearing twelve hats, with two others twirling on his fingers.

Bodley thrusts the pommel of his cane playfully at one of the prostitutes waving at them from the doorways. A small half-asleep boy, minding a cart of worthless jugs and pots he's been instructed to sell, flinches for fear the cane is a projectile about to smack into his snot-encrusted nose.

'We couldn't find anyone willing to publish our next book—' Bodley explains.

'—*Art As Understood by the Working Man*—'

'—so we're going to damn well publish it ourselves.'

'*Art as* . . .? Publish it yourselves . . .? But why . . .?' asks William, shaking his head in amused befuddlement. 'From the title, it sounds to be a . . . a less contentious book than your previous ones . . .'

'Don't you believe it!' crows Ashwell.

'It's a brilliantly simple idea!' declares Bodley. 'We got hold of a wide variety of rude working folk – chimneysweeps, fish merchants, kitchen-maids, tobacconists, match-sellers, and so forth – and we read them bits of Ruskin's *Academy Notes* . . .'

'. . . and showed them engravings of the paintings . . .'

'. . . and then asked them their opinion!' Bodley contorts his face in a caricature of donkeyish intellect, and pretends to be examining an engraving held at arm's length. 'Wot you say dis one's name wos? Afferdighty?'

'A Greek lady, sir,' mock-explains Ashwell, instantly playing the straight man to Bodley's buffoon. 'A goddess.'

'Greek? Blimey. Where's 'er black moustache, then?'

Whereupon Bodley re-composes his face into a different character, a more thoughtful man, scratching his head doubtfully. 'Whe-e-ell, maybe I'm hignorant – but this Afferdighty 'as got mighty queer dugs in my hopinion. She's got 'em where I never seen dugs on any woman down *my* street – an' I seen plenty!'

Rackham laughs uproariously – a good belly laugh such as he's not enjoyed since . . . well, not since he was *last* out with his friends.

'But why on earth,' he demands, 'are your usual publishers refusing to publish this one? It'll make them just as much money, I'm sure!'

'That's precisely the problem,' smirks Bodley.

'Every one of our books has lost money!' declares Ashwell proudly.

'No!' protests William.

'Yes!' cries Ashwell. 'Oodles!' And he laughs like a hyena.

William reels to one side, misjudging his footing on the cobbles, and Bodley catches him. He's a little drunker than he'd thought.

'Lost money? But that's impossible!' he insists. 'I've met so many people who've read your books . . .'

'Oh, no doubt you've met every single one of 'em,' says Ashwell breezily. Not twenty feet away, a gin-sozzled old woman slaps her elfin pigeon-chested husband hard against his sparse-haired skull. He falls like a ninepin, to a scattered chorus of guffaws.

'*The Great Social Evil* will recoup its costs, in time,' qualifies Bodley, 'thanks to masturbating students and frustrated widows like Emmeline Fox . . .'

'But nobody bought *The Efficacy of Prayer* except the miserable old nincompoops we quoted in it.'

William is still grinning, but his mind, honed by his long year's experience as a businessman, is having some difficulty with the sums.

'So let me see if I understand you,' he says. 'Instead of letting a publisher lose money, you mean to lose money yourselves . . .'

Bodley and Ashwell make identical dismissive hand gestures, to show they've considered this matter carefully.

'We'll publish pornography too,' declares Ashwell, 'to cover the losses incurred by our worthier books. Pornography of the rankest order. The demand is immense, Bill; the whole of England is desperate for sodomy!'

'Yes, the *arse*-whole!' puns Bodley.

'We'll publish a guide for men-about-town that's updated each month!' continues Ashwell, his cheeks flushed with enthusiasm. 'Not like that damned useless *More Sprees*, which gives you a cockstand reading about some girl, and you go to the house, only to find she's dead, or the place has gone to the dogs, or it's full of Pentecostals!'

William's smile fades. The reference to *More Sprees in London* has reminded him of another reason why he and his chums became estranged in the first place: Bodley and Ashwell were aware of a prostitute called Sugar, a prostitute who abruptly disappeared from circulation. What might they think if they visited the Rackham house and heard the name 'Miss Sugar' mentioned by a servant? Highly unlikely, but still William changes the subject.

'You know,' he says, 'I've been chained to my desk so long, it's bliss to be out on the town with my old friends.' (His stutter, he notes, is completely gone: all it takes is a few drinks and the right company!)

'*Fidus Achates*!' cries Bodley, slapping William on the back. 'Remember the time the bullers chased us all the way from Parker's Piece to our set?'

'Remember the time the proctor found that pretty slut Lizzie sleeping in the Master's Lodge?'

'Happy days, happy days,' says William, though he has no memory of the incident.

'That's the spirit,' beams Ashwell. 'But *these* days can be every bit as happy, Bill, if you let 'em. Your perfume business is locomoting along at fearsome speed, I hear. You don't need to be stoking it every minute of the day, what?'

'Ah, you'd be surprised,' sighs William. 'Everything threatens to fall apart constantly. Everything. Constantly! Nothing in this damn world takes care of itself.'

'Steady man, steady. Some things are wonderfully uncomplicated. Shove any old cock into any old cunt, and the rest happens automatically.'

William grunts agreement, but in his heart he's far from sure. Lately, he has come to dread Sugar's overtures of love, for his pego has remained flaccid when he would most wish to have use of it. Is it still in working order? It gets stiff at inconvenient times, particularly in his sleep, but lets him down when the moment is ripe. How much longer can he keep Sugar ignorant of the fact that he's ceased, it seems, to be fully a man? How many more nights can he plead exhaustion or the lateness of the hour?

'If I don't keep my wits about me,' he complains, 'Rackham Perfumeries will be extinct by the time the century's out. And it's not as if I have anyone to pass it on to.'

Ashwell pauses to buy an apple from a girl he likes the look of. He gives her sixpence, much more than she's asking, and she bows, almost spilling her remaining apples out of her basket.

'Thank you, poppet,' he winks, biting into the firm flesh, and walks on. 'So . . .' he remarks to William, his mouth mumbly with pulp, 'So you don't want to marry Constance, is that it?'

William stops in his tracks, astounded.

'Constance?'

'Our dear Lady Bridgelow,' says Ashwell, making the effort to enunciate clearly, as if Rackham's bafflement may be nothing more than a problem with diction.

William sways forward, contemplates the ground, his vision blurring in and out of focus. A criss-cross pattern of furry muck is stuck to the cobbles, either horse-dung with a high quotient of thistles or the much-dispersed vestiges of a squashed dog's pelt.

'I . . . I wasn't aware that Constance had any desire to marry me.'

Bodley and Ashwell groan good-naturedly, and Bodley grabs him by the shoulder of his coat, jerking it in exasperation.

'Come on, Bill, d'you expect her to get down on her bended knee and ask you herself? She has her pride.'

William digests this as they walk on. They've turned the corner into King Street, a somewhat wider thoroughfare. Prostitutes on both sides wave to them, confident that this evening's policeman has been amply persuaded to spend his energies on pickpockets and brawlers.

'Best fuck in London 'ere!' shouts a tipsy trollop.

'Getcher roast chestnuts 'ere!' bawls a man on the opposite footpath.

Bodley pauses, not for the chestnuts or the trollop, but because he's just stepped on something squishy. He lifts his left shoe and peers down at the sole, trying to determine whether the thing – now mingled with the oily mud between the cobblestones – was a turd or merely a lump of rotten fruit.

'What do you think, Philip?' says Ashwell, grinning over his shoulder at the drunken lass who's still blowing him kisses. 'Ready for a bit of fun?'

'Always, Edward, always. What about the lovely Apollonia?' As an aside to William, he explains: 'We've found a cracker of a girl, Bill, an absolute cracker – a woolly-haired African. She's at Mrs Jardine's house. Her cunt is dark purple, like a passionfruit, and they've taught her to speak like a debutante from Belgravia: it's the most comical thing!'

'Try her while the trying's good, Bill: she'll be snaffled by some diplomat or ambassador soon, and disappear into the bowels of Westminster!'

Bodley and Ashwell stand topper to topper and consult their fob-watches, briefly conferring over the possibility of going to Mrs Jardine's, but they soon agree that Apollonia is unlikely to be available at this hour. In any case, William gets the impression that, despite singing the praises of her exotic flavour, they've sampled it too recently, and hanker for something different.

'So what do you fancy?' says Ashwell. 'Mrs Terence's is nearby . . .'

'It's half past nine,' says Bodley. 'Bess and . . . whatsername – the Welsh one – will be taken, and I don't much care for the others. And you know what Mrs Terence is like: she won't let you leave once you're in.'

'Mrs Ford's?'

'Expensive,' sniffs Bodley, 'for what you get.'

'Yes, but prompt.'

'Yes, but it's in Panton Street. If fast service is what we're after, we could pop in to Madame Audrey's just around the corner.'

Listening to them, William realises that his fears were in vain: these men have already forgotten Sugar, forgotten her entirely. She is ancient history, her name erased by a hundred other names since; the girl who once seemed to shine like a beacon in the murky vastness of London has been reduced to a glimmering pinprick of light in amongst countless similar glimmers. Life goes on, and there is never an end to the people surging through it.

'What about those three over there?' says Bodley. 'They have a cheerful air about 'em.' He nods towards a trio of whores giggling in the window-light of a chandler's shop. 'I'm not in the mood for hoity-toity pretensions tonight, or misery.'

The two men walk over to the waving women, and William, fearful of being left stranded and unprotected, tags along. He tries to keep his eyes on the dark street to the left and right of the women, but he's helplessly drawn to their vulgar display of lamp-lit taffeta and pink bosom. They're a cheeky threesome, well-groomed in an overdressed way, with masses of hair spilling out from under their too-elaborate bonnets. William has the uneasy feeling he's met them before.

'Nice weather we're 'avin',' simpers one.

'You never 'ad no one like me, ducks,' says another.

'Nor me neither,' says the third.

Are these the same three women who pestered him in The Fireside, when he first met Sugar? They look younger, thinner, and their dresses are less ornate, but there's something about them . . . Dear Heaven, could Fate really throw up such a hideous coincidence? Does one of these powdered doxies have it on the tip of her tongue to hail him as 'Mr Hunt' and ask him how his books are faring, or demand to know how his tryst with Sugar ended?

'In the mouth, how much?' Bodley is enquiring of the woman with the fullest lips. She leans forward and murmurs in his ear, smoothly settling her forearms on his shoulders.

Within seconds, the transaction has begun. Ashwell, Bodley and an unwilling William have entered a shadowy cul-de-sac scarcely wide enough to accommodate the combined bulk of a squatting woman and a standing man. Ashwell watches Bodley being serviced, and gropes under the skirts of another woman while she strokes his exposed prick, whose size and firm-ness impress William, even at a glimpse, as demoralisingly superior to his own. The third woman stands with her back to William, facing out towards the open street, watching for unwanted company. By now William is certain – as certain as he can be – that he's never seen these three women before. He stares at the back of the one keeping watch, and tries to imagine himself lifting up her bustle, pulling down her drawers, and fucking her, but she seems to him devoid of erotic allure, a darkened Madame Tussaud's manikin of indifferently stitched dress material, a horse-hair bustle, a neck that's too thick, a glinting spine of buttons one of which, annoyingly, dangles loose from its buttonhole. His manhood is soft and damp; he has left his best years far behind him; he will spend the rest of his life worrying about Rackham Perfumeries; his daughter will grow up ugly and unmarried and ungrateful, the laughing-stock of his dwindling circle; and then, one day, in the middle of penning a futile letter with his crippled hand, he'll clutch at his heart and die. When did it all go wrong? It all went wrong when he married Agnes. It all went wrong when—

Suddenly he becomes aware of Bodley groaning in satisfaction. The woman is almost finished with him; as he approaches orgasm, he agitates one trembling hand in the air, and makes as if to clamp hold of the back of her head. She intercepts him in mid-swing, grabbing his arm first by the wrist, then curling her fingers inside his, so that she and Bodley are holding hands. It's a peculiar gesture of control, of checkmated forces, which has the appearance of utmost tenderness and mutual urgency. William is instantly, powerfully aroused, and what seemed impossible a minute ago now feels imperative.

'Oh God!' cries Bodley as he spends. The girl keeps hold of him, squeezing his hand tight, nuzzling her brow against his belly. Only when Bodley slumps against the alley wall does she let him go and tip her head back, licking her lips.

Now! The moment is now! William steps forward, fetching his swollen manhood out of his trousers.

'Now me!' he commands hoarsely, his whole body prickling with anxious sweat, for already he can feel his organ's rigid flesh begin to lose its charge of blood. Mercifully, the prostitute delays no longer than an eye's-blink before taking him in her mouth and clapping her palms on his buttocks. William sways, momentarily off-balance; oh God, a pratfall at this juncture would be the end of him! But it's all right, she has him secure, her fingers dig into his flesh, her mouth and tongue are expert.

'Go on, sir, stick it in,' says another female voice from behind him, addressing Ashwell. 'You can afford it, sir, and you won't be sorry.'

'I haven't a sheath on me.'

'I take good care of meself, sir. I've been to the doctor only last week, sir, and he says I'm clean as a kitten.'

'Even so . . .' says Ashwell, panting, 'let it spill . . .'

'It's a fine silky cunt I 'ave, sir. A connoisseur's cunt.'

'Even so . . .'

William, dizzy with mounting excitement, cannot understand Ashwell's qualms. Fuck the girl and have done with it! Fuck all the females in the world while the fucking is good! He feels as though he could spend like a geyser, filling first one woman, then the next, in their mouths, their cunts, their arses, leaving a great mound of them lolling and rumpled . . . Ah!

A few seconds later William Rackham is lying flat on the ground, unconscious, with five people standing over him.

'Give him air,' says Ashwell.

'What's the matter with him?' says one of the whores anxiously.

'Too much to drink,' says Bodley, but he sounds none too sure.

'He was given a terrible beating by bughunters not so long ago,' says Ashwell. 'They cracked his head open, I believe.'

'Oh, poor lamb!' coos the woman with the full lips. 'Will 'e be like this always?'

'Come on, Bodley, help me with him.'

The two men seize their friend under the armpits, and heave him a few inches off the ground. Taking umbrage at being ignored, the ringleader whore tugs at their sleeves, to regain the gentlemen's attention before they become too preoccupied.

'I've only been paid for one,' she reminds them. 'Fair's fair.'

'And I ain't been paid at all,' bleats the girl who kept watch, as though, of the three, the most debauched use has been made of her. The third woman frowns, unable to think how to add her voice to the grievances, given that Ashwell was interrupted before reaching the fulfilment he'd paid for.

'Here's . . . here's . . .' Ashwell claws a handful of coins, mostly shillings, from his pocket, and pushes them into her hands, while the other two crane their necks to see. 'You can do the arithmetic between you, can't you?' Fretful now about the unconscious Rackham, he has no appetite for haggling. Christ almighty: first Henry, then Agnes . . . If there's one more death in this wretched family . . . ! And what a beastly stroke of fate, if those eminent swells Philip Bodley and Edward Ashwell should be forced to inaugurate their new career as publishers by carrying a corpse through the streets of Soho in search of the nearest police station!

'Bill! Bill! Are you with us?' Ashwell barks, patting William roughly on the cheek.

'I . . . I'm with you,' Rackham replies, whereupon, from the mouths of five onlookers – yes, even from the whores, for they've not found it in their hearts to scarper – issues a profound and wholly mutual sigh of relief.

'Well . . .' says the eldest woman, adjusting her bonnet and casting an eye on the flickering lights of the thoroughfare. 'Good night, then, all.' And she leads her sisters out of the dark.

For another few seconds Bodley and Ashwell loiter in the cul-de-sac, tidying their clothing, combing their hair, using each other as a mirror. You'll not see them again, so take a good last look at them now.

'Take me home,' groans a voice from somewhere near their trouser-cuffs. 'I want to go to bed.'

THIRTY-THREE

ent up to her room in disgrace, Sugar indulges, at long last, in a tantrum. A solitary, silent tantrum, in the privacy of her drab little bed-chamber, but no less a tantrum for that.

How dare William tell her it's none of her business what hour he comes home! How dare he tell her the mud on his clothing is his own affair, and that he owes her no explanation! How dare he tell her he's perfectly capable of handling his own correspondence, and has no further need of her flatteries and her forgeries! How dare he tell her that instead of lurking in wait for his return from an innocent visit on old friends, she'd be much better off sleeping, as her eyes are constantly bloodshot and ugli-fied by the dark rings under them!

Sugar kneels at her bedside in the candlelight, William's expensive Christmas gift of Shakespeare's *Tragedies* in her lap, and tears out the pages by the handful, illustrations and all, clawing at the fragile paper with her brittle, jagged nails. How thin and smooth the pages are, like the pages of a Bible or a dictionary, as if made from glazed starch, or the stuff that ciga-rettes are wrapped in. She scrunches them inside her fist, *Macbeth*, *Lear*, *Hamlet*, *Romeo and Juliet*, *Antony and Cleopatra*, all of them shredding under her nails, useless blather about ancient aristocracies. She'd thought William bought them for her in recognition – in *honour* – of her intellect, a coded message in front of his servants that he knew her soul to be a much finer thing than theirs. Tripe! He's an empty vulgarian, a crass oaf who might as soon have bought her a gilded elephant's foot or a jewelled chamber-pot had his eye not been diverted by this 'hand-tooled' assortment of Shakespeare. Damn him! *This* is what she thinks of his oily attempts to buy her gratitude!

As she rips and rends, her body convulses with infantile sobs, an inces-
sant rapid spasming, and the tears run down her cheeks. Does he think
she's blind, and without a sense of smell? He stank of more than mud
when he stumbled into the house, supported on either side by Bodley and
Ashwell; he stank of cheap perfume, the sort worn by whores. He stank
of sexual connection – a connection he'd probably say (in his favourite
phrase lately) had 'nothing to do with' her! Damn him, snoring off his
debauches in that bedroom where she's never been invited! She ought to
burst in on him with a knife, slit his belly open and watch the contents
spill out in a torrent of gore!

After a while, her sobs subside, and her hands grow weary of clawing
the pages. She slumps against her dresser, surrounded by crumpled wads
of paper, her naked toes lost under them. What if William should come in
and find her like this? She crawls forward on her knees and picks up the
paper-balls, tossing them into the fireplace. They're consumed at once,
flaring for the merest instant before shrivelling into ash.

Better she should be burning Agnes's diaries than her Christmas gifts
from William. The volumes of Shakespeare are harmless, whereas the diaries
could betray her any day or night. Where's the good in continuing to hide
them under her bed, when she's gleaned all she can from them, and they
can only cause trouble? Agnes won't be back to reclaim them, that's for
certain.

Sugar fetches one of the diaries into the light. Over the months, every
speck of dried mud has been rubbed off, so that the delicate volume no
longer looks as though it was rescued from a grave of damp earth, but
merely looks ancient, like a relic of a bygone century. Sugar opens it, and
the ruined fragments of its absurdly dainty padlock and silver chain dangle
like jewellery over her knuckles.

> *Dear Diary,*
> *I do hope we shall be good friends.*

Sugar flips the pages, witnessing once more Agnes Pigott's struggles to
be reconciled to her new name.

> *It's only what my governess calls an appelation, after all, for the conveniance of the*
> *World At Large. I am foolish to fret so. <u>GOD</u> knows what my real name is,*
> *doesn't He?*

Sugar lays the diary to one side; she'll destroy all of them but *this* one, the very first, which is small enough to be hidden out of harm's way. She can't help thinking there would be something . . . *evil* about destroying the first words Agnes entrusted to posterity. It would be like pretending she never existed; or, no: that she began to exist only when her death provided the meat for a newspaper obituary.

Sugar extracts another diary from under the bed. It happens to be the final Abbots Langley chronicle, written by a fifteen-year-old Agnes preparing to go home and nurse her mother back to health. Dried flower-petals flutter out of its pages to the floor, crimson and white, weightless. Agnes Unwin's valedictory poem reads thus:

> *Our happy Joys of Sisterhood are done*
> *The Sun is through the redd'ning Heavens pushing*
> *Our little race of Learning now is run —*
> *For none can thwart the Future onward rushing!*

Squaring her jaw, Sugar consigns the diary to the flames. It smoulders and hisses softly. She looks away.

Another diary is fetched from its hiding-place. Its first entry relates that there has been no reply from 'the Swiss Post Office' on the matter of where to send Miss Eugenie Soon-To-Be-Schleswig's scrapbook of kittens. This volume, too, can go on the flames, when the first is consumed.

Sugar picks up a third volume. *Liebes Tagebuch . . .* it announces on its opening page. Another for the fire.

She picks up a fourth volume. It dates from the early years of Agnes's marriage to William, and begins with an unreadable hallucination of demonic harassment, decorated in the margins with hieroglyphical eyes scrawled in clotted menstrual blood.

A few pages further on, a convalescing Agnes reflects:

> *I had thought, while I was being schooled, that my old Life was being kept warm for me, like a favourite dish steaming under a silver cover, waiting for my return Home. I now know that this was a tragic dillusion. My step-father was plotting all the while, to kill my dear Mother inchmeal with his cruelty, and to sell my poor Self to the first man that would take me off his hands. He chose William <u>on purpose</u>, I can see that now! Had he selected a suitor of a loftier Class, he would have been for ever running in to me, at the places where the Upper Ten Thousand*

meet. But he <u>knew</u> that William would drag me down from the heights, and that once I was sunk as low as I am now, he need never set eyes on me again!

Well, I'm glad! Yes, glad! He wasn't my father anyway. Admittance to the grandest Ball would not be reward enough to quell my <u>revulsion</u> at his company.

All through the ages it has been like this: Females the pawns of male treach-ery. But one day, the Truth will be told.

The odour of perfumed paper turning to punk begins to permeate the room. Sugar glances at the fireplace. The diary's shape is still intact, but glows livid orange at the edges. She fetches another from under the bed, and opens it at random. It's an entry she hasn't read before, undated, but its ink is rich blue and fresh-looking.

> *Dear Holy Sister,*
> *I know You have been watching over me, and please dont think I'm not grate-ful. In my sleep You assure me All will be well, and I am comforted and rest in peace against your breast; yet on waking I am once again afraid, and all Your words melt away from me as if they were snowflakes fallen in the night. I yearn for our next meeting, a <u>bodily</u> meeting in the world outside my dreams. Will it be soon? Will it be soon? Make a mark upon this page — a touch of Your lips, a finger-print, <u>any</u> sign of Your presence — and I will know not to give up Hope.*

With a grunt of distress, Sugar throws the diary into the fireplace. Its impact sends a shower of sparks flying, and it comes to rest on top of the still-smouldering carcass of the other one, but standing precariously upright. This, as far as the scientific principle of ignition is concerned, is by far the more efficient posture: the pages are licked into flame at once.

She scrabbles under her bed once more, and what emerges is not another of Agnes's diaries, but her own novel. How her heart sinks to see it! This raggedy thing, bulging out of its stiff cardboard jacket: it's the embodi-ment of futility. All its crossed-out titles — *Scenes from the Streets*, *A Cry from the Streets*, *An Angry Cry from an Unmarked Grave*, *Women Against Men*, *Death in the House of Ill Repute*, *Who Has Now the Upper Hand?*, *The Phoenix*, *The Claws of the Phoenix*, *The Embrace of the Phoenix*, *All Ye Who Enter Here*, *The Wages of Sin*, *Come Kiss the Mouth of Hell*, and, finally, *The Fall and Rise of Sugar* — are tainted by her own juvenile delusions.

She balances the sheaf of papers on its torn and frayed spine and allows it to fall open where it will.

'But I am a father!' pleads one of the novel's doomed males, struggling impotently against the bonds the heroine has tied around his wrists and ankles. *'I have a son and a daughter, waiting for me at home!'*

'Better you had thought of that before,' said I, cutting through his shirt with my razor-sharp dress-making shears. Very intent I was upon my work, swivelling the scissors back and forth across his hairy belly.

'See?' I said, holding up a limp scrap of white cotton in the shape of a butter-fly, its two halves held together by a shirt-button. 'Isn't that pretty?'

'For pity's sake, think of my children!'

I leaned upon his chest, digging my elbows as hard as I could into his flesh, while speaking directly into his face, so close that my hot breath caused his eyes to blink. 'There is no hope for children in this world,' I informed him, hissing with fury. 'If male, they will become filthy swine like you. If female, they will be defiled by filthy swine like you. The best thing for children is not to be born; the next-best thing is to die while they are still innocent.'

Sugar groans in shame at the ravings of her old self. She ought to throw them on the flames, but she can't. And the two sacrificed diaries of Agnes's are still burning oh-so-slowly, giving off a pungent smell and smothering the coals with a veil of wilting black card. There's simply too great a volume of illicit paper here; it would take hours, days, to burn it all, and the smoke and stench would attract attention from the household beyond. With a sigh of resignation, Sugar shoves her novel, and the handful of diaries she'd condemned to extinction, back under the bed.

In the middle of the night, from the heart of the dark, a hand is laid on Sugar's thigh and shakes her gently from her sleep. She groans anxiously, anticipating her mother's words: 'You needn't shiver any more . . .' But her mother is silent. Instead, a deep male voice whispers through the gloom.

'I'm sorry, Sugar,' he is saying. 'Please forgive me.'

She opens her eyes, but finds she's burrowed wholly under the sheets, her head wrapped up in linen, her arms wrapped around her abdomen. Gasping, she emerges into the air, squinting into the radiance of an oil lamp.

'What? What?' she mutters.

'Forgive me for my oafish behaviour,' repeats William. 'I wasn't myself.'

Sugar sits up in bed and runs one hand through her tangled hair. Her palm is hot and sweaty, the hidden flesh of her belly feels suddenly cool for the lack of her hands upon it. William places the lamp on top of her dresser, then sits at the foot of her bed, his brow and nose casting black shadows over his eyes and mouth as he speaks.

'I collapsed in town. Too much too drink. You must forgive me.'

His voice, for all its imperative message, sounds flat and morbid, as if he's counselling her against thinking ill of the dead.

'Yes, yes of course, my love,' she replies, leaning forward to take his hand.

'I've been considering your opinion,' he continues dully, 'that it would be beneficial for Sophie to have more . . . outings in the company of . . . of us both.'

'Oh, yes?' says Sugar. She notes the time on the clock above his head: it's half past two in the morning. What in God's name does he have in mind at this hour? A spin in the carriage, the three of them in their night-gowns, admiring the gas-lit streets of suburbia while Cheesman serenades them with a lewd ditty?

'So, I've a-arranged . . .' says William, extracting his hand from hers and fiddling with his beard as his stammer begins to take hold. 'I-I've arranged a visit to m-my s-soap factory. For you and S-Sophie. Tomorrow a-afternoon.'

For an instant, Sugar's spirits are buoyed up on a wave of dizzy optimism almost indistinguishable from her usual morning nausea. Everything is falling into place! He's seen the light at last! He's realised that the only way to snatch happiness from the jaws of misery is to stay together, and damn what the world thinks! *Now* is the moment to throw herself into his arms, guide the palm of his hand to the curve of her belly, and tell him that immortality for the Rackham name – *his* immortality – is assured. *You think there are only two of us here in this room,* she could say. *But there are three!*

Hesitating on the brink of this outburst, the words on the tip of her tongue, she seeks out his eyes in the inky shadows of his brow, and sees only a fugitive glint. Then the last thing he said begins to niggle at her wakening brain.

'Tomorrow afternoon . . .' she echoes. 'You mean . . . today?'

'Yes.'

She blinks repeatedly. Her eyelids feel like they're lined with grit.

'Couldn't it be another day?' she suggests, very soft, to keep her voice sweet. 'You'd benefit from a lie-in, don't you think, after . . . well, after the night you've had?'

'Yes,' he concedes, 'but this visit was a-a-arranged qu-quite some time ago.'

Sugar, still blinking, strains to comprehend. 'But surely it's for *you* to decide—'

'There's another p-person coming too. S-someone whom I'm loath to i-inconvenience.'

'Oh?'

'Yes.' He cannot look her in the eye.

'I see.'

'I . . . I hoped you would.'

He reaches out to touch her. The aroma of alcohol still exudes from his pores, released in a waft from his armpits as he leans across the bed to lay his palm on her shoulder. His stubby fingers smell of semen and the perfume of street-walkers.

'I haven't told you o-often enough,' he says hoarsely, 'w-what a treasure you are.'

She sighs, and squeezes his hand briefly, letting it go before he has a chance to lock his fingers into hers.

'We'd better sleep, then,' she says, turning her face away and dropping her cheek against the pillow. 'My eyes, as you've pointed out, are bloodshot and ugly.'

She keeps still, feigning cataleptic exhaustion, staring at his shadow on the wall. She sees the magnified black shape of his hand hovering in the space above her, trembling in its arrested impulse to soothe the anger from her flesh. The stale air of her little bedroom, already muggy with burnt writing-paper, burnt book-binding thread, and the scent of betrayal, grows intolerable with the tension of his yearning to make amends. If she could force herself to sit up for just one second, ruffle his hair and kiss him on the forehead, that would probably do the trick. She nuzzles her cheek harder into her pillow, and closes her fist under it.

'Good night,' says William, getting to his feet. She doesn't reply. He picks up the lamp and carries its light out of her room, closing the door gently behind him.

★　★　★

Next day, shortly after lunch, Sophie emerges from the school-room, ready to accompany her father and Miss Sugar to the factory where soap is made. Her face has been washed with that same soap this morning, by Rose (for Miss Sugar is slightly too crippled to wash and dress anyone just at the moment). Rose has a different way of combing and pinning Sophie's hair and when Miss Sugar sees it she looks as though she wants to take the pins out and begin from the beginning. But she can't because Rose is watching and Father is waiting and Miss Sugar is wrestling with her crutch, trying to walk in such a way as to pretend she hardly needs it and is just taking it along in case she gets tired.

Sophie has been thinking a lot about Miss Sugar lately. She has come to the conclusion that Miss Sugar has another life beyond her duties as a governess and a secretary to Father, and that this other life is rather complicated and unhappy. This conclusion came to her quite suddenly, a few days ago, when Sophie peeked through the crack in her school-room door and witnessed her governess being carried up the stairs by Papa and Rose. Once long ago, on an occasion when Sophie disobeyed Nurse's command not to peek out of the nursery door, she saw her Mama being carried up those same stairs, looking remarkably similar to Miss Sugar: unladylike, all rumpled skirts and dangly limbs, with only the whites of her eyes showing. There exist, Sophie has decided, two Miss Sugars: the self-possessed custodian of all knowledge, and an overgrown child in trouble.

When the time comes to descend the stairs, Miss Sugar attempts two or three steps with the crutch, then hands the crutch to Sophie to hold while she leans heavily on the banister the rest of the way. Her face has no expression on it except for a half or perhaps a quarter smile (Sophie has just been introduced to fractions) and she gets to the bottom without showing much effort, although her forehead is twinkly with sweat.

'No, I'm quite all right,' she says to Father as he looks her up and down. He nods and allows Letty to dress him in his overcoat, then strides out of the door without a backward glance.

Father is seated inside the carriage before you can say Jack Robinson. Sophie and Miss Sugar approach more slowly, the governess limping across the carriage-way with that same quarter-smile on her reddening face. Cheesman stares at her with his big head tilted to one side, his hands in the pockets of his greatcoat. His eyes and Miss Sugar's meet, and Sophie understands at once that Miss Sugar hates him.

''Ere now, Miss Sophie,' says Cheesman when Sophie comes within arm's length and, reaching down, he snatches her off the carriage-way, through the cabin door and onto her seat, with a single sweep of his strong arms.

'Allow me, Miss Sugar,' he grins, as if he means to sweep her up too, but he merely extends a steadying hand as Miss Sugar climbs into the cabin. She's *almost* safely inside, when she sways back a little – and instantly Cheesman's hands are on her waist, then they disappear behind her bottom. A rustling sound issues from Miss Sugar's horse-hair bustle as the coachman pushes her up.

'Take care, Cheesman,' hisses Miss Sugar as she claws the coach's upholstery and pulls herself inside.

'Oh, I always do, Miss Sugar,' he replies, bowing so that his smirk is hidden in the upturned collars of his coat.

In a jiffy, they're on the move, with horse-harness jingling and the ground shaking the frame of the carriage. They're going all the way to a place called Lambeth! Miss Sugar has shown it to her on a map (not a very good or clear map, it must be admitted; it seems that the persons who make school-books are more interested in drawing ancient Mesopotamia at the time of Asshurbanipal than the London of today). Anyway, Lambeth is on the *other* side of the River Thames, the side that doesn't have the Rackham house and the church and the park and the fountain and Mister Scofield & Tophie's photography shop and Lockheart's Cocoa Rooms where she ate the cake that made her sick, and all the rest of the known world.

'You are turned out very nicely, Sophie,' says her Father. She blushes with pleasure, even though Miss Sugar frowns and looks down at her own shoes. One of those shoes is very tight, swollen by the sore foot inside. The leather is stretched and shiny, like a ham. Miss Sugar needs new shoes, or at least one. Sophie needs new shoes, too; her feet are very pinched, even though she hasn't fallen downstairs or anything of that sort: only grown bigger, from age. Wouldn't it be good if Miss Sugar suggested a visit to a shoe shop, after the visit to Papa's soap factory? If time is short, it would be a sensibler place to go than a Cocoa Room, because food ceases to exist as soon as you swallow it, whereas a well-fitting pair of shoes is a lasting boon for the feet.

'And after you've seen my factory, we'll go to Lockhart's Cocoa Rooms,' says Father, nodding across to Sophie with his eyes exaggeratedly wide. 'You'll like that, won't you?'

'Yes, Papa,' Sophie says. Merely to be addressed by him is a privilege worth any disappointment.

'I have told that fool Paltock he's to sort himself out by the thirty-first of this month,' he goes on. 'It was high time, don't you think?'

Sophie ponders this for a moment, then realises that her role in the conversation has come to an end.

Miss Sugar draws a deep breath and looks out of the window.

'You know best, I'm sure,' she says.

'When I say "that fool", I didn't call him that in my letter, of course.'

'No, I should hope not.' Sugar pauses, chewing at tiny flakes of dry skin on her lips. Then: 'He'll transfer his allegiances to your competitors without the slightest scruple, I'm sure, and at a time when it inconveniences you to the maximum degree.'

'All the more reason to give him a nudge now, before the Season.'

Sophie turns her head to the window. If her father should feel any further need to speak to her, he'll no doubt summon her attention.

The journey through the city is wonderfully interesting. Apart from Kensington Gardens and Hyde Park, whose trees she recognises in passing, and the big marble arch, everything is new to her. Cheesman has been instructed 'not to get us snarled in traffic', and so he steers the carriage through all sorts of unfamiliar thoroughfares, re-joining Oxford Street only when unavoidable. When he comes to the so-called circus at which, on their previous outing, Sophie was disappointed not to witness any lions or elephants, he doesn't turn right towards the bright commotion, but keeps going straight.

Soon the buildings and shops are looking neither grand nor cheerful – indeed, they look shabby, and so do the people on the footpaths. All the men bear a strange resemblance to Mr Woburn the knife-sharpener who comes to the Rackham house, and all the women look like Letty except not as neat and clean, and nobody sings or shouts or whistles or declares they've something that only costs a ha'penny and is worth half a crown. They move like dreary phantoms through the grey chill, and when they lift their faces to note the passing of the Rackham carriage, their eyes are black as coals.

The paving under the wheels of the carriage becomes more and more uneven, and the streets narrower. The houses now are in a frightful state, all jumbled together and falling apart, with long sagging lines of people's underclothes and bed-sheets hung in plain view, as if no one here is the least bit ashamed of wetting the bed. There's a horrid smell of dirty things, substances that Shears might use to make plants grow or kill them, and the women and children have hardly any clothes on.

As they rattle through the worst street yet, Sophie notices a little girl standing barefoot by a large iron bucket. The child, dressed in a buttonless blouse so large that its ragged hem clings to her filthy ankles, taps the bucket idly with a stick. Yet, although in these respects the girl is as different from Sophie as the trolls in Uncle Henry's fairytale book, their faces – the girl's face, and Sophie's face – share such a striking resemblance that Sophie is agog, and leans her head out of the carriage window to stare.

The urchin child, finding herself the object of unwelcome attention, reaches down into her bucket and with a single unhesitating motion hurls a small missile. Sophie doesn't pull her head back; she can't quite believe that the dark thing flashing through the air exists in the same world as her own body and the carriage in which she sits; rather, she's entranced by the expression of stubborn malevolence on her twin's face . . . entranced for an instant only. Then the projectile hits her right between the eyes.

'What the devil . . . !' yelps William, as his daughter sprawls backwards onto the cabin floor.

'Sophie!' cries Sugar, lurching violently as Cheesman reins the carriage to a halt. She scoops the child into her arms, relieved to see only bewilderment, no blood. No serious harm has been done, thank God: there's a mucky brown mark on Sophie's brow, and in her flailings for balance she has (with the unerring bad luck that attends such mishaps) squashed the fallen dog turd between her palm and the toe of Father's left shoe.

Instinctively, Sugar grabs the nearest loose cloth – the embroidered antimacassar from the seat next to William's – and begins to wipe Sophie's face with it.

'Haven't you got a handkerchief!' barks William, in a state of furious agitation. His fists are clenched, his chest heaves, he thrusts his angry face out of the window, but the urchin has vanished like a rat. Then, noticing that Sophie's hand is still dark with dogshit, he recoils against the wall of the cabin, away from any further besmirching.

'Stop thrashing about, you stupid child!' he yells. 'Sugar, take her glove off first! God almighty, can't you see . . . !' The two females, cowed by his rage, fumble to obey. 'And what were you doing,' he bawls at Sophie, 'poking your head out like that, like an imbecile? Have you no sense whatsoever?'

He's trembling, and Sugar knows his outburst is as much from distress as anything else; his nerves have never quite recovered from his beating. She cleans Sophie as best she can, while William jumps out of the cabin and washes his shoe, with the help of a rag supplied by Cheesman.

'A splash of beer's the remedy for that, sir,' chirrups the coachman. 'I always keep some 'andy for just such a purpose.'

While the men are busy, Sugar examines Sophie's face. The child is sobbing almost imperceptibly, her breaths shallow and quick, but there are no tears, and not so much as a whimper of complaint.

'Are you hurt, Sophie?' whispers Sugar, licking the tip of her thumb and wiping one vestigial smudge of muck from the child's pale flesh.

Sophie juts her jaw forward, and her eyes blink hard.

'No, Miss.'

For the continuation of the journey, Sophie sits as still as a waxwork or a parcel, responding only to the joltings of the carriage wheels. William, once his explosion of temper has settled, becomes aware of what he's done, and shows his contrition with such offerings as 'Well, *that* was a n-narrow escape, w-wasn't it, Sophie?' and 'We sh-shall have to get you some n-new gloves now, sh-shan't we?' – all delivered in a jolly tone that's pitiful and irritating in equal measure.

'Yes, Papa,' says Sophie quietly, displaying her good manners but nothing more. Her gaze is unfocused; or rather, it is focused upon some layer of the cosmos that's invisible to gross creatures called William Rackham. Never has her resemblance to Agnes been as remarkable as it is now.

'Look, Sophie!' says William. 'We're about to cross Waterloo Bridge!'

Obediently, Sophie looks out of the window, her head pulled well back from the aperture. After a minute or two, though – to William's palpable relief – the magic of a vast body of water viewed from a great height does its work, and Sophie leans forward, her elbow resting on the window-ledge.

'What do you see, hmm?' says William, clownishly attentive. 'Barges, I expect?'

'Yes, Papa,' says Sophie, staring down into the churning grey-green expanse. It's scarcely recognisable as the neat blue ribbon on the map that Miss Sugar showed her this morning, but if this bridge they're crossing is Waterloo Bridge then they must be very near Waterloo Station, where her

Mama got lost while searching for the Music School. Sophie peers down into the distant water and wonders which bit of it, exactly, is the bit where her mother sank under the waves and drank more water than a living body can hold.

Outside the iron gates of the Rackham soap factory in Lambeth, a carriage stands waiting, shackled to two placid grey horses. In this coach, behold: Lady Bridgelow. Ensconced snugly in the burnished cabin, like an aquamarine pearl in a four-wheeled shell, she draws all eyes to her even before she alights.

'Lord, look at that smoke . . .' tuts William, as he steps out of his own carriage and peers regretfully into a sky tainted with the murky efflux from Doulton & Co, Stiff & Sons, and various other potteries, glass-makers, breweries and soap-makers in the neighbourhood. He guiltily appraises his own chimneys, and is reassured to note that the smoke issuing from them is wispy and clean.

'Oh, William, *there* you are!' Inside the coach, a pale starfish of pigskin fingers wiggles.

Approaching Lady Bridgelow after he's motioned the watchman to throw the gates wide, William apologises profusely for any inconvenience she may have suffered, to which she responds by insisting that it's *her* fault for arriving earlier than they'd agreed.

'I've been looking forward to it so much, you see,' she trills, allowing herself to be helped out onto the footpath.

'Difficult for me to believe . . .' says William, gesturing vaguely at the utilitarian ugliness of the factory's immediate locale, so different from the glittering pleasure gardens he imagines are Lady Bridgelow's natural habitat.

'Oh, so you doubt my word!' she teases him, feigning offence with a limp diminutive hand laid on her satiny blue breast. 'No but really, William, you mustn't take me for an old relic. I've no desire to spend the rest of my days pining for things that are about to pass into history. Honestly, can you imagine me following a herd of doddery aristocrats around the countryside while they shoot pheasants and bemoan the evils of Reform Bills? A fate worse than death!'

'Well,' says William, bowing in mock-obeisance, 'if I can save you from such a fate, by showing you my humble factory . . .'

'Nothing would amuse me more!'

And they proceed through the gates.

(What about Sugar, you ask? Oh well, yes, *she* enters too, hobbling on her crutch, with Sophie close by her side. How odd that Lady Bridgelow, for all her playful repudiation of patrician snobbery, appears not even to have noticed the governess's existence – or perhaps her innate grace and tact don't permit her to remark on the misfortune of a person's physical disability. Yes, that must be the reason: she doesn't wish to embarrass the hapless governess by enquiring how she came by her unsightly limp.)

Sugar watches in dismay as William and Lady Bridgelow walk side by side, cutting a path through the toadies and sycophants who cringe to give them room. By contrast, those same employees edge inwards again after Mr Rackham and his distinguished guest have passed, as though primed to eject from the premises any interlopers who might be skulking in their wake. Sugar does her best to walk tall and hold her head high, putting as little weight as possible on her crutch, but she's plagued by the additional pain of indigestion, and it's all she can do not to grip her stomach and whimper.

The factory itself, when the little party enters its fiercely lit interior, is nothing like Sugar had anticipated. She'd pictured a building of grand proportions, a cavernous, echoing structure like a railway station or a church, filled with monstrous machines that hum and gleam. She'd imagined the processes happening invisibly inside tubes and vessels, each feeding the other, while dwarfish human attendants oiled the moving parts. But Rackham's Soap Factory isn't that sort of set-up at all; it's an intimate affair, conducted under ceilings as low as a tavern's, with so much polished wood on show that it might almost be The Fireside.

Stunted girls with pinched faces and red hands – a dozen of them, like manufactured replicas of Janey the scullery maid – are working in an atmosphere thick with the mingled odours of lavender, carnation, rose and almond. They wear rustic wooden clogs with roughened soles, for the stone floors are iced with a waxy, pellucid patina of soap.

'Watch your step!' says William, as he escorts his visitors into his fragrant domain. Under the glowing lights, his face is scarcely recognisable; his skin is golden, his lips silver, as he assumes the role of the master of ceremonies. Forgetting his reticence, free of his stutter, he points here, he points there, and explains everything.

'Of course, what you see here is not strictly soap *manufacture* – that's a dirty business, not worthy of a perfumer. The correct word for our far more fragrant procedures is *re-melting*.' He enunciates the word with exaggerated clarity, as if he expects his guests to scribble it on a notepad. Lady Bridgelow swivels her head in polite wonder; Sophie looks from her Papa to Lady Bridgelow and back to her Papa, puzzling over the mysterious chemistry that imbues the atmosphere between them.

The bars of soap, which Sugar had imagined tumbling fully-formed out of a chute or a nozzle at the very end of a complex automaton, exist only as puddles of gelatinous ooze, twinkling in wooden moulds. Wire frames are poised above the aromatic goo, to guillotine it into rectangles when it stiffens. Each mould contains a different colour of mucus, with a different scent.

'This yellow one is – or will be – Rackham's Honeysuckle,' says William. 'It relieves itching, and the demand for it has grown five-fold this year.' He dips a finger into the glimmering emulsion, and reveals two distinct layers. 'This cream that's risen, we skim off. It's pure alkali, which in my father's day was allowed to remain, thus making the soap irritating to sensitive skin.'

He moves on to a different mould, whose contents are bluish and sweet-smelling.

'And here we have what will become Rackham's Puressence, a blend of sage, lavender and sandalwood oil. And here' (moving on again) 'is Rackham's Jeunesse Eternelle. The green colour comes from cucumber, and the lemon and chamomile act as an astringent, restoring smoothness to the face.'

Next he takes them to the curing chamber, where hundreds of bars of soap lie nestled on beds of metal and oak.

'A full twenty-one days they'll lie here, and not a day less!' declares Rackham, as if malicious whisperers have claimed otherwise.

In the wrapping room, twenty girls in lavender smocks sit at a massive table, ten on either side, overseen by a vulpine fellow who paces slowly around them, his ginger-haired hands hooked in his waistcoat pockets. The girls lean forward in formation, their brows almost touching as they enfold the soap in waxed paper parcels. Each of the parcels is printed with an engraving of William Rackham's benevolent visage, as well as a minuscule text authored by Sugar one late night in May, while she and William sat side by side in bed.

'Good morning, girls!' says William, and they respond in chorus: 'Good morning, Mr Rackham.'

'Often they sing to themselves,' says William to Lady Bridgelow and his other guests, with a wink. 'But we've made them shy, you see.'

He approaches the table, and gives the lavender lassies a smile. 'Let's hear a song, girls. This is my little daughter come to see you, and a very fine lady as well. You needn't be bashful; we're moving on to the crating hall now, and shan't be watching you, but if we could only hear your sweet voices, why, that would be capital.' Then, dropping his voice to a conspiratorial tone, he murmurs, 'Do your best for me,' while rolling his eyes meaningfully in the direction of Sophie, to appeal to their collective maternal nature.

William and his visitors then proceed to a large vestibule at the rear of the factory, where sinewy shirt-sleeved men are packing loose piles of finished soaps into flimsy wooden caskets. Sure enough, no sooner have Lady Bridgelow, Sugar and Sophie stepped across the threshold than a melodious chanting starts up in the room they've just left: first one timorous voice, then three, then a dozen.

'Lavender's blue, diddle diddle,
Rosemary's green, diddle diddle,
When I am king, diddle diddle,
you shall be queen . . .'

'And here,' says William, pointing at two massive doors beyond which, through a crack, they can glimpse the world outside, 'is where the factory ends – and the rest of the story begins.'

Sugar, who has been preoccupied with the triple challenge of keeping her limp as unobtrusive as possible, restraining her urge to groan as her stomach gripes wickedly, and suppressing the temptation to punch Lady Bridgelow's simpering face, becomes aware of a discreet tugging at her skirts.

'Yes, what is it, Sophie?' she whispers, bending down clumsily to allow the child to whisper in her ear.

'I need to do a piddle, Miss,' says the child.

Keep it in, can't you? thinks Sugar, but then she realises that she, too, is bursting to go.

'Pardon me, Mr Rackham,' she says. 'Is there, on the premises, a room with . . . washing facilities?'

William blinks in disbelief: is this some sort of obtuse enquiry about soap production, a gauche attempt to reprise her performance in his lavender fields, or is she requesting a formal tour of the factory's water-closets? Then, mercifully, he understands, and commandeers an employee to show Miss Sugar and Miss Sophie the way to the conveniences, while Lady Bridgelow affects a consuming interest in the list of far-flung destinations chalked upon the delivery slate.

("I heard one say, diddle diddle
since I came hither
that you and I, diddle diddle,
must lie together . . .")

Lady Bridgelow ignores the child's indiscretion with the grace of one whose pedigree exempts her from such gross frailties. Instead, she picks up an individual soap and studies the curious text on its wrapper.

The employees' latrine has a much more modern and streamlined appearance, in Sophie and Sugar's eyes, than the rest of the soapworks. A row of identical white glazed stoneware pedestals, each attached to a brilliant metal cistern bracketed under the ceiling, exhibit themselves like a phalanx of futuristic mechanisms, all proudly engraved with the name of their maker. The seats are a rich brown, glossy with lacquer, brand new it seems; but then, according to the address inscribed on all the cisterns, the Doulton factory is only a few hundred yards down the road.

The pedestals are so tall that Sophie, having clambered onto one, dangles her feet in space, several inches from the eggshell-blue ceramic floor. Sugar turns her back and walks a few steps farther along, studying the wall-tiles while Sophie's pee trickles into the bowl. The pain in her guts is so sharp now that it catches her breath and makes her shiver; she longs to relieve herself, but the prospect of doing it in front of the child worries her, and she wonders if, by superhuman force of will, she can wait until later.

Merely piddling in Sophie's presence wouldn't be so bad: a shared intimacy that might compensate, to some extent, for the erosion of dignity. But the pangs in her bowels are fearsome, and she's loath to unleash a noisy flux of stink into the room, for *that* would ruin beyond repair the image of Miss Sugar the serene custodian of knowledge, and brand upon Sophie's mind (and nose!) the gross reality of . . . of Miss Sugar the sick animal.

Hugging herself tight and biting her lip to suppress the cramps, she stares at the wall. A disgruntled employee has attempted to gouge a message into the ceramic:

W. R. is

but the hardness of the surface has proved too obdurate.

Suddenly she must – absolutely *must* – sit down. Her stomach is skewered with agony, and every inch of her skin prickles with cold sweat; the flesh of her buttocks, bared in desperate haste as she claws handfuls of her dress onto her bent back and yanks down her pantalettes, is wet and slippery as a peeled pear. She lets herself drop heavily onto the seat, and with a stifled cry of anguish she slumps forward, her bonnet falling to the tiled floor, her hair unravelling after it. Blood and other hot, slick material erupts and slithers between her thighs.

'Oh God!' she cries. 'God help me . . . !' and a flush of dizziness seems to flip her upside down before she loses consciousness altogether.

A moment later – *surely* only a moment later? – she wakes on the floor, sprawled on the chilly damp tiles, her thighs slimy, her heartbeat shaking her body, her ankle throbbing as if caught in a steel trap. Craning her head, she sees Sophie cowering in a corner, face white as the stoneware, eyes huge and terrified.

'Help me, Sophie!' she calls, in an anxious hiss.

The child jerks forward, like a doll pulled by a string, but her expression is contorted by impotence. 'I–I'll go and fetch someone, Miss,' she stammers, pointing at the door, beyond which lurk all the strong men and serviceable ladies with which her Papa's factory is so well-stocked.

'No! No! Sophie, *please*,' begs Sugar in a frantic whisper, thrusting up her hands as she flounders in a tangle of her own skirts. '*You* must try.'

For another instant, Sophie looks to the outside world for rescue. Then she runs forwards, seizes her governess by the wrists, and heaves with all her strength.

'Well,' says William, when the goodbyes have been spoken and Lady Bridgelow has been borne away. 'How did you like *that*, Sophie?'

'It was most wondrous, Papa,' replies the child, in a spiritless voice.

They're seated in the Rackham carriage, their clothing exhaling the sweet scent of soap into the confines of the cabin, their knees almost touching, as Cheesman ferries them away from Lambeth. The visit has been a resounding success, at least in the estimation of Lady Bridgelow, who confided in William that she'd never had an experience that thrilled quite so many of her senses at once, and she could well imagine how it might overwhelm a person in less than robust health. Now he is left with Sugar, who does indeed look green around the gills, and Sophie, who looks as if she's been subjected to an ordeal rather than given the treat of her life.

William settles back in his seat, rubbing his knuckles ruefully. How perverse his daughter is! One cross word and she's sullen for the rest of the day. Disheartening though it may be to admit it, it's highly likely the child has inherited Agnes's unforgiving streak.

As for Sugar, she's dozing where she sits – actually dozing! Her head lolls backward, her mouth is slack, it's frankly disagreeable to behold. Her dress is rumpled, her hair is haloed with loose wisps, her bonnet's slightly askew. Sugar would do well to take a page from the book of Lady Bridgelow, who, from the moment she alighted from her carriage to the moment she waved William adieu, was immaculate and bright as a button. What an unusual person Constance is! A model of dignity and poise, and yet so full of life! A woman in a million . . .

'Waterloo Bridge again, Sophie,' says William, offering his daughter the marvels of the world's greatest river a second time that day.

Sophie looks out of the window. Once more she rests her chin on her forearms and examines those turbulent waters in which even big boats don't look quite safe.

Then, glancing up, she sees something genuinely miraculous: an elephant floating through the sky, an elephant keeping still as a statue. *SALMON'S TEA* is the message emblazoned on its bulbous flank, and it dawdles above the rooftops and chimneys on its way to those parts of the city where all the people are.

'What do you think, Sophie?' says William, squinting up at the balloon. 'Should Rackham's get one of those?'

That evening, while William makes a start on the day's accumulated correspondence, the remainder of his household does its best to return to normal.

A few doors farther along the landing, Sugar has refused, as gracefully as she can, Rose's offer to put Sophie to bed. Instead, she asks for a tub of hot water to be delivered to her own bedroom, a request which Rose has no difficulty understanding, having noted that Miss Sugar looks like she's been dragged through a hedge backwards.

The day has been long, long, long. Oh God, how can a man be so blind to the needs of others? Cruelly oblivious to how much Sugar and Sophie yearned to go home, William protracted the outing to an unbearable length. First: lunch in a restaurant in the Strand, where Sugar almost fainted in the airless heat and was obliged to eat underdone lamb cutlets that William praised, from previous acquaintance, as divine; then a visit to a glover; then a visit to *another* glover, when the first one couldn't provide Sophie with a soft enough kidskin; then a visit to a shoe-maker, where William was finally rewarded with a smile from his daughter, when she stood up in her new boots and took three steps to the looking-glass. If only he'd left it at that! But no, encouraged by that smile, he took her to Berry & Rudd, the wine merchants in James Street, to get her weighed on their great scales. 'Six generations of royal families, both English and French, have been weighed on these, Sophie!' he told her, while the proprietors leered in the background. 'They're only for persons of great consequence!' Then, as a final treat, the promised climax to the afternoon: a visit to Lockhart's Cocoa Rooms.

'What a jolly threesome we are today!' he declared, for an instant the very image of his own father, dangerously over-filled with the gas of bonhomie at Christmas. Then, when Sophie was occupied with the earnest study of a dessert menu the size of her upper body, he leaned forward and murmured close to Sugar's ear, 'D'you think she's happy now?'

'Very happy, I'm sure,' Sugar replied. Only when leaning forward in her seat was she made aware, by a sharp sting of pain, that the hair of her genitals was glued to her pantalettes with dried blood. 'But I think she's had enough.'

'Enough of what?'

'Enough pleasure for one day.'

Even when they were back in the Rackham house, the ordeal was not quite over. In a virtual replication of the aftermath of her *first* visit to the city weeks before, Sophie was violently ill, vomiting up the same mixture of cocoa, cake and undigested dinner, and then, inevitably, there were tears.

'Are you sure, Miss Sugar,' said Rose at bedtime, hesitating at the door of Miss Rackham's room, 'you wouldn't like me to help you?'

'No thank you, Rose,' she said.

Whereupon – *finally* – seven hours and forty minutes after Sugar's fall from a blood-spattered earthenware basin onto the floor of the latrine of the Rackham Soap Works – she and Sophie are allowed to go to bed.

Other than holding Sophie's nightshift and handing it over, there's nothing Sugar can do to assist; she leans heavily against the bed while the child undresses and climbs in.

'I am very grateful to you, Sophie,' she says hoarsely. 'You are my little rescuer.' As soon as the words have left her lips, she despises herself for making light of the child's courage. It's the sort of patronising remark William might make, treating Sophie as if she were a clever little dog performing an amusing trick.

Sophie lays her head back on her pillow. Her cheeks are mottled with exhaustion, her nose bright red. She hasn't even said her prayers. Her lips twitch to ask a question.

'What's an imbecile, Miss?'

Sugar strokes Sophie's hair, smoothing it back from her hot forehead.

'It's a person who's very stupid,' she replies. Burning to ask a couple of questions of her own – *Did you look into the water-closet's basin before you pulled the handle to flush it? And what did you see?* – she manages to resist. 'Your father didn't mean to call you that,' she says. 'He was angry. And he hasn't been well.'

Sophie shuts her eyes. She doesn't want to hear any more about grown-ups who aren't well. It's high time the universe was restored to its normal function.

'You mustn't worry about anything, little one,' says Sugar, blinking tears off her eye-lashes. 'Everything will be all right now.'

Sophie turns her head aside, burying her cheek deep in her pillow.

'You won't fall down again, will you, Miss Sugar?' she demands, in a strange tone between a sulk and a croon.

'I'll be very careful from now on, Sophie. I promise.'

She touches Sophie lightly on the shoulder, a forlorn gesture before turning to leave, but suddenly the child rears up in bed and throws her arms tight around Sugar's neck.

'Don't die, Miss Sugar! Don't die!' she wails, as Sugar, poorly balanced, almost pitches headlong into the child's bed.

'I won't die,' she swears, staggering, kissing Sophie's hair. 'I won't die, I promise!'

Not ten minutes later, with Sophie soundly asleep, Sugar sits in a large tub of steaming warm water in front of the fire. The room no longer smells of burnt paper and glue, but of lavender soap and wet earth: Rose, God bless her, has finally managed to prise the window open, breaking the stubborn seal of paint.

Sugar washes thoroughly, repetitiously, doggedly. She squeezes spongefuls of soothing water over her back and bosom, squeezes the sea creature's porous skeleton until it's like a damp powder puff, then presses it to her eyes. The rims are sore from weeping: she really must stop.

Every now and then she looks down, fearing what she might see, but there's a reassuring film of suds that disguises the pinkish tinge of the water, and any clots of blood have either sunk to the bottom or are hidden inside the froth. Her injured foot is very swollen, she knows, but it's invisible to her, and she fancies it hurts less than it ought to. Her cracked ribs (she strokes a lathered palm over them) are almost healed, the bruises vivid. The worst is over, the crisis has passed.

She reclines into the tub as deeply as its circumference allows, snivelling again. She bites her lower lip until the flesh throbs, and finally she has her sorrow under control; the convulsing water settles into stillness – or as still as water can be with a living body in it. In the opaque moat that shimmers between her legs, every heartbeat makes the water quiver like the lapping of a tide.

A few doors along the landing, at the same time as Sugar is taking herself to bed, William opens a letter from Doctor Curlew that begins thus:

Dear Rackham,

I've deliberated long and hard whether to write or keep silent. I don't doubt you are sick to death of my "meddling". Nevertheless there is something I could scarcely fail to notice when I attended your daughter's governess after her mishap, and my resolution to hold my tongue about it has caused me no little botheration since . . .

This preamble is longer than the story itself, which takes only one sentence to tell.

★   ★   ★

In Sugar's bed, in the dark, many people are under the sheets with her, talking to her in her sleep.

Tell us a story, Shush, in that fancy voice of yours.

What sort of story? she asks, peering into the dappled waters of her dream, trying to put names to the indistinct faces submerged beneath.

Something with revenge in it, the voices giggle, irredeemably coarse, doomed to live out their lives in Hell. *And bad words. Bad words sound funny when you say them, Sugar.*

The giggles echo and re-echo, accumulating on top of one another until they're a cacophony. Sugar swims away from them, swims through the streets of an underwater city, and even in her dream she thinks this odd because she has never learned to swim. Yet it seems a skill that comes without teaching, and she can do it without taking her night-gown off, propelling her body through sewer-like alleyways and bright transparent thoroughfares. If this is London, its population has floated away like debris, and has ended up somewhere far above, a scum of human flotsam tarnishing the sky. Only those people who are of consequence to Sugar have remained below, it seems.

Clara? calls a voice from a nearby, quite the loveliest and most musical voice Sugar has ever heard.

No, Agnes, she replies, turning a corner. *I'm not Clara.*

Who are you, then?

Don't look in my face. I will help you, but don't look in my face.

Agnes is lying supine on the cobbles of a narrow lane, naked, her flesh white as marble. One thin arm is draped across her bosom, the other crosses it downwards, hiding her pubic triangle under her childish hand.

Here, says Sugar, shedding her night-gown and draping it over Agnes. *Let this be our secret.*

Bless you, bless you, says Agnes, and suddenly the watery world of London disappears, and the two of them are in bed together, warm and dry, tucked up snug as sisters, gazing into each other's faces.

William says you are a fantasy, murmurs Agnes, reaching forward to touch Sugar's flesh, to banish her doubt. *A trick of my imagination.*

Never mind what William says.

Please, my dear Sister: tell me your name.

Sugar feels a hand between her legs, gently cupping the sore part.

My name is Sugar, she says.

THIRTY-FOUR

here is no name written on either of the two envelopes that Sugar finds slipped under the door of her bedroom the following day; one is blank, the other marked 'To Whom It May Concern'.

It's half past twelve in the afternoon. She has just returned from the morning's lessons in the school-room, where Sophie let her know from the outset that there must be no disruption, distraction or idleness to spoil the serious business of learning. Yesterday was all very interesting, but today must be different – or rather, today must be the same as any other day.

'The fifteenth century,' recited Sophie, with the air of one who has been entrusted with the responsibility for saving that epoch from slatternly neglect, 'was an age of five principal events: printing was invented; Consternople was taken by the Turks; there was in England a civil war that lasted thirty years; the Spaniards drove the Moors back to Africa; and America was discovered by Christopher . . . Christopher . . .' At which point she looked up at Sugar, wanting nothing more nor less than the name of an Italian explorer.

'Columbus, Sophie.'

All morning, despite being tempted a dozen times to burst into tears, and despite the steady leak of blood into the makeshift chauffoir pinned to her pantaloons, Sugar has been the perfect governess, playing the role exactly as her pupil required. And, in a fitting conclusion to the morning's business, she and Sophie have just shared a meal of sieved vegetables and milky rice pudding, the blandest lunch they've yet been served, evidence that someone must have informed the kitchen staff of Miss Rackham's distressed digestion. The disappointed look that Sugar and Sophie exchanged when Rose put this steaming pap in front of them was by far the most intimate moment they've shared since the day began.

Now Sugar returns to her room, anticipating the blessed relief of removing the blood-stained cloth from between her legs and replacing it with a clean one. Last night's washtub, sadly, has been removed, although she could hardly have expected Rose to leave it sitting there, a body of cold water with a glutinous red sediment on the bottom.

Postponing her creature comforts for a minute, she stoops clumsily to pick up the envelopes. The unmarked one, she expects, is a note from Rose informing her, in case she hadn't noticed, that the window is unsealed. Sugar opens the envelope, and finds a bank-note for ten pounds and an unsigned message scrawled on plain paper. In a majuscule, childish script that might have been written left-handed, it says:

It has come to my notice that you are with child. It is therefore impossible for you to remain as my daughter's governess. Your wages are enclosed; please be prepared to leave your room, with all belongings and effects, on the first of March of this year (1/3/76). I hope the Letter of Introduction (see other envelope) may be of some use to you in the future; you will note I have taken a liberty re your identity. The fact is that in my opinion, if you are to get anywhere in life, it is necessary to have a proper name. So, I have given you one.

Further discussion of this matter is out of the question. Do not attempt to come and see me. Kindly keep to your room whenever the house is visited.

Sugar re-folds the sheet of paper in its original order of creases and, with some difficulty, for her fingers have become cold and numb, she replaces it in its envelope. Then she opens the lavender-tinted envelope marked 'To Whom It May Concern', sliding her thumb along its flap to avoid tearing its formal integrity. The sharp edge of the paper cuts her flesh, but she doesn't feel it; she worries only that she'll stain the envelope or its contents. Balanced on her crutch, licking her thumb every few seconds before the hair-fine line of blood has a chance to well into a loose droplet, she extracts the letter and reads it. It is written, with care, on Rackham letterhead, and signed with William's name, as neatly as any of her forgeries.

To whom it may concern.

I, William Rackham, am pleased to introduce Miss Elizabeth Sugar, who was in my employ for five months from November 3rd, 1875 to March 1st, 1876, in the capacity of governess to my six-year-old daughter. I have no doubt that Miss Sugar discharged her duties with the greatest competence, sensitivity and enthusiasm. Under her management, my daughter has blossomed into a young lady.

Miss Sugar's decision to leave my employ is, I am given to understand, due to a close relative's ill-health and in no way derogates from my satisfaction with her abilities. Indeed, I can hardly recommend her too highly.

Yours,

William Rackham

This letter, too, Sugar re-folds along its original creases, and returns to its envelope. She sucks her thumb one last time, but the cut is already healing. She places both letters on top of her dresser, and hobbles over to the window, where she transfers her weight from the crutch to the window-sill. Down in the Rackham grounds, Shears is happily pottering, fussing around saplings that have survived the winter. With a snicker-snack of his metal namesake he severs a loop of twine that was holding a slender trunk aligned with a stake: it needs no such mollycoddling anymore. Visibly proud, he stands back, fists poised on his leather-aproned hips.

Sugar, after some consideration, decides that driving her fists through the glass of the window-panes would land her in terrible bother and give her only momentary relief from her anguish. Instead, she fetches pen and paper and, still standing, with the window-sill serving as a writing-desk, she forces herself to be reasonable.

Dear William,

Forgive me saying so, but you are mistaken. I was briefly afflicted with a painful swelling, which has since passed, and I now have my monthly courses, as you can discover to your own satisfaction if you come to me.

Your loving Sugar

She reads and re-reads this missive, listening to its tone reverberate in her head. Will William take it the right way? In his state of alarm, will he interpret the phrase 'as you can discover to your own satisfaction' as argumentative, or can she rely on him to perceive the bawdy suggestion behind it? She draws a deep breath, counselling herself that of all the things she has ever written, *this* must not fail to hit the mark. Would the saucy humour be clearer if she inserted the word 'perfect' between 'own' and 'satisfaction'? On the other hand, is sauciness what's needed here, or should she substitute a more soothing, blandishing tone?

Within seconds, she realises she's far too agitated to write a second message, and that she had better deliver this one before she does something foolish. So, she folds the paper in half, limps out onto the landing, proceeds straight to William's door, and slips the letter under it.

In the afternoon, governess and pupil perform arithmetic, check that the achievements of the fifteenth century are not already forgotten, and make a start on mineralogy. The hands of the clock advance fraction by fraction, as the map of the world is lit up, little by little, by the progress of the sun through the sky. A window-shaped beam of sunlight glows on the pastel seas and autumnal continents, clarifying some, obscuring others in shadow.

Sugar has chosen the topic of mineralogy at random from Mangnall's *Questions*, judging it to be a safe, unemotional subject that will satisfy Sophie's need for orderly tangibles. She recites the principal metals, and has Sophie repeat them: gold, silver, platina, quicksilver, copper, iron, lead, tin, aluminium. Gold the heaviest; tin the lightest; iron the most useful.

Looking ahead to the next question, *What are the principal Properties of Metals?*, Sugar already wishes she'd prepared for the lesson as usual, and lets slip a small groan of exasperation.

'It will take me a little while to translate these words into language you can understand, dear,' she explains, turning away from Sophie's upturned, expectant face.

'Are they not in English, Miss?'

'Yes, but I must make them simpler for you.'

A flash of offence crosses Sophie's face. 'Let me try to understand them, Miss.'

Sugar knows she ought to decline this challenge with a soft, tactful answer, but can't think of one just now. Instead, in a dry, oratorical voice, she reads aloud:

'Brilliancy, opacity, weight, malleability, ductility, porosity, solubility.'

There is a pause.

'Weight is how heavy things are, Miss,' says Sophie.

'Yes, Sophie,' Sugar replies, contritely ready to supply the explanations that eluded her before. 'Brilliancy means that they shine; opacity that we can't see through them; malleability that we can beat them into any shape we wish; ductility . . . I don't know myself what that is, I shall have to find it in a dictionary. Porosity means that it has tiny holes in it, although that doesn't sound right, does it, for metals? Solubility . . .'

Sugar shuts her mouth, observing at a glance that this faltering, head-scratching variety of teaching is not to Sophie's taste at all. Instead, she skips ahead to the part where Mrs Mangnall cites the discovery of an inexhaustible abundance of gold in Australia, which allows Sugar to extemporise a description of a poor gold-digger, hacking at the hard ground while his hungry wife and children look hopelessly on, until one day . . . !

'Why are there such long words in the world, Miss?' enquires Sophie, when the mineralogy lesson is over.

'One long difficult word is the same as a whole sentence full of short easy ones, Sophie,' says Sugar. 'It saves time and paper.' Seeing that the child is unconvinced, she adds, 'If books were written in such a way that every person, no matter how young, could understand everything in them, they would be enormously long books. Would *you* wish to read a book that was a thousand pages long, Sophie?'

Sophie answers without hesitation.

'I would read a thousand million pages, Miss, if all the words were words I could understand.'

Back in her bedroom during the hiatus between the end of the day's lessons and dinner, Sugar is shocked to find no reply to her message. How is this possible? All she can think of is that William's mind has been put at rest but that, in his selfishness, he sees no urgency to let her know. Again she seizes hold of pen and paper, and writes:

> *Dear William,*
> *Please — every hour I wait for your reply is a torture — please give me your reassurance that our household can go on as before. Stability is what we all need now — Rackham Perfumeries no less than Sophie and myself. Please remember that I am devoted to assisting you and sparing you inconvenience.*
> *Your loving Sugar*

Re-reading this communiqué, she frowns. One too many 'pleases', perhaps. And William may not take kindly to the suggestion that he's torturing her. But, again, she hasn't the heart to compose another version. As before, she hurries to the door of his study and slips the letter under it.

Dinner for Sugar and Sophie consists of mercilessly sieved rhubarb soup, poached fillet of salmon and a serving of rather watery jelly; Cook is still worried, evidently, that little Miss Rackham's digestion has not yet recovered its equilibrium.

Afterwards, Rose brings a cup of tea to wash the dinner down – full strength for Miss Sugar, two-thirds milk for Miss Rackham – and Sugar, having taken one sip, excuses herself for a minute. While the piping-hot tea cools, she might as well check her room, to see if William has finally been jogged from his self-absorption.

She leaves the school-room, hurries along the landing, opens the door of her bedroom. There's nothing in there that wasn't there before.

She returns to the school-room, and resumes drinking her tea. Her hands are trembling ever-so-slightly; she's convinced that William is, or was, on the very point of responding, but that he's been delayed by unforeseen demands, or by the chore of eating his own dinner. If she can only make the next hour pass quickly, she'll save herself futile fretting.

Sophie, although more settled than she was at the beginning of the day, is not overly sociable now that the lessons are over; she has moved to the far corner of the room and is playing with her doll, trying, with the insertion of crumpled balls of paper under its skirts, to change the outmoded crinoline into a bustle. Sugar can tell, from her expression of earnest concentration, that she wishes to be left alone until bedtime. What to do, to make the time pass? Twiddle her thumbs in her bedroom? Read what's left of Shakespeare? Prepare for tomorrow's lessons?

Suddenly inspired, Sugar picks up the dishes, cutlery and tea-cups, arranges them in as stable a stack as she can devise, and hobbles out of the room with them, leaving her crutch leaning against the doorjamb. She has plenty of time; no one will be watching how slowly she descends the stairs.

She grips the banister with one hand, resting her whole forearm hard against the polished wood; her other hand grips the dishes, pressing the sharp rim of the dinner-plates under her breast. Then, one stair at a time, she escorts her body downwards, alternating one painful swivel of the injured foot with a heavy painless step of the good one. With each six-inch drop, the crockery rattles slightly, but she keeps the stack balanced.

Once she's safe on the ground floor, she advances carefully along the hall, pleased at the steady if inelegant rhythm of her progress. Without mishap, she passes through a succession of doors until, finally, she crosses the threshold of the kitchen.

'Miss Sugar!' says Rose in great surprise. She's been caught red-handed eating a leftover triangle of toast and butter, her legitimate supper not being due for another few hours. Her sleeves are rolled up, and she leans against the great slab-like table in the centre of the room. Harriet, the kitchenmaid, is farther back, fashioning some ox tongues into the required shape for glazing. Through the scullery door the dowdy skirt, wet shoes and swollen ankles of Janey can be glimpsed as she scrubs in the sink.

'I thought I'd return these,' says Sugar, proffering the dirty dishes. 'To save you the trouble.'

Rose looks flabbergasted, as if she's just witnessed a flamboyant somersault by a stark naked acrobat who now stands waiting for applause.

'Much obliged, Miss Sugar,' she says, and swallows the half-chewed bread.

'Please, call me Sugar,' says Sugar, handing the plates over. 'We've worked together on quite a few things by now, haven't we, Rose?' She considers reminding Rose specifically of Christmas, and the way they were both powdered up to the elbows in flour, but judges that this might appear a little fawning.

'Yes, Miss Sugar.'

Harriet and Rose exchange nervous glances. The kitchenmaid doesn't know whether to stand to attention with her hands folded across her apron, or continue moulding and pinioning the ox tongues, one of which has unrolled and threatens to stiffen in quite the wrong shape.

'How hard you all work!' remarks Sugar, determined to break the ice. 'Wi— why, Mr Rackham can scarcely imagine, I'm sure, how constant your labours are.'

Rose watches with widening eyes while the governess limps all the way into the kitchen and lowers herself stiffly into a chair. Both Rose and Harriet are only too well aware that their labours have been far from 'constant' since the death of Mrs Rackham and the total cessation of dinner parties; indeed, unless the master marries again in the near future, he must soon come to the conclusion that he's employing more servants than he needs.

'We've no complaints, Miss Sugar.'

There is a pause. Sugar looks around the kitchen in the harsh mortuary light. Harriet has folded her hands, allowing the ox tongue to do what it will. Rose is folding her sleeves down to her wrists, her lips pursed in an apprehensive half-smile. Janey's rump gyrates as she scrubs dishes, the haphazard pleats of her skirts swaying to and fro.

'So,' Sugar pipes up, as companionably as she can manage, 'what are you all going to have for supper? And where's Cook? And do you all eat here, at the table? I expect you get interrupted by bells at the worst possible moment.'

Rose's eyes go in and out of focus as she swallows this indigestible quadruple spoonful of questions.

'Cook's gone upstairs, and . . . and we'll have some jelly, Miss. And there's roast beef left from yesterday, and . . . And would you like some plum cake, Miss Sugar?'

'Oh yes,' says Sugar. 'If you can spare it.'

The plum cake is fetched, and the servants stand by and watch the governess eat. Janey, finished stowing the dishes in the racks, comes to the doorway to see what's going on in the wider world.

'Hello, Janey,' says Sugar, in between bites of plum cake. 'We haven't seen each other since Christmas, have we? What a shame it is, don't you think, the way one part of the household is hidden from the other?'

Janey blushes so red that her cheeks almost match the colour of her lobsterish hands and forearms. She half-curtsies, her eyes bulging, but utters not a sound. Having landed in mischief twice already for incidents involving members of the Rackham household with whom she oughtn't to have had any intimacy – first Miss Sophie, on the day she got a bloody nose, and then poor mad Mrs Rackham, on the day she barged into the scullery offering to help – she's determined to stay out of trouble this time.

'Well,' says Sugar brightly, when she's consumed her last morsel of plum cake and the servants are still staring at her in mistrust and bafflement. 'I suppose I must be going. Sophie's bedtime shortly. Goodbye, Rose; goodbye, Harriet; goodbye, Janey.'

And she heaves herself to her feet, wishing that she could ascend through the air, painlessly and instantaneously, like a spirit whisked away from the scene of its own corporeal demise; or else that the kitchen's stone floor could open up and swallow her down into merciful extinction.

On her return to her room, there's a letter from William after all. If 'letter' is the right word for a note saying simply:

No further discussion.

Sugar crumples this note in her fist, and is again tempted to smash windows, scream her lungs raw, hammer on William's door. But she knows this is not the way to change his mind. Instead, her hopes shift to Sophie. William has reckoned without his daughter. He has only the vaguest conception of the loyalty that's developed between governess and child, and he'll soon find out. Sophie will change his mind for him: men can never stand to be the cause of female weeping!

At bedtime, Sugar tucks Sophie in as usual, and smooths her fine golden hair evenly over the pillow until it radiates like a picture-book illustration of the sun.

'Sophie?' she says, her voice hoarse with hesitation.

The child looks up, aware at once that a matter more momentous than the sewing of dolls' clothes is being raised.

'Yes, Miss?'

'Sophie, your father . . . Your father is likely to have some news for you. Quite soon, I think.'

'Yes, Miss,' says Sophie, blinking hard to keep sleep from claiming her before Miss Sugar arrives at the point.

Sugar licks her lips, which are as dry and rough-textured as sackcloth. She's loath to repeat William's ultimatum aloud, for fear that this will give it an indelible reality, like writing in ink over pencil.

'Most probably,' she flounders, 'he will have you brought to see him . . . And then he will tell you something.'

'Yes, Miss,' says Sophie, puzzled.

'Well . . .' Sugar presses on, summoning courage by taking hold of Sophie's hands. 'Well, when he does, I . . . I want you to tell him something, in return.'

'Yes, Miss,' promises Sophie.

'I want you to tell him . . .' wheezes Sugar, blinking against tears. 'I want you to tell him . . . how you feel about me!'

For answer, Sophie reaches up and embraces her just as she did yesterday, except that this time, to Sugar's astonishment, she strokes and pats her governess's hair in an infantile approximation of a mother's tenderness.

'Good night, Miss,' she says sleepily. 'And tomorrow: America.'

There being nothing more she can do but wait, Sugar waits. William has retreated from a firm resolution before – many times. He has threatened to tell Swan & Edgar to go hang; he has threatened to travel to the East India docks and grab a certain merchant by the collar and shake him till he gibbers; he has threatened to tell Grover Pankey to use better elephants for his pots. All bluster. If she leaves him alone, his tumescent resolve will wilt and shrivel to nothing. All it requires from her is . . . superhuman forbearance.

The morning of the next day passes without incident. Everything is exactly as normal. The Pilgrims have landed on American soil, and made peace with the savages. Homesteads are being built from felled trees. The luncheon, when served, is less bland than yesterday's: smoked haddock kedgeree, and more of the plum cake.

On Sugar's return to her room at midday, she finds a parcel waiting for her: a long, thin parcel, wrapped in brown paper and string. A conciliatory gift from William? No. A small *carte-de-visite* is attached to the end with string; she fetches it close to her eyes and reads what it has to say.

Dear Miss Sugar,

I heard about your misfortune from my father. Please accept this token of my good wishes. It needn't be returned; I find I have no use for it anymore, and I hope that you will very soon be in the same position.

Yours truly,

Emmeline Fox

Sugar unwraps the parcel, and brings to light a polished, sturdy walking-stick.

On her return to the school-room, keen to show Sophie her new tool, which allows her to walk with a much more dignified gait than the crutch, Sugar finds the child huddled over her writing-desk, sobbing and weeping uncontrollably.

'What's the matter? What's the matter?' she demands, her stick thumping against the floorboards as she limps across the room.

'You're going to be suh-suh-sent a*way*,' wails Sophie, almost accusingly.

'Was William – your father . . . here just now?' Sugar can't help asking the question, even though she smells his hair-oil in the air.

Sophie nods, bright tears jumping off her glistening chin.

'I *told* him, Miss,' she pleads shrilly. 'I *told* him I luh-luh-love you.'

'Yes? Yes?' prompts Sugar, stroking her palms ineffectually over Sophie's cheeks until the salty wetness stings the cracks in her flesh. 'What did he say?'

'H-he di'nt suh-suh-say *anything*,' sobs the child, her shoulders convulsing. 'But he luh-luh-looked very angry with muh-muh-me.'

With a cry of rage, Sugar pulls Sophie to her breast and kisses her over and over, murmuring inarticulate reassurances.

How dare he do this, she thinks, *to* my *child*.

The full story, when Sophie has been sufficiently calmed to tell it, is this: Miss Sugar is a very good governess, but there are a great many things that a lady needs to know that Miss Sugar doesn't know, like Dancing, Playing the Piano, German, Watercolours, and other accomplishments whose names Sophie can't recall. If Sophie is to be a proper lady, she'll need a different governess, and quite soon. Lady Bridgelow, a lady who knows all about these things, has confirmed that this is necessary.

For the rest of the afternoon, Sugar and Sophie labour under a suffocating cloud of grief. They carry on with the lessons – arithmetic, the Pilgrim Fathers, the properties of gold – with a sorrowful awareness that none of these subjects is quite what's required of a young lady in the making. And at bedtime, neither of them can look the other in the eye.

'Mr Rackham asked me to tell you, Miss,' says Rose, standing in the door of Sugar's bedroom at supper-time, 'that you needn't get up tomorrow morning.'

Sugar grips her cup of cocoa tight to keep it from spilling.

'Needn't get up?' she echoes stupidly.

'You needn't come out until the afternoon, he says. Miss Sophie is not to have any lessons in the morning.'

'No lessons?' echoes Sugar again. 'Did he say why not?'

'Yes, Miss,' says Rose, fidgeting to be released. 'Miss Sophie is going to have a visitor, in the school-room; I don't know who, or when exactly, Miss.'

'I see. Thank you, Rose.' And Sugar lets the servant go.

Minutes later, she's standing outside William's study door, breathing hard in the unlit stillness of the landing. A glimmer of light is visible through the key-hole; a rustle of activity (or does she imagine this?) is audible through the thick wood, when she presses her ear against it.

She knocks.

'Who is it?' His voice.

'Sugar,' she says, trying to suffuse that one word with all the affection, all the familiarity, all the companionship, all the promises of erotic fulfilment, that a single whispered sound can possibly embody: a thousand and one nights of carnal bliss that will see him through until he's an old, old man.

There is no reply. Silence. She stands shivering, urging herself to knock again, to appeal to him more persuasively, more cleverly, more insistently. If she yells, he'll be forced to open up to her, to keep the servants from gossiping. She opens her mouth, and her tongue squirms like that of a dumb half-wit selling broken china in the street. Then she walks barefoot back to her bedroom, teeth chattering, choked.

In her sleep, four hours later, she's back in Mrs Castaway's house, aged fifteen but with a book's worth of carnal knowledge already written into her. In the midnight hush after the last man has stumbled homewards, Mrs Castaway sits perusing her latest consignment of religious pamphlets all the way from Providence, Rhode Island. Before her mother can become too engrossed in her snipping, Sugar summons the pluck to ask a question.

'Mother . . . ? Are we *very* poor now?'

'Oh no,' Mrs Castaway smirks. 'We are *quite* comfortable now.'

'We aren't about to be thrown into the street, or anything like that?'

'No, no, no.'

'Then why must I . . . Why must I . . .' Sugar is unable to finish the question. In the dream no less than in life, her courage falters in the face of Mrs Castaway's arch sarcasm.

'Really now, child: I couldn't permit you to grow up *idle*, could I? That would leave you open to the temptation of Vice.'

'Mother, *please*: I—I'm in earnest! If we aren't in desperate straits, then why . . . ?'

Mrs Castaway looks up from her pamphlets, and fixes Sugar with a look of pure malevolence; her eyeballs seem to be effervescing with spite.

'Child: be reasonable,' she smiles. 'Why should *my* downfall be *your* rise? Why should *I* burn in Hell while *you* flap around in Heaven? In short, why should the world be a better place for *you* than it has been for *me*?' And, with a flourish, she dips her glue-brush into the pot, twirls it around, and deposits a translucent pearl of slime on a page already crowded with magdalens.

Next morning, Sugar tries the handle of a door she's never touched before, and, thank God, it opens. She slips inside.

It's the room Sophie once referred to as 'the room that hasn't got anyone living in it, Miss, only things.' A storage-room, in other words, immediately adjacent to the school-room, and crowded with dusty objects.

Agnes's sewing-machine is here, its brassy lustre dulled with the subtle powder of neglect. Behind that, there are strange apparatuses that Sugar recognises, after some study, to be photographic in nature. Boxes of chemicals, too; further evidence of William's former passion for the art. An easel leans against the far wall. William's, or Agnes's? Sugar isn't sure. An archery bow hangs by its string from one of the easel's wing-nuts: a folly of Agnes's that she found herself too weak to pursue. A rowing oar inscribed *Downing Boat Club 1864* has toppled to the carpet. Stacked on the floor, in front of book-cases that are too full for any more, are books: books about photography, books about art, books about philosophy. Religion, too: many about religion. Surprised by this, Sugar picks one off the stack – *"Winter afore Harvest", or the Soul's Growth in Grace*, by J. C. Philpot – and reads its flyleaf.

Dear Brother, I'm confident this will interest you,

Henry.

On the window-sill, covered with cobwebs, yet another stack of books: *Ancient Wisdom Comprehensively Explained*, by Melampus Blyton, *Miracles and Their Mechanisms*, by Mrs Tanner, *Primitive Christianity Identical with Spiritualism*, by Dr Crowell, several novels by Florence Marryat, and a large number of much slimmer volumes, among them *The Ladies' Hand-Book of the Toilet, The Elixir of Beauty, How to Preserve Good Looks*, and *Health, Beauty and the Toilet: Letters to Ladies from a Lady Doctor*. Sugar opens this last one, finds that Agnes has defaced the margins with remarks like: *Not in the least effective!, No benefit whatso-ever!* and *Fraud!*

I'm sorry, Agnes, thinks Sugar, replacing the book on the pile. *I tried.*

A large wooden edifice like an outsize wardrobe, but backless and fastened directly to the wall, serves as a wooden mausoleum for Agnes's less frequently worn dresses. When Sugar opens the doors, an aroma of lavender moth-repellent escapes. This wardrobe, Sugar's certain, is as close as she can get to the school-room wall on the other side. She takes a deep breath, and steps in.

The splendid array of Agnes's gowns hangs undisturbed and pungent. No moth could hope to survive within this wonderland of expensive cloth, this efflorescent interleaving of sleeves, bodices and bustled skirts, and indeed one such insect lies dead on the floor, inches away from a translucent bar of soap-shaped poison embossed, predictably enough, with the Rackham 'R'.

All the Agneses Sugar remembers are here. She has followed these costumes – when they contained Agnes's compact little body in their silky embrace – through crowded theatre foyers, sunny gardens and lantern-lit pavilions. Now here they hang; neat, incorrupt and empty. Impulsively Sugar buries her nose in the nearest bodice, to exclude the dominant odour of poison in favour of some faint residue of Agnes's personal perfume, but there's no escaping the heady odour of preservative. Released from Sugar's grasp, the costume swings back on its hook with a squeak.

Sugar steps deeper into the shadowy recess, and her feet are entangled in soft whispery cloth. She bends down to investigate, picks up a voluminous jumble of purple velvet, is startled to find her own fingers poking through holes in it. The dress has been mutilated in ten, twenty, thirty places by scissors; cannibalised as if to provide fabric animals for a velvet Noah's-ark tableau. The other dresses beneath it are similarly butchered. Why? She can't imagine. It's too late to understand Agnes now. Too late to understand anything.

At the very rear of the closet, Sugar lowers herself to a sitting position, her bad foot stretched out gingerly before her, her backside resting on a pillow of Agnes's ruined gowns, her cheek and ear leaning against the wall. She shuts her eyes, and waits.

Half an hour later, when she's nodding off to sleep, and almost sick from the reek of poisoned lavender, she hears what she's come for: a strange woman's voice from the school-room beyond, interspersed with William's.

'Stand straight, Sophie,' he commands, benignly enough. 'You aren't a . . .' A what? Inaudible, this last word. Sugar presses her ear harder to the wall, presses so hard it hurts.

'Tell me, child, and don't be shy,' urges the strange woman's voice. 'What have you learned all this time?'

Sophie's reply is too soft for Sugar to hear any of it, but (bless her!) it's quite lengthy.

'And have you any French, child?'

Silence for a few seconds, then William butts in:

'French was not one of Miss Sugar's accomplishments.'

'And what about the piano, Sophie? Do you know where to put your fingers on the piano?' Sugar pictures a face to match the voice: a sharp-nosed face, with crow-black eyes and a predatory mouth. So vivid is the picture that she imagines her own fist colliding with that sharp nose, snapping it into a bloody mash of splintered bone. 'And do you know how to dance, child?'

Again William speaks up, mentioning Miss Sugar's incompetence in this regard. Damn him! How she would love to shove a knife into his – But what's this? He's coming to her defence after all. He's venturing to enquire if Sophie is not perhaps a little *young* to be initiated into such skills as piano-playing and dancing. Aren't they useless, after all, until she's nearer courting age?

'That may be true, sir,' admits the new governess sweetly, 'but it is my belief that they have a virtue in themselves. Some teachers under-estimate how much a child can learn, and how early she can learn it. *I* believe that if a little girl can be encouraged to flower a few years earlier than the rest . . . Why then, all the better!'

Sugar bites her lip and placates herself with fantasies of hacking this woman to gory fragments.

'Would you like to play a tune on the piano, Sophie? It really is simpler than you could possibly imagine. I can teach you one in five minutes. Would you like that, Sophie?'

She's shoving herself forward, this woman: showing off everything she has to offer, begging to be the one chosen. Sophie's reply is inaudible, but what else can the child say but yes? William, Sophie and the new governess leave the school-room, and descend the stairs. The pact has been made; there's no pulling out of it now; it's like the moment when a man takes a whore by the hand.

A minute later, Sugar stands at the door of the storage-room, listening for what happens next. She hasn't long to wait: an unfamiliar sound strikes up from the parlour: a simple two-finger melody. It's played first in a confident, deliberate manner, three or four times over, then copied, haltingly and imprecisely, by hands that must be Sophie's.

The tune? Well, it's not 'Hearts of Oak', but it might as well be. As surely as Sugar used to know it was time to leave The Fireside when 'Hearts of Oak' was sung, she knows that this melody Sophie is playing on the piano is her cue to leave the Rackham house forever.

Sugar returns to her bedroom and begins packing at once. What's the point of waiting until the first of March for the hammer to fall, when the minuscule hammers inside the parlour piano have already delivered the blow? Every hour that she remains offers William sixty opportunities to humiliate and torment her; every minute that she must teach Sophie under the looming shadow of their imminent separation is unbearable.

She'll survive, she'll find a way to keep off the streets. The ten pounds William gave her yesterday was an insult, a mockery of what she's done for his daughter, but hidden in her dressing-cabinet she has plenty of money. Plenty! Crammed amid the jumble of stockings and underwear are the crumpled envelopes she accumulated during her sojourn in Priory Close. So generous was William then, and so disinclined was she to waste money on anything unconnected with winning his love, that she spent only a fraction of the wages that his bank, regular as clockwork, posted to her. Most of these envelopes, coming to light as she scrabbles them out from under frivolous unmentionables she hasn't worn in months, are unopened, and crackle with a fortune beyond the imaginings of servants. Why, even the loose coins she's carelessly tossed into these drawers amount to more than the likes of Janey would earn in a full year.

Stowing her hoard of cash into safe places – her purse for the coins, a pocket of an overcoat for the bank-notes – she appreciates for the first time that she's spent less since coming to live in the Rackham house than she spent in her first forty-eight hours in Priory Close. To the prostitute she was then, these sums seemed no great fortune, a flow of largesse which could be swallowed up any day by the purchase of a particularly sumptuous dress or a few too many restaurant meals. Now, looking at all this money through the eyes of a respectable woman, she realises it's wealth enough to launch her into any future she chooses, if only she's frugal and finds some work. It's wealth enough to take her to the ends of the Earth.

As Sugar packs, she wrestles with her conscience. Should she, *can* she, tell Sophie the truth? Is it merciful, or is it cruel, not to explain the circumstances of her departure? Will Sophie suffer terribly from being deprived of the chance to say goodbye? Sugar frets, half-convinced she's genuinely considering changing her mind, but deeper inside she knows she has no intention of telling the truth. Instead, she continues to pack as if by brute instinct, and the voice of reason is lost like a sparrow-cheep in a gale.

One travelling case is all she needs. The crates of clothes that William organised to be fetched from Mrs Castaway's are still in storage somewhere, in a place whose whereabouts he never did get around to telling her. Not that it matters: she doesn't want them now. They're whore's weeds, the lavish plumage of a demi-monde. The dress she has on, and one or two others (this dark-green one, her favourite): that's all she needs. A couple of shifts, some clean pantalettes, stockings, a spare pair of shoes: a suitcase is soon full. Her wretched novel and Agnes's diaries she stuffs into a tartan bag.

She lifts the suitcase in one hand – her good side – and loops the bag over the shoulder of the arm that must lean on the cane. She takes three or four steps, shambling like a circus animal forced to walk on hind-legs at the threat of a whip. Then she hangs her head, lowers her unmanageable burdens to the floor, and weeps.

'Let's have our afternoon lessons outside today,' she suggests to Sophie, not long afterward. 'The house is stuffy, and the air is fresh.'

Sophie springs up from her writing-desk, visibly cheered by the prospect. She hastens to dress for an outing; education *en plein air* is what she likes best, especially if it involves a visit to the fountain, or a glimpse of ducks, rooks, dogs, cats, or indeed any breed of creature other than human.

'I'm ready, Miss,' she declares in a trice, and so she is, needing only a small adjustment to the tilt and fastening of her bonnet.

'Go downstairs, little one; I'll follow on behind.'

Sophie does as she's told, and Sugar lingers in the school-room for a little while longer, gathering together the necessaries for the lesson, and a few other items besides, which she shoves into a leather satchel. Then she descends the stairs, her cane clacking against the banisters as she goes.

Outside, the weather is windy, rather bleak, but not bitter. The sky is dim, steel-grey, imbued with the sort of light that makes everything, be it grassy lawn, cobbled street, iron fence or human flesh, appear as shades of the same colour.

Sugar would have preferred to walk directly out of the front gate, but unlucky coincidence has placed Shears there, hard at work transplanting a rose bush so that passers-by can no longer reach through the railings and steal the flowers of his labour. He has his back to Sugar and Sophie but, being a sociable soul, he'll no doubt turn and speak to them if they try to pass him, and Sugar doesn't want that. So, with a gentle tug at Sophie's wrist, she makes a *volte-face* and they move around the side of the house.

'Are we going with Cheesman, Miss?' Sophie enquires, a logical question in view of the carriage-way looming up. The coachman and the horse are out of sight, but the unshackled coach stands in front of its little house, twinkling with soapy water, ready for another foray into the dirty, smoky world beyond the Rackham confines.

'No, dear,' replies Sugar without looking down, her eyes fixed on the mews gate to the right of the stable. 'This way is nicer, that's all.'

The gate is bolted, but not locked; the padlock hangs open on its loop, thank God. Clumsily juggling her walking stick and Sophie's hand, Sugar removes the lock and slides the long iron rod out of its shaft.

'Good afternoon to yer, Miss Sugar.'

With a violent start Sugar spins around on her good heel, almost overbalancing from the weight of her bags – the tartan Gladstone on one shoulder, the satchel on her other arm. Cheesman is standing very close, his stubbly face impassive except for an impudent gleam in his eyes. In the dreary light, and without the sartorial props of his greatcoat and hat, he looks shabby and thin; the chill breeze has blown several locks of his hair, stiff with stale oil, over his shining forehead, and there are circular tankard stains in the lap of his trousers.

'Good afternoon to *you*, Cheesman,' Sugar nods dismissively, her voice vinegar.

'I'll open the gate for yer, Miss,' offers the coachman, extending a thickly-haired hand and forearm, 'if you and Miss Rackham would care to take yerselves to the carriage.'

For an instant Sugar considers taking him up on his offer. A ride in the carriage would be easier than walking, and now that Cheesman has accosted her anyway, she may as well make use of him. He could deliver them to the nearest park, and they could proceed from there . . . Yes, for an instant Sugar reconsiders, but when she looks again at the man himself, she sees the dark grime under the fingernails of the hand he extends towards her, and remembers how he dug those fingers into her waist and bustle not so long ago.

'I shan't be needing you, Cheesman,' she says firmly, gathering Sophie against her hip. 'We're not going far.'

Cheesman retracts his arm and, positioning his palm on the back of his hairy neck in a caricature of bemusement, he appraises Sugar from head to foot.

'Big 'eavy bags yer got there, Miss,' he remarks, squinting at her mis-shapen Gladstone, 'if I may say so. 'Eaps of fings in there, for a short walk.'

'I've told you, Cheesman,' insists Sugar, a quaver of anxiousness skewing the flint-edge of her voice. 'We've just decided to stretch our legs a little.'

Cheesman lowers his eyes to the level of Sugar's skirts and leers. 'I don't see as *your* legs need any stretchin', Miss Sugar.'

Anger lends Sugar courage. 'You're impertinent, Cheesman,' she snaps. 'I shall speak to Mr Rackham about you immediately on my return.'

But, much as she hoped he'd be cowed by this threat, Cheesman is unmoved, except for his eyebrows.

'Speak to Mr Rackham, you say? On yer return? And when might *that* be, exackly, Miss Sugar?'

Cheesman steps forward, so close that she can smell the spirits on his breath, and blocks the gate through which she longs to pass.

'Seems to me, Miss Sugar,' he muses, folding his arms across his chest and peering up into the dismal heavens, 'meanin' no disrespect . . . but it's sure to rain, any minute now I reckon. Them clouds . . .' He shakes his head mistrustfully. 'Foul, wouldn't yer agree?'

'What are you about, Cheesman?' demands Sugar, removing her hand from Sophie's shoulder lest, in her terror, she should squeeze it too hard. 'Step out of the way!'

'Now, now, Miss,' cautions the coachman, in a reasonable tone. 'What would Mr Rackham say if *Miss* Rackham 'ere' – he indicates Sophie with an amiable nod - 'was to come 'ome wiv a chill? Or ain't that likely, in your opinion?'

'For the last time, Cheesman: stand aside,' commands Sugar, knowing that if he doesn't yield now, she won't have the strength to muster this imperious tone again. 'Sophie's welfare is *my* domain.'

But Cheesman is sucking his teeth reflectively, looking back towards the carriage.

'Well now, Miss Sugar,' he says. 'I fink the *uvver* governess, what was 'ere this mornin', might not see eye to eye wiv you there.'

Barely pausing to savour the effect of this statement, he raises his palms skywards and enquires dramatically, 'Now was that a drop a' rain?' He examines each palm with a frown. 'I truly ask meself, would Mr Rackham want 'is daughter to be took out in the rain? And why's a governess that's 'avin' to be replaced for reasons of bad 'ealth so keen to do it?'

Seeing him posed there, his palms open to whatever might fall into them, Sugar thinks she sees what he's angling for.

'Let's discuss this in private,' she says, trying to keep the defeat out of her voice. Maybe if Sophie doesn't actually witness money changing hands she'll be none the wiser. 'I'm sure we can come to an understanding that will benefit us both.'

'I never doubted it, Miss,' agrees the coachman cheerfully, bouncing away from the gate. 'Is be'ind the coach private enough for yer?'

'Stay here a moment, Sophie,' says Sugar, setting her bags down but avoiding the child's gaze.

Once hidden from Sophie behind the carriage, Sugar hastily delves into the pocket of her overcoat and fetches out a crumpled bank-note.

'Seems we're beginnin' to unnerstand one anuvver now, Miss Sugar,' murmurs Cheesman in bright-eyed approval.

'Here, Cheesman,' says Sugar, pressing the money into his outstretched hand. 'Ten pounds. A small fortune, for you.'

Cheesman crushes the note in his fist and stuffs it into his trousers.

'Oh yes,' he affirms. 'This will buy a beer or two. Or three . . .'

'Good,' sighs Sugar, turning to leave. 'Much joy may you—'

'. . . but really, Miss Sugar,' he goes on, laying a detaining finger on her shoulder, 'money ain't much use to me. I mean, Mr Rackham knows the wage 'e pays me, and 'e knows what it buys and what it don't buy. I can't very well turn up wearin' a fancy suit o' clothes, can I, or a gold chain on me watch? So, to me, ten pounds is . . . well . . . it's really only a powerful lot o' beer, don't yer see?'

Sugar stares at him, weak with loathing. If there is one man she would wish to see shackled to the murderous bed of her novel's heroine, pleading for his life while she slices him open like a fish, it's him.

'You won't let us go, then?' she croaks.

Grinning widely, Cheesman waggles his forefinger like a kindly demagogue chiding a thoughtless pupil.

'I didn't say that, now did I?'

Ignoring how she bridles with fright as he seizes hold of her arms, he pulls her close, so that her cheek collides with the meaty shovel of his jaw.

'All I want,' he says, speaking softly and with exaggeratedly clear diction, 'is a little somefink *more* than money. Somefink to remember you by.'

Sugar's stomach shrinks as if doused with ice-water; her mouth goes dry as ash. *What do you take me for?* she wants to rebuke him. *I'm a lady: a lady!* But the first utterance that emerges from her tight throat is, 'There isn't time.'

Cheesman laughs and, guiding her against the wheel of his coach, gathers up her skirts in his hands.

Once the Rackham gate is shut behind them, Sugar and Sophie walk out of the house's sight unhindered and unobserved.

'Where are we going, Miss?' says Sophie as they hurry along the narrow passageway that connects the mews with the main road.

'Somewhere nice,' says Sugar, panting as she hobbles, her Gladstone bag and satchel lolling to and fro, her walking-stick hitting the cobbles with such force that the end is beginning to fray.

'Shall I carry one of the bags, Miss?'

'They're too heavy for you.'

Sophie frowns, looks worried, looks back towards the house, but it's already lost to view. The skies have darkened considerably, and big raindrops are falling from the clouds, hitting the ground – and Sophie's bonnet – like small pebbles. Sophie examines the universe for further clues as to the wisdom or foolishness of this little outing. Although she hasn't the words to express it, she feels she has an instinct for cosmological messages that others fail to divine.

In a neighbour's back garden (can one refer to neighbours if one hasn't ever met them?) a man is digging a hole; he stops for a moment and waves to Sophie, his face lit up by a smile. A little farther along, the mongrel dog who has, on other occasions, barked at them, regards their approach with serene composure. These are good omens. One more such omen, and who knows?: the skies may clear.

An omnibus is rolling into view, advancing along Kensington Park Road towards the city.

'Walk faster, Sophie,' says Miss Sugar breathlessly. 'Let's . . . let's take a ride in the omnibus.'

Sophie obediently quickens her pace, though it's doubtful Miss Sugar is capable of moving any faster herself. The misshapen bags on her shoulders are jogging and slewing most inelegantly as Miss Sugar stumps forward, fist trembling on the handle of her stick.

'Run ahead, Sophie, so the conductor sees we want to get on!'

Sophie scoots ahead and, an instant later, Sugar stumbles on a loose cobble and almost sprawls head over heels. The Gladstone bag falls to the ground, disgorging its contents all over the footpath: Agnes's diaries, tumbling in more directions than seems scientifically possible, opening their pages like the froth of milk boiling over, a spillage of wind-blown paper releasing a confetti of dried flower petals and faded prayer cards. And Sugar's novel, spewed out of its cardboard jacket all along the street for three body-lengths or more, its densely-inked pages whipped up into the breeze in unbelievably rapid succession.

For one second, Sugar jerks her hands towards the fluttering mess, then she reels round and lollops in pursuit of Sophie.

Sugar and Sophie sit inside the crowded omnibus, not speaking, only breathing. It's as much as Sugar can manage not to gasp and wheeze. She dabs surreptitiously at her crimson, sweaty face with a silk white handkerchief. The other passengers — the usual miscellany of frumpy old women, benign schoolmastery-looking men in top hats, fashionable young ladies with pedigree lap-dogs, furry-bearded artisans, snoozy matrons half-buried under straw baskets, umbrellas, elaborate hats, bouquets, sleeping infants — behave as if Sugar and Sophie don't exist, as if no one exists, as if the omnibus is an empty conveyance rattling towards London for its own amusement. They keep their eyes on the newspaper, or their own gloved hands folded in their laps or, when all else fails, the advertisements posted above the heads of the passengers opposite.

Sugar raises her chin, fearing to look at Sophie. Above the feathery summit of a dowager's hat, printed in two colours on a pasted handbill, hovers William Rackham's face, framed between other bills advertising tea and cough lozenges.

Rain begins to pelt against the windows, turning the sky grey as twilight. Sugar seeks out a vacant interval between two heads, and peers through the rain-spattered glass. Out on the street, would-be passengers are hurrying through the silvery gloom.

'High Street Corr-*nerrr*!' yells the conductor, but no one disembarks. 'Room for one more!' And he helps a half-drenched pilgrim aboard.

All the way along the Bayswater Road, Sugar keeps her eye on any pedestrians who look as if they may be approaching the omnibus. No policemen, thank God. Strange, though, how she's convinced – just for a second – that she recognises almost every upturned face she glimpses! Isn't that Emmeline Fox, trotting along under a parapluie? No, of course it isn't . . . But look there: surely that's Doctor Curlew? Again, no. And those two swells, punching each other roguishly on the shoulder – could they be Ashley and Bodwell – or whatever their names were? No, these are younger men, barely out of school. But there! Sugar's fists clench in fear as she spies an angry-looking man running towards her through the rain, his wayward, fleecy hair bobbing absurdly on his hatless head. But no: William's hair was shorn almost to the scalp long ago, and this man dashes across the street to the other side.

Farther along, between Hyde Park's riding promenades and St George's burial ground, a woman hurries to catch the omnibus, gliding along the footpath as if likewise mounted on wheels. Her head is obscured beneath her umbrella, but despite this, she impresses Sugar as the very embodiment of Agnes. Her dress is pink – perhaps that's the reason – pink as Rackham's Carnation Cream Soap – although the driving rain has discoloured the skirts with darker rivulets, giving them the appearance of striped confectionery.

'Are you with us, ma'am?' yells the conductor, but this appeal to the lady to join the common throng seems to offend her delicate sensibilities, and she slows her pace, stops, and pirouettes in the opposite direction.

'Where are we going to have our lesson, Miss?' enquires Sophie softly.

'I haven't decided yet,' says Sugar. She continues to stare out the window, avoiding Sophie's face as anxiously as she would avoid the edge of a precipice.

At Marble Arch, a man boards the omnibus, drenched to the skin. He takes his seat between two ladies, mortified to impose his sodden form upon their dry persons, hunching up in a futile effort to contract his tall, wide-shouldered body into a smaller physical space.

'Forgive me,' he mumbles, his handsome face blushing bright as a lamp.

It's Henry Rackham, thinks Sugar.

All the way in to the centre of the city, the drenched man stares stonily ahead of him, his blush scarcely fading, his hands awkwardly patting his knees. By the time the omnibus reaches Oxford Circus, he can stand it no longer: his shoulders have begun to exude a subtle halo of steam, and he knows it. With another muttered apology, he lurches out of his seat and flees back into the rain. Sugar watches him disappear into the deluge and, despite her own state of anxiety, finds it in her heart to wish him a speedy arrival at his destination, wherever that may be.

'We must get out here, Sophie,' she says a minute later, and rises to her feet. The child does likewise, grasping a fold of adult skirt as Sugar limps out of the omnibus into a swirling great cloud of rain.

Is this a park they see before them? No, it isn't a park. Almost as soon as their feet have settled on solid ground, Miss Sugar has hailed a cab, called some instructions up to the driver, and hurriedly ushered Sophie into the cigar-smoky cabin. The cabman, though drenched to the skin, is a jovial soul, and he flicks the streaming rump of his reluctant horse with a whip.

'Make yer choice, you old nag,' he jokes. 'The knacker's yard, or King's Cross Station!'

'Will we be home for supper, Miss?' asks Sophie, as the carriage jolts into motion.

'Are you hungry, dear?' Sugar replies.

'No, Miss.'

Feeling she can put it off no longer, Sugar permits herself to look at Sophie's face for just a moment. The child is wide-eyed, slightly bewildered, unmistakably worried – but not, as far as Sugar can tell, tensed for flight.

'Here, I'll give you your spyglass,' says Sugar, and hoists the satchel up against her bosom, keeping it out of range of the child's vision. She hunches forward to make extra-sure Sophie won't be able to see the satchel's contents – a history book, an atlas, clean underwear, the framed photograph of Miss Sophie Rackham signed *Tovey & Scholefield*, a higgledy-piggledy assortment of combs and hair-brushes, pencils and crayons, *Alice's Adventures in Wonderland*, the poems of Mr Lear, a crumpled shawl, a jar of talcum powder, a Manila envelope stuffed full of Sophie's own home-made Christmas cards, the book of fairytales donated with fond wishes by a 'tiresome' uncle and, nestled in the very bottom, the spyglass.

'Here,' she says, handing the metal cylinder down to Sophie, who accepts the object unhesitatingly, but lays it in her lap without looking at it.

'Where are we going, Miss?'

'Somewhere very interesting, I promise,' says Sugar.

'Will I be home in time for bed?'

Sugar wraps one arm around Sophie's small body, her hand cupping the swell of the child's hip.

'We have a very, very long journey ahead of us, Sophie,' she responds, dizzy with relief when Sophie relaxes, wriggles closer, and lays her own hand on Sugar's belly. 'But when it's over, I'll make sure you have a bed. The warmest, cleanest, softest, driest, nicest bed in the whole world.'

THIRTY-FIVE

illiam Rackham, head of Rackham Perfumeries, slightly the worse for the several stiff brandies he drank after the departure of the police, stands in his parlour staring out at the rain, wondering how many bits of paper are still unaccounted for: how many are still fluttering through the evening air, or plastered to the windows of his Notting Hill neighbours, or being read by astounded pedestrians when they pluck them off hedges and fence-railings.

'This is all we could find, sir,' says Letty, raising her voice to compete with the howl of the wind and the susurrating din of the downpour. She adds a handful of muddy pages to the sodden heap in the middle of the parlour carpet, then straightens up, wondering if her master really means to dry out all these wet sheets of paper and read them, or whether he's merely concerned to keep the streets of his neighbourhood clean.

William waves her away, a gesture of grudging thanks and dismissal all in one. These last few salvages from the writings Sugar strewed so spitefully to the wind can't add anything to what he's read already.

Outside the parlour door, a musical murmur of feminine apology suggests that the departing Letty has collided, or almost collided, with Rose. What a household! A full complement of women scurrying upstairs and downstairs, and no one left for them to serve but William Rackham, a man disconsolately circling a mound of muddy paper. A man who, in the space of a year, has gained an abundance of onerous responsibilities, but lost his wife, his brother, his mistress and now — God grant that it not be true! — his only-begotten daughter. Is there nothing more effectual he can do in the circumstances, than scour the streets for lost pages of a tale in which men are tortured to death?

Maybe he was remiss not to have shown Sugar's scribblings to the police, but it seemed a waste of time, in such an urgent case, to delay the search by even a minute. The absurdity of the thought: to keep barely literate policemen sitting in his parlour, frowning in earnest concentration over the feverish fictions of a madwoman, when they could be out *there*, in the streets of London, hunting for her in the flesh!

William falls into an armchair, and the whuff of air sends one of Agnes's intricately embroidered squares of fabric flying off the armrest. He retrieves it from the floor and replaces it on the chair, useless though it is. Then he fetches up a page of Sugar's writings, the page he read first of all, when the first armful of this bizarre debris was delivered to the house. It was flaccid and fragile then, dripping with water, and liable to tear in his hands, but the warmth of the parlour has since dried it, so that it crackles between his fingers like an autumn leaf.

All men are the same, declares the thin, evil-looking scrawl. *If there is one thing I have learned in my time on this Earth, it is this. All men are the same.*

How can I assert this with such conviction? Surely I have not known all the men there are to know? On the contrary, dear reader, perhaps I have!

Again William purses his lips in distaste at this admission of Sugar's promiscuity. Again he frowns at the accusation that follows, where he is denounced as *Vile man, eternal Adam*. Yet, fascinated by the sleazy charisma of slander, he reads on.

How smug you are, Reader, if you are a member of the sex that boasts a scrag of gristle in your trousers! You fancy that this book will amuse you, thrill you, rescue you from the horror of boredom (the profoundest horror that your privileged sex must endure) and that, having consumed it like a sweetmeat, you will be left at liberty to carry on exactly as before! Exactly as you have done since Eve was first betrayed in the Garden! But this book is different, dear Reader. This book is a KNIFE. Keep your wits about you; you will need them!

Oh God, oh God: how is it possible that his daughter has fallen into the clutches of such a viper? Ought he to have guessed sooner than today? Would another man have come to his senses faster? It's so obvious now, so terrifyingly self-evident, that Sugar was a madwoman: her unnatural intellect, her sexual depravity, her masculine appetite for business, her reptilian skin . . . Oh God, and what about the time she crawled, crablike, in pursuit of him, squirting water from her quim! What was he thinking of, to take this for an arousing bit of tomfoolery, an erotic parlour frolic, when any fool would recognise it as the bestial cavortings of a monster!

How is it possible, though, that God saw fit to install *two* madwomen in the bosom of his household, when other men are altogether spared? What has he done to deserve—? But no, such questions are a self-indulgence, and fail to solve the problem at hand. His daughter has been abducted, and is being conveyed, likely as not, towards a pitiful fate. Even if Sophie manages to slip out of her captor's grasp, how long can a defence-less innocent survive in the nefarious maze of London? There are preda-tors on every street corner . . . Not a week goes by that *The Times* doesn't print reports of a well-dressed child being lured into an alleyway by a kindly-looking matron, then 'skinned' – stripped of its boots and clothes – and left for dead. Better by far if Sugar holds Sophie to ransom; what-ever she asks, short of ruining him altogether, he will gladly pay!

William presses his thumbs against his eyes, and squeezes. Haunting his brain like a lurid lantern-slide is his recollection of his daughter weep-ing, her face contorted with grief as she beseeched him not to send Miss Sugar away. Her tiny hands, too fearful to clutch at him, clutched instead at the edges of her little writing-desk, as if it were a flimsy boat being tossed upon a tumultuous sea. Is *this* the picture he must carry with him to the grave? The photograph of Sophie taken at Scholefield & Tovey's studio, which he offered to hand over to the police for the purposes of a 'WANTED' poster, is nowhere to be found – stolen by Sugar, evidently. Instead, he's had to take scissors to the 'family' portrait, and snip Sophie's face from it, despite knowing from his own photographic experience that an image of such tiny dimensions, when enlarged and retouched by care-less strangers, is unlikely to bear much resemblance to his daughter . . .

But again, these are secondary considerations, mere details and distrac-tions, which skirt around the central horror of his predicament. Yesterday his daughter was safely present and accounted for, shyly playing a tune on the piano, taking her first hesitant steps towards forgiving him, towards understanding that he did have her best interests at heart after all; today, she is gone, and his skull resounds with the memory of her weeping.

It's beyond belief, how easily Sugar has committed this crime! Was there really *no one* to stand in her way? He's interrogated his entire house-hold, interrogated them no less thoroughly than the police, he'll wager. The female servants know nothing, saw nothing, heard nothing, swear they were too busy with their appointed tasks to notice the abduction. How can they have the temerity, the gall to assert this? The house is virtually unpeopled, yet it's swarming with servants – what do they *do* all day, if not laze in armchairs and read tuppenny books in front of the kitchen fire? Could not *one* of their number be spared from these arduous activities to make sure that the last female Rackham didn't get spirited away by a lunatic?

The males were only marginally more helpful. Shears confirmed that Miss Sugar didn't leave by the front gate: a thousand thanks, Mr Shears, for this vital information! Cheesman said that he saw, at a distance, Miss Sugar and Miss Sophie go out for a walk, but thought nothing of it, since they often did so in the afternoons. Hearing this, William was sorely tempted to berate the fellow for his lack of imagination, especially since Cheesman knew damn well that this governess was no governess at all. Ah, but there's the rub: Cheesman's illicit knowledge. As the only Rackham employee with a prior awareness of Sugar's true origins, Cheesman could make things damn awkward for him now that the police are involved. So, instead of suggesting that any man with a grain of sense would have asked Sugar a few penetrating questions, William contented himself with enquir-ing if Cheesman had happened to notice how the governess was dressed, and if she was carrying any luggage.

'I ain't much of a one for noticing the clothes on a woman, sir,' said Cheesman, scratching his sandpapery chin. 'An' as for luggidge . . . I didn't see none o' that, neither.'

A search of Sugar's bedroom confirmed the coachman's impression: a full suitcase was found standing abandoned near the door. Its contents, when disgorged all over the floor by an incensed William, proved to be everything a woman might need if leaving home: grooming utensils, night-gown, underwear, toiletries (Rackham's), the green dress she wore when first she met him. No clue, however, to where she might have gone.

William's hand has begun to tremble, and he hears the fluttery rustle of paper in his lap – the maiden page of Sugar's manuscript he still holds gripped between his fingers. He casts it from him, and butts his head back on the armchair. Another of Agnes's embroidered trifles – an antimacassar

decorated with robins and ornamental 'R's in honour of her new husband
– is nudged off its perch and falls onto his shoulder. Irritably, he tosses it
aside; it lands on the piano lid and slips off the lustrously polished wood.
A pretty tune it was, that issued from that piano yesterday – and today
the body that sat upon that stool has been sucked into a terrifying vacuum.

He grits his teeth, fighting back despair. Sugar and Sophie are out there
somewhere. If only he could be granted, for just one hour, a God's-eye-view,
an aerial perspective far above the city's rooftops but short of the obscuring clouds; and if only Sugar could be carrying on her person, unknow-
ingly, a halo of guilt, an incandescent mark of criminality that made her
glow like a beacon below, so that he could point down from the sky and
cry: *There! There she goes!*

But no, such fantasies are not the way the world is. An unspecified
number of policemen are dawdling through the streets, seeing no farther
than the next corner, distracted by brawling hawkers and scurrying thieves,
keeping their eyes half-open for a lady with a small child who, unlike all
the hundreds of innocent respectable ladies with small children strolling
the metropolis, must be arrested. Is this the best they can do, when the
daughter of William Rackham is in danger of her life?

He leaps up, lights a cigarette and sucks on the smoke, pacing the room.
His fury and agitation are worsened by his awareness that there's nothing
to distinguish him from any other man in this situation: he is behaving
exactly the same as they would, pacing and smoking, waiting for other
people to bring him news that's unlikely to be good, and wishing he hadn't
drunk so much brandy.

The muddle of wet papers on the carpet is starting to steam faintly.
With a grunt of disgust, he skims a page off the top, finds it unreadably
blurred by rain, snatches up another.

'*But I am a father!*' is what his eyes light upon. '*I have a son and a daughter, waiting for me at home!*'

'*Better you had thought of that before,*' *said I, cutting through his shirt with
my razor-sharp dress-making shears. Very intent I was upon my work, swivelling the
scissors back and forth across his hairy belly.*

The stomach within William's own hairy belly churns in horror and he
can read no further. Glowing in his mind is a vision of Sugar as she was
when they first met, a gently smiling advocate of the bloodiest revenges.

'*Titus Andronicus*, now *there's* a play,' she cooed to him across the table in The Fireside, and he failed to hear the warning bell, thinking only that she was making conversation. Bewitched by her precocious intellect, he imagined there was more to her than that – he took her to be a tender soul, cursed with loneliness, genuinely eager to please. Was he altogether mistaken? Pray God that *some* of what he saw in her was real; pray God she has a streak of kindness in her, or Sophie is doomed!

Letting the page fall, William stares at the French windows, whose panes rattle and stream with rain. A trickle of water has entered the room through the join, and trembles on the periphery of the floorboards. The carpenter gave his solemn oath that would never happen again! He said those windows were 'sealed snug as a lady's locket', damn him! William still has the blackguard's business card; he'll call him back and make him do the job properly!

'If you please, sir,' says Letty, rousing him from his impotent wrath with a jolt. 'Will you be having any supper?'

Supper? *Supper?* How can this imbecile imagine he has the stomach for supper on a night like this? He opens his mouth to scold her, to let her know that it's precisely her numbskulled inability to understand there's more to the world than plum-cake and cocoa that's allowed this calamity to happen in the first place. But then he observes the look of fright on Letty's face, and perceives her honest, canine desperation to please him. Poor girl: she may be a half-wit, but she means well, and the wickedness of women like Sugar isn't her fault.

'Thank you, Letty,' he sighs, rubbing his face with his palms. 'Some coffee, perhaps. And some bread and butter. Or . . . or asparagus on toast, if you can manage it.'

'No trouble at all, Mr Rackham,' chirps Letty, pink with gratitude that here, at last, is something that's in her power to deliver.

Next morning, Rose brings William the silver tray of post, and he rifles through the envelopes, searching for ransom notes. In amongst the business correspondence, there are only three letters without a return address on the back. Too impatient for the nicety of the paper-knife, he rips them open with his fingernails.

One is an appeal on behalf of India's lepers who, according to a Mrs Eccles of Peckham Rye, can be wholly cured if each businessman in Britain earning in excess of a thousand pounds per annum donates just one of those pounds to the post office box address below. Another is from the William Whiteley emporium in Bayswater, expressing confidence that every Notting Hill resident will by now be aware that Whiteley's has added iron-mongery to its cornucopia of departments, and that ladies shopping without a male escort and requiring luncheon can safely visit the refurbished refreshment room. The third is from a gentleman living a few hundred yards away in Pembridge Villas, enclosing a filthy sheet of paper decorated with hollyhock emblems and an ornate letterhead too damaged by muddy shoeprints to decipher. Inscribed in *faux*-Gothic calligraphy is the following list:

> *Minuet:* 10
> *Gavotte:* 9¹/₂
> *Cachucha:* 8¹/₂
> *Mazurka:* 10
> *Tarantella:* 10
> *Deportment during engagements/partings:* 10
> *Deportment during lulls:* 9¹/₂
> *Well done, Agnes!*

To which the gentleman from Pembridge Villas adds, on a separate clean sheet:

> *My wife is of the opinion that this may once have belonged to you.*

Rose, when she brings her master the second mail, is discomposed to find him hunched over his study desk, sobbing into his hands.

'Where is she, Rose?' he groans. 'Where is she hiding?'

The servant, unaccustomed to such intimacy from him, is caught off-guard.

'Could she have gone home, sir?' she suggests, nervously fingering the empty silver tray.

'Home?' he echoes, removing his hands from his face.

'To her mother, sir.'

He stares at her, open-mouthed.

★   ★   ★

Having made himself sweaty and breathless by running from where he left Cheesman's carriage ensnared in the Regent Street traffic, William Rackham knocks at the door of the house in Silver Street – the house that never was, despite the claims of *More Sprees in London*, in Silver Street proper.

After a long pause, during which he inhales deeply and attempts to calm the beating of his heart, the door is opened a crack. A beautiful brown eye peeps out at him, the focal point of a long, thin plumb-line vignette of alabaster skin, crisp white shirt, and coffee-coloured suit.

A woman's silky voice speaks. 'Have you an appointment?'

'I w-wish to see Mrs Castaway.'

The eye half-shuts, displaying a luxurious eyelash. 'Whether you'll see her or not,' replies the voice, honeyed with insolence, 'depends on how bad a boy you've been.'

'What!' William cries. 'Open the door, madam!'

The strange woman widens the slit until the steel chain that's hung across it is stretched taut. Her mannish hair, oiled flat to her scalp, her coat and trousers – as smart as any swell's – and her Mornington shirt-collar complete with cravat, send a chill of disgust down William's spine.

'I w-want a few w-words with Mrs Castaway,' he reiterates.

'You're behind the times, sir,' says the Sapphist, bringing a cigarette holder into view, and taking a puff on it, quick as a kiss. 'Mrs Castaway is dead. Miss Jennifer Pearce is the proprietress here now.'

'It's . . . it's a-actually news of Sugar that I'm after.'

'Sugar's gone, and so are the rest of last year's girls,' the woman retorts, smoke leaking from her nostrils. 'Out with the old, in with the new, that's our philosophy.' And indeed, what Rackham can see of the house's interior is renovated beyond recognition. An unfamiliar face peeks out of the parlour, followed by a body: an exquisitely dressed apparition in blue and gold Algerine.

'It's m-most important I find Sugar,' he insists. 'If you have any inkling of her w-w-whereabouts, I implore you tell me. I'll pay you w-whatever you ask.'

The madam dawdles nearer, lazily swinging a tightly-furled fan as if it were a whip.

'I have two things to say to you, sir,' she declares, 'and you needn't pay for them. Firstly, the girl you call Sugar has renounced the gay life, as far as we know: you may care to rummage around for her in the kennels of the Rescue Society. Secondly, in our opinion, your soaps and ointments are not improved by having your image stamped upon them. Lord grant us *some* places where we don't have to see a man's face. Close the door, Amelia.'

And the door closes.

For a few moments following this outrage, William considers knocking afresh and this time demanding satisfaction, on pain of police escort. But then he cautions himself that these vile creatures may well be telling the truth about Sugar. She isn't in *this* house, that's clear enough; and if not here, then where? Is it really conceivable that Sugar might throw herself on the mercy of the Rescue Society? How else to explain the curious coincidence of Emmeline Fox sending Sugar a parcel only a few days ago? Is this yet another example of a clammy collusion between two tragically misguided females? Determined not to let anger cloud his reason, he wanders away from Mrs Castaway's, back to the hurly-burly of Silver Street.

'Missis play the piano, sir?'

After an excruciating omnibus ride, in which he sat face to face with a smirking dowager – she with an advertisement for Rackham's Damask Rose Drops above her head, he with an advertisement for Rimmel's Eau de Benzoin above his – William disembarks in Bayswater, and proceeds directly to the long row of modest little houses in Caroline Place. There he steels himself for his next struggle against the tightening bonds of tragedy.

Having received no answer the first time, William knocks louder and more insistently at the door of Mrs Emmeline Fox. The front window is shrouded with curtains, but he has seen two auras – auroras? – of lamplight glowing through the layers of faded lace. Henry's cat, roused by the commotion, has leapt onto the sill and now butts and strokes his furry snout against the cobwebby cross-piece of the window-frame. He looks fully twice the size he was when Mrs Fox first bore him away from the Rackham house.

'Who is it, please?' Through the wooden barrier comes Mrs Fox's voice, sounding sleepy, although it's two in the afternoon.

'It's William Rackham. May I speak with you?'

There is a pause. William, windblown and conspicuous in the street, fidgets in frustration; he's well aware that a visit of this kind –

unaccompanied man upon lone woman – offends propriety, but surely Mrs Fox, of all people, ought to be prepared to bend the rules?

'I'm not decent,' comes her voice again.

William blinks at the brass number on her door, dumbstruck. At the street corner, a dog yaps joyously at a mongrel companion on the other side, and a boy in shirtsleeves casts a suspicious glance at the tubby bearded man with the angry face.

'Couldn't *I* come to see *you*,' Mrs Fox goes on, 'a little later this morning? Or afternoon?'

'It's a matter of great urgency!' protests William.

Another pause, while Henry's cat stretches himself to his full height against the window-panes, revealing a heroic girth and two downy balls.

'Please wait a minute,' says Mrs Fox.

William waits. What the devil is she doing? Ushering Sugar and Sophie out of her back door? Stowing them in a wardrobe? Now that he's made the effort to come here, his initial suspicion that Mrs Fox might hold a clue to Sugar's whereabouts has swollen into the manic conviction that she's harbouring the fugitives herself.

After what seems an age, Mrs Fox opens up to him, and he steps inside her vestibule before she has a chance to object.

'How can I help you, Mr Rackham?'

With a glance he appraises the state of her house – the musty smell, the subtle patina of dust, the iron bed-frame leaning against the wall, the piles of books on the stairs, the burlap sack marked *GLOVES FOR IRELAND* blocking access to the broom-cupboard. Mrs Fox stares at him tolerantly, only the slightest bit shamed by her poorly kept house, waiting for him to offer her an explanation for his boorish imposition. She's dressed in a calf-length winter coat with a black fur collar and cuffs, buttoned up to the breastbone. Under that, instead of a blouse or a bodice, she's wearing a man's shirt that's none too clean and far too big for her. Her boots are buttoned only so much as will prevent them sagging like black banana peels off her naked ankles.

'My daughter has been abducted,' William declares, 'by Miss Sugar.'

Mrs Fox's eyes widen, but not nearly as much as such shocking news *ought* to widen them. Indeed, she looks half-asleep.

'How . . . extraordinary,' she breathes.

'Extraordinary!' he echoes, bewildered at her sang-froid. Why the devil doesn't she swoon, or drop to her knees with her hands clasped to her bosom, or lift her feeble fist to her brow and cry 'Oh!'?

'She impressed me as such a nice, well-meaning girl.'

Her placid leniency provokes him to anger. 'You were deceived. She's a madwoman, a vicious madwoman, and she has my daughter.'

'They seemed fond of each other . . .'

'Mrs Fox, I don't wish to argue with you. I–I . . .' He swallows hard, wondering if there's a way to broach his intentions that doesn't make him out to be an utter barbarian. There isn't. 'Mrs Fox, I wish to satisfy myself that Sugar – that Miss Sugar and my daughter are not in this house.'

Emmeline's lips part in astonishment.

'I cannot consent to that,' she murmurs.

'Forgive me, Mrs Fox,' he replies hoarsely, 'but I must.' And, before her glare of disapproval can unman him, he stumps past her, into the kitchen, where he immediately collides with an interlocked bale of Henry's chairs. The room, small to begin with, is bizarrely cluttered with two of everything: two stoves, two crockery cupboards, two ice pails, two kettles, and so on and so on. There's a bread-loaf with a knife stuck in it, and fifteen, twenty tins of salmon and corned beef, lined up like soldiers on a bench that's been sponged clean but still shows rosy-yellow stains of blood. There's barely room to stand, let alone conceal a tall woman and a substantial infant. The garden, clearly visible through the rain-washed kitchen window, is a wilderness of lush, inedible greenery.

Already knowing himself to be in the wrong, but unable to stop, William lurches out of the kitchen and inspects the other rooms. Henry's cat follows at his heels, excited by so much physical activity in a house whose pace is usually so sedate. William dodges the ricks of dusty furniture and does his best to avoid kicking boxes, mounds of books, neatly addressed parcels awaiting only postage stamps, bulbous sacks. Mrs Fox's parlour shows evidence of devoted industry, with dozens of envelopes filled and ready for sending, a map of the metropolis spread open on the writing-desk, and numerous receptacles containing glue, ink, water, tea, and a dark-brown substance with a milky scum on top.

He thunders up the stairs, blushing as much from shame as effort. At the door of the bedroom, a cardboard box is littered with cat turds. Inside, Mrs Fox's bed is rumpled, and a pair of male trousers, much sullied by cat fur, lies prone on its coverlet. Hanging from a hat-stand is an immaculate and neatly ironed outfit of bodice, jacket and dress, in the sober colours that suit Mrs Fox best.

William can bear it no longer; his fantasy of wrenching open a wardrobe and, with a cry of triumphal relief, pulling Sugar and his terrified daughter into the light has withered utterly. He returns downstairs, where Mrs Fox stands waiting for him, her face upturned, her eyes gleaming with reproach.

'Mrs Fox,' he says, feeling dirtier than the contents of the cardboard box on the landing. 'I–I . . . How . . . This violation of your p-privacy. How can you ever f-forgive me?'

She folds her arms around her chest, and squares her jaw.

'It's not for me to forgive you, Mr Rackham,' she remarks coolly, as though merely reminding him that the Christian faith they nominally share is not of the Catholic brand.

'I was . . . not in m-my right m-mind,' pleads William, shuffling towards the front door, worried that – on top of everything else – he'll step on Henry's cat, which is cavorting around his ankles, biting his trousers. 'I-is there n-nothing I can do to redeem m-m-myself in your estimation?'

Mrs Fox blinks slowly, hugging her bosom harder. Her long face has, William notices belatedly, an odd beauty about it, and – God in heaven, can it be? – is that a *smile* teasing the corners of her lips?

'Thank you, Mr Rackham,' she says suavely. 'I'll give your offer serious thought. After all, a man of your resources is ideally matched with the many worthy things that need doing in this world.' She gestures towards the philanthropic jumble of her house. 'I've taken on more work than I can manage, as I'm sure you've noticed. So . . . Yes, Mr Rackham, I look forward to your assistance in the future.'

And, unorthodox to the last, she – not he – opens the door, and bids him good day.

'Miaow!' concurs Henry's cat, prostrating himself happily at his mistress's feet.

Chastened to the point where he would welcome a thunderbolt from heaven to blast him painlessly to a cinder, William returns to his own house. Have the police called? No, the police haven't called. Does he want his luncheon warmed? No, he does not want his luncheon warmed. Coffee, bring him coffee.

Unendurable though the tension is, he has no choice but to endure it, and to carry on his business as normal. More mail has arrived, none of it regarding Sugar or his daughter. One letter is from Grover Pankey, Esq., calling him ill-bred, and severing all connexion with him. So deranged are William's spirits that he considers challenging Pankey to a duel: the ugly old cur is probably a crack shot, and would put William out of his misery with one puff from his pistol. But no, he must keep his head about him, and make overtures to that Cheadle fellow in Glamorgan. Cheadle's ivory pots are light as sea-shells, but strong enough to survive being squeezed hard in one's fist. William knows: he's tried it.

He tears open a letter with an unfamiliar name and address on the back: Mrs F. De Lusignan, 2, Fir-street, Sydenham.

Dear Mr Rackham, the good lady hails him,

My hair went grey through trouble and sickness, but one bottle of your Raven Oil brought it back to a splendid black, as nice as it was in my young days. All my friends remark upon it. You may make what use you like of this letter.

William blinks stupidly, poised on the brink of laughter and convulsive weeping. This is the sort of devout testimonial he and Sugar have invented out of thin air for Rackham advertisements, and here it is: 100 per cent genuine. Mrs F. De Lusignan, admiring her dyed hair in a looking-glass in Sydenham, God bless her! She deserves a whole box of Raven Oil – or perhaps that's what she's tickling him for.

The remainder of the mail is strictly business, yet he forces himself to chew through it, each finished letter wearying him a little more like a spoonful of ash swallowed with the greatest difficulty. But then, in the middle of replying to Miss Baynton in the Toilet Department of Harrod's, he suddenly realises, in a blinding flash of revelation, where Sugar must have gone, and where, even now, his daughter tremblingly awaits her fate.

By the time William finally reaches Mrs Leek's house in Church Lane, St Giles, the sun is low in the sky, casting an incongruous golden glow on the ancient, ramshackle buildings. The convoluted exoskeletons of iron piping shine like monstrous necklaces, the poultices of stucco are butter-yellow on the walls, the clothes-lines flap their ragged burden like courtly pennants. Even the cracked attic windows tilting skew-whiff under the roofs blaze with reflected light – a light that's doomed to fade in a matter of minutes.

However, William is not inclined to admire the view. His immediate concern is whether the address from which a coachman, once upon a time, was instructed to pick up an old man in a wheelchair for the onward journey to Rackham's lavender farm in Mitcham, is the self-same address at whose door he stands now, rapping the blistered wood with his fist. He only has Sugar's word, after all, that the old man really lived here, and this is not the sort of street where a well-dressed man can safely ask for directions.

After an eternity, the door swings open, and there, squinting through clouded pince-nez in the gloom, sits Colonel Leek.

'Forgotten something?' he wheezes, taking William to be a recently departed customer. Then: 'Oh, it's *you*.'

'May I come in?' says William, concerned that even now, Sugar may be shepherding Sophie through the filthy interior of this house towards a back exit.

'Oh, by all means, by all *means*,' declares the old man, with exaggerated *politesse*. 'We'd be honoured. A man as exalted as you, sir. Mr Forty Acres! Glorious, glorious . . .' And he spins on his axles, then wheels himself along a rancid runway of carpet that sighs with damp. '1813: prospects for farmers never better! 1814, 1815, 1816: frosts the like of which was never seen before, ruined crops from shore to shore, bankruptcy aplenty! Adam Tipton, of South Carolina, known in 1863 as the Cotton King! In 1864, after the coming of the weevil, found with a bullet in his brain!'

'I've come to see Sugar,' blurts William, following on behind. Maybe if he states his wish forthrightly, like a no-nonsense requisition, he'll jolt the old blackguard into divulging more than he should.

'She never came back for me, the trollop,' scoffs Colonel Leek. 'A woman's promise is like a Pathan's ceasefire. I never got my snuff, never got a second look at your *glorious* lavender farm, sir.'

'I thought you disliked the experience,' remarks William, momentarily peering up the ill-lit stairwell before stepping across the threshold of the parlour. 'I seem to recall you complaining you were as good as . . . *abducted*.'

'Och, it made a nice change,' bleats the old man, showing neither discomposure nor inclination to nibble at the bait. He has come to rest in a snug corner of the room, adding his shabby bulk to the general clutter of outmoded china and military junk. 'My very first lavender farm! Powerful educ*a-a-ay*tional.' He bares dark ruminant teeth in an ingratiating leer.

A woman has descended the creaking stairs and now pokes her face into the room. She's a pretty little thing, no spring chicken but well-preserved, with a good-humoured kindly face and a shapely body, clad in the fashionable colours of two Seasons ago.

'Was you lookin' for me, sir?' she enquires of the stranger, somewhat surprised at the phenomenon of trade coming to her rather than she soliciting it.

'I'm looking for Sugar,' says William. 'A regular visitor to this house, I believe.'

The woman shrugs sadly. 'That was a long time ago, sir. Sugar's found a rich man to take care of 'er.'

William Rackham stands straight and balls his fists. 'She has stolen my daughter.'

Caroline ponders a moment, wondering if this man means what he says, or if 'stolen my daughter' is one of those fancy turns of phrase that educated people use to signify some loftier notion.

'Your daughter, sir?'

'My daughter has been abducted. Taken by your friend Sugar.'

'Did you know,' interjects Colonel Leek with lugubrious enthusiasm, 'that of every ten persons drowned in England and Wales, six will be children aged ten years or less?'

Caroline watches the well-dressed stranger's eyes widen in offence, and just as she's thinking how much he reminds her of someone she once knew, she twigs that this fellow is the perfumer Rackham, the brother of her gentle parson. The memory of that sweet man fetches her a sly blow in the pit of her stomach, for she's had no warning, and memories can be cruel when they give you no warning. She flinches, claps one hand protectively to her breast, and cannot meet the accusing glower of the man who stands before her.

'I'll not be taken for a fool!' yells Rackham. 'You know more than you admit to, I can tell!'

'Please, sir . . .' she says, turning her head away.

As surely as if a lid had been lifted from a vat, William detects the heady stench of a secret that can no longer be kept hidden. At last he's on the right track! At last this affair is moving towards the explosive dénouement he has been craving – the revelation, the release of tension, that will shake the universe in one fierce convulsion, and then allow everything to fall back into its rightful place, restored to normality! With a grunt of determination, he pushes past the woman, strides out of the parlour, and begins to stamp up the stairs.

'Yaaarrr! Sevenpence!' shouts Colonel Leek, clawing the air after him.

'Watch yer step, sir!' shouts Caroline. 'Some o' them stairs—'

But already it's too late.

Night has fallen over St Giles, over London, over England, over a fair fraction of the world. Lamp-lighters are roaming the streets, solemnly igniting, like an army of Catholic worshippers, innumerable votive candles fifteen feet in height. It's a magical sight, for anyone looking down on it from above, which, sadly, no one is.

Yes, night has fallen, and only those creatures who are of no consequence are still working. Chop-houses are coming to life, serving ox cheeks and potatoes to slop-shop drudges. Taverns, ale-houses and gin palaces are humming with custom. The respectable shop-keepers are shutting up their premises, locking the stanchions and bolting the latches; they snuff out the lights, condemning their unsold merchandise to the penance of another dismal night of self-contemplation. In the lower reaches of society, poorer, shabbier creatures labour on in their homes, gluing matchboxes, sewing trousers, making tin toys by candlelight, pushing neighbours' washing through the mangle, squatting over basins with their skirts rucked up to their shoulders. Let them toil, let them grub, let them disappear into obscurity, you haven't time to see any more.

Refined society basks in a warm atmosphere of gas and paraffin, and its servants are stoking fires for the comfort of those souls who'll now while away the remaining hours till bedtime with embroidery, dining, scrapbook-pasting, letter-writing, novel-reading, parlour games, prayers. Formal calls of an intimate nature have ended with the toll of a bell, and the conversations thus interrupted, however interesting they may have grown, cannot be resumed until the appointed time tomorrow. Well-behaved infants are being led by nurses into the presence of their mothers, to be petted for an hour or two before being whisked upstairs again to waiting beds. Unmarried gentlemen like Bodley and Ashwell, not in the least disadvantaged by not having wives, are spreading napkins over their knees in the Café Royal, or reclining into armchairs at their clubs with a sherry. In the grandest houses, cooks, kitchenmaids and footmen are limbering up for the complicated challenge of delivering piping hot food through long draughty corridors to dining-rooms at exactly the correct junctures. In humbler households, small families accept what is set down before them, and thank God for it.

In Church Lane, St Giles, where no Gods are being thanked, and no children are being bathed, and gas-lamps are few and far between, William Rackham is being led along in near-blackness, stumbling and limping on wet, mucky cobble-stones. He has his arm slung around the shoulder of a woman, and with every step, he groans in pain and mortification. One trouser-leg is torn and sopping-wet with blood.

'I'm all right!' he cries, rearing away from the woman, only to seize hold of her again when his injured leg fails to support him.

'Just a little further, sir,' pants Caroline. 'We're almost there.'

'Hail me a cab,' says William, blundering forward in a haze of his own spent breath. 'All I need is a cab.'

'Cabs don't come 'ere, sir,' says Caroline. 'Just a little further.'

A sudden gust of wind is seeded with sleet, stinging William's cheeks. His ears are throbbing, swollen, as though he's been boxed across them by an angry parent.

'Let me go!' he groans, but it's he who's hanging on.

'You need a doctor, sir,' Caroline points out, taking his peevishness in her stride. 'You'll go to a doctor, won't you?'

'Yes, yes, yes,' he groans, incredulous at how one rotten stair could have reduced him to this state.

The lights of New Oxford Street shine up ahead. Muffled voices swirl through the wind, weary babble from the Horseshoe Brewery's workers being discharged into the night. Their scarecrow silhouettes loom through the drizzle as they cross the boundary from Bloomsbury to where they belong.

'Oi, parson!' someone shouts, and there's raucous laughter.

Caroline escorts William Rackham to the edge of the great thoroughfare, under a street-lamp, then tugs him back so that he doesn't stumble into the gutter.

'I'll stay with you, sir,' she says matter-of-factly, 'till a cab comes. Else you'll get yerself killed.'

In the brighter light, William takes stock of his leg – ragged and revolt-ingly clammy with blood – and then of the woman beside him. Her face is impassive, a mask; she has every reason to despise him; yet here she is, showing him charity.

'Here – take this,' he says, clumsily pulling a handful of coins from his pocket – shillings, sovereigns, small change – and pressing them upon her. Wordlessly she accepts, and secretes the money in a slit in her skirts, but still she stays by his side.

Shamed, he tries to stand on both feet, and a shock of pain shoots up through one leg, as if a vengeful phantom lurking underground has fired a bullet straight through his heel towards his heart. He reels, and feels the woman's arm hard around his waist.

Tears spring to his eyes; the lights of New Oxford Street blur to an ectoplasmic shiver. His body shivers too, in fear of its own injuries: what sort of shape will he be in when this is all over? Is he destined to be a crip-ple, a figure of fun who lurches lamely from armchair to armchair, who writes like a child, and stutters like an imbecile? What has become of the man he once was? A wraith-like shadow passes by on the opposite side of the street, purposefully fleet, pallbearer-black.

He shuts his eyes tight, but the apparitions continue to come: a tall thin woman wrapped in green silk, hurrying through the rain without a bonnet or umbrella. For an instant, as she passes under a street-lamp, her luxuriant surplus of hair glows orange like a flame, and he fancies her smell is flicked towards him on the breeze, like no other odour on earth. Even as she passes, she trails her fingers behind her, wiggling them as if invit-ing him to take hold. *Trust me*, she appears to be telling him, and Lord, how he longs to trust her again, to press his feverish face between her breasts. But no: it's Sophie she's beckoning to – his daughter, unrecognis-ably filthy, dressed in rags, a barefoot guttersnipe from a cautionary slide-show. Steady, steady: it's only a fantasy, a trick of the imagination: he'll have her back yet, safe in the bosom of the family.

Next to pass is a grisly female phantasm, a naked corpse of white flesh much disfigured with crimson gashes and lavender bruises. Her chest gapes open, revealing a palpitating heart between her full breasts, and she dances gracefully on the smutty cobble-stones. Though his eyes are still shut, William turns his face away and buries it in the soft shoulder beside his cheek.

'Don't go to sleep on me, sir,' Caroline warns him amiably, adjusting her stance, squeezing him hard until he rouses. He looks into her face again; it's not quite so impassive now; he detects a weary half-smile. Her shawl has slipped, and the sweat of exertion twinkles in the hollows of her collar-bones; her flesh, though firm, reveals some wrinkles at the neck. Peeping up from the swell of her left breast is a vivid scar, an old burn or scald, shaped like an arrowhead. There's a story behind that scar, no doubt, if she had a mind to tell it.

Ach, how warm she is, and how firmly her hand is pressed in the small of his back! How thick and glossy her hair is, for a woman no longer young! Now that they've been at rest here for a while, he's aware of her body breathing against his own – how divinely she breathes! Helplessly, he adjusts the rhythm of his own inhalations to coincide with hers. They stand together under the street-lamp, veiled inside a gently swirling column of light, their short shadows joined indistinguishably, a strange black chimera cast upon the cobbles, female on the left side, male on the right.

'You really are m-m-most kind,' he tells her, longing to be lying down in a cosy bed. 'I don't know how to—'

'Here's yer cab, sir!' Caroline says cheerfully, patting his arse as rescue comes trundling into view at last. And before he has a chance to make her life too complicated, she nimbly slips from his embrace and hurries back towards Church Lane, out of his reach, out of yours.

'Goodbye!' sings her voice, for her body is already gone, blotted into the unreadable darkness.

nd to you also: goodbye.

An abrupt parting, I know, but that's the way it always is, isn't it? You imagine you can make it last for ever, then suddenly it's over. I'm glad you chose me, even so; I hope I satisfied all your desires, or at least showed you a good time. How very long we've been together, and how very much we've lived through, and still I don't even know your name!

But now it's time to let me go.

ACKNOWLEDGEMENTS

I was far too young in the 1870s to pay proper attention to everything I should, so this account is no doubt riddled with inaccuracies. In fact, *The Crimson Petal* would have been complete and utter fiction had I not been aided in my researches by a great many people. I thank them for sharing their memories with me, and accept responsibility for any falsehoods that remain. Some of these, like the re-scheduling of the Abbots Ripton rail disaster and the shameless embezzlement of what properly belongs to Le Petomane, are deliberate; others are mere ignorance, from which the following erudite folk were powerless to save me:

Chris Baggs, Clare Bainbridge, Paul Barlow, Francis Barnard, Lucinda Becker, Cynthia Behrman, Gemma Bentley, Alex Bernson, Marjorie Bloy, Nancy Booth, Nicola Bown, Trev Broughton, Arthur Burns, Jamie Byng, Rosemary Campbell, Roger Cline, Ken Collins, Betty Cortus, Eileen M. Curran, Frederick Denny, Patrizia di Bello, Jonathan Dore, Gail Edwards, K Eldron, Marguerite Finnigan, Holly Forsythe, Judy Geater, Grayson Gerrard, Sheldon Goldfarb, Kerryn Goldsworthy, Valerie Gorman, Jill Grey, Lesley Hall, Beth Harris, Kay Heath, Sarah J. Heidt, Toni Johnson-Woods, Ellen Jordan, Iveta Jusova, Katie Karrick, Gillian Kemp, Andrew King, Ivo Klaver, Patrick Leary, Paul Lewis, Janet Loengard, Margot Louis, Michael Martin, Chris Ann Matteo, Liz McCausland, Hugh MacDougall, Kirsten MacLeod, Deborah McMillion, Terry L. Meyers, Sally Mitchell, Ellen Moody, Barbara Mortimer, Jess Nevins, Rosemary Oakeshott, Judy Oberhausen, Jeanne Peterson, Siân Preece, Angela Richardson, Cynthia Rogerson, Mario Rups, Herb Schlossberg, Barbara Schulz, Malcolm Shifrin,

Helen Simpson, Carolyn Smith, Rebecca Steinitz, Matthew Sweet, Ruth Symes, Carol L. Thomas, George H. Thomson, Maria Torres, Audrey Verdin, Trina Wallace, Robert Ward, Stephen Wildman, Peter Wilkins, Perry Willett, Chris Willis, Michael Wolff and Karen Wolven.

I'm indebted to Patrick Leary for setting up the excellent VICTORIA internet discussion group, and to Cathy Edgar for directing me to it.

Mindful of the necessity to keep this book nice and slim, I can't list all the publications I've consulted, though special mention must be made of Jennifer Davies' *The Victorian Kitchen*. Thanks to all the folk who've written about the era, and especially to those who photographed and painted it.

Several brave souls volunteered to read the manuscript. Kenneth Fielden's sound advice at an early stage steered me away from blind alleys and pitfalls, and gave me a push in the right direction. Mary Ellen Kappler read the text in weekly instalments sent through the ether, and worked more closely on it than I had any right to expect. Her rare combination of scholarship and insight was not merely useful but inspirational.

Thanks also to my editor Judy Moir, who combed through the manuscript with the same care, dedication and good humour that she has shown in editing my previous books.

Most of all I'd like to thank my wife Eva for her incisive criticisms of *The Crimson Petal* in its radically different drafts over the years. Her high expectations and her ability to communicate her vision of the book's potential have enriched it no end.

Michel Faber
April, 2002